AKÉ • ÌSARÀ

Wole Soyinka was born in Nigeria in 1934. Educated
there and at Leeds University, he worked in the
British theatre before returning to West Africa in
1960, where he has since been based. In 1986 he
became the first African writer to win the Nobel Prize
for Literature. His plays include *The Jero Plays* (1960,
1966), *The Road* (1965), *The Lion and the Jewel* (1966),
Madmen and Specialists (1971) and *A Play of Giants*
(1984). His novels include *The Interpreters* (1973) and
Season of Anomy (1980) and his three collections of
poetry are *Idanre* (1967), *A Shuttle in the Crypt* (1972)
and *Mandela's Earth* (1989).

WOLE SOYINKA

AKÉ

The Years of Childhood

and

ÌSARÀ

A Voyage Around Essay

Minerva

A Minerva Paperback
AKÉ ● ÌSARÀ

Aké first published in Great Britain 1981
by Rex Collings Ltd
First published in Minerva in 1991

Ìsarà first published in Great Britain 1990
by Methuen London
First published in Minerva in 1991

This Minerva edition published 1994
by Mandarin Paperbacks
an imprint of Reed Consumer Books Ltd
Michelin House, 81 Fulham Road, London SW3 6RB
and Auckland, Melbourne, Singapore and Toronto

A CIP catalogue record for this title
is available from the British Library
ISBN 0 7493 9641 5

Typeset by Deltatype Ltd, Ellesmere Port, Cheshire
Printed and bound in Great Britain by
Cox & Wyman Ltd, Reading, Berks

Contents

AKÉ

For Eniola (the 'Wild Christian'),
and to the memory of 'Essay'.
Also for Yeside, Koyode and Folabo
who do not inhabit the memory span
of the years recounted in these pages.

I

The sprawling, undulating terrain is all of Aké. More than mere loyalty to the parsonage gave birth to a puzzle, and a resentment, that God should choose to look down on his own pious station, the parsonage compound, from the profane heights of Itoko. There was of course the mystery of the Chief's stable with live horses near the crest of the hill, but beyond that, this dizzying road only sheered upwards from one noisy market to the other, looking down across Ibàràpa and Ita Aké into the most secret recesses of the parsonage itself.

On a misty day, the steep rise towards Itoko would join the sky. If God did not actually live there, there was little doubt that he descended first on its crest, then took his one gigantic stride over those babbling markets – which dared to sell on Sundays – into St Peter's Church, afterwards visiting the parsonage for tea with the Canon. There was the small consolation that, in spite of the temptation to arrive on horseback, he never stopped first at the Chief's, who was known to be a pagan; certainly the Chief was never seen at a church service except at the anniversaries of the Alake's coronation. Instead God strode straight into St Peter's for morning service, paused briefly at the afternoon service, but reserved his most formal, exotic presence for the evening service which, in his honour, was always held in the English tongue. The organ took on a dark, smoky sonority at evening service, and there was no doubt that the organ was adapting its normal sounds to accompany God's own sepulchral responses, with its timbre of the *egúngún*,* to those prayers that were offered to him.

Only the Canon's residence could have housed the weekly Guest. For one thing, it was the only storey-building in the parsonage, square and solid as the Canon himself, riddled with black wooden-framed windows. BishopsCourt was also a storey-building but only pupils lived in it, so it was not a house. From the upper floor of the Canon's home one *almost* looked the top of Itoko straight in its pagan eye. It stood at the highest lived-in point of the parsonage, just missing overlooking the gate. Its back

---

* Ancestral masquerade.

was turned to the world of spirits and ghommids who inhabited the thick woods and chased home children who had wandered too deeply in them for firewood, mushrooms and snails. The Canon's square, white building was a bulwark against the menace and the siege of the wood spirits. Its rear wall demarcated their territory, stopped them from taking liberties with the world of humans.

Only the school-rooms of the primary school shared this closeness to the woods, and they were empty at night. Fenced by rough plastered walls, by the windowless rear walls of its houses, by tumuli of rocks which the giant trees tried vainly to obscure, Aké parsonage with its corrugated roofs gave off an air of fortifications. Secure within it, we descended or climbed at will into overlapping, interleaved planes, sheer rock-face drops, undergrowths and sudden hide-outs of cultivated fruit groves. The hibiscus was rampant. The air hung heavy with the perfumes of lemon leaves, guavas, mangoes, sticky with the sap of *boum-boum* and the secretions of the rain-tree. The school-compounds were lined with these rain-trees with widespread shade filled branches. Needle-pines rose above the acacia and forests of bamboos kept us permanently nervous; if monster snakes had a choice, the bamboo clumps would be their ideal habitation.

Between the left flank of the Canon's house and the School playing-fields was – the Orchard. It was too varied, much too profuse to be called a garden, even a fruit-garden. And there were plants and fruits in it which made the orchard an extension of scripture classes, church lessons or sermons. A leaf-plant, mottled white-and-red was called the Cana lily. As Christ was nailed to the Cross and his wounds spurted blood, a few drops stuck to the leaves of the lily stigmatizing it for ever. No one bothered to explain the cause of the abundant white spots which also appeared on every leaf. Perhaps it had to do with the washing of sins in the blood of Christ, leaving even the most mottled spots in a person's soul, snow-white. There was the Passion fruit also, born of another part of that same history, not however a favourite of any of us children. Its lush green skin was pleasant to fondle in one's palm, but it ripened into a desiccated yellow, collapsing like the faces of the old men and women we knew. And it barely managed to be sweet, thus failing the infallible test of a real fruit. But the queen of the orchard was the pomegranate which grew, not so much from a seed of the stone church, as of the lyrical Sunday School. For it was at the Sunday School that the real stories were told, stories that lived in the events themselves, crossed the time-border of Sundays or leaves of the Bible and entered the world of fabled lands, men and women. The pomegranate was most niggardly in producing. It yielded us outwardly hardy fruit only once in a while, tended with patience by the thick-veined hands and face which belonged to someone we only knew as Gardener. Only Gardener could be trusted to share the occasional fruit among the small, dedicated band of pomegranate watchers, yet even the tiniest wedge transported us to the illustrated world of the Biblical Tales Retold. The pomegranate was the Queen of Sheba, rebellions and wars, the passion of Salome, the siege of Troy, the Praise of beauty in the Song of Solomon. This fruit with its stone-hearted look and feel unlocked the cellars of Ali Baba, extracted the genie from Aladdin's lamp, plucked the strings of the harp that restored David to sanity, parted the waters of the Nile and filled our parsonage with incense from the dim temple of Jerusalem.

It grew only in the Orchard, Gardener said. The pomegranate was foreign to the black man's soil, but some previous bishop, a white man, had brought the seeds and planted them in the Orchard. We asked if it was *the* apple but Gardener only laughed and said No. Nor, he added, would that apple be found on the black man's soil. Gardener was adjudged ignorant. It was clear that only the pomegranate could be the apple that lost Adam and Eve the joys of paradise. There existed yet another fruit that was locally called apple, soft yet crisp, a soft pink skin and reasonably juicy. Before the advent of the pomegranate it had assumed the identity of the apple that undid the naked pair. The first taste of the pomegranate unmasked that impostor and took its place.

Swarms of bats inhabited the fig tree, their seed-pocked droppings would cake the stones, lawns, paths and bushes before dawn. An evergreen tree, soft and rampant, bordered the playing-field on the side of the bookseller's compound, defying the Harmattan; it filled the parsonage with a tireless concert of weaver-birds.

An evil thing has happened to Aké parsonage. The land is eroded, the lawns are bared and mystery driven from its once secretive combs. Once, each new day opened up an unseen closure, a pocket of rocks, a clump of bush and a colony snails. The motor-hulk has not moved from its staging-point where children clambered into it for journeys to fabled places; now it is only a derelict, its eyes rusted sockets, its dragon face collapsed with a progressive loss of teeth. The abandoned incinerator with its lush weeds and glistening snakes is marked by a mound of mud. The surviving houses, houses which formed the battlements of Aké parsonage, are now packing cases on a depleted landscape, full of creaks, exposed and nerveless.

And the moods are gone. Even the open lawns and broad paths, bordered with whitewashed stones, lilies and lemon grass clumps, changed nature from season to season, from weekday to Sunday and between noon and nightfall. And the echoes off the walls in Lower Parsonage acquired new tonalities with the seasons, changed with the emptying of the lawns as the schools dispersed for holidays.

If I lay across the lawn before our house, face upwards to the sky, my head towards BishopsCourt, each spread-out leg would point to the inner compounds of Lower Parsonage. Half of the Anglican Girls' School occupied one of these lower spaces, the other half had taken over BishopsCourt. The lower area contained the school's junior classrooms, a dormitory, a small fruit-garden of pawpaws, guava, some bamboo and wild undergrowth. There were always snails to be found in the rainy season. In the other lower compound was the mission bookseller, a shrivelled man with a serene wife on whose ample back we all, at one time or the other slept, or reviewed the world. His compound became a short cut to the road that led to Ibarà, Lafenwà or Igbèin and its Grammar School over which Ransome-Kuti presided and lived with his family. The bookseller's compound contained the only well in the parsonage; in the dry season, his place was never empty. And his soil appeared to produce the only coconut trees.

BishopsCourt, of Upper Parsonage, is no more. Bishop Ajayi Crowther would sometimes emerge from the cluster of hydrangea and bougain-villaea, a gnomic face with popping eyes whose formal photograph had first stared at us from the frontispiece of his life history. He had lived, the teacher said, in BishopsCourt and from that moment, he peered out from among the creeping plants whenever I passed by the house on an errand to our Great Aunt, Mrs Lijadu. BishopsCourt had become a boarding house for the girls' school and an extra playground for us during the holidays. The Bishop sat, silently, on the bench beneath the wooden porch over the entrance, his robes twined through and through with the lengthening tendrils of the bougainvillaea. I moved closer when his eyes turned to sockets. My mind wandered then to another photograph in which he wore a clerical suit with waistcoat and I wondered what he really kept at the end of the silver chain that vanished into the pocket. He grinned and said, Come nearer, I'll show you. As I moved towards the porch he drew on the chain until he had lifted out a wholly round pocket-watch that gleamed of solid silver. He pressed a button and the lid opened, revealing, not the glass and the face-dial but a deep cloud-filled space. Then he winked one eye, and it fell from his face into the bowl of the watch. He winked the other and this joined its partner in the watch. He snapped back the lid,

8

nodded again and his head went bald, his teeth disappeared and the skin pulled backward till the whitened cheekbones were exposed. Then he stood up and, tucking the watch back into the waistcoat pocket, moved a step towards me. I fled homewards.

BishopsCourt appeared sometimes to want to rival the Canon's house. It looked a house-boat despite its guard of whitewashed stones and luxuriant flowers, its wooden fretwork frontage almost wholly immersed in bougainvillaea. And it was shadowed also by those omnipresent rocks from whose clefts tall, stout-boled trees miraculously grew. Clouds gathered and the rocks merged into their accustomed grey turbulence, then the trees were carried to and fro until they stayed suspended over BishopsCourt. This happened only in heavy storms. BishopsCourt, unlike the Canon's house, did not actually border the rocks or the woods. The girls' playing-fields separated them and we knew that this buffer had always been there. Obviously bishops were not inclined to challenge the spirits. Only the vicars could. That Bishop Ajayi Crowther frightened me out of that compound by his strange transformations only confirmed that the Bishops, once they were dead, joined the world of spirits and ghosts. I could not see the Canon decaying like that in front of my eyes, nor the Rev J.J. who had once occupied the house, many years before, when my mother was still like us. J.J. Ransome-Kuti had actually ordered back several ghommids in his life-time; my mother confirmed it. She was his grand niece and, before she came to live at our house, she had lived in the Rev J.J.'s household. Her brother Sanya also lived there and he was acknowledged by all to be an *òrò*,* which made him at home in the woods, even at night. On one occasion however, he must have gone too far.

'They had visited us before,' she said, 'to complain. Mind you, they wouldn't actually come into the compound, they stood far off at the edge, where the woods ended. Their leader, the one who spoke, emitted wild sparks from a head that seemed to be an entire ball of embers – no, I'm mixing up two occasions – that was the second time when he chased us home. The first time, they had merely sent an emissary. He was quite dark, short and swarthy. He came right to the backyard and stood there while he ordered us to call the Reverend.

'It was as if Uncle had been expecting the visit. He came out of the house and asked him what he wanted. We all huddled in the kitchen, peeping out.'

'What was his voice like? Did he speak like an *egúngún*?'

* A kind of tree daemon.

9

'I'm coming to it. This man, well, I suppose one should call him a man. He wasn't quite human, we could see that. Much too large a head, and he kept his eyes on the ground. So, he said he had come to report us. They didn't mind our coming to the woods, even at night, but we were to stay off any area beyond the rocks and that clump of bamboo by the stream.'

'Well, what did Uncle say? And you haven't said what his voice was like.'

Tinu turned her elder sister's eye on me. 'Let Mama finish the story.'

'You want to know everything. All right, he spoke just like your father. Are you satisfied?'

I did not believe that but I let it pass. 'Go on. What did Grand Uncle do?'

'He called everyone together and warned us to keep away from the place.'

'And yet you went back!'

'Well, you know your Uncle Sanya. He was angry. For one thing the best snails are on the other side of that stream. So he continued to complain that those òrò were just being selfish, and he was going to show them who he was. Well, he did. About a week later he led us back. And he was right, you know. We gathered a full basket and a half of the biggest snails you ever saw. Well, by this time we had all forgotten about the warning, there was plenty of moonlight and anyway, I've told you Sanya is an òrò himself. . . .'

'But why? He looks normal like you and us.'

'You won't understand yet. Anyway, he is òrò. So with him we felt quite safe. Until suddenly this sort of light, like a ball of fire, began to glow in the distance. Even while it was still far we kept hearing voices, as if a lot of people around us were grumbling the same words together. They were saying something like, "You stubborn, stiff-necked children, we've warned you and warned you but you just won't listen. . . ." '

Wild Christian looked above our heads, frowning to recollect the better. 'One can't even say, "they". It was only this figure of fire that I saw and he was still very distant. Yet I heard him distinctly, as if he had many mouths which were pressed against my ears. Every moment, the fireball loomed larger and larger.'

'What did Uncle Sanya do? Did he fight him?'

'Sanya wo ni yen? He was the first to break and run. Bo o ló o yǎ mi, o di kítìpà kítìpà!* No one remembered all those fat snails. That iwin† followed

---

* If you aren't moving, get out of my way!
† A 'ghommid'; a wood sprite which is also believed to live in the ground.

us all the way to the house. Our screams had arrived long before us and the whole household was – well, you can imagine the turmoil. Uncle had already dashed down the stairs and was in the backyard. We ran past him while he went out to meet the creature. This time that *iwin* actually passed the line of the woods, he continued as if he meant to chase us right into the house, you know, he wasn't running, just pursuing us steadily.' We waited. This was it! Wild Christian mused while we remained in suspense. Then she breathed deeply and shook her head with a strange sadness.

'The period of faith is gone. There was faith among our early Christians, real faith, not just church-going and hymn-singing. Faith. *Igbàgbó*. And it is out of that faith that real power comes. Uncle stood there like a rock, he held out his Bible and ordered, "Go back! Go back to that forest which is your home. Back, I said, in the name of God." Hm. And that was it. The creature simply turned and fled, those sparks falling off faster and faster until there was just a faint glow receding into the woods.' She sighed. 'Of course, after prayers that evening, there was the price to be paid. Six of the best on every one's back. Sanya got twelve. And we all cut grass every day for the next week.'

I could not help feeling that the fright should have sufficed as punishment. Her eyes gazing in the direction of the square house, Wild Christian nonetheless appeared to sense what was going on in my mind. She added, 'Faith and – Discipline. That is what made those early believers. Psheeaw! God doesn't make them like that any more. When I think of that one who now occupies that house . . .'

Then she appeared to recall herself to our presence. 'What are you both still sitting here for? Isn't it time for your evening bath? Lawanle!' 'Auntie' Lawanle replied 'Ma' from a distant part of the house. Before she appeared I reminded Wild Christian, 'But you haven't told us why Uncle Sanya is *òrò*.'

She shrugged, 'He is. I saw it with my own eyes.'

We both clamoured. 'When? When?'

She smiled. 'You won't understand. But I'll tell you about it some other time. Or let him tell you himself next time he is here.'

'You mean you saw him turn into an *òrò*?'

Lawanle came in just then and she prepared to hand us over, 'Isn't it time for these children's bath?'

I pleaded, 'No, wait Auntie Lawanle,' knowing it was a waste of time. She had already gripped us both, one arm each. I shouted back, 'Was Bishop Crowther an *òrò*?'

Wild Christian laughed. 'What next are you going to ask? Oh, I see. They have taught you about him in Sunday school, have they?'

'I saw him.' I pulled back at the door, forcing Lawanle to stop. 'I see him all the time. He comes and sits under the porch of the Girls' School. I've seen him when crossing the compound to Auntie Mrs Lijadu.'

'All right,' sighed Wild Christian. 'Go and have your bath.'

'He hides among the bougainvillaea. . . .' Lawanle dragged me out of hearing.

Later that evening, she told us the rest of the story. On that occasion, Rev J.J. was away on one of his many mission tours. He travelled a lot, on foot and on bicycle, keeping in touch with all the branches of his diocese and spreading the Word of God. There was frequent opposition but nothing deterred him. One frightening experience occurred in one of the villages in Ijebu. He had been warned not to preach on a particular day, which was the day for an *egúngún* outing, but he persisted and held a service. The *egúngún* procession passed while the service was in progress and, using his ancestral voice, called on the preacher to stop at once, disperse his people and come out to pay obeisance. Rev J.J. ignored him. The *egúngún* then left, taking his followers with him but, on passing the main door, he tapped on it with his wand, three times. Hardly had the last member of his procession left the church premises than the building collapsed. The walls simply fell down and the roof disintegrated. Miraculously however, the walls fell outwards while the roof supports fell among the aisles or flew outwards – anywhere but on the congregation itself. Rev J.J. calmed the worshippers, paused in his preaching to render a thanksgiving prayer, then continued his sermon.

Perhaps this was what Wild Christian meant by Faith. And this tended to confuse things because, after all, the *egúngún* did make the church building collapse. Wild Christian made no attempt to explain how that happened, so that feat tended to be of the same order of Faith which moved mountains or enabled Wild Christian to pour ground-nut oil from a broad-rimmed bowl into an empty bottle without spilling a drop. She had the strange habit of sighing with a kind of rapture, crediting her steadiness of hand to Faith and thanking God. If however the basin slipped and she lost a drop or two, she murmured that her sins had become heavy and that she needed to pray more.

If Rev J.J. had Faith however, he also appeared to have Stubbornness in common with our Uncle Sanya. Stubbornness was one of the earliest sins we easily recognized, and no matter how much Wild Christian tried to explain the Rev J.J. preaching on the *egúngún*'s outing day, despite warnings, it sounded much like stubbornness. As for Uncle Sanya there was no doubt about his own case; hardly did the Rev J.J. pedal out of sight on his pastoral duties than he was off into the woods on one pretext or the other, and making for the very areas which the *òrò* had declared out of bounds. Mushrooms and snails were the real goals, with the gathering of firewood used as the dutiful excuse.

Even Sanya had however stopped venturing into the woods at night, accepting the fact that it was far too risky; daytime and early dusk carried little danger as most wood spirits only came out at night. Mother told us that on this occasion she and Sanya had been picking mushrooms, separated by only a few clumps of bushes. She could hear his movements quite clearly, indeed, they took the precaution of staying very close together.

Suddenly, she said, she heard Sanya's voice talking animatedly with someone. After listening for some time she called out his name but he did not respond. There was no voice apart from his, yet he appeared to be chatting in friendly, excited tones with some other person. So she peeped through the bushes and there was Uncle Sanya seated on the ground chattering away to no one that she could see. She tried to penetrate the surrounding bushes with her gaze but the woods remained empty except for the two of them. And then her eyes came to rest on his basket.

It was something she had observed before, she said. It was the same, no matter how many of the children in the household went to gather snails, berries or whatever, Sanya would spend most of the time playing and climbing rocks and trees. He would wander off by himself, leaving his basket anywhere. And yet, whenever they prepared to return home, his basket was always fuller than the others'. This time was no different. She came closer, startling our Uncle who snapped off his chatter and pretended to be hunting snails in the undergrowth.

Mother said that she was frightened. The basket was filled to the brim, impossibly bursting. She was also discouraged, so she picked up her near empty basket and insisted that they return home at once. She led the way but after some distance, when she looked back, Sanya appeared to be trying to follow her but was being prevented, as if he was being pulled back by invisible hands. From time to time he would snatch forward his arm and snap,

'Leave me alone. Can't you see I have to go home? I said I have to go.'
She broke into a run and Sanya did the same. They ran all the way home.

That evening, Sanya took ill. He broke into a sweat, tossed on his mat all night and muttered to himself. By the following day the household was thoroughly frightened. His forehead was burning to the touch and no one could get a coherent word out of him. Finally, an elderly woman, one of

13

J.J.'s converts, turned up at the house on a routine visit. When she learnt of Sanya's condition, she nodded wisely and acted like one who knew exactly what to do. Having first found out what things he last did before his illness, she summoned my mother and questioned her. She told her everything while the old woman kept on nodding with understanding. Then she gave instructions:

'I want a basket of *àgìdi*, containing 50 wraps. Then prepare some *èkuru* in a large bowl. Make sure the *èkuru* stew is prepared with plenty of locust bean and crayfish. It must smell as appetizing as possible.'

The children were dispersed in various directions, some to the market to obtain the *àgìdi*, others to begin grinding the beans for the amount of *èkuru* which was needed to accompany 50 wraps of *àgìdi*. The children's mouths watered, assuming at once that this was to be an appeasement feast, a *sàarà** for some offended spirits.

When all was prepared however, the old woman took everything to Sanya's sick-room, plus a pot of cold water and cups, locked the door on him and ordered everybody away.

'Just go about your normal business and don't go anywhere near the room. If you want your brother to recover, do as I say. Don't attempt to speak to him and don't peep through the keyhole.'

She locked the windows too and went herself to a distant end of the courtyard where she could monitor the movements of the children. She dozed off soon after however, so that mother and the other children were able to glue their ears to the door and windows, even if they could not see the invalid himself. Uncle Sanya sounded as if he was no longer alone. They heard him saying things like:

'Behave yourself, there is enough for everybody. All right you take this, have an extra wrap . . . Open your mouth . . . here . . . you don't have to fight over that bit, here's another piece of crayfish . . . behave, I said . . .'

And they would hear what sounded like the slapping of wrists, a scrape of dishes on the ground or water slopping into a cup.

When the woman judged it was time, which was well after dusk, nearly six hours after Sanya was first locked up, she went and opened the door. There was Sanya fast asleep but, this time, very peacefully. She touched his forehead and appeared to be satisfied by the change. The household who had crowded in with her had no interest in Sanya however. All they could see, with astonished faces, were the scattered leaves of 50 wraps of *àgìdi*, with the contents gone, a large empty dish which was earlier filled with *èkuru*, and a water-pot nearly empty.

* An offering, food shared out as offering.

14

No, there was no question about it, our Uncle Sanya was an *òrò*; Wild
Christian had seen and heard proofs of it many times over. His companions
were obviously the more benevolent type or he would have come to serious
harm on more than one occasion, J.J.'s protecting Faith notwithstanding.
Uncle Sanya was very rarely with us at this time, so we could not ask him
any of the questions which Wild Christian refused to answer. When he
next visited us at the parsonage, I noticed his strange eyes which hardly
ever seemed to blink but looked straight over our heads even when he
talked to us. But he seemed far too active to be an *òrò*; indeed for a long
time I confused him with a local scoutmaster who was nicknamed Activity.
So I began to watch the Wolf Cubs who seemed nearest to the kind of secret
company which our Uncle Sanya may have kept as a child. As their tight
little faces formed circles on the lawns of Aké, building little fires,
exchanging secret signs with hands and twigs, with stones specially placed
against one another during their jamboree, I felt I had detected the hidden
companions who crept in unseen through chinks in the door and even from
the ground, right under the aggrieved noses of Wild Christian and the
other children in J.J.'s household, and feasted on 50 wraps of *àgìdi* and a
huge bowl of *èkuru*.

The Mission left the parsonage just a vicar and his catechist: Aké was no
longer worth a bishop. But even the Vicar's 'court' is a mere shell of itself.
The orchard has vanished, the rows of lemon grass have long been eaten by
goats. Lemon grass, the cure of fevers and headaches – an aspirin or two, a
cup of hot lemon grass tea and bed. But its effusion was really fragrant and
we drank it normally as a variant of the common tea. Stark, shrunk with
time is that white square monument which, framed against the rocks
dominated the parsonage, focussing the eye on itself as a visitor entered the
parsonage gate. The master of that house was a chunk from those rocks,
black, huge, granite head and enormous feet.

Mostly, they called him Pastor. Or Vicar, Canon, Reverend. Or, like my
mother, simply Pa Delumo. Father's choice was Canon and this also
became my own, but only because of a visit to Ibara. We made several of
those outings; visit to relations, accompanying Wild Christian on her
shopping expeditions or for some other purpose which we could never
grasp. At the end of such outings however, we were left with a vague
notion of having been taken out to see something, to experience
something. We were left with exhilaration – and of course exhaustion,
since we walked most of the way. But sometimes it was difficult to recall
what concrete things we had seen, what had been the purpose of our

setting out, specially dressed and neatly combed. And with much bustle and preparation.

We had climbed a steep road and come on the imposing entrance – the white pillars and plaque which said: THE RESIDENCY. Some white man clearly lived there, the gate was patrolled by a policeman in baggy shorts who stared over our heads. The house itself was set well back up a hill, part hidden by trees. But the objects on which my eyes were fastened were two black heavy-snouted tubes mounted on wooden wheels. They stood against the pillars, pointed at us, and beside each one was a pile of round metallic balls, nearly as big as footballs. They are guns, my mother said, they are called cannons, and they are used to fight wars.

'But why does Papa call Pa Delumo a cannon?'

She explained the difference but I had already found my own answer. It was the head, Pa Delumo's head was like a cannon ball, that was why father called him Canon. Everything about the guns recalled the man's presence, his strength and solidity. The cannons looked immobile, indestructible, and so did he. He seemed to overwhelm everything; when he came to visit us he filled the front room completely. Only the parlour appeared to suit him, once he was sunk in one of the armchairs he became easier to contain. I felt sorry for his catechists, junior vicar or curate – his assistants seemed to have different names also – they appeared insipid, starved parodies of himself, so seemingly poor in spirit that I would later think of them as church mice. Of the men who came to our house wearing a round collar, only our uncle Ransome-Kuti – whom everyone called Daodu – matched and even exceeded his personality. Pa Delumo's presence awed me, he dominated not merely the parsonage but Aké itself, and did this more effectively than Kabiyesi, our Oba at whose feet I often saw men fall prostrate. Occasionally I met far more mysterious clerics, elusive, with their own very private awesomeness, such as Bishop Howells who lived in retirement not far from our house. But the Canon was the vicar of St Peter's and he filled the paths and lawns completely as he strode downhill to visit his flock or deliver his booming sermons.

The Canon came often for discussions with father. Sometimes the talk was serious, other times his laughter resounded throughout the house. But they never argued. Certainly I never heard them argue about God the way my father carried on with the bookseller or his other friends. It was frightening at first to hear them discuss God in this way. The bookseller especially, with his shrill voice and turkey neck, he seemed to be poorly equipped, physically, for such flippant statements about such a Power. The Canon sometimes seemed to be that Power, so the contest, conducted though it was indirectly, seemed very unequal and risky for the bookseller. My father of course I assumed to be specially invulnerable. Once, the Canon was walking across the parsonage while they argued on something which had to do with the birth of Christ. They spoke at the top of their voices, sometimes all at once. The Canon was separated from them by no further than the lawn outside and I wondered, when he stopped suddenly, if he had overheard and was about to come and rebuke them.

But he had only stopped to talk to a little boy held by the hand by a woman, perhaps his mother. He stooped to pat him on the head, his large mouth opened in an endless smile and the corners of his eyes broke into wrinkles. His forehead creased – sometimes it was difficult to tell whether he was pleased at something or he had a sudden headache. His jacket was far too small, the trousers stopped some distance above his ankles and his round collar seemed about to choke him. The broad-brimmed clerical hat squashed his giant figure – I glanced quickly to see if he had suddenly diminished in size and was reassured by his enormous shoes which, I learnt from a cousin, were called No-Size-in-London. I obtained a last flash of his vast bottom before he straightened up and the woman's hand vanished totally from sight as he encased it in his own. These alternations between superhuman possibilities and ordinary ill-fitting clothes unsettled me, I wished he would remain constantly in his cassock and surplice.

Essay's favourite position in all arguments was the devil's advocate – he was called S.A. from his initials, HM or Headmaster, or Es-Ay-Sho by his more rumbustious friends. For some reason, few called him by his own name and, for a long time, I wondered if he had any. It did not take long for him to enter my consciousness simply as Essay, as one of those careful stylistic exercises in prose which follow set rules of composition, are products of fastidiousness and elegance, set down in beautiful calligraphy that would be the envy of most copyists of any age. His despair was real that he should give birth to a son who, from the beginning, showed clearly that he had inherited nothing of his own handwriting. He displayed the same elegance in his dressing. His eating habits were a source of marvel to mother, who by contrast I soon named The Wild Christian. When Essay dissected a piece of yam, weighed it carefully, transferred it to his plate, paused, turned it around, sliced off a piece and returned it to the dish, then commenced the same ritual with the meat and stew, she would shake her head and ask,

'Does that extra piece really matter?'

Essay merely smiled, proceeded to chew methodically, slicing off each piece of meat, yam, like a geometric exercise, lifting a scoop of stew with the edge of his knife and plastering the slice of yam like a master mason. He never drank between mouthfuls, not even a sip. At debate time however, he soon grew as excitable as the bookseller, the shrillest of them all with his tiny twinkling eyes. He appeared to have the sun permanently beamed in his eyes. The bookseller brought into the house that aura of guinea-fowl, turkeys, sheep and goats all of which he raised in his abundant compound. The sheep were always being rounded up; either the gates had been left carelessly open by a visitor or the stubborn animals had found yet another gap in the stone-and-mud walls. Thin and peppery, leather-taut cheek-bones thrust out restlessly, he punctuated his discourse with bird-like gestures. Even at his most aggressive his shoulders slouched, his fingers refused to release the cloth-cap which, outside, never left his head, perhaps because he was completely bald. We could tell his laughter apart, shrill and raspy, revealing gapped teeth which imparted to his face, finally, the look of an old wicker-chair.

The bookseller's wife was one of our many mothers; if we had taken a vote on the question, she would be in the forefront of all the others, including our real one. With a bovine beauty, jet-black skin and inexhaustible goodness, she nevertheless put disquieting thoughts in my head, and all because of her husband. By contrast to him, she was ample, and sometimes when the bookseller disappeared for days, I felt certain that she had just swallowed him up. It was with great relief that I would encounter his bald head bobbing about in animation somewhere in his house or in the bookshop. Of all the women on whose backs I was carried, none was as secure and comfortable at Mrs B.'s. It was capacious, soft and reassuring, it radiated the same repose and kindliness that we had observed in her face.

We slept often at the bookseller's. Mrs B. would send a maid to inform our house that we would eat and sleep at their own house for the night, and that was that. When we got into trouble we ran behind her and she shielded us:

'No no, I take the beating on myself. . . .'

Wild Christian tried to reach round her with the stick, but there was simply too much of her. Unless the offence was particularly serious, that was the end of the matter.

Her only daughter, Bukola, was not of our world. When we threw our voices against the school walls of Lower Parsonage and listened to them echo from a long distance, it seemed to me that Bukola was one of the denizens of that other world where the voice was caught, sieved, re-spun and cast back in diminishing copies. Amulets, bangles, tiny rattles and dark copper-twist rings earthed her through ankles, fingers, wrists and waist. She knew she was *àbiku*.* The two tiny cicatrices on her face were also part of the many counters to enticements by her companions in the other world. Like all *àbiku* she was privileged, apart. Her parents dared not scold her for long or earnestly.

Suddenly her eyes would turn inwards, showing nothing but the whites. She would do it for our benefit whenever we asked her. Tinu stood at a distance ready to run away, somehow she expected terrible things to follow. I asked Bukola:

'Can you see when you do that with your eyes?'

'Only darkness.'

'Do you remember anything of the other world?'

'No. But that is where I go when I fall in a trance.'

'Can you fall into a trance now?'

From her safe distance Tinu threatened to report to our parents if I encouraged her. Bukola merely replied that she could, but only if I was sure I could call her back.

I was not very sure I could do that. Looking at her, I wondered how Mrs B. coped with such a supernatural being who died, was re-born, died again and kept going and coming as often as she pleased. As we walked, the bells on her anklets jingled, driving off her companions from the other world who pestered her incessantly, pleading that she should rejoin them.

'Do you actually hear them?'

'Often.'

'What do they say?'

'Simply that I should come and play with them.'

'Haven't they got anyone to play with? Why do they bother you?'

She shrugged. I felt resentful. Bukola was after all our own playmate. Then I had an idea.

'Why don't you bring them over here? Next time they call you, invite them to come and play with us in our own compound.'

She shook her head. 'They can't do that.'

'Why not?'

'They cannot move as we do. Just as you cannot go over there.'

She was so rare, this privileged being who, unlike Tinu and me, and even her companions in that other place, could pass easily from one sphere to another. I had seen her once during her fainting spell, her eyes rolled

* A child which is born, dies, is born again and dies in a repetitive cycle.

19

upwards, teeth tightly clenched while her body went limp. Mrs B. kept wailing:

'Egbà mi, ara è ma ntutu! Ara è ma ntutu!'* desperately chafing her limbs to bring her back to life. The bookseller ran from the shop through the adjoining door and forced her teeth open. The maid had already snatched a bottle from a cupboard and together some liquid was forced down her throat. The *àbikú* did not immediately regain consciousness but I could tell, after a little while, that the danger had passed. The household grew less tense, they stretched her on the bed and she relaxed totally, her face suffused with an unnatural beauty. We sat beside her, Tinu and I, watching until she woke. Her mother then made her drink some light fish-soup which she had busied herself preparing while she slept. Normally we would all eat from the same bowl but this time, Mrs B. transferred some of the soup to a smaller pot to which she then added some thick liquid from a bottle. It was brackish and had a pungent smell. While we spooned up our soup from a separate bowl, Mrs B. held her daughter's head back and made her drink her own soup in one go. Bukola evidently expected it; she drank her potion without any complaint.

Afterwards, we went out to play. The crisis was completely over. Mrs B. however insisted that we remain within their compound. I reminded Bukola of that spell. 'Was it your other playmates who called you then?'

'I don't remember.'

'But you can do it any time you want.'

'Yes, especially if my parents do something to annoy me. Or the maid.'

'But how do you do it? How do you actually *do* it? I know your eyes first of all turn white. . . .'

'Do they? All I know is that if . . . let us say I want something, and my mother says No. It isn't all the time mind you, but sometimes my father and mother will deny me something. So then I may hear my other companions saying, "You see, they don't want you there, that is what we've been telling you." They may say that and then I get a feeling of wanting to go away. I really *want* to go away. I always tell my parents, I will go, I will go if you don't do so and so. If they don't, I just faint.'

'What happens if you don't come back.'

'But I always come back.'

It made me uneasy. Mrs B. was too kind a woman to be plagued with such an awkward child. Yet we knew she was not being cruel; an *àbikú* was that way, they could not help their nature. I thought of all the things

* Help me, she is getting cold all over!

20

Bukola could ask for, things which would be beyond the power of her parents to grant.

'Suppose one day you ask something they cannot give you. Like the Alake's motor-car.'

'They have to give me what I ask,' she insisted.

'But there are things they don't have. Even a king doesn't have everything.'

'The last time it happened I only asked for a *sàarà*. My father refused. He said I had one not so long ago, so I fainted. I was really going.'

Tinu protested. 'But one cannot have a *sàarà* every day.'

'I don't have a *sàarà* every day,' she persisted. 'And the *sàarà* I asked for that time was not for me, it was for my companions. They told me that if I couldn't come to play with them just yet, I should make them *sàarà*. I told my mother and she agreed, but father refused.' She shrugged. 'That is what happens when the grown-ups refuse to understand. Papa had to kill an extra fowl because it took longer than usual for me to come back.'

Her oval, solemn face changed from innocence to authority as she spoke. I watched her intently, wondering if she was scheming another departure. Natural as it all seemed, there was also a vague disquiet that this was too much power for a child to wield over her parents. I went over all the faces at the *sàarà*, the movement of food and drinks, the sudden disputes that rose as we ate, and the peacemaking voices of the grown-ups; nothing unusual appeared to have happened. It had been a *sàarà* like any other. We sat in groups on mats spread out in the garden, all in outing dresses. Bukola especially gorgeously dressed. Her eyes were deeply marked in antimony and her face powdered. She ate at our mat, from the same dish, there was nothing other-worldly about her; certainly I had not seen her giving food secretly to unseen companions, yet the *sàarà* was for them.

I wondered sometimes if Mr B. took refuge in our house to escape the tyranny of this child. Fond of arguments as father was, on any subject on earth or in heaven, it was the bookseller who usually prolonged their disputations far into the night. He would worry the dead flesh of an argument with hawk-like talons, conceding a point with the greatest reluctance, only to return to a position long discarded or overtaken by new arguments. Even I could tell that, and the exaggerated patience in Essay's voice only served to confirm it.

And sometimes their arguments took frightening turns. One day the bookseller, Fowokan the junior headmaster of the primary school, the catechist and one other of Essay's cronies followed him home from church service. Osibo the pharmacist enjoyed sitting on these sessions but took little part in them. Their voices had long preceded them into the house, they were all hotly wrapped in the debate, talking all at once and refusing to yield a point. It went on right through bottles of warm beer and soft drinks, exhausted Wild Christian's stock of chin-chin and sweet biscuits and carried over into lunch. Even as she shook her head in despair at 'these friends of your father', wondering why he always managed to attract to himself friends with such stomachs for arguments and food, it was obvious that Wild Christian enjoyed the rôle played by the Headmaster's house as the intellectual watering-hole of Aké and its environs.

Towards late afternoon, tea and sandwiches or cakes refuelled their vocal powers for the final rally, for by then it was approaching the hour of evening service and they all had to return home for a change of clothing. It was usually at this time that Bukola's father seemed in the greatest danger. The arguments would take a physical turn with the bookseller, always the bookseller, about to be made the sacrificial proof of some point of disagreement. My loyalty to his wife created a terrible dilemma. I felt it was my duty to run and warn her that her husband was about to be sold into slavery, banished from Abeokuta, dropped from an aeroplane, hurled from the church tower, tied to a tree in the dead of night alone with evil spirits, sent on an investigation mission to hell or on a peace mission to Hitler . . . always some dangerous consequence of a going argument, and the only way, they would all decide, in which it could be resolved. That day, these friends actually wanted to cut off one of Mr B.'s limbs.

'All right, shall I tell Joseph to sharpen the cutlass?'

The argument had started from that morning's sermon. It had gone a hundred different ways at different times and, as usual, the bookseller's gesticulating arms had fanned the embers back to life when every point had been exhausted. Now he seemed about to lose the arm. Still, he fought back. He always did.

'Did I tell you that my right arm had offended me?'

Amidst laughter – and this was the strangest part, they always laughed – Essay called out to Joseph to bring the cutlass.

Mr Fowokan offered, 'Or an axe. Whichever is sharper.'

Mr B.'s hands flapped about even more desperately, 'Wait, wait. Did I tell you that my arm had offended me?'

'Are you now saying that you are without sin?' the Catechist countered.

'No, but who is to say definitely that it was my hand which committed the sin? And which arm are you going to cut off, left or right?'

'Well . . .' My father gave the matter some thought. 'You are left-handed. So the probability is that your left hand committed the sin. Joseph!'

'Not so fast. Let's go over God's injunction again . . . if thine right hand offendeth thee . . . note, *offended thee* . . . it says nothing about committing a sin. My right hand may commit a sin, or my left. That makes it an offence against God. But that does not mean that *I* am offended. God may be offended, but it is up to him to take whatever action he pleases.'

Essay looked shocked. 'You are now claiming that an offence against God is not to be regarded as an offence against man? You refuse to take God's side against sin?'

Hastily, the bookseller reassured God. 'No, don't put words into my mouth. I never said such a thing. . . .'

With one accord they shouted, 'Good. In that case let's waste no more time.'

Joseph had already arrived and was waiting in the wings. My father took the cutlass, the others seized the bookseller.

'Wait, wait,' the man pleaded. I turned to Tinu with whom I eavesdropped from the corner of the parlour: 'One of us had better run and fetch Mrs B.' But then she was never really interested in the discussions, so she could not see when an argument had to be put to a dangerous test.

Essay tested the edge of the cutlass with the tip of his thumb. The bookseller shouted: 'But I tell you neither my left nor right hand has offended me.'

My father sighed. 'Today is a Sunday, God's own day. Imagine you are standing before him. You are his servant, a respected sidesman in his church at St Peter's. You insist that Christ's injunctions are meant to be taken literally. All right, God is now asking you, has your right hand *ever* offended thee? Yes or no.'

It was the sort of language which frightened me even more than the violence about to be visited on the bookseller. My father had the habit of speaking as if he was on first-name terms with God. Why should he suggest that God would come into our front-room just to prosecute the bookseller! I expected any moment a Visitation worse than the bookseller would ever experience from this unequal contest.

Tinu slipped away. The crowd in the front room were laughing at the bookseller who struggled furiously, especially with his voice. Their laughter made it all the more wicked. Essay scraped the cutlass along the concrete floor and advanced one step. The bookseller suddenly wriggled free, flung open the door and escaped. Yelling 'After him! Catch him' they all dispersed, remembering to fling back their thanks to Wild Christian for

23

the Sunday feast. I dashed through the dining-room and the backyard to our gate so I could watch the chase through the parsonage. It ended where the paths separated, one towards the bookseller's compound, the other to the parsonage gate through which the others would regain their own homes. Their laughter ran through the compound as they waved good-bye to one another. I did not appreciate their levity in the least, feeling too deeply thankful that Mrs B. would not have to cope with a one-armed husband in addition to that wilful *àbikú*.

II

Every morning before I woke up, Tinu was gone. She returned about midday carrying a slate with its marker attached to it. And she was dressed in the same khaki uniform as the hordes of children, of different sizes, who milled around the compound from morning till afternoon, occupied in a hundred ways.

At a set hour in the morning one of the bigger ones seized the chain which dangled from the bell-house, tugged at it with a motion which gave the appearance of a dance and the bell began pealing. Instantly, the various jostling, tumbling, racing and fighting pupils rushed in different directions around the school buildings, the smaller in size towards the schoolroom at the further end of the compound where I could no longer see them. The bigger pupils remained within sight, near the main building. They split into several groups, each group lined up under the watchful eye of a teacher. When all was orderly, I saw father appear from nowhere at the top of the steps. He made a speech to the assembly, then stood aside. One member of the very biggest group stepped forward and raised a song. The others took it up and they marched into the school-building in twos, to the rhythm of the song.

The song changed every day, chosen from the constant group of five or six. That I came to have a favourite among them was because this was the same one which they sang with more zest than others. I noticed that on the days when it was the turn of this tune, they danced rather than marched. Even the teachers seemed affected, they had an indulgent smile on their faces and would even point out a pupil who on a certain changed beat in the tune would dip his shoulders in a most curious way, yet march without breaking the rhythm. It was an unusual song too, since the main song was in English but the chorus was sung in Yoruba; I could only catch the words of the latter:

> B'ina njo ma je'ko
> B'ole nja, ma je'ko
> Eni ebi npa, omo wi ti're.*

* If the house is on fire, I must eat
  If the house is being robbed, I must eat
  The child who is hungry, let him speak.

25

I never heard any such lively singing from the other school, indeed that group simply vanished from sight, yet this was where my sister went. I never saw her anywhere among the marching group; in any case, there was nobody her size in that section. My curiosity grew every day. She sensed this and played on it, refusing to answer my questions or else throwing off incomplete fragments which only fed my curiosity.

'I am going to school,' I announced one day. It became a joke to be passed from mouth to mouth, producing instant guffaws. Mother appeasingly said, 'Wait till you are as old as your sister.'

The hum of voices, once the pupils were within the buildings, took mysterious overtones. Through the open windows of the schoolroom I saw heads in concentration, the majestic figure of a teacher who passed in and out of vision, mumbling incantations over the heads of his attentive audience. Different chants broke out from different parts of each building, sometimes there was even direct singing, accompanied by a harmonium. When the indoor rites were over, they came out in different groups, played games, ran races, they spread over the compound picking up litter, sweeping the paths, clipping lawns and weeding flower-beds. They roamed about with hoes, cutlasses, brooms and sticks, retired into open workshop sheds where they wove baskets, carved bits of wood and bamboo, kneaded clay and transformed them into odd-shaped objects.

Under the anxious eyes of 'Auntie' Lawanle, I played by myself on the pavement of our house and observed these varied activities. The tools of the open air were again transformed into books, exercise books, slates, books under armpits, in little tin or wooden boxes, books in raffia bags, tied together with string and carried on the head, slung over shoulders in cloth pouches. Directly in front of our home was the lawn which was used exclusively by girls from the other school. They formed circles, chased one another in and out of the circles, struggled for a ball and tossed it through an iron hoop stuck on a board. Then they also vanished into classrooms, books were produced and they commenced their own observances of the mystery rites.

Tinu became even more smug. My erstwhile playmate had entered a new world and, though we still played together, she now had a new terrain to draw upon. Every morning she was woken earlier than I, scrubbed, fed and led to school by one of the older children of the house. My toys and games soon palled but the laughter still rankled, so I no longer demanded that I join Tinu in school.

Instead, I got up one morning as she was being woken up, demanded my bath at the same time, ate, selected the clothing which I thought came closest to the uniforms I had seen, and insisted on being dressed in them. I had marked down a number of books on father's table but did not yet remove them. I waited in the front room. When Tinu passed through with her escort, I let them leave the house, waited a few moments, then seized the books I had earlier selected and followed them. Both parents were still in the dining-room. I followed at a discreet distance, so I was not noticed until we arrived at the infant school. I waited at the door, watched where Tinu was seated, then went and climbed on to the bench beside her.

Only then did Lawanle, Tinu's escort that day, see me. She let out a cry of alarm and asked me what I thought I was doing. I ignored her. The teachers heard the commotion and came into the room. I appeared to be everybody's object of fun. They looked at me, pointed and they held their sides, rocked forwards and backwards with laughter. A man who appeared to be in charge of the infant section next came in, he was also our father's friend and came often to the house. I recognized him, and I was pleased that he was not laughing with the others. Instead he stood in front of me and asked,

'Have you come to keep your sister company?'

'No. I have come to school.'

Then he looked down at the books I had plucked from father's table.

'Aren't these your father's books?'

'Yes. I want to learn them.'

'But you are not old enough, Wole.'

'I am three years old.'

Lawanle cut in, 'Three years old *wo*? Don't mind him sir, he won't be three until July.'

'I am nearly three. Anyway, I have come to school. I have books.'

He turned to the class-teacher and said, 'Enter his name in the register.' He then turned to me and said, 'Of course you needn't come to school everyday – come only when you feel like it. You may wake up tomorrow morning and feel that you would prefer to play at home. . . .'

I looked at him in some astonishment. Not feel like coming to school! The coloured maps, pictures and other hangings on the walls, the coloured counters, markers, slates, inkwells in neat round holes, crayons and drawing-books, a shelf laden with modelled objects – animals, human beings, implements – raffia and basket-work in various stages of completion, even the blackboards, chalk and duster. . . . I had yet to see a more inviting playroom! In addition, I had made some vague, intuitive connection between school and the piles of books with which my father appeared to commune so religiously in the front room, and which had constantly to be snatched from me as soon as my hands grew long enough to reach them on the table.

'I shall come everyday,' I confidently declared.

Mr Olagbaju's bachelor house behind the school became a second lunch-hour home. His favourite food appeared to be the pounded yam, *iyan*, at which I soon became his keen accomplice. Through the same *iyan*, I made my first close school friend, Osiki, simply by discovering that he was an even more ardent lover of the pounded yam than either Mr Olagbaju or I. It seemed a simple matter of course that I should take him home or to Mr Olagbaju's whenever the meal was *iyan*; moreover, Mr Olagbaju was also teaching me to play *ayo*,* and this required a partner to play with. It was with some surprise that I heard my mother remark:

'This one is going to be like his father. He brings home friends at meal-times without any notice.'

I saw nothing to remark in it at all; it was the most natural thing in the world to bring a friend home at his favourite meal-time. So Osiki became an inseparable companion and a regular feature of the house, especially on *iyan* days. One of the house helps composed a song on him:

> Osiki oko oniyan
> A ti nwa e, a ko ri e†

which she began singing as soon as we appeared, hand in hand, on the path leading from the school. But the pounded yam was also to provide the first test of our friendship.

There were far too many aspects of the schoolroom and the compound to absorb in the regular school hours, moreover, an empty schoolroom appeared to acquire a totally different character which changed from day to day. And so, new discoveries began to keep me behind at lunch-time after everyone had gone. I began to stay longer and longer, pausing over objects which became endowed with new meanings, forms, even dimensions as soon as silence descended on their environment. Sometimes I simply wandered off among the rocks intending merely to climb a challenging surface when no one was around. Finally, Osiki lost patience. He would usually wait for me at home even while Tinu had her own food. On this day however, being perhaps more hungry than usual, Osiki decided not to wait. Afterwards he tried to explain that he had only meant

---

* A game played on a wooden board with dug-out holes, and seeds.
† Osiki, lord of the pounded-yam seller
  We have sought you everywhere but failed to find you.

28

to eat half of the food but had been unable to stop himself. I returned home to encounter empty dishes and was just in time to see Osiki disappearing behind the croton bush in the backyard, meaning no doubt to escape through the rear gate. I rushed through the parlour and the front room, empty dishes in hand, hid behind the door until he came past, then pelted him with the dishes. A chase followed, with Osiki instantly in front by almost the full length of the school compound while I followed doggedly, inconsolable at the sight of the increasing gap, yet unable to make my legs emulate Osiki's pace.

Finally, I stopped. I no longer saw Osiki but – Speed, Swiftness! I had not given any thought before then to the phenomenon of human swiftness and Osiki's passage through the compound seemed little short of the magical. The effect of his *dansiki* which flowed like wings from his sides also added to the illusion of him flying over the ground. This, more than anything else, made it easy enough for the quarrel to be settled by my mother. It was very difficult to cut oneself off from a school friend who could fly at will from one end of the compound to the other. Even so, some weeks elapsed before he returned to the pounded-yam table, only to follow up his perfidy by putting me out of school for the first time in my career.

There was a birthday party for one of the Canon's children. Only the children of the parsonage were expected but I passed the secret to Osiki and he turned up at the party in his best *buba*. The entertainments had been set up out of doors in front of the house. I noticed that one of the benches was not properly placed, so that it acted like a see-saw when we sat on it close to the two ends. It was an obvious idea for a game, so, with the help of some of the other children, we carried it to an even more uneven ground, rested its middle leg on a low rock outcrop and turned it into a proper see-saw. We all took turns to ride on it.

For a long time it all went without mishap. Then Osiki got carried away. He was a bigger boy than I, so that I had to exert a lot of energy to raise him up, lifting myself on both hands and landing with all possible weight on my seat. Suddenly, while he was up in his turn, it entered his head to do the same. The result was that I was catapulted up very sharply while he landed with such force that the leg of the bench broke on his side. I was flung in the air, sailed over his head and saw, for one long moment, the Canon's square residence rushing out to meet me.

It was only after I had landed that I took much notice of what I had worn to the party. It was a yellow silk *dansiki*, and I now saw with some surprise that it had turned a bright crimson, though not yet entirely. But the remaining yellow was rapidly taking on the new colour. My hair on the left side was matted with blood and dirt and, just before the afternoon was shut out and I fell asleep, I wondered if it was going to be possible to squeeze the blood out of the *dansiki* and pump it back through the gash which I had located beneath my hair.

The house was still and quiet when I woke up. One moment there had been the noise, the shouts and laughter and the bumpy ride of the see-saw, now silence and semi-darkness and the familiar walls of mother's bedroom. Despite mishaps, I reflected that there was something to be said for birthdays and began to look forward to mine. My only worry now was whether I would have recovered sufficiently to go to school and invite all my friends. Sending Tinu seemed a risky business, she might choose to invite all her friends and pack my birthday with girls I hardly even knew or played with. Then there was another worry. I had noticed that some of the pupils had been kept back in my earlier class and were still going through the same lessons as we had all learnt during my first year in school. I developed a fear that if I remained too long at home, I would also be sent back to join them. When I thought again of all the blood I had lost, it seemed to me that I might actually be bed-ridden for the rest of the year. Everything depended on whether or not the blood on my *dansiki* had been saved up and restored to my head. I raised it now and turned towards the mirror; it was difficult to tell because of the heavy bandage but I felt quite certain that my head had not shrunk to any alarming degree.

The bedroom door opened and mother peeped in. Seeing me awake she entered, and was followed in by father. When I asked for Osiki, she gave me a peculiar look and turned to say something to father. I was not too sure, but it sounded as if she wanted father to tell Osiki that killing me was not going to guarantee him my share of *iyan*. I studied their faces intently as they asked me how I felt, if I had a headache or a fever and if I would like some tea. Neither would touch on the crucial question, so finally I decided to put an end to my suspense. I asked them what they had done with my *dansiki*.

'It's going to be washed,' mother said, and began to crush a half-tablet in a spoon for me to take.

'What did you do with the blood?'

She stopped, they looked at each other. Father frowned a little and reached forward to place his hand on my forehead. I shook my head anxiously, ignoring the throb of pain this provoked.

'Have you washed it away?' I persisted.

Again they looked at each other. Mother seemed about to speak but fell silent as my father raised his hand and sat on the bed, close to my head. Keeping his eyes on me he drew out a long, 'No-o-o-o-o.'

I sank back in relief. 'Because, you see, you mustn't. It wouldn't matter if I had merely cut my hand or stubbed my toe or something like that – not much blood comes out when that happens. But I saw this one, it was too much. And it comes from my head. So you must squeeze it out and pump it back into my head. That way I can go back to school at once.'

My father nodded agreement, smiling. 'How did you know that was the right thing to do?'

I looked at him in some surprise, 'But everybody knows.'

Then he wagged his finger at me, 'Ah-ha, but what you don't know is that we have already done it. It's all back in there, while you were asleep. I used Dipo's feeding-bottle to pour it back.'

I was satisfied. 'I'll be ready for school tomorrow,' I announced.

I was kept home another three days. I resumed classes with my head still swathed in a bandage and proceeded to inform my favourite classmates that the next important event in the parsonage was going to be my birthday, still some months away. Birthdays were not new. I had shared one with Tinu the previous year and even little Dipo had had his first year of existence confirmed a few weeks before the fateful one at the Canon's house. But now, with the daily dressing of my head prolonging the aura of the last, the Birthday acquired a new status, a special and personal significance which I assumed was recognized by everyone. Indeed I thought that this was a routine knowledge into which one entered in the normal way of growing up. Understanding the functioning of the calendar became part of the order of birthdays and I dutifully watched Essay cancel one date after the other on the IBUKUN OLU STORES 1938 Almanac alias The Blessed Jacob, the alias of which was printed, for some reason, in a slanting form, rather like my father's handwriting.

All was ready on the thirteenth of July. I headed home after school with about a dozen of the favoured friends, led by Osiki. They all stacked their slates in the front room and took over the parlour. On the faces of the guests, everyone on his best behaviour, was a keen anticipation of food and drinks, of some music from the gramophone and games and excitement. Now that they were home, I became a little uncertain of my rôle as celebrant and host; still, I took my place among the others and awaited the parade of good things.

We had settled down for a while before I noticed the silence of the house. Essay was still at school, mother was obviously at her shop with Dipo who would probably be strapped to the back of Auntie Lawanle. But where were the others? Come to think of it I had expected mother to be home to welcome my friends even if she had to go back to the shop to attend to her customers. It occurred to me also that Tinu had not come home at all, perhaps she went straight to the shop – she was considered old enough by now to do this on her own. That looked promising; any moment now I expected our mother to rush through the doors, making up for the delay with all sorts of unexpected delights.

I went out to the backyard, expecting to find at least one of our cousins or detect signs of preparations for the Birthday. There was nobody. The kitchen was empty and there was no aroma from recent cooking. I called out, announcing that I was home with guests and where was everybody? Really puzzled now, I returned to the dining-room, inspected the cupboards, the table – beyond the usual items there was nothing at all, no jars of *chin-chin*, no *akara*, no glasses or mugs obviously set aside, no pancakes, jollof rice . . . there was simply nothing out of the ordinary. This was not how Birthdays normally behaved but, there did not seem to be any cause for alarm. I checked the date on Ibukun Olu Stores once more, satisfied myself that there was no mistake, then settled down with my guests to wait for Birthday to happen.

My mother rushed in not long afterwards, Dipo strapped to her back, Auntie Lawanle and others following, carrying the usual assorted items which accompanied them to the shop every morning. This was impressive because it meant that the shop had been closed for the day and it was still early afternoon – obviously Birthday was really about to happen in earnest. But she came in shaking her head and casting up her eyes in a rather strange manner. She stopped in the parlour, took a long look at my friends, looked at me again, shook her head repeatedly and passed through to the kitchen from where I heard her giving rapid orders to the welcome ring of pots and pans and the creak of the kitchen door. I nodded with satisfaction to the guests and assured them.

'The Birthday is beginning to come.'

A moment later Tinu came in to say I was wanted by mother in the kitchen. I found her with her arms elbow deep in flour which she was kneading as if possessed. Without taking her eye off the dough she began,

'Now Wole, tell me, what have your friends come for?'

It was a strange question but I replied, 'We've come to eat Birthday.'

'You came to eat Birthday,' she repeated. For some reason, Lawanle and the others had already burst out laughing. Mother continued, 'Do you realize that you and your friends would still be sitting in that parlour, waiting to "eat your birthday" if Tinu hadn't come and told me?'

'But today is my birthday,' I pointed out to her.

Patiently she explained, 'No one is denying that. I had planned to cook something special tonight but . . . look, you just don't invite people home without letting us know. How was I to know you were bringing friends? Now look at us rushing around, your friends have been sitting there, nearly starving to death, and you say you've brought them to eat birthday. You see, you have to let people know. . . .'

The Birthday proved to be all that was expected once it had got over the one disappointing limitation – Birthday did not just happen but needed to be reminded to happen. That aspect of its character bothered me for a while, it was a shortcoming for which I tried to find excuses, without success. The Birthday lost a lot in stature after this, almost as if it had slid down from the raised end of that fateful see-saw to the lower end and landed in a heap, among other humdrum incidents in the parsonage. Still, it had added the calendar to my repertoire of knowledge. When it came to my turn to entertain the gathering, I sang:

> Ogbon'jo ni September
> April, June ati November
> February ni meji din l'ogbon
> Awon iyoku le okan l'ogbon.

The others took it up, Osiki supplying a ko-ko-ti-ko-ko . . . ko-ko-ti-ko-ko beat on the table so fluently that my mother asked him jokingly if he had been drumming for the masqueraders. To everybody's surprise he said, Yes. Their *agbole*,* he revealed, even possessed its own mask which paraded the town with others at the yearly festival of the *egúngún*. When Osiki promised to lead their *egúngún* on a visit to our house at the next festival, I could not help feeling that the Birthday had more than made up for its earlier shortcoming. I had watched them before over the wall of the backyard, seated on Joseph's shoulders. I knew that the *egúngún* were spirits of the dead. They spoke in guttural voices and were to be feared even more than kidnappers. And yet I had noticed that many of them were also playful and would joke with children. I had very nearly been startled off Joseph's shoulders once when one of them passed directly beneath the wall, looked up and waved, calling out in the familiar throaty manner,

'Nle o, omo Tisa Agba.'†

But Joseph explained that it was only natural that the dead should know

* Family compound.
† Greetings, son of the Senior Teacher.

all about the living ones. After all, they once lived like us and that friendly one might even have been in the compound before. Now, discovering that Osiki had an *egúngún* which emerged from their compound every year was almost the same as if we also had one of our own. We crowded round him and I asked if he knew which of his dead ancestors it was.

He shook his head. 'I only know it is one of our ancient people.'

'Are you actually there when he emerges from the bottom of the earth?'

He nodded yes. 'Any of us can watch. As long as you are male of course. Women mustn't come near.'

'Then you must come and call me the next time,' I said. 'I want to watch.'

'You want to what?' It was mother, her voice raised in alarm. 'Did I hear you say you want to go and watch *egúngún* in his compound?'

'Osiki will take me,' I said.

'Osiki is taking you nowhere. Better not even let your father hear you.'

'Why not?' I said, 'he can come too. Osiki, we can take him can't we? He is not like Mama, he is a man too.'

My mother gave a sigh, shook her head and left us to listen to Osiki's tales of the different kinds of *egúngún*, the dangerous ones with bad charms who could strike a man with epilepsy and worse, the violent ones who had to be restrained with powerful ropes, the *opidan* with their magical tricks. They would transform themselves into alligators, snakes, tigers and rams and turn back again into *egúngún*. Then there were the acrobats – I had seen those myself over the wall, performing in a circle of spectators near the cenotaph. They did forward and backward somersaults, doubled up their limbs in the strangest manner, squeezed their lower trunks into mortars and then bounced up and down in the mortar along short distances as if they were doing a mortar race. Apart from Giro, the crippled contortionist to whose performance we had once been taken in the palace compound, only these *egúngún* appeared to be able to tie up their limbs in any manner they pleased.

'Can I come back as an *egúngún* if I die?' I asked Osiki.

'I don't think so,' he said. 'I've never heard of any Christian becoming an *egúngún*.'

'Do they speak English in the *egúngún* world?' I now wanted to know.

Osiki shrugged. 'I don't know. Our own *egúngún* doesn't speak English.'

It seemed important to find out. The stained-glass windows behind the altar of St Peter's church displayed the figures of three white men, dressed in robes which were very clearly *egúngún* robes. Their faces were exposed, which was very unlike our own *egúngún*, but I felt that this was something

34

peculiar to the country from which those white people came. After all, Osiki had explained that there were many different kinds of *egúngún*. I sought his opinion on the three figures only to have Tinu interrupt.

'They are not *egúngún*,' she said, 'those are pictures of two missionaries and one of St Peter himself.'

'Then why are they wearing dresses like *egúngún*?'

'They are Christians, not masqueraders. Just let Mama hear you.'

'They are dead, aren't they; they've become *egúngún*, that is why they are wearing those robes. Let's ask Osiki.'

Osiki continued to look uncertain. 'I still haven't heard of any Christian becoming *egúngún*. I've never heard of it.' Then he suddenly brightened. 'Wait a minute, I've just remembered. My father told me that some years ago, they carried the *egúngún* of an *ajele*, you know, the District Officer who was here before.'

I rounded on Tinu triumphantly. 'You see. Now I can speak to those *egúngún* in the church window whenever they come. I am sure they only speak English.'

'You don't know what you are talking about. You are just a child.' She turned scornfully away and left us alone.

'Don't mind her,' I told Osiki. 'She knows I've always liked the one in the middle, the St Peter. I've told her before that he is my special *egúngún*. If I come first to your compound, perhaps we can go next to the church cemetery and make him come out of the ground in the same way.'

'With his face bared like that?' Osiki sounded scandalized.

'Of course not,' I assured him. 'That is only his picture. When he comes out of the ground he will be properly dressed. And I'll be able to talk to him.'

Osiki looked troubled. 'I don't know. I don't really know if he will be a real *egúngún*.'

'But you've just said that the *egúngún* of the District Officer came out in procession before.'

'It is not the same thing. . . .' Osiki tried to explain, but finally admitted that he did not really understand. Somehow, it was not going to be possible but, why it should be that way, he didn't know. I reminded him that the District Officer was both white and Christian, that St Peter's had the advantage because he was near a cemetery. In addition, anyone with eyes could see that he was already in his *egúngún* robes, which meant that he had joined in such festivals before. Osiki continued to be undecided, to my intense disappointment. Without his experience, I did not even know how to begin to bring out *egúngún* St Peter without whom,

35

from then on, the parade of ancestral masquerades at Aké would always seem incomplete.

When I again lay bleeding on the lawns of the infant school, barely a year later, I tried to see myself as a one-eyed masquerade, led by Osiki along the paths of the parsonage to visit my old home and surprise Tinu and Dipo by calling out their names. The accident occurred during a grass-cutting session by the bigger boys. The rest of us simply played around the school grounds or went home for the rest of the day. Osiki should have been cutting grass with the others but he had become my unofficial guardian, taking me home or to Mr Olagbaju's house after school or fetching me from home, as if I had not walked to school all by myself nearly two years before. On that afternoon we were playing together, he chasing me round and round the infant school building. I was already developing a sense of speed, nothing to match his, but could dodge faster than he could turn whenever his arms reached out to grab me. I had just rounded the corner of the schoolroom when I saw, through the corner of my eye, the upward flash of a blade. Beneath it was a crouching form, its back turned towards me. That was all I had time to see. The next instant I felt the blade bite deep into the corner of my eye, the day was blotted out in a flush of redness and I collapsed forward on my face, blinded. I heard screams from everywhere. When I rolled over and put my hands to my face they were instantly drenched in the same warm thick flood which had accompanied my somersault in the Canon's garden.

I lay still, unaware of any pain. My only thought was that if I did not remain like that, on my back, my eye would fall out on to the ground. Then I thought perhaps I would actually die this time; since I had obviously lost an eye, I tried to recall if I had ever seen a one-eyed masquerade among the *egúngún* whom we watched over the wall. There were sounds of heavier feet running towards me. I recognized the voices of teachers, felt myself raised up and carried into the schoolroom, then laid on a table. I heard Mr Olagbaju send someone to fetch my father.

Through the noise and confusion I gathered that I had run straight into the upward stroke of a cutlass wielded by a pupil who was busy cutting grass, his back turned to me. I heard the confused boy calling on God to save him from the stigma of becoming a murderer in his lifetime. One of the teachers told him to shut up and eventually pushed him out. When I heard my father's voice, it occurred to me to open the undamaged eye – I had not, until then, acted on the fact that I was only hit in one eye, not both. Wiping the blood from the left eye, I blinked it open. Standing round the table was a semi-circle of teachers, looking at me as if I was

36

already a masquerade, the *opidan* type, about to transform himself into something else. I touched myself to ensure that this had not already happened, so strangely watchful were all the pairs of eyes.

'How did it happen?' my father demanded even as he examined the wound. A babble of voices rose in explanation.

I asked him, 'Am I blind?'

Everyone shouted at once, 'Keep still, Wole. Don't move!'

I repeated my question, feeling now that I was not dying but wondering if I would be obliged to become a beggar like those blind men who sometimes came into the parsonage, led by a small child, sometimes no bigger than I. It occurred to me then that I had never seen a small child leading a blind child.

Someone asked, 'Where is that Osiki?'

But Osiki was gone. Osiki, when I was struck down, had simply continued running in the direction which he was facing at the time. He ran, I was sure, at a speed which surpassed even his usual phenomenal swiftness. Some of the bigger boys had tried to catch him – why, I did not know – but Osiki outstripped them running lean and light in the wind. I could see him, and the sight brought a smile to my face. It also made me open the injured eye and, to my surprise, I could see with it. There were loud gasps from the anxious faces who now crowded closer to see for themselves. The skin was split right into the corner of the eye but the eyeball itself was unscathed. Even the bleeding appeared to have stopped. I heard one teacher breathe 'Impossible!' while another shouted, 'Olorun ku ise!'* My father simply stood back and stared, his mouth agape in disbelief.

And then I felt very tired, a mist appeared to cover my eyes, and I fell asleep.

* God's work be praised!

III

I could not climb the ladder by myself, but I already knew where it was. Simply by following the rush of feet, I knew where to go whenever the sounds from an event carried into the house of Aké. It was an iron ladder and sometimes four or five of the household would stand on it at once gazing out, throwing off comments on the event. They ignored my efforts to come on the ladder with them, claiming it was dangerous.

Then one day Joseph relented and hoisted me up on his shoulders and I obtained my first look over the wall of our yard. I followed the group of dancers from the road which went past the cenotaph, behind the church, then disappeared in the direction, Joseph said, of the palace. I had recognized the church and the cenotaph. I had also recognized another feature of the landscape, and this was the large gate of the parsonage itself. I understood then that the outer walls of the parsonage were joined continuously, giving way in places to gates or windows. Seated on Joseph's shoulder, I traced the wall against which our bodies were pressed leftwards, saw it melt into the wall of the storeroom where the pots – both for cooking and for father's gardening – were kept, then vanish into the wall of the barn for firewood and chicken, after which it became the wall of a small recess which served as father's garden nursery, then the wall of the bathroom, and finally the kitchen. From there it moved to encase the catechist's compound, wrapped round the rest of his house, then changed back into a plain wall until it was broken into by the parsonage gate. It then ran into the wall of the lower Girls' School before sheering off at the corner into the frontage of the bookshop, the only building in the parsonage which faced outwards on to the street.

Along the way, there were a few windows here and there, token ventilations, set high in the wall, almost against the iron sheet roof. Mostly however, the walls ran smoothly, varied in places by overflowing banana leaves, guava, or the bitter-leaf plant such as the luxuriant one whose leaves brushed my face at that moment. It became clear then that we in the parsonage were living in a separate town by ourselves, and that Aké was the rest of what I could see. That other town, Aké, was linked by rusted roofs just as ours was joined by walls. Only special buildings like the church or the cenotaph stood by themselves. Everything else was joined in one continuous seam.

And so the next time that the sounds came, I did not bother to contest a place on the ladder, which I could not climb anyway. I had recognized now where that gate was, through which I passed on the way to church, clutching Lawanle's, Joseph's or Mama's hand. I had realized also that one would obtain a much clearer view simply by going outside the gates and watching from there. On reaching the gate, I was surprised to find it latched; it was even more annoying that I could not reach the wooden peg which would release the latch. Then I heard excited voices on the outside, obviously there were others before me who had the same idea. I banged on the gate and someone opened it.

They were all strangers. I had seen none of the faces before. I wondered if they were passers-by who had climbed the steps leading up to the gate for an even clearer view. I thought they looked at me in some rather uncertain way, but they made way for me to come to the front and we ignored each other's presence at the sight of the police band, the cause of the excitement. They had on bright sashes, bright red fez caps with dangling tassels and what looked like embroidered waistcoats. The drum which was strapped to the man in front was unbelievable in its size; at every step I expected him to topple over, but he pounded its white skin with complete mastery, his gaze set rigidly to the front. His arms made flourishes in the air, giving the heavy-ended drumsticks a twirl, then dashing them against the sides. The man in the lead juggled an enormous mace, threw it in the air, spun around and caught it as it descended. Once, he even caught it backwards, earning a roar from the crowd. A gleaming brass funnel rose between the players; the face which blew into it looked as if it would burst. It gave off notes which were nearly as deep as the big drum but the strain on the player's face far exceeded that of the drummers.

I had a strange sensation. Each time the big drum was hit, it seemed that the vibrations entered my stomach, echoed around its walls, then went out again to re-join the drum. I listened and *felt* each time the *boom* came and I was left in no doubt about it; obviously it was the way of the big drum. I had no doubt that it affected everyone in the same way. I noticed little boys following the band, some walked directly behind, imitating the march of the policemen, others walked alongside, at the extreme edges of the road. They seemed not much bigger than I, and I soon joined them. Unlike the strangers at the gate, none of them seemed to notice me. I stayed with the group at the back, taking care however not to mimic the swagger of the others. It did not seem a decorous thing to do and the policemen looked stern enough to take offence.

We marched past the bookshop and I felt vindicated. The frontage was exactly where I had gauged it while seated on Joseph's shoulder. But then the curious thing happened; after the bookseller's, the wall rolled away into a different area I had never seen before. Soon it moved away altogether, was covered up by houses and shops and disappeared for ever. It upset my previous understanding of the close relationship between the parsonage and Aké. I expected the wall to be everywhere; by now I should have been on the outside of the walls of the school playing-fields, the roof of the primary school should be visible, then the infant, the corn-field of the school farms and perhaps the cemetery. None of this happened. Instead there were shops and storey-buildings. And there were inscriptions everywhere: AKINS PHOTO STUDIO: LONDON-TRAINED PORTRAITIST, then, in smaller letters: A Trial Will Convince You. Photos lined the two halves of the open door of the studio, while the photographer himself sat outside on a bench with crossed legs, a scarf around his neck, smoking a pipe. I recognized him because he had been in our house before to take photographs of Dipo when he was born. I thought that photographers did all their work in people's homes and was surprised to discover that they also ran their own shops.

I made a note to start learning how to ride a bicycle as we marched past a bicycle hirer, busy mending a tube. A learner whose feet barely touched the pedals was just taking off, supported by a teacher who was no bigger but who appeared very full of instructions. The parsonage wall had vanished for ever but it no longer mattered. Those token bits and pieces of Aké which had entered our home on occasions, or which gave off hints of their nature in those Sunday encounters at church, were beginning to emerge in their proper shapes and sizes.

Every week, sometimes more often, Lawanle or Joseph would go off with a large basin of corn and return with it crushed, a layer of water over it. Then would begin a series of operations with calabashes, strainers, baskets and huge pots. It ended with those pots being placed in a dark corner of the kitchen, covered. As the days passed they would give off an ever ripening smell of fermentation. A week would pass and after several tests, tasting and sniffing, one pot would emerge from the darkness, and from it was scooped the smooth white paste which in turn was stirred in hot water to provide the morning *ogi*, a neutral mixture which everyone seemed to enjoy but I. The *akara* which went with it, the *jogi*, *moinmoin* or *leki** was a different matter. My mouth was watering even as I thought of

* Delicacies made from black-eyed beans.

it. But I could not understand how *ogi*, which took so much mysterious labour, could appeal to any taste.

Now I saw that the labour involved was even much greater than I knew, which only made matters worse for *ogi*, in my estimate of its pretensions. We were passing by a small shop in which a machine whirled, propelling a belt with enough noise to match the music of the police band. A cluster of women waited by the door with their corn-filled basins and I realized that this was where Joseph or Lawanle came on those weekly excursions. There was a basin placed under a wide funnel which opened downwards. Suddenly the whitish mixture was flushed through into the basin, of the same coarse mix that Lawanle would bring home. Then they would all commence the task of refining it and leaving it for some days to settle. Mother loved the *'omi'kan*, the sour, fermented liquid which formed at the top after its period of rest. It had some curative powers, she claimed, a suggestion which I found unappealing. Medicine and food led separate lives and should never be mixed up.

The starched, cowled, white lady who visited us sometimes with bags of lozenges apparently also lived in a compound. For there, boldly etched on the gates in a stone-fenced wall were the words: Miss McCutter's Maternity Clinic. This was the first word that day to give me any trouble. We knew her simply as Miss Makota, and there had been no previous hint that her name might be spelt differently. Nevertheless the 'Maternity Clinic' left me in no doubt that this was where the lady lived. I wondered if I should surprise her with a visit, but decided against it, fearful that I might not be able to catch up with the band.

Once or twice I did wonder if I was not being carried too far from home. There was however the reassurance that one part of my observation about the town remained intact – the houses remained linked together. We encountered more and more houses which stood on their own, like the church and the cenotaph, but they continued to be linked, if not along the roofs, then by the fences which surrounded them. At one point or the other, they touched. Why this should prove so reassuring, I did not know, but I continued to feel much at home with every step.

We came on the police station not far from McCutter's and I expected the band to stop there. They did not even glance in the direction of the station but marched straight past, trumpets blaring and the trombones flashing in the sun. The composition of the group of children around me appeared to change all the time. Suddenly one face or group disappeared, only to be replaced by a new crop which surfaced along the way, as if by pre-arrangement. It crossed my mind that I was perhaps depriving someone of his place in the procession by remaining, but no one said anything; on the contrary every face appeared wrapped up in the music, the marching, in simply enjoying themselves. I marched along with the rest.

Near the first road-junction we came to yet another sign over which I pored. It read: MRS T. BANJOKO. LONDON-TRAINED SEWING MISTRESS. I looked for 'A Trial Will Convince You' in vain. In its place was an invitation to 'Enquire Within for the Proprietress, Banjoko Sewing Academy'. It seemed unnecessary to enquire 'within', since the sewing school was taking place right before us, on the pavement. The girls all wore uniforms of blue, shapeless dresses which made me think that the first task of the pupils was to sew their own dresses before they learnt how. Mama made dresses for us, and I could not remember seeing anything so shapeless on Tinu. The lady who sat at the machine appeared to fit the role of the proprietress, at whose meaning I could only guess. I had not encountered such a difficult word before and I made a note to ask my father how it differed from the simpler one of a school-mistress.

There were quite a number of them. The proprietress had her back stolidly turned on the passing excitement and the girls sensed that they were obliged to do the same. Just the same, I caught them all, without exception, dart excited glances towards the road. Their obedient faces flashed a momentary conspiracy with the band of us marching behind and beside the column, I felt I was lifted in the air, secretively bonded to those poor slaves of the sewing machine. The termagant at the instruction desk knew nothing of our furtive contacts; I knew however that she must have sensed a loss of attention because she turned round, appeared to see the procession for the first time, then rounded on her pupils in a manner which was clearly angry and reprimanding. The girls clustered together, giggling but attentive. One, who had giggled the most, waved her hand at us behind her back and most of us waved back, some of the bolder even shouting a greeting or a mild abuse at the tyrant who would not let them join the troupe. The band remained impervious to the goings-on around them and behind their back. They blew and drummed stolidly ahead, the brass cymbals flashed and clashed, sweat covered the unfortunate one who was encased in the fat network of tubes which curved skywards and opened flat-lipped and wide-mouthed over the player's shoulder.

I knew now where I had encountered such a funnel. It was the same as the picture on our gramophone into which a dog barked, below which was written: HIS MASTER'S VOICE. Tinu and I had long rejected the story that the music which came from the gramophone was made by a special singing dog locked in the machine. We never saw it fed, so it would have long starved to death. I had not yet found a means of opening up the machine, so the mystery remained.

At the road-junction one arm of the signpost read: To LAFENWA; the other – IGBEIN, IBARA. The procession followed the latter. There was a market before we got to Ibara. There, women were waiting by the road, more were flocking from their stalls by the time we got there. Their stalls stretched endlessly from the right side of the road, goods piled up on low stools or on specially laid trestles. I hesitated; it did not seem possible that there was so much *thing* in the world! I moved to the side of the band so that I could see beyond them – there were no crossroads in sight and anyway, I reasoned that if I did not stay too long in the market, I could find my way back to the procession by the sound. I turned into the market, wide-eyed. Peppers of all shapes and sizes rose in profusion from wooden and enamel trays. There were mounds of gari which beggared those cupfuls that were brought out at cooking-time to be turned to *eba* in hot water. The earthy smell of yam powder assailed my nostrils long before I came on it, piled high in calabash trays. And SALT! Nobody surely, not even the whole of Aké could eat so much salt in a hundred years, yet I came on the piles stall after stall. It gave way to a variety of tubers, vegetables, dried fish and crayfish, then the stalls of meat with men flashing long, two-edged knives among slabs of meat, brushing away flies with one hand or hitting a small boy on the head for dozing off while flies landed on the meat. The butcher was as magical in his own field as the policeman who performed the juggling with the mace. Each moment he looked as if he would cut his fingers but no, the knife flashed just between two fingers and down on the table landed two neatly sliced pieces of meat.

It seemed a long time before the foods stopped altogether, giving way to clothes, sewing materials, toys, even small bookstalls with pens, rubbers, inkwells and notebooks neatly laid out.

And then I came to a sudden stop and backed away. Staring me in the eye was a shrunken head of an animal, dangling from a low wooden shelf beneath a stall. Only then did I notice that it was still attached to the body. It had been dried and preserved. And there were more. My eyes continued along the shelf, dropped to the trestle-table below and encountered skulls, just the plain, whitened skull, without any skin or flesh, large empty sockets and holes for noses. And there were dried barks, leaves. It was the strangest line of stalls in the entire market, with its assortment of stones, beads, pieces of iron, coloured powders in little heaps, small parcels tied up in leaves, bottles filled with the strangest liquids, and barks and leaves visible within the bottles. There were also the dried snakes and mice. The women were much older in these stalls, they sat impassively, obviously unmoved by the music of the band which had driven the younger ones on to the street. From time to time, a wizened hand rose from the dark interior of the stalls, fly-whisk in hand, and described in a slow circle through the stall. I experienced shock at their flat, emptied breasts and remembered suddenly that it was wrong to stare. I looked away.

Were these the witches we heard so much about? No breast that I had seen before had appeared so flat, it did not seem human. Yet when I looked in the trays again I recognized barks and roots similar to those which were bought by father, stuffed into bottles and jars where they were left to soak for days. They were given to us for some ailments. Some we simply drank at periods mysteriously communicated to either parent. And there were other barks bred in huge pots. Once, after a fever, I broke out in a rash. I remembered being washed every day with the contents from such pots. The herbs and roots were brought home in baskets, boiled and allowed to cool, I was scrubbed in them, given pungent liquids from other stuffed jars to drink, and put to bed. Or there were pills from Miss McCutter's, Oke Padi or some other place, and teaspoonfuls of unpleasant fluids from neatly labelled bottles. Often both forms of remedies were administered together, or took turns from day to day. It did not seem to matter if one was ill or not, we always had to take something or the other, only the intervals varied. I was not reassured by the appearance of these women who appeared every bit as crinkled as the herbs and roots on their trays. The potions seemed now to be fluids from their own bodies since I could not conceive of blood flowing in them, certainly not blood of the same colour as I saw when I cut my feet on a stone.

The nearest looked up suddenly at me and I returned her gaze. Then she smiled. If she hadn't, I may have asked her the questions which were racing through my mind. But her face, which did not look like the face of the living while it was at rest, suddenly turned into the face of the shrunken heads which dangled just above her head. I turned and fled, running all the way until I caught up with the band. My head was pounding more from fright than from the exertion, for the thought had occurred to me that there was no certainty whatsoever that the skulls were really the skulls of animals. They could have been the skulls of young children who had been foolish enough to wander too close to the witches' stalls. I reflected that I had never liked those potions we were made to drink anyway; now I had a good reason for refusing them.

44

To my surprise, the signpost that we next encountered also read, LAFENWA. It was at a cross-roads, not a fork like the last one. Two other hands read IGBEIN, IBARA, then LANTORO, while AKÉ pointed the way we had marched from. We had already passed the road to Lafenwa; I did not know what to make of such misleading signposting but it was something else to ask my father when I returned home.

It was only appropriate that the Ransome-Kuti should live in a school compound like my father. Kuti was a principal and I recognized from the sign ABEOKUTA GRAMMAR SCHOOL that we were passing the compound where he taught. I tried now to recollect how my father had explained the difference between Principal and Headmaster, but the only fact that remained with me was that I would go to the Grammar School after I had finished in St Peter's. Marching past the stone walls of the compound, I saw no reason why I should wait. The main building was set back into the compound and a wide path swept towards this stone mansion which stood on wide, arched pillars and was profusely covered in bougainvillaea like BishopsCourt of the parsonage. But it was far more imposing than that building, more imposing than BishopsCourt and Pa Delumo's own residence joined together. I pressed my face against the iron gates and wondered if I should not go in at once and resume my schooling there. Then I remembered it was a Saturday, so there would be no schooling. Monday however was a different matter, I would find my way back without difficulty.

As I rejoined the procession, however, I thought I now understood the difference between a principal and a headmaster. Only a principal could preside over a school as huge and imposing as the one which I had just seen. Still, I hoped that the fact that I was only the son of a headmaster would not prevent me from obtaining a place there; in any case the principal was a frequent guest at our house. Mother called him Uncle and we were encouraged to do the same. I preferred his other name, Daodu. It fitted the man's appearance, his deep voice and energetic gestures. He rode about on the only motorized bicycle I had ever seen, his agbada billowing on either side of him.

One day, he fell off, right near us, at Aké. If we had been peeping over the wall at the time we would have seen it happen. He was brought into our house where I heard someone explaining that his agbada had billowed out as usual until the sleeve was caught in the spokes of the wheel. They all disappeared into father's room while mother flew all over the house. Water was boiled, bandages and lints prepared but then a nurse arrived, disappeared into the room and came out again with my father.

'We must take him to the hospital. The burn at the thigh is quite bad.'

I heard father mutter something about the machine falling on top of him, so that the hot exhaust must have done the damage. The nurse said my father had done the right thing by smearing the injury in vaseline. The nurse left the house again, we were herded into the back of the house and the parlour door locked on us. There were heavy movements, doors opening and shutting, then silence. When we emerged, the patient had gone, father and mother with him. When Daodu emerged from hospital he bought a car and never rode on the motorped again. Koye, his first son whom we were told to call Cousin Koye because he was much older than Tinu and I, soon began to turn up on it at our house on errands or visits. Daodu's car, we learnt, was the third in the whole town. The first was owned by the Alake himself, another belonged to a wealthy Chief who lived in Itoku. Even the English District Officer did not appear to own one; he rode a motor-cycle or went on horseback.

I felt rather uplifted as I marched away from the Grammar School; I was going there, that was settled. But I also discovered that I liked the Kutis. Schooling under Daodu promised to be an adventure. This light-headed feeling helped me up the road towards Ibara which was so steep that my legs, for the first time, gave a hint of tiring. I had begun to think that I would have to sit down beside the road and rest when we came to yet another compound with neat rows of houses, small hut-like houses which were however built with concrete and roofed with iron sheets. The sergeant at the top of the column barked out an order and the band wheeled into the compound and entered. They marched straight towards the longest of these buildings, on to the grounds in front of it and re-grouped themselves to different orders from the sergeant. They were still in two lines, but now they stood shoulder to shoulder and marked time on one spot. I kept the same distance from them as I was when they began to line the grounds, indeed, I had slowed down when they entered the compound so that I was not really far from the gate. An order was given, the music stopped with a final drum-roll and a violent clash of cymbals. The air was very still.

And then I made a discovery. I was alone. The ragged, motley group of children who had followed, clowning, mimicking, even calling out orders had fallen off one by one. It occurred to me now that I had seen no one nor heard any of their festive voices for a while. They had all vanished, leaving no one but me. And then I made another discovery. In a matter-of-fact way, I realized that I did not know where I was.

The sergeant spun round on his heels, barked out some sentences in a

46

very strange language to somebody hidden within the building. That person now came out, smartly uniformed. The first thing that struck me about him was that he was albino. Then the next moment I realized that he was not an albino at all but a white man. Also that, unlike the marching policemen, he wore shoes. He was dressed simply in khaki, so I knew that he was also a policeman. His appearance however bore very little resemblance to that of the band. He stood on the steps of his office while the sergeant called out yet another order which made the lines stiffen up. Another was called and they appeared to relax. The sergeant then continued in the same language within which I succeeded in catching a few English words and name-places. He appeared to be 'reporting' something, the 'Oba's palace' was involved in it, and it all ended with 'all correct' and 'further orders'. The white man spoke a few words, the sergeant gave two more barks and the parade broke up and went their different ways, all except the sergeant. He stayed with the white officer and they spoke some more; it was during this dialogue that the white man looked up and saw me.

I was tired, I was sure of that now. The thought of running away at once when the man looked up, saw me, pointed and said something to the sergeant therefore remained just a thought. I had no idea in which direction to run. The sergeant also looked up, turned and began to march towards me. I probably would have run then, tiredness and all, but the white officer restrained him and came forward himself, the sergeant following close. Instinctively I backed one step towards the gate, but the man smiled, held out both hands in a gesture I did not quite understand, and approached. When he had come quite close, he bent down and, using the most unlikely accent I had ever heard asked,

'Kini o fe nibi yen?'*

I knew the words were supposed to be in my own language but they made no sense to me, so I looked at the sergeant helplessly and said,

'I don't understand. What is he saying?'

The officer's eyes opened wide. 'Oh, you speak English.'

I nodded.

'Good. That is venhrry clenver. I was asking, what do you want? What can I doon for you?'

'I want to go home.'

He exchanged looks with the sergeant. 'Well, that seems vum-vum-vum. And where is home?'

* Literally: what do you want there?

47

I could not understand why he should choose to speak through his nose. It made it difficult to understand him all the time but by straining hard, I could make sense of his questions. I told him that I lived in Aké.

'It has a big church,' I added, 'just outside our walls.'

'Ah-ah, near the church. Tell me, whaznname?' I guessed that he was asking what my name was, so I told him, 'My name is Wole.'

'Wonlay. Good. And your father's name?'

'My father's name is Headmaster.'

'What?'

'My father's name is Headmaster. Sometimes his name is Essay.'

For some reason this amused him immensely, which I found offensive. There was no reason why my father's names should be the cause for such laughter. But the sergeant had reacted differently. His eyes nearly popped out of his head. I noticed then that he was very different from the grownups whom I had seen around. He had long marks on his face, quite different from the usual kind we encountered in Aké. And when he spoke, his voice sounded like that of the Hausa traders who brought wares to our house for bartering with old clothes and strange assortments of items. It was a strange procedure, one which made little sense to me. They spread their wares in front of the house and I had to be prised off them. There were brass figures, horses, camels, trays, bowls, ornaments. Human figures spun on a podium, balanced by weights at the end of curved light metal rods. We spun them round and round, yet they never fell off their narrow perch. The smell of fresh leather filled the house as pouffes, handbags, slippers and worked scabbards were unpacked. There were bottles encased in leather, with leather stoppers, amulets on leather thongs, scrolls, glass beads, bottles of scent with exotic names – I never forgot, from the first moment I read it on the label – Bint el Sudan, with its picture of a turbanned warrior by a kneeling camel. A veiled maiden offered him a bowl of fruits. They looked unlike anything in the Orchard and Essay said they were called dates. I did not believe him; dates were the figures which appeared on a calendar on the wall, so I took it as one of his jokes.

Once or twice my father tried to offer money but the trader proved difficult. 'No, I can like to take changey-changey.' Out came old shirts, trousers, discarded jackets with holes under the armpit, yet Changey-changey – as we now called him – actually received these clothing derelicts in return for his genuine 'morocco' leather. 'Look'am master, a no be lie. Look, genuine morocco leather. 'E fit you, big man like you must have leather brief-case for carry file. 'E be genuine. Put 'am one more shirt. Or torosa.'

Their voices were so similar that they could only be brothers. I was even more convinced of it when I heard him say, 'If na headmaster of Aké be in father, I sabbe the place. But what 'im doing here?'

They both turned to me. I had no answer to the question. Then the white man asked, 'Are you lost?'

'I followed the band,' I replied.

The officer nodded sagely, as if everything had fallen in place. He turned to the sergeant and asked him to get his bicycle. The man saluted and went off. Something continued to puzzle the officer however. He put his hand on my shoulder and guided me towards the office.

'How old are you?'

'I am four years and a half.'

He let out a loud 'What!', stopped, and looked at me again. 'Are you sure?' I nodded. He looked at me more closely, said, 'Yes of course. Of course. And you walked from Aké? Where did you start from?'

'At the cenotaph. There were other children, but they left me.'

We reached his office and he lifted me on to a chair. 'Are you thirsty?' already producing a bottle of orange squash. There was a jar of water on the table and he mixed me a drink in a glass. I drank it to the last drop.

'Do you want another glass?' He did not wait for a reply before mixing another and handing it to me. It followed its predecessor just as rapidly. I began to feel better. I looked round the office for the first time, stretched my legs and took an interest in the papers on the table. I recognized a journal on it which came every week to my father. I looked at the man with greater interest.

'You are reading my father's paper.'

He looked startled. 'Which one?'

'That one. *In Leisure Hours*.'

'Really! You say it's your father's paper?'

'Yes. He has a new one every week.'

He opened it rapidly, looking for something on its pages. 'You mean he is the editor?'

I could not understand him. I repeated, 'He has it every week.'

And then the man grinned and nodded. 'I see, I see.'

I was feeling drowsy. The sergeant arrived with his bicycle. Half-awake, I felt myself lifted on to the cross-bar and the bumpy ride began. I barely sensed the arrival back home, hands lifting me up, passing me to other arms. My head appeared to weigh a ton when I tried to come awake and respond to the babble of voices I heard around me. I felt the immense expanse of the bed in mother's bedroom coming up to meet me, the room

49

easily recognized by the smell of *òri** - and-camphor. Then I dropped into oblivion.

I woke up in a hazy semi-darkness. A short while later, I realized where I was. I also felt a huge pit in my stomach and climbed down from the bed, heading for the kitchen to see what hour of meal it was. When I opened the door, a wave of human voices engulfed me. The entire front room was crowded with grown-ups and they all seemed to be speaking with excitement. So I turned and walked towards the sound. As I came through the parlour I pushed open the curtain in the intervening door and suddenly everything went silent. A hundred pairs of eyes were turned on me, and I wondered what the matter was. In the silence I spoke out the only thing on my mind:

'I am hungry.'

Mouths opened wide. Then the silence was broken by the bookseller's wife. She struck her palms together in a gesture of amazement and exclaimed, 'E-eh! Omo nla! Did you hear him? He is hungry.'

A babble of voices ensued, mostly echoing the bookseller's wife. I could not understand that there should be such excitement over the fact of my hunger. It looked like evening in any case, and I had not eaten all day. Then I heard my father's voice cutting in, and he appeared to be smiling.

'Well, it seems only natural that he should be hungry. Wouldn't you be, after a walk from Aké to Ibara?'

I heard someone say, 'Yes, but the way he said it!' before I was swept up by the bookseller's wife, and nearly smothered against her ample breasts. 'Give my child food!' she shouted. 'Mama, why are you starving him? My lord and husband says he is hungry and you haven't jumped to give him food. All right, I'll take him home and feed him.'

And before I knew what was happening, she had swung me on to her back, slipped her wrapper round to secure me tightly and was singing and dancing. And suddenly everyone was singing with her, laughing and shouting at the top of their voices. Only one person sat in her chair, seemingly unmoved by it all, this was mother, sitting with her chin rested on her palm, staring at me. From time to time she shook her head, sighed deeply and nodded to herself. Mrs Bookseller said,

'Look at her. I suppose she would still prefer him to be wandering through the wilds of Abeokuta. HM, please give me a stick. I think a dose of her favourite medicine will do her good.'

* Shea-butter.

Father laughed and said, 'Good idea. I'll get the stick.' He whipped it out from its corner by his chair and handed it to the bookseller's wife. The next moment, Mama was up and bounding through the parlour. Everybody seemed in such high spirits, it was strange to see grown-up men and women prancing through the house like the urchins who had marched to the music of the police band until they chose to abandon me. I never knew when the meal was set out at last because I had again fallen asleep on the back of the bookseller's wife. I woke up in her bed the following morning, light-headed and strangely exhilarated. At the back of my mind, even as I sat down to the biggest breakfast I had ever set eyes on, was a feeling that I had somehow been the cause of the excitement of the previous night and had, in some way, become markedly different from whatever I was before the march.

IV

I spluttered, grabbed Nubi's hand and fought for the sponge with all my strength. At first I had merely pushed her hand away, again and again, only to find her yet again suffocating me with water, soapsuds and gritty strands of fibre. Nubi would not yield. Now if it had been Joseph . . .

I wiped one eye free of soapsuds and found Nubi standing back, looking at me.

'Are you going to let me wash you or not?'

'Let me do the face myself.'

'You!' Her laughter was scornful. 'Put your hand over your head, let me see.'

I obeyed her. It appeared to be some kind of test. Perhaps if I passed she would leave my face alone.

'Right over. Like this.'

I placed my arm right over the top of my head, doing my best to follow her. Now her fingers were playing with the lobe of her left ear, she covered the ear completely, made it disappear in her palm.

'Now, do you see a difference?'

I asked, 'Am I not doing it right?'

More scornful laughter. 'Don't you notice any difference?'

'What am I not doing right?'

'It is not what you are not doing right. It is what you are not doing at all. Look at my hand. It reaches over my head and covers this ear completely. See? Now look at yours. It hardly reaches over the top of your head.'

It sounded very significant, but I could not see what she was getting at. I kept staring at her hand, and the ear that kept appearing and disappearing under it.

'That difference explains why I have to bathe you. If you think because they allowed you in school you are now a big boy in the house you still have a lot to learn. There are things they can't teach you in school. Now, come on.'

She advanced, sponge in hand. 'Joseph lets me do my face,' I persisted.

'Mama says I should bathe you, that is all I know. She didn't divide your body into bits, some for you and some for me.'

Her left hand now dipped the bowl into the bucket, scooped up the water and moved to douse my head. I ducked.

'Look at you! You are wasting water. You know what Mama is going to do to you when I tell her?'

I moved to the corner of the bathroom. Too late, I realized I was trapped.

Even so, I fought for my life. As the bowl looped over my head with its contents, I reached out and deflected it. Nubi was drenched and it seemed to make her angry.

'Now you see what you have done!' The movement was so fast, I had no time to protect my face. From out of nowhere a huge wad of moistness slammed into my face, traversing every pore rapidly but most especially blocking my nostrils.

Her fingers dug into my skull, pressing it down while she scrubbed my face without once letting in air. When I tried to bite I only got a mouthful of the sponge, so I did my desperate routine, let my knee buckle and, in that brief respite, butted her in the stomach. I heard her scream. 'O pa mi o'* and the next moment there were cries of 'Tani yen?'* from all over the house.

'Tani lo' gun nbe yen? Tani?'* And then there were running feet.

Hastily wiping off soapsuds with both hands, I blinked my eyes open and saw Wild Christian framed against the opening. She shook her head from side to side, baffled as always. Now I was really scared that she was going to take over.

'She has finished,' I said. 'I've had my bath.'

'He butted me with his head,' Nubi complained, clutching her stomach.

'Stop exaggerating,' Mama snapped.

'Yes, Ma.' And Nubi straightened up at once.

'Screaming down the whole house. Are you trying to scare everybody?'

'No, Ma. But he wouldn't let me scrub his face.'

'You've scrubbed it,' I reminded everyone at large. 'You've done nothing but scrub it since I came to have my bath. You've nearly scrubbed it to death, what more do you want to scrub? Tinu is still waiting for her bath.'

---

* Murder!
  Who is that?
  Who screamed just now? Who?

53

Suddenly I felt secure; there was a smile on Wild Christian's face. She said to Nubi, 'All right, call Tinu. In any case they are both old enough to start bathing themselves now.'

'Yes, yes. I've said it before. I don't need her or Joseph.'

'But you must bathe in their presence, so they can make sure you do a proper job.'

I nodded. It seemed a little enough concession to make. Just the same, I added, 'I don't really need them. In fact I have scrubbed myself before when Joseph was too busy. Joseph inspects me afterwards and he says I am quite clean.'

'All right then. Although I can never understand how you come to be so afraid of water, you, a July-born.'

I was now rinsing off the rest of the soap. 'But I am not afraid of water,' I protested.

'No? Just look at the way you are rinsing yourself. There is soap all over your face but you haven't even touched it.'

I quickly threw the next bowlful over my head. As usual, something went wrong. It usually did when water was cast over my head or face. The next moment I was spluttering and fisting the stinging rivulets off my face, fighting for breath.

Even through the wasps' nest that had erupted about my ears as the water commenced its habitual torture of my senses I heard Wild Christian laughing as she walked away.

At breakfast they discussed it. 'That son of yours . . .' she began, 'I don't know what he has done to water, but they don't appear to get on very well. Do you know what happened this morning?'

They discussed it as if I was not present. It was another of their strange habits, but I had also noticed that it seemed peculiar to most grown-ups; they would discuss their children as if the children were not there. We never discussed them when they were within hearing. As I listened to them from our own table I shook my head in strong denial. Yes, they had missed the point; I was confident, as usual, that I had discovered the loophole in their argument.

'Wole is shaking his head,' Essay observed.

My mother laughed. 'Are you going to deny that even when you yourself poured water on your head . . .'

'No, but I am not afraid of water. If I were, how is it I like to go out and bathe in the rain?' I slapped my spoon into the bowl of *eko* making it send up a small splash.

'Be careful, Mr Lawyer. Don't waste your food,' my mother admonished.

'I am not going to be a lawyer. I am going to marry Mrs Odufuwa and be a pastor.'

'Oh, it is Mrs Odufuwa now, is it? What happened to Auntie Gbosere?'

'She hasn't come to visit us,' I explained. 'Mrs Odufuwa spent plenty of time with us at Easter. She is very fine.'

Essay took some time pondering the challenge. 'Well,' he said at last, 'maybe you are not afraid of rain. But it doesn't mean you are not afraid of water.'

Mother looked from one to the other, said, 'To ò,'* and prepared to leave for her shop. Her attitude indicated that she knew just how long the see-saw argument would take and that she had better things to do.

'Is rain not the same as water?' I demanded.

'Rain means water, but water does not necessarily mean rain.'

With suitably solemn nods, Wild Christian sighed, 'Ngh-hunnh!', called for her wosi-wosi† bag to be brought to her bedroom in preparation for the shop.

'But there can be no rain without water,' I protested.

Father nodded. 'True. But there can be water without rain.'

'The water came from rain in the first place didn't it?'

'Ah, that is where you are wrong. Rain actually comes from water. It is because of the water that rain is caused.'

I was getting in deep waters. My early triumph had long dissipated; then I remembered the Bible. 'What happened in the Bible?' I asked. 'Didn't God create them both separately?'

'Well, let's see. Go and bring the Bible from the parlour.'

I climbed down from the bench, my mind tried to race ahead to what the Bible had to say on the subject. The choice of passage picked for us to learn by rote had not included verses from Genesis, at least, none surfaced.

I picked up the Bible and returned to the dining-room. After handing it to him I returned to my table to pick up my bowl of *eko*, then joined him at his table, sitting in mother's chair. My *akara* was long finished and I eyed the corracle-shaped dish which still contained four or five of his *akara*. He caught the glance and smiled, pushing the dish towards me.

'Mind you,' he continued, 'you will find that the Bible tells only one part of the story. After God created this and that, he still left them to react with one another in their own ways. There are what we call the laws of nature, that is where the question of how rain is formed comes in.'

* Well, well!
† Odds-and-ends.

It seemed an unnecessary complication. I sucked air through my lips as I bit into fresh green *atarodo** that the Wild Christian had fried into the *akara*. The entire issue should have been resolved by the order in which rain and water were created. Then I remembered:

'All right. Why has the whole town been saying prayers for rain? Does that not mean God is still creating rain when he likes?'

He reflected briefly. 'Remember this. Even after he has created things on earth and given them their own working laws, as the Creator he can still interfere; for instance he can quicken up the processes or slow them down.'

The Wild Christian came out of her bedroom into the parlour just then to say good-bye and heard what Essay had just said. She came out shaking her head with that perpetual wonder at the infinite patience of Essay. 'But dear, are you sure he can understand all these arguments you indulge him in?'

She came in then fully into view, saw that I had changed tables and also appropriated Essay's left-over *akara*. In one swift movement she had snatched up the dish, closed it and placed it in the basket now on the maid's head. As I knew only too well, that would form part of her 'elevenses'.

'I did think the argument was getting rather lively. I didn't know that akaralogics and atarodimensis were making his tongue dance.' She hauled me off the chair. 'Carry this!' She plunked a bag in my hand and I knew what it meant. It was Saturday. Since there was no school, she meant to make me do my share at the shop.

'I have some homework,' I protested.

'Bring it to the shop with you.'

I put down the bag, disappeared into the 'pantry' for my books.

'You shouldn't encourage him too much, dear. He is too argumentative. You know what he said to the sexton? Last Sunday, during afternoon service. He was chattering away, he and that new friend of his, Edun's son. So the sexton went over and rebuked them. Do you know what this your son replied?'

'What did he say?'

'He said, of all the crowd in the church who were singing and praying, how could the sexton prove that he was talking? Can you imagine? Asking the sexton to prove that he was talking! I'm sure if the sexton had obliged they would still be in the pews arguing it out, that's the sort of child he is.'

---

* Fresh peppers, a round type.

56

I paused behind the door, horrified. Essay did not trifle with reports of mischief in church or Sunday school. How could the sexton have done this to me? Telling the Wild Christian was simply making sure that Essay got to hear it sooner or later. I remained motionless, glued my eye to the gap in the door, listening.

'We-e-ell,' I heard him say, 'it would be a rather difficult thing to prove, you know . . .'

Wild Christian sighed. 'I knew it. I knew you would defend him when it came to a matter of argument. I don't know why I even bothered to tell you. After all, he got it from you. Where is he? Has he taken my bag?'

'That's it on your chair.'

'O ya, let's go.' She pushed the maid forward. 'I'll leave him to plague you with his arguments. In any case he only embarrasses me at the shop with all his foolish questions. Why is your stomach bigger than my father's? Are you pregnant like the organist? Yes, that's the sort of thing he asks, in case no one has told you.'

'Really.' His mouth opened wide with laughter. 'When was this?'

'Ask him. He's your son. Ọmọ,* let's go. My customers are waiting.' She gave the maid a shove and was gone from the house.

I stayed on the spot. Essay's laughter did not mean that there was definitely no reprimand to come. He remained in his chair, very still. I felt him listening. Through the crack in the door I could only see a thin line of his back, yet I knew he was listening for sounds of my movement in the 'pantry'. We both knew the game. Why, I could not tell, but Essay would make no move until I made mine. A footfall, cough, something knocked over, a creak in the door. Until I announced my existence, he would simply sit still, probably reach out a hand for a toothpick and, with a faraway look, long distanced from his surround, commence picking his teeth. Elegantly. I glued myself to the ground, hardly breathing.

And of course, the prayers began. There was one other way the contest could end, and that was with the arrival of a visitor. Essay had a long, even deliberately spun-out memory. It was part of his wicked patience. Days, weeks after the culprit had forgotten his misdemeanour, after many weeks in which Essay had even patted him on the back for some especial conduct, some achievement or initiative, an errand delivered accurately in spite of the complexity, high marks in school etc. etc., Essay would summon the oblivious one:

'Er . . . oh yes, Bunmi.'

* Child.

'Sir?'

'Mm. You were sent to Itoku three weeks ago, not so? You remember?'

'Yes, sir.'

'Mm-hm. And the road to Itoku passes these days through the bookseller's compound, not so?'

Silence. Resignation or the commencement of sweat.

'Have you lost your tongue? I said, to get to Itoku, you now have to pass through the bookseller's compound, and of course one is not allowed to leave the bookseller's compound without spending some time plucking his mangoes?'

Silently I tried to work out the scale of my offence, measuring talking during a church service to taking time off on an errand to pluck mangoes. The graduation was not reassuring. I prayed harder for a visitor, aware though I was that this might prove to be no more than a postponement of a painful reckoning. And then I had to sneeze!

'Wole!'

'Sir.'

And at that moment came the sound of a heavy step on the outside pavement. The voice of Wild Christian followed through. 'Dear, are you still home?'

'Yes, I'm here.'

She spoke to someone outside. 'Come in, come in. Take a seat, I'll call him for you.' She came through the parlour while I squeezed myself back behind the door, doubtful that this was exactly the respite I had prayed for. Not for the first time, I noticed that God had a habit of either not answering one's prayers at all, or answering them in a way that was not straight-forward.

'God so good, I met Mr Adesina on the way. He was asking if you would be in this evening because he wanted to see you . . . I thought he might as well see you now, is that all right?'

'Is it about his job with the Synod?'

'What else does he ever think about? He keeps pestering me at the shop and I always tell him to see you. Is he scared to come? This time I dragged him back with me. If I had left him to come by himself he would be circling the parsonage till dark.'

'Why did you bring him? The answer is still the same – I won't plead for him. He cannot be trusted with funds.'

'All right, you tell him, dear. I have told him a hundred times but he won't accept it. Let him hear it from your own mouth.'

They both went to the front room. I followed after all was silent in the dining-room, paused to flick a crumb of *akara* off Essay's plate into my mouth.

In the same practised move my hand swept to the wash-basin which stood on the left wall, facing into the dining-room. The hand dived smoothly into the basin, flicked up a tiny amount of water and brushed my lips in one fluid movement. Almost at once a powerful blow landed on the side of my head knocking me almost into Essay's chair.

'Good.'

She stood glowering over me. 'I thought we had cured you of that habit.'

Wild Christian had a habit of levitating from nowhere. For a moment I dwelt on the unfairness of it. I had cured the habit. My movement was, admittedly, the same as when it was a 'problem', but this time, I had merely rinsed my fingers of the *akara*, a movement which was normally completed by also wiping the mouth. Then, on a moment's reflection, I felt relieved. The blow could easily have been for eating that crumb of *akara* which, for her, could have meant GREED and would call for something more than a mere blow to the head. I did not even whimper as she proceeded to seize my right hand between hers and squeeze the fingers together until they hurt.

'Just let me catch you at it again.'

She then set about the purpose which had brought her back, got out a tea-mug for the visitor and removed the tea-cosy. I quietly reminded myself never again to give the appearance of reviving the ritual which I once repeatedly enacted with the Wash-Hand Basin, driving the household mad.

I also admonished the Wash-Hand Basin by kicking it; after all, it was the source of the 'habit' that took the entire household to cure. This basin was yet another of the mysterious presences in the house, full of myriad recesses, shelves and ledges. Amidst the scampering of cockroaches, salt sachets, tablets, mini-bottles, soaps and chipped china jostled with packets of potassium permanganate, pieces of alum, glucose and a variety of yeasts. Like every other item of furniture, it served more than the purpose for which it was known. And more than all other items, it was – a LANDMARK. The interior of the house was defined by its location . . . it's in the corner of the Wash-Hand Basin . . . underneath the Wash-Hand Basin . . . I was going past the Wash-Hand Basin when . . . go and fetch me the stick by the Wash-Hand Basin . . . he pushed me against the Wash-Hand Basin . . . I was polishing the Wash-Hand Basin . . .

Even the mice had picked up the habit of escaping from the pantry by one undeviating path which took them behind or under the Wash-Hand Basin.

It was higher behind than in front, so that when Essay raised the lid on the few occasions when it was closed, lifting it backwards on its hinges, it rose and rose to his height, then exceeded it – and Essay to us was a very tall man. I thought it was fortunate that the stand was where it was. If there were no wall for the lid to rest against, nothing would have saved the rest of the stand from toppling over backwards from the sheer weight of the lid.

The basin itself sat in a big hole on the flat shelf which formed the cover of the interior, below the main lid, and it always seemed to me, frowning into the darkness of the lower cupboard, that the view of cockroaches looking up at this big, white enamel protrusion, must be quite like the view of the rats which scuppered about in the big dug-out latrine whenever any grown-up buttocks filled the hole in the box above them. Both holes appeared about the same in size, but beyond that, there were no further similarities. The lower cupboard had a separate door which opened along a horizontal axis and was secured by a flimsy, metallic hook. Its two shelves housed every object that was missing from the pantry or which could not find space on the dining-table, the dresser in Wild Christian's bedroom, the window-sill by my father's place at the dining-table, or the small cupboard behind his head where he kept his Epsom Salts, tooth-brush, a bottle of the mysterious 'Alcool' which he occasionally substituted for a chewing stick when cleaning his teeth, and cotton wads. Every other item of that domestic family of objects resided in the Wash-Hand Basin.

After a lot of pondering over the peculiar angle of the lid, I came to the conclusion that the extra inches at the back were to allow for that extra ledge on which were placed, in addition to the cake of soap, all other objects which could find no room in the lower cupboard. The search for any member of a particular family of objects, objects such as a bottle of aspirin or an exotic cake of soap, usually began and ended in the Wash-Hand Basin.

The 'habit' had developed unnoticed by me. As for Essay – nothing escaped him. One day I was walking from the front room to the pantry, a course which took me between the Wash-Hand Basin and his dining-table when he shouted:

'Stop!'

I froze.

'Why did you do that?'

I did not know what I had done.

He studied me intently. 'All right. Where did you just come from?'

'Iwaju-ile.'*

'And you were going to the pantry, not so?'

'Yes, sir. I needed to fetch a book.'

'I see.' He thought for a moment. 'Now go back. Sit at your desk for a minute. At the end of a minute, walk to the pantry exactly as you normally do.'

At the end of a minute I was taking that ninety-degree turn past the Wash-Hand Basin when the order came again, 'Stop!'

I froze. Fast as the order had come, it was too late for whatever purpose he had in mind. Again he studied me intently.

'Go back again. This time, when I say stop, stay exactly in whatever position you are. Don't move your head, shoulder, anything. If one foot is before the other, remain exactly like that. Do you understand?'

'Yes, sir.'

'I don't even want you to turn and face me. Walk as you normally walk to the pantry. Don't change your pace or anything. I may not even stop you this time, if I do, it may not be at the same place. I may shout STOP any time at all along the way. Now, is that clear?'

Clear, but highly mysterious. I could not understand what this was about and tried hard to recollect how I walked. It seemed to me that nothing had changed in my way of walking, but who could tell? Only Essay.

I expected the order to be given in a different place this time but no. It came at precisely the same spot and I obeyed his instructions, I hoped, to the letter. Now what?

On his face was a glint of satisfaction. He leant back and contemplated my existence for a long moment. He nodded slowly.

'What is your hand doing on your mouth?'

My hand? Mouth? I thought backwards rapidly.

It was true. My hand was resting lightly on my mouth, somewhat to the left of the face. And the strange thing was that it was wet. I held it away from my face. There was no doubt about it; my fingers were wet.

'Don't you know what you do every time you pass that wash-hand basin?'

'No, sir.' Although now, glimmerings of a peculiar cleansing rite had begun to surface in my mind. There was a recollection of an arm snaking out of its own volition, dipping in the basin . . . yes, I thought I now knew what Essay had patiently observed. The fresh, moist feel of my lips

---

* Front room, house frontage.

61

confirmed the rest of the motion. Passing by the Wash-Hand Basin, my hand flew to the basin, dipped, flashed over my lips, left to right. Catching myself at it several times after this, I wondered if it could be a form of madness.

It had been going on for a long time; the cure took just as long. Every member of the house was ordered to watch me, shout on me just before, or report me if it was too late. Then I would be made to walk past the basin several times over. Joseph took delight in tiptoeing after me, making me leap out of my skin as he imitated Essay's voice and shouted on me to stop. If neither parent was in, Lawanle or Nubi or indeed any of the 'cousins' tried to assume their role of drill-master. Even Tinu, older by a mere year and some months, got into the act. I felt a fervent need to lock them all up, beginning with her, in the dark interior of the Wash-Hand Basin and pour the slop from the basin over their heads.

The rains set in again. Harmattan, when the skin chapped and the vaseline, metholatun and pomade jars rapidly emptied, vanished from memory until the following year. A habit which had begun with the Harmattan, when I would linger by the wash-basin and moist the cracked skin of my lips also disappeared with that season, never to return. How it had grown into such an unthinking, streamlined motion did not puzzle me for long; there were other habits to be picked up, then abandoned forcibly or be replaced by others before they came to the attention of the ever-watchful Essay or The Wild Christian.

I never did discover how Adesina had lost his position with the Synod, and if he ever got it back. He left the house, like so many others before him, dejected, tearful. His eyes cast a last appealing look at Wild Christian who had stayed on the periphery of the discussion; normally she would not even remain there, but the Synod somehow involved her as well since it was a church affair. To the man who could not be trusted with funds, I heard her play the same dutiful role I had now learnt to expect:

'Well you know, it's the Headmaster's decision. I couldn't ask him to act against his conscience.'

V

Even the baobab has shrunk with time, yet I had imagined that this bulwark would be eternal, beyond the growing perspectives of a vanished childhood. Its girth has dwindled with time and the branches now give only a little shade. There was a name for the school bell-house, a description at least, a place in the family of physical things – it came back without effort – the Only Child of the Distant Church-Tower. Only now, even the distance between the bell-house and the church-tower has shrunk. White as a pillar of salt, the church-tower still dominates mango trees, the *orombeje* tree in the churchyard, the cenotaph also which, although placed outside the church walls, seemed to belong to the same extended family of St Peter's church. The church-tower is sometimes framed against the steep road towards Iberekodo, nudging dwarf rusted roofs along its sides. Aké, Ibarapa, Itoko, then over the hill into Mokola, the Hausa quarter, before Iberekodo itself. The hive of brown shacks, pink and orange bordered houses, stops abruptly before the crest and gives away to the ordered wall and broad gates of the chief's stable. Hidden within the hillside on either side of the road are the twin-markets of Ibarapa, night and day markets, the night to the right, the day, left. None of this has changed.

But the more intimate things have. Baobab, bell-houses, playing-fields and paths. Even Jonah. At Sunday School the teacher looked through the window for inspiration, waved at a nearby clump of rocks but rejected them. On the other side of the school building, hidden from us was a rock that was smoothed by our feet. It appeared to cover the earth – at least from where the junior schoolroom ended, to the cemetery outside the parsonage at the higher end, the furthest point from the main gates.

'You know where the school does its clay modelling? The whale that swallowed Jonah was bigger than that rock.'

The eager ones nodded assent. 'Yes, whales are enormous.'

'Bigger than houses.'

'Even ships.'

'Bigger than aeroplanes.'

We had heard the occasional drone of an aeroplane, even seen its

63

moving speck in the sky. A hand pushed a piece of paper towards me. I read,

'My father's house is bigger than a whale.'

I was really indifferent but replied, 'Liar!'

I would not read his response, feeling sufficiently crushed. That was my rock. My own very private rock. And now the Sunday School teacher had turned it into the common property of these lying, boastful, querulous others. She had intruded into a private abode, one of many. Different from that sleeping, eating, living place which belonged equally to Essay, Wild Christian, siblings, vague relations or 'ọmọ ọdọ' – a vague expression for something between servant and family appendage – Jonah was my own very secret habitat. And now the Sunday School teacher had turned Jonah into something from the Bible.

For after that, the patient, placid presence, hitherto unnamed, became Jonah. Permanently. Its mystery became complicated in a world of biblical tall tales whereas before, it had remained unaffected even by the weekday activity of mixing clay on its vast body, using rain water that had gathered in numerous oval holes. Who made those, we did ask, not that we were really curious. But the modelling classes never touched the intimate lives Jonah and I lived at weekends, for the school went home while I remained in the parsonage and could walk over to climb up its steep sides and sink through its broad back into deep immobility. There were other rocks in the compound, rocks with clumps of bamboos, smooth inclines down which we all slid and yelled. Jonah was bare, solitary and private. Until the school teacher turned it into a fairy tale. Swallowed and sealed up in a whale's belly! It did not sound wholly improbable but it did belong in a world of fables, of the imagination, of Aladdin's lamp and Open Sesame. Whereas before . . . I experienced the passing of a unique confidant, the loss of a replete, subsuming presence.

The guava tree was another, not the luxuriant, generous tree beside the communal water-tap, overlooked by the pastor's square, squat residence. This other was some distance away, near the infant school building. It was protected from stones and sticks because its fruits were usually closer to the ground and, in any case, it did not give off much fruit. But it had large, dark-green and fleshy leaves and one of its branches was weighted almost to the ground. This guava tree had an affinity with the rainy season, nothing really tangible, except that it did not seem to be itself except in the rainy season. Under brooding clouds it performed the double feat of existing yet retreating into an inner world of benevolent foliage spirits, moist yet filled with a crisp vitality, silent yet wisely communicative. It was also without time. So was Jonah in a way, but the guava had this indefinable assurance of swallowing time, making it cease to exist. I sneaked out of our house in the morning and suddenly it was dusk, yet I had no recollection of any action beyond being among the branches. I watched Joseph, or Nubi walking up the stone-lined path. Nubi was of course later baptized like all non-Christians who came into the household. After that, we had to call her by her Christian name, Mary. She would come up the broad path and turn first towards the pond where she knew we often played, flicking flat pebbles to skim off the slime-covered surface or simply watching the ducks. She walked up wiping her brow with the loose tip of her wrapper, calling out my name. She belonged to another world, one which however became real enough when she yanked me expertly from my perch.

'You are going to eat the cane tonight, you wait.'

I stumbled all the way, keeping up with her speed. She looked at me at last with some concern.

'Can't you start shivering?'

'I am not cold.'

'Who asked you if you were cold?'

'You said, couldn't I start shivering?'

'Idiot. Ọ̀dẹ̀. It rained this afternoon. Anyone could have caught a cold.'

'But I haven't.' It had rained too. I now remembered taking refuge in the deserted schoolroom. She felt my clothes.

'You haven't got wet anyway. That would have made things worse for you. Still I don't understand why you didn't come home after it stopped raining, instead of going to sit up in that tree.'

I understood at last. 'I could say I was trapped by the rain, couldn't I?'

'What an idiot! It stopped raining over two hours ago. That's why Mama sent me for you. We all thought you were in the house all that time.'

'But I told Joseph I was going to the school compound.'

'He told her. But you've stayed so late. Pity you haven't got a fever. It's standing in the corner for you at least.'

Nubi was wily, that much was becoming clear. Had she played that game before? Timidly, I inquired.

She chuckled. 'You forget, Mama's medicines are not very pleasant.'

'But you have faked a fever before, not so?'

'Listen, you silly. You ask too many questions.'

'No, tell me.' I really wanted to know.

'I don't have to fake shivering when I see I'm going to receive Mama's flogging. I start shivering from the moment I know she is just waiting to let loose. You'd be surprised, but it is actually she who says, have you got a fever? She's never realized that one can start shivering from the thought of that *pasan*.'*

'So you say yes?'

'Of course, you idiot. Wouldn't you?'

'But you always have a temperature,' I insisted. Temperature was again one of those magic words. If the Wild Christian said you had Temperature you had Temperature. Since we cooked on an open hearth I always wondered how, if you put a palm against the forehead of any of us in that unventilated kitchen, you would not discover Temperature. Essay, I sometimes observed, was not that impressed by Temperature.

Nubi conceded that she had never fully understood Temperature. But it helped to have it, and she always had it at the right time.

'Do you think I have Temperature?' Vaguely I felt that it might be possible, since I had been running to keep up with her. She felt my forehead.

'Not a chance. I think you are going to feel that stick.'

But the walls have retained their voices. Familiar voices break on the air, voices from the other side of the rafters. Isara was second home – Essay's natal home. All the grandparents were Father and Mother – and somehow we said these as if with capital letters. There the rafters were smoky, bare of the usual ceiling mat. There were objects in corners of the roof, wrapped in leaves, in leather. Some were not so mysterious, since Father would often reach up into such a bundle, one that seemed caked with the accumulation of a hundred years' drought. Yet out of it would come nothing more puzzling than kolanuts, or snuff. Isara was another kind of home, several steps into the past. Age hung from every corner, the patina of ancestry glossed all objects, all human faces. Our older relations were differently aged from those in Abeokuta, relations on our mother's side. Laterite, mud houses, floors of dung plaster, indigo dye on old women's hands – I did not like that, I hated the touch of hands transformed by the indigo gloss. And it was in Isara also that we saw so much indigo-green tattoo on the arms and bodies of women.

New Year meant Isara. Smoked pork, the flavour of wood smoke, red dust of a dry season, dry thatch. New Year was palm wine, *ebiripo*, *ikokore* . . . a firmer, earth-aged kind of love and protection. Isara was filled with unsuspected treats, as when Father pulled down yet another ominous

* Whip.

66

bundle from the rafters and it turned out to be smoked game, ageless in its preservation. Our women were darker in Isara, much darker. Buba, wrapper and shawls were also of those varied shades of indigo, though occasionally one would encounter the white shawl, or a bright yellow headgear which further receded the wearer's face into an ancient shadow.

I could not understand why Father's rafters in Isara should be so bare, yet so full of surprises, while the ceiling at the parsonage, though sealed up was, beyond the scuttling of mice, devoid of mystery. Occasionally the termites took a hand. Suddenly the ceiling mat fell on our heads – the termites had long been silently busy and no one suspected they were everywhere. A long-forgotten box of papers was pulled out from under the bed and we found its contents ruined by termites. They travelled into the roof from along a hidden crack in the wall and went to work. Suddenly the iron sheets were exposed; between the zinc roof and the mat – nothing. In fact, the ceiling often bred tantalizing thoughts of a nocturnal visit by Father, impatient for our New Year visit, secreting his mystery parcels in the ceiling to last the long wait. It was a teasing, unsettling thought. So finally, I had to make a hole in it.

I had no planned to, though I often intently pierced the matting with my expectations. A loud, truly deafening noise was the first awareness I had that anything was wrong. It brought the world to an end. Something smacked against the mat, an instant later another sound, dull yet crisp announced that something had passed through and hit the metal sheeting of the roof.

But the definition of those sounds came much later, for I was at this point on the floor, the explosion having startled me off my chair. I believed also that I was paralysed and refused to move: I had been shot to death, there was no other explanation for the suddenness of my descent to earth, none other for the lack of pain or the full clarity of my senses. Obviously, I had attained a heavenly dimension. Moreover, HM was in his bedroom at the time; I was waiting for him to emerge when it happened. There was no motion, so it could not be his bedroom whose door still seemed so plain to the eye.

The preceding moments regained focus. Yes, I had been sitting in the front room, under the porcelain clock. I occupied the chair where visitors sat who had business with my father. His air-gun leant against the wall and I sat in the chair by the door, waiting for him to come out so as to accompany him, as usual. Like Jonah, like the Guava Tree and the bell-house, Essay-on-the-hunt was another private existence. He never spoke. I followed him, sometimes carrying his gun, picking up the birds he shot, mostly wood pigeons. Sometimes a hawk or kestrel, a squirrel – once, even a small *emo*.* I recalled the excitement that followed the shooting of a rare bird, hitherto unseen, perhaps a migrant. We went through the deserted school compound and into the surrounding bush. Rocks loomed before us and he climbed carefully, first handing me the gun. When he reached a firm ledge he reached out for his gun and I climbed after him. We sat and waited. Or we climbed down the other side, then we might make the return by a wholly different route, walking down the path that ran along the school wall on the outside and entering by the main gate. Perhaps the bookseller or the catechist would stop him then while I went ahead with the day's bag.

Huddled close against the floor, scenes of past excursions flashed through my mind, so certain was I that I was dead. I had drifted off perhaps into a frequent reverie while caressing the stock of the rifle. My hand must have found the trigger. Then it became clear to me that I was not dead, so, naturally, a different terror took its place. Indeed only then did any fear intrude. Acceptance of my death had come easily: very different was the thought of my father's reaction to my carelessness.

I scrambled up, but slowly. Still no movement from the bedroom. Was it mere imagination? I was certain I heard the door creak. It would be like him, I thought, to peer through and watch my reactions. The gun still leant against the wall, in pulling the trigger I had not even knocked it down. A whiff of something burning stung my nostrils and I forced back a sneeze, scraping against a chair. This time there was no doubt in my mind – something moved behind the door. I fixed my gaze on the porcelain clock, marvelling that it had not been hit. The muzzle of the gun still pointed directly at its base. Its face was decorated by a windmill and two women with hooped skirts and strange, tight-fitting caps. On the other side of the diamond-shaped face, a flock of birds flew over some fields. For the first time, and for a very brief moment, I wondered if my father had bought that clock because of the birds. All the design was blue. The porcelain looked fragile. Would I escape a beating?

He is watching, I thought. Perhaps he thinks I am wounded. So that also became a possibility and I began to look for traces of blood. None. Still no movement from his bedroom. But I knew him. He was the opposite of Wild Christian who would by now have rushed out. First consideration: is he wounded? Finding him intact, a barrage of blows ten times more lethal than I could imagine a bullet through the flesh. Certainly more disorientat-

* A wild rodent, rat family.

ing. By contrast HM might pursue his original plans as if nothing had happened. The hunting excursion, home, supper, small talk, visitors, disputation on predestination or the War. Evening prayers, then . . .

'Wole!'

No, I was not going on any hunt with him, let him formulate his punishment as he wished but I was not going to be kept in suspense, trotting by his side, carrying his gun and picking up fallen game as if nothing was going to happen. Whatever he was planning behind that door . . . I leapt up and was out through the door before he could even gather up his voice. A few moments later I lay panting on the back of Jonah, keeping a watchful eye on the path through which he must pass if he still meant to hunt.

At different times, something was always going to be the death of 'that son of yours' – this appeared to be my mother's fervent belief. And the most persistent threat to my existence at Aké appeared to be day-dreaming or brooding. How she described it depended, I found, on the seriousness of whatever lapse had been caused by the ailment. She lost no chance to remind Essay of the need to cure me of it before it was too late, so now I conjured up her presence and watched her react to the news that her prophecy had nearly been fulfilled. I told you before, I heard her say, so I won't say anything more. Only to expand, a few moments later, on the dangerous effects of so much brooding in a child. She was not alone. We knew of parents who took their children to 'native doctors' for a cure for the same complaint.

I was now truly worried; it seemed as if Wild Christian might after all be right. Only one other event had succeeded in my paying any attention to her complaint – this was the incident of the rose-bush. We were all in the backyard, she was cooking, which meant that the entire household was occupied with running trivial errands for her, holding a spoon or a cup, receiving a slap if the fire had burnt down or the pot had over-boiled. Unless I was especially picked upon, I would manage to escape being a part of the disorder, usually by going to read in the front room, or even simply from being seen just completing my lessons in the front room. It was recognized that I had special chores in the house. I took some share in the cooking but it was really a token share, much less than that of Tinu for instance, or of any of the 'cousins' who lived with us. One of these special chores, one which I chose for myself and enjoyed doing, was looking after Essay's garden. I watered the plants, pruned dead stalks and discouraged the spiders from spinning their webs across the crotons. The roses came in for the most careful tending. I was murderous with the goats which sometimes succeeded in penetrating our defences to nibble at the flowers. Nothing would do but to lock the gate on them, then drub them thoroughly with stones and cudgels. Once we nearly beat a goat to death. He lay panting and bleeding in the narrow path leading to the gate. The aim of one of our cousins had been a little too true and the stone had been much larger than the ones which, by unspoken agreement, we normally used.

When we opened the gate at last, the goat was too weak to climb out. Terrified now, we doused it with cold water, then heaved the wretched animal over the step. We locked the door and watched it through a gap while we prayed that it would recover and go away before Essay returned. He approved of us chasing out goats, not locking them up and murdering them. It was with immense relief that the tortured animal staggered up at last and wobbled off unsteadily. The following day it was back again, in the parsonage. If it had come into our garden again, I would have killed it.

Only my father himself surpassed the jealousy with which I guarded the flowers, as one of HM's staff discovered, painfully. He acquired a name from his harsh encounter with this jealous regard – 'Lè móọ' – Stick it back on! – an episode which also made our neighbours, and Essay's colleagues, marvel at the nature of that strange being the Headmaster, who would pursue an impossible demand with such single-mindedness.

Odejimi, the teacher, thought at first that it was a typical HM joke, a mistake which many people committed because of the Headmaster's fussless way of meaning what he said. The teacher had arrived in school, a pink rose stuck in the button-hole of his jacket. My father admired the rose, then asked him, very ordinarily, where he had obtained it.

'Oh, in your garden of course, Headmaster.'

Essay did not change his tone when he said, 'Ah, I thought I recognized it. You like roses, I see.'

'Oh yes indeed, sir. And I must congratulate you. Really, you have a wonderful garden. I never knew it or I would have visited it more often.'

'Oh? So how did you discover I had a garden?'

'I was passing by, sir, and your back gate was open. I saw the blooms through the opening and I could not believe my eyes. You hide your light under a bushel, Headmaster.'

'Thank you,' said Essay. And there the matter was left.

School over, he sent for Odejimi. 'Ah yes, your rose. I can't quite remember who you said gave you permission to pluck a rose from the garden.'

Odejimi looked puzzled, then corrected the mistake. 'Oh no, I never said that anyone gave me permission.'

My father looked surprised. 'Really? You mean you just went into the garden and helped yourself.'

'Precisely, sir. I mean, I hope you don't mind.' Very belatedly, Mr Odejimi was beginning to get a message.

'Not at all,' my father assured him. 'But I would like you to return it now. You know, to the place where you found it.'

There was a long silence. Odejimi briefly lost his syntax and appeared to stammer. 'Er . . . to returning it, sir? You mean return it to the er . . . to your garden.'

'Yes please, that is, if you do not mind.'

'Of course, Headmaster. I am er . . . really sorry that you took offence. I should have asked your permission.'

'That's all right. Just return it where it belongs and we will forget the matter.'

Odejimi smiled broadly, relieved that no direr consequences were to follow. He picked up his books and marched briskly towards our house. Essay watched him cover half the distance, then followed him. His uncanny sense of timing ensured that both he and Odejimi met exactly at the back gate, Odejimi already on his way out, beaming.

'Oh, I see you've finished,' Essay remarked.

'Yes indeed, sir, I've left it in the flower-pot.'

'Good. Let's just go and see how it's doing, shall we?'

A baffled Odejimi followed his boss to the scene of crime. There, slumped over the rim of the pot was the wilting rose. Essay took a long look at the object, then craned his neck a little to the side to discover the stalk from which it had been cut.

'But it came from that stalk originally, didn't it?'

'Oh yes,' confirmed Odejimi, his voice most sprightly in his eagerness not to contradict. 'That was the precise stalk from which I er . . . removed it.'

'Good. Lè móọ!'

'Beg your pardon, sir?'

'I said, Lè móọ.' And with that final instruction, Essay turned and walked into the house. He calmly set about the tasks he would normally perform at that hour, paying no further attention to the teacher.

I had raced ahead from school to brief Tinu and Dipo. Together we now watched the hapless man open and shut his mouth as the fishes did when

71

they were brought to the house for sale, still alive. His rechristening was instant – he was now Mr Lè-móọ

Lè-móọ made a move at last. Holding the rose in his hand with great tenderness he entered the house. My father was in his bedroom. Lè-móọ stood in the front room, faced the door which led to the bedroom. For one moment we thought he would commit the ultimate folly of following my father into the room, he looked sufficiently confused to have done anything in that moment. However, he merely coughed to attract attention.

'Excuse me, sir. Er, sir . . . . Headmaster sir.'

Essay made no attempt to conceal his movements in the room. For almost an hour Lè-móọ remained on the spot, the dead flower in his hand. From time to time he punctuated his wait with, 'Sir, if I may just explain, sir . . .', 'if I could just have a word with you, sir'; 'Please, Headmaster, I wonder if . . . I mean, if I could only . . .'

An hour passed before Essay emerged from the room. The space between his table in the front room and the chairs arranged against the wall next to the parlour was not wide enough to take two people at a time, and his eyes opened in measured exasperation of finding a total stranger blocking a passage in his own home. Lè-móọ flattened himself against the edge of the table, but Essay did not attempt to pass. Instead, he waited. It took another full second before the teacher realized that he was about to add to his catalogue of sins and he leapt backwards, apologizing profusely, stumbling over his words and feet. Essay ignored him and went to the backyard. He took one look at the flower-pot, looked at Odejimi who had followed him there, and gave a thin pitying smile that sent the teacher licking his lips in fright. It was a smile we all knew, it was accompanied by a movement of his head from side to side. We turned cartwheels in the pantry in a fever of excitement, for we had recognized the commencement of a long, difficult lesson for the erring teacher. We settled deeper into our ringside seats, speculating on the possible lines of development.

Lè-móọ underwent a mental transformation at some point during the next hour, because his next specific act was to try and hold the dismembered rose to the stalk. He began by freezing a long time, staring into vacancy. Then he turned towards the flower-pot, his movement like a sleep-walker's, and again he held the rose to its parent stalk, pressing the two severed points together. When he let go, the rose fell into the bed. It was a big disappointment. Seeing his fixed stare into nowhere, watching his lips working in some strange fashion, we had come to the conclusion that he was working a spell, either on Essay or on the rose. It became clear that it was the latter when he held the flower against the stalk and we were set to cheer, thinking that it would work. It failed, and Lè-móọ stared into the pot, then raised his head up with his hands, clutching both sides, and bellowed in anguish:

'Ye e! Mo k'éran!*

I suddenly felt pity for him.

The next moment, he was standing stiff-backed, animated. His eyes had lit up with a GREAT IDEA and he bolted from the house as if from hell. We felt profoundly disappointed. Surely Odejimi, a teacher under the HM, should know better than that. Could this be the great idea that had occurred to him? Running away? No one escaped Essay, certainly not someone who had tampered with his roses.

It was not until the return of Wild Christian from the shop, with Odejimi in tow, that we learnt the true nature of his inspiration. He had gone to solicit the aid of mother in appeasing the wrath of the Headmaster. The journey from the shop to the house, a mere ten minutes' walk, must have taken an hour, since Lè-móọ insisted on prostrating himself to her at every step, wringing his hands and repeating that he was a doomed man unless my mother could do something for him. The slow procession continued right into the backyard where Wild Christian commenced her preparations for the evening meal. She promised a hundred times that she would do her best but nothing would satisfy Odejimi unless she somehow produced Essay on the spot and got him to say that all was forgiven. Wild Christian sent off at least four of the children in all directions to spy out Essay's movements; only then did the poor man relax, getting in the way of mother's cooking by offering to do every chore including stirring the soup. He had to be prised from the grinding stone and was finally expelled to the furthest corner of the top of the yard with a bottle of lemonade and a sauceful of chin-chin. I took them to him and, assessing full well his state of mind, spoke kindly to him.

'You don't feel like eating at all, I'm sure.'

'Oh yes, no, I mean yes, I don't. Please, thank Mama but yes, I mean tell her no thank you. Very kind of her. Kind woman. Is HM in yet!'

Tinu was waiting round the corner. We shared the chin-chin and drank the lemonade. For me, he had now paid his dues and I had no further interest in his agony. We could not after all chase him round the yard like a goat.

It was close to midnight when Odejimi left the house that day, an

* Ah, I'm in trouble!

exhausted, chastened teacher. Wild Christian did not broach the subject immediately; she merely served Essay his dinner, pretending not to understand the purpose of the quick survey which he made of the backyard when he returned, and the tight pursing of his lips on failing to see Lè-mọ́ọ anywhere. Afterwards, she remained closeted with him for about an hour. When she came out, she sent some food to Lè-mọ́ọ who had not moved from his hide-out in the yard. She had to go out herself and force him to eat, to our intense disappointment.

The bell rang for evening prayers. I had no doubt whatsoever that Lè-mọ́ọ was on his knees, praying hard with the family but on his own behalf. After prayers, Essay sat in the front room, reading. Of his knowledge of Lè-mọ́ọ's presence in his backyard, he betrayed no sign. I did not sleep. When the house had fallen completely silent, Essay went through the parlour to the yard. I heard him shout,

'Is Odejimi there?'

Startled from his doze, the ill-starred man snapped out a 'Present, sir' and stumbled over objects towards Essay. He repeated, 'Present, sir, I'm right here, sir, very sorry, sir.'

Then followed the cool, measured voice of Essay,

'Don't you have a bed to sleep in?' There was silence, then, 'Well, good-night. Secure the gate after you.'

When I heard *my* name forced through a choked pipe, the sound of it near-identical with the first escape attempts of piped water after the long drought of Harmattan, I knew that an unbelievable disaster had befallen the house. I came back to earth thoroughly frightened, for Essay had appeared at the outer door and his face was going through unaccustomed changes of horror, incredulity, intense agitation. Essay, the cool, deliberate HM pointed a shaking finger in my direction and I had to acknowledge that, unbelievable though it was, the voice that had called out my name was indeed his.

In my hand was a stalk of *ewedu*.* I leant against the half-barrel filled with earth, the bed of the new rose-bushes on which I had lavished much time and care. The buds were appearing for the first time, two or three had actually begun to open. The strange aspect was that they now lay in shreds, flogged to death by my own hands. If Wild Christian had not had her helpers constantly passing or awaiting orders in front of her, she would have seen the action long before and called me to my senses. But she was

* A vegetable.

seated on a low stool, fussing with her pots and pans, while the children mostly had their backs to me. When Essay stepped on the threshold of the outer dining-room door, the sight that confronted him over the cooking group was this: his Number One Gardening Assistant, leaning against the barrel, the *ewedu* stalk in his left hand going gently up and down into the rose plant, a hypnotized stare into nowhere on his face. The fresh young petals lay wounded on the bed, caught among the thorns and branches. Even the leaves were broken, stamens were cut in half at the filaments, the crop lay piteously on the leaves of the calyx, the younger stalks had been slightly bruised by the gentle but persistent strokes of an *ewedu* baton which had been conducting some music in my head. The disaster was total. In broad daylight, in the presence of a large number of people who, as if through the wiles of the devil – nothing else could account for it – had been so positioned that they could not even see or suspect and warn, I had physically assaulted Essay's roses and inflicted mortal wounds on them.

At least Lè-móọ had something to attempt to glue back on the plant; where did one begin in all this?

I had never loved Wild Christian as I did at that moment. Responding to her husband's bellow of pain, she looked up and took in the situation. She breathed a soft 'A-ah' and her eyes filled with pity. The next moment Essay charged across the intervening space and his fingers affixed themselves to his favourite spot, the lobe of my ear, only this time, he was not merely pinching it to hurt but was trying to lift me up with it. Wild Christian moved very swiftly. It was one of the few times in her life that she interfered with Essay's punitive decisions, going as far as detaching my ear from his fingers and pleading with him.

'Dear, you must *know*. He must have been dreaming. Ah-ah, isn't he the one who spends all his time looking after the garden. His mind wasn't here. He didn't know what he was doing.'

Essay's snorts diminished to heavy breathing, then became regular. He appeared to calm down. He took one more look at the battered plant, shook his head in self-pity, and strolled away from the scene.

Wild Christian sighed. 'Something just has to be done before you kill yourself or set fire to the house.'

VI

I lay on the mat pretending to be still asleep. It had become a morning pastime, watching him exercise by the window. A chart was pinned to the wall, next to the mirror. Essay did his best to imitate the white gymnast who was photographed in a variety of postures and contortions on that chart. There was a precise fusslessness even in the most strenuous movements. In . . . Out . . . In . . . Out . . . breathing deeply. He bent over, touched his toes, slewed from one side to the other, rotated his body on its axis. He opened his hands and clenched them, raising one arm after the other as if invisible weights were suspended from them. Sweat prickles emerged in agreed order, joined together in disciplined rivulets. Finally, he picked up the towel – the session was over.

From the window-sill he next picked up his chewing-stick and a cup, the stick moved over an impeccable set of teeth, scrubbed deep into the corners, up and down the front teeth. He spat neatly into the cup. From time to time he grunted a response to the greeting of a passer-by. Once or twice he would actually consent to return a half phrase to a passing neighbour, a phrase with discernible words, but I felt that this caused him an effort.

After a while he picked up his towel, rolled the ends of his wrapper in a lump about his waist or tied them around the back of his neck and went out of the bedroom. I followed the sound of his slippers through the house and into the backyard where he would stroll, pausing to examine his roses and pick off some withered petals. Occasionally his voice would ring out, summoning someone to perform an errand, probably calling for his clippers to snip off a withered branch. Often, simply standing still among his plants, gazing through the flowers into his distances.

The room gave off an ordered mustiness, in contrast to Wild Christian's bedroom. Hers was a riot of smells, a permanent redolence of births, illnesses, cakes, biscuits and petty merchandise. This varied from the rich earth-smell of *aṣọ òkè*,* to camphor balls and hundreds of unguents. Some

---

* A hand-woven cloth, much valued.

of the household, including a grown-up maid, still wetted their mats at night, so there was a permanent tang of urine in the air. In any case a sick child was instantly transferred from the mat on the floor to her enormous, four-poster bed where the mattress further absorbed the effects of a bladder whose training had become temporarily slackened by strange fevers. Afterwards the mattress would be turned over to the sun for a whole day, but it never completely lost that acrid tang which suffused the room even with both windows fully open.

Wild Christian's bed was twice the size of Essay's, at least it always appeared so. It had huge brass knobs on all four posts and the railings at the head and feet of the bed had little brass spheres which could be unscrewed. For some reason, the railing at the foot was removed altogether, which saved us quite a lot of punishment. Now when we unscrewed the tiny spheres at the surviving end, played with them and lost them, we could obtain spares from the discarded railing which lay hidden in the big store-room.

The four-poster with those shiny knobs, and the enormous dresser were the only items in the room which aspired to any definable form or shape. Everything else in the bedroom was resolutely, even fanatically set against order or permanence in any form. Bundles were piled underneath the bed, baskets of soap, trayloads of tinned sardines, pilchards, packets of sugar, bolts of cloth, round camphors and square, leaf-wrapped parcels of shea-butter or black, local soap. Jars of sweets, home-made and imported, such as Trebor mints, rested on the window-sills side by side with odd pamphlets, bibles, hymn-books and tattered books. Tightly sealed tins of kerosene, palm-oil, groundnut oil, enamel bowls of *gari*, beans and dried corn were stacked in a corner . . . my father would come into the room in search of something, look around, give up and go out shaking his head in patient despair.

The top of the chest of drawers was marked by the same profusion of disorder, only, its inhabitants were of a different species from the insatiable cavern beneath the bed, the wall corners or the window-sills. Jewellery boxes, isolated beads, bracelets, ear-rings and other ornaments, a leather-bound bible, hymn and prayer books all with silk ribbon markers were the approved residents. There were also china pieces decorated in high relief like the cicatrix on the face of an *ara-oke*,* and other ornate curios which multiplied at festivals, or with the arrival of visitors from outlandish places. Yet, at night, sufficient space was created on the floor

* Someone from the hinterland, considered 'bush'.

77

where a mat was spread to sleep a constantly varying assortment of children – sometimes as many as twelve – there being no more avid a collector of strays than Wild Christian, tacitly aided by her husband. We never knew her to say No to any of those parents, guardians or relations who brought their ward for 'training', or simply to be cared for. Some ran away, only to be brought back again. Some arrived with their heads full of ringworms, their stomachs distended from poor diet, their feet eaten by yaws and with lice in their hair. Others came well trimmed and groomed, their boxes full of new clothes, their pockets full of spending money.

'What are all those portmanteaux for?' Wild Christian would ask, her face deceptive in its innocence, but fooling no one.

'Oh, just a few changes of clothing.'

'I see. Well, leave him two shirts and a couple of shorts, leave him a *dansiki* for church, and take the rest back. As for money, make sure you leave him with none of his own. If he needs pocket money, let him come to me.'

Wild Christian's bedroom manifested the very nature of the children whom she took under her wing; it waged war against itself yet created a sense of belonging. The bedroom, not their parents, appeared to have given birth to this family, spewed them out only to resorb them and make them children of the house. In the calm and privacy of my father's bedroom I would wonder about these parents who willingly abandoned them to the home of 'headmaster' and his wife. I wondered what my sister felt about it all, unable to enjoy the intimacy which I derived from my privileged position in father's bedroom. Dipo was still a baby. Since he was a boy, I expected that he would later join me in *our* room; that seemed only right.

It was a room whose mustiness came from accumulated papers – frayed journals, notebooks, files, seasoned leather cases and metallic trunks, leather shoes carefully laid out. Twice a year Essay reduced the volume of papers by holding a bonfire from which we snatched glossy catalogues and intriguing journals, over which we pored. They belonged to a different, unreal world. By lifting the hanging bedspread, my eyes could rove at ground-level round the cardboard cases and trunks, all awaiting the next disgorgement, wondering if they knew of their fated end in a bonfire.

The room was full of dust-motes, caught in the beam of sunlight that came through the window. Through it I reviewed the bookcase with its neatly stacked shelves. I had already sampled several of their hoard, leaving even Essay astonished at my appetite for books, yet even he did not know how deeply I had burrowed into his bookcase. I had casually drifted into dusting his bedroom, finally easing out Joseph whose duty it was. Half of my working hour was spent devouring his shelves. Wild Christian lost no opportunity to show me off to her visitors and, at the beginning, I needed no prompting to begin showing off. But then she had to bring Tinu into the act, disparaging her comparative lack of attainment. In place of my delight at being invited to read came discomfort, then resentment. Tinu was the closest playmate I knew and a protective bond had grown between us which only showed when she was hurt or threatened. Helping her with her homework I regarded the same as doing my own; I could not see the difference nor understand that Essay found it necessary to ask questions which were so obviously designed to catch her out. Reducing her before strangers was, however, the ultimate crime.

Wild Christian's sense of the ultimate crime was different; it consisted very simply of manifesting 'èmí èsù', the spirit of the devil, at any time, but most unpardonably in front of visitors. The catalogue of 'èmí èsù' was quite sweeping, and it included showing even the slightest evidence of 'unwilling' in the face of the parental order. No child of HM and his wife, no ward, no 'omo odo' was about to commit such a crime; alas, a few had faces which betrayed them even before the thought was formed. Wild Christian constantly impressed upon me that I was principal of these. Thus I resorted to failing to find the books through which I was to demonstrate my cleverness to visitors, I developed sudden fevers, which unfortunately were not believed, since they were not accompanied by 'Temperature'. Bukola was the only child I knew who could effortlessly manipulate 'Temperature', and hers was always in the opposite direction – her body would simply go cold. Lacking her talent, I took to vanishing when ordered to find a book and perform to visitors.

I had an ally. It was no more than a fleeting expression, and Essay never permitted himself more than that once to show disapproval. It was also likely that he did not really mind when the exhibition took place among his 'own people' – like his debating circle – but once at least I caught him wince in discomfort, then turn away to hide his distaste. My disappearances took on a bolder turn, books vanished, Essay's bedroom door somehow got mysteriously locked and the key was missing. I grew reckless, and it seemed the normal order of things.

Now I sought ways to let the household know that father and I belonged in a separate world. Wild Christian watched the progressive abandonment of participation in the general household ordering and let it go. 'Papa gave me some homework' was final, it brooked no argument. But the seeming triumph did not come without its rooted fears. I sensed, not battle, but demarcation lines being drawn, yet even these required a measure of defiance which escalated every day. I would deny it to myself, yet I knew that it was taking place; the treatment of my own sister was merely the first event to bring it to my uneasy notice.

Deep down, I felt I was headed towards a terrible punishment. I could not define how I had deserved it, nor how to avert it. The song in the story which my father had told me the previous night came back to mind like a special warning,

> Igba o l'ọwọ
> Tere gungun maja gungun
> tere
> Igba o lẹsẹ
> Tere gungun maja gungun
> tere
> Igba mi l'awun o
> Tere gungun maja gungun
> tere.*

The Tortoise was lying of course. Claiming he knew neither hand nor foot of the cause of his terror was quite typical of his deceitful nature. But the sight of gourds which broke off their moorings on the farm and began to chase him over rocks and rivers must have been most unnerving. The song appeared far more suitably applied to me: every time Wild Christian accused me of being possessed of 'ẹmí èṣù', I was simply puzzled that no one else appeared to share my deep sense of injustice. I had not, after all, provoked the situation. I roved through the woods on the next expedition with one fearful eye on anything bulbous. There were no gourds on the farms or in the woods of the parsonage but there were the baobab trees with their velvet-cased oval fruits, the shape and size of grinding stones. I saw them raining down on me, then pursuing me through the woods. If Wild Christian prayed hard enough, perhaps it could happen.

My eyes fell on the exercise chart; that offered some escape from disturbing thoughts. I stood up and began to strike some of the postures of the callisthenist.

'What do you think you are up to?'

---

* The gourd has no arms.
  Tere gungun etc.
  The gourd has no legs
  Yet the gourd is pursuing the tortoise.

Lawanle had just come in. The intrusion was unpardonable. 'Don't you know you are supposed to knock before entering Papa's room?'

'Since when did you become Papa?' And she came further into the room.

'It is still *our* room,' I insisted.

'It won't be much longer,' she said. 'You are getting older, you know.'

'What difference does that make?'

'You'll find out when it's time.' She shrugged. 'Now come on. Mama is asking what you are still doing in the room. Why haven't you had your bath?'

'What am I going to find out?'

'Oh God, come on. Must you always follow one question with another question? That is what is wrong with you, you like arguments too much, you fancy yourself another Papa, don't you?'

'What am I going to find out?'

She half-sung, 'That there will be some CHANGES in this house.'

'What changes?'

Lawanle let loose her derisive laughter. 'Someone is going to find out very soon.'

'All right, I am no longer interested. Keep your secrets.'

Pulling me into a corner of the parlour, she asked, 'Didn't Papa tell you he was travelling?'

'Where to?'

'You see. It is always a mistake to answer even one question of yours. All one gets in return is another question.'

I lied. 'I knew he was travelling because he told me an extra story last night. He does that when he is going to be away for some time. In fact he told me two more but I fell asleep in the middle of the last.'

'Then he should have told you where he was travelling to.'

By now we were crossing the parlour and approaching the backyard, so further conversation was impossible.

As I scrubbed myself in the bathroom I felt ill with apprehension. Lawanle's words had merely increased the unease which was lately surreptitiously transmitted to me – those sentences that began on mother's tongue, but were never completed. The fleeting disapproval of some privilege extended to me by Essay, the pursing of the mouth as I made off with my mat to his room while Tinu, cousins and all retired to the common mat. I hated the communal mat, I realized quite suddenly; it went beyond merely feeling special in Essay's room. I hated it with a vehemence that went beyond the fact that some of the others, much older than I, still continued to wet the mat. I simply preferred to be on my own.

My father travelled; I moved into Wild Christian's bedroom. I awaited his return with a different kind of anxiety – his return would be testing time. On the first night of his return I made to resume my normal sleeping-place but was prevented by mother's casual voice saying,

'Wole, why don't you sleep with the others tonight? You shouldn't abandon them just because your father is back. And your baby brother is getting used to climbing down to sleep with you.'

In the dark, I dissected the tone. Was this to be just a token expression of me caring about being with others? I did not for one moment believe in Wild Christian's concern for Ladipo's feelings; even so, I permitted myself to hope that my reinstatement was only deferred a night. Normal relations would resume the following night.

That following night, I lay on my mat in the dark and cried. My transfer was permanent. And there could be no mistaking the rather guilty half-smile of confirmation on my father's face.

Ladipo was growing fast in his cot. He was born with a noisy, excessive energy which constituted another reason for keeping clear of that maternal dormitory. He had long begun his efforts to climb over the cot and had succeeded once or twice, chiefly by falling down from the top of the cot, so desperate was he to get on the mat with us. It occurred to me then that this child was born with no sense at all, if he actually wanted to leave the sheltered peace of his cot to join that medley of bodies on the mat. Sleeping there brought on the wildest dreams. A tree would fall over my body and I would struggle awake; it was an arm or a leg flung over me. Some of the other sleepers were veteran warriors of sleep – they went to sleep only to *ja'run'pa*, to fight tremendous wars which took them from one corner of the mat to its extreme opposite, rolling and mowing down bodies on the way, ending up in the morning upside down in the wrong place or miraculously back in their original position. I would wake up in the night after a violent struggle with pythons that had tied up all my limbs, suffocating under slimy monsters from a mythical past, unable to utter the scream for help which rose in my throat.

Nothing disturbed the blissful repose of these warriors and other victims of their campaigns. They slept and snored soundly through it all, led from the bed by the stentorian bassoon of Wild Christian. On waking up in the middle of night, the sounds in the room approached the sounds in the Blaize Memorial Canning factory where we were once taken to watch the grapefruits, oranges, guavas and pears being cleaned, sliced, pulped, canned by a series of monstrous guillotines, motors and flapping belts, pistons and steaming boilers which spluttered, belched, spat, thundered and emitted measured jets of liquids that went into the cans and bottles.

In the mornings there would often be the argument about who had actually left the wet patch or two on the mat. Wild Christian was a specialist in unravelling that short-lived puzzle. She pronounced on the matter with such detective ease that she verged on the mystical, considering the unpredictable positions in which the suspects found themselves in the morning, far from the scene of crime. Gradually it dawned on me that there was a characteristic shape and smell formed by the puddle of every human being, the secret of which could only be known to parents, including surrogate parents. Of the latter, my only doubts were whether the secret was mystically transmitted or formed part of the character-notes brought by the actual parents of the 'cousin' when he or she was handed over.

'You have to watch him, Ma'am. He doesn't steal, no, I have never caught him with that terrible habit. But he is lazy, ah, he is lazy. That pawpaw hanging from your tree over there, which doesn't even have enough energy to move out of the way of a bird's beak, is not half as lazy as this wretch you see before you.' And with her finger jabbing in the head of the totally bewildered youth, 'You see that half-eaten pawpaw, that is what children's brains become when they don't use them. We say Study, but you won't study. You want to become an *alaaru* carrying loads for half-pennies at Iddo station. Look, you won't even have a head to put the load on if you don't exert your brain now, because it will just collapse. Your brain would have turned to pulp, pecked by birds in your sleep like that pawpaw mash you see over there. . . .'

It was the mother's last public duty before washing her hands of the reluctant student. But then, as she departed, she would invariably remember one final detail which always had to be whispered. No amount of eavesdropping by Tinu or me ever caught what this strictly-between-parents secret was. The truant mother would, almost guiltily, certainly with much furtiveness, draw Wild Christian aside and a brief, intense, one-sided conversation would follow, with direct glances at the changeling. After giving much thought to the problem of the communal mat, I was left with only the one conclusion that it was at this secret session that characteristics of the new entrant's urine puddle were passed from one mother to the other.

The diversions of the public streets frequently spilled into the parsonage. The sounds carried well before; we followed its course and could tell within minutes if the event would pass us by, in which case we rushed to the ladder and other improvised stands which provided us with a panorama of Aké, over the churchside wall that had nearly proved my undoing. I could now race up the ladder with the rest. If the spectacle poured over the crest of Itoko's sky-grazing road towards Aké, it would turn the corner of the church compound towards the palace; retain a straight course past the cenotaph of the warrior Okenla and round the bookshop towards Igbein and Kuti's Grammar School; or best of all, pass right under our noses along the untarred road between the church compound and our wall, to turn either left towards the Aafin or right in the direction of the General Hospital. Depending on what occasion it was, the parsonage would also receive the noisy guests; funeral processions however did not pay courtesy calls on us, though they were often just like weddings, or outings of dance societies.

The hearse led the way, drawn by pall-bearers; sometimes a horse took their place but this was not very often. The coffin was smothered in wreaths made of plaited palm branches into which flowers had been woven. If it was headed for St Peter's, the church-bell began tolling some minutes before the cortege came within sight, solemn, single strokes at intervals of between thirty and sixty seconds. We could almost feel the slow tramp of feet through the ground, accompanied by creaky turns of the hearse wheels. Often they appeared silently, each face set with grief, compassion, or the sense of occasion – these last we easily detected. They were the ones who fussed over a card which had become displaced from the wreath, their lips were pursed in an unchanging manner and they turned to whisper something or the other to the actual mourners at exact intervals. At the church, the hearse was relieved of its burden which was then taken by a group of men into the church. It always seemed strange that, in spite of all the funerals at St Peter's, no one had ever worked out a comfortable way of taking the coffin from the hearse, carrying it up the few steps, through the aisle between the pews and on to the two cross-benches in front of the altar. The coffin appeared inordinately heavy no matter who had died, the bearers staggered under the load and we always waited for one of them to stumble and bring the coffin down with the crash. It never did happen.

Some processions however arrived for the church service already hymning or chanting refrains to prayers or other mutterings by a robed cleric who led the procession or brought up the rear. Such singing was soft, appropriately restrained. It was nothing beside the scene that followed after the actual interment which followed directly after the church service.

The file of solemn, weeping women and their stiff companions broke formation and spilled over the street in ecstatic dances. Hands which had been clasped so formally in front of the mourners waved cheerful goodbyes to anyone along the road as if each person stood for the relation they had just buried. Trumpets appeared from nowhere, clarinets, drums, tambourines and trombones – it all depended on how elderly or important the deceased had been. Even the empty hearse appeared to be affected by the mad gyrating, not surprisingly, as the two men who were still attached to its handle had also thrown themselves with energy into the dance. They appeared to have their own special motions; a few steps to the right, then the left, back again into a straightforward course, then up went the handle and before it came down they had turned to face the rest of the procession and thus continued to dance backwards, pulling the hearse along. The women's lungs were the more powerful, pumping energy into the singing without diminishing the manipulations of their buttocks:

> Ile o, ile o
> Ile o, ile o
> Baba (Iya) re'le re
> Ile lo lo tarara
> Baba re'le re
> Ile lo lo, ko s'ina.*

One spectacle we did not relish. Indeed, except for the urchins who followed them, this kind of spectacle had nothing of the festive about it. Whatever form it took, its principal feature was this: a youthful culprit with evidence of his or her transgression tied to the neck or carried on the head. Next came the guardian or parent, wielding the corrective whip from time to time. As they went through the streets, layabouts and urchins were encouraged to swell the numbers, jeering and singing at the top of their voice. They picked up tins and boxes along the way and added an assortment of rhythm to which the culprit was expected to dance; often it was the offender who supplied the lead while the mob provided the refrain. Most of the time, the tired, humiliated wretch was a young woman, a fact which made some impression on me.

* Home, Home
  The elder has gone home
  Directly
  The elder has gone home
  Home is he bound, he will not miss his way.

It was perhaps the only time that the kindly Mrs B. earned my silent rebuke. Her maid was suffering from the same incontinence as afflicted the majority of the cousins and house helps in our house. One morning we looked out, attracted by the sounds of the familiar stick-on-can beat within the parsonage itself. The sound came from the bookseller's compound and we soon made out the words:

Tòólé, Tòóle, a f'òkò ìtò borí
Suúlé ṣuúlé fóko nùdi.*

And then she came in sight. The offending mat was rolled and borne on her head, the procession went from house to house where a stop was made and the girl had to dance her dance of shame. At each house, Mrs B. gestured and the music stopped briefly:

'Look at her. Sixteen and she still wets the mat like a newly-born. I don't know what to do with her, Auntie, I just don't know what to do with her. She is old enough to be preparing for the matrimonial home, but is she to go there with wet mat and coverlet? Look at the ungainly, gormless, unprepossessing object. In any case, who is going to look at it and want to put it in the house? She doesn't even seem to know that the market for husbands is not open to such as it . . . Shut up!' Down came the whip on the blubbering mess, about her shoulders, back, then legs making her skip, so that without any further prompting, the orchestral jangle was resumed to the skipping of her feet.

'Did I ask you to blubber? Dance, atoo'le! You really think anyone is impressed with all that crying? Come on, sing out! Those fit to be your children are drumming for you, they stopped pissing in their beds ages ago. But you have no shame, so dance when they beat for you.'

How long it lasted depended on the stamina of the guardian, or on a chance meeting with a capable pleader, at home or on the street. When they came to our house, Wild Christian stood and watched until she judged that Mrs B. was ready for appeasement. Then she stopped the drumming and singing and beckoned to the maid to come nearer.

'Is this a good thing for you?' she demanded.

The maid appeared to be confused, or maybe she did not even hear the question. Mrs B. raised the whip. 'I think she has gone deaf and dumb. Let me open up her ears a little.'

* Bed-wetter, bed-wetter,
  With a piss-pot for a head-cover
  Excretes on the mat and cleans her anus with fibre.

86

Wild Christian gestured restraint. Mrs B. let fall her arm and the admonition was resumed:

'Is this a good thing for you? At your age, to be paraded through the streets like this. A grown woman, still wetting her mat, is this good? That is what I asked you.'

'No, ma, it is not good.'

'SPEAK UP!'

The maid skipped in anticipation and found her long-distance voice. 'No, ma, it is not good. It is not a good thing.'

'Good. But do you know that this is all for your own good? That you are being helped so that you will not go and disgrace yourself elsewhere?'

'Yes, ma, I know it is for my own good.'

'Are you going to make an effort to change?'

'I will change, ma. By God's power I promise to change.'

The exchange lasted a while, ending with a short sermon. Wild Christian then turned to Mrs B., 'took the rest of the punishment on herself.' Mrs B. curtsied, the maid knelt fully on the ground and said her thanks, the urchins had begun to drift away, knowing that the fun had ended. I watched Mrs B. and maid, the former leading, walk back in the silence that had descended once more on the parsonage and wondered if the maid was still going to wet her mat that night. Lawanle said the treatment always worked, but only if in addition, she roasted the egg-nest of the praying mantis and ate it. Lawanle claimed to have made a particular cousin eat at least a dozen egg-nests of the praying mantis plus a special potion prepared according to the recipe of an old woman at Ibarapa. She had used it successfully for her own cure several years before. All of them were agreed that at home Wild Christian was doing it all wrong. Sending the offenders supperless to bed was not going to solve anything; they only ate more during their last meal, which was not permitted later than five in the evening. And anyway who could keep an eye on them throughout to make sure they didn't drink water to shore up their bedtime hunger? It was a matter for the *babalawo** and he, Lawanle insisted, would probably prescribe the very method employed by Mrs B.

Mrs B., when she brought her road-show to our house, had actually succeeded in redeeming herself in my eyes. One did not have to look closely to see that she actually pulled her blows with the whip. If I was in any doubt about it, one look at Wild Christian confirmed it; she was plainly amused by what Mrs B. considered corrective lashes. In any case, she *knew*

* Oracle-priest; diviner.

Mrs B. If Wild Christian had been wielding the whip, that maid would not have skipped, she would have leapt out of her skin and continued dancing even when asked to stop.

In a similar spectacle where the offence was more serious, such as stealing, the urchins were encouraged to participate in whipping the culprit. Stealing meat from a soup-pot was considered particularly heinous, though why, I could not understand. If the thief, when caught, had already swallowed the evidence of his crime, he was made to carry the soup-pot on his head, and his mouth was smeared with oil from the pot. The outing could go on day after day after day. The complainants never seemed to have enough, such was the outrage of these soup-pot guardians. I thought, after all he has eaten the meat, no amount of dancing and flogging would bring it back. And a piece of meat always seemed too small and insignificant to conjure up the number of people who turned out on parade. As Wild Christian prepared dinner that evening while we hung around fetching and holding for her, conversation turned to the morning's exhibition. Wild Christian threatened similar cures for our own mat-wetters and other types of miscreants. Because she expected it, she read disapproval on my face.

'Wole is planning to dip his hand in the pot, that's why he disapproves.'

I denied that I disapproved.

'Or maybe he has been doing it already, only we haven't caught him.'

'If you caught him he would lawyer his way out,' Joseph warned.

'Not with me,' Wild Christian promised. 'It's his father who has all that patience. When I clobber him as he opens his mouth he would soon discover I don't stand for any nonsense.'

'Anyway,' contributed a cousin, 'Wole is more likely to steal toffee or sugar or powdered milk, Ovaltine and things like that.'

I glared a challenge at that cousin. His face betrayed nothing but I wondered what he knew. Obviously nothing. By now he would have blackmailed me if he had known that I had been dipping regularly into the tin of Lactogen. After Dipo was weaned and had begun to eat solids, the big tin of Lactogen lay in a corner of the pantry, forgotten. I had developed a passion for the powdered delicacy, it seemed the most exquisite taste in the world, soft, melty, light on the tongue. It was not merely a question of stealing a handful at a time; I had appropriated the entire tin which nobody remembered, secreted it among other bric-à-brac in the pantry, from where it emerged from time to time to satisfy my craving.

It was at least a month later before the tin was discovered, but by then nobody knew how much had remained in it in the one year or more since it was last opened. If I had not been so desperately hooked, I would have known that Wild Christian would be suspicious of its long disappearance and would keep watch on the level of powder it contained. Her suspicions were soon confirmed, so she summoned everyone, asked questions and issued a general warning. That should have been sufficient. It was not only that she was on the war-path, she was clearly planning something exemplary for the foolhardy thief whenever he was caught. Perhaps she already knew the milk-thief and knew that it was now a habit. Inspired guesses came mysteriously to Wild Christian. But I was hooked. Still, a week passed before I abandoned all further resistance, watched the physical disposition of everybody else and homed on the tin. Wild Christian, whom I had last seen preparing vegetables further up the yard, opened the pantry-door a little and nodded:

'Good. So it's you. I thought so. I've always known it.'

I believed her. Normally she would by then have drowned out the external world with a barrage of blows. This time she was unusually calm. And she visibly gloated as if a long-awaited moment had been reached. Her self-satisfaction bothered me, it appeared to go beyond the crime. Again I had the uneasy feeling that I had foolishly walked into a trap.

'We will wait until your father comes. When he has finished with you, you will then come and eat my own punishment.'

Alone in the pantry, I began to plan to run away. It was not just a question of getting caught, there was something much too pat about the whole act, as if everyone had been waiting for just this moment and had in some way played a small role in bringing it about. One thing was not going to happen: I was not providing a spectacle for anyone, neither within the parsonage nor on the streets of Aké. Once again I was struck with the disproportionate attention paid to a tin of powdered milk whose existence had long been forgotten. I had placed it under my personal protection for nearly two months and had grown to regard it as my private booty. My mind was made up; I would run away, first emptying the Lactogen on the floor as a final protest.

I moved furtively from the pantry to the bedroom, to the front room where most of my books were, packed them into a small bag and awaited the right moment to escape. Essay returned from school and, as I expected, Wild Christian immediately ensconced herself with him in his room to report the terrible discovery. It was the right moment, and I tip-toed through the parlour and into the front room. A moment later and I would have gone, but the voices were coming out loud and clear from the bedroom and I hesitated, then settled down to listen. My mother was evidently displeased that Essay would not personally deal with the offence. I heard him grumble,

'You should have flogged him. Why bother me?'

I heard her reply, 'But he must have finished half that tin. I remember very well what level it was when I last used it for Dipo. It was very nearly full. I had just opened it before he lost all interest in milk or anything like that.'

Unperturbed, Essay insisted, 'Then punish him for the whole tin. I still don't understand why you didn't just beat him on the spot.'

Wild Christian knew when she was getting nowhere. She whirled out of the room so fast that I had just enough time to fling the bag over the lower-door on to the pavement outside. As she hauled me into the backyard with her, all I could think of was the tell-tale bundle lying on the front pavement, containing my favourite books and clothing. She shouted for her stick and even before its arrival I found myself leaping about the backyard, dodging wild blows from fist and feet, felled by some and rolling with others. Till the last moment, I kept fearing, and hoping that she would attempt to transfer the event outside our own backyard; in my mind I rehearsed the swift movement down, the bundle of my possessions snatched up and then – a continuous run through the parsonage, through the streets, heading nowhere but everywhere, away from the household whose subtle hostilities had begun to prickle my skin. I now blamed the entire household for my banishment from Essay's room. Of the many strange thoughts which crowded my mind under the beating was one which claimed with complete assurance that I was being proved right, I had for long suspected that my place was no longer in that house. The certainty simply came and stayed with a host of others. They crowded my head without any particular order, without any attempt to resolve themselves, probably simply to help me forget the actual pain of the beating. Only, they proved far more painful than the blows. By the time it was over I had decided that it would be best to pursue my original plans, pick up my bundle and seek my fortune away from the parsonage.

When I sneaked out later, not much later, the bundle was gone. Joseph had found it, had picked it up and resorted its contents where they belonged. I did not know what to make of his action after he admitted to it, but it seemed a natural thing for him to have done.

That same night, when the whole house was asleep and Wild Christian was shaking the roof with her snores, I tiptoed into the pantry, filled my mouth with powdered milk. In another second I was back on the mat. In the dark, I let the powder melt, dissolve slowly and slide down the back of my throat in small doses. In the morning I felt no pain whatsoever from the pounding of the previous evening.

VII

Change was impossible to predict. A tempo, a mood would have settled over the house, over guests, relations, casual visitors, poor relations, 'cousins', strays – all recognized within a tangible pattern of feeling – and then it would happen! A small event or, more frequently, nothing happened at all, nothing that I could notice much less grasp and – suddenly it all changed! The familiar faces looked and acted differently. Features appeared where they had not been, vanished where before they had become inseparable from our existence. Every human being with whom we came in contact, Tinu and I, would CHANGE! Even Tinu changed, and I began to wonder if I also changed, without knowing it, the same as everybody else.

'If I begin to change, you will tell me, won't you?'

She said, 'What are you talking about?'

'Haven't you noticed? Joseph, Lawanle, Nubi, everybody is changing. Papa and Mama have changed. Even Mr Adelu has changed.'

Mr Adelu was one of our most frequent visitors. Compared with some others, there was nothing remarkable about him. This made it all the worse that Mr Adelu should change. From the bookseller now, I expected no better.

But occasionally, I did detect the cause. The birth of Dipo brought about such a CHANGE, indeed, it began long before his arrival. There was nothing whatever to remark about Wild Christian, who was then anything but wild, except that she had begun to bulge. I could not then tell whether she ate a lot or not, but it appeared normal that grown-ups should grow in whichever direction suited them. I hoped myself to grow some day towards my father's height, but I was in no hurry about it. What was curious was that Essay appeared to change far more – in his habits – than Wild Christian who simply bulged and bulged. Still, a howling brother, endowed with superabundant energy, appeared at the end of that change, and somehow that explained all that had gone before. Essay's worried looks disappeared, to be replaced by endless smiles and chuckles. The house appeared to loosen up in every way. Visitors streamed into the house and I sought the refuge of Jonah more and more to escape the noisy changes.

The changes sometimes were mundane, domestic. The parlour furniture would suddenly affect Wild Christian in some way and then it would vanish, only to re-appear in a new arrangement. The intervening hours would be spent hunting bed-bugs which had made a home in the parlour cushions. Seams of the cushion-covers were carefully explored, a needle was heated over a candle and then – a sizzling sound, the end of a bed-bug. Next, to find their eggs, brush the flame lightly over them and hear them give off brief crackles, dull explosions, ending in a charred spot. When the arm-chairs and the drink stools went back, a CHANGE had taken place. Some never went back, demoted to the store-house in the upper backyard or to the front room where visitors first rested, while Essay was summoned. Even the immutable homilies, embroidered, framed and glazed, would be transposed around the walls. I looked up expecting to see REMEMBER NOW THY CREATOR IN THE DAYS OF THY YOUTH only to find EBENEZER: HITHERTO HATH THE LORD HELPED US.

Somtimes, the nail from which the homily was hung had merely been moved a foot or two towards or away from the front room. The consequences were serious. It meant that Essay could no longer be seen reflected long in advance of his arrival home, from the moment when he stepped through the door of the primary school on to the broad path that led almost straight down to the gate of the parsonage. He was visible until two-thirds way down the path, when he was picked up by HONOUR THY FATHER AND THY MOTHER – this was the moment to abandon all mischief. Within the house itself, REMEMBER NOW THY CREATOR picked up his reflection as he emerged from the bedroom, the ageless curtains flapping. This put an end to whatever we were doing wrong at meal-time in the dining-room. We often studied in the front room, where the material that really held our interest was quickly hidden in the desk the moment Essay, having finished his gardening in the backyard, appeared within THE LORD IS MY SHEPHERD, suitably surrounded by the crotons that grew in profusion just outside the dining-room window. The framed homilies were a lifesaver and we worked hard to restore them to their spying functions. Unable to tamper with the nail itself, we resorted to tilting the frame, shortening the cord on one side or placing clumps of the nest of a home-wasp behind the frame. The piece of dried mud, if discovered, would evoke no surprise, as wasps built their nests in the ceilings where they remained until someone felt an inclination to prise them off.

There was the CHANGE in sleeping arrangements. Not mine alone. Suddenly everyone was banished from Wild Christian's bedroom. The parlour became the new bedroom; chairs were moved aside, the centre-table was placed in the corner, mats were spread out and pillows placed in position for those who used them. At night Essay had to pick his way through the sprawling bodies to get a drink of water. That was a pleasant change. There was a lot more room in the parlour and one no longer woke up with his nose pressed against a sack of black-eyed beans.

The CHANGES sometimes came from reports. Even without meaning to eavesdrop, it was nearly impossible not to listen to conversations going on in any part of the house. Visitors came, spoke, argued or cajoled, sought something from or offered something to Essay, usually Essay, but sometimes also Wild Christian. Some were total strangers; they came within HM's orbit once and disappeared for ever. Yet they took away with them a part of those motions of reliance, accustomed gestures, codes and confidences which secured us within the walls of HM's home. Imperceptible at first, we found that attention had been withdrawn from or was now being trained on some of us. There was a new language to be learnt, a new physical relationship in things and people. Once or twice, I felt that the entire household was about to prepare for a journey, to be uprooted from Aké in its entirety. Yet no one could tell me where to, how or why, and we never moved.

Yet, even CHANGE often acted inconsistently. Until the birth of Folasade, I had believed that Change was something that one or more of the household caught, then discarded – like Temperature. Folasade's was permanent. She came after Dipo; unlike him, she was a quiet child. And then, from morning till night, she cried, rolled about in her cot, and kept the whole house awake. She did not reject food outright but ate with great difficulty. We could see the effort in her eyes, barely ten months old. When we reached for her hand through the railings of the cot, she clutched the offered finger with all her strength, holding on. Then suddenly she would twitch, her eyes changed as the pain washed over them, she began to cry all over again.

Our parents spent hours in Essay's bedroom; we could hear them talking but could make out no words. They spoke very softly. The maid was sent for, questioned. Her voice was clear enough, whatever she was being asked, she denied. She was vehement, called on God to witness. She repeated over and over again 'Nothing happened, nothing happened at all, sir.' She came out of the bedroom, her face set, aggrieved by false suspicion or accusation.

Folasade was taken to hospital. She went in the morning and did not return until late afternoon. Her little trunk was encased in plaster from beneath the arm-pits to her buttocks. Wild Christian carried her, not on her back, but in her arms, wrapped up in a shawl.

She still cried from time to time. But many nights she merely lay awake. I got up from the mat, knelt by the cot and looked into the silent pools of her eyes. She did not appear to acknowledge me. Day after day Folasade lay on her back, was brought out to be fed, changed, then returned to her cot or increasingly on to our mother's bed, propped with pillows on both sides. She was so still that the pillows seemed superfluous. Folasade simply lay still and stared at the ceiling.

One day, I came on the maid sitting by herself, crying. I had noticed for some time that she was to be found more and more by herself. The others would not talk to her. I saw a plate of food beside her, untouched. When I asked her what was the matter she frightened me by a sudden intensification of her weeping so that it took a long time before I made out that she was actually saying between sobs:

'I swear I did not drop her. I swear by God I did not drop her any time. I looked after her, at no time did she drop from my hands, I swear.'

She was seated on the steps which led to the store-room of the Upper Backyard, overlooked by one of the windows of mother's bedroom. I now heard that window being opened. When I looked up there was the face of Wild Christian; never before or since then would I see such a concentration of grief and rage all at once as she stared straight at the weeping maid. The window had been flung open, there was nothing furtive about it. I saw then that she must have heard the maid, had been keeping her eye on the girl. What made her decide to confront her, even silently, just then, could have been the sound of my voice. The maid looked up and saw her. Her tears dried instantly.

Later that evening, the maid was summoned again. This time the questioning took hours. Before it was over, I had fallen asleep. By the morning the maid was gone, she and her luggage.

So were Essay and Wild Christian. So was Folasade. Whatever they finally extracted from the girl had sent them straight back to the Catholic hospital at Ita Padi. There was little gaiety in the home during their absence, only anxiety. The maid's departure, the disappearance of both parents with the baby foretold some momentous development but we did not know what it was. It was Joseph who revealed that the maid had packed her things that night and been escorted out of the house by him, on Essay's instructions. Where they had gone with the baby he did not know,

95

but he had looked over the wall under which they passed and the direction suggested the hospital at Ita Padi.

There was no change in Folasade's appearance when they returned, no change whatever in her motions when she was placed in her cot. Wild Christian spent more and more time in Essay's room even when he was at school. She simply lay in bed or was on her knees, praying. She prayed a lot.

One morning, her motions appeared somewhat more purposeful than before. A man whom we knew simply as Carpenter – he had his workshop at the corner of the road along our churchside wall – came into the house with a small wooden box, square-shaped. My father took it into Wild Christian's bedroom.

Through the door, I heard her say, 'I think the children should see her first, don't you?'

There was a brief, mumbled discussion, and then we were summoned.

Folasade was laid out in a long white dress which covered her plaster and stretched over her feet. Her eyes were closed and she was just as still as she had been for several weeks past. I looked at Tinu who stood there impassively. Wild Christian stood by, a sad sweet smile on her face, saying things which I could not understand, only that we were not to feel sad about anything, because Folasade was now out of pain. 'You see, she does not suffer any more.'

Again I looked at Tinu. I expected her to do or say something, mostly do something, after all she was the elder. But Tinu kept her eyes on the body, looked once slowly at both parents, then turned to continue her mute, expressionless study of our sister.

Suddenly, it all broke up within me. A force from nowhere pressed me against the bed and I howled. As I was picked up I struggled against my father's soothing voice, tears all over me. I was sucked into a place of loss whose cause or definition remained elusive. I did not comprehend it yet, and even through those tears I saw the astonished face of Wild Christian, and heard her voice saying,

'But what does he understand of it? What does he understand?'

There was no CHANGE after Folasade's departure, none whatever. I daily expected a cataclysm of unthinkable proportions but it never happened. If the house had picked itself up by the roots and floated skywards, I would have shown no surprise, but nothing happened. The normality was almost overbearing and I began to suspect a conspiracy between our parents to ensure that this time when CHANGE would be so reasonable, even necessary, it did not happen.

As if it did not matter, as if it signified nothing at all that Folasade had not only died, but had chosen to go on her very first birthday.

The flimsier structures of Aké, built of unbaked mud, could not stand up to the rains of July and August. The corrugated iron sheets were penetrated by the wind which ripped them off, flung them over other roofs, leaving the rain to find the weakest point in the walls, dissolve the mud and flush out the household. But sometimes the rain acted first; it found the crack in the thin cement coating, soaked it to its foundations, then the house collapsed on its inmates. A wet, shivering survivor, a growing pool about his feet, stood in the front room and told the tale of disaster. He was escorted to the back room, stripped while Essay rummaged in his trunks for some old clothing and Wild Christian prepared a steaming mug of tea, almost treacly with sugar and milk, and a chunk of white bread liberally spread with butter.

Although the house had crashed in Aké itself, far from the parsonage, the *agbara* which flowed past our raised pavement now brought with it all the debris of that house, and the faces of its victims one after the other. Smoke-caked rafters jostled with medicine bottles, a chamber pot followed, astride it was a child's doll, white, blue-eyed and flaxen-haired. She sat with one leg slightly raised and one arm pointed to the sky.

Mrs Adetunmbi came all the way from Ikereku, disconsolate. Even in the front room she ran from spot to spot, wringing her shawl, indeed her motion was closer to attempting to wash her hands in the shawl. 'E gba mi, e gba mi'* . . . she said that she was going to fetch firewood, she hasn't been back. The rains stopped over four hours ago but still she is not yet back . . . e gba mi o, Headmaster, e gba mi . . .'

But what do you want Headmaster to do? The rains may have stopped but the agbara *is still rushing and swelling. Mama, I have just seen the face of your daughter floating past our doorstep; I did nothing to stop her.*

'Where are you going?' Wild Christian opened the window as I sneaked past.

'Only to the school compound.'

'To do what?'

'To pick some guavas. They'll be plenty on the ground after this rain.'

'Tell Bunmi to go. You will only catch a cold.'

'She can't. It's my guava tree.'

* Save me, save me . . .

97

'Are you mad?' Wild Christian nearly exploded. 'I said you are going nowhere. Come back here!'

I returned, stood with my legs apart. She continued to stare, so I put my hands behind my back.

'Did you hear what I said?'

'I heard, Ma. I was returning to read my book.'

'And what do you say when you are talked to?'

'Yes, Ma.'

A long baleful glance. 'Take yourself out of my sight.'

'Yes, Ma.'

I caught Bunmi as she came out of the back gate. 'If you touch my guava tree, their *iwin* will visit you at night.'

'Go away, you see you don't even know anything about spirits. It is *òrò* which lives in trees, not *iwin*.'

'Just touch the tree and see who is right. I've warned you.'

'You are only jealous because Mama wouldn't let you go and pick the guava.'

'Even the ones on the ground, I warn you. Touch them and you'll see.'

When she returned, she reported my threats to Wild Christian. Later that evening at dinner, I saw her glance at me from time to time. When Essay had finished his meal, she announced quite loudly, looking at me all the while,

'I'll come with you now to discuss . . .'

Essay grunted, 'Oh, all right.'

Bunmi jabbed her finger in the direction of my nose. 'Now we shall see who is going to chop that stick tonight.'

'For what? What offence did I commit?'

'Stubborn. When I told her what you said she said you were getting too stubborn. She said she was going to tell Papa.'

'For telling her, both the *iwin* and *òrò* will get you tonight.'

I went to the front room to read, expected the summons to come any time. I found I did not much worry about it.

'What are you staring at?'

'Your nose.'

'I shall tell Mama you have been rude again.'

'One can only be rude to one's elders. Who do you think you are?'

'Rudeness is rudeness. Mama says we are to report you if you are ever rude again.'

'Did I abuse you?' I demanded.

Bunmi stared at me, the same look of puzzlement came into her eyes. 'What is the matter with you, Wole? Why do you want to quarrel with everybody?'

'Leave me alone.'

But they would not. Acting on instructions it seemed, but they simply would not. Alone, Bukola suited my mood. I escaped to the bookseller's as often as I could. Bukola knew how to be silent. Even when she spoke, she transmitted a world of silence into which I fitted. She picked up pebbles and weighed them in her hands, thoughtfully. She ate as if she ate with *other* people. I watched her intently, seeking something that would answer barely formed questions. She glided over the earth like a being who barely deigned to accommodate the presence of others. With her, I found some peace.

I always knew when Wild Christian was going to discuss me with Essay, it very simply transmitted itself to me on a wave of hostility. I would not hesitate, I went and eavesdropped. Sometimes it was Tinu who came to call me. At other times Nubi or Joseph would inform me, gleefully, as if to terrify me. I strolled casually past them, then went and pinned my ear to the curtain.

'It is not new,' Wild Christian was saying, 'he has always tended to brood.'

'Then there is nothing to worry about.'

'But it is not healthy. It is not natural in a child. When he had only Tinu for a playmate it wasn't too bad. But for some years now he has tended to wander off by himself. And now this . . .'

'If it has to do with Folasade,' counselled Essay, 'it will wear off.'

'And then spending so much time alone with you. That really cut him off the rest of the family.'

'So I am now to blame . . .'

'I wasn't blaming you, dear. I am just trying to see that we mustn't encourage him any more. Especially as it is making him headstrong.'

'I hadn't noticed he was headstrong.'

'You are away most of the time, you don't notice. And of course these children won't come to you and tell you.'

It would end with Essay promising to watch me more closely.

'We must take him out of himself,' my mother persisted.

'All right, all right.'

The Odufuwa came to visit, but it only lifted my spirits a little. Mrs Odufuwa was quite simply and without dispute from any but the blindest man with the coarsest sensibilities, the most beautiful woman in the world.

I bore her husband no grudge, after all, he was my godfather, so he should prove no obstacle to my marrying this goddess once I had grown to manhood. I followed her about as she strolled in the garden with her husband.

She had nicknames for everyone for she could not, as a 'wife' of the house, call us children by name, at least not those who were born into the house before she became a wife of the family. And so Tinu was 'Obinrin Jeje', the gentle woman – which I considered a most observant choice, and it only confirmed Mrs Odufuwa's cleverness. I came next, and I was Lagilagi, the Log-Splitter. Before I could even wield a vegetable knife, I had insisted on helping Joseph with the splitting of firewood, employing an axe. The goddess had observed me at my exertions, and the name stuck. Hitler's world power thrust had just begun to percolate to us. The German race had acquired a fearsome, bellicose reputation – it was inevitable, Dipo could only acquire one name – Jamani!'

The goddess and her husband were moving leisurely through the flowers; I followed them. Joseph was in the vicinity, preparing logs for chopping. Wild Christian was somewhere on the periphery. I simply followed, stopped when Odufuwa stopped, touched the roses at the stalk where she had briefly sniffed them, brushed the croton with my hand where her sleeve had brushed. Then from nowhere came Jamani to ruin it all, not so much walking as preening and turning cartwheels, leaping out in front, falling behind only to re-emerge far ahead of the evening strollers. I watched his antics with an older brother's indulgent amusement.

Mrs Odufuwa turned round, looked at me and said, 'Lagilagi, I understand you work as hard on these flowers as your father.'

I savoured the moment, rolling the sound of her voice all over again through my head. Then came Joseph's jarring voice saying,

'Which Lagilagi? You shouldn't call him that name again, Madam. He cannot *la* anything. He is so lazy he can't move a fly off his nose until it has begun to produce maggots.'

First, I wondered how Joseph, a Benin, had suddenly picked up such earthy Yoruba argot. He was *kobokobo*,* still spoke Yoruba with his individual quaintness even after several years with us. Yet there he was tongue-bashing me in true Yoruba market style without any strain. And for no reason. I stared at him, open-mouthed.

'Is that true, my Lagilagi?'

Dipo came bounding in view and Joseph pointed at him. 'Look at his

* Rude expression for those who do not speak the local language.

brother, almost three years his junior. He is far tougher than the one you've named Lagilagi. I bet Dipo can already lift that axe and split wood with it.'

I moved forward without one moment's hesitation, lifted the axe and stuck in it a nearby log.

Then Wild Christian joined in. 'All he does is sneak off into corners by himself – reading, always reading. He pretends to be busy with books because he cannot tackle anything else.'

I was hurt. What had I done? Why did they try to reduce me in the eye of my future wife? I looked from one to the other and they were grinning, laughing at me.

Nubi emerged from nowhere. Something was building up, something prepared outside of me, yet I was at the centre of it. Nubi now said,

'If he sees a fight he will run. He cries when he is touched as if everyone wants to beat him.' She sniggered. 'Hm, who wants to commit murder? If you touch him he will faint, then die altogether of fright. Me? No thank you, let him run under the skirts of his books.'

Who were they talking about, I wondered. Everything said around me sounded like the findings of a serious study, so they could only be talking about someone and of specific deeds, or non-deeds. That someone appeared to be me yet I could not recognize myself in what they said. Joseph suddenly stopped Dipo mid-somersault and held him, turned his head to face me:

'I bet Dipo can give him a thorough beating.'

'Of course he can,' said Wild Christian. 'He'll beat him until he begs for mercy.'

My only concern was to see what Mrs Odufuwa was making of this. Did she believe any of it? She stood with her husband beside the dwarf guava tree with a puzzled smile on her face, and I only thought how unfair it was to subject her to such an unbecoming spectacle.

Nubi suggested, 'Why don't we see for ourselves? Dipo will beat him soundly.'

Dipo, never one to resist any invitation to action, began to square his little fists. He struck a fighting pose and leapt from side to side in a war-dance all his own creation. I had never seen such excitement on his face! Cheers rang out from all sides while I stood limply, patronizingly amused by his antics. He was like a gnome, so frisky and so full of joy at being alive and among attentive grown-ups. But then, with no warning at all, only the sound of Joseph's 'Come on, Dipo, show him,' this compact little creature launched himself at me, fists flying. I was borne backwards by the sheer weight of the charge and could no longer separate the different causes of the ringing in my ears.

From far distances I heard voices, protests, admonitions. Time had passed, how much time I did not know. There was a period of total emptiness in which I remembered nothing, only a storm of rage in my veins. But now I felt hands under my arms, strong hands, desperate, even trembling hands under my arms against which I struggled with equal desperation. Then I recognized Joseph's voice:

'Wole, o to, o to?* Do you want to kill him?' spoken with his quaint Benin accent.

And Wild Christian's voice, more soothing and disturbed than I had ever heard it. 'Wole, we were only teasing you. You should have remembered that he is only your junior brother. Ah ah, whatever it was, you should not have got violent with him.'

The skies fell on me. I shivered so violently that Wild Christian put her hand on my forehead and looked anxious. In the background were Dipo's howls. He had been carried into the dining-room where he was now being consoled with sweets and fruit juice. Wild Christian turned her head towards the sound and once again, a strange look came into her eyes. There was such deep pain and confusion, there was fright also, I thought. Anyway it was a different mother from whatever it was I last saw in her.

'But why?' she repeated, more to herself. 'It was all a joke. Did you want to kill him? He's only a baby, you know, you shouldn't have taken him so seriously.'

Dipo's howls had gone down, and Joseph came out. It could have been my imagination, but I felt that he deliberately gave me a wide berth. His words however left me in no doubt about how he felt. To ensure that he was at his most cutting, he did not even deign to address me directly; indeed I now understood why he had cut such a wide curve around me. 'I suppose,' he said to no one in particular, 'the big brother is feeling pleased with himself. I don't even know why we bothered. We should have let him kill his own brother, which was what he wanted.' He let out a deliberately prolonged hiss, 'Shee-aaw? Some people don't even know how to conduct themselves as elders.'

Wild Christian shushed him, but I saw no difference in both their attitudes. I was overwhelmed by only one fact – there was neither justice nor logic in the world of grown-ups. I had imagined that I was the aggrieved one. What did occur I still was not sure of, beyond the fact that I

* Enough, that will do.

102

had come to being violently prised off a squawking bundle that was my brother. But I also recollected clearly enough that I had not provoked the situation. I had joined the others in enjoying the clowning of Dipo – until he launched himself at me like a rocket. Where was I at fault? Still, I was faced with the fact – the entire world was united in finding me guilty of attempted fratricide, and there was nowhere I could seek redress.

Whatever it was all about, it was enough for Wild Christian to exert herself to make me understand something in connection with the episode. After the normal evening prayers she called me into the bedroom and, as she usually did over any trivial to critical problem with a child, made me kneel and pray especially with her. Then she spoke to me. There were warnings on the dangers of allowing the devil to come between one and his natural love and care for the rest of the family. It was so easy to be possessed by the devil, she said. The phrase *emi esu* occurred repeatedly and I really began to wonder if I had not truly become possessed by the soul of the devil. There was that 'black-out' period of which I remembered little.

Dipo was a favourite of both Tinu and me. His energy and humour left us constantly entertained. Moreover, he was considered not yet old enough for punishment, so we foisted on him many of our own mischiefs. He was always ready to own up to breaking a vase which Tinu or I had knocked down in a fight or admit to leaving a door ajar which let in the goats. Later, as he became wiser, he demanded payment for his services – a piece of meat, a toffee or an extra piece of yam. He became so adept at extracting payment – preferably in advance – that we decided that he would end up in charge of Wild Christian's shop and be gaoled for profiteering. Could that Dipo have angered me so much that I no longer knew what I was doing? The thought was deeply alarming.

From Joseph and the others I eventually gathered that I continued hitting him long after he was down, crying, and beyond defending himself. I denied this heatedly. But then, there was that *emi esu* which Wild Christian tried to exorcise with her constant prayers; could this really take a child over without his knowing? If only there was a way of sensing when one was being taken over, one could take necessary precautions. I had long lost faith in the efficacy of Wild Christian's prayers. There were several of her wards over whom she prayed night and day. She took them into the church and prayed over them, found any excuse, any opportunity at all to drag them before the altar and pray over them. They continued to steal, lie, fight or do whatever it was she prayed against. The scale of such perversity, it seemed, must be beyond the remedy of prayers since the two had the entire church to themselves and God was not being distracted by other voices from that same direction. I had no doubt that prayers worked for Wild Christian herself, she seemed to thrive on it and she claimed her prayers were always answered. It was different for the rest of us who had allowed entry to *emi esu*, and there was little even she could do about it.

I resolved to guard against it in the future, at least, to guard against what seemed a kind of blacked-out violence. And indeed, a less distressing explanation surfaced in my mind: that I had merely lashed out against the whole world of tormentors and that Dipo had been unlucky to time his war-dance for that moment. There was another solace. I waited with some anxiety for the moment when Essay would be given a report of the event, but he never was. On the contrary I obtained a distinct feeling that every care was taken to ensure that he was kept in ignorance of what had occurred.

VIII

Workmen came into the house. They knocked lines of thin nails with narrow clasps into walls. The lines turned with corners and doorways and joined up with outside wires which were strung across poles. The presence of these workmen reminded me of another invasion. At the end of those earlier activities we no longer needed the oil-lamps, kerosene lanterns and candles, at least not within the house. We pressed down a switch and the room was flooded with light. Essay's instructions were strict – only he, or Wild Christian could give the order for the pressing of those switches. I recalled that it took a while to connect the phenomenon of the glowing bulb with the switch, so thoroughly did Essay keep up the deception. He pretended it was magic, he easily directed our gaze at the glass bulb while he muttered his magic spell. Then he solemnly intoned:

'Let there be light.'

Afterwards he blew in the direction of the bulb and the light went out.

But finally, we caught him out. It was not too difficult to notice that he always stood at the same spot, that that spot was conveniently near a small white-and-black object which had sprouted on the wall after the workmen had gone. Still, the stricture continued. The magic light was expensive and must be wisely used.

Now the workmen were threading the walls again, we wondered what the new magic would produce. This time there was no bulb, no extra switches on the wall. Instead, a large wooden box was brought into the house and installed at the very top of the tallboy, displacing the old gramophone which now had to be content with one of the lower shelves on the same furniture. The face of the box appeared to be made of thick plaited silk.

But the functions continued to be the same. True, there was no need to put on a black disc, no need to crank a handle or change a needle, it only required that the knob be turned for sounds to come on. Unlike the gramophone however, the box could not be made to speak or sing at any time of the day. It began its monologue early in the morning, first playing 'God Save the King'. The box went silent some time in the afternoon, resumed late afternoon, then, around ten or eleven in the evening, sang 'God Save the King' once more and went to sleep.

Because the box spoke incessantly and appeared to have no interest in a response, it soon earned the name *As'oromagb'esi*.* An additional line was added to a jingle which had been formed at the time of the arrival of electricity. Belatedly, that jingle had also done honour to Lagos where the sacred monopoly of the umbrella by royalty had first been broken;

Elektiriki ina oba
Umbrella el'eko
As'oromagb'esi, iro oyinbo.†

At certain set hours, the box delivered THE NEWS. The News soon became an object of worship to Essay and a number of his friends. When the hour approached, something happened to this club. It did not matter what they were doing, they rushed to our house to hear the Oracle. It was enough to watch Essay's face to know that the skin would be peeled off the back of any child who spoke when he was listening to The News. When his friends were present, the parlour with its normal gloom resembled a shrine, rapt faces listened intently, hardly breathing. When The Voice fell silent all faces turned instinctively to the priest himself. Essay reflected for a moment, made a brief or long comment and a babble of excited voices followed.

The gramophone fell into disuse. The voices of Denge, Ayinde Bakare, Ambrose Campbell; a voice which was so deep that I believed it could only have been produced by a special trick of His Master's Voice, but which father assured me belonged to a black man called Paul Robeson – they all were relegated to the cocoon of dust which gathered in the gramophone section. Christmas carols, the songs of Marian Anderson; oddities, such as as record in which a man did nothing but laugh throughout, and the one concession to a massed choir of European voices – the Hallelujah Chorus – all were permanently interned in the same cupboard. Now voices sang, unasked, from the new box. Once that old friend the Hallelujah Chorus burst through the webbed face of the box and we had to concede that it sounded richer and fuller than the old gramophone had ever succeeded in rendering it. Most curious of all the fare provided by the radio however were the wranglings of a family group which were relayed every morning, to the amusement of a crowd, whose laughter shook the box. We tried to

* One who speaks without expecting a reply.
† Electricity, government light
  Umbrella, for the Lagos elite
  Rediffusion, white man's lies.

imagine where this took place. Did this family go into the streets to carry on their interminable bickering or did the idle crowd simply hang around their home, peeping through the windows and cheering them on? We tried to imagine any of the Aké families we knew exposing themselves this way – the idea was unthinkable. It was some time, and only by listening intently, before I began to wonder if this daily affair was that dissimilar from the short plays which we sometimes acted in school on prize-giving day. And I began also to respond to the outlandish idiom of their humour.

Hitler monopolized the box. He had his own special programme and somehow, far off as this war of his whim appeared to be, we were drawn more and more into the expanding arena of menace. Hitler came nearer home every day. Before long the greeting, Win-The-War replaced some of the boisterous exchanges which took place between Essay and his friends. The local barbers invented a new style which joined the repertory of Bentigo, Girls-Follow-Me, Oju-Aba, Missionary Cut and others. The women also added Win-de-woh to their hair-plaits, and those of them who presided over the local food-stalls used it as a standard response to complaints of a shortage in the quantity they served. Essay and his correspondents vied with one another to see how many times the same envelope could be used between them. Windows were blacked over, leaving just tiny spots to peep through, perhaps in order to obtain an early warning when Hitler came marching up the path. Household heads were dragged to court and fined for showing a naked light to the night. To reinforce the charged atmosphere of expectations, the first aeroplane flew over Abeokuta; it had a heavy drone which spoke of Armageddon and sent Christians fleeing into churches to pray and stay the wrath of God. Others simply locked their doors and windows and waited for the end of the world. Only those who had heard about these things, and flocks of children watched in fascination, ran about the fields and the streets, following the flying miracle as far as they could, shouting greetings, waving to it long after it had gone and returning home to await its next advent.

One morning The News reported that a ship had blown up in Lagos harbour taking some of its crew with it. The explosion had rocked the island, blown out windows and shaken off roofs. The lagoon was in flames and Lagosians lined the edges of the lagoon, marvelling at the strange omen – tall fires leaping frenziedly on the surface of water. Hitler was really coming close. No one however appeared to be very certain what to do when he finally appeared.

There was one exception: Paa Adatan. Every morning, Paa Adatan appeared in front of Wild Christian's shop opposite the Aafin, before whose walls he passed the entire day. Strapped to his waist was a long cutlass in its scabbard, and belts of amulets. A small Hausa knife, also in its sheath, was secured to his left arm above the elbow and on his fingers were blackened twisted wire and copper rings – we knew they were of different kinds – *onde, akaraba* and others. If Paa Adatan slapped an opponent with one of his hands, that man would fall at his feet and foam at the mouth. The other hand was reserved for situations where he was outnumbered. It only required that Paa Adatan slap one or more of his attackers and they would fall to fighting among themselves. The belt of amulets ensured of course that any bullet would be deflected from him, returning to hit the marksman at the very spot on his body where he had thought to hit the immortal warrior of Adatan.

Paa Adatan patrolled the Aafin area, furious that no one would take him into the Army and send him to confront Hitler, personally, and end the war once and for all.

'Ah, Mama Wole, this English people just wan' the glory for den self. Den no wan' blackman to win dis war and finish off dat nonsense-yeye Hitler one time! Now look them. Hitler dey bombing us for Lagos already and they no fit defend we.' He spat his red kola-nut juice on the ground, raging,

'When dey come, Mama, dem go know say there be black man medicine. I go pile dem corpse alongside the wall of dis palace, dem go know say we done dey fight war here, long time before dey know wetin be war for den foolish land. Oh er . . . Mama,' he rummaged deep in the pouches of his clothing, 'Mama Wole, I forget bring my purse enh, look, big man like myself, I forget my purse for house. And I no chop at all at all since morning time . . .'

A penny changed hands, Paa Adatan saluted, drew out his sword and drew a line on the ground around the shop frontage. 'Dat na in case they come while I dey chop my eba for buka. If they try cross this line, guns go turn to broom for dem hand. Dem go begin dey sweeping dis very ground till I come back. Make dem try am make I see.'

I followed Paa Adatan once to watch him at breakfast. The food-seller already knew what he wanted and set before him four leaf-wrapped mounds of eba, lots of stew and one solitary piece of meat which sat like a half-submerged island in the middle of the stew. Paa Adatan left the meat untouched until he had demolished this prodigious amount of eba, each morsel larger than anything I could eat for an entire meal. Halfway through, the stew had dried up. Paa Adatan hemmed and hawed, but the woman took no notice. Finally,

'Hm. Iyawo.'

Silence.

'Iyawo.'

The food-seller spun round angrily. 'You want to ruin me. Everyday the same thing. If everybody swallowed the stew the way you do, how do you think a food-seller can make a living from selling eba?'

'Ah, no vex for me, Iyawo. But na Win-de-war amount of stew you give me today.'

She spun round on her stool, ladle ready filled, and slopped its contents into his dish. 'Only na you dey complain. Same thing every day.'

'God bless you, God bless you. Na dis bastard Hitler. When war finish you go see. You go see me as I am, a man of myself.'

The woman sniffed, accustomed to the promise. Paa Adatan set to, finished the remaining mounds, then held up the piece of meat and suddenly threw it into his mouth, snatching at it with his teeth like a dog at whom a lump of raw meat had been thrown. His jaw and neck muscles tensed as he chewed on the meat, banged on the low table and issued his challenge:

'Let him come! Make him step anywhere near this palace of Alake and that is how I go take in head for my mouth and bite am off.'

He rose, adjusted the rope which strung his trousers and turned to leave.

'By the way, Iyawo, make you no worry for dem if den come, I don taking your buka for my protection – Aafin, de shop of Headmaster in wife, Centenary Hall, my friend the barber in shop and that cigarette shop of Iya Aniwura. If any of Hitler man come near any of you, he will smell pepper. Tell them na dis me Papa Adatan talk am!'

Head erect, chest defiant, he resumed his patrol.

One day, a convoy of army trucks stopped by the road, just in front of the row of shops which included ours. Instantly children and women fled in all directions, mothers snatching up their and others' toddlers who happened to be by. The men retreated into shops and doorways and peeped out, prepared for the worst, ready to run or beg for their lives. These were not the regular soldiers who were stationed at Lafenwa barracks. They were the notorious 'Bọtẹ', recognizable by their caps. They were said to come from the Congo, and were reputed wild and lawless. People claimed that they descended on shops, took what they needed and left without paying, abducted women and children – raping the former and eating the latter. To call a man Bọtẹ became an unpardonable insult; to await their approach was the height of folly.

I was in the shop with Wild Christian who of course had no interest in the Boṭes' reputation. As every other shop in the vicinity had either shut its doors or been abandoned, they made for ours and asked to purchase the items they required – biscuits, cigarettes, tinned foods, bottled drinks and sweets. I climbed up to take down jars from the shelves, handed them down to Wild Christian. Suddenly I heard a sound which could only be defined as the roar of a dozen outraged lions. Through the space between the soldiers' heads and the top of the wide door I saw the figure of Paa Adatan, his face transfigured by a set, do-or-die expression. He was naked to the waist, his usually bulbous trousers had been pulled up from the calves and tucked into his trouser-band. In one hand I beheld the drawn sword, in the other, a *sere** into which he muttered, then waved it round in a slow circle before him.

The soldiers turned, stared, and looked at one another.

Wild Christian had heard and recognized the cause of the commotion but was paying it no heed.

Paa Adatan cursed them. 'Bastards! Beasts of no nation! Boṭe Banza. You no better pass Hitler. Commot for that shop make you fight like men!'

The soldiers did not appear to understand a word, but the gestures could not be mistaken. They whispered among themselves in their strange language, raised their eyebrows and shrugged their shoulders. Then they turned back into the shop and continued with their purchases. Three or four sat on the pavement before the shop and watched.

Wild Christian, her view blocked by the soldiers, could not see Paa Adatan at all. At the intensification of Paa Adatan's curses, she grew worried, asked me what was happening.

'He is dancing now,' I reported.

Paa Adatan had indeed begun a war-dance. He sang at the top of his voice,

Ogun Hitila d' Aké
Eni la o pa Bote.†

Some of the soldiers stayed on to watch him while others continued to buy up every eatable item in the shop. Wild Christian inflated the prices by at least twice what she normally charged, but they did not mind at all. On the contrary, they even gave me a packet of their own biscuits which were thick, sweet and crunchy. We spoke in sign language throughout, with plenty of smiling, shrugging and hand-waving.

* A mini-gourd with magical powers.
† Hitler's war arrives in Aké.
 Today we shall kill these Bote.

The trouble began when they attempted to leave. Paa Adatan stopped singing, drew a line across the ground and dared them to step over it. He himself retreated some way back from the line, leapt up and made a wild rush at the line, sword outstretched, came to an abrupt stop at the line – on one leg – rocked his body for some moments on the leg, spun round and returned to starting-point from where he repeated the process over and over again.

The soldiers were now bewildered. Wild Christian finally pushed her way out, remonstrated with Paa Adatan.

'Enough, Paa, enough! They are our friends. You are stopping them from going to fight Hitler.'

'Dey be Bote,' Paa Adatan replied. 'They and Hitler na the same. Look them. Cowards!' He shook his *sere* at them. 'Put down those goods wey you tief or I go give you message take go Hitler.'

It was all over a short while later. Two of the soldiers left in the trucks had crept up behind Paa Adatan. They seized his arms from behind and disarmed him both of sword and *sere*, pinioned his arms to his sides. Paa Adatan fought back like the true warrior he was. He threw them off, fought through the waves of bodies that engulfed him, bore them to the ground with him and continued to struggle. No blows appeared to be struck, it was all wrestling, and a titanic struggle it proved. Paa Adatan fought like one who knew that the entire safety of Aké resided in his arms, legs and torso. He was a rugged terrain which had to be captured, then secured tree by tree, hill by hill, boulder by boulder. They sat on each limb, breathing and perspiring heavily, shouting orders and curses in their strange language. Then they brought some rope and bound him. Even then, he did not give in.

The soldiers then stood in a circle, wiping off perspiration and watching him. They marvelled, shook their heads, looked for some explanation from all the faces that had emerged one by one from shops, windows, nooks and corners after Paa Adatan had begun his act. No one however could speak to them, though some nodded affirmation when a soldier turned to the watchers, touched a finger to his head and raised his eyebrows.

Paa Adatan, in his bonds, struggled to a sitting position, looked at his captors and shook his head.

'O ma se o.* The glory of Egbaland is lay low inside dust.'

Some *ogboni* were now seen rushing from the palace, having heard of the incident. Their appearance seemed to convey to the soldiers some

* How pitiful!

semblance of authority so, with signs and gestures, they transferred all responsibility for Paa Adatan to them, handed over his sword and *sere* and climbed back into their lorries and drove off.

A debate then began. Should the police be called? Was it safe to untie Paa Adatan? Should he be transferred to the Mental Hospital at Aro? They argued at the top of their voices while Paa Adatan sat in his bonds, impassive.

Finally, Wild Christian had had enough. She left her shop and calling on me to help her we began to untie Paa Adatan's bonds. There were immediate cries of fear and protest but we ignored them. One of the men made to restrain her physically. She rose, drew up her body to its fullest height and dared him to touch her just once more. I bristled to her side and called the man names which would have earned me an immediate slap from Wild Christian in other circumstances. An *ogboni* chief intervened, however, told the man off and himself completed the task of loosening the remaining knots in the ropes.

Paa Adatan, freed, rose slowly. The crowd retreated several steps. He stretched out his hand for his sword and replaced it in his scabbard. Next he took his *sere*, dropped it on the ground and crushed it with his heel. The explosion was loud; it startled the watchers who moved even further back, frightened. He walked slowly away. He moved with a sad, quiet dignity. He walked in the direction of Iporo, vanished bit by bit as the road dipped downwards before it turned sharply away, round the Centenary Hall. I never saw him again.

About this time also, another feature of our lives disappeared for ever. Essay and Wild Christian collected strays. It seemed a permanent aspect of our life at Aké; with very few lapses, there was always an adult who appeared without warning seemingly from nowhere, became part of our lives and then disappeared with no explanation from anyone. Sometimes it would happen that mother had something to do with the sudden evaporation of Essay's strays.

Wild Christian stayed at her shop most of the day and, for some of Essay's strays, this was the sensible period to descend on their protector and friend. Before she left she ensured that her husband's breakfast was on the table – *akara* balls and *ogi*; *moin-moin* and *agidi*; bread, omelette and tea; or boiled yams and omelette or fish stew – one or more of these combinations served for breakfast. But the real treat was the rarest of delicacies – *leki* – made of crushed and skinned black-eyed beans and melon-seed oil, a teaspoonful of which, in the sharing, could cause week-long hostilities in the household. I had a place of observation between the legs of the tallboy. It was understood in the household that when I occupied that position, I took care of his plate and whatever was left in it. The dish itself was, however, sacrosanct. That is, until You-Mean-Mayself entered the household.

We all became practised in his unique accent and would entertain ourselves and Wild Christian with mimicries that sent her friends falling over with laughter. Strangely enough, I considered Mayself's incursion into our lives sufficient compensation for the diminution of those choice morsels which father left on his plate, whenever he observed me with my eyes fastened on his jaw movements from between the legs of the tallboy. There was an emotional wrench when the dish was *leki* but generally, Mayself's constant replenishment of our repertoire of his vocal nuances and eyelid flutter more than made up for it. Tinu and I, the cousins, and later even Dipo vied for honours in reproducing his variations on the reaction of startled surprise to a normal hospitable question:

'Have you had your breakfast?'

'Mayself? Nyou.'

He was short, rather light-complexioned and had a small, box-like head. HM's regimen was to go to the school to conduct the opening, then return home for a leisurely breakfast. By then, Wild Christian would be in her shop. Mayself was at the house either before my father went off to school or was home awaiting his return. He sat in the chair below the porcelain clock in the front room, picked up a magazine or a book and browsed. When Mother was out of town, he would arrive even earlier, perhaps while my father was doing his exercises in the room. We hid our giggles from HM, knowing very well what would be the consequences of making fun of a guest. Later of course, we mimicked him openly.

Eventually, from his bedroom, the bathroom, his stroll in the garden or from school, father would return, greet his guest courteously and go about his business. There were times, especially during the holidays, when he breakfasted late, sat a long time at his front-room desk to finish some work, then proceeded to a breakfast already turned cold. He chatted sometimes with his guest, engaged in some mild-to-passionate debate on the politics of the day, the news and rumours of war or some local agitation. We waited. Sometimes, tired of waiting for Mayself's act we sent someone to remind Essay that his breakfast was ready. Or to ask if his *ogi* or bean pottage should be re-heated. We never doubted that he knew the reasons for our solicitude, nevertheless he reacted normally, inquired what there was for breakfast, then, before issuing instructions for extra *moin-moin* or *akara* to be placed on the table, he turned to his guest and enquired:

'Have you had your breakfast?'

Mayself's face then rose from the journal in which he had buried it during Essay's planning of breakfast. He looked up, startled, stared at first in any direction except the one from which the question had so clearly emanated. Suddenly he realized his mistake, turned to the questioner, registered visibly that the question had, surprisingly, been directed at him. There followed a quick intake of breath as the novelty of the question, one which could never before have been pronounced in his hearing, etched a huge surprise on his face. Only then came the predictable, ritual answer:

'Oh, you-mean-mayself? Ny-ou.'

The first section emerged clipped in spite of a full exaggeration of the vowels. The second, the 'Ny-ou' by contrast, which faded into an upper register, was like the mewing of our cat and it was this I think which sent us into paroxysms of laughter, burying our faces in cushions of armchairs behind which we were hidden. You-mean-mayself resumed his browsing, father his work until the supplemented breakfast was announced. Essay then rose, paused for him, and they proceeded solemnly into the dining-room where, displaying every sign of being as fastidious an eater as his host, Mayself nevertheless proceeded to eradicate any ideas in our minds that elegance of table manners was necessarily inimical to a hearty appetite – a fallacy into which we had fallen from Essay's own eating patterns. Then again I would wonder if it was worth it, this ephemeral entertainment, especially on days when the price was a loss of left-overs in the shape of bean-paste in melon-seed oil!

Wild Christian habitually served out both man and wife portions in the same dish even when she would eat separately. She had an aesthetic feel for food; certain dishes went with certain foods and, for *leki* she always used a coracle-shaped, flowery porcelain of a near-luminous whiteness. She piled it about three-quarters high, carefully wiped the edges of any smear before sending it to the table. Since she had to be at the shop early she had her breakfast sent on to her, her *real* breakfast, that is. For Wild Christian took no chances with her stomach. She began the day with a kind of tasting-breakfast, a pre-breakfast which matched, in quantity, what my father would eat for the entire morning. The maid then prepared her real breakfast according to her instructions. About two hours later came what could be called her elevenses, a sort of Consolation Snack. This consisted of whatever was left in the dishes from father's breakfast, plus anything that caught her fancy from nearby foodsellers. On *leki* days she looked heartily forward to the Consolidation Snack.

Alas, one day there was no Consolidation Snack. Mayself had seen to it.

Until now You-mean-mayself had been a joke. Wild Christian had still to meet him, being kept from home by her shop, debt-collecting, purchasing trips both within and out of town. Our portrayal of him became so much part of household life that Wild Christian would even call Essay to come and watch his children perform. Now it was different. Wild Christian was patient. She raised the matter in her usual innocent manner; a wife whose domestic routine had been disturbed, merely wanted to enquire what might have caused such a thing. Half-way through supper she said,

'I hope the *leki* was all right this morning?'

That morning, father had returned from school only to be summoned back before he could begin his breakfast. He left his guest at the table who then proceeded to finish the *leki* to the last lick. An outraged Nubi reported this gluttonous limit to Wild Christian.

HM had not even known what was served for breakfast. 'Oh, was it *leki*? I had the children prepare me something. I had to rush back to school . . .'

She pretended surprise. 'But how stupid of them. The *leki* was there all the time. Joseph!'

Joseph ran in. 'Joseph, where is the breakfast I prepared for your father? Why wasn't it placed on the table?'

Against father's 'Em-em-em-em-em' Nubi's voice rang out, 'We put it on the table, Ma. Papa's guest ate it all.'

Her eyes rounded. 'Oh? You didn't tell me you had a guest, dear. I would have prepared some more.'

'Oh it's all right. I was no longer hungry when I returned anyway.'

They continued with supper. Some moments later she asked, 'Who was he, dear? Is it someone I know?'

'Oh er . . . an old friend. I doubt if you've met.'

She shook her head good-humouredly. 'He must be a very strange friend. Do you mean a friend ate all your breakfast and left you nothing.'

'Oh it didn't matter.' Essay tried to shrug it off. 'The children prepared something for me.'

Wild Christian was too shrewd to pursue the matter further. But she had given notice. When she was ready, she would deal with that inconsiderate friend.

He became a fixture during the mid-year holiday. The rains provided sufficient excuse – not that he needed any – sometimes it would rain without once stopping for weeks. No one would dream of turning out a guest in such weather, anyway Mayself was not very anxious to leave. He began to stay for lunch, then dinner whenever mother travelled anywhere or was not back in time for Essay's dinner. But matters came to a head, finally.

Wild Christian had served lunch both for Essay, herself, and allowed for the unexpected guest or two. Mayself was no longer regarded by us as a guest so that when she was confronted by empty dishes and she asked what guests had called on Essay, we replied truthfully, None. Essay was not yet home.

'Are you children trying to tell me that your father ate all the food in these dishes by himself?' she threatened.

Eyebrows raised in the Mayself surprise curve, we chorused, 'Papa himself? Ny-ou.'

'I see,' sighed Wild Christian. 'So it's him again.'

And we went into a performance of the latest variations.

'Are you ready for some lunch?'

'Mayself? Oh, net reilly. But perhaps you are . . .'

'In that case let's have some lunch.'

'Oh er . . . yes Headmaster.'

'Would you like some supper?'

'Mayself . . . oh er . . . net unless . . .'

'I'll just see what the children have set up . . .'

But Wild Christian was no longer amused. We saw the battle-light in her eyes and felt a twinge of pity for Mayself who had permitted a touch of greed to ruin the real pleasure we derived from his presence in the house. It was now a little more than the fact that this guest deprived her even of her own specialities. Essay, she knew, was a spare eater and an exceedingly polite host; it followed therefore that he was not getting enough to eat. At their next meal-time together she glanced at father and asked,

'But dear, are you sure you are getting enough to eat?'

'Of course. Do I look underfed?'

'No but . . . Well, I want to make you that kind of yam pottage you like so much tomorrow. What do you think?'

'Which one is that?'

'Made with *ororo* and a bit runny. And of course I'll use some of that smoked pork Father has just sent us from Isara . . .'

'Oh yes, yes.'

'Dear, are you listening? I want to be sure you get enough of it to eat.'

*

The first we knew of the existence of our Uncle Dipo was when a smart-looking bespectacled man in army officer's uniform came upon us unannounced in the yard. We fled. Nothing like it had ever happened and, with all the war alarms, there was little doubt in anyone's minds that Hitler had indeed arrived and was about to ship us off into slavery. Essay had travelled out of town. Wild Christian was at her shop; neither had warned us of an impending visitor. We did not hear him come through the front door, the front room and the parlour, so we scattered to Upper Backyard, barricaded ourselves in the storeroom, others in the latrine. Two cousins and I raced up the ladder and threw ourselves flat on the roof, ready to dive over into the street on the other side if Hitler pursued up there. We did nothing of the sort for the moment however. Instead we dragged on our bellies until we could look over the other edge of the roof into the yard.

The stranger did not give chase. Instead he remained on the spot and seemed to sway a little. His eyes appeared to be fused with his spectacles so that what struck me most was that his face glowed centrally through a pair of head lamps, like a motor-car. His gentle, swaying motion added to his air of the unreal, and I began to change my opinion about his real identity; I now thought that he was perhaps a ghost. And then he raised his head, rocked forwards and backwards with a more distinct motion and exploded:

'Bastards! Where are they?'

The stranger moved forward and there was no longer any room for error; we had seen a few drunks before. Hitler, ghost or the devil himself, the stranger was clearly drunk. He moved forward, coming up the yard in the same direction we had fled. His eyes fell then on one of our huge water-pots, buried deep in the ground and partly opened. This was the favourite pot of the house. It was sheltered both by a wall and two luxuriant crotons on either side; at all times of the day, its water was cool and refreshing. The stranger went towards the pot, swayed, unbuttoned his fly and began to urinate in it.

Cries of outrage were torn from me and the two cousins who, from our vantage point, had witnessed this unspeakable act of desecration. It was wholly outside the range of our imagination. We had seen the occasional guest staggering in the yard from rose-bush to rose-bush, trying to rejoin his companions in the front room through the kitchen-door, even keeling over as he tried to unbutton his flaps in the bathroom. But to urinate in a water-pot!

The next moment we were scaling down the ladder as fast as we had climbed up it. Shouting abuses on him we tugged at him, pummelling him with all our strength. With the one hand which was not busy guiding his member he swiped us off easily.

'Get away from me you Burmese imps!'

It was the first time I had ever heard such an expression, but I did not wait to puzzle out what Burmese imps were. I sprang for his back, landing with such force that it catapulted him forward. The lid of the waterpot was knocked backward and his face went into the pot which was half-empty, the same motion however bounced me over his head so that I landed in a heap and was wedged between the pot and the wall. The cousins had seized hold of one of his legs and were dragging him backwards, screaming for help.

Neighbours arrived almost at the same time as the other children who had hidden in Upper Yard. They saw the uniformed man sprawled over the water-pot and fell back. I had scrambled up from my brief imprisonment and was screaming at the top of my voice:

'It's this Hitler! He is urinating in our pot!'

But Hitler was motionless. When the neighbours finally approached and lifted up his head he had passed clean out. They kept him there and stood guard.

Mother arrived from the shop soon after – someone had sent for her. She recognized the stranger at once and exclaimed,

'But I thought he was still in Burma!'

The neighbours helped to get him to bed, having first chased us off so that he could be made to look decent. Wild Christian shook her head all through supper, refusing to answer our questions beyond saying,

'He is your Uncle. He enlisted over the objections of his entire family – he has always been a wild one.' But she would not tell us his name.

The following morning, by the time we woke up, our Uncle Dipo was already awake. Cleaned, he looked spruce and commanding even in civilian clothes, and was eating breakfast, seated in Essay's chair. When we returned from school, he was gone. To all our questions Wild Christian would only reply that he had returned on leave unexpectedly and had now gone back to his new station. The water-pot was emptied, scrubbed, an entire bottle of Dettol was then scrubbed into it, and the pot neglected for some days. Then it was scrubbed with soap all over again, rinsed out, then left to dry. Only then did it resume its place as the water-cooler of the household, but I never again drank water from it without inwardly grimacing.

Our own Dipo continued to grow in energy and mischief, nothing could daunt him. One day, he vanished. For several hours his absence remained unnoticed. At home, it was mostly thought that he was in the shop with Wild Christian; she of course had no idea that he was anywhere but home. He vanished shortly after breakfast, soon after he had received a few mild strokes for some offence. It was a new world for our brother, this world of beatings, facing the corner, 'stooping down' which required that the culprit stand on one leg and raise the other and stoop over forwards, resting one finger on the ground. The other arm was placed penitently on the curved back. Another favourite punishment was standing up with arms outstretched, parallel to the ground. The cane descended sharply on the knuckles of the miscreant if either arm flagged, just as, in stooping, an attempt to change the leg earned the offender severe strokes on the back. We had a 'cousin' whose offences somehow constantly earned him the stoop. He became so inured to the posture that he sometimes fell asleep under punishment.

Dipo had witnessed every member of the household undergo one form of punishment or another as a matter of course. The beleaguered population of children had trained his innocence to own up to offences which he never committed because he was still too young to be punished. When the induction came, Dipo did not at first realize that it was the end of his immunity; to him, it must have seemed a mistake. Then it happened a few more times and he sensed that the period of charmed existence was gone for ever. Dipo vanished. The household was thrown into turmoil for a few hours before he was brought home by a would-be traveller. Dipo, after roaming through Abeokuta for the greater part of the day had found his way to a motor park. When he tried to board the lorry however, both the driver and the passengers could not help observing that he appeared too young to be travelling by himself. Inquiries began, a policeman was fetched – in the meantime, the child had been tricked out of the park into a nearby shop – finally, Dipo was returned home accompanied by the sympathetic traveller.

What either parent made of the adventure we did not know or care; to the rest of the household, Dipo was an instant hero. He looked so vulnerable when he returned in tow of these two adults that my first feeling was one of fright for him. No one looking so defenceless should have been driven to the dangers of such an adventure. Then I took to wondering if our parents would let this affect their over-ready recourse to the cane for every infraction; they did not. As for Dipo, by the following day he was bouncing irrepressibly around as if nothing had ever occurred. No trace of the adventure or its after-effects showed in his demeanour. We began to look on him then as a species of being apart, obviously indestructible. Perhaps a year later, long after the visit of the mystery Uncle, Wild Christian announced that Dipo's name was to be changed to Femi. She explained that it had been on her mind for some time because children named Dipo always turned out wild and ungovernable. The change of name left us mostly indifferent, but I hid my own astonishment. Once again I felt a helpless confusion – did these grown-ups ever know what they wanted? It did not seem possible that this was the same Wild Christian who had egged on Dipo not so long before, who, with the conniving of Joseph and Nubi had set him on me. Now she was changing his name because he had responded only too well to their own proddings? I mused on the problem for weeks afterwards; each time his new name was called, I was mystified anew.

But the soldier-of-fortune had a name at last. In spite of Wild Christian's careful silence on that theme, I decided that his name could be none other than Dipo. As the new entity, Femi, joined the household, Uncle Dipo joined the procession of strangers who marked our lives with their vivid presence, then departed, never to be seen again. His duration was the briefest, but like a true Dipo, the most sudden and tempestuous.

IX

It was understood in Isara that the children of the Headmaster did not
prostrate themselves in greeting; our chaperon always saw to that. The
children of Headmaster on arrival for Christmas and New Year had to be
taken round to every house whose inmates would be mortally offended
otherwise. On the streets we met relations, family friends, gnarled and
ancient figures of Isara, chiefs, king-makers, cult priests and priestesses,
the elders of *osugbo* who pierced one through and through with their eyes,
then stood back to await the accustomed homage. We were introduced –
the children of Ayo – at long last we were in one place where Essay's name
was called as a matter of course – the children of Ayo, just arrived to
celebrate *odun*. The elder waited, our chaperon smiled and explained.

'They don't know how to prostrate, please don't take offence.'

Reactions varied. Some were so overawed by these aliens who actually
had been heard to converse with their parents in the whiteman's tongue
that they quickly denied that they had ever expected such a provincial
form of greeting. A smaller number, especially the ancient ones whose
skins had acquired the gloss of those dark beaten *età** merely drew
themselves up higher, snorted and walked away. Later, they would be
mollified by the Odemo, the titled head of Isara, to whose ears their
complaints might come. Perhaps the fact that we were related to this royal
house eased their sense of being slighted, we only observed that when we
met the same ancients again, they smiled more indulgently, their frowns
eased to amused wrinkles at the strange objects whom their own son of the
soil had spawned in some far-off land. And perhaps news of an
embarrassing encounter at the palace had spread to them.

After church service one Sunday, our first, I accompanied Essay to the
Odemo's palace. When we came into the parlour, a number of the chiefs
were already seated, so were some faces I had never seen before, including
a heavily-beaded and coralled stranger, in a wrapper of *aso-oke*, who was
very clearly not of Isara. He spoke and acted more like a brother-chief to

* Locally woven cloth, much valued.

the most senior of the chiefs, even carried himself as if he was the Ọdẹmọ's equal.

We entered, the Ọdẹmọ hoisted me on his knees and asked me a number of questions about school. The usual cries went up 'A-ah ọmọ Soyinka, wa nube wa gbowo'* and they stretched out their hands.

Kabiyesi put me down, I went and shook hands round the assembly. The tall, self-consciously regal man was standing by a cupboard, lazily waving a fan across his face. When I came to him, he looked down on me from his great height and boomed out in so loud a voice that I was rocked backwards on my feet.

'What is this? Ọmọ tani?'†

A chorus of voices replied, 'Ọmọ Soyinka' pointing to my father who was already in close conversation with Ọdẹmọ. The stranger's lip turned up in a sneer; in the same disorientating boom as before he ordered,

'Dòbalè!'‡

The response from the parlour was good-humoured, bantering . . . of course you don't know, they are these 'ara Egba', the children of Teacher, they don't even know how to prostrate.

The stranger's eyes flashed fire. He looked from me to Essay, to the chiefs, back to me and then to Ọdẹmọ. 'Why NOT?'

I had recovered from the onslaught of his voice and his truly intimidating presence. In place of it, I felt only a cold resentment of his presence in that place and finally, his choice of Essay as his enemy. I had never given the question of prostration much thought except that, on the red dusty roads of Isara and its frequent dollops of dog and children's faeces, prostration did not seem a very clean form of salutation. I would not, I knew, have minded in the least prostrating to Father, or to the Ọdẹmọ, or indeed to some of the elders seated in Ọdẹmọ's reception room or those others who flocked to Father's house to drink their thanks to the gods for our safe arrival. But I would have tried every dodge in the world to avoid prostrating on those streets whose dust stuck to one's clothes, hair, skin, even without dragging oneself on the ground or placing one's nose to a patch of urine, human or canine. To this arrogant stranger however, not even Essay and his Wild Christian could make me prostrate, even if they had a change of mind!

Coming directly from the Sunday service probably brought the response to my head, certainly it was no justification which I had ever thought out

* Ah, Son of Soyinka, come over and shake hands.
† Whose child is this?
‡ Prostrate yourself!

124

before, or heard used in any argument. I heard myself saying, with a sense of simply pointing out the obvious,

'If I don't prostrate myself to God, why should I prostrate to you? You are just a man like my father aren't you?'

There followed the longest silence I had ever heard in an assembly of grown-ups. Ọdẹmọ broke the silence with a long-drawn whistle ending by swearing: 'O-o-o-o-o-oro baba o!' And turning to Essay, 'E mi ṣu' wọ re ko?'*

My father shook his head, gestured with open hands that he had nothing to do with it. Ọdẹmọ's voice had made me turn to look at him, then round the room at a surprising identity of expressions on the faces of all the guests. Suddenly confused, I fled from the room and ran all the way back home.

At the end of that vacation, Essay decreed that full prostration should commence, not only in Isara, but in our Aké home.

The Ọdẹmọ visited us frequently at Aké, his visits were one prolonged excitement. Essay was so wrapped up with him that we took the utmost liberties, knowing that he had little time for us. Daodu was one other visitor – except that he never stayed overnight – who earned Essay's undivided attention. To us however, the Ọdẹmọ was simply Essay's close friend, he meant little else. It was the women traders who brought the flavour, the smell and touch of Isara to Aké. They frequently arrived late at night like a weather-beaten caravan, heavy-laden baskets and fibre sacks on their heads. They were filled with smoked meats, woven cloths and local ointments, *gari*, yam flour, even tins of palm oil. They arrived close to midnight, lit their fires in the backyard, cooked and kept to themselves. Wild Christian would take them extra food and Essay would visit them in turn to receive messages and news from home. Their self-containment made a deep impression on us for they made no attempt to become part of the household. Only two of them ever came into the front room to talk with Essay, and we found out later that they were his aunts. It was incredible that Essay should have aunts, it did not seem possible that he could be encumbered by such extra relationships. Anyway, he never called them Auntie.

A new sound would enter the house, the deep dialect of Ijebu, which we did our best to imitate. When Essay conversed with the visitors, we were lucky to understand a sentence or two. They appeared to speak a new language, not the Yoruba we spoke so thoughtlessly. Around their fires in

* By my Oro ancestors! Did you teach him that?

the yard, this sound filled the night like a weird cultic dirge not dissimilar from the chanting of the *ogboni* which sometimes reached our house from their meeting-house at the Aafin. The storehouse in Upper Backyard was cleared out and given over to them for their stay but, unless the weather was bad, they spread their mats out in the open air, and slept.

In the morning they were gone before we woke. They returned with depleted sacks and baskets, all their produce sold in the market for whose day they had timed their arrival. The following day they would visit the shops, buying other forms of goods which they would take back and sell in Isara. They departed at dawn the day after, leaving behind a tang of smoke and indigo.

I had expected to walk to Isara; instead we went to the motor-park with our loads and entered a lorry. The lorry was not bound for Isara however, it stopped at Iperu, leaving the journey uncompleted by some seven miles. After waiting nearly half the day for further transport, Essay decided that we should walk. The luggage was divided up among us and we set off. Only then did I remember why I had imagined that it was a mere casual walk all the way from Abeokuta to Isara – it was what the traders did every market-day! They set out at dawn with their heavy loads and walked the whole day, arriving at our house at night. It did not seem possible! I asked my father if the women had been telling me the truth and he said Yes, they did walk. Occasionally, he said, they would take two days, especially if they had too much merchandise to carry. They stopped at a village on the way and rested the night. I tried to think how long the journey had taken us by lorry but had no idea. I no longer felt tired. Dipo was strapped to the back of a maid. My excitement rose as we drew near our other home, the home of those dark women who trudged all day to dispose of smoked meats and woven cloth and spoke in a language of dirges. We were almost at the entrance of Isara when a lorry appeared but we still piled in gratefully and entered Isara in a cloud of the reddest dust that could possibly exist on the surface of the earth.

It was these itinerant traders, our shadowy guests at Aké who now rushed to become our guides, explaining us to their world. They basked in their contact with us on our own grounds, proudly explaining us to the bewildered and soothing our passage with the resentful. They fought over us, became fiercely possessive. They would have fed us morning till night but here, Wild Christian was at her most unbending about our accepting food outside the walls of our grandfather. This went beyond the mere censure on GREED. She was morbidly afraid that we would be poisoned.

Our Ijebu relations, it seemed, had a reputation for poisoning, or for a hundred and one forms of injuring an enemy through magical means. We were drilled in ways and means of avoiding a handshake, for various forms of injury could be operated through the hands. One would return home and simply wither away. Thus we perfected the technique of bowing with our hands at the back; the more persistently a chance acquaintance proffered his hands, the more resolutely we kept our hands behind, bowing respectfully and looking permanently on the ground. It became a game, Tinu and I would compare notes afterwards on evasion tactics.

No amount of strictures could keep us from the caravanserai when they came to Aké. Wild Christian did not know of the many nocturnal visits we paid to them in the yard, the questions with which we plied them, and our relishing of both smoked meat and the smoky stories they told us, far different in tone from even the most exciting of Essay's stories. Now visiting them in their own homes, I sadly watched much of their mystery dissipate. Father's mud-huts were very sparsely furnished, his wardrobe consisted of no more than two or three agbada, a few buba and trousers for casual wear, caps and his chieftaincy robes, but none except his farming or hunting gear was patched or threadbare. The homes of those traders depressed us, their shabbiness could not be disguised. Beneath their joy at our presence we now sensed the strain of sheer survival, a life made up of forty-mile treks laden with merchandise. Their one 'dress of pride' was worn in our honour whenever they came to take us out, and the same dress would appear again at the most important festival of the year, the New Year itself, then disappear, we knew, until the next festival.

Isara was not the most sanitary of places. There were communal *salanga*, deep latrine-pits, usually well-kept. But it seemed to be accepted that children's excrement could be passed anywhere, after which the mongrel dogs which roamed about in abundance were summoned to eat it up. If they were not available, flies swarmed them until they finally dried up, were scattered by unwary feet at night, churned through by bicycles and the occasional motor lorry. And there were uncultivated patches in between dwellings into which faeces were flung or expelled directly by squatting adults. For us it was a constant source of astonishment that these grown-ups did not mind that they were perceived, in broad daylight, with buttocks bared to the bush. Coming from an afternoon spent watching the gold and silver smiths, the paths and streets became a contamination of the visual feast I had partaken in the workshops of Isara's craftsmen. I displaced their apprentices at the bellows and held crucibles for their molten metals. Back in the streets, the noise and stench were a startling descent from the silence and the purity of their motions. Often, the thought of the obstacles to be avoided kept me at home or at Father's. His simple mud-house was clean, which for us meant normal. Once I asked Essay why we could not bring to Isara those Sanitary Inspectors who descended unannounced on Aké households, if only for the duration of our stay. Essay appeared to look round nervously, as if to ensure that no one had heard me. Then he made me promise only to remind him of it after we were back in the parsonage.

Father had promised often to take me to his farm but he had several duties in connection with the festive season, so he suggested that I ask Broda Pupa to take me to his. It was an outing I was not to be denied and life became a torment for Broda Pupa until he agreed to tackle Wild Christian for permission. He was our neighbour, owned a barber's shop a few doors from where we stayed. Harmful medicines could also be passed through the head, so it was a measure of his closeness to the family that Wild Christian sent us to Broda Pupa for our Christmas-and-New Year hair-cut special. Getting her to agree that I go with him to his farm for a whole day was not so easy however, but Broda Pupa had a flexible sense of humour that soon adjusted itself to Wild Christian's vulnerable sides. And of course there was Father's own authority which counted for much, as long as he was around at the right moment. So finally, with the additional security of a genuine cousin, who was as close to manhood as any of my Isara companions, we set off one early dawn for Broda Pupa's farm.

'Come on, ara Aké,' he shouted as he waited outside the door. 'I am taking you to school.' He handed me a cutlass to carry saying, 'Here is your pencil. Your exercise book is waiting for you at the end of an hour's walk. Are you ready?'

I was never more ready. I jumped down and fell in between him and Yemi, drawing the morning dew into my lungs. The dust was not yet stirred, the Harmattan dew disguised the smell of the streets which would grow rank by noon.

Broda Pupa's timing was accurate, the walk lasted just about an hour. There was a hut on the farm and its contents provided us with a quick breakfast before we set out to work clearing a fresh patch of land, shoring up ridges with the hoe and gathering fruits into a large basket. Harmattan was a period of drought and I could not understand why everything here should be so green, the ground soft and rich. Broda Pupa explained that the area was drained by a large stream, one of whose tributaries we had crossed on the way. From time to time he would fake a mock alarm: 'Watch that scorpion!', making me leap out of my skin.

When that no longer worked, he vanished silently into the bush, reappeared behind me and drew a slithery branch along the back of my neck.

'All right,' I said. 'Don't blame me if I think you are a snake and lash at you with my cutlass.'

It was Yemi who went up to meet the only snake we encountered that day. He had climbed up a kola-nut tree to crop down some pods. He had hardly begun, was still shinning towards the branch where the heaviest pods were clustered when we heard him call out, so softly that we just managed to catch it.

'Broda!'

'Did you call? Yemi!'

There was silence for some moments, then we heard Yemi moving among the branches, with obvious stealthiness, and in a different direction. Brother Pupa was puzzled and shouted angrily.

'What are you doing? The kola-nuts are not in that direction.'

A few more moments passed and then we heard Yemi, by now totally hidden by the luxuriant branches.

'There is a snake, a monstrosity coiled round the branch where those kola-nuts are. I think it's an *agbadu*.'

I glanced panic-stricken at Broda Pupa. He was by no means ruffled. He called out to Yemi, 'Is it moving?'

'No, but it's watching me.'

Broda Pupa laughed. 'What else do you expect him to do? See you climbing towards him and then take a nap? Now listen, you've moved away from the trunk now, haven't you?'

'Of course,' and I thought Yemi sounded testy. 'He is in that direction on the other side of the trunk.'

'All right. Listen to me. Don't move back towards the trunk. Just look down and tell me if there is a branch below you which can take your weight.'

There was a pause, we heard the rustle of leaves as Yemi parted the branches. 'Yes, there is.'

'Good. Then you don't have to jump all the way down and break your neck. Lower yourself on to that branch, and don't make any sudden move. Just climb down as you would if there were no snake watching you.'

Yemi made the required manœuvre. I couldn't help feeling scared for Yemi and resentful towards Brother Pupa. He could afford to make light of the whole thing, he wasn't up in the tree.

The next moment a body came crashing through the leaves. Yemi had missed his footing or the branch had proved not as strong as he thought. Fortunately he landed on a soft piece of ground and he soon picked himself up, babbling:

'Broda, it is huge. It is monstrous! That isn't a snake at all, it's a sorcerer up there, I swear. It's a sorcerer.'

Broda Pupa snorted. 'Is it? Just gather me a pile of stones, will you? But first show me where it is exactly so I can keep my eye on it.'

We followed Yemi to a point below the cluster of kola-nuts. Yemi was right. It didn't take long for me to identify it because it was just like another thick branch of the tree, except that it was black, jet glistening black and its body pulsed a little, but that could have been my imagination.

Broda Pupa nodded with satisfaction. 'Good. I was just wondering what we would eat with our yam for lunch.'

I thought he was joking. 'Nobody eats snakes,' I said.

He looked at me, a slow dawning in his eyes. 'Ah, I forgot, ọmọ Teacher. The teacher's children don't eat things like that. They eat bread and butter.'

'No, that is not what we eat. But nobody eat snakes.'

'Well, we'll soon see. Yemi, get me that cutlass and you, ọmọ Teacher, keep an eye on the snake. I think I'll cut the kind of sticks we need myself. Yemi, you gather the stones.'

'Suppose it jumps down?' I asked.

'Speak English to it,' Broda Pupa said, and left me alone.

I spent the ten minutes they were gone contemplating the snake. It was fat and unruffled. It did not look as if it was going to come down in a hurry, but I did not really know the habits of snakes. Those we had encountered at Aké were usually killed by grown-ups, long before I came on the scene. I had seen some live ones slither past and had simply fled, reporting their presence to grown-ups. In any case, none of them had ever approached anything this size.

They returned at last. I watched Broda Pupa's methodical preparations. I could not help reflecting that he had applied the same approach to obtaining Wild Christian's consent for my day's excursion to his farm. Essay was already preoccupied with so many civic matters, people were always calling on him or he was attending meetings somewhere, so it was largely left to Wild Christian to veto even the most innocuous proposals. But Broda Pupa was determined, in any case I gave him no peace of mind. He applied the same deliberation now to plucking that snake off its perch, first grading the stones by size, rejecting some, setting some aside – as it turned out – for me. He performed the same service for the sticks, weighing them in his hand, cutting some down to shorter lengths, then putting aside one long, heavy-ended sapling.

Satisfied, he selected the throwing point, explaining, 'We don't want Wole's stones bouncing back on that branch and hitting us on the head, do we?'

I turned to him but he quickly snapped, 'Keep your eye on the animal.'

Satisfied at last, he directed me to the pile of small-size stones and gave final instructions:

'I'll throw first. Yemi follows with his stones, and Wole finishes off the snake with his pebble. We repeat the process until that snake falls down to the reception committee. Is everybody clear on that?'

I nodded, already infected with the excitement.

Broda Pupa launched the first cudgel. It flew through the few intervening leaves and thudded against the mid-section of the snake, shaking it out of its complacency and nearly taking it off its perch. As the snake propelled itself forward in fright, it was stopped short by the smack of Yemi's stone against a branch just in front of it. Almost at once Broda Pupa's stick whistled through the air, without awaiting my own turn.

'Come on, Teacher, you are too slow.'

I launched my pebble at the same time as Yemi threw his, saw mine rise barely up to the level of the lowest branch before commencing its journey back to earth.

'Very good, very good. With our big English hunter around no farmer need ever lack for meat.'

The pair kept up the incessant barrage. The snake was disorientated, moved backwards and forwards, climbed to the very highest perch but the stones and sticks found him there. I had long given up trying to contribute my pebbles, convinced that Broda Pupa never intended more than that I should not feel left out. I occupied myself with watching the futile efforts of the snake to escape. Finally, it plunged downwards. I noticed then that Brother Pupa had already picked up the heavy sapling with his left hand. As the snake fell downwards he transferred it to his right and was on top of the snake before it could recover its reflexes. A blow landed on its body and the next thunked squarely on its head. It writhed with incredible energy, lashed out in all directions. Broda Pupa banged it once more on the head, then stood a few feet away.

'Give me the cutlass,' he ordered.

Yemi moved to give it to him but he said, 'No, no, give it to Wole to bring to me.'

He stood too close for my liking to where the snake was writhing. I took the cutlass and hesitated. Then I saw that he stood between me and the snake anyway. Before the snake could lash at me – which it seemed to want to do very much – it would have to go through Broda Pupa. Nonetheless I stretched out the cutlass to him at arms-length.

He shook his head. 'No, no, ọmọ Teacher. When you hand over a cutlass or a knife to someone, always hold it by the blade. I mean hold it so that you don't cut yourself with it, but make sure that you present the handle to him, not the blade. That is how we do it on the farm.'

I obeyed him. 'That's it. We'll make a farmer of you yet.'

'I am going to be a doctor,' I said.

'Nothing wrong with that,' he said, cutting off the snake's head with one blow. 'But you can still keep a farm. I am a barber after all, and I keep a farm.'

I had never thought of that. And then I thought of Essay. 'Papa is a Headmaster, but he is also a gardener.'

'You see. He was raised here.' He tossed the cutlass to Yemi who knew what to do without being told. He scooped up the head with the flat of the cutlass, went to one side and began to dig a hole.

'Why are you planting it?' I demanded.

'Always remember this. A snake's head is still dangerous even after you've cut it off. Someone may step on it and the poison will go into his body the same as if a living snake had bitten him. Always bury it deep in the ground, and preferably away from used paths.'

Yemi's choice was the base of a large tree, between its roots. Brother Pupa next selected a yam from his barn and gave it to me.

'Can you peel yams?'

'I cook at home sometimes. For the whole family.'

'Good. Yemi will build a fire while I skin the snake. Since you don't eat snake meat you'll have to eat your yam with palm oil.'

We busied ourselves with preparations for the meal. Peppers were plucked from the farm, a few vegetables were prepared, a bottle of palm oil and other condiments emerged from the well-stocked barn and, within an hour, a sizzling fragrance of snake meat ragout had overcome the smell of green leaves on the farm. When the stew was nearly ready, Yemi looked up.

'Broda, why don't we use the mortar?'

'You mean, pounded yam?' Brother Pupa put on a look of innocence.

Yemi looked. 'I know some people who can fight their best friends for pounded yam.'

'Oh, I don't know anyone like that. But, yes, let's go the whole way. It's some people's first day on a farm.'

I protested. 'We have a farm on the way to Osiele, just outside the town.' That was true. I had accompanied Essay there once or twice but it was mostly cared for by a farmer whom he employed.

'Well, as I said, your father was raised here. He is a farmer's son. But I know his work doesn't give him much time to have a farm like this one. I mean, have you ever spent weeks on your farm?'

I shook my head.

'You see. What about a night?'

'Never,' I admitted.

'Or cooked a pot of strew like this or eaten pounded yam on the farm?'

'We don't have an *abule** on it like you do.'

'Ah-ha, that is what I am talking about. If Teacher's wife had agreed, we would have spent the night here.'

I clutched eagerly at the idea. 'We can. You can say tomorrow that it grew too dark and we decided to pass the night here.'

Brother Pupa shook his head. 'She will have a search party after us if we are not back by nightfall. Come on, help Yemi with the hot water and let's pound this yam. I am hungry.'

So indeed was I. When we began eating, I had been certain that I would not touch the snake meat. When the stew was poured into a dish however, I was astonished to find that the meat was not slimy and mottled but an attractive white, firm yet tender-looking, with the consistency of either chicken or rabbit. I decided to taste a little and was again astonished that it tasted in between rabbit and chicken meat. I gave silent thanks for narrowly failing to deprive myself of such an unexpected treat. It was also something to boast about when I returned to Aké, feeling certain that it was a rare pupil indeed who would claim that he had ever feasted on a snake. Broda Pupa nodded approval at the appetite with which I now attacked the meat, pushed more pieces to my side of the dish.

A short rest after lunch, to give the sun some time to 'burn itself down', and we completed the weeding of the plot, baring the young cassava to light. Then we set off home with bundles of yams, a basket of oranges, some vegetables and peppers.

'School' was not over for the day however. We were half-way home and close to a crossing of paths when we heard a human cry. Broda Pupa stopped, signalled to us for silence and listened. It was a continuous cry of someone in pain. It drifted out nervelessly and the distance between the sound and us lessened gradually. I could hear that it drifted closer and

* Hut (or village, farmstead).

closer along the path which was about to cross ours, that it was a man's voice and that it sounded like the cry of a child long after it had been beaten, a long continuous moan of a suffering whose acuteness had passed.

The wailer finally came in view and we gasped. His face, arms and neck were swollen to twice their normal size. It was not an even swell, but a series of close lumps, the size of *awuje*.* The man shuffled rather than walked along the path. He stared ahead of him and did not even seem to notice us. From his half-open lips drooled the incessant moan as if his mouth, his vocal chords had themselves become debilitated.

Brother Pupa shook his head in pity. 'He is from the village over there. He has only a short distance to go.'

'What on earth did that to his face?' I asked.

'Bees,' they both replied. 'He must have run,' Yemi added.

'Well, what should he have done?' I asked. 'Wouldn't you have run?'

'Oh no. You must never do that. Just fling yourself on the ground fast and roll away from the spot.'

'Suppose it's thick bush and you can't roll.'

'Get down as low as you can to the ground,' Broda Pupa advised. 'Get right down to the earth as close as you can, and roll away. Don't stand up and don't run. Get yourself flat on the ground and roll. Even if you land on thorns, stay on the ground, and roll.'

Towards the end of our stay, by pretending to be with our new kinswomen, the trading chaperons, I succeeded in joining a hunting party of my own age-group. They were as usual all much older than I. Our weapons were catapults, stones, sticks, whatever else was handy. Jimo was the leader. He divided the group into beaters and marksmen, I being naturally among the beaters. I had brought down a lizard or two, even a small bird with a catapult at Aké, but I could not pretend to be in the class of Jimo and his mates who frequently knocked down a running squirrel with a shot from the catapult. I was nevertheless determined to excel myself as a beater. As we moved through the bush in a line, I poked in every hole with a stick, thrashed every suspicious-looking clump of bush and shook down saplings. My lungs expanded to match the rousing cry of the others;

'*Gbo, gbo, gbo, gbo; gba, gba, gba, gba.*'

Jimo and the sharpshooters, catapults, stones and cudgels at the ready, waited at the other end of the demarcated grounds. I moved towards yet

* A broad bean.

another shrub, shook it and was instantly rewarded with a sharp pain on my forehead. Another followed almost at once, and then I saw them. An angry nest of hornets, swooping down to punish the intruder. Even as I hit the earth, I felt that Broda Pupa would have been proud of me. His instructions resounded clearly in my head and I obeyed them as if in a practice drill, thinking how provident it was that, barely two weeks before, we had met the victim with the puffed-up face, I again experienced the elation of feeling that I was under some special protection; in Isara, this was a constant, unquestioned state of mind, nothing could even threaten to unsettle it.

Jimo cancelled the rest of the hunt. I had received none other than the first two stings and I protested, but he was not to be deterred. It could lead to a fever, he said, and then he would get blamed. Everyone, it seemed, was eager not to be responsible for any mishap to the children of Teacher. I was however too full of having saved myself, by a lesson whose timing bordered on omens, on the supernatural, to mind this irritating attitude which befell us from the singular misfortune of being 'Teacher's children'. I bore my wounds proudly home and displayed them – not to Teacher and Wife – but to that other parent who had become a fellow conspirator, who truly embodied the male Isara for me in its rugged, mysterious strength, the female complement of which I had earlier obtained from the trading women.

Except that his was smaller, Father's head was almost identical with the Canon's, but he made up for its size by the energy it radiated. It looked hard, truly impregnable, I really did believe that not even a gunshot could penetrate that head, that any bullet would simply bounce off its round, hermetic casting. In spite of the quantity of hair on it, Father's head nevertheless gave an impression of being smooth, the smoothness of iron-plating. He was also a much smaller person than his son, but every inch of him gave off such power that he effortlessly dominated all who came near him. The fact was barely discussed but I knew that he belonged in that same province of beliefs as the *ogboni* of Aké, as the priests and priestesses of various cults and mysteries against whom Wild Christian and her co-religionists sometimes marched on some special week-end of the year, preaching the word of God to them in market-places, on the streets, in their homes. The occasion chosen for such a forage was the anniversary of the missionaries' arrival in Egbaland; their mission was to perpetuate the spirit of those missionaries and bring a few more pagans into the christian fold.

In my secret heart, I feared for Father. I did not see how he would escape

135

the religious onslaught of Aké once the forces began to close on him – from Essay simply by example and the occasional quiet discussion, from Wild Christian by pointed silences, ostentatious preparations for those celebrations of Christmas which belonged only to Christians. New Year embraced everyone, but Christmas had its own hundred-and-one gatherings, worships, communions, prayer-meetings both at home and in closed and open spaces from which outsiders were excluded. Wild Christian had a way of 'leaving out' the unbeliever, especially one in whose household she belonged.

For the moment, however, Father appeared indifferent to the Word of God. When I narrated the incident of the bees, and the coincidence of the earlier warning, he did not say, as Wild Christian would have done, 'God moves in mysterious ways'; he remarked instead:

'Ogun protects his own.'

I had heard that name before. I said to him, 'Ogun is the pagans' devil who kills people and fights everybody.'

'Is that what they teach you?' he asked.

'Yes. Isn't it true?'

Father scratched his chin, pierced me with his eyes. Then he asked me the most unexpected question,

'Do your playmates ever beat you up?'

I told him, 'Sometimes. But mostly they are afraid to touch me because I am the Headmaster's son.'

'So that 's what you tell them when they want to fight you? You mustn't touch me because I am Teacher's son.'

'No, I don't say it, they say it themselves.'

'What do you mean? How do they say it?'

'They snap their fingers at me and say, "You're lucky. If you weren't the Headmaster's son, you would have smelt pepper today." I think they are afraid they would be dismissed from school if they touch me.'

'And you. Do you think Ayo would do that?'

'No. What some of them don't know is that if we fight, we get punished. Any time we return home with torn clothes or somebody reports that we have been in a fight we get punished.' And then I wondered what he must think of this situation which had always struck me as manifestly unfair. 'What do you think of it, Father? We get beaten outside, and then we return home only to get beaten. It's not right, is it?'

Father's eyes twinkled with inward merriment. Except that his eyes were much larger and brighter, he had the same trick with his eyes as the Canon, they wrinkled at the corners almost half-way to his ears when he

136

was amused. He got up now and headed towards the cool corner where he pulled out a keg of palm wine. I did not wait to be asked to fetch the calabashes from the cupboard. I continued to explain,

'They say only children who lack training fight, that it is Satan's work. And to make matters worse, the whole of Aké knows that we get flogged if we get in a fight, so, the ones who do not attend our school, they don't care. They are not afraid of being punished in school. They provoke us saying, fight back if you dare. They land a quick blow and run away. Or else we run away.'

He looked at me intently. 'Are you sure you don't run away because they are bigger?'

'Oh, they are all bigger anyway. I don't think I have ever quarrelled with anyone my size.' Then I remembered, and added, 'Except once with Dipo.' I was overcome with embarrassment. 'But they provoked me, Mama included.' The whole scene was replayed through my mind and I recounted it to him. I asked, 'Father, they are not very consistent, are they? Punishing us when we fight outside, then provoking my brother against me!'

Father scratched the stubble of his chin. 'You will understand that later. They were trying hard to do the right thing, but the wrong way.'

He filled my calabash halfway and filled his to the brim. He blew the froth away and drank it all down. I sipped from mine, watched his face for comments. It grimaced.

'That man is lazy. I've told him, if he doesn't go further up the stream for my wine, I shall stop him bringing any more wine to this house. The tree from which he got this is over-tired, in fact all the trees at the bottom of Larelu's farm are over-tired, but he is too lazy to go half a mile further upstream.' He shook his head in emphasis, 'All right, I'll see to him. *Alakori!*'*

Just the same, he refilled his calabash, took out an *orogbo*,† crumbled its thin skin between his fingers, and bit into it, 'That should hide the taste a little. Now, let's continue. Your father wants you to go to that white man's school in Ibadan. Did you know that?'

'Government College? Yes, he has said so. But I'm just finishing Standard Three. So that is still a long time away.'

'Not so long in your father's planning. Ayo doesn't believe in letting

---

* Hopeless character.
† A hard nut with stimulant properties.

children ripen in the body before he begins to force their brains.' He frowned suddenly. 'Wait. Did you say you were in Standard Three?'

'Well, I have just passed into Standard Four.'

His armoured head went up and down slowly, like a male lizard's. 'Yes. That is what your father was talking about. At the end of the next year you will have finished Four. After that, he wants you to go to the secondary school. He says it is in this New Year, this one we are entering now that you must take the test for your new school.'

'Yes. I will take both the tests for Abeokuta Grammar School and Government College.'

He nodded again. 'And unless my memory is playing me tricks, you are now exactly eight and a half. Is that right?'

'Yes, Father.'

'So, if you pass into this Government College, you will leave home and enter a boarding school. You will be on your own for the first time, away from your parents, at the age of nine and a half – am I right? Is my counting correct so far?'

I assured him that it was, beginning to sense where all this was leading. I got ready to disagree with him, to assure him that I was not afraid to leave home, indeed, that I was anxious, even desperate to leave home. I did not want him protesting to Essay that I was far too young.

'You think that is far too young to leave home, don't you, Father?'

'No. Children leave home for other things too, not just for books. No, I was just thinking that you might find the others too old. Look, even in Ayo's school, in Abeokuta where the people have had their eyes opened much longer than here by the white man, haven't you noticed how much older your classmates are?'

I agreed that I had. 'But I kept beating them all in class,' I assured him. 'I have no trouble at all.'

'Yes, your father tells me that. But you have not got my point yet. Here, people don't go to secondary school straight from primary. They can't afford to. Very often they go on to Standard VI Primary where they get this certificate they call Asamende.'

'As Amended' had entered the folklore of education as the ultimate goal in book striving for would-be pupil teachers, sanitary inspectors, railway conductors and so on. I smiled, but Father misunderstood.

'It's no laughing matter. With Asamende they go to work, save up enough, then go to secondary school where they try, try, try to reach Standard Eight. That is where most of them stop. Few manage to reach the ultimate Ten Books. Now, do you see what I am getting at? If you think your mates in primary school are now much older than you, think what they will be like in the secondary schools. They will be men – *garapa-garapa*! A few would have got married already and will even be hiding a child or two round the corner. You will be sharing desks with MEN, not boys!' He rubbed the stubble on his chin and chuckled. 'They will arrive with their shaving-soap and razor.'

When his chuckles had subsided, he grew solemn again. 'Now, here is Ayo, very ambitious for you. He wants to send his son into battle and believe me, the world of books is a battlefield, it is an even tougher battlefield than the ones we used to know. So how does he prepare him? By stuffing his head with books. But book-learning, and especially success in book-learning only creates other battles. Do you know that? You think those men are going to be pleased when you, whom they are nearly old enough to spawn, start defeating them? Hm? Tell me that. Has Ayo ever discussed that with you?'

I was now thoroughly alarmed. A straightforward occupation like sticking one's head in books and passing examinations was taking on ominous proportions. Father saw that he had made an impression on me and re-filled my calabash. 'Drink your wine, it's quite weak. Even if you drink the whole gourd Eniola can't complain that I am turning you into a drunkard.'

That was the other thing. Father was one of the few people who called Wild Christian by that name. The two Ransome-Kuti, Daodu and Bere and the Odemo also called her that, or Moroun, so did one or two relations who popped up from nowhere from time to time and vanished just as abruptly. To others she was Mama Tinu or Mama Wole, or Iyawo Headmaster. Father continued watching me intently.

'Human beings are what they are. Some are good, some evil. Others turn to evil simply because they are desperate. Envy, hm, you mustn't make the mistake of thinking that envy is not a powerful force for the action of many men. It is a disease you'll find everywhere, yes everywhere. Your mother knows that too. I have seen that much. The only trouble with her is that she thinks she knows what to do about it. What does she think I am alive for?'

I was puzzled at this, I did not understand him and I said so.

He tucked his chin into his neck and shook it about like a battling cockerel, 'O-oh, you think I simply bring you all here for the New Year without looking out for you? O-oh, if that is how you do things at Aké, that is not how we take life here. There is more to the world than the world of Christians, or books. So, enough for today. You and I have business tomorrow.'

I felt a thrill of expectations. Perhaps another outing to the farm, this time Father's own farm. As usual I could not help asking, 'What business, Father?'

He stood up. 'Oh yes, I forgot. They say you never stop asking questions. Go on and play with your friends. I've arranged it all with your father, only I had not decided on the day. Now I think we'll get it over with tomorrow.'

He saw on my face that I was too intrigued now to leave without some further explanation but, he shook his head. 'Tomorrow. But you will come back and sleep here tonight. Go on.'

In Isara we occupied a house by ourselves. Wild Christian that is, and the children. Essay slept in Father's house. From the moment of our arrival in Isara he ceased, in effect, to be part of the Aké family, the Mr & Mrs ended and he moved back into the Isara fold, and the obligations of his hometown. There were constant consultations, town meetings, family meetings, church council sessions, Obaship affairs . . . a hundred duties that a whole year, sometimes less, had kept waiting for him. He spent much of his time with the Odemo but it was not merely duties that kept him there. The Odemo, with one or two others such as my godfather who was the husband of my wife-to-be, obviously relieved the narrowness of discourse which Essay now experienced in Isara. I often wondered if the Odemo was not equally desperate for his kind of company.

It was not a rigid arrangement; often one or more of us would simply camp down at Father's and sleep there. There were always mats and space on the dung-plastered floor of what served as the living-room. In spite of Wild Christian's emissaries, I spent half the nights of Isara in Father's house; this was however the first time that I received a direct order to sleep there. My curiosity was intense as I went to sleep – which did not come until well into the night.

I woke up early to find Father bent over me, an oil-lamp in his hand. It was not yet daylight but there were already two other figures in the house. I saw their forms in a corner of the room, one was clearly an elderly man, the other a young boy, only slightly taller than I was. Instinctively I looked round to see if my father was around but he wasn't. I assumed that he was still fast asleep in the inner room.

My mind still on a planned excursion I asked, 'Where are we going?'

'Are you fully awake?'

I nodded. 'Go and have a wash, I've left a pail of water in the yard.'

I obeyed. As I walked past the two figures I noticed, on the floor between them, a clay dish, a bottle of palm oil, several small tin containers filled with powders, mostly dark colours. A flat plate contained some metal implements and what looked like the fragment of a shell. Puzzled, I had my bath, shivering from the coolness of the morning air and a sense of foreboding.

When I returned, I noticed that the stools and chairs had been re-arranged. The palm-stalk upright had been moved from its position against the wall to near centre of the room. A low stool, an *ipeku*, was placed before it and on this, the elderly stranger was just positioning himself. The boy knelt by his side, re-arranging bottles, jars, trays and the strange assortment of implements.

'Come and sit here,' Father commanded, pointing to the palm-stalk chair. I obeyed.

He moved from the door to face me. 'You remember what we talked about yesterday?'

I replied, 'Yes.'

'Good. Now listen very carefully. What you are about to undergo will give you pain but . . . LOOK AT ME!'

I snatched my eyes back from the sinister tray and looked into his burning eyes. 'That's better. Keep your mind away always from a source of pain. Now, this boy here, he is your own age. It is up to you to decide if you want to shame yourself by crying before him.' He paused, boring into me with his eyes. Since he appeared to expect a reply, I said,

'No, I won't cry.'

'I know you won't. I just wanted to remind you, in case you forget. It will pain you of course, you are not wood, so it must pain you. But you are not to cry.'

I was now wholly paralysed by fear, but that did not stop my heart racing. I waited for the worst. I still had no idea what was in store, only that I was expected not to cry, however painful it was. And then I remembered something.

'When Folasade died, I cried.'

Father stopped in his tracks. The stranger paused also, looked at Father in some puzzled way. I saw that Father was taken aback, not knowing what to make of this. Finally,

'Folasade? Ah, yes. Hm.' And he went off in a private reverie. 'That child was *abami*. I told Ayo at the time – *abami gidi*!* Going off like that, on

---

* A weird child, veritably weird.

her very day of birth, hm. Anyway, that was different. A man cannot argue with his soul. Ibanuję, ko m'omode, ko m'agba.'*

He nodded abruptly to the stranger. I felt my right ankle suddenly in the grip of a vice, the heel pressed against the ground. Just as swiftly, the hand moved to the ball of my foot, pressing downward and maintaining the pressure of the heel against the ground. The little boy swabbed the ankle with a wad soaked in something, the next moment the elderly man had seized the most scalpel-like of the metal objects, dipped it in the clay dish and a sharp pain began at my ankle and shot up my body to the brain. I yelped! The left hand kept my foot firmly fixed to the ground. As I cried out I would have twisted my body, only there were now two strong hands, Father's, keeping my shoulders pressed against the backrest of the chair.

As if in a dream, I looked down and saw the same blade flash into the dish and out again, until the pain in my flesh was no longer defined by moments. The bites of the blade merged into one another and I stared down at the arc of incisions in fascination, at the anklet of blood oozes which progressed round my ankle. After that first sharp cry, my body bound itself to silence, but the tears that were forced out in that moment continued unchecked as I gritted my teeth together and forced back every sound. Father's fingers dug into my shoulders as my body contracted with every incision. I could no longer look down. I shut my eyes, glued my teeth together and waited for the end of the ordeal. The tears ran, unchecked.

A soothing band encased my ankle. When I looked down I noticed a wide swathe in the mixture of the dish. Binding my ankle now was the strip of cloth which had been soaked in that mixture. The boy was quite gentle. Even as I sank into the luxury of the cessation of pain, the blade had bitten into my other ankle. But the shock had passed, and taken the surprise of the pain with it. After the ankles both wrists underwent similar incisions. I winced from time to time but my jaws were at least unclenched. I watched every move, even began to admire the neat, precision skill of the wielder of the knife.

When it was over, I disbelieved what a short time it had all taken. Outside, the sun was beginning to cast shadows on our doorstep. The stranger spoke in low tones in the corner of the room while Father nodded and grunted in apparent agreement. Then the elder came back and began to pack his instruments, the boy rinsing out the dish just outside the door while the elder cleaned out his blades, poured the rest of the powders into

* Sorrow knows neither child nor elder.

small jars which he transferred to a bottomless bag which I now saw hanging by the door. Father saw them off, and shut the door.

He came towards me, sat on the vacated stool and said, 'Wole, you did – strong. You acted like a true Akin. And now listen to me. Listen very carefully, and this in spite of anything anyone, ANYONE tells you . . . If they tell you the contrary, tell them I said it . . .'

Unhurriedly, taking his time as if the taking of snuff was the most hazardous operation in the world, he reached sideways to the lower ledge of the small table, took out his tin of snuff, opened it, shook some into his left hand, replaced the cover, taking care to keep his left hand cupped to avoid spillage, replaced the tin on the ledge, then proceeded to take a pinch from the palm and treat either nostril to an equal amount of snuff. For some reason, probably because of the unprepared-for immersion I had just undergone, every sense was painfully tuned and the slightest detail of his motions took on a life of its own, so that I seemed to be seeing him for the first time.

My hearing also had acquired a wild tuning. When he sneezed I leapt up from the chair and my head continued to echo with the sound, even while he spoke.

'Whoever offers you food, take it. Eat it. Don't be afraid, *as long as your heart says, Eat*. If your mind misgives, even for a moment, don't take it, and never step in that house again. Do you understand what I have just said?'

I could only nod, dumbly.

'I said, anyone offers you food or drink, if your mind does not hesitate, go ahead. It is I that say so. If, however, you experience even one moment of doubt, turn your back on that place and never go back. Next, don't ever turn your back on a fight. Where you are going, maybe next year, maybe the year after the next, I don't know. For all I know they may not let you back here before you go to that school but it does not matter. Wherever you find yourself, don't run away from a fight. Your adversary will probably be bigger, he will trounce you the first time. Next time you meet him, challenge him again. He will beat you all over again. The third time, I promise you this, you will either defeat him, or he will run away. Are you listening to what I am telling you?'

'Yes, Father.'

'First time, second time, never mind that he beats you. But keep going back. In the end you will put him to shame – either you will trounce him soundly, or he will run away.'

He rose. 'I sent your parents and the other children away to Sagamu.

They should have gone by now, there are plenty of people there they haven't visited. So we are by ourselves.'

I turned towards the room. 'I thought Papa was in there.'

He smiled and shook his head. 'Oh no, this is just between the two of us. Now I must go to a meeting. Somebody will bring you your breakfast. Don't eat anything else. Don't eat anything today and tomorrow except what I send you. Do you understand?'

I assured him that I did. I felt drained, my head was in confusion and my wrists and ankles throbbed. There was a strange distance from my hands as if they no longer belonged to me.

Then I heard myself ask, 'Did Papa get his ankles cut too? I mean, when he was like me.'

Father raised his eyes to the rafters. 'They said it. Ayo warned me, and so did Eniola. When I said they should leave you with me today, they warned, Be careful. He will kill you with questions.'

He went into his room. I could still hear him chuckling to himself as he changed, letting out his single prolonged yell of wonder which had a neatly regulated tailing off at the end. For a long while I sat still, trying to work out if my ankles would take my weight or if they would fall off the moment I lifted my feet. It was as if my quandary had transmitted itself to him in the room because his voice came ringing out almost at once:

'Try walking on the outer edge of your feet, then on the inside edge. When both have failed, you might try walking as you normally do – squarely on both feet, only a little more gently. That usually works best.'

And then, as I stood up, I found myself grinning, because I was certain that Father did not think that I would understand.

X

The smells are all gone. In their place, mostly sounds, and even these are frenzied distortions of the spare, intimate voices of humans and objects alike which filled Aké from dawn to dusk, whose muted versions through the night sometimes provided us with puzzles of recognition as we lay on our mats resisting sleep. Even the least pleasant smell, such as the faintly nauseating smell of a smashed bed-bug, tinged with the whiff of camphor that should have prevented its appearance in the first place was part of the invisible network of Aké's extended persona; it was of the same order as the nocturnal rumblings of Sorowanke, the madwoman who lived by the mango tree, talking in her sleep. This was the mango tree in the square, nearly opposite the church. At night we would hear her distinctly exorcising her demons or bickering with her lunatic lover Yokolu. Even as the sizzle of the heated needle was heard from Wild Christian's nocturnal battles against the bugs, the crickets and cicadas engaged in their own challenge to the prolonged choir practice from St Peter's church, probably on the eve of a Church festival. Sorowanke punctuated the anthem in rehearsal with her sudden yelps and slaps against cracked, emaciated thighs as the tower-clock solemnly chimed the twelve strokes of midnight. Over it all, as we drifted asleep, coursed the pungent ferment of pulped corn from the dark corner of the kitchen, the smell of *ojojo* from the frying-pot of a woman who served the late night-farers, of palm-wine from the same night-stall which dispensed a late supper of *eko*-and-*ojojo* and, at week-ends especially, the sound of the lazy strings of Dayisi, the juju-band guitarist returning from an engagement, or simply serenading the night.

The smells have been overcome. And their conqueror, sound, is not even the measured chimes of the tower-clock or the parade of *egúngún*, police band, market cries or bicycle-bell but a medley of electronic bands and the raucous clang of hand-bells advertising bargain sales of imported wares. The dusty road which once grandly intervened between our backyard wall and the church wall is now shrunken; a half, pressed against St Peter's parsonage wall, is shared among a variety of stores peddling the products of a global waste industry – fly-blown shawls, combs, mirrors, flaring radio antennae, chrome or foam-and-rubber motor-car decorations, ornamented flasks, drinking-glasses disguised as floral arrangements, oriental table-mats stamped Manchester, clocks, 'gold' jewellery, photo-frames with a backing of white voluptuous bodies . . . Raquel Welch, Marilyn Monroe, Diana Dors, Jane Russell, Greta Garbo. Sometimes the figures are mincing males, also stars of the celluloid world. They strike a pose of conscious masculinity but, even with their aggressive moustaches, the sum is – androgynous. Along the same midnight walk of Dayisi the guitarist now darts the young hawker, releasing into the faces of passers-by through his finger on the caller's button, the dulcet chimes of Made-in-Hong-Kong doorbells.

Along Dayisi's Promenade I also sang, but only on those occasional late evenings when I was sent on an errand to Pa Solatan or some other member of our parents' circle in the direction of Aafin or Iporo, or to our Auntie Mrs Lijadu. I sang to buoy up my spirits against the dangers of the dark, against figures who drifted past in the dark and who, for all I knew, might be spirits or kidnappers. There had accrued to me a formidable weapon in my armoury of incantations against the unknown, after my role as The Magician on prize-giving day at St Peter's in Standard III. Even if most dangerous spirits did not converse in English, there was no way that they could mistake the ferocious will of the counter-force marching along Dayisi's Promenade and singing at the top of his voice:

> For I'm a magician
> You all must know
> You'll hear about me wherever you go
> You can see my name in letters large
> You can see me perform for a poultry large
> For Anthony Peter Zachary White
> Is a man who always gives delight . . .
> My friends I bid you come and see
> What sort of wizard I may be
> Come one and all
> And join the crowd
> And lift your voice in praises loud . . .

Why poultry? It was one of the baffling details of that children's opera. The power of the magician was no stranger however, even though it belonged among the mysterious.

Centenary Hall was constantly host to a procession of magicians who were invariably 'trained in India'. They burnt incense, transfixed volunteers from the audience and sliced their assistants in half. Once there was a terrifying encounter between a member of the audience, a near duplicate of Paa Adatan. He had answered the call for volunteers from the audience on whom the magician would demonstrate his hypnotic powers. This aggressive, muscular volunteer had however refused to be hypnotized. The Doctor Magician exerted all his powers, burnt coils and coils of incense, muttered a hundred Abracadabras and recited the terrifying pronouncements of – someone whispered near us – the Seventh and Ninth Books of Moses; the volunteer simply turned towards the audience, half-rose from his couch and sneered. The Doctor sprinkled his mystic water from Jerusalem around the couch, flicked his fingers at the recumbent form and fanned the air around the volunteer's face with down-facing palms; the stubborn Egba man refused to go to sleep. But finally the deed was done, the volunteer's eyes glazed over and the Doctor stood over his inert form, triumphant. But then, his face turned ugly. The confrontation had reduced his status and competence in the eyes of the audience and he began to prowl round the stage in a fury. He shouted words to the effect that the defeated man and he had been engaged in a life-and-death duel and thus the contest could only be concluded on those terms. The audience appeared nervous. Suddenly he dived on the sleeping figure, pulled up his *dansiki*. Sure enough, around his waist was a leather thong of amulets. This he ripped off and held out to the audience; we understood this to be the Doctor's explanation of the man's prolonged resistance. His next motion was the most terrifying moment of the entire evening. He pounced on the long sword with which he had sliced his assistant in half and, raising it, darted towards the couch with an intent that no one could mistake. Some of the audience fled, others covered their eyes and screamed. I was merely open-mouthed in horror, unable to believe that an evening's entertainment of magic could be about to end in such a violent manner. The commotion was so complete that I neither saw, nor could anyone explain to me how it all ended.

That contest unravelled itself for me, even as it took place, as a simple contest between the magician and the *osó*, the wizard or sorcerer. The magician was the agent of the mysterious Orient – India, Egypt, the Three Wise Men, Moses and Pharaoh and the Plagues. The wizard was our own challenger, armed with local charms against the alien forces of the Orient. But he had been defeated and, for all I knew, had been vengefully cut in half by the enraged man of the Orient. The smell of incense hung permanently over my memory of that encounter, linking up in some undefined way with the aura of those three kings who had approached the infant child with gifts of gold, frankincense and myrrh. It was, without doubt, an evil, vengeful force, terrifying and pitiless in application. Playing the role of The Magician, self-declared both 'magician' and 'wizard', was therefore a rather baffling contradiction but the songs were all the more potent for that. It was the language of a dual force which the witches and the kidnappers would understand. Songs from that operetta became my regular guard whenever I had to brave the passage between our backyard wall and the churchyard where, to add to the menace of the dark, there was also a cemetery, not to mention the huge mango tree whose bole was large enough to house a hundred ewèlè, òrò, iwin and other ànjònnú!

But the seasonal anthems rehearsed by the choir also exerted my voice. The tunes came out clearly enough, but not the words. These emerged as some strange language, a mixture of English, Yoruba and some celestial language that could only be what was spoken by those cherubs in the stained-glass windows, whose mouths sprouted leaves and branches as they circled the beatific faces of saints and archangels. These indecipherable lyrics led to strange interpretations, and I was engaged in belting out some of these when I bumped into Mr Orija the organist who was just emerging from the rear-gate of the church compound. I was checked in stride by the apparition of the untidy man who always looked, wherever he was, as if he was still enveloped in his cassock and surplice and was racing towards the church with only seconds to spare before the beginning of service. I stopped, muttered a Good Evening sir in a panic and fled. I could no longer remember what jumbled version of the Easter Cantata I had been singing but I hoped that it had not sounded blasphemous enough to lead to a report to Essay the following day.

I was wrong. Mr Orija visited the house almost with the crowing of the cock the following morning. But he had not come to report any transgression, only to ask Essay if I could join the choir. There followed a somewhat prolonged discussion – I eavesdropped, from the moment I saw the lumbering figure of the organist approaching the front door. Essay thought that I was far too small but Mr Orija insisted that my voice was just right for the soprano. In the end it was agreed. Special robes would have to be made for me when the time came, but I was to join in the choir practices immediately.

Edun, who lived on the other side of Ibarapa morning market was inducted at the same time. We celebrated the occasion as yet another liberating step from the demands of our households. In addition to lessons, scouting, and a few fictions, there was now the legitimate escape through

'Of course. Why not? I'm not going anywhere tomorrow. Yes, a good idea.'

A short silence. She moved closer to the bone. 'Are you expecting visitors tomorrow at lunch?'

Our whisper was deliberately audible: 'Mayself? Ny-ou.' HM pretended he had heard nothing.

'No-o-o. No. Mr Adelu might call of course but . . . No, I'm not expecting anyone.'

'Well, if you do have anyone at lunchtime could you send for me at the shop? I mean you could always have something else in the afternoon and reserve the pottage for the evening. I am making it specially, and it is, after all, Father's smoked pork from Isara.'

'Yes, yes, by all means. As you like.'

She plotted it all with Nubi. As soon as Mayself arrived Nubi ran to inform her and took mother's place in the shop. That day, we waited in the front room assiduously engaged in studies. Not a page was turned over. Wild Christian arrived. Mayself leapt up from his chair, the model of old-world courtesy. He bowed low over her hand:

'Gyud meerning, Madam.'

Thin-smiling, Madam exchanged courtesies. Essay, on the other side of the table, smothered a very fractional smile; he was intuitive about plots. We guessed he would simply let matters take their course.

'I thought I would come and see to your pottage myself,' she explained. 'These children might spoil it and Father did send that delicacy specially for you.'

'But the shop . . . ?'

'Oh, Nubi can handle most things now. In any case today is a slack day, with all this rain. I'll just go and get it ready.'

Not a flicker of anticipation betrayed Mayself's interest in the conversation, his face remained buried in the book in deep concentration. Under the desk we pinched one another. What strategy had she decided on?

The bustle and smell of preparations reached us in the front room but it was doubtful if any mouth among ours watered that day. Heads bent resolutely down, our eyes were nevertheless fixed on the little man before us. At long last the voice from the kitchen rang in summons:

'Woleee.'

'Ma.'

I received nudges as I squeezed past others, each saying, this is it. When I reached the dining-room I saw that the table was already laid – for two.

There was also a small tray containing a small saucer of biscuits, and a glass.

'Go and ask the gentleman whether he prefers ginger-ale or orange squash.'

I did as I was told. This time his surprise was genuine.

'Mayself? Eouh, derzn matter. Tell madam anything thank you.'

So Wild Christian chose for him. As she handed me the tray she herself prepared to follow. That puzzled me. Mayself again sprung to attention. I lay the tray down on the table beside him.

'Oh, Medm is so kind, so kind. And you must help me thank Headmaster too. Mr Soyinka is really most hospitable, a real gentleman if I may say so.'

She smiled sweetly. 'Please don't mention it.'

'Oh, but I must, I must. A very kind soul, his qualities are very rare.'

Mother indulged him with some further five minutes of pleasantries, then interrupted: 'I hope you will excuse him just for a short while . . .'

'Of course, madam, of course . . .'

'Some rather important family matters have come up . . .'

'Oooh, ooh . . .'

'Family problems.' She smiled, then looked at father. 'Dear, I know you are busy today so perhaps we can discuss things over your lunch.'

I had regained my seat by then. A cousin wrote in his notebook – 10/10 – grading her performance as superlative, a verdict which we all endorsed. Essay rose, acknowledging defeat and murmured an Excuse me. Mayself sprang to his feet – Quite, quite – and did not resume his seat until they had both passed from the room.

She kept Essay in the dining-room for nearly two hours, bringing up every possible subject under the earth. Mayself munched his biscuits with his habitual daintiness, yet they disappeared with that contradicting speed whose mechanics remained a mystery we tried to solve long after Mayself had disappeared from our lives. He did not of course give up so readily. He turned up again the following day and the day after, but his adversary had left instructions and she would be summoned. She entered the house from then on through the backdoor so that the first intimation that Mayself had of her presence was her voice summoning one of us. That presaged the arrival of a tray of biscuits and orange juice. She no longer turned up in the front room at all but simply sent word to father to 'spare her a moment'. Mayself's conduct was correct to the last, profuse in his thanks, yet partaking of what hospitality he received as a pleasant incident in his life. He disappeared finally, and the house became the poorer for his absence.

choir practice. And although I lived nearer to the church, it was somehow accepted that it was I who should go past the church, cross the street between Aké square and Ibarapa market, go through the market, pick my way through the intervening *agbole* and return with Edun through the same passages to the church for choir practice and, when we began to robe, for church services.

We varied the course. The evening market was normally out of our way since it lay on the other side of the road to Iberekodo, but the morning market was mostly bare and devoid of interest by the hour of choir practice. Going through the sister market only added some ten or fifteen minutes to the walk and I made sure that I set out early enough to make up the time for it. The flavours of the market rose fully in the evenings, beckoning us to a depletion of the *onini* and halfpennies which we had succeeded in saving up during the week. For there they all were, together, the *jogi* seller who passed, in full lyrical cry beneath the backyard wall at a regular hour of the morning, followed only moments later by the *akara* seller, her fried bean-cakes still surreptitiously oozing and perfuming the air with groundnut oil. In the market we stood and gazed on the deftly cupped fingers of the old women and their trainee wards scooping out the white bean-paste from a mortar in carefully gauged quantities, into the wide-rimmed, shallow pots of frying oil. The lump sank immediately in the oil but no deeper than an inch or two, bobbed instantly to the surface and turned pinkish in the oil. It spurted fat globules upwards and sometimes beyond the rim of the pot if the mix had too much water. Then slowly forming, the outer crust of crisp, gritty light brownness which masked the inner core of baked bean-paste, filled with green and red peppers, ground crayfish or chopped.

Even when the *akara* was fried without any frills, its oil-impregnated flavours filled the markets and jostled for attention with the tang of roasting coconut slices within farina cakes which we called *kasada*; with the hard-fried lean meat of *tinko*; the 'high', rotted-cheese smell of *ogiri*; roasting corn, fresh vegetables or *gbegiri*. *Akàmu*, the evening corn pap, was scooped into waiting bowls from a smooth, brown gourd sitting in enamelled trays on bamboo trestles, presided over by women who daily improvised new praise-chants. An *onini*, even a halfpenny did not fulfil every craving but the sights and the smells were free. Choir practice became inseparable from the excursion through Ibarapa's sumptuous resurrection of flavours every evening. When, a few months later, our apprenticeship was over and we became full-fledged choristers, I continued to leave early on Sundays and other church seasons to call on Edun for both morning and evening services. The morning market was not open on Sundays but there was a woman who appeared to have converted all the smells and textures of both morning and evening markets in her pot of stew, a crayfish and locust-bean biased concoction which queened it over rice and a variety of yams. Apart from a few stalls of fresh vegetables, she alone defied the claims of Sunday to a market-free gesture of respect. The consequence was predictable. Breakfast at home was not niggardly, so it was not a question of hunger. It was even special on Sundays – yams, fish stew, omelette, bread, butter and the inevitable tea or lemon grass infusion. But it was not yet breakfast on Sunday until I had picked my way through the stalls of Ibarapa, cassock and surplice thrown over the shoulder, rescued Edun from his home and, robbing God to pay Iya Ibarapa, used up the pennies we were given for offering on the steaming, peppery, glutinous riot of liver, of chunks and twists of cows' insides served by the old woman as church bells signalled the half-hour before confronting God. Once or twice, probably a little oftener, we were struck by the fear that God might object to this weekly deprivation of his rightful dues, but I think I lightened our apprehensions by suggesting that we sang better after the richness of the markets in our throats than we ever did with the delicacies of the parsonage alone. In any case, we watched for signs of disapproval from the designated owner of those Sunday pennies, but received none.

When I asked Ibidun, Mrs Lijadu's niece, what our Aunt put in her stews to make it taste so peculiar she said, *pasmenja*. It was a strange word but one which was perfectly suited to the flavour of the meals we had with our Aunt who, we had decided, belonged to the vague Brazilian side of our relations. An axis of tastes and smells was formed between her and our grandmother, Daodu's sister, who lived alone in Igbein almost on the other side of Abeokuta. We did not visit her much but, when we did, I would realize with a start – and not just at mealtime – that I was not at Mrs Lijadu's but in the home of our maternal grandmother, the mysterious elder sister of Rev A. O. Ransome-Kuti. It remained one of the mysteries of the family relationships over which Wild Christian spent so much time trying to educate us. Were the Olubi our cousins and did this mean blood or marriage relations? I listened, understanding none of the elaborate and intricate family history. Links were formed of far more tangible matters. Our Igbein grandmother had nothing in common, as far as I ever discerned, with her formidable brother Daodu. Equally stern and just as affectionate perhaps, but I was more ready to accept, and indeed continued to believe for a long time that she was Beere's mother. And I thought that she and Mrs Lijadu were sisters because they both cooked with *pasmenja*, both homes were constantly wreathed in the smell of *pasmenja*. Even their buns and *chin-chin* had identical flavours; as for food in both homes, it could only have been cooked, not merely by sisters, but by two people who had been sisters all their lives. Daodu's wife, Beere, I never associated with any form of cooking. Eating, that was a different matter.

Beere had a passion for *moin-moin* and she was so fond of *moin-moin* made by Wild Christian that she often sent one of her elder children, Koye or Dolupo, all the way from Igbein to Aké for Wild Christian's *moin-moin*. When she came in person and joined our parents at table, a shriek of outrage was wrung from her if an over-zealous maid had unwrapped the steamed delicacy from the leaves. For her, the sublime parts of *moin-moin* were those wafer-thin truants which leaked into the folds of leaves and were now steamed into light, independent slivers, to be peeled leisurely from their veined beds and sucked smoothly through the lips in between, or, as a finale to the chunky mouthfuls of the full-bodied *moin-moin*. The hapless maid produced *moin-moin* paraded in all its steamy, but naked glory and Beere would confidently insist that the leaves be retrieved. There was no danger; she knew very well that they had not been thrown into the dust-bin. We watched her glide meticulously through every leaf, prise through the stuck-together leaves with a skin-surgeon's care. She levered apart the baked veins of the leaf-wraps, casually picking up the oiled wafers along the way and licking her lips in ostentatious enjoyment. She acknowledged our unvoiced stares of protest by remarking loudly – if she happened to be in the mood – that anyone who really believed that such tidbits should be left to children was either a fool or an Englishman. Then, with a roguish look on her bespectacled face, she measured off a slice from the centre of the *moin-moin*, pushed it aside for us and winked, remarking afterwards that she would sooner forgo the main lump than lose those insubstantial slivers with their Wild-Christian flavour, sealed in secret corners cunningly pinched by her practised fingers.

The hawkers' lyrics of leaf-wrapped *moin-moin* still resound in parts of Aké and the rest of the town but along Dayisi's Walk is also a shop which sells *moin-moin* from a glass case, lit by sea-green neon lamps. It lies side by side with McDonald's hamburgers, Kentucky Fried Chicken, hot dogs and dehydrated sausage-rolls. It has been cooked in emptied milk-tins and similar containers, scooped out and sliced in neat geometric shapes like cakes of soap. And the newly-rich homes stuff it full of eggs, tinned sardines from Portugal and corned beef from the Argentine. The fate of *wara*, among others, is however one without even this dubious reprieve. The vendor of milk-curds, floated in outsize gourds has been banished by chromium boxes with sleek spouts which dispense yellowish fluids into brittle cones. If it were, at least, ice *cream*! But no. The quick-profit importer of instant machines is content to foist a bed-pan slop of diabetic kittens on his youthful customers and watch them lick it noisily, biting deeper into the cone. Even Pa Delumo's Sunday school children knew better; the ice cream king of Dayisi's Walk would have been dethroned, through neglect, by the *wara* queen.

Our teeth were cut on *robo*, hard-fried balls of crushed melon seeds, and on *guguru-and-epa*, the friend and sustainer of workers on the critical countdown towards pay day. A handful of *guguru* was washed down in water, palm-wine or pito and hunger was staved off for the rest of the working day. Evening, and *konkere* department took over, a bean-pottage with a sauce of the darkest palm-oil and peppers, and of a soundly uncompromising density. Mixed with *gari*, it fully justified the name of concrete whose corrupted version it proudly bore. The Hausa women who sold *guguru* carefully graded their corn; we combined in our purchases the hard-roasted teeth-breakers, the fluffy, off-white floaters and the half-and-half, inducing variations into taste-buds with slices of coconut or measures of groundnuts. Today's jaws on Dayisi's Walk appear no less hard-worked, indeed they champ endlessly – on chewing-gum. Among the fantasy stores lit by neon and batteries of coloured bulbs a machine also dispenses popcorn, uniformly fluffed. Urchins thrust the new commodity, clean-wrapped, in plastic bags in faces of passengers whose vehicles pause even one moment along the route. The blare of motor-horns competes with a high-decibel outpouring of rock and funk and punk and other thunk-thunk from lands of instant-culture heroes. Eyes glazed, jaws in constant, automated motion, the new habituees mouth the confusion of lyrics belted out from every store, their arms flapping up and down like wounded bush-fowl. Singly, or in groups of identical twins, quad- or quintuplets they wander into the stereo stores, caress the latest record sleeves and sigh. A trio emerge with an outsize radio-cassette player in full blast, setting up mobile competition with the already noise-demented line of stores.

They move on to the trinket-and-cosmetic shop, their jaws implacably churning through the gummed-up troughs of synthesized feed in every conceivable idiom, pause at McDonald's, bury corpses of sausage-rolls in their mouths and drown the mash in Coca-Cola. A girl decides at last on one of several competing brands of 'skin-tone' creams, already picturing her skin bleached lighter, if the glossy poster on the wall fulfilled its promises. There is a welcome intrusion of a more localized noise, or so it seems at the beginning. Alas, it is only yet another local imitation of foreign pop, incongruously clothed in some pious, beatitudinal phrases and left-over morsels of traditional proverbs and saws. But these musicians have the measure of their audiences – the newly rich, importers and contractors, the managers of 'groups of companies'. Bathed in the glow of such instant piety, their minds and senses untasked by linear melodic lines and the single all-purpose chord, they embrace and ostentatiously patronize the new music, barely recognizing the identicality of the new 'Fuji', 'Fuji-Rock', 'apola-disco', 'Afro-Reggae' with their equally vapid precursors.

Their choices equally untroubled but tuned to distant mentors, the children of the new professionals – doctors, lawyers, engineers, bureau-crats and clerics – pass behind the parsonage along Dayisi's Walk clutching the very latest cassettes from 'the abroad' and congregate at Kentucky Fried Chicken to compare notes. A girl pauses at the hair-dressers' and soon, the sound of sizzling joins the disco sounds, followed by the smell of frying hair as the hot comb heats up the brain of the young consumer without firing her imagination. At the end of the operation the belle of St Peter's examines the magazine floss on her head, touches it lightly here and there and approves her new appearance. It is time to join the others at the Colonel's for a share of the 'finger-lickin' goodness'.

Sometimes Dayisi's promenade merged with strange cruelties. In the mango season Aké Square was particularly heady with smells. It was not just the fruits, though these gave off their own sticky perfumes, in addition to attracting a plague of butterflies, swarms of flies and bluebottles once the sticks and stones began to fell the ripened fruits. The tree in season was however so lush with shade that food-sellers stayed willingly beneath it. All day, the workers, office staff from nearby local government offices, schoolboys and lorry passengers squatted among the roots of the tree, on improvised benches, or simply stood while they made combination meals out of a hundred varieties. Sorowanke was an additional attraction. Sometimes they would give her food, even occasional clothing, other times she was the subject of abuse, good-natured teasing, and the occasional anonymous missile.

Sorowanke had built her shack against bushes some distance from the mango tree – a few thin strips of corrugated iron sheets, some cardboard, rags and sticks were sufficient for the makeshift home. Yokolu her lover had no fixed abode; he patrolled all of Abeokuta and could be encountered at all hours in any corner of the town. One day, we saw him sharing a meal with Sorowanke. He came more and more frequently, until we noticed that among the rags which Sorowanke now spread out to dry after washing were some that belonged obviously to a man. Yokolu wandered off less and less, spending most of the day around the mango tree and sharing the food that was habitually given to Sorowanke.

The event created some consternation among the mango-tree population. Our own pupils at St Peter's brought back daily news of the progress of this liaison between the two outcasts, and the reactions of the food-sellers and their customers. Imperceptibly at first, the crowd around the mango tree began to diminish in spite of the deep and broadening shade around the tree. The food-sellers who remained moved further away from the tree-trunk towards the church, opting for new positions almost on the perimeter of the shade. Sorowanke and her lover took over the abandoned space. Their tins, cans, frayed baskets began to appear among the roots where customers used to eat. Their laundry appeared on the lower branches of the tree. Soon, Sorowanke and Yokolu followed their possessions into the base of the tree. At high noon they could be seen dozing with their backs against the tree; their hearth was now permanently positioned in a convenient triangle formed by two exposed roots of the tree, the concoctions from their pots vying in pungency with the familiar smells of fried pork and yam pottage, *leki* and the myriad other delicacies of the regular food-sellers. There were grumblings, but it seemed as if the new demarcation of territory was now tacitly conceded.

And then, Sorowanke's stomach began to swell. It grew bigger and bigger and Sorowanke talked less and less, even at night, sitting on her haunches among the roots, drawing deeper and deeper into the shadows. No longer ranting to the universe as she was wont, especially when Yokolu went on his mysterious voyages round the world, she contented herself with muttering incantations which no one could decipher. One day, her consort disappeared. Sorowanke grew even more withdrawn from the world. Since she always looked downwards when muttering, it appeared that she was speaking to the swelling in her belly. Abruptly, one morning, we heard shouts, screams, the sounds of missiles clattering on iron sheets. I rushed to the ladder with others and there we saw some of our schoolmates pelting Sorowanke with stones and sticks. The food hawkers joined in while some men on their way to work simply stopped and watched, jeering and calling her witch. Only a few days before, she had returned from an unaccustomed absence – a few hours at the most – to find her shack smouldering, her belongings scattered, flung far from the base of the tree. Since then she would sit in the same position, muttering, barely eating. In any case there was not much food or money – perhaps it was this which took her away for a few hours in the first place. And now the stones were flying at her. A well-aimed cudgel knocked off her remaining tin-pot from the crude hearth beneath which she had lit a fire, spilling nothing but plain water. I saw her bleeding from the temple, waving a hand across her face as if she was trying to swat a fly. But they were hard stones, and sticks, and Sorowanke suddenly felt along the tree-trunk and staggered up. The children moved in, scattered her fire, threw the remaining rags and cardboard boxes into the bush where her shack once stood. The food-sellers completed the work, swept the grounds clean and moved back to their former stations. It took no more than a week before Aké completely forgot the pregnant madwoman, Sorowanke.

XI

All that I observed was that he kept more and more to his room, that he ate less often, and then, mostly in his room and that when he emerged, he appeared to look more keenly at us and shake his head sadly. Nothing changed in his appearance. Visitors came less frequently. When they did they stayed for only a short while, sometimes not seeing Essay, simply being told, 'Headmaster is resting.'

Wild Christian spent more time in the house, abandoning the shop to the maid and the cousins. She spent much of the day in and out of his room, taking him food, tea, conversing with him in low voices. Our little infringements went unpunished by either of them, and these in turn diminished so that there was really nothing to rebuke. A blanket of general somnolence hung over the house, a peaceful dispensation which repelled harsh voices. No one had to ask us not to raise our voices, to avoid knocking things over. We had no inclination to play truant, to dawdle on errands or join our other playmates in furtive dares. After school, I hastened home, unconsciously impelled by a need to be with the family, to share the quiet intimacy of touch, looks, a drawing together which was tangible in every simple action.

And yet I barely understood. Not even when I came upon him unnoticed among his flowers, his gaze more and more frequently floated on distances. I turned a corner of the house, and surprised him speaking softly to himself with an annoyed shake of the head.

'Oh dear, what a pitiful death.'

It happened a number of times. There was no mistaking the words. On his face played his smile of half-regret, half-annoyance, perhaps also, a touch of curious anticipation, but the words were unmistakable. Sometime he tossed his head, smiling with a touch of indulgence, as if he was chiding a wayward, precocious child.

'Yes, what a pitiful death.'

Then, one day, he called me into his room. He was sitting up in bed and made me sit down in his chair, by the window. I had never seen him smile so much, so insistently.

'You are not to let anything defeat you,' he began, 'because you are the man of the family, and if you are not strong, what would you expect Tinu and the others to do? What you must pursue at all times is your education. Don't neglect that. Now you know I've always wanted you to go to Government College.'

Mystified, but now deeply troubled, I nodded yes.

'It is true you are now in the Grammar School. But you must continue to sit the exams for Government College. And not merely sit to pass, but win a scholarship. The government colleges have several scholarships for the deserving child, which is what you must strive to be. Aim for a place in Government College. You see, no matter what happens, the government will support its scholar – always bear that in mind.'

I promised to aim for a scholarship. It seemed so important to him and suddenly I was caught up in the feeling that I was making an important transition through a promise that was eternally binding. It was plain that I must let nothing come between me and the fulfilment of this promise, which was made between two people on an unfamiliar, hitherto un-explored plane. He nodded, as if he had recognized my own act of recognition, and was content.

'Things do not always happen as one plans. There are many disappoint-ments in life. There is always the unexpected. You plan carefully, you decide on one step after another, and then . . . well, that is life. We are not God. So you see, one cannot afford to be weighed down by the unexpected. You will find that only determination will bring one through, sheer determination. And a faith in God – don't ever neglect your prayers. You are the man of the family, remember that others will look up to you. You must never let them down.' He shook his head for emphasis, 'Never, never let them down!'

That evening, I developed a high fever. It raged throughout the night and through the following day. Not until the third day did it begin to abate. Throughout the delirium I was conscious of only the two faces – father and mother – bent down anxiously over the bed. And the voice of Wild Christian saying, when the fever began to drop,

'What is the matter? Is it because of the talk you had with your father?'

I said nothing, knowing that what she had suggested was the truth, but failing to see how one thing could possibly have led to the other.

When I recovered, I found the photographer hovering around the house. My illness had, it seemed, delayed a planned fiesta of photography which now commenced with a kind of calm intensity. Essay had turned out his wardrobe for his finest *aso oke*. He was photographed singly, with every

157

shrubbery of his garden, the crotons and the roses, he was photographed with Wild Christian, with each one of his children, then with all of us, then in several family groupings. He went back to his room and changed, was photographed against the setting sun, against the walls of the bedroom, seated, standing . . . but always with that wide smile on his face. He moved about cheerfully, giving the photographer instructions, positioning each of us exactly as he wanted us, first on his knees, then standing beside him – I wondered what the photographer made of this sudden orgy of portraiture. Essay's last instruction to him that evening was that he should hurry the results. Over the photographer's amazed protests, he insisted that the plates must be developed, printed and brought to the house the following evening.

I went back to bed, fatigued, suffering a mild relapse of the fever.

Then, so gradually that I did not really notice it, the shadow passed. Little by little I began to observe a return of the old routine, an increase in noise, cheerfulness, jokes, front-room visits and the normal shop-keeping absences of Wild Christian from the house. When the house was normal again, I began to think that it had all been a hallucination of my fever. The inert spell of seeming to wait – for what I did not know – had lifted. The days regained definition and pattern. A sense of liberation, a deep psychic relief, a sense of a lasting reprieve took over. Beyond a few times when I caught myself watching Essay with a baffled intensity, beyond the evidence of the photographs which had been framed and now hung on the walls, I accepted the new dispensation as a matter of course, with perhaps a sense of gratitude to an unseen Force for a deliverance from the suspected but unnamed Menace.

XII

Grandfather was right, they were not all men at Abeokuta Grammar School – AGS to most of Abeokuta – but there were numbers whose only distinguishing feature from teachers was that they wore the blue shirts and khaki-khaki uniforms of the schoolboys. In every other aspect they were ready to be heads of their own households, and some of them already were.

Nearly half of my beautiful new text books, exercise books, pencils, rubbers, blotters and other equipment vanished in the first week in AGS. The deepest loss however was a gleaming mathematics set, the first I had ever held or seen. It opened up vistas of a totally new form of scholarship and promised great excitement. That it should vanish before I even had the time to understand what the dividers, the compasses, the set square and the translucent half-circle with strange markings were meant to impart was far more painful than the punishment which accompanied their loss. Not even the replacement – with an equally new set – could compensate for the loss of that first flat metal box to which I had accorded such reverence that, I ignored all advice and refused to deface it by carving my name on it. The big boy who had stolen it, who everybody knew had stolen it and who knew that we all knew, had already scratched his name across the box inside and out. It established his ownership and there was little that anyone could do, not even the class-teacher to whom I reported the loss, and my suspicions.

There were a few more acts of initiation into the new world and, before the year was out, I did not need to overhear Wild Christian's remarks to acknowledge that I was now inclined to day-dream far less and was responding with some enthusiasm to a noisy environment. My mathematics set had been stolen right under my nose, even as a lesson was in progress. Such an event would have been unthinkable at St Peter's. I began instinctively to study my new companions very closely and devise ways to survive among them. I looked forward to my next visit to Isara: even the prescient old man, I felt, had something to learn about the natives of AGS who moved in and out of its mansion in pursuit of knowledge.

Daodu was away when I joined the school. He had joined a mission of educationists selected from all over West Africa to England: in his absence Mr Kuforiji, a mathematics teacher, acted as principal. His nickname was Wèé-wèé, a name which meant nothing until one encountered the thin, piping-voiced Acting Principal in his tight-fitting gabardine suit, spectacles which placed his gaze above the head of whoever he conversed with, and a gait which suggested a hen interrupted in the act of pecking scattered corn. When he went on his rounds of the school, appearing suddenly in the classroom where he remained for minutes to monitor the lesson, he was never without his cane. Apart from whatever report the class-teacher had to make on individual performance and conduct, Wèé-wèé also made his own on-the-spot assessment of appearances and application, picked out those who fell short of his requirements and administered his corrective before the class.

Even so, he was considered only an average disciplinarian. He could be managed, even manipulated, and many succeeded in getting away with close to murder with him. Even the dramatic height of his Acting career, a scandal which involved a prefect, ended with the wrong climax, and not even with a whimper.

AGS was justly called a toughening school, a training ground for later survival in life. It appeared often to be managed, not by the teachers but by a combination of anonymous forces which were located somewhere in the huge dormitory of the boarding school, in the cellars and corridors of the arched stone mansion and along the perimeter of trees and bushes and copses round the playing-fields. Transactions of an obscure nature took place over those fences with the outside world during sports periods, during breaks in lessons and after classes. I obtained the feeling early that it was in these places, not in the schoolrooms or assembly hall, not in the principal's office, that the real running of the school took place. School bounds did not exist for some of the boarders who had perfected a system for confounding any housemaster who found, on his nightly rounds, an empty bed that remained empty until morning. At the end of the enquiry he more than often became uncertain that he had ever seen such a bed, or that the bed which he saw so starkly empty had been in that particular row of beds.

It was not uncommon to see a senior boy dispensing fortunes to his friends; he had simply broken into his father's strongbox and emptied it. An agitated father would arrive, the future Public Enemy No. 1 was summoned into Wèé-wèé's presence for the commencement of a moral siege. When the father was lucky, the remainder of his fortune was recovered in the stuffing of his son's mattress, in one of the individual 'safes' within the walls of the various buildings or buried in a termite-proof box beneath a tree on the school farm. Once, the entire savings of a cocoa-farmer were stolen in this way. The bereaved man arrived in a state of collapse, and had to be carried up the stairs into the principal's office. On learning that his father was in the school, the son simply packed his box and fled. He never returned to the school and neither, we learnt, did he return to his home. He disappeared to Lagos, took a job and paid occasional visits to his old school dressed in the latest fashionable suits, dispensing largesse to his former classmates. One day he came to say a final good-bye. His father had saved up again and was now sending him to England for 'further studies'.

But the real scandal came when a Senior boy, and a prefect, made a girl pregnant. It was not unusual, but it was the first time that the girl's parents had insisted on the offender's dismissal from school. Normally the matter was taken up and settled by the parents of the two people concerned. The prefect was popular. He had a game leg which did not inhibit him in any way. His firm handling of the school was so full of humour that no one bore him any resentment. Always fastidious even in his school uniform, he had even developed a way of walking with his handicap so that it looked more like a dandyish 'style' than a disability. Some of the junior boys actually tried to imitate, in a milder form, the unique swank which he gave his body as he walked up to the platform to cries of his nickname – A-Keenzy – to make announcements, or to prepare the assembly for the arrival of the Acting Principal. It was sheer bad luck that he had to pick on an 'important' family in Abeokuta who demanded their pound of flesh. Mr Kuforiji was reluctant to blight the career of any student by dismissal, especially in his final year, yet the offence was grave enough to merit some exemplary punishment. He hit on public caning – before the entire school assembly. For a school prefect this was, even for AGS, a serious humiliation. And the number of strokes was an unprecedented – thirty-six!

A special assembly was summoned. The staff filed solemnly into the front row of the auditorium and Mr Kuforiji mounted the platform. In appropriately formal tones, he announced the purpose of the meeting, expressed the shock of the entire school community at the disgrace brought upon us, and the unhappiness visited on the girl's family by the thoughtless act of one of our own members. He then named the offender, ordered him to rise and come to the platform. Kuforiji turned to him and intoned that he had resolved to give him another chance in life by offering him a choice. He could leave the school in dismissal, with his

161

name tarnished for ever, or he could receive thirty-six strokes of the cane before the assembly. The young man chose the latter.

Three canes had been laid on the table. The prefect was ordered to 'touch his toes' and the punishment began. One of the teachers was appointed to keep count.

Wèé-wèé changed canes at the end of the first twelve; A-Keenzy did not move a muscle. Halfway through the second dozen, Wèé-wèé had begun to sweat. When he changed canes at the count of twenty-four, we noticed that he took longer before he resumed, and that his strokes had begun to lose their bite. There was stillness in the hall, punctuated only by the falling strokes. I sensed that history was being made. All eyes were glued to A-Keenzy's body, unable to believe that any man could absorb twenty-four strokes on his back and buttocks without once shifting position, without the slightest noticeable twitch of a muscle. I began to wonder if A-Keenzy had padded himself in some way when I recalled that Wèé-wèé had first pulled back the perfect's trousers and peeped down them to ensure that there was no cheating. Kuforiji administered the last six strokes through sheer will-power. Sweat covered him profusely. A-Keenzy rose, calm, unruffled, bowed with impeccable grace and intoned the ritual response to the administration of correction:

'Thank you, Principal': and then the roof of the assembly hall was solidly pounded with a thunderous applause. In vain did the principal, having first recovered from the shock, bang on the table for order. His assistant grabbed the bell and swung it furiously. It only added to the sounds of jubilation. All staff joined in the attempt to staunch the spontaneous outburst of applause, it went on and on, wave after wave until it wore itself out. For minutes after the silence, Wèé-wèé was too scandalized to speak. He glared over the heads of his wayward charges, looking for appropriate words. Finally he spluttered,

'Eyin omo Satani!* Shameless incorrigible idiots, you really think that that was something to applaud? Awon omo alaileko!† Your souls must be corrupted in and out – Get out! Assembly dismissed!'

Wèé-wèé sank gratefully back into the mathematics classroom when Daodu returned from his mission in England. He was welcomed back into Abeokuta by crowds which must have emptied every home in the town. Daodu rode on a white horse into Aké for a Thanksgiving service at St Peter's church, flanked by royal buglers, drummers, and a column of boy

* Satanic children . . .
† Lacking in home-training.

scouts. His agbada looked, if anything, more voluminous than usual, as if it had been designed specially to arc outwards on the broad back of a horse in contrast to the leaner girth of the motorped which had put him in hospital two or three years before. His exploits in England had become known largely through word of mouth – how he had forcefully ranged himself against the British plans to establish only one university for all of their West African Colonies, he insisting instead on one university for each country. His stubborn, nearly isolated opposition was highly acclaimed; only our Daodu could have done it.

For most of us however the implication went over our heads, though it was not difficult to grasp the principle that more schools were better than one. What mattered however was that Daodu had braved Hitler's submarines which, from all reports, did not discriminate between warlike and peaceful ships. Daodu had survived Hitler's demon bombers, had safely crossed the seas, twice, in spite of the infamous mines which dotted the shipping-lanes. He rode into Aké, a towering ebullient presence which – it was rumoured – had frequently overawed even the District Officer of the colonial government and the Alake of Abeokuta before whom, in his own turn, men prostrated themselves as he passed and women knelt. An anthem of welcome was composed by the music-teacher; I sang it constantly at home.

A week after his return, I began to wonder why Hitler had committed the unforgivable blunder of letting the Rev A. O. Ransome-Kuti escape, unharmed, when he had him at his mercy. I did not go so far as to wish him at the bottom of the seas but, we had heard of prisoners being taken after merchantships were bombed or intercepted. Surely there was no reason why the same fate should not have befallen Daodu. From all accounts, he had neglected his priestly profession for the sake of education; I felt that God had missed an opportune moment for redress, that he should have arranged Daodu's itinerary to include a few years' spell as chaplain to a prisoner-of-war camp.

Mowing the grass of the compound at Aké was an integral part of schooling, as indeed it was in any school of our knowledge. It was a simple, regulated occupation with fixed hours, with demarcated plots for every class. From time to time also a student might earn extra hours of grass-cutting as a punishment. Exceptionally, the entire school population was turned out, *oja agba** in hand, to crop the school compound from end to end, moving like a well-drilled army in straight lines and leaving nothing

* Cutlass made from barrel hoops.

behind that could flutter to the heaviest movement of the wind. The teachers followed afterwards, looking out for patches that had not been cropped close enough to the ground.

True, I had done less of grass-cutting than most in the formative years but this had been due to the unlucky accident which had nearly taken off my right eye. It had left a permanent scar, a visible reminder to every teacher of what, to everyone, was nothing short of a miracle. Overawed by this singular mark of divine protection and, reluctant to tempt fate all over again, the teachers simply ordered me back into the classroom whenever it was time for mowing the grass. I had therefore a retarded education in the art of the *oja agba* but, I did catch up in my last year in the primary school when the incident had become all but forgotten.

Grass mowing was as it should be – without any mystique. The blade had to be kept sharp, stones must be avoided in order to keep the edge even, the mower bent low to the ground, knee flexed, the arm swung the *oja agba* in a smooth, unbroken arc and the stroke ended on the opposite side of the body, slicing through the measured space and leaving its batch of green slivers at the mower's feet. The masters of the art were of course prisoners. I had often watched them at work on the lawns before the Alake's palace. One, sometimes two of them would be appointed the song-master. Using a piece of metal and a can, or a long nail on his *oja agba*, he provided a rhythm to which the rest wielded their blades:

> N'ijo itoro – Gbim!
> N'ijo i sisi – Gbim!
> O o ni lo l'oni – Gbim!
> O o ni se b'emo – Gbim!
> Won gba e l'eti – Gbim!
> Ewon re d'ola – Gbim!
> Tin tinni gba tin tin tin gba
> Tin tinni gba tin tin tin gba . . .*

In AGS however, grass took on 'good' and 'bad' definitions. It was not just a question of weeds or dangerous kinds of grass with thorns or with sharp or stubbly roots. Grass, ordinary smooth, green luscious grass which I had taken for granted on the lawns and playing-fields of Aké was now

* On the day of threepence
  On the day of sixpence (i.e., stolen)
  You are tightly held
  You won't ever repeat it
  You are soundly slapped
  Your sentence begins tomorrow.

split into two categories – good, and bad. The care of our fields was therefore carried out, not with *oja agba* or hoes, but meticulously with one's fingers. Every clump of bad grass had to be uprooted one by one. Recognizing good and bad grass was easy enough after a while, but discriminating between them, and therefore acting upon them as required proved increasingly difficult for me. I could not understand it! What was more, the effect of this strange procedure, which was not complemented by the re-planting of good grass in the stripped areas, had turned every lawn and field into a patchwork of grass and desert. Looking down from the upper floor of the building, the football field especially appeared to be under the attack of a fungoid growth or some other kind of communicable skin disease.

Invisible lines criss-crossed the football field, dividing it into plots for every class. Then further divisions within each plot marked the allotments for each group of three or four. It was evident that Wèè-wèé did not share Daodu's unique obsession in grasses; his inspection on Friday afternoons consisted of walking through the fields like a brisk sleepwalker, looking above the head of all the students, certainly never down at the grass. With the announcement of Daodu's impending arrival however, attitudes changed. Class teachers were given instructions. Many hitherto neglected chores and rituals were re-introduced. Leaning on walls, especially with one's hands, brought down unaccustomed punishment. Most of these were irritating, some irksome, but none produced that special block which the treatment of grass had constructed in me. I infected a few others in my class and my own group dawdled while others clawed into the ground for their lives. We were new to the school, had never encountered Daodu professionally and we sensed much exaggeration in all of this. No monster could be as thorough as he was made out to be – was he not the same Daodu who had fallen off his moped, been carried into my father's bed and then hospitalized? I could not see him being so ill-occupied as to go sniffing the ground for every single blade of so-called bad grass and creating a fuss because of a stray one here and there.

Ransome-Kuti resumed his duties as if he had merely gone away a day or two. This created my first misgiving – that a man who had just run the gauntlet of bombs should move straight to presiding over the school assembly, inspecting ceilings for cobwebs and complaining of the singing. And his first Friday found him also routinely on the open grounds, doing just what no man fresh from international adventures should be expected to do. Followed by the entire staff, Daodu was carefully criss-crossing the field and, while he did not actually get down on all fours, he walked slightly bent forward, his hands folded behind him, his alert eyes sweeping yards to the right and left like a searchlight. Abruptly he would stop, look more intently. Then he gave his signature chuckle, which I now heard for the first time. It was, I discovered too late, a world of meanings apart from those beefy Daodu chuckles to which I was accustomed. This began in the region of his lower chest, rose to his lower jaw and stayed there, to be released throatily, in deep contented measures through lips that were parted in a mirthless half-melon smile. It was a chuckle which said,

'A-ah, they thought they could get away with it but they simply do not know me. After all these years, they still do not know the one and only Daodu!'

It was apparently also a cue for the school. When the sound of that chuckle was heard, I was astonished to hear also, from all corners of the field, a chorused response. It took the form of just one word lengthily intoned. 'Dao-o-o-o-o-o-o-o-o-o-o!'

Beyond a mere glance in his direction to see who the victim was, Daodu's schoolboys paid no further attention. He had in the meantime pounced on the offending spot, uprooted and held up the 'bad' example.

'And who was in charge of this?'

The criminal stepped forward. Daodu looked around to see if there were any further oversights in the same area, nodded satisfaction and announced,

'Three!'

The boy knew what to do. He bent over, Daodu stretched out his hand and a cane was placed in it. The *Ta-a, ta-a, ta-a* of the switch over a tautened skin menaced our ears, followed by the boy's mandatory, 'Thank you, Principal', and the tour continued.

The desperate efforts which my group now put into extracting Daodu's unfavourite grass came too late. We uprooted what we could, stuffed our pockets with them, tried to smooth the blades of the 'good' grass over its objectionable bedfellows but finally had to stop as the entourage came closer. The lenses of Daodu's glasses positively twinkled with delight when he came on our plot. The chuckle rose from its usual starting-point, came up to his throat, then descended into his stomach and bubbled there for a while before it travelled back for its sadistic release through his half-melon, mirthless smile. From every spot on the field the salutation rose in the air:

'Dao-o-o-o-o-o-o-o!' On and on it went, as if it would never end, measured out in proportion to the intensity of Daodu's own chuckle. He had no need to ask who were responsible for the offending plot, guilt was written unmistakably on a group of four freshers who stood apart, waiting for the worst. When he announced it, I felt ready to bolt. I was convinced that this man was a potential murderer and could already see me being carried off the field, dead.

'Twenty-four,' he said, and we all gasped in disbelief. He paused, looked along the line of the four of us. His eyes came to rest on me, then moved to the biggest boy of the four who was almost twice my size. 'Now,' he resumed, 'here we have four partners in crime. How do they normally share their things – may we know? Equally? Or according to size?'

Such was my relief at discovering that we were not to receive twenty-four each but share it between us that I did not hesitate to insist,

'Equally.' Stepping forward at the same time. One thing I was not prepared to share with the others was the agony of watching and awaiting my turn. The bigger boys could have it to themselves. By keeping my eyes and my mind on the grass and reflecting on the absurdity of the distinction I was required to make between them, I was able to take my mind off much of the pain, apart from the first which sent a shock through my body. Daodu clearly wielded a massive stroke. I allowed myself to hear only the count, not the stokes themselves. It was soon over, I straightened up and remembered just in time to say,

'Thank you, Principal,' feeling anything towards him but gratitude.

It was the only time Daodu would flex his cane against my back and the last I would wish him in Hitler's concentration camp. Not even a week passed after this before he resumed his usual place in my admiration. Everything that Daodu did was not merely larger than size, he made trivia itself larger than life and made drama of every event. 'Discipline' was turned into an adventure. Sometimes it seemed that the code, 'Innocent until proved Guilty' was created specially for him or by him – he carried it to the length of absurdity. It was not enough to admit an offence; it had to be proved against the accused. Or else the accused was required to prove it against himself, arguing extenuating circumstances along the way. If he made a forceful plea, he not only went scot-free but his accuser might earn what would have been his punishment, especially if his presentation of the case was adjudged inept.

Once, the principal himself caught three boys red-handed in one of the many copses at the bottom of the field. One was the notorious 'Iku'. They were roasting a freshly killed chicken over a small fire. The head and feathers lay beside them, so Daodu had no difficulty whatsoever in identifying the source of the chicken. Daodu kept the most massive poultry I had ever seen anywhere and I had heard the bigger boys say often how they would love to get their hands on one of them. These three had obviously managed it at last.

Court was held in the usual place, the dining-room corridor which ran the full length of the front of the mansion. The corridor which opened into this at ninety degrees served as classrooms for what appeared to be the primary section of AGS but was in fact an independent section run by Mrs Kuti and known as Mrs Kuti's Class. The Kuti lived in the part of the building which began halfway down the front corridor, the earlier half serving as dining-room for Mrs Kuti's own boarders. The boarding and teaching sections, and the living quarters of the Kuti thus flowed into one another, a screen separating the boarders' dining-room from the dining section of the Kuti.

Preceded by the evidence of offence, the head, feathers and half-roasted chicken, the accused tapped on the screen and were admitted. The screen was then moved aside so that any interested watcher could observe or participate in the proceedings from the dining section of the boarders. Since Daodu was himself the principal accuser, the boys were required to present the charges themselves, prosecute themselves and make their own defence.

'Iku', as we expected, was the spokesman. The nickname, Death was one of the most appropriate nicknames coined for any boy in that school. Iku constantly defied death by his choice of routes for nightly escapes from the dormitory, any one of which could have resulted in a broken neck. He looked confident.

'It was this way, principal. There was I at the lower perimeter of the fields, principal, with my friends about to engage in a scholastic experiment, Chemistry to be exact, principal, relating to the phlogiston theory of spontaneous combustion. It succeeded, principal. To our scientific delight a small fire erupted among the twigs and *oguso** which we had gathered for the purpose, principal. We were about to put out his fire, it having served its purpose of proving a scientific point when along came a cockerel, whose patination and regal bearing identified it beyond doubt as having emerged from no other place than from the private poultry yard of Mrs herself.

'The second accused, Bode here, principal, said to me, "Iku, there promenades a chicken belonging to principal's Mrs. How did it get here?" To which I replied, principal, "I am as ignorant as you are on the subject matter." Upon which the third accused – Akinrinde, principal – said, "Ours not to reason why, but to act, using our initiative as the principal

* Fibre kindling.

168

himself constantly teaches us." I concurred, principal, and there being no time like now because action speaks louder than words time and tide waiteth for no man opportunity once lost cannot be regained a stitch in time saves nine, principal, and finally, one good turn deserves another so, with these thoughts for our guide, we spread out, closed in on this cock in order to catch it and restore it to the poultry yard from which it had escaped.

'Principal, it was a frisky cockerel. It was not one of those mangy, timid fowl which one meets in most houses. It was a spirited cockerel, principal, a well-nourished, aggressive, independent-minded cockerel, principal – how could it be otherwise when it was raised, reared and nurtured under the very hands of the principal and his wife, Beere? The cock flew against the second accused, knocking him down – you may like to examine his battle-scars, principal. That fearsome cockerel simply batted him with his wings, scratched his outstretched wrists – second accused, will you please step forward and exhibit your scratches.'

Bode stepped forward, held out his wrists to Daodu and turned them over. They were indeed marked by what appeared to be long scratches which could have been inflicted by talons. Daodu inspected them solemnly, nodded to Iku to resume.

'Now, principal, upon the second accused falling backwards to protect himself, the impetus with which the deceased had launched itself naturally carried it forward, inflicting, as we have said, principal, the aforesaid wounds on the outstretched wrists of the second accused. Now, principal, it is possible to conjecture what would have happened if this had been an ordinary fire. But it was not, principal. This was a fire built on the phlogiston theory of total, spontaneous combustion. It followed therefore that it was extremely, and evenly hot. The cockerel's impetus carried it right into the centre of that inferno, where it instantly lost consciousness, overpowered by the intense heat, and itself contributing to the validity of the experiment which had taken us to the seclusion of the field in search of scientific truth, thus leaving us without any outside witnesses, principal.

'Our offence therefore, principal, lies not in any wilful, overt act, but in the passive misdemeanour of concealment, principal. But the deed was done, there was no use crying over spilt milk, in every cloud there is a silver lining and like thoughts, not to mention our fear to report ourselves and maybe, be misunderstood, kept us back. For this slight error of judgement, speaking for myself the first, and the second and third accused here, principal, we throw ourselves on the mercy of the court.'

All was silent. The accused awaited their fate. Daodu sipped at his now tepid tea and thought hard. I thought I had never heard such an impudent rigmarôle and waited confidently for a series of punishments to be pronounced which would begin, at the least, with eighteen strokes apiece. I had much to learn from Daodu's schema of evidence and guilt. It was not enough to dismiss any defence, however fantastic or derisive as a piece of impudence: the onus was for the acuser to *disprove* it. Even the explanation for the existence of the fire – what was the phlogiston theory anyway? I doubt if principal knew himself, physics was not his field. He looked up finally without a trace of a smile.

'Case dismissed.'

'Thank you, prin-ci-pa-a-a-a-a-a-l.'

He interrupted by holding up his hand. 'I refer however only to the case with which you were originally charged, which was . . . ?' He waited.

'Unlawfully stealing a chicken, property of Rev and Mrs Ransome-Kuti and knowingly roasting same with the intention of secretly consuming it, principal.'

'Good. But you raised a new charge in your defence. Concealment, failing to report an accident.'

'Correct, principal.'

'To which you also, at the same time, pleaded guilty.'

'The principal is again correct.'

'So that it now remains for me to pass judgement.'

'Yes, thank you, principal.'

'Then this is the sentence. You will all three take back the chicken and complete what you were doing with it. That will be your entire diet – for all three of you – for the next week.'

'Thank you, principa-a-a-a-a-a-l.'

'The kitchen should be instructed accordingly. Court adjourned.'

'Thank you, prin-ci-pa-a-a-a-a-l!'

One chicken between three fully grown boys for seven days? It sounded inadequate. I wondered if they wouldn't have preferred to be beaten and given other tasks to perform. However, I did not think he really expected them to starve, he knew only too well that they would live by their wits and with the aid of others. Iku, I later discovered, was a veteran of many argued cases. Indeed, he would never plead before any teacher, insisting on his right to be heard by the principal. The teachers had long given him up and left him to do pretty much as he liked. The other two were his regular accomplices in hundreds of escapades, some of which took place in the town, leading to identification parades which never succeeded in picking him out.

Daodu was manic in his treatment of music. When he conducted the school in one of the many anthems we performed periodically, his massive frame was galvanized, and a patch of wetness emerged beneath the armpit of his jacket, widening its circle until it reached his chest. His ears picked up unerringly the source of a wrong sound. I was mystified however by his failure to simply weed out those who were obviously tone-deaf. Instead, he picked out the offending row, or class, and caned them after a faulty performance. The solution was obvious, very simple, but he never seemed to consider it. The school was required to sing; any portion of it which could not sing well had to be punished. I spent my lunch-hours with the family, upstairs, eating with the boarders at meal-times. One afternoon I was tinkering with the piano when Daodu asked my why I did not learn the piano properly, offering to give me lessons. I hurriedly assured him that my father had already begun, dreading the impact of his cane whenever I fluffed a note. This was less than a half truth but the cause justified it even if it had been an entire lie. I had now assumed a definite position with regards to the rational shortcomings of grown-ups, marvelling how, for instance, an educationist and experienced traveller like Daodu could behave like Wild Christian who obtained all her authority from that section of the Bible which said, 'Spare the rod . . .'

Before Daodu's return, a group had grown up around Mrs Kuti. It was an informal gathering which began with three of four women, then increased in numbers. They met, discussed problems which had to do with the community and matters relating also to their homes. Wild Christian was a member of this group and whenever she came to the Kuti for a meeting, I simply waited after school and later returned home with her. They ignored my presence near abouts as they chatted and drank tea. They were all Christian, wives of 'professionals' – teachers, pastors, pharmacists, and so on. When they were not discussing problems of sanitation, the shortages or rise in price of some commodity, plans for some kind of anniversary, their absorbing concern appeared to centre on the plight of young women who were just entering a phase of domestic responsibility. Over and over again came the observation that 'they don't know what to do'; 'they seem not to understand how to take their place in society'; 'they don't know how to receive visitors'; 'even the wedding of such and such was a deep embarrassment'; 'some of them don't know about sanitation or even child care'; and more in that vein. Attempts to help individually often met with abuse, they complained. It was suggested that they could jointly visit the homes of such newly-weds and discreetly offer advice. Another suggested that such 'problem' ladies should be invited casually to their meetings and duly instructed.

I felt I knew just the sort of women they were talking about. My mind went back to the saddest wedding I had ever witnessed at St Peter's, Aké. It was a white wedding – gloves, veil, hat, bouquet, gown etc. Itemized, there was nothing missing in the colonial ensemble of the occasion. The bridegroom wore a matching suit with his best man, pocket handkerchief and carnation in place. The chief bridesmaid, pages and other bridesmaids were spread out on either side of the bridal pair in all the correct attire, shoes gleamed and stockings were spotless white. The bridal train spread a long way behind them on the cobbled yard of St Peter's as they stood on the steps for a photograph. There was only one thing wrong – not one item of attire fitted anyone. The clothing appeared to have been picked off an assortment of shops and dumped on the backs of a random choice of children, men and women who had never set eyes on a city or heard an organ peal. The bride looked as if she would deliver her child any moment, her pregnancy stuck out before her like an explanation of the misery on the face of the bridegroom, and of the bored, uncomfortable stance of the pages and maids. There was a shabbiness about the spectacle which went beyond the ill-fitting clothes; it was the lack of joy anywhere, a guilty furtiveness in spite of, indeed reinforced by the depressing attempt to impose an outward covering – and an alien one – on a ceremony that lacked heart or love or indeed, identity.

I seriously hoped that the group of women had this on their mind, I waited for them to refer to it specifically, to make their disapprobation felt for a scene which had troubled me for days afterwards. No one brought it up however, and I had to be content with hoping that they all had it in mind. They were however equally concerned with the problems of infant deaths, how to get women to use the post-natal clinics more, rely less on patent medicines picked up at random. They also, in some vague, general way, wanted women to involve themselves in more civic activities, such as philanthropic work.

Daodu was strolling past the 'Group' one afternoon when he stopped to listen. Then he interrupted:

'You know, you women have quite good aims but you don't seem to know how you want to implement them. You've been meeting now for some time and all I see all the time are *oníkaba*.* The people who really need your help are the *aróso*,† yet they are not here. Forget the problems of

* Gown wearers.
† Wrapper wearers.

172

social graces for newly-weds. Concentrate on the *aróṣọ*. Bring them in on your meetings. They are the ones who need your help.'

And he continued his stroll.

The white-haired lady, the most venerable-looking among them was the first to speak after he left them.

'Daodu has just spoken a truth of the first importance. We are incomplete. The next time, let each one of us bring at least one *aróṣọ* to the meeting.'

XIII

Wild Christian took her friend, Mama Aduni, to the meeting of the Group. The meetings had now outgrown the dining-room of Mrs Kuti's Class and shifted into the courtyard below. On the faces of the women who now flocked to the meeting, market women who dealt in peppers, gari, palm oil, and homemade wares, I identified the same inward tiredness as I had seen in our itinerant traders from Isara, our chaperons who, in their own homes, placed their meagre resources at our disposal. The wide arched balcony windows looked directly on to the yard.

On the days of their meetings I went upstairs, listened and watched. There was always some little drama going on, some dispute which had to be settled – usually by Beere, the White-haired Lady whom I now knew as Ma Igbore, or Wild Christian. Sometimes, one of the women would burst into song or tell some ribald story. The meeting might take on the atmosphere of a Counselling Court, or a spontaneous festival. Some of them arrived early to prepare the food.

The movement into the courtyard began after another suggestion by Daodu. He now made it a routine to stroll past the group and listen for some moments. His bedroom and study were within earshot in any case, and I suspected that he took his 'casual' stroll only after the discussions had reached a point which gave him an idea, for he hardly ever passed without contributing something. One day he said,

'Do you know the real trouble with the aróṣọ? They are illiterate. They don't know how to read and write, that is why they get exploited. If you set aside half an hour at these meetings, you could end up making all the women in Egbaland literate by the end of a year!' He chuckled at his own wild optimism, strolled on.

The idea was taken. Mama Aduni and the handful of aróṣọ who had by now joined the Group were told to spread the word. Slates and markers were bought, pencils and exercise books. When the trickle became a flood, they shifted into the courtyard. Each oníkaba took on a group which she coached intensely for half-hour to an hour at each meeting. Then, while the discussions continued on hygiene, community development, self-help programmes, market and commodity prices, they continued to copy the letters, the figures, pausing only to join in the talking. From the top of the balcony, one saw only a series of backs humped in concentration, topped by head-ties which showed in some cases, wads of white hair. For that first half-hour they worked in almost total silence with sudden outbursts of laughter, laboriously making one stroke, then another. Often it was Wild Christian's bantering voice which caused the laughter. She would, for instance, seize an agonized hand in hers and guide it along the slate, instructing loudly:

'Like this. Look, put down this stick, no no, make it a straight piece of wood like an electric pole not a crooked one. Or do you think it's your husband's leg you are drawing? Now, put something like a curved road on it – no, no, not like that. Don't you even know what your belly looks like when you and your husband have been getting up to God knows what? En-hen. I know that would do it. Now that is a "b". One electric pole, and your big belly resting at the bottom of it – "b" bente-bente . . . asikun bente-bente . . . bente-bente, asikun bente-bente . . .' moving smoothly into an improvised song-and-dance.

The courtyard erupted with laughter while Mama Aduni or the white-haired lady went and dragged her away complaining, 'For a teacher's wife, you are remarkably good at disrupting the concentration of pupils!'

They were keen pupils, mostly young, and it was these keen ones who set in motion in Igbein, the Great Upheaval that ended in Aké. They were always the first to arrive, they helped in setting up the benches and chairs, sweeping the yard when necessary, getting in an extra hour of practice to themselves before the others arrived. I accidentally became a proud teacher at those pre-meeting sessions. Dolupo and Koye, the two eldest of the Kuti children, had long been conscripted into service. I was already in my usual place on the balcony when I saw them struggling with words – they had reached the stage of putting the letters together, mostly in the wrong order. I shouted a correction, they shouted back, asking if I was too lazy to come down and show them. I was down the stairs in a flash. I found that they were mostly from outlying villages, not from the main town of Abeokuta itself; perhaps that explained their eagerness.

And then they stopped coming; even to the main session they would come late. Sometimes they never turned up at all. It was not only the eager pupils, there were others too, and not only from the suburbs. It was harvest time; these were mostly farmers' wives, so the leaders assumed for a while that the chores of the farms kept them away. They took their places with apologies, tried to catch up on their lessons as the meeting progressed. Finally however the right question was asked, or the leaders listened more keenly to those excuses that the late comers mumbled through an ongoing debate. The gatherings of mutual self-improvement changed character from that moment when one voice followed the other to explain:

'I was arrested by the Tax people.'

'The *Parakoyi** took half of my farm produce for market toll. I went to the local councillors to seek their help.'

'We were waylaid on the way to the farm. The Local Police asked us to contribute one-fifth of every item as duty.'

'I tried to dodge the uniformed men. I turned into a path I thought I knew and got lost. Only God saved me or I would still be wandering in the forests.'

'They have no heart, those men. They look at you like they have no flesh and blood until you give them what they want.'

'We spent the night in a police cell. They seized all our goods and will continue to hold them until we bring them our Tax papers. But we have not been to the market, how can we pay when they have taken the goods we are going to sell?'

'It is those chiefs. They are in this together. They set the *adana*† to do their dirty work because they daren't levy a toll on farm produce.'

'No, it's the Alake; I heard one of the *adana* say we shouldn't complain to him. "Go to Kabiyesi who sent us," he said.'

'Our own tormentors said it was the white man. He said the order came to the *ajele*‡ from his fellow white man in Lagos. They are just servants of the white man in Lagos.'

'ENOUGH!'

The voice was none other than Kemberi's. The junior 'wives' of a household and a mischievous lot, I reflected, to so name a woman whose real name, and a Christian one at that, was Amelia. To the women's gathering this highly feared, fearless and voluble woman might be Madame Amelia, but about the time that I became a limpet on the group, I heard both Wild Christian and Beere refer to her as Kemberi. When I delivered a message soon after and referred to her as Madame Kemberi, my head nearly flew off from a swipe from Wild Christian's backhand. Beere protested, pointed out that I could hardly be blamed for repeating a name I had heard. Only then was it explained to me that Kemberi was a

* Market wardens.
† Agents who waylay farmers or market women.
‡ An administering agent, thus, the District Officer.

176

special nickname given to her by the 'wives' of her compound. Only really close comrades such as Beere and Wild Christian ever called her by that nickname, and only when they were all by themselves.

'Enough!' Kemberi repeated and the murmurs of indignation began to subside. 'What you are all saying in so many words, is that the women of Egbaland are no longer free to walk the streets of their own land, or pursue their living from farm to home and farm to market without being molested by these bloodsuckers – am I right?'

'What else have we been saying?'

She held up her hands, then turned to Mrs Ransome-Kuti. 'Beere, you heard them. What are we doing about it? You said, teach them ABC; we have been doing that. And we also said to them, give your children a clean home, and strain every bone in your body to give them a good education. And they have been doing that. It is because of these children that they refuse to sit at home, waiting for some idle drunkard of a husband to learn the same lesson. After all, the women of Egbaland are not unaccustomed to hard work. But now we gave them a new reason – their children. And they began to work and they gave their little savings to the education of their children. And because of the little we have learnt together, these good-for-nothing children no longer come home and lie that they have come first in class when all they have been doing is staying away from school and scoring the round, fish-eye of Zero. At least, some of us now know the difference between 100 and Zero, between 1st and 34th. When the school report comes home, even if some of our women cannot read everything, they can read enough on that card to know if that child is wasting their money. And if they cannot read, they know where they can bring the card – right HERE!

'Now these same women are telling us that they can no longer come here freely. The streets of Egba are blocked by the very people against whom we have tried to give them protection. Tax! Tax on what? What is left after the woman has fed children, put school uniform on his back and paid his school fees? Just what are they taxing?'

A roar went up from outraged voices. Kemberi again commanded silence. 'It is time we told them, No more taxes. They want to bleed us dry, let us tell them, No more Taxes.'

A tumult of approbation overspilled the courtyard. Order was resumed. Mrs Ransome-Kuti was empowered to give notice of a demand for the abolition of tax for women, both to the District Officer and the Alake of Abeokuta and his Council of Chiefs. It was the longest meeting so far of the women, and the 'Group' remained upstairs long after the crowd had departed. There was no question of my going home that night; I sensed the beginning of an unusual event and was gripped by the excitement. On a par with the Sanitary Inspector, the Tax Officer was perhaps the most feared individual in Abeokuta – without however the tolerance which generally attached to the former. The Tax Officers had invaded our house on occasion. Although their conduct was polite, even routine, they did succeed in conveying such an aura of power that I was constantly relieved when Wild Christian opened one of the smaller top drawers and produced the yellow receipt. Once, in a sweep of the petty shops, an over-zealous type had even accompanied her home to verify that she had indeed paid her tax. The bigger cousins wanted to chase him out. Kemberi's pronouncement therefore sounded like an ally's declaration of one of those civil wars which appeared to make up both Yoruba and English histories in the text-books. There was also the memory of the women from Isara, trudging the forty plus miles from Isara laden like *omolanke*,* the push-carts which had begun to compete with the human *alaaru*.† I saw them waylaid by the *adana*, forced to disgorge a portion of their merchandise at the gates of Abeokuta, after carrying them an inhuman distance. And of course the immediate outrage against my own prize pupils who could no longer come early to their lessons because of the taxman's harassment became a personal affront. Before I fell asleep, I had made up my mind that when I grew up, no khakied official was going to extract one penny in tax from my hard-earned salary.

The Group met till late. I had long fallen asleep on the bench in the dining-room and woke up the following morning in a bed in the dormitory of Mrs Kuti's Class. On the following morning at breakfast I heard, for the first time, the expression Egba Women's Union. There appeared to be some further bandying around of alternative titles but, finally, a new movement appeared to have emerged, formally, with that name – Egba Women's Union.

Beere left for England shortly after this – war or no war, there appeared to be conferences to attend; if it was not the Christian Mission, it was the Colonial Mission. Wild Christian's shop at Aké became a focus for women from every corner of Abeokuta. Mama Aduni became a kind of Roving Marshal, showing up at all hours with women of every occupation – the cloth-dyers, weavers, basket makers and the usual petty traders of the markets – they arrived in ones, twos, in groups, they came from near and

* Push-cart.
† Porter.

distant compounds, town sectors and far villages whose names I had never heard. They smelt of the sweat of the journey, of dyes, of dried fish, yam flour, of laterite and the coconut oil of their plaits. Some were tattooed on arms and legs, with cicatrices on their faces. In addition to the head-tie, their shoulder shawls, neatly folded were placed lightly on their heads for additional protection from the sun.

Far from dodging the chore of keeping shop, I could now hardly be kept away from it. Some of these women came first to the parsonage, as this was easier to find than the shop. Before they had even stated their business I had jumped from my books and was escorting them to the shop. In the distance between the house and the shop, freed from the usual reproving glances to check the 'compulsive' questioner, I shamelessly indulged my curiosity. Only one of them unwittingly betrayed me. Unable to take my eyes off her stooped shoulders which, I was convinced, had been caused by carrying merchandise through distances as far as Isara, I suggested,

'Why don't you take the horses of that chief at Itoko? They can carry your loads for you.'

The woman laughed and promised to ask Mama Aduni to put it forward at their next meeting. But she told Wild Christian within minutes of their meeting. To my surprise she only shook her head, saying, 'I should have known.'

There was a long lull. No one could tell me whether the women had actually stopped paying taxes or not. I now listened, without any attempt at subterfuge to discussions between Essay and Wild Christian – she sought his advice on many of the problems which the women brought to her. The daily routine at the parsonage increasingly revolved around the new Women's Movement. Wild Christian travelled, addressed groups, received her womenfolk at all hours. Sometimes their visit to the shop lasted no longer than a minute: the next moment, Wild Christian had picked up her shawl, flung a head-tie over her head, snatched up her bag with an 'O ya', and to me, 'Mind the shop,' ushered out the complainants before her to the source of the trouble. Invariably I locked up the shop as it fell dark. She often returned late, yet, even then, over a late meal that lasted hours, she and Essay would discuss her tactics on the immediate problem and a further strategy for resolving it definitively in favour of the victimized women.

Essay became a grass widower though, from what I could see, he thrived on it. He would mull over a new approach to some problem, then send a note to Wild Christian in the shop. I could always tell when it was a 'crisis note'. If she was away from the shop at the time, I opened it and read it. If I knew where she had gone, it provided the perfect excuse to keep the courier in the shop while I went after her, remarking in as off-handed a manner as I could manage that I considered it urgent. Sometimes I tried to recollect how I had slipped into the habit and wondered at the fact that Wild Christian never raised any objection. However, she never voluntarily took me along to these trouble spots while my curiosity was uncontrollably aroused whenever she made her lightning departures with the complainants. Simply by paying close attention to the brief conversation, I easily located these trouble spots after their departure. When there were no notes from Essay, any *aróṣọ* visitor provided an even better excuse. I simply locked up the shop, took them in tow, and went after her.

For the first time, I travelled out of Abeokuta without either parent. In spite of his increased involvement with the Women's Movement, father had never lowered his sights on GCI, the government college in Ibadan where he had scheduled me for a scholarship. I scored him surprisingly insensitive for his attempt to prise me off Abeokuta at a time of such absorbing events. However, he had taken good care to see that my homework preparations were never interrupted. In between trailing Wild Chistian to her crisis points, there were pages of exercises to be completed and brought home after shop. I sat the examinations, weeks passed, then the letter arrived summoning me for an interview in Ibadan. I gained a new acquaintance in Oye, who had also qualified for an interview, and, we planned the Big Adventure together, only to have my parents reduce its dimensions by insisting on a chaperon for me. In vain I reminded them that I was now ten, a veteran of six months survival course at AGS – nothing would budge them, not even my record as Oddjob man with the Women's Movement. The other boy was admittedly older, but Oye's parents had consented to his travelling alone only when they learnt that he would be going together with the Headmaster's son. I argued the lack of sense of it with Joseph who had been appointed my guard. If it was considered by this boy's parents sufficient guarantee of his safety, wasn't that all the greater proof that I could be trusted to look after myself?

Joseph looked at me with something akin to pity. 'I hope those white men at your new school like argumentative brats.'

When the final results were published, my name appeared on the list. I had won admission but no scholarship. It meant waiting another year for another try. Joseph took it to heart, he brooded for a long time, then went to Wild Christian. 'Mama, please beg him not to argue with the white man. You see, they had to admit him, they know he is clever. But do you think the white man will give food to a native who will only get strength to chop his head off with a cutlass?'

I was disappointed. Before I attended the interview the idea of Government College was no more than a curiosity which lurked in the back of my mind. Winning an interview and travelling on my own to Ibadan would have been a satisfactory climax, but I had not counted on the physical lure of the school. My parsonage was dwarfed by its sheer expanse, so was AGS. What it lacked in Abeokuta rocks was more than made up with woods, orchards, brooks, farms and small game. The candidates were drawn from every corner of the country – at least, so it seemed. We arrived as instructed, with our own blankets and pillows, were housed together in one long dormitory where friendships developed fast and lasting from first encounters. Appalled by my ignorance of such a diversity of names, facial types, places and temperaments, I became tongue-tied and for once, asked no questions. And again, Father was right – they were mostly MEN. But the proportion of those nearer my age was comfortingly high. This group instinctively banded together, eyed resentfully by the 'papas' among them. One of them had a moustache.

Two other boys had travelled together from the same town. They were also Ijebu, but not from Isara. We were hardly two hours old in Apataganga, the suburb of Ibadan where the school was sited, before we were cautioned by others to beware of them. They had come with *oogun** which was designed to throw all others into confusion while they took, uncontested, the top places. A boy from Edo swore that he had seen them burying something in the corner of the schoolroom where we would sit the exams. A further proof of their sinister intent was that they had arrived one day earlier than required. While this was to be expected from those who had to travel long distances – Benin, Awka, Makurdi etc., there was no excuse for someone from the near Ijebu province to leave his station on any day other than the day before the Interview. There could only be one reason – they had come to 'spoil the ground' for others!

This last argument was exceedingly persuasive, and there could be only one response. Someone proposed that we search their luggage during their absence and was vociferously cheered. I had not really believed we would, but we found an assortment of strange objects – amulets, black powder wrapped in a piece of paper, the kind of rings which I had seen on Paa Adatan and, a sheet of paper with strange diagrams and words which seemed to me distortions of some biblical names from the Old Testament.

* Medicine (supernatural, magical).

181

It was a grim reception awaiting the boy in whose luggage these items had been found. While I was a willing participant in the search, I was rather dubious about the rightness of actually confrontng the pair with our trophy. I *knew* we had no right to search their luggage, yet I accepted that we *needed* to do it. Confronting them with our discoveries was another matter – for a start, what did these things mean? Why shouldn't anyone be in possession of amulets, black powder and a paper filled with cabalistic signs? I thought of Bukola, the *abiku*, and my fingers went round my own wrist where Father's visitor had incised mysterious potions into my bloodstream. There did not appear to be a qualitative difference between these varied 'possessions'.

The two boys saw the grim circle of accusers, but only one pair of eyes flew directly to the corner to behold the laid-out items on the bed. His face worked, enraged, he ended up spluttering.

'You can all go to gaol for this. You are robbers, thieves. When I report you to the police you will see.'

The Edo boy who had alerted us in the first place said, 'My father is a police officer. Last month he arrested somebody for using bad juju against another man. That man nearly died.'

The beleaguered boy reacted to this challenge by turning to his townsman, as if for help. His friend looked confused, not quite knowing what to do. The next moment the juju-maker spun round and walked fast into the night.

'Don't let him escape!' his main accuser shouted and they all sped after him. I did not move. The pace of events left me in as great an uncertainty as the other Ijebu boy with whom, apart from two or three others, I found myself alone in the room. I walked up to him.

'Do you believe in this juju?'

He shrugged. 'He does,' nodding toward the exit through which everybody had just departed.

'But what about you?'

'I don't know. I swot hard. I need a scholarship or I'll never get any education.'

'But your father doesn't make you any juju?'

He shook his head. 'He used to be a Moslem. Now he is a Christian. As far as I know he has never used juju. Maybe that's why he is so poor.'

He had picked up a book, preparatory to reading. I decided to risk bothering him with one more question. 'What did he bury in the corner of the classroom?'

'Oh, so they saw us.'

'You mean you buried it with him?'

He shook his head. 'No, but I watched him.'

'And you didn't try to stop him?'

'Why should I? Do you believe in it?'

I shrugged in turn. 'I am not really sure.'

'Well, there are you. Nobody is sure.'

They trooped back later, having lost him in the dark. I told the Edo boy what the fugitive's friend had told me.

'Right,' he said, 'we'll get a priest to say prayers over it tomorrow morning.'

I looked at him in surprise. 'What will that do?'

'It would destroy its power,' he replied.

I was not satisfied. 'How will he know what kind of prayer to say? He doesn't know what kind of juju it is.'

Someone else offered. 'There are only two kinds of *oogun* – the bad and the good. Any prayer can undo the power of the former.'

Then another voice suggested that it was safer if we dug it up altogether and threw it on some rubbish heap.

There were other voices raised in terror. 'You don't know what you are saying. Who is going to take such a chance? Go near a thing like that and have your hands wither? Count me out.'

Before I knew what I was saying, I had boasted, 'My hands won't wither.'

'Yes?' came back the sneer. 'I suppose your father has "baked and seasoned" you?'

'No, not my father. My grandfather did.'

I immediately earned some strange looks. Some of the boys drew further away from me, while others crowded round in curiosity. 'Are you serious or joking?'

'Let's go and dig up that thing and you'll see.'

I felt quite light-headed as I picked up the lantern. The Edo boy followed and soon I was heading a procession of five or six boys to the schoolroom. The Edo boy directed us to the corner, we picked up some sticks and dug.

We had hardly scraped down to three inches before we came on the white bundle, about the size of an orange. I picked it up by the tip of its tie and took it over to the pavement in the middle of the lawn.

Someone asked, 'What do we do with it?' to which the Edo boy promptly replied, 'Burn it of course. That's what they do in court with the bad juju which gets seized.'

So we unscrewed the cover of the lantern, soaked the bundle in kerosene and threw a lighted match on it. The cloth caught fire immediately, burnt for a while and then commenced a series of small explosions from within. A particle of something was flung out, landing quite close to the feet of one of the boys. While the rest of us simply drew back instinctively, he panicked and shouted,

'Epe lo fo ja'de yen!'*

and fled. The infection was instant. We all turned and raced back to the dormitory, some screaming 'Jesu, Jesu Gbami' all the way. Even through the tumult however, I heard the Edo boy muttering, repeatedly, 'S.M.O.G., S.M.O.G. . . .' like a mystic incantation. When we had all regained some measure of sanity back in the dormitory, I asked him what he had been reciting.

'S.M.O.G.,' he replied. 'Have you never heard it? It stands for Save Me O God. When you are really in a hurry, it is quickest to use the initials.'

The cause of all the excitement must have returned during the night. When morning came his luggage was gone and his bed was not slept in. We never saw him at the interview. Good riddance, was all I thought to myself, but the Edo boy sat up in his bed, both hands clutching his head. I asked him, 'Were you still thinking of having him arrested?'

He shook his head in a most troubled manner. 'You don't see. Just see what careless fools we were, going to sleep like that. He could have killed us with his juju during the night! If my father got to hear of this . . .'

'Why, what would he do?'

'He would beat me for carelessness. That is how to get yourself killed. Or maimed for life.' He looked round slowly, sank into utter despair and even turned to broken English.

'Look how we sleep like munmu. We no even sabbe wetin that bastard done leave behind.'

'What are you worrying about? Keep saying S.M.O.G.'

He brightened up, nodded eagerly and we went out for our showers.

Ransome-Kuti's curiosity knew no bounds. He admired the government schools for some things but was, in the main, dubious about the ability of the white teachers to impart a worthy education to an African.

'For one thing,' he said to me, 'they cannot impart character to a pupil. Not the right *character*. What a school like AGS does is to give our boys

---

* That's dangerous spells spurting from its mouth.

character. No other school can touch it. What did you think of those white teachers?'

I reminded him that we had not been taught, only interviewed and made to sit further examinations.

'Yes, yes, but they spoke to you. You spoke with them. What opinion did you form?'

'They seemed nice enough. But I still found it difficult to understand them all the time – we all did. This speaking through the nose . . . '

'You'll get used to that. I got used to it myself. Hm. I know the white man at home, which is really where to get to know them. I am glad I went to England. Makes one better fitted to cope with the small boys they send here as their colonial officers. Some are not bad though. But as teachers . . . no, I still don't know why Ayo wants to send you to their school.'

Disloyally, I blurted out, 'I like the place now.'

His eyes widened, 'You really do? You prefer it to being here.'

'I think I am going to like it, uncle.'

He looked at me as if he was seeing me anew. 'Amazing. Now that is amazing. You really prefer . . .' And then he recovered quickly, 'But then you haven't even completed a year here. You haven't really become a Grammarian.'

'I like the school,' I insisted. 'I hope I can get a scholarship.'

'Now that's it!' he exploded. 'I was trying to remember the one advantage which could possibly speak for that school. Yes, they do award scholarships. Right, if you obtain a scholarship, all right, that will be good for Ayo. But you must see me every holiday. I want to know how they go about their teaching.'

I promised I would.

'They teach you to say "Sir" in those schools. Only slaves say Sir. That is one of their ways of removing character from boys at an impressionable age – Sir, sir, sir, sir, sir! Very bad. So you must come and see us during the vacation . . .' Another shortcoming struck him and he looked rather wistful, shaking his head. 'And they hardly ever use the cane there – now that is a serious mistake.'

'I don't think so, principal.'

'No. You don't believe that caning is good for character?'

'No, principal.'

'Oh dear, oh dear, oh dear. You of all people, Eniola's son?'

'No, principal.'

He sighed, shook his head dolefully once more and continued down the corridor.

Beere was on the high seas, heading home. One morning the newspapers were filled with denunciations of her activities in England. At a conference – or a public lecture – she had claimed that the women of Egbaland led a pauper's existence. They were wretched, underprivileged and ruthlessly exploited. The four-page newspaper carried a long letter contesting her statements and upbraiding her temerity in telling such lies against the noble women of Egba. It was a disgrace and Beere was a traitor to her own countrywomen. The letter invited the British people to visit Abeokuta for themselves. There they would see prosperous women, even the average Egba woman lived in comfort and splendour. There were hospitals galore, the town was spotlessly clean and housing was sumptuous. Mrs Ransome-Kuti was advised to stick her nose in whatever business took her to England, and leave the concern for the welfare of Egba womanhood to the one man who had always made it his benevolent concern, the father of all Ebga himself – the Alake of Abeokuta.

Even as the women were gathering for a meeting arranged by the Group to decide what reply to make to this attack, the same journal published a letter in her defence by someone who signed himself 'Onlooker'. This writer confirmed Beere's claims in detail, referred his readers to the numerous hovels hidden away in Ikereku, Iberekodo, Ago-owu etc., where the women burrowed like rats to eke out a miserable existence. At the meeting, the new copy was passed from hand to hand. Even those who could not read wanted to see it. Finally, Ma Igbore, the white-haired lady took the paper and read it out, translating the contents. Shouts of approval rent the air. Then Kemberi took the floor.

'The other letter, that one which says that you are all millionaires, was signed by Atupa Parlour and some of those prostitutes of the Alake. Because a mere handful of them have accumulated some *jibiti** wealth and mince in and out of the palace dripping with gold trinkets, they forget that they are still living among those who cannot even give their children two square meals a day. Well, Beere is on her way. When she arrives, Egba people will know who is the real *odale*.† But there is one thing you must all keep in mind – the hand is the hand of Jacob but . . . we know who Esau is!'

Another rose. 'Of course. I can confirm that. The Alake put them up to it and it was the D.O. who put it in the Alake's head. The D.O. was still at

* Fraudulent.
† Traitor.

the palace when Kabiyesi sent for Atupa and her wealthy friends. The letter was waiting for them when they arrived, all they had to do was put their fingerprint at the bottom – Atupa can't read A from B. They did not write that letter themselves. Since when has Atupa Parlour been able to put two words together except to say, "Wait, let me take off my wrapper." '

In the midst of the gales of derisive laughter which followed, Daodu strolled in, holding also a copy of the Onlooker's statement.

'What you women should do,' he said, 'is print a hundred copies of this. Take them with you when you go to meet Beere and distribute it at the port.'

The idea was acclaimed. Daodu resumed his stroll while the meeting continued. He was back ten minutes later.

'Make it a thousand. Yes, one thousand. Hand them to all the people just disembarking and distribute them among those who have come to meet them.'

Again the women chorused their approval. Daodu did not reach the end of the path before he turned yet again, his face set, and walked briskly back to the meeting. 'Make it ten thousand. Yes, print TEN THOUSAND. We'll find the money somehow. Scatter them in the air, spread them right under the nose of the colonial government in Lagos. Yes, print ten thousand!'

There was no time to lose. Daodu now took over the direction of arrangements for welcoming back his Beere from England. He overlooked no detail. He ordered huge water-pots, the same size as ours in Aké, to be bought, buried all over the compound and filled with water. He conferred with Wild Christian and the other leaders in the Group over the feeding of the crowd of well-wishers who were bound to descend on the compound. I caught, I believed, a glimpse of the workings of his mind – Daodu wanted his wife's homecoming to be an even greater triumphal entry than his, beginning in Lagos and swelling in magnitude to envelop her detractors and overwhelm them completely.

XIV

Mrs Kuti's return changed the AGS compound into festival grounds. In addition to the water-pots, Daodu had ordered hundreds of oil-lamps. Bamboo poles were cut in four foot lengths and buried along the paths, round the fields, in the kitchen compounds and the oil-lamps were placed in their hollows. The corridors of the vast mansion, the ledges on the arched pillars, benches, garden tables also had their quota of lamps. When they were lit at night, the compound looked as if it had been invaded by millions of giant fire-flies. Huge trays, pots and basins and baskets moved in and out of the rows of light, loaded with food. There were songs, sudden roars of 'Dao-o-o-o-o-o-o-o . . . Bee-re-e-e-e-e-e-e-e . . .' as one or the other of the couple appeared in some part of the compound. Groups of women poured endlessly into the compound, some of them preceded by their own drummers. They had no sooner passed then another entered from a wholly different direction. Two or three would meet along the same path, there would be a medley of rhythms and melodies, then they would merge or simply separate again, retaining their own identities, filter through the crowds or dance upstairs to greet the newly arrived. From time to time a group would fall silent. Above the sounds of singing and shouting in other areas of the compound would rise the voice of a priest, offering yet another prayer of thanksgiving for Beere's safe return. I had never seen Daodu so proud, a big man already, he was visibly bursting with satisfaction and pride at the occasion. I watched him closely whenever I came close to him; it seemed to me that I was looking at a rare event – a grown man who was unabashedly happy. His barrel chest was, if anything, thrust further outwards than I had ever seen it. His shoulder appeared to have gained a few more inches, he rolled from side to side, filling out the huge *agaada* which he had selected for the occasion. He remained mostly upstairs, but would often look out of different windows, his eyes taking in everything, turning to give orders and point in a particular direction. It was clear that the Women's Union had a truly formidable ally in Daodu.

Towards midnight the crowd appeared to diminish; strolling through the compound however, I found that what had happened was that the women had reduced their activities. They were seated or sleeping in every nook and corner, in every corridor, resolved to keep vigil till daybreak. I went to sleep sometime later but was soon woken up by a commotion at the gates. I heard shouts, and rushing feet. When I leapt out of bed and rushed to a window, I found a man already there, swathed in a big dressing-gown. It was Daodu. His eyes were trained on the crowd just outside the gate where the trouble was taking place. He called out. The crowd turned, then parted. In the middle, helpless in the grip of other women was a young woman, stark naked. Her captors began to lead her towards the building, heaping abuses and blows on her. On her head was a calabash of *ebo*.* In the flickering lights I saw that it contained the body of a dog, cloven in two from head to tail. It was covered in a mess that could have been made up of blood, palm-oil, ashes or some kind of powder. Around it were kola-nuts, some coins – mostly pennies and *onini*,† cowrie shells and palm kernel husks. The woman's body was already covered in weals where she had been beaten. But it was her face which held me riveted. There was an unearthly quality about it so that, just as her body did not appear to take any notice of the blows, her face registered nothing of the pain. It shone vividly in the light of the oil-lamps but it registered nothing. Her luminous eyes stared straight before her except once, when a screaming woman moved directly in front of her and screamed:

'Dahun! Tani ran e?'‡

Then she stopped, turned her eyes on the woman and rested them on her, without expression, until the procession moved on again towards us.

When they were below the window, Daodu asked them again what the matter was, ordering them to stop further blows on the woman. He reminded them that Beere was fatigued after her journey and the strain of the welcome, and urged them to keep their voices down. The male night guard provided details of what had happened? He had found the woman inside the compound, with the *igba ebo*§ on her head. He had actually found her close to the house, not far from where he was then standing – he pointed out the place. When he challenged her, she fled, escaped through a gap in the fence and ran to the front of the gate where she tried again to deposit the *ebo*. By this time his shouts had aroused the other women and they helped him capture the intruder. That was all.

Daodu turned to the women. 'Does anybody know her?'

* Sacrifice, a ritual offering.
† A coin, equivalent to a cent, no longer in use.
‡ Answer! Who sent you?
§ Calabash of sacrifice.

The women looked at one another, at the captive, shook their heads. They struck their palms across each other, hissed, sighed and cursed. The mystery of her sudden materialization had disconcerted them. The path was broad, was more than effectively lit. There were people everywhere one stepped in the compound that night. Yet this woman, stark naked, with a conspicuous *igba ebo* on her head had penetrated right up to the walls of the mansion where she would have deposited her evil load but for the vigilance of the night guard. No one knew her, and she would not speak. I noticed in fact that no further effort was being made to make her speak. It was as if, at some moment, all the women knew for certain that the woman could not be made to speak.

One woman said, 'Atupa Parlour must have sent her.'

The suggestion became an accepted fact even before the utterance was completed. Voices were raised in execration of this diabolical plot to injure Beere through satanic means. The Alake also came into it at some point but the general verdict was that Atupa Parlour had sent the woman.

Daodu looked nonplussed. It was only four o'clock in the morning and he had not quite solved what to do with the naked woman standing below him. I could see that there would be no more sleep for me that night, so I hoped that he would decide to hold court as he normally did with his school offenders. I tried to phrase the charges but they all fell short, incomplete. I had never known any case of a naked woman caught prowling in AGS with an *igba ebo* on her head. I wondered how Iku would handle her defence.

Finally Daodu ordered them to keep her under close guard until daybreak, then send for the police.

The women led her away to the lawn behind the kitchen. They formed a ring around her and made her stand, the calabash on her head, until daybreak. Then they prodded her forward and led her through the streets, still naked, to the police station singing,

> Atupa Parlour on ngb'ebo ru
> Gbogbo oloye n'tagbure.*

Obviously, before dawn they had also decided that the Egba chiefs had something to do with the attempt. Even with the coming of daylight, the neutral expression on the woman's face did not change.

Explanations were numerous throughout the following day and for days

---

* Atupa Parlour is carrying round offerings
All titled chiefs are selling vegetables.

afterwards. The commonest appeared to be that the carrier had been bathed in a potion which rendered her invisible – it was for this reason that she had to be naked. The potion must have been defective however, making its effect wear off before her mission was completed, hence her sudden appearance from nowhere at all in front of the walls of the mansion. What the *ebo* was meant to do, no one could say, except that it was directed against Beere and was certainly not a friendly, welcoming gesture from whoever had sent it. On their way back from the police station the women made a detour past Atupa Parlour's house at Ikereku. They smashed more windows there and threw debris through the windows into her famous 'parlour'. She herself was rumoured to have now taken permanent refuge at the Aafin.

The meetings of the women, probably as a result of the attempt on Beere's health – or even her life – became galvanized by a new sense of urgency. Leaflets were printed almost every other day on one subject or the other. Wild Christian drafted some or, to be more accurate, she spoke her ideas aloud to Essay who then made notes, rewrote everything in his neat longhand, then pushed the sheets of paper towards her saying, why don't you get the women to discuss that tomorrow? I had now settled fully into my role as Special Courier, moving swiftly between Igbein and Aké, the shop, Mama Aduni's, Mama Igbore and Kemberi, settling down longest wherever there appeared to be some promise of action. The general meetings continued, the reading and writing lessons had been resumed and I had begun to wonder if one of my pupils would not make a better wife than Mrs Odufuwa. She was younger, lively and teased me incessantly. She was also unmarried, which, I had then discovered, was rather important in the making of such decisions. And she also had the habit of saying that she was eager to learn, so that she could speak grammar to me when we were married. Since I had not mentioned the subject to her, I felt that this was a point in her favour, responding without any prompting to what was already going on in my mind. Unfortunately some of the others had also declared their intention to marry their 'young teacher'. Wild Christian was constantly urged by them to feed me properly so that I could grow up quicker and catch up with them and continue their lessons in a secure, matrimonial home. They had a habit of gesturing in very secretive ways when they said this, so that the women around roared with laughter. They would look wise and knowing, including my favourite pupil, in ways which my first wife-to-be would never have permitted herself. It was at once embarrassing and intriguing, I never quite knew what to make of them and yet I guessed that they were referring to the secret rites that went

191

on between husband and wife. They had inexhaustible energy and appeared to be intimidated by no one, not even Beere, Wild Christian, or Daodu. In the 'classroom' however, they were transformed. When one of them became too high-spirited, the others were quick to reprove her, the favourite proving the most constant ally. I decided that we would get married after I became a doctor.

The Group now held their own regular meetings apart from the general one. At one such meeting it must have been decided that, just as an hour had been set aside for reading, writing and arithmetic, another for health questions and so on, a period should also be set aside for the airing of tax problems. I arrived at my observation post one day to find the gathering engaged at one of these sessions. It started out like any other, but culminated in the first of the women's marches on the Aafin.

Several women had spoken of their experiences with the Tax officers. The women's original resolution had been turned down, it seemed, or simply ignored. At every meeting, a report was given about the course of the No More Taxation demand. It was hardly necessary; reality was manifested in their continuing harassment on the roads, in the markets, in their petty businesses. These were recounted in great detail, to cries of indignation. New texts were drafted. New delegations were chosen. The District Officer was bombarded with petitions, demands and threats. Mrs Kuti had travelled to Lagos countless times and toured the country to gain support for the women's demands. At some point, much later, we heard of the formation of the Nigerian Women's Union. The movement of the *onikaba*, begun over cups of tea and sandwiches to resolve the problem of newly-weds who lacked the necessary social graces, was becoming popular and nation-wide. And it became all tangled up in the move to put an end to the rule of white men in the country.

For suddenly there was Oge-e-e-e-ed!*

And there was Ze-e-e-e-e-ek!† His oratory, we learnt, could move mountains.

Some young, radical nationalists were being gaoled for sedition, and sedition had become equivalent to demanding that the white man leave us to rule ourselves. New names came more and more to the fore.

A new grouping was preparing to visit England, just as Daodu and Beere had done. They would demand, not just higher institutions for all the colonial countries, but an end to the white man's rule. Their people were

* Ogendengbe Macaulay, nationalist leader.
† Nnamdi Azikiwe, nationalist leader.

going round the whole country to collect money for this purpose. The Women's Union threw its forces behind the efforts. Concerts were held. We surrendered our pocket monies, knowing somehow that even our half-pennies mattered in the great cause. Oged, Zeek, Tony, Ibiam, Ojike – these were simply names, but in Abeokuta, everyone knew Beere and the Women's Union. And both their *onikaba* and their *aroso̩* had said Yes to a certain movement with the longest-winded name any of us had ever heard – The National Council of Nigeria and the Cameroons. We were anxious to speed them on their way.

But the Women's Union still faced the Tax Problem. At the hour for the recital of experiences, an old woman got up to speak. She was so old that she had to be assisted up. The meeting was her first, and she had dragged her feeble body to the assembly as a last hope for the menace now hanging over her head.

'I come from near Owu,' she began, 'I heard that some people here are doing something about the suffering which the Tax people are putting on our heads. Perhaps you can help.'

She began to rummage in the folds of her wrapper, at the end of which a knot was tied. Her fingers fumbled at the knot, obviously incapable of fully untying it, so other hands rushed to help her. The knot was unravelled and a piece of paper was taken out.

'There it is,' she said, 'that is the cause of the whole trouble. I have brought all the disaster on my own head . . . I will tell you. I had a son, my only son, and he died about three years ago. He left thirteen children do you hear? thirteen children from different wives. They are all young children. When the children were brought to me, I said, what am I to do with these children? I have no husband, and that was my only surviving son. Even I now have to think of how to live.

'Well, to cut a long story short, it happened that my son had a farm, that was where he derived his livelihood. So people said to me, Iya, don't just sit there and watch these children suffer. Go and take over the farm. Take with you those of the wives who are not afraid of hard work, get help from anywhere, cultivate the farm and use its produce to educate the children. So I said, well, it is better to work than to beg. I went to the farm. We have just been managing to make a living from it, just a living, nothing more. Even the education of the children is stop and go. They can only go to school one at a time.

'Well, I thought that life was hard enough on me at my age. That was until two weeks ago. The Tax people brought this paper, they say that, because I have a large farm, I am to get a special assessment. They say that

I am *gbajumo** because I have a large farm, but they say nothing about the thirteen children and four women who depend on the farm for *gari*, no. They say I am *gbajumo* with a large farm. So, that is the paper before you. Where am I supposed to get the money they have written on that paper? I want you to tell me where. Just tell me where the money is so I can go and look for it because I tell you, in the three years we have been taking our food from that farm, I have never seen that kind of money. Me, my "wives", my children, none of us has ever seen that kind of money in our lives.'

In the hush of the gathering, the old woman was helped down on her seat. Among the Group who sat at their usual table facing the assembly, there was no deliberation, just the piece of paper moving from hand to hand, then being laid on the table and smoothed flat slowly by Mrs Kuti, a frown on her face. The silence went on and on, mocking the spate of resolutions, delegations, consultations, the high-sounding organizations in and around the existence of the gathering. Not unpredictably, it was Kemberi who erupted into the silence. She was suddenly up behind the table, pushing back her chair with her body. Mrs Amelia Osimosu, known to the junior wives of the Osimosu compound as Kemberi looked round the table, and forced her way out from behind it:

'Enough! We've heard enough. O ya, e nso l'Aké!'†

The women rose in a body. Hands flew to heads and off came the head-ties, unfurling in the air like hundreds of banners. The head-ties flew downwards, turned into sashes and arced round the waists to be secured with a grim decisiveness. Kemberi leading the way, they poured out of the grammar school compound, filled the streets and marched towards the palace at Aké.

There is a public frontage at the palace of the Alake; it consists of a broad field which is almost square in shape and runs the entire length of the palace. The field acts as a kind of buffer between the palace walls and the public street. Wild Christian's shop was situated opposite the Aké end of this field, on the other side of the street. The field was well-kept, bordered by the usual whitewashed stones and shaded by trees which stood at precise intervals along the perimeter of the field, and on either side of a broad drive from the arched gate to the palace building itself. Over the

---

* Well-to-do, well-known.
† It's time. Let us march on Aké.

arch was the figure of an elephant in repose, the symbol of royalty of Egbaland.

Bordering the field at right angles on the Aké end was a long, low structure of wood and clay. It was broken at neat intervals by uneven archways which were sealed two-thirds of the way up by wooden crosswork and topped by a low-slung corrugated iron roof. One side ran along the same public road as the palace field; the other, at right angles, simply vanished into a warren of mud horses and compounds. These two walls hid, from the streets, the corridors of the *ogboni* enclave. From the shop we saw them pass at all hours of the day on their way to attend a meeting of chiefs at the Aafin or their own periodic sessions within the *ogboni* compound. Age appeared to be the condition for this numinous society, yet a number of them also strode by in crude, vigorous health, called out their greetings in robust voices, looking more like warriors than participants at sessions of cunning, experience and wisdom.

Each *ogboni* was invariably to be seen in a single broad cloth which he wore like a toga, one shoulder covered by the end loops. On the other shoulder, otherwise bare, was thrown the distinctive shawl, a narrow piece of cloth of coarse weave, tasselled at the ends, with a mid-section of fluffed-out multi-coloured patterns. Some, especially the older *ogboni* wore a *buba* beneath the covering broad cloth. Some passed barefoot or bare-headed, some in leather or woven slippers, in the casual headgear of a soft cloth-cap whose pouch fell over one ear. An iron or brass staff of office was carried in the right hand or borne before them by a servant. The broad, circular stiff-leather fan appeared to belong to their formal attire, but the most distinctive feature of the Egba *ogboni* was the broad-rimmed hat, usually of stiffened leather, decorated with coloured leather or raffia strips, cloths or beads. The *ogboni* slid through Aké like ancient wraiths, silent, dark and wise, a tanned pouch of Egba history, of its mysteries, memories and insights, or thudded through on warriors' feet, defiant and raucous, broad and compact with unspoken violence. We were afraid of them. Among other furtive hints and whispers we heard that they sent out child kidnappers whose haul was essential to some of their rites and ceremonies. Certainly they controlled the *oro** cult whose bull-roarer sent all women into the first available indoor refuge. It was unusual for the bull-roarer to be heard in daylight, and without warning, but it happened once when I was in the shop with Wild Christian. She quickly locked the shop doors on us until the danger was past. Their weird chants drifted

* A secret male cult with the task of carrying out sentences.

many evenings into the parsonage, punctuated by concerted thuds which, we learnt, was the sound of their staffs striking the clay floor as they circled round in their secret enclave. There was no formal teaching in such matters, but we came to know that in the *ogboni* reposed the real power of the king and land, not that power which seemed to be manifested in the prostration of men and women at the feet of the king, but the *real* power, both supernatural and cabalistic, the intriguing, midnight power which could make even the king wake up one morning and find that his houseposts had been eaten through during his sleep. We looked on them with a mixture of fear and fascination.

To reach their own enclave however, the *ogboni* had to pass through the central elephant-topped archway, then turn left into the private path which led into their sector. The central driveway led directly into the palace complex, through a passageway under the long, two-storey building which formed the outer line of the palace structures. This building housed the offices and council rooms of the Native Administration, presided over by the Alake. And at the inner wall of that building, emerging from the tunnel beneath it into a courtyard, the outer world stopped.

This brief, low tunnel, roofed by the upper floor of the offices, was a time capsule which ejected us into an arcane space fringed by the watchful, luminous eyeballs of petrified ancients and deities. For this was my first impression on emerging from the brief shadow of the tunnel into the sunlit courtyard. From the humane succession of bookshop, church, cenotaph, sewing academies, bicycle repair shacks, barbers' shops, petty trader stalls, the stone and concrete bulk of the Centenary Hall, stray goats and noisy hawkers, tree-lined field and office buildings, we were thrust suddenly on this arc of silent watchers, mounted warriors – single and clustered, kneeling priestesses, sacrificial scenes, royal processions. Knowledge of the names came later – the eyes of Ifa, Sango, divination priests, Ogun, Obatala, Erinle, Osanyin iron staffs with their rings of mounted divination birds . . . even the *ogboni* in procession, frozen in motion. They surrounded the courtyard on a low wall which formed the half-circle of the courtyard and was shielded by an outjutting roof held up in turn by houseposts, elaborately carved in human and animal figures. The low wall was only the outer line of a curved passageway whose inner wall housed grottoes filled with more carved denizens of the ancestral world. Passageways opened into it from various interiors of the palace, radially, and these were again filled with intervals of votive presences, progressively shadowy as the passages receded.

One of these passages, to the left, facing inwards from the tunnel, was broader than others. It rose on wider, staggered planes and vanished into a pillared space over which rose an independent unit with a wooden fretwork verandah which overlooked the main courtyard – these were the living quarters of the Alake. At his hour of public audience the crowd gathered in the courtyard below. When the Alake appeared up in the verandah, men prostrated themselves flat on the ground and the women would *yinrinka*, a motion which involved getting on their knees with their elbows on the ground, then tilting until they touched the ground with one side, then the other before returning to their half-crouch position. The petitioners or complainants were then called upon in turn by one of the Alake's clerks or chiefs, judgements were awarded, advice given, settlements and arbitrations recommended or instituted on the spot.

I had witnessed the scene several times. We were first taken to visit the Alake, Tinu and I, one day after church. I had hardly begun school then, and the lasting impression was one of a cemetery with no headstones, no marbles and whitewashed graves, only wooden figures which did not quite conform to the usual shapes of angels and cherubs such as filled the graveyard beside the church. But there had also been the familiar surrounding of the Alake's private garden which was nearly as luxuriant as Essay's, but boasted a number of plants that I had not seen before. Most memorable of all however was his aquarium, the first I had encountered. It was at the bottom of a series of flagstones, in a kind of indoor courtyard, and contained both grey and coloured fishes. One of them, we were warned, would give an unpleasant sensation if touched. At the first opportunity I slipped out from the parlour and went and touched it, nearly falling in. The sensation was a frightening one; I had no choice but to keep it to myself for fear that I would never be allowed inside the palace again. The Alake made much of the Headmaster's family, largely on account of our mother, of whom he was very fond. During later visits, he held Tinu and me by either hand, pestered us with questions and referred to us as his 'yekan'. When I asked mother what 'yekan' meant, I was most unprepared for the news that it meant that we were his relations. The world of the parsonage and the Aafin were so far apart, I could not see how the two could be linked in any way. The king, in spite of his periodic appearances in church where he had his own pew, was compelled by his position to follow the *orisa*. Becoming a king was to 'je oba', and this, we informally gathered, was to be taken literally. When the old king died, his heart and liver were removed and the new king was required to eat them. Nothing upset me more than to learn, so casually, that the man who had taken me on his lap and claimed I was his *yekan* had actually eaten human flesh, even for the sake of kingship. For some time after this I would watch the Alake on our visits, wondering if I could detect the stain of human blood on his lips, and doubly puzzled to find there nothing but a warm, crinkly smile. I never found the courage to ask him directly; it seemed to be one of those very few things in the world which one dared not ask about, I could not find the courage to do it!

I knew the hour of the Alake's audience and sometimes when we were two at the shop, I risked going over to watch the various petitioners. Once he saw me and beckoned to me at the end of the audience. Afraid that he perhaps wanted to send a message to Wild Christian, thus exposing my presence there, I fled. After that I went very rarely, taking great care not to be detected. The cases were varied, and many of them were filled with comic drama. Some had nothing of the humorous about them, except for the retainers or some attendant chiefs who seemed to quarry belly-laughs out of any situation. It was at these sessions also that I found, for the first time, that one of those passages which led away from the arced corridor was lined with detention cells. I had seen 'native' police around the mouth of this passage but assumed that they were merely part of the palace guard. At one of these sessions however, a door in the passage was unlocked and a group of offenders – men and women – were led out by the policemen. They were flung down in the dust of the courtyard below the Alake whose thin, plaintive voice then floated down from the balcony asking them,

'Why is it you people always have to be made to pay your tax?'

It was this scene that came most clearly to mind as I turned aside half a mile before the CMS bookshop to take a short cut which took me to the rear of St Peter's parsonage, through the cemetery, then through the school compound, through BishopsCourt, emerging by the nearer gate opposite Pa Solotan's house, then round the back of the church to Wild Christian's shop, stopping to pass the news to Bunmi who was on duty at the time. I secured myself a good observation position a full five minutes before the advance-guard of the women crowd burst on the palace and into the courtyard to demand an immediate audience with their 'Baba'. The *akoda* at the tunnel entrance began by confronting them with an attitude of extreme haughtiness.

'Who are you? Who sent you? What do you mean? Have you ever known Kabiyesi grant audience at this hour? Go back and warn those noisy people coming behind you that . . .'

When the 'noisy people' swarmed through the gates and spilled into the fore field of the palace, filling it completely, the rest of the *akoda*'s questions and commands stuck in his throat. He goggled and began to walk backwards into the palace, to be replaced by a hurrying squad of junior chiefs. I recognized them as the retainers, some of them with some minor palace titles, who usually lounged on mats in the courtyard before the passage that led to the Alake's quarters. Some of them I had also seen as functioneers during the king's audiences, selecting the next petitioner to be heard and running errands like clerks of a court. Their urgent mission seemed to be to persuade the advance-guard to keep the women from entering the main courtyard of the palace. The women replied that the crowd would remain peacefully in the field as long as Kabiyesi emerged to receive the delegation of women who were then on their way. The chiefs thanked them, returned to deliver their message to the king.

Not long after, the formal leaders arrived – Mama Igbore who astonished me by keeping pace with the others to arrive so quickly, Wild Christian, Mama Aduni, two or three other women and of course – Kemberi. When the Alake appeared, they curtsied, going down on their knees, but no more. The Alake had obviously resolved to receive the emissaries courteously. He spoke to them with urbane fatherliness, his high-pitched voice coated with a persuasive concern, addressed them as his own daughters, friends or relations, inviting them to share their civic concerns.

'Ah-ah, Moroun, *yekan mi* . . . And Mrs Owodunni . . . I see Igbore is here too, not to mention the clergy . . . well, the matter must be heavy. But even the very composition of you here, who in effect make up the city, assures me that there is nothing we cannot solve. Nothing can be beyond solution with the group I see before me, so let's get to it. What is the matter in our beloved Egbaland?'

Kemberi knelt again, greeting him, 'Kabiyesi o, Kabiyesi', shifted from one knee to the other, then stood up. 'Kabiyesi, the message which I bring you today is the message of all the women who have left their stalls, their homes and children, their farms and petty affairs to come and visit you today. They are the suffering crowd who are gathered on your front lawn – you can see them yourself, Kabiyesi, they are all the womanhood of Egba, and they have come to say – Enough is Enough. The voice with which I speak is the voice of our Beere, Mrs Kuti. The words which you hear from me are the words of Mrs Kuti. She asked me to tell you, on behalf of those women you see outside, that the women of Egba have had enough. They are starving, their children are starving, they are diseased, they have no hope of education or a better future, and yet their mothers have more and more burdens placed on them. Now the woman are saying, Enough.

'Once upon a time, Kabiyesi, the *parakoyi* in the markets formed an honoured, revered institution. They kept the peace, their presence gave us a sense of security, even a sense of being in our own homes during the long hours of keeping market. What we gave, we gave gladly. We set ourselves a toll which we contributed to keep them fed and clothed. Now, in these past years, they have grown beyond the level of greed. They dip their hands in our *gari*, in our *elubo*, our salt, vegetables, in our corn and oil, right up to the elbow and do it as of right. They say they are empowered to do this by the chiefs, by the council or whatever comes into their minds. It doesn't matter where they get this new power, we say Enough is Enough. We don't want them in the markets any more. We want them moved out. They bring *akoda* and police to arrest our women, lock them up and even flog them. We don't want to see them in the markets any more.

'And then, after the *parakoyi* have filled their fat bellies, in return for which they do nothing, the Tax people waylay our women on the roads, raid them in the markets, in their homes, carry them off – even nursing mothers – to lock-ups until they pay their tax. Mrs Kuti says I am to tell you we have written petitions, held meetings, protested everywhere about the injustice of many of these assessments which are used to oppress our women. She says we have told the council to keep their officers in check, to look into this matter of demanding tax where the breadwinner has nothing with which to feed the family. Now, the matter has reached *gongo*. Special o, ordinary o, levy o, or poll o, our Beere says I am to tell you – no more. The women of Egba say, NO MORE TAX. Of any kind! Simply – NO MORE TAX. Beginning from today, we reject all forms of taxation!'

Her voice had risen at this point, carrying to the nearer women in the field. Immediately they took up her cry which gathered volume and rolled through the field, filling all of Aké with that one cry:

'No more tax! We women say – No More Taxation!'

The Alake waited for a lull, sitting thoughtfully, weighing the problem in rapt concentration as if it was the first time he had encountered it. Finally he spoke:

'Enh, it is a matter you have put very capably, Amelia – I thank you very much, I thank all of you and I thank Mrs Kuti who is not here.'

'She herself is on the way,' Kemberi assured him.

'Is she?' And I thought the Alake looked momentarily worried but recovered quickly. 'Ah well, then we will have even more heads to put together over the issue. But right now, let me ask you women – do you think it can be done? Taxation is as old as human society, can one simply do away with it just like that?'

Wild Christian replied, 'Kabiyesi, over this matter, I wish to implore you to reflect very carefully. *Very* carefully. The women are saying, No more Tax. It is no time to start asking whether taxation began with our forefathers or not. Our women today, those women whom we meet everyday, they are the ones we are talking about. They cannot afford the tax.'

'That may be true,' the Alake replied. 'I am not saying that I am not in sympathy with their plight. But my question still remains – can it be done? Is it really possible to have a society today where women will not pay tax? In any case, this is not a decision which I can take. It is not the Alake who imposes taxation, it is a council of government. The matter has to be laid before them. And what I am asking all of you is – do you really see a body which must run a community, using not sand but money – do you really think it can be done, abolishing tax just like that?'

Kemberi burst in, shaking her head vigorously. 'Ngh-ngh, Kabiyesi, ngh-ngh. We have come to you as our Baba, as the one we know. We do not know any council of government other than you. You are the government and the government is you. It is you we have come to talk to, not to any chiefs or council. It is you who must reflect on this matter very carefully. As *Aya* Headmaster has said, reflect *very* carefully.'

'I will, I will,' Alake assured her. 'But I have to summon a council meeting. I have already done so. I have even sent for the *ajele* because you see, that is all part of what I am saying – this matter extends beyond the palace, it is not a thing we can do alone. And it cannot be done overnight. So, give us time. Tell your people, I have promised to look into it. The council will meet, and we will consider everything.'

He sighed then turned, somewhat wistfully I thought, in the direction of Wild Christian. 'Moroun,' he said, 'let me ask you something. You are the wife of a teacher, the Headmaster of a school. He is in charge of the school, he supervises activities, he decides policies and so on. Now imagine a situation which calls for a decision which will profoundly affect the normal direction of the school. I mean, not just a question of changing the style of marching or of holding the morning assembly or even whether to declare a school holiday or not. I am speaking of something which goes to the root of administering the school – increasing or decreasing school fees, changing the education curriculum – things like that. I want to ask you, can the Headmaster do it alone?'

My mother replied, 'No, Kabiyesi. He would call a meeting of his staff.'

The Alake nodded carefully. 'We are all in agreement so far. Now comes the more difficult one. Suppose, at the meeting, whatever measure is proposed by the Headmaster is opposed by all his staff. This is something he believes in very much, something he sees as necessary, perhaps a demand by the pupils' parents which he believes in wholeheartedly. The meeting goes on all day, continues into the next, goes on for a whole week. He argues his points carefully, he tries to win them over but they won't agree. Nothing he says can make them change their minds. True, he is the boss, but he is only one. He has done his best, his conscience is satisfied. Well, what should a wise man do at that point?'

Wild Christian kept her eyes on the ground and shook her head sadly. 'Kabiyesi,' she said, 'this question you have asked me is one which should really have been put to *agba-igba*,* not to a child, which is what we are before you.'

'But I asked it as a question between husband and wife,' the Alake said.

'Well,' said Wild Christian, 'in that case, and since you have spoken of satisfying one's conscience, I would say to him, if you cannot follow your conscience, then the job is not worth clinging to. That is what I would say to the Headmaster.'

All the women in the Group nodded, gravely. The Alake stared ahead in the absolute stillness of the courtyard. An endless moment elapsed and then he sighed, rose and entered the house.

The end of the audience was separately signalled from the outside by the arrival of Beere which let off the familiar cry 'Bee-e-e-e-e-e-re' from the multitude on the fields. She was hemmed in on all sides and, for a while, passage into the main courtyard was impossible. As if to complicate matters the District Officer arrived, accompanied by policemen who vainly tried to clear a path for him. The women at the outer fringe, that is, near the arched gate recognized him and, in a good-natured way, began to tease him. In fact, their attitude was extremely friendly, as if they felt that, with his arrival, the sinister operations of the Alake's oppressive agents would be fully exposed. The young Englishman however grew redder and redder in the face, recognizing that he was being made fun of and resenting this slight to his authority. He ordered the policemen to clear a way forcibly through the crowd, which they did easily because the women co-operated. But then he came to where Mrs Kuti was, surrounded with anxious women who plied her with questions.

Those women around Mrs Kuti were not as patient as the earlier ones. They remained stolidly where they were, evidently expecting the District Officer's group to do the same. When the policemen tried to exert pressure

* A well-seasoned elder.

on them in order to clear the way, they turned angry, let up a continuous shout of derision at the officer. His face and neck now approaching the colour of camwood, he ran the gauntlet of insults until he gained – and only through Beere's intervention – access to the palace courtyard. It was, I felt certain, this lingering sense of humiliation which made him, once he had gained the security of the palace, mount the balcony of the offices which overlooked the field and shout to Mrs Kuti:

'Look here, Mrs Kuti, we are trying to hold a serious meeting here. Will you kindly keep your women in order.'

Mrs Kuti replied, 'So are we, holding a serious meeting. Or do you think we are here to play?'

Further infuriated, the man shouted, 'Well, tell them to shut up!'

There was a pause. Mrs Kuti blinked through her glasses upward at the man, then inquired, 'Excuse me, were you talking to me?'

'Yes of course I am. SHUT UP YOUR WOMEN!'

In the sudden silence which fell over the shocked women, Mrs Kuti made the response which flew round Abeokuta for weeks afterwards, as the 'grammar' which hammered the ill-starred District Officer into submission. It was referred to sometimes as the grammatical TKO of the entire uprising, sometimes the episode was simply described as one in which Mrs Kuti 'fi grammar re l'epa' or 'o gba n'stud', 'o gbe fun' and a number of other variations. It was undeniable that the District Officer was rendered speechless by Mrs Kuti's angry riposte which rang through the hush:

'You may have been born, you were not bred. Could you speak to your mother like that?'

The District Officer's open-mouthed retreat was accompanied by a welling of the women's angry murmur. There were shouts on the Alake to get rid of the insolent white man at once, within minutes. If he was not out, they would come in, cut off his genitals and post them to his mother. Chiefs appeared on the same balcony, were hooted away with only one demand – that white man was to leave the precincts of the palace immediately as his very presence was an abomination not merely to the women but to the palace which belonged to the people of Egbaland. The mood was now violent, the Group was lost amidst the multitude, vainly attempting to placate the women.

What would have happened next, was impossible to predict. I had retreated to the edge of the field but remained close to the office blocks, fearful now of being trampled to death. I passed Mrs Kuti once in the crush and saw her smile for the first time that day saying,

'Hm, l'oogun, o ti ya de'bi.'*

She asked me where my mother was, little realizing that she and Mama Aduni had been within arm's length of her during the exchange, before the surge of the crowd prised them apart again.

The tension was not immediately relieved, but its focus was shifted away – fortunately for the white man – by the arrival of one of the *ologboni*. They had been arriving in ones and twos to confer with the Alake on the crisis and their passage had been quite uneventful. Now came the Balogun of one of the Egba districts, an arrogant, puffed-up individual, or perhaps it was simply that he felt it his duty to act in accordance with his title, which was that of a war-leader, in face of this civil disturbance. Undaunted by the sheer mass and mood of the gathering, indeed, probably provoked by it, he decided to assert his manhood authority, hissing as he strutted through the rear section of the crowd, accompanied by his retainers. In a voice as burly as his figure he hissed:

'Hm-hm-hm, pshee-aw! The world is spoilt, the world is coming to an end when these women, these *agb'eyin-to*,† can lay siege to the palace and disturb the peace.' And he raised his voice further, 'Go on, go home and mind your kitchens and food and feed your children. What do you know about the running of state affairs? Not pay tax indeed! What you need is a good kick on your idle rumps.'

What happened next constituted the second high point of the uprising on that day. After that, no one could doubt the collective psychic force of the women and, specifically, of the Beere. She was now rumoured to exert supernatural powers – to which indeed was already credited the exposure of that carrier whose invisibility had worn off as she was about to set down the evil load at Beere's doorstep. For something happened to the Balogun's thigh as he suited action to his threat and delivered a kick in the general direction of the women. As he set that leg down, it simply gave way under him and he collapsed. Embarrassed, he very quickly scrambled up, only to half-collapse again as he attempted to set his weight on it. He had come with about six retainers – perhaps it was this also which gave him so much daring – and they now rushed about him in a practised way and bore him off. It happened very quickly and smoothly, like a familiar exercise, reminding me of the accounts of civil war in Yorubaland when the war-leader's attendants would rush to rescue him, when wounded, even in the face of fire. The women were of course also spellbound – momentarily at

* Hm, man of strife, here already?
† Who urinate from the rear.

least – by his collapse. In fact, those nearest to him had shrunk back, not knowing the nature of his sudden seizure. By the time they had recovered, the Balogun had been swept away, leaving his brother *ogboni* in trouble.

For from then on, any figure in an attire which remotely resembled an *ogboni* was set upon. His shawl was snatched, shredded, his wrapping cloth was stripped off him – fan, office staff, cap all had long disappeared. The *ogboni* were flogged with their shawls, fans, and were left only with their undershorts when finally let through a gauntlet of abuse into the palace or back in the direction of their homes.

And then I heard the ultimate challenge of the women, for this was not just a rallying-song, even an ordinary war-song, but the appropriation of the man-exclusive cult – *oro* – by women in a dare to all men, *ogboni* or not. I could not be sure whether the women would regard me as a 'man', or that, if they did, they would at least recall their 'young teacher', courier extraordinary, scout and general factotum. When I saw stocky, middle-aged and elderly, grizzled men, the fearsome *ogboni*, abandoning their hats, shawls, staffs of office and run on the wind faster than I ever saw Osiki perform, and beheld even the non-*ogboni* men skirting the palace environs, moving deeper into their shops, and finally picked out the wording of their new chant:

> Oro o, a fe s'oro
> Oro o, a fe s'oro
> E ti'lekun mo'kunrin
> A fe s'oro.*

I decided to move closer to the sanctuary of Wild Christian's shop without further delay!

I found her already there, issuing instructions about closing up the shop. She looked worried, very worried. Since the beginning of the women's movement I had never seen her so downcast. Only then did I make an incredible discovery – Wild Christian deeply abhorred violence! It was an astounding revelation. Her entire temperament, her violent outbursts on our hapless heads had led me to assume that she would be in the midst of the tumult – which I had myself very reluctantly abandoned, and only for fear of my own safety. Indeed I had expected her to return home with trophies gathered from the comic apparitions of those deflated terror figures. She mentioned then that she had been looking for me in

---

* *Òrò-o*, we are about to perform *òrò*
  Lock up all the men, we are bringing out *òrò*.

order to send me to Bunmi to lock up the shop and, speaking more to herself than to me, remarked that the situation had got out of hand, the women no longer distinguished between the Balogun type, and those other *ogboni* who had actually given them help, had encouraged their fight against taxation and were going to the palace to speak on their behalf. But it wasn't those friendly ones she was concerned with, the entire scene of violence sickened her.

Even as she supervised the packing up of the wares which were laid out in front of the shop, a late *ogboni*, completely unaware of what was going on, marched confidently past the shop towards the Aafin. Wild Christian stared at him, unbelieving, for some moments, then cried out:

'Baba! Baba, where are you going?'

The leader stopped, assured himself that he was the one spoken to and announced, 'To the Aafin. We have been summoned to sort out some trouble there – yes, I can even hear it from here.'

'Baba, get back quickly. If they catch sight of you . . .'

Something in the renewed noise from the palace gate made me realize that the women there had seen the old man. Wild Christian heard it too. She rushed out and dragged him into the shop, shut one half of the door on him and said, 'Quickly, Baba. Remove your robes, remove all your *ogboni* gear.'

The urgency in her voice only made him more confused. 'Enh? Enh? Ewo lo tun de yi? Enh?'*

She reached behind the door, snatched off his shawl and hat and threw them behind the counter. 'Baba, kia-kia, your wrapper – take it off. Throw it behind with the rest. Leave only your shorts.'

The women arrived moments later, about twenty of them. There was only one direction in which the *ogboni* they had seen so clearly could have disappeared and this was Wild Christian's shop. They gathered in front while we continued packing up goods from the display mats and trestles. Wild Christian did not attempt to deny that the man was in the shop.

'If it is that old man you are looking for, he is inside changing. He is not an *ogboni*.'

There was a chorus of disapproval. 'Ah, Mama Wole, how can you tell us that when we saw him with our own eyes.'

'Well, when you saw him, he was, but now he is changing. I've told him to take his *ogboni* things off because the *ogboni* are no longer wanted here today. What more do you want?'

---

* What new development is this?

'They are still enemies,' interjected one of the women, 'in or out of their silly shawls they are our enemies. Are they not the ones who have been taxing us? Mama, let's apportion this one his own *seria* before we let him go.'

The rest raised shouts of support. Another added, 'Today is the day of reckoning for all of them, Mama, bring him out.'

And yet another voice. 'We are the *agb'eyin-to*, not so? They forget that they were all born by these same *agb'eyin-to*. Including the very oldest among them! Well, let their mothers teach them something today.'

Wild Christian burst out laughing. 'Is that all that is paining you? Because one stupid *ogboni* called us *agb'eyin-to*! Listen, did we come here for that or weightier matters? The man who insulted you has been carried home, half-paralysed – that is heaven's justice for you. I don't know this man, one of you can go inside and ask him. At the most I know only two or three of the *ogboni*, so don't think I am protecting him because he is my *ibatan*.* But I do not like trouble, I don't like all this violence. It is not what we set out to do.'

They looked a little mollified, in any case, their initial ardour had cooled somewhat. Still one of them demanded, 'Let him take off all his paraphernalia. We don't want to see any of it on the streets of Abeokuta today or tomorrow, even forever.'

Wild Christian pushed in her head, 'Baba, fold all your attire neatly and tie it up in his cloth and go home.'

The man sighed, 'Ah, I'm in no hurry. I will stay here until all is quiet, then go home exactly as you say.'

Wild Christian turned to his pursuers. 'You see, what more do you want? The Baba is still suspicious of you. Go on. I'll see him off when you have gone.'

Still they insisted, 'We want to see his face. There are a number of them for whom we are specially on the lookout. Let's see his face and make sure he is not one of them.'

So the old man had to show his face, introduce himself, and swear that he had never done a thing against women, was going to cast his voice on the side of the abolition of tax and the women could count on him on any measures they wanted. As for the *parakoyi* he had told Kabiyesi times without number that they were leeches and parasites – and this was no hearsay, he had gone by the evidence of his own wife who was a market trader like most of those he was then talking to . . .

---

* Relation.

They left at last, the old man prostrated himself repeatedly, thanked and blessed Wild Christian profusely. He sped off in his shorts, bundle in hand, leaving his staff behind. He would fetch it the following day, he said.

Calm began to descend as it neared dusk. At some point, a decision had been taken that the women would lay siege to the palace until all their demands were granted. The calm was hastened by what seemed an orchestrated movement from all roads and byways which led towards the palace. This movement contrasted deeply with the earlier violence and chaos, yet did not appear to be a separate event; one thing flowed into another, affected what it replaced and gave birth to a new mood, a new atmosphere of communion and cohesion.

They came from the direction of Iporo, Iberekodo, Ibara, Lantoro and Adatan, from other byways within the heart of the city itself. The lines of humanity curled through hidden *agbole* to swell the other throngs on a final approach along the road that led to the gates of the palace. They were like the caravans from Isara, laden with stocks and foods, only there were streams and streams of them. From about an hour before sunset, as if they had been signalled in, processions of women brought food and greetings from outlying villages, market women arrived, having closed their stalls for the day, hastening to partake of the events at the palace. The cries of welcome began to overcome those of outrage and pursuit. The newcomers recognized faces, reported their arrival to the leaders who, by these means, now began to regain control of their followership. Mats arrived on the heads of the women. There began a transformation, not only of the physical terrain, but of the shapes and motions of the gathering. Fires were lit; for the first time, water and food were thought upon. The younger women were rounded up and assigned to different chores.

Evening had settled on the field when, as if to further enhance and consolidate this new mood, word came that a woman was in labour. Wild Christian, who had by now dispatched Bunmi home with the shop basket and returned to the field, hastened there with her lieutenant, Mama Aduni. They examined the woman and decided that she must be rushed to hospital. It was too late. The excitement of the previous hours, the rush, the noise, the shoving and pushing, had been too much for the baby which, no one was at all surprised to learn, was a girl. It was nearly my first chance to watch a live birth but, after being ignored in the panic and excitement Mrs Kuti, who was hurrying in after news had reached her, saw me standing placidly among the ring of women and chased me off. Still, I watched them bury the after-birth under one of the trees on the lawn. Nothing could have happened of such a profound propitiousness as the birth of the child – and a female! The mood, which had already subsided into one of quiescent in-gathering now became radiant with joy. The baby was cleaned, the umbilical cord tied – I was allowed to see none of this but the running commentaries, instructions, advices were more than enough vivid transmission – and finally, both the mother and child were taken to the Catholic Hospital a hundred yards away – Oke Padi.

And yet more and more caravans arrived. As yet another group was welcomed, Mama Igbore shook her head and said,

'It is as if the heavens themselves have opened up, as if the graveyards have opened and all the dead and forgotten peoples of other worlds are pouring to join us here.'

From a swiftly shifting point in the various groupings, a voice would rise in song, but now it was all rapture and plain festivity. The outwardly religious songs – inspired by the *orisa*, by Allah or Christ – were begun by the adherents of the particular religion but were taken up by everyone irrespective of their leanings and chanted into the night.

> La–illah–il–allah
> Anobi gb'owo o wa
> On'ise nla gb'owo o wa
> Anobi gb'owo wa
> A te'le ni ma ya gb'owo o wa
> Anobi gb'owo o wa.*

---

* La-illah-il-allah
  Lord, take our hands
  Doer of great deeds, take our hands
  He who follows without deserting, take our hands
  Lord, take our hands.

XV

The women now dug in for a long siege. Shock squads roamed the city, mobilizing all womanhood. Markets and women's shops were ordered closed. Those who defied the order had their goods confiscated and sent to the field before the palace. Even before the concession was formalized, the *parakoyi* had vanished from the markets, the tardiest only catching a glimpse of the approaching militants before abandoning their positions and seeking other predatory grounds. The men became more fully involved, at least, they became more openly involved. At every step, they had shouted their encouragement of the women's actions and even in some cases, driven their hesitant wives from home, angry that such wives did not know that the cause concerned them also, and that its victory would bring them much-needed relief. One physically dragged his wife to the palace one morning, gave her money to spend on food and assured her that he would look after the children until the strife was over. There were also many women there with their young who camped out in the open with them and shared the hardship. But the movement of laden lines towards the Aafin now included men. They stopped by on the way from their farms; many had even journeyed to the farm to bring the women yams, fruits, palm wine. A hunter or two stopped to drop the day's catch of bushmeat and share jokes with the women.

Beere and The Group negotiated with the new District Officer, the former having been recalled. They held meetings with the Alake's Council, most of which ended in deadlocks. At the end of each meeting they reported back to the assembly who responded with songs and dances of defiance.

Reinforcements of armed police had been sent from Lagos the morning after the initial riots. They stayed away from the palace but within sight, camped in the Centenary Hall and drilled ostentatiously on its grounds. A group of young women moved on to the road next to the drill grounds and mimicked their actions in comic formations. Crowds gathered and turned the police 'showing the flag' exercises into a farce. The drill-major sweated in the morning sun, striving in vain to retain some dignity and cower the women with his authority. He gave up finally, gave the order and the police dispersed and retreated to the other side of the hall, keeping only an observation post on the steps of the hall to monitor the activities of the women.

And yet another shock squad had moved to Ikereku, to the two-storey building of Atupa Parlour. They sacked it completely, having first put to flight the half-dozen policemen who were posted there on guard. Fortunately Atupa had not returned to the house since the episode of the *ebo*. They returned to the camp waving a few underwear looted from her house and singing with coarse relish yet another song:

Obo Atupa lo d'ija s'ile
Alake oloko ese.*

Obviously, some time since the first courteous exchanges, the women had cast the Alake fully in the role of the arch-villain; there was to be no more diplomacy. When the raiding team arrived, they were joined by the massed camp who milled round the trophies borne aloft on poles, laughing and slapping palms, punctuating the song with obscene gestures. I tried to picture their prisoner, the Alake, sealed up with his aquarium and electric fish, unable to stop the sound of this and other derogatory songs which the women had made up about him, and saw a frightened, lonely man. I could not imagine him eating the heart or liver of anyone and failed to understand why he refused to take the simple course of granting every single request of the women. I concluded somehow that he was perhaps as much the slave of the District Officer – if not the present one, at least of the earlier, insolent one – as he was a prisoner of the women.

The gathering now moved to isolate him further. At some point a decision was taken and announced loudly so that everyone, including casual passers-by could hear it: no woman must be seen, for any reason whatever, within the palace. Even The Group did not exempt themselves, having, as I later discovered, taken the step of appointing a male chief as their future go-between. The truth was, Mrs Kuti and her colleagues had now reached a point where they felt that there was nothing further to be gained from future discussions with the palace. It had now become a war of wills.

And the negotiations went on, but they now took a form in which the

* Atupa's vagina started the strife
  Alake, with penis of a poison rat.

211

results could only be known afterwards. To my disappointment, I could no longer be present at any of these meetings, even of those taking place among The Group by themselves. The veteran messenger continued to run errands between Beere and Wild Christian especially, but was now only left with vague notions of contacts being made, negotiations and draft agreements being signed to be put later to the entire assembly, processes which took place at unstated hours and places. For instance, The Group and some of the chiefs held a meeting with the new District Officer at his office. It was at this meeting, it was later revealed, that the abolition of the Special Assessment on all women was first proposed by the 'other side', also that the *parakoyi* were to be disbanded. The Group announced these to the assembly even while assuring them that they considered the concessions derisive.

And there was another secret session, a report of which was not shouted from the rooftops but which nevertheless percolated through the rank and file within minutes of the session. It had taken place in the *ogboni* enclave. The elders had sent a message to Mrs Kuti, their humiliations at the hands of the women forgiven.

'Come and talk to us,' they said. 'We consider ourselves the sons of Majeobaje;* we cannot sit back and watch things get worse and spoil totally in our hands. Come and see us with a list of all the things the women want. You'll be surprised how closely our minds agree.'

At the meeting, the *ogboni* assured them that everything was happening as it had been written, nothing was strange to them, the elders, because Ifa had seen and spoken it all. Wild Christian recited their speeches to Essay during dinner on the following day, the first dinner at home at which I had been present – with her and Essay – in days, even weeks.

'They were very nice, very courteous. They didn't even want us to apologize over their rough treatment at the hands of our wild ones. They only warned us to be cautious, to know where we were going, to be sure where we actually wanted all this to take us. "As for us," they said, "we are not surprised or alarmed. Ifa said it all before and, when it started, we went back to consult again and Ifa said – now is happening what I told you before." Those *ogboni* said it comes in cycles – every fourteenth king – or was it thirteenth? I've forgotten – I feel so tired. They said that after every thirteenth or fourteenth king to sit on the throne of Egbaland, it always comes about like that. They said so many things, so many strange things. But the main thing they wanted to say to us was that we should rest assured

* Let-things-not-come-to-ruin.

that they would not allow things to spoil in Egbaland. They didn't want us to think that they were sitting down doing nothing.'

They were locked up together a long time that night, speaking in low voices. I did not really think that Wild Christian was physically tired. Something had happened at the *ogboni* enclave to move her profoundly – it showed in the manner in which she recounted the events. Her weariness appeared not to belong to the body but to her mind, to some new form, or hint of understanding or maybe simply of viewing events. I reflected on the little I had heard, and concluded that the *ogboni* must be very careless or forgetful people. If everything was already predicted and they knew it – as they claimed – then why had they not anticipated their treatment at the hands of the women? And I wondered if the Balogun had anticipated his fate – matters were worse for him, he had become fully paralysed on one side and was now receiving treatment at the clinic of a traditional healer, far from Abeokuta. I did not think much of the claims to prescience of the *ogboni*.

It was time again to make another assault on the broad fields and orchards of Government College. During the turmoil I had again sat the examinations; once again I was summoned for an interview. Essay coached me relentlessly – but for the thought of the consequences, I would have said to him, Don't worry, I shall win that scholarship this time – I know it. But he had already begun to upbraid me for over-confidence, wrongfully I thought. There was no way of explaining to him that there were certain things of which I would, without any reason, suddenly become assured. For instance, as the women's struggle wore on and Essay pinned me to the front desk of the house after returning from school, I often sat there and studied without feeling that I was missing anything of importance. When he returned, looked at me with a glint of mockery in his eye and asked how the women's war was getting on without me, I often replied without thinking,

'Oh, nothing is happening right now. Nothing will happen for the next two days.'

I never knew just why I had said that, but I was more often proved right than wrong. I had a feeling that this used to irritate him immensely.

After a week-end closing assembly at school, I went upstairs to say good-bye to Daodu and Beere as I was to leave for Ibadan the following day. Formerly, the assembly alternated between two anthems as the final song – one was the Egba National Anthem, the other was a kind of 'God Save the King', the king being the Alake of course, not the other one on the other side of the ocean. For some weeks now, the latter anthem had been abandoned. As we trooped out of the hall however, I heard it being rendered unofficially by several independent groups. For a moment I thought that it was an act of defiance against Daodu, then I heard the words. A different verse had been substituted for the former words of salutation and loyalty:

> Kabiyesi, oba on'ike
> Ademola k'eran
> Omo eran j'ogun ila
> Omo ote lo l'obe
> Kabiyesi, baba eran
> Kabiyesi o
> Kabiyesi oba iwin
> Kabiyesi o.*

Poor Alake, I thought, his rout was really complete!

When I came upstairs, Beere was at the telephone, one of the three or four telephones in the whole of Abeokuta. Her tone was angry, I had never seen her so furious with anyone.

'Let me tell you, Mr District Officer, we are not impressed. We are by no means impressed – no, not surprised either. I knew it was coming and when I heard it on the radio all I could think was, just like them, just like the white race. You had to drop it on Japan, didn't you? Why didn't you drop it on Germany? Tell me that. Answer my question honestly if you can – why not Germany?'

There was a pause while she listened to what the other speaker had to reply.

She laughed – a dry, bitter sound. 'I give you credit for intelligence, but not for honesty. That was a merely clever answer, it was not honest. You know bloody well why. Because Germany is a white race, the Germans are your kinsmen while the Japanese are just a dirty yellow people. Yes, that *is* right, that is the truth, don't deny it! You dropped that inhuman weapon on human beings, on densely populated cities. . . .'

Her face became more and more agitated as she listened, then broke in

---

* Hail, king of hunchbacks
  Ademola has carried trouble
  Son of a beast who inherits okro
  Child of intrigue who takes the soup-pot
  Hail, father of beasts
  Hail, king of wood daemons.

again, 'Yes, you know damned well what you should have done if you sincerely desired their surrender. You could have dropped it on one of their mountains, even in the sea, anywhere they could see what would happen if they persisted in the war, but you chose instead to drop it on peopled cities. I know you, the white mentality: Japanese, Chinese, Africans, we are all subhuman. You would drop an atom bomb on Abeokuta or any of the colonies if it suited you!'

This time I heard the laughter of the other speaker over the ear-piece. He spoke for a long time while I watched the various changes of expression on Mrs Kuti's face. It relaxed, smiled, then became taut, even grim again as she resumed speaking.

'No, I did not ring you up for that, I just wanted to pass a message to the so-called Allies, and you were their nearest representative. But now, since you bring the matter up, let me tell you this. Your king – this one here, I mean . . . no, don't interrupt me, I have a right to say he is yours because you saved his head this time. As far as we women are concerned, he is already gone. But listen to me, there really isn't much to discuss. I have sent you our list of complaints. He has gone back on every word, every promise and agreement which he signed before we decided not to press on for his abdication. Well, just tell him from me, that if he hasn't learnt his lesson from Hitler . . . comparison or not, never mind that now . . . just tell him he should take his lesson from Hitler. As for you, that is, as for the Colonial Government, better get your atomic bomb ready because the next time round, he is going. Tell them Beere said so, his days are numbered. He is GOING!'

I saw her listen some moments longer, shrug and simply add, 'Well, I've warned you. Good-bye,' and she replaced the phone.

She turned to me and stared for a long moment. 'Yes, I remember you are leaving us for Government College. Wait here, I have something for you.'

She disappeared into the bedroom, returned with a small, flat parcel – it looked like a shirt but I never got to see what it was because I had to correct her at once.

'I am not leaving yet. I am only going for an interview. Schools don't start a new year until January.'

She thought briefly. 'Of course. How could I have made such a mistake? In that case I can't give you this yet.' And she replaced the shirt on the dining table.

'Suppose I don't get selected after all?' I asked.

Smiling, she pretended to give that also some thought. 'Hm, that would

215

be a difficulty. I've been keeping this for your departure. Well, let's see . . . all right, let's begin from the beginning. How long will you be away for this interview?'

'Three days.'

She fished out a sixpence. 'That's for you to buy something with. Now, suppose you are admitted . . . wait, aren't you also supposed to win a scholarship?'

I nodded, and she resumed. 'Good. If you gain admission but no scholarship I shall give you the shirt. Right? Now, if you win a scholarship, guess what.'

'A pair of shoes,' I replied promptly.

She exclaimed, 'What!' and then remembered and laughed. 'Oh yes, I remember now. All right, a pair of shoes.'

One day I had tackled our parents over the fact that we were never bought shoes. It was particularly galling at Harvest, Christmas and New Year when special outfits were made, to find that shoes were one item most resolutely omitted in the HM household. This I could not understand, since both parents wore shoes and slippers as a matter of course. I picked the occasion of a festive meal-time when the dining hall was full – Tinu, Femi and I, the various cousins and even some of the neighbouring children. 'Why,' I asked loudly, but of no one in particular, 'does no one ever buy us shoes?'

Essay blinked, turned on his deaf ear while Wild Christian simply declared:

'Children do not wear shoes.'

I felt the eyes of both on me, expectant, for some time afterwards but I said nothing further. Eventually, Essay said,

'Wole, don't you even want to know why children do not wear shoes?' I shook my head. 'No,' knowing full well that he must have thought up a good answer to be so persistent. I much preferred the grounds which Wild Christian had carelessly selected and only awaited my opportunity.

The moment came not long after, at the Kuti residence, on a Sunday where we had gone visiting. Wild Christian was sitting to lunch with Daodu and Beere while, at a table across from them Tinu and I sat with our cousins who had just returned from church and were still variously attired in jackets, long dress, ties, shoes and socks. I picked a moment of silence in the brisk conversation – which was difficult, because Daodu was an incessant conversationalist – and said loudly,

'Mama, I thought you said that children do not wear shoes?' and continued eating.

Conversation died for some moments. Then Daodu threw back his head, slapped his thigh and let out the most deafening roar of laughter the corridor had ever heard. He laughed and wiped his eyes, spluttered, took a sip of water and continued chuckling sporadically for a long time after. Mrs Kuti simply smiled and said,

'Eniola, owo ba e l'ote yi.'* She then added, to me, 'Wole, any time you find a pair of shoes you like, come and tell me. I shall give you the money for it.'

Koye immediately offered, 'I have some which I have outgrown. I'll take him to my room after lunch and we'll see if any of them fits him.'

Dolupo offered to take Tinu along. I looked at Wild Christian. The smile on her face looked more like a trapped scowl but I was past caring at that moment. In any case, even if we returned home with bags bulging with shoes, I knew that we would never wear them. Essay was inflexible on that score – to him, shoes on the feet of children was the ultimate gesture in the spoiling of the young. The children of relations and acquaintances who had been packed off to the Headmaster's house for 'training' discovered that, to their intense unhappiness. Their shoes gathered mould in their boxes, and eventually they outgrew them. In his school, a new pupil who had transferred from Lagos turned up one day in a pair of canvas shoes. He was not merely suspended, his real parents had to travel from Lagos and plead for the entire day before he was taken back.

Mrs Kuti delighted in small conspiracies; she understood very well what I meant and so we went into the strategies of the operation. Clearly, the shoes could only be worn during term at Government College; they would have to remain there during vacations and would never be produced at home. And of course I had to ensure that they were kept out of sight in Ibadan whenever my parents came to visit me – at least at the beginning. She was confident that it would no longer matter once I became a senior boy.

That problem out of the way, I asked her why she had been angry about the bombing of the Japanese. Were they not Hitler's friends?

'The white man is a racist,' she said. 'You know your history of the slave trade, well, to him the black man is only a beast of burden, a work-donkey. As for Asians – and that includes the Indians, Japanese, Chinese and so on, they are only a small grade above us. So, dropping that terrible weapon, experimenting with such a horrifying thing on human beings – as long as they are not white – is for them the same as experimenting on cattle.'

* Eniola, you have really caught it this time.

Daodu returned from the office during the conversation, deposited some files on a shelf and, catching the trend of the animated lecture, came over and poured himself some tea, nodding at several of Mrs Kuti's points. He stabbed the air in my direction:

'I would never send Koye or any of his brothers to a school run by white men. But you must understand this, it is not merely because they are white, it is also because they are colonizers. They try to destroy character in our boys . . . remember what I told you, last year when you were going off for your first interview?'

'Yes, Uncle.'

'Right. Was I right or not?'

'But I told you, Uncle, the school was on holidays, it was empty. All we did was sit exams.'

He turned to Beere. 'Do you know what I found out? Those teachers don't allow pockets in their shorts!'

Beere was clearly startled. 'Is that true?' she asked me.

I confirmed it.

'Now, why do you think they do that? Why on earth should a young man not have pockets in his shorts? You know,' he shook his head in a really worried manner, 'the white man is a strange creature. In his country, in his own schools – and remember, I visited a number of public schools during our conference – Eton, Harrow etc. – well, their boarders wear suits, all with pockets. From the most junior form. And the question I ask myself is this – why should one of them come here as a principal and forbid pockets in the shorts of his black schoolboys, WHY!'

I gave it some thought. Something which I had remarked about the pair of them – Daodu especially, struck me all over again. With them, I never needed to ask so many questions. They were always ready to talk to me – or indeed to any willing child – as they would to their fellow adults. Daodu would often collar me, even if I was quietly reading in the parlour or dining-room and ask me if I had heard some recent item of news from Lagos or elsewhere, and ask my opinion. It could be labour unrest, the formation of an association, some projected alliances as the war progressed, a new scientific invention . . . if I had not yet encountered the item of news he would shake his head reprovingly.

'You must take an interest! Don't just stick your nose in that dead book you are reading. Don't you see, if Mussolini could undermine the independence of Abyssinia, what chance has the new National Council of Nigeria and the Cameroons got with their demand for some measure of self-government? These people who have managed to defeat Mussolini, is

it likely that they will ever surrender what they already have? What do you think of Winston Churchill?'

I blurted out on that occasion, 'Actually, you remind me very much of him.'

I had not really considered it before but a strong resemblance did strike me at that moment, very forcefully. He stopped in his stride, folded his arms across his chest and tucked his hands under his armpits as if he was hugging himself. I could see the inside of his head working out all the elements which must have combined to make me give such a forceful declaration.

'Amazing, amazing. I have always found children's powers of observation remarkable. Now you have to tell me *why* you hold such an opinion. No, not right now. But you must remind me. I want every single detail of what has given you that opinion.'

It was that persistent, bulldog expression on his face again as he asked – why? Why would a white principal forbid pockets in the shorts of the GC boys? I had some ideas on the matter but first I had some good news to give him:

'We learnt that Powell will be leaving shortly. He's retiring. The new principal may let us have pockets.'

Daodu turned to his wife and explained, 'Powell is the present principal. A very keen Boy Scout. A-ha! Now that is an even greater indictment. A boy scout needs as many pockets as he can use. Have you ever been a boy scout?'

'Well, I was a cub at St Peter's. We had a teacher who was a keen scoutmaster. His name was Activity.'

They both laughed. I added, 'But he left, and no one else took his place.'

Daodu nodded approvingly. 'Now scouting also develops character. It would be interesting to see if this scouting enthusiast, who does not provide pockets for his schoolboys, at least encourages scouting in his school.'

I was able to fulfil his worst fears – GCI had no scouting programme. At my previous interview, I had marked down Scouting in that section of our questionnaire which required us to state our hobbies. One of the white faces who sat on the panel had smiled and regretted that there was no scouting in the school. When I passed this information to Daodu, he raised his arms in genuine concern, looking at me with something akin to commiseration.

'See? Do you see now? This Powell, Mr V. P. V. . . . no, what are those peculiar initials of his again?'

'V.B.V.P.'

'That's right, V. B. V. Powell . . .' He shook his head. 'Heaven knows what those letters stand for . . .'

'Very Bad Very Poor,' I briskly announced, and he and Beere chuckled loud and long. I told them that one of the candidates who already had a brother in the school had informed us of that secret interpretation of Powell's initials.

'A fair enough judgement,' Daodu commented. 'He is always posing at the head of the national scout jamborees with his scout uniform stuck all over with labels and decorations. So, there we have the keen scoutmaster, yet he does not encourage scouting in his school.' He pursued his lips and looked me up and down as if I was walking into some mortal danger. Even Beere seemed to be equally infected by the sudden pessimistic outlook on my future. She commented:

'Double standards of course. It's just what I was telling that District Officer before you came in – dropping the atom bomb over Hiroshima but not over white Germany. There is a racist in every white man.'

Reverend Kuti sighed. His countenance was really doleful and I began to wonder if I had not made a mistake in wanting to go to Government College. Then he brightened up somewhat, asking, 'You are now what? How old, how old?'

'Eleven,' I replied.

'Mm . . . well, that's not too bad. You'll be eleven and a half when you join them in January. And you've had two years as a Grammarian . . . that ought to have done it, I think. Don't you think so?' Turning to Beere for confirmation.

'Oh yes, yes,' she assured him. 'Not forgetting the fact that he's been brought up by Ayo and Eniola. I think he'll be able to cope with them over there.'

Daodu nodded. He was visibly cheering up, and he gave a defiant snort. 'Yes, we'll see. An ex-public schoolmaster who sews up his students' pockets and makes them say Sir-Sir-Sir, like slaves. A scoutmaster who discourages scouting. And no caning either – at most maybe two or three instances in any year – oh yes, so I've discovered. Mostly ceremonial caning – I doubt if any pupil from that school has ever taken home a single scar on his back! How on earth do they hope to train our boys properly that way? Oh . . . I nearly forgot – no shoes.'

It was my turn to be startled. 'Are you sure, Uncle?'

Firmly, he repeated, pressing his lips, 'No shoes. Since your first interview I have become very interested in that school. They have very strange ideas of character building. No shoes. Except for the senior prefects – they are allowed to wear tennis shoes. Or sandals. Otherwise, No pockets, No shoes . . . aha, there is yet another one, no underpants. Why it should be a school policy I don't know. As long as the uniform is clean and neat, I fail to understand why the housemasters should concern themselves with making sure that the boys wear no underpants. Especially the bigger boys . . .'

I was no longer paying attention. My eyes had swivelled slowly to encounter Beere's who was grinning with her eyebrows raised in mock distress. The sight was so comical that I burst out laughing and she joined in, leaving Daodu glancing from one to the other, frowning in his attempt to recollect what he had said that was so funny. Tilting her voice in sympathy Beere queried,

'No shoes?'

'No shoes,' I sighed, feeling the oppressive weight of my years. It was time to commence the mental shifts for admittance to yet another irrational world of adults and their discipline.

ÌSARÀ

Author's Note

I have borrowed *Ìsarà*'s subtitle from John Mortimer's play *A Voyage Round My Father*. The expression captures in essence what I have tried to do with the contents of a tin box which I opened some four years ago, that is, about two years after *Aké* was written. The completion of that childhood biography, rather than assuage a curiosity about a vanishing period of one's existence, only fuelled it, fragments of an incomplete memory returning to haunt one again and again in the personae of representative protagonists of such a period. Of course my own case may have been especially acute; I was in political exile when 'Essay' died. All plans to return home for the funeral were abruptly cancelled when I received a message from the 'Wild Christian' urging me to return home indeed if I wished to bury her with her lifelong partner. I recorded a message, which was played at the funeral, and stayed put in an indifferent clime.

Years later, I opened the metallic box, scraped off the cockroach eggs, and browsed through a handful of letters, old journals with marked pages and annotations, notebook jottings, tax and other levy receipts, minutes of meetings and school reports, programme notes of special events, and so on. A tantalising experience, eavesdropping on this very special class of teachers of our colonial period; inevitably I would become drawn to attempting to flesh out these glimpses on a very different level of awareness and empathy from that of *Aké*.

I have not only taken liberties with chronology, I have deliberately ruptured it. After all, the period covered here actively is no more than fifteen years, and its significance for me is that it represents the period when a pattern of their lives was set – for better for worse – under the compelling impact of the major events in their times, both local and global, the uneasy love-hate relationship with the colonial presence, and its own ambiguous attitudes to the Western-educated elite of the Nigerian protectorate.

Life, it would appear, was lived robustly, but was marked also by an intense quest for a place in the new order, and one of a far more soul-searching dimension than the generation they spawned would later undertake. Their options were excruciatingly limited. A comparison between this aspect of their time and their offsprings', when coupled with the inversely proportionate weight of extended family demands and expectations, assumes quite a heroic dimension.

Ìsarà then is simply a tribute to 'Essay' and his friends and times. My decision not to continue with real names, as in *Aké*, except in a few cases, is to eliminate any pretence to factual accuracy in this attempted reconstruction of their times, thoughts, and feelings. Like most voyages, this one has not followed the itinerary I so confidently mapped out for it; indeed it proved an almost impossible journey which came close to being abandoned more than once. 'Ilesa' is of course not simply one such institution nor Ìsarà one such community. I hope the surviving 'ex-Ilés' all over the nation will understand this compulsion to acknowledge in some form, and however tenuously, their seminal role in the development of present-day Nigerian minds, and will overlook the obvious lapses and areas of dissatisfaction.

W. S.
November 1988

I

EX-ILÉ

Ashtabula! Soditan eased out the envelope with foreign stamps, addressed in a bold, sweeping cursive. It was already slit open, and as he released the neatly folded sheets, his spare frame responded to the emerging treat and he visibly relaxed. The luxury of reading and re-reading his private correspondence was one in which he indulged whenever possible in the privacy of Ìsarà, especially when he returned there out of season. Season was New Year, Harvest, or Easter; or whenever the ex-Ilés agreed to meet in the hometown for a special occasion, usually a wedding, a grand funeral, or a house-warming for one of The Circle who had finally 'returned to sender.' This meant more than a simple homecoming; it was homecoming in a manner (and on a scale) that finally fulfilled the hopes and prayers, the nursed dreams and burdensome aspirations, of that close community from which they were dispersed to nearly every region of the country. Success, and its embodiment on their natal soil, preferably in the form of a modest but 'modern' house, was a 'return to sender.'

In a seasonal re-entry one was never alone; Ado, Ibadan, Jos, Ede, Benin – all places of exile descended on the small community, retailing accounts of the intervening months, swapping anecdotes, doctoring failures, and decking out successes. Off-season visits were peaceful; there were hours of quiet intimacy with Mariam, his mother, and Pa Soditan, his father. Hours to pick his way between recumbent sheep and sunken waterpots which lined the shadowy passages, ducking beneath low trestles from which indigo-dyed cloths would drip on busier days; to acknowledge the few greetings without their usual accompanying impositions, the demands and enquiries. It was as if the town had evolved a tacit understanding. No one bothered 'Tisa,' or *omo* Josiah, with the casual request for monetary help, a letter of introduction for a job-seeker, assistance with admission to a school – all this was somehow restricted to the seasonal visits. Of course most of the inhabitants were out on their farms, living in makeshift homes for weeks, even months, at a time, or had travelled to Lagos, Ibadan, and Kano farther north on trading forays. No matter, Ìsarà out of season was without the usual incursions on his presence, peaceful, and somewhat lonely, steeped in an unshakable languor which spread even over the marketplace. The Oba's palace, despite the lounging figures of the royal retinue in the verandah and the rare appearance of a brace of chiefs in robes and shawl, appeared curiously untenanted. The few public centres, such as the clinic, tax office, and Native Authority court, exuded a mere symbolic air, languishing for lack of patronage. The gates to the *iledi* would creak open only once or twice; a priest would emerge, shut the gate carefully behind him, and shuffle homewards with eyes cast to the ground, greeted by and greeting none, his silence inviolate as the heart of divination. Only the primary school, St James's where Akinyode himself began his journey to adulthood, seemed to contest the general lethargy, yet even here the teachers merely led in muted voices their pupils' rote responses, no different from the small clumps of pupils in the open-air Koranic school on the other side of the market from the palace – bored voices, vacant stares, stirring to life only when the *mallam*'s sporadic whip beat a slow tattoo on their docile heads. Nothing really stirred, not the sheep with huge pregnancies hugging the shadows of red mud walls. The solitary hawker made the rounds of the few tenanted passages, her hawking cries more dirged than full-throated, no rousing accent to entice the indifferent. Built into the hillsides of red laterite, Ìsarà at such periods was neither hostile nor welcoming; it was simply indifferent, the stone shrapnels of its walls and rust of corrugated roofs belying the lushness of the valley below, which wove a moist sash round the town on nearly every side. Why, Akinyode sometimes wondered, had his ancestors chosen to build on such inclement soil? Was it a need for safety in those earlier, uncertain times? Yet the town looked exposed to any determined incursion. The wooded valleys were perfect hiding places for an enemy; he could lay indefinite siege to these bird-cages tucked precariously against the naked sides and ridges of a nature cantilevered hill.

One did not notice these features when the town came to life in season. Then Ìsarà metamorphosed into a giddy butterfly, and even the harsh-grained walls turned soft and coquettish, overwhelmed by new voices, incessant taps on open doors and the rattle of latches, yells of children and the hum of the lone corn mill. The narrow streets broadened overnight to receive their sons and daughters, heedless of the constant cloud of dust that swiftly coloured their skin, finery, and hair a brilliant red. But that was not now, and the schoolteacher did not mind their absence. The distant clang of the blacksmith's anvil was truly music to his ears, and his letters kept him company. Contentedly he communed with distant friends while he waited to be summoned for the final rites of the event that brought him unseasonally into town – the 'outing' of the first motor lorry to be owned by an indigene of Ìsarà. The pioneer was his father's friend Node, sadly paralysed – by the evil machinations of a treacherous friend, as all Ìsarà knew, but that matter had long been settled, the culprit (or suspect, the teacher persisted in saying) ostracised. It was the least he could do, to be present, since he had himself to blame or praise for bringing the monumental project to fruition. His fellow ex-Ilés would be here as well if Node were of their generation, but Node was a stay-at-home successful farmer of his father's age, illiterate but shrewd. Negotiations had begun before his illness and he had relied on the schoolteacher's contacts with the world of forms and legal mazes. The lorry would be used to transport timber – for that he also required a special licence. This was one point on which Akinyode had failed to move him – Node would have nothing to do with passengers. Nor did that parsimonious mind make the mistake of launching his vehicle 'in season.' He knew what this would have meant – feasting the entire Ìsarà, streams of mendicant drummers and praise-singers, and even uninvited out-of-town well-wishers come to celebrate (and squander) his good fortune. No, a small ceremony it had to be, *etutu* rituals performed by Jagun, a Christian blessing by Pa Josiah, and a Koranic reading by the imam. The day would be rounded off by a modest feast – just for Node's household and Jagun's and Soditan's families, and of course those whom he had invited to officiate and launch the vehicle into a career of luck and profit.

Even as the schoolteacher settled more snugly into his father's fibre-cane chair, a crude guttural bleat pierced the afternoon haze, and Akinyode, irritated, glanced angrily through the window in the direction of Node's compound. Again the bleat was repeated, if anything reinforced with a desperate vigour, shattering the accustomed peace of an unseasonal day. Node would not skimp on the girth and soundness of the sacrificial ram, the teacher knew, so it was certain that this bleat, quite unlike the perfunctory sounds that emerged from the native quadrupeds of Ìsarà, could only be that of the doomed animal. The schoolteacher chuckled to himself – all right, I give you till dawn tomorrow; then Node will ride on your back to Ashtabula!

It had taken quite a while before the schoolteacher brought himself to accept the word as yet another place-name. Like Ìsarà. Or Kaura Namoda. That had made him pause. What would the natives of Ashtabula think of that one? Or Olomitutu? How did it sound in their ears? Even so, as a name for white people – Ashtabula? This hand from beyond the seas had stretched the bounds of place-naming beyond easy acceptance. What spirits had presided over the naming ceremonies of such a place? A settlement was no different from a child; you recognised its essence in the name. That was the problem – there was nothing remotely European about the name Ashtabula! Or were Americans now far removed from white stock and breeding? And Wade Cudeback – that name was also striking – rough, rugged, no doubt a disciplinarian of the old school. His handwriting did its best to extend Ashtabula beyond plain images of a small provincial town – *90 degrees Fahr., whereas our average for this date is merely 55 degrees*. That reminded Akinyode that he should take the readings of the school thermometer and barometer and record them as soon as he returned to Abeokuta. The rain gauge was, like the school, on pre-harmattan vacation; there would be not one inch to record for another three months, possibly four. No moisture but the morning dew.

Cudeback used a thick nib, he noted. And the notepaper? He held it to his nose – yes, the faint smell was not too dissimilar from that of his favoured Quink ink. There were suggestions also of pinewood, river moss, possibly gum arabica. With this last, however, he suspected that he had merely foisted that much-remarked smell from his own desk in Aké onto a stranger's remote corner of the world. It was the man's handwriting that evoked such fancies. Each exclamation mark was like the housepost of the *ogboni* shrine, or a Corinthian column in the Illustrated Bible (Authorized Version). His *I* had generous loops both up and down, resulting in a coracle shape, mildly unbalanced by a wave, akin to a fat cowrie, or a curled-up millipede. Each *D* was consistently like the cauliflower ear of Osibo, the pharmacist, while the *W* was just like an *abetiaja*,* or the starched, bristling headgear of the Reverend Sisters from Oke Padi hospital. And so it went on: The lower-case *y* had its downward tail reversed and looped so far upwards that it became a hangman's noose, while an ultimate *t*, contrasted with the ordinariness of his *t* at the start of a word, was slashed downwards with a vicious, decapitating stroke which, extended far below the base of the letter, turned it into an amputee, a cheerful acrobat dancing on its one leg, amusing the rest of its alphabetic audience with that near-magical turn of the *iguniko* as it shoots up skywards on one stilt.

The teacher absolved himself of envy. It was a different calligraphy from his, that was all, not necessarily a better one. It needed no bias at all to see that his own handwriting was more disciplined, more consistent. There were some self-indulgent quirks in Cudeback's penmanship; perhaps it

* A Yoruba dress-cap.

had to do with the sometimes erratic, sometimes magical scenes he described as he proceeded through the vast continent of America on his restless vacations.

There was this also about the man's narrative: a bias? No, perhaps a slant, an unintended flavouring, maybe no more than the Ashtabulan essence of the man himself, which brought the schoolteacher down to the favourite gibe of the ex-Ilés at themselves: 'You can take an Ìsaràman out of Ìsarà, but you cannot take Ìsarà out of an Ìsaràman.' Wherever his pen pal went, all through *the four provinces of Canada and six states of the United States, a scintillating 3,500-mile trip in my jallopie*, it seemed as if this traveller was never really out of Ashtabula. How this feat was wrought, Akinyode could not quite decide, but it seemed Wade Cudeback always humped Ashtabula with him in his rucksack. . . . *The Thousand Islands Bridge, the Chateau de Ramezay, a bell which weighed 24,780 pounds and is probably the largest bell in America, the lowlands and sandstone landscapes. St Joseph's shrines where many come to be cured, a three-mile walled city, upstream tides of the Petitcodiac River* . . . Petticodiac! And yes, this was the fact that had briefly slipped his mind. The Indians were the real owners of the American continent, and it explained everything, even the name Ashtabula. Little wonder their spirits still roamed the continent at will: Ashtabula was everywhere. Perhaps even in the name Cudeback? No matter, Akinyode settled for a kindred spirit. A teacher too, no wonder at all. Did he suffer from this compulsion to instruct? Mr Cudeback and his single-spaced seven-page letter filled with rare scenic details would provide a departure in next year's geography classes. Or general knowledge. A passionate traveller, his friend; even as he narrated his adventures of the summer of thirty-seven, he was already planning an excursion for the following year, singing his signature tune:

> I never see a map but I'm away
> On all the errands that I long to do
> Up all the rivers that are painted blue
> And all the ranges that are painted gray . . .

Would they ever meet? And where? Ìsarà or Ashtabula? What had moved the man to send a letter to the *Gazette*? And he in turn, in far-off Ìsarà, had been moved to write – and post (a very different step!) – a reply. Then commenced the exchange of letters, sometimes personal, sometimes, as in the case of these 'tales of adventure,' circulated among others. Even as he read his letters, Akinyode would begin to compose his reply, mostly laudatory, but with the occasional reprimand. *Sir, how could you devote so many lines to 'the famous Montmorency Falls,' picturesque and charming though they may be, yet they are but a norm of nature, while the Magnetic Mountain, which deserves to be the Eighth Wonder of the World, is given such scant attention. Perhaps, my dear Mr Cudeback, such sights are commonplace in Ashtabula (and environs), yet I must tell you that in Ìsarà there are no such wonders seen. I must therefore request that you devote an entire letter to describing again this phenomenon of nature which, I assure you, I shall be hard put to convince my pupils thereof, even as my own circle to whom I read this portion of your letter have expressed the greatest scepticism, suggesting that this is twin-fantasy to the tales of* A Thousand and One Nights *or the* Adventures of Sindbad the Sailor.

Was that last too long a sentence? He would review it later, but first to re-read the passage that had so much whetted his appetite, fired his imagination, and provoked his protest. *From Moncton we drove to Magnetic Hill. To get the thrill of this phenomenon I drove my car down the hill to a certain spot at the foot, shut off the motor, put the gears in neutral, released the brakes, and my car started slowly backing up the hill, gaining speed as it ascended. Thus my car backed up the hill without power!* Nothing more? Tucked within a seven-page letter, tightly spaced? And there was the issue of the quotation marks – what did they signify? Was Cudeback interjecting the experience of some other traveller? Apart from the breathtaking impossibility of this eerie power, there were far too many other questions unanswered. Under no scale of values, even for a society with scientific explanations for every freak of nature, could such a phenomenon be worth less than three exclamation marks! This portion being for circulation to others, it was typed, so perhaps one should not judge Cudeback too hastily. If it had been handwritten, that exclamation mark would perhaps have revealed more of the traveller's state of mind by its girth, by the agitated impression left by Cudeback's favoured nib.

The letter was lavishly interlaced with snippets of verses – were they his own composition? The references to plants and flowers received Akinyode's neat question marks on the margin, betraying none of his inner excitement, for the schoolteacher was a nature fiend. For instance, were his water lilies in Ashtabula the same species as those in Ìsarà's lush vegetation?

> The water lilies beckon in the cove
> I snatch just one, to breathe its heady spice
> For we must on, beyond the point, to find

A wooded shore all virgin in its solitude
And skirt the hoary rock that turns around . . .

Even the rocky parsonage at Abeokuta had its share of water lilies. As for
Ìsarà, the deepened, walled-in section of the stream where every
household fetched its water was filled with ferns and lilies, many of them
species unknown in the much-tended gardens of the parsonage. And what
a strange man, this Cudeback. *It seems to me that you also are smitten by the
travel bug* – that was surely an understatement to bring the year to a close.
Was it by chance he brought all Cudeback's letters to Ìsarà to read and re-
read even when he had yet no intention of replying? *Take the adventure,
heed the call now, ere the irrevocable moment passes. 'Tis but the banging of the
door behind you, a blithesome step forward, and you are out of the old life into
the new.* Again his friend had placed that in quotation marks – it was
frustrating. Were they his words, something he had written before to
others? He made a note to demand the source and, if possible, the book
from which it had been quoted.

Ashtabula was a private world, one which he kept secure even from the
close circle of the ex-Ilés. From time to time he would 'lend' them a portion
of that world, a portion too immense to keep within Ìsarà. The Magnetic
Mountain was one – no one could be expected to guard such a revelation
selfishly beneath his pillow. And to Sipe, the other adventurer, the
would-be merchant prince, he passed on tidbits that could guide his
constant search for new commercial chances. Like the paper mill in
Dalhousie, yes, that was something in which he could, as teacher, not now
as the business tycoon into which Sipe would convert him, devote his
energies and even his school and personal resources. Books. This was
where books began, at least the material which made them books, not the
mere facts and fancies of nature and experience, of reality and imagination.
His neat hand copied the description, eyes aglow with the prospect of a
paper mill in his hometown of Ìsarà. Timber was everywhere. The
'Gbororbe stream would be damned – he knew the very spot, just where a
tiny waterfall cascaded twenty feet down deep-pocketed red-ochre
laterite. . . . *Wood supply held nearby, sent to the mill, cut in two-foot lengths,
these forced thru crushes by pressure broadside against the face of the wood by
rapidly revolving stones. Water is added during the process to reduce the heat
created by the friction, and to see the material after the log has been crushed, one
would think that hot water had been added, but our guide plainly told us the
steam was caused by the friction. The pulp thus made is passed thru screens
which remove the coarse particles and then run on rotary screens to allow the*

water to be drawn off by means of a vacuum suction. Near the end of the process it passes over several rollers for further drying of the pulp and is then rolled, weighed, and bound for shipping. Akinyode nodded his approval. So simple. What, after all, was the value of all the training at St Simeon's, whose constant sermon was self-reliance? If they could not now harness their environment to the end of such a basic product, why were they Simeonites? Was all the material needed for that potential industry not already in place in Ìsarà, the stagnant backwater that flung its sons far inland to St Simeon's Teacher Training Seminary at Ilesa? Another backwater, Ilesa; its sole claim to note was the seminary itself and the young elites it trained.

But now Akinyode re-examined their status – were they really frogs in such inert, anonymous ponds? These places also had their history. The Fulani wars raged through their earth, razing and dividing the old Kingdom of Oyo, pitting warlord against warlord; their petty calculations, greed, ambition, alliances of convenience, the ravages of slavers and fanatic hordes . . . and Ìsarà, harassing and harassed in turn by Egba, Ijaiye, sometimes Ibadan, but never subdued. How else did the town obtain its praise-name, Afotamodi – they whose city ramparts are raised on ammunition? He conceded it – the reminiscences of a Wade Cudeback, strolling through his own history and others', did provoke these envious thoughts. Why, even Mr Cudeback motoring into a place called Salem – strange, the name should be a prerogative of the Bible – even Cudeback had found, faithfully preserved, the famous Witches' House. If there was one commodity Ìsarà had no shortage of, it was witches! His own grandfather's name translated as 'surrounded by sorcerers.' So where was Ìsarà's Witches' or Sorcerers' House? Was it by any chance the *iledi*?

That could be, come to think of it, an equivalent of sorts. Akinyode felt slightly relieved, then moved to other paths and monuments of history trodden and touched by his wandering friend. *We saw the Plains of Abraham famed for the battle in 1759 between Wolfe and Montcalm which ended in the defeat of Montcalm and the fall of Quebec. Later we saw Montcalm's house, one of the oldest houses in the city, where he is supposed to have been taken after the battle and which is now used for a souvenir store.* Well, a mere 1759? Ijaiye, Kiriji, Basorun Gaha, those belligerent Aare ona Kakanfo, and Okenla, Lisabi . . . the worthy Dr Johnson had chronicled their era, and many of these wars were even more recent. The aged survivors – and some not so ancient – would sometimes recount their own participation, bringing the scenes of courage and terror to life. So where were the trails, the spots, the landmarks? Where could he take his senior pupils – assuming he could persuade the mission to such a bold extension of the history classroom? And yet why not? It was the kind of excursion that was endorsed in principle by *The Nigerian Teacher* – so where could he take even a handful of pupils on such an exercise? Then sit them down to write the story of their passage among the ghosts of their own history. He would pick out the best essay and send it off to Wade Cudeback – yes, here is something in return for your Magnetic Mountains and Reversing Falls and the marathon runner Paul Revere. The thought depressed him: Where did the seminarian tutors of St Simeon's ever take him? Yet in his youth had he not often traversed those grounds, those battle-contested grounds of Yoruba kingdoms? From Ìsarà to Ilesa, at least four times a year – twice only as he grew older and became inured to a prolonged exile – passing through Saki, Iseyin, and the ancient city of Oyo, walking, cycling, entombed in a dust-filled rickety transport. Through the years of training, were the seminarians ever taught to look? Had his youth truly vanished through so much history without even knowing that one had to *look*!

Still, there was more than enough time now to make up for lost time. He had made his tentative beginning with his adventurous return to Iseyin, so different from his 'unseeing' passages through that hilly town of weavers during his seminarian days. And the musical pageant planned to celebrate the centenary of the first Christian mission in Egbaland – that was indeed part of the process – what better way could one find to recall history? Travelling would unearth more material. Now the roads were better, one could even learn to drive. Maybe acquire a 'jallopie' like Wade Cudeback. The teacher gave a derisive laugh – when? On his schoolteacher's salary? Such ambition! Best to limit such plans to what he could accomplish on his new Raleigh bicycle. And of course the railway. Ah yes, the railway. Muted echoes of his raucous first encounter with the railway circled his skull in the silent afternoon, punctuated by the motto he had adopted, before leaving home, as his guiding homily. Together with the railway song all children knew by heart, even those who had never seen the powerful monster, it began once again to play a contrapuntal rhythm to the turns of the carriage wheels – *He has no future . . . who fails to affect his present . . . who fails to affect his present . . . who fails to affect his present . . . Mo ti gun'ke, mo ti so . . . mo ti gun'ke mo ti so . . . who fails to affect his present . . . faka fiki faka fi . . . who fails to affect his future . . . oke ti alajapa ko le gun . . . mo ti gun . . . mo ti so . . . faka fiki faka fi . . . who fails to affect his present* – and he found that he was afraid. Have I climbed that hill? Is my pace like the tortoise of the song? Have I climbed? Would I slip? *Faka fiki faka fii . . .*

It had not made much sense at the time, but this first-ever departure, bound for enrollment at the seminary in Ilesa, simply had to be done by railway. It was both curiosity and adventure. The motor vehicle was already commonplace; one saw the lorries at least every other day, and the occasional sedan when an important visitor came into town. But the railway was mere legend to many like him in Ìsarà; it had chosen most cruelly to bypass all of Ijebu area, snake through Ifo and Abeokuta to Ibadan and the north. So to Abeokuta he half-trekked with his companion, Damian, and joined a passenger lorry in Owode – all for the lure of a ride on rails between Abeokuta, Ibadan, and Ede. There would be no choice after that but to tramp the distance between Ede and Iwo, mostly on footpaths, with his earthly possessions – including parting gifts – carried in turn by him and his not-much-older companion, who was also his guide and protector. More bush paths led to Oyo, but the path would sometimes broaden, revealing tracks of an intrepid lorry – passenger, goods, or timber. Between Oyo and Iseyin, motorisation was routine. Thereafter, it would be desultory, with Iseyin to Shaki most likely a measured dialogue with their feet. The intervening distance to Ilesa was also on foot, although his father had been assured that there were donkeys there for hire, and possibly bicycles and hammock bearers. They would both ride the hired bicycle to Ilesa; then Damian would stay overnight and return it to its place of hire the following day, leaving Yode alone in school.

Damian, the Edo boy, had somehow lost his way into Ìsarà and stayed on, hoping to learn the trade of printing by annexing himself to Josiah. His reasoning hinged on the obvious: Josiah was a Christian and a church elder. The Christians used books. Bought books. They even owned bookshops. Books were the result of printing. Proven: Sooner or later Josiah would lead him to the path of his printing trade. In the meantime, he farmed with him and looked after his house. Damian had a dark history, so Yode eyed him from time to time, wondering whether or not to reveal that he had somehow unearthed that secret. He was a little apprehensive of Damian, who spoke such a weirdly toned version of his Ìsarà dialect. He had left Benin, fleeing a taskmaster of an uncle, lived off motor parks, and eked out a living as one of the army of porters to be found at railway stations. The fare that brought him to Ìsarà had been saved, despite days of hunger, for such a final act of desperation. He had sought no destination, merely entered the lorry that rumbled towards its take-off as his own stomach signalled its pangs of privation and the limits of its endurance. The lorry stopped at Ìsarà; Damian disembarked and lay across the road.

Between them, the pact was sealed. The only question was how soon they could dodge the straggle of well-wishers who had escorted them to the boundary, nearly half the population of Ìsarà. They headed into a ring road – no more than a footpath – which circled Ìsarà, then joined up with the track that would take them into Egbaland, to Owode, and then the railway station at Lafenwa. And Akinyode, as yet ignorant of the existence of Ashtabula and Montcalm's battlegrounds, sank into the exotic world of a railway carriage. The noise, the chaos of every station enraptured him, the railway bridges, the water pumps at which the railway stopped to 'drink,' the piercing whistle, which was almost drowned by the rhythmic, measured grind of wheels accelerating and decelerating downhill and uphill, the ceremonial approaches and departures from stations. The one-armed blue-red signals by the tracks snapped into new positions seemingly without human agency – until Damian, amused, pointed out the little concrete hut mounted high above the landscape, and the sweaty arms that pulled at levers. Later, he saw similar levers on ground level, among the coils of rail, manned by peak-capped signalsmen in stiff khaki jackets and shorts.

Damian's accounts had fallen short of this railway world of iron and steel and fat wooden slippers; nothing could match the flag in the hand of the station guard, his censorious eye sweeping up and down the platform, flag upraised, smartly dropped, followed by a nod of acknowledgment from the grimy, sweat-soaked engine driver, who leaned so casually, so confidently, so fully 'in control' of this monster, in which they could actually stretch their legs and walk, unlike the cooped-up journeys in motor lorries. Everything was excessive! Shrieking children amid farm produce; the *akowe** clans, complete with Madam and children and portmanteaus, all probably on tranfer; the coat and tie, the occasional trilby hat or bowler, the arrogant condescending glances at the spluttering, squalling mass of the 'other' humanity. Nothing of Damian's description ever prepared him for the wooden benches with comfortable space between them and a wide passage the length and breadth of the carriages, right down the middle, quite unlike any of the passenger lorries he had ever entered; nothing prepared him for the stamped reels of tickets! – paid for through the little grille in the window of Lafenwa station – or for the sure-footed train guard, who seemed to defy the rolling and pitching of the train, touching the back of the benches only from time to time when the train gave an unusual lurch. Nothing prepared him for the rumble of the

* White-collar workers.

iron girders as the rolling wheels took on their timbre and augmented it, wrapping it round his head and filling up the carriage with sounds just short of prolonged thunder; and Damian had said nothing at all of the tunnel into which the train suddenly disappeared – it was a mere culvert over which a motor road did pass but it filled Yode with instant terror until in the dim light he saw Damian's mouth again open in mocking laughter, so he half-shut his eyes. The train clung to its sooty shroud even after it had emerged, close wrapped into the after-spew of its dark, pungent smoke, which had collected as the train gained entry beneath the culvert. That avalanche of grit forced backwards as the archway of the culvert received its first blast passed harmlessly through the carriage for most of the passengers, the practised ones, who knew that they must shut their eyes at that point. But it stuck to their hair and clothing, and some hastily covered up the food they were eating and their drinks, put their hands over the children's eyes, or forced the babies' heads into their laps. The monster steadily belched out its own entrails and was in turn swallowed by them. When the grit stung Yode's eyeball, he knew he had heeded Damian's warning too late – mind you, Damian had only warned him about the moments when the train went down a steep incline and the carriages caught up with the smoke before it dispersed. Then also when those brisk harmattan winds chose to blow in the wrong direction. But nothing at all about tunnels, however short. People went blind with the grit, Damian and his father's travelling friends who lived up north had explained countless times – that was why there were many blind beggars from the north; the grit from the train damaged their retinas. They travelled in open freight trains with their cattle or simply sneaked a ride, and that was the result – blindness. Yode had wanted to ask if the cattle went blind too, but he was much too awed by the power of these seasoned travellers from the exotic foreign territory of the railway line – Enugu, Makurdi, Kano, Oshogbo – and anyway, who gave children the right to ask questions in the presence of elders when a child was not even part of the discussion? And Damian had never been farther north than Ibadan. The grit stung him as it slid beneath the eyelid and Yode panicked, rubbing it hard.

'Don't!'

Damian forced his hand away and prised open the eyelid with thumb and forefinger. It stung like mad and he tried to close it but Damian's Edo fingers were stronger.

'Roll your eyeball to the right.' He did and tears flowed freely while the stubborn grit stung him like a thousand wasps. 'Now to the left.'

Damian murmured curses on the elusive piece of grit, took off his fingers, thinking that it had somehow fallen out. Yode blinked hard once, then twice, and back came the pain again and he yelped. So Damian glued his fingers to the eyelids yet again, ordering, 'Keep them as wide open as you can,' and blew a wad of hot air across the eyeball. 'Got it,' he screamed in triumph. 'It has swum right into the centre of the eye.' He yanked out the tail of Yode's shirt, expertly dabbed the eye, and – instant relief – there it was. He held it out to Yode, who was alarmed at the sheer size of the charcoal piece, moistened by his tears. The relief was enormous; he leaned back in his seat and inhaled deeply the pungent smell of the smoke, which he quite liked. A faint suspicion that this odour might prove unhealthy if inhaled for long periods did not stop him from enjoying the tang of raw indigo dye. His mind went back to the sounds and sensations of the passage through the tunnel and across the bridges. It seemed no different from the *igbale*** into which real humans disappeared, to re-emerge as *alagemo*.† Slyly opening his eye, he inspected Damian. No, he did not think that he had turned into *alagemo* himself. The thought of *agemo*‡ had merely aroused his urge to ask THE QUESTION. Even to phrase it in his mind seemed far too huge an undertaking – yet until it was asked, it hung between them like an ominous bat suspended from the rafters. Going to St Simeon's seminary, leaving home for the first time and for such a prolonged period, was a rite of passage; he would not return the same child as he went. Had his father not called him and told him: You are going into a man's world. Remember that. You must make your world there, your friends, your future companions. As for the white man, remember he is very powerful, but he is only a man; so be like a man towards him, but a respectful man, because he is your teacher, and he is the one who rules your father's land. And then the farmer became confused and drove him out of the living room.

But one became a man in stages, not all at once. And a question like this . . . suppose it had to do with some shameful family secret, a silted-up well which was wisely kept covered up in the family compound? Tangled with weeds, its still, brackish water left stagnant for generation after generation? This would be no abandoned quarry-turned-playground into which a child could cast stones or drop a casual bucket. Not even one indulged as he was by his outlandish companion, who looked on Yode as one destined for great things in life and therefore entitled to be treated with some deference. At the time of the event, Yode had stored it away as an awesome

* Secret robing room for masquerades; subterranean house of the ancestral mask.
† Of the spirit-mask family.
‡ Same as *alagemo*.

thing whose real meaning he would demand as soon as he was old enough. After that, the only question that remained was: When would he be old enough? If leaving home for the first time – not merely leaving briefly but separating from home with one's entire belongings in a wooden box, nuzzling one's bare feet – if that was not being old enough, well, when would he be old enough? Suppose at this new abode a schoolfriend also attempted to kill himself, what should he do?

If the worst came to the worst, Damian would simply never speak to him again. It was best to wait until the journey was nearly over, thus shortening the period of his silent punishment.

Damian would leave him to his fate in the seminary and return to his parents. Perhaps he would report him for broaching the forbidden subject. Still, there was nothing his father could do until the first holidays. Again Yode considered waiting until the very last station before Ede, then posing the question. They had taken Damian away; he came back with his head shaven, looking drugged. There was certain to be a long story behind it, not something to be rushed, otherwise what was the point? So he divided up the risks. Either Damian would tell him the terrible secret, giving him time to elaborate on any details – or the rest of the journey would be passed in spoken rebuke, or in silence. He hoped, in the latter case, that Damian would choose silence. At least he would have tried his best to find out why a youth, only two years above his own fourteen years, had tried to kill himself.

The train kept up its ponderous progress, bearing him away to a new grouping, putting an end to neighbourhood and sibling fights, family pressures, the iron fists of teachers, and the uncertain faith of both parents struggling against the silent pull of their abandoned deities. Yode already felt that he was acquiring a new status. He assessed Damian opposite him more critically and felt that it was only a matter of time before he became just as old. Perhaps THE QUESTION ought to wait until he was as old, with that faint swathe of darkness covering his upper lip. But then, Damian might return to his own hometown while he was away. He had, after all, come to Ìsarà by running away. There was this also, and it became Yode's primary concern – there was the question of one's Christian duty. Damian might try it again, finish off what he had begun, what everyone – his father, the Jagun, Pa Node – had been so appalled about. It would all be over. He would not even be home to be part of the disruption of routine, to eavesdrop on the stream of witnesses, accusers, counsellors, hushed gossip . . . All he would be left with was guilt, guilt for his failure to make Damian confide in him. He had to ask now, before this final separation from home, for a length of time that had already begun to weigh on him like a first intimation of eternity.

> *Mo ti gun'ke, mo ti so*
> *Mo ti gun'ke mo ti so*
> *Oke ti alajapa ko le gun*
> *Mo ti gun, mo ti so*
> *Faka fiki faka fii . . .*

'What do you find so amusing?'

'This train. In fact, trains in general.'

'And what is so amusing about trains? You would have preferred to go all the way by lorry?'

Yode did not bother to admit that it was the children's railway song which had suddenly drummed itself through his mind. More than likely his companion would only remark that a boy of his age should not even think of children's games, not when he was about to become a boarder in an *oyinbo** seminary. In any case, Yode wanted some time to think, to decide how he would phrase this all-consuming question.

A long blast from the train rescued him from the need to elaborate. This would mean they were approaching a level crossing, going round a sharp curve, approaching a station – or simply that the driver was feeling bored. From his window seat he leaned out cautiously – *NEVER LEAN OUT OF THE WINDOWS! A tree branch might sweep you out through the window or a telegraph pole brain you* – but he did not need to lean too far out as his bench was on the inside of the train's curved spine, a monstrous millipede it seemed at such moments. Yode began to count the coaches, a methodical instinct taking over, as if anticipating and preparing himself for the lessons ahead, but only expressing traits that had already been remarked at St James's primary school, just on the outskirts of the market near the Odemo's palace. He squinted to reduce his eyeball surface, more respectful now of coal dust and smoke. Sinuous coaches wrapped themselves around the vegetation as if to deny their mechanical world. Yode had long decided that if there was a horned species of the snake, like the horned beetle, for instance, the railway train was surely modelled on it.

Olodo station, and the noise was overwhelming; it looked like market day. Hawkers swarmed over the train even as it pulled properly to a stop. The human traffic struggled in both directions – women laden with trays of trinkets, bundles of cloth strangled by ropes at midriff, but tidily,

---

* White man.

243

balanced freely on a young girl's head, textures and colours madly at variance with the staid wooden interior of the coaches. Hen coops and dangling guinea fowl, the squawks and spirals of feathers, occasional fights with beak and claws, quickly stifled, result of their own confusion and uncertain fate. The heady smell of palm wine, dirt-speckled froth in the broiling sun, vegetables by the basketful; a sudden bundle, tied at the stalks, would be thrust through the windows, forced into a complaisant hand, which weighed it thoughtfully, returned it as another, deemed fuller, fresher, or simply different, was thrust in the face of the hesitant buyer; the reek of raw eggs, some already smashed, yolk congealed or seeping through the base of the baskets; the boiled eggs, a choice offered between farm hens' and wild guinea fowls', the difference apparent in the speckles; fried *sawa-sawa* and the inevitable bowl of fried peppers; the halfpenny loaves of Shackleford, or 'sugar bread,' which would be sliced in half, the whitebait tucked in the slit, the peppery paste sealing off the midday snack. Headties and screaming faces, the racing feet of eager sellers, leaping from window to window, stair to stair, strapped-on babies bobbing up and down with loudly exhaled breaths, threatening to fall off, their hands dangling helplessly and lips flapping from the mother-bounces, yet miraculously secured. A huge basin was raised, covered with layers of sacking, the sacking was pulled aside, and a full blast of steam rivalling the railway engine's hit Yode in the face; beneath, re-heated lumps of yam or boiled corn on the cob. Farther away on the platform you could see the blackened half-barrels or basins on improvised hearths from which the mobile stock had been replenished, then covered in sacking to keep warm for the traveller. The curses and banter; anger one moment vanishes magically, re-emerges in laughter and teasing offers: I'll follow you home if you like, or you can take my daughter. You're sure you are not too young for her? The next basin of boiled yam floated past their window, sweeping along the route of the fruits, vegetables and peppers, *odunkun*, coco yam, *esuru*, and innumerable other species of the yam tuber, and Damian had had enough. If Yode chose to stare open-mouthed for flies to enter, he had better ideas for his jaws.

'Wouldn't you like some boiled yam?'

'Hm? Oh, yams. Yes, yes, in fact I think I am feeling quite hungry.'

'I should think so. Just think when last we ate. And that was quite some walking distance, from the motor park to Lafenwa.'

'*Abiamo . . .*'*

* Nursing mother.

Swift motions as the woman stopped in mid-stride, set the bowl down, her baby tossed forward as if to fly over her head but stoutly secured by the shawl around her waist. She asked how many pieces, the sharp practised blade already slicing through a whole tuber, while Yode wondered if Damian meant him to pay also for his share, when his father had provided them both with money for the journey.

'Don't forget the salt, Iyawo.' Damian, very sternly, man of the world in his own element, ignoring the woman's protests, her insistence that she had already sprinkled salt on the creamy interior of the yam. But Damian shook his head, unbending. 'Salt, put extra salt on the leaf. Then we can sprinkle it on to our tastes.' And to Yode, 'Never let these women cheat you. You had better learn how to deal with them if you are going to do more of these travels.' He shut up Yode, who protested that he was no novice at the market, by reminding him that this was not a market nor was it Ìsarà. This was THE WORLD. The railway denizens are different from the rest of humanity. 'Mark my words and save yourself later grief.' When the woman reached out her hand for payment, Damian further showed who was in charge. He pointed down the platform to where his hungry eyes had spied the seller of roast pork – something to go with the yam was needed. 'Iyawo, if you don't mind, that pork-seller over there.' The woman knew she had no choice; she cast an anxious look at faces poked through other windows, prospective customers, let out her best hawker's high-pitched yell: '*Iya! Gb'elede wa.*'* Yode succumbed immediately and took out the coins to pay her off, seeing her eagerness to be gone, her body rocking on the balls of her feet while a hand cupped itself around the bottom of the restless baby on her back. She half-turned in a practised manoeuvre, raising her left arm and jerking her buttocks, and the child half-slewed leftward, its head bobbing up beneath the raised armpit. She pasted a small sliver of yam between its lips and looked very pleased to have the money waiting for her when she next turned round. And so it was the turn of the roast pork and the game of haggling began, moving from one tempting piece to the other.

'I'll be back in a moment,' Damian said. 'I'll leave the choice to you; I want to stretch my legs a little on the platform before I attack the yam.'

Wrong, of course. Totally wrong. The lesson, repeated for at least a week by the ragtag preparatory committee, was: *NEVER GET OFF A TRAIN AT THE STATION!* He stared at Damian, who, affecting the utmost casualness, strolled down the carriage corridor, disappeared round

---

* Woman, bring the roasted pork.

the door, and re-emerged moments later among the teaming traders on the platform. Yode stared, was hesitating to cry out a caution, when the pork-seller seized back the portion still undergoing absent-minded weighing in his hand and made to go. 'No, no, wait.' He dug into his pocket and brought out the asking price, without haggling. So much for Damian's lesson, and he the cause of this carelessness.

Pushing his way through with his long arms, on short bandy legs, Damian was already at the entrance to the station building, but he did not remain within it, since Yode saw him shortly reappear behind the building, duck beneath an open window, thinking he was unobserved, then vanish altogether between what looked like a row of kiosks and prefabricated dwellings.

The terrified scream startled his neighbours in the carriage: 'Demiyen!'

But Damian was already beyond hearing, his face, lightly cicatrixed on the forecheeks close to his nostrils, was wreathed in the contented smile of homecoming, home being anywhere that rendered due recognition and adult service in exchange for his penny. The apprentice farmer puffed out his chest, ready to transform himself among strangers into an experienced printer BY ROYAL APPOINTMENT to – well, why not? – the Odemo of Ìsarà. He soon found what he was seeking; his nose had led him unerringly. As he took his seat he studied his companions and prepared to improvise a superior status.

Within Akinyode's breast, a sudden descent of calm, and resignation. He was alone, cast on the wide, wild world, facing a new life by himself. As he slowly bit into his food he felt suitably old, filled with the certainty that he had seen Damian for the last time, that he had taken his leave as whimsically as he had appeared in Ìsarà, found lying in the red dust of Ìsarà road, just outside the makeshift motor park, just lying there, resigned to any fate that might overtake him. The night guards had come upon the stranger – the lorry arrived at dusk – and when they challenged him he merely stared at them, not even deigning to respond to their presence. A night marauder, no doubt, waiting for full darkness to link up with his gang, perhaps the advance scout who would sneak into a compound in full darkness, then open the doors to his waiting comrades skulking among crooked passages of the township. So they tied his hands together and blew their whistles. The other guards came and they discussed him. When dawn came they took him to Jagun, and he sent for his friend Josiah. The stranger's emaciated frame and hollowed cheeks, not to mention the manner of his appearance in the town, swiftly adjusted the drama-laden babbling of the night guards; and when a bowl of *eko* and a wrap of *moin-*

moin were set before him, his ravenous assault on the meal confirmed the surmises of the two men. The guards were thanked for their vigilance, and Josiah assigned him to the Oba's household. As he picked up a few more words in the language of his hosts, Damian – which was the name he had bestowed upon himself when he first ran away from Benin – confided that his ambition was to learn a trade, and that printing was his choice. And could he go and work for that benign papa who had first suggested that he be fed after his apprehension and who, he learned, was a Christian? He confessed to being disturbed by the pagan carvings that surrounded the Oba's courtyard. They frightened him, he said, they gave him nightmares. The Oba's attendant to whom he spoke promised to pass on his wishes. Later, Damian heard raucous laughter from a corner of the courtyard where the attendant had gathered his cronies and was regaling them with the tale of this *kobokobo** beggar who had nightmares in the Oba's palace. They made no attempt to hide the fact that he was the butt of their ridicule, tried to rival one another for the funniest imitation of his accent. They did not stop even when they saw him watching; rather, they took their show towards him, tugged at his clothing, danced and staggered round, and collapsed on their backs with laughter.

Late afternoon of the same day, a hushed gathering in the audience room of the Odemo, Jagun in attendance, and Josiah. There was a woman also, seated on the patterned oval matting, her legs drawn up sideways. A little girl stood by the door, somewhat frightened by the array of elders, and then the culprit was led in by two palace stalwarts. He cast a glance round the room, which he was entering for the first time, then dropped his gaze to a spot before his feet as he recognised the woman seated on the ground. A tap behind his right shoulder reminded him of the custom of his adopted place; he threw himself on the ground in prostration and remained there. Pa Josiah spoke.

'Do you know that woman, Demiyen?'

What did they want him to say? How did this woman find out that he lived here? What brought her along to disrupt his plans?

'Demiyen, we are asking you – look at that woman. Have you seen her before?'

Jagun was impatient. 'Someone get me the *koboko*. We shall see if that does not open his mouth.'

An attendant ran off while Josiah made one more attempt. 'Did you

---

* Alien; speaker of an incomprehensible language.

leave the palace today? Did you go out to make a purchase from this woman?'

And Damian burst into huge, racking sobs. Nothing could be said or done, no amount of shaking could staunch it – threats, pleas, the raised *koboko* in the hand of Jagun, not even the intimidating thwack as he brought it down expertly on the floor, just missing Damian's prostrate back by a mere hairsbreadth. Frustrated, the Odemo gestured and his attendants half-dragged, half-carried the jellied form away, his sobs still echoing in their ears. Josiah turned to the woman: 'Tell Kabiyesi what happened exactly.'

The woman made obeisance to the Oba anew. 'Kabiyesi, *k'i e pe*. It was surely the watchfulness of our ancestors that prevented what would have happened today, within the hallowed walls of our own father in this town. Usually I am alone in the stall, but today I took Ajike with me. That was how I was able to send someone to follow him and find out where he lives. Caustic soda! First Ajike offered him the soap when he said he wanted soda. She held out the tin of soap to him but he said, no, it was the caustic soda he wanted, the powder, not the ready-made soap. I was inside the stall and I overheard him. So I came out. I said to myself, Who is the *kobokobo* coming here to ask for caustic soda? I didn't know of any soap-maker in Ìsarà who was a *kobokobo*. I asked him where he came from but he wouldn't tell me. That was when I became suspicious. I had heard about one stranger who had been picked up by the night guards, but I thought they had long sent him away to prison. So I asked him, What do you want with caustic soda? He was staring at me, no, not even staring at me but at something else in front of him. I said, Is this a lunatic? As if my mind knew what he was about to do, he started singing.'

She was interrupted by exclamations round the room. Eyes widened in a mixture of wonder and anticipation, and it was the Odemo himself who asked, 'Singing? Did you say singing?'

'In that *kobokai* language of his which no one could understand. People were passing by, stopping, then moving away. He went on singing for some time, without even looking at me. Then, I don't know, maybe the song was finished or he was tired. Anyway, he turned as if he was seeing me for the first time and asked me, "Where is that soda?" So I repeated what I said before – "What do you want the soda for?" That was when he said, "What is the matter with this woman? Do you have a law here against a man doing away with his life?" Kabiyesi, can you imagine how I felt? I shouted "What?" but he went on as if he had not even heard me. He said, "You are here to serve customers, not so? So just give me the powder and

248

take your money. Or do you think you're the only market woman in this world?" *E gbani e l'aja!* Kabiyesi, my blood was running cold; I didn't know what to do. So, I think when he saw that he would not get what he wanted from my stall – I mean, my fathers, God forbid! In this town? That was when he started to walk away.'

The length and breadth of the chamber expelled a long sigh; knowing looks flew from one grizzled head to another. Jagun snapped his finger around his head to ward off the intended evil, while the attendants snapped their thumbs against each other, murmuring '*To, to, to . . .*' Josiah contented himself with a silent prayer of thanksgiving, which he divided evenly between the presiding spirits of *osugbo** and Christ the Son of God, ensuring in his now-practised way that he gave precedence to neither. He had perfected this even-handed style of communion – but only in crisis, when he was not truly at ease with the direction he must choose. Church service were simpler, so were Christian prayer meetings, but there were too many ambiguities in the matter of life and death, a grayness of attribution which, despite his faith, still lingered. Still, he managed to conceal it from all new converts who came to him for counsel, but not from his son.

'Praise be, Ajike was with me. Tell me, what could I have done if she had not been there? I let the man go off till he was nearly hidden by the corner of the market, then I whispered to Ajike, "Follow that man quickly, don't let him see you, just follow him from a distance and find out where he lives. Don't come back unless you have seen him to his home." Node's girl is a sharp one, I can tell you, and thank God she takes after her father. Or what do you think I felt when she came back and said to me – my knees simply collapsed when she told me – she said she had followed him into Kabiyesi's courtyard! I shouted, "Are you sure?" and she said to me, "I know the Aafin, that is where the Odemo lives, not so?" I tell you, that child is simply too old for her years.'

Mo ti gun'ke mo ti so, mo ti gun'ke mo ti so . . .

'Feeling homesick already?'

The train picked that moment to roll, and a familiar figure was pitched forwards against him. So quickly attuned had he become to the motions of the train that, busy also with his thoughts, he had missed all the ritual of station-leaving, had been oblivious to whistle, scampering feet, the last-minute hawking cries of the tradeswomen, had missed even Damian's 'rascal leap' onto the moving train. His astonishment at his return was

* Meeting-house of a council of elders.

249

overwhelmed by a strong feeling of resentment, tinged only absent-mindedly with relief. He had become fully reconciled to his abandonment and was feeling no further anxiety about the immediate future. Worse still, Damian's loss of balance had been somewhat excessive, really spectacular, and when he opened his mouth to speak, barely an inch from Yode's face, he let loose an introductory belch whose smell revealed just where he had been since his disappearance.

'You were drinking,' he accused.

Damian made valiant efforts to regain his balance, then sank into his seat. 'Only *burukutu*,' he admitted. 'Very cheap at this station. They brew it right behind the station building, fresh-fresh from guinea corn. And you know, the woman remembered me. She remembered me! She was so happy to welcome me, she did not even take payment. I tell you, railway people . . .'

'You did not invite me to come.' Akinyode found that he was very resentful.

Damian's eyes opened wide. 'Ask you to come? You! Do you know where you are going? Let me tell you, you think they have *pito* there? Ho, let me tell you, my brother is in one of those places, there is one in Ughelli, not much different from the one you'll be attending, judging from what I hear. Let me tell you, Josiah's son, you must forget things like *burukutu*. Or *pito*. In that place, you will drink only BEVERAGES. Yes, beverages. Ovaltine, cocoa, tea, and coffee. Beverages. You think they have even palm wine there? Your father warned me, he said he would thrash me if I let you have anything on the way except bread and tinned sardines. O-oh, because I let you eat some yam and roast pork – by the way, where is . . . ?' Yode thrust the parcel at him. 'Good. Well, I was only being nice, because we are old friends. But he has told me all about the school rules, you know, he talks of nothing but this seminary when we are alone on the farm. For instance, I know by heart the list of all the things you must bring with you –'

'I know everything, thank you,' Yode snapped.

'O-oh. So you do. And you know you will not be allowed to speak that Ijebu language in there. And you can only keep milk and sugar in your cupboard. And BEVERAGES. No *gari*. No *ebiripo*. No *robo*, *aadun* . . .' He crammed the yam in his mouth, tearing at the pork and speaking with his mouth full.

Irritated, Akinyode tried to change the subject. 'I did not see you coming in.'

A look of infinite disappointment suffused Damian's face. 'You did not . . . do you mean . . . ?'

'I did not.' Akinyode was puzzled by this look akin to pain on his companion's face.

'But I waved at you,' Damian accused. 'I thought you were watching me.'

'I saw you only just now.'

'You mean you did not see me wait until the wheels had begun to roll and gather speed . . . ?'

'Well, you were inside by then, weren't you?'

'Of course not,' Damian exploded. 'I was on the platform. What is the point waving at you just to watch me climb onto a stationary train? I caught it in motion. That's the way we do it.'

Akinyode was appalled. This was exactly what should not be done. On the list of rail-travel taboos was this very one, above even the leaning-out-of-windows prohibition. Those leg amputees on Beggars' Row in the cities, how do you think they got their legs cut off? Slipping under the train, of course, as they tried to trainhop after the train had moved. Showing off. Expensive *omo ita*.* Rascality is one thing, but at the cost of a leg? And sometimes even loss of life?

'I suppose,' said Akinyode slowly, 'it would not have mattered to you anyway.'

A flicker of suspicion passed over Damian's eyes; his tipsiness appeared to be suspended, if only for some moments. 'What would not matter?'

Akinyode pressed on. 'Whether you killed yourself or not.'

Damian's eyes went vacant and Akinyode found he had nearly bitten his tongue. But it was now too late to draw back. 'You tried to kill yourself. With caustic soda. I heard Baba and Chief Jagun discussing it. Didn't Jagun shave your head and make incisions on it?'

Involuntarily, Damian's hand shot up towards his head. But he stopped before it touched. He let the arm fall slowly, then dropped his head against the carriage wall. He let his eyelids shut slowly, uttering no sound. Until they reached Ibadan his young companion could not swear whether he was asleep or was merely pretending.

Akinyode's heels struck the box of possessions beneath the bench. It was stuffed also with gifts, some of them coming in at the last minute: a shirt, a pocket knife, a book – it was a text of Christian homilies – a disguised wallet which contained the most valued items – the threepenny and sixpenny pieces, the few shillings, all with the head of King Edward, the king of England, that nation whose history, albeit bowdlerised, they all

* Rascality.

251

knew by heart. The box contained a bed sheet, two embroidered pillowcases, a coverlet of local weave – Ilesa was quite chilly in the harmattan, the seminarian circular had warned them. His notebook of guiding precepts was already beside him on the bench. And of course Damian was right, there was the packet of sugar, tins of evaporated milk, sweetened cocoa, which he preferred to Ovaltine in any case, and – a decision which his father had left to him – a tiny jar containing 'protection,' made by the hand of Jagun himself. He was free to throw that in the bush before he entered the hallowed precincts of St Simeon's Seminary, or to keep it with him. The choice was his. For the teacher-trainee, it was not too much of a dilemma; he had already resolved to hand it to Damian, hopeful that it would shield him from any more suicidal impulses.

It seemed to have worked. At least, Damian never again attempted suicide. And it was only appropriate that Damian should be the one to sit behind the steering wheel and launch Node's gleaming motor on its maiden voyage. First, he was no longer Damian. His transformation was so complete that no one even remembered the name he had brought into Ìsarà, one which he had shed as easily as he had first acquired it. Not that anyone ever called him Damian. Demiyen it was from the first rendition. De-mi-yen, his new townspeople assumed, was how he himself would have pronounced his name if only he spoke Ijebu. But Demiyen was no longer even that. Challenged to a fight by a truculent layabout on the playing fields of St James's primary school one Saturday, he had replied to his aggressor's taunts with his own war cries and self-boosting in his native Edo tongue. Then, infected by the many sounds around him, some urging on the fight, some mocking the *kobokobo*, others attempting to break it up, he had, without even being aware of it, suddenly shed his Edo rallying cries and broken into the Ìsarà dialect. It was one word only, and the contrast with his earlier barrage in Edo was so startling that the crowd was momentarily transfixed. The taunt came out perfectly, urged by the flow of adrenaline – '*Wemuja!*'* It became his sole response to the prolonged verbal prances of his opponent – '*Wemuja!*' And the crowd swung over to his side and urged him on with shouts of '*Wemuja!*' After the combatants had been separated – the contest being more or less even – he was carried shoulder-high and accompanied home with a rhythmic chant of '*We-mu-jaa, We-mu-jaa!*' Pa Josiah came out of his cottage to see the cause of the

* You know nothing of a real fight.

252

commotion, saw his farmhand floating over a sea of heads and arms, dancing up the steep incline. When they saw him standing with arms on his hips, legs set wide apart, and thunder in his eyes, they hurriedly set down their hero and vanished, leaving Damian to face the wrath of his master for his desecration of a peaceful afternoon. One sideways swipe as he tried to sneak around Josiah into the backyard sent him reeling in the dust. But he was beyond pain, still borne on the wave of his unplanned acceptance by his age-group in Ìsarà. Two weeks later, even Pa Josiah had begun to call him Wemuja.

Wemuja had changed in other ways. He had filled out; no extra inches to his height, only to his arms and his chest and his leg muscles, which seemed content to make up in girth what they lacked in length. His arms were disproportionately long. But it was the bandyness of the legs which astonished Akinyode. He simply had not known that his former companion's legs were that bowed. Yet this new appearance fitted him for the role of driver of the timber lorry. The short limbs sprouted from the same tangle of growth that produced the giant boles which weighed down the lorry and threatened to up-end the novel contraption as it strained against invisible leashes holding it to the foot of the hill. The lorry had taken on its first-ever load the night before, hewn down from Node's concession between Ìsarà and Sagamu, then driven into Ìsarà in the morning for its formal baptism. The reception group waited at the top of the hill, looking down on the lorry's approach. Wemuja's head would have been missed but for the broad-brimmed scoutmaster or ex-army hat he sported, pinned up on one side. And even this was barely visible over the steering wheel. He drove with his arms wrapped around the circumference, hugging the wheel. Drummers had appeared miraculously from passages which opened into the road along the gradient. Akinyode smiled; it was futile to try to keep such things from them. They joined the vehicle, hopped and pranced uphill with it, easily keeping pace with its slow speed. Node had been lifted outdoors and a smile of contentment struggled to alter the shape of his nearly immobile lips.

The proudest man however was Wemuja. He had long given up his ambition to be a printer, switching his allegiance, after that rail journey with Akinyode, to driving a railway engine. The route to that profession, he reasoned, lay in understudying the lorry drivers who plied the Ìsarà route, and he spent his meagre earnings from Josiah to pay for lessons over the years. Then he overheard the schoolteacher and his father discussing Node's plans to go into the timber business and even to purchase a lorry. His mind was made up; the entire course of his existence was mapped definitively that very moment. He, and no one else, would drive that lorry. He intensified his lessons, and soon even Pa Josiah could no longer deny that there was a driver in the extended family. Did not his own son advocate the timber trade as a first step to the printing of books? To his new friends, Wemuja boasted that he was not just a lorry driver but was in the book-production business. And if the schoolteacher was also around, he winked at him and said, 'Mr Teacher and I, we are in the same profession.'

As Wemuja expertly parked the lorry on the tiny plateau above Node's compound and leapt down from the driver's cabin, Akinyode looked at his beaming, contented face with a hint of envy. Had he reached his Ashtabula? He had probably risen much earlier than the teacher had that morning, full of anticipation for the initial step. He would check all those mysterious gauges in the engine and fill the radiator with water. His assistant, Alanko, would secure the wooden blocks that would serve as wedges between the load and the platform of the lorry. Wemuja, he was certain, would himself test the tyre pressures, the hawser. A breakfast of *eba* certainly, a terrifying mound in which he would make a deep scoop to create space for the vegetable stew from a tin container, meat, and perhaps a bit of stockfish. Cool water from a jar chilled overnight in the dew, far from the Reversing Falls of Ashtabula or its underground streams, and certainly more refreshing.

A voice cut through his reverie. It was Jagun, commenting, 'So it was Commer you decided upon after all.'

Akinyode nodded. 'It is more expensive but our Lagos people say it is the best.'

'Very strong they say.'

'Ve-ry. Much stronger than Ford, which was the one we thought of to begin with.'

Wemuja intervened with definitive authority. 'Ford is all right for passenger lorry, Baba, or Bedford. But for timber, you need engine like Commer.' He turned, shouted an order to his mate to bring down the gourd of palm wine which they had collected on their way. Alanko was a contrast to his boss, weedy, tufts of hair patchily strewn around his skull as if he had been a porter at the railway station carrying baskets of eggs and bags of kola nuts on his bare head. Wemuja strolled to the side of the lorry to relieve him of the gourd; he looked as if he only had to vault on the back of the heavy log, wrap his bandy legs around it, and he would ride the entire lorry without any use of the engine, a veritable cowboy on a timber horse galloping to Ashtabula!

A strong hand gripped his shoulder. It was again Jagun, and he drew him away from the others, towards where his father was standing. 'It is good that you came,' he said, as they walked. 'I would have sent Josiah to you but now that you are here . . .' He paused until they arrived where the elder Soditan was waiting. He grinned at his crony. 'I have begun the *oro awo** with our Tisa.' His father, he noticed, did not change expression. 'Well, *omo* Josiah, the long and short of the matter is, our king is ailing. We have consulted Ifa, and it seems we have not long to search for a new king.'

Akinyode looked from one to the other. Surely this had nothing to do with him. For another thing, it was a mild break in the unwritten etiquette. There was one relief for which he was always grateful during those unseasonal visits – a lack of demands, of impositions. This matter, however, sounded as if it might prove the father of all impositions. So he waited, apprehensive.

'I know what you must be thinking,' Jagun continued. 'This is not an affair of children. You are thinking that it has nothing to do with you, but you are wrong, Tisa. Times are changing. The white man is here and he pokes his nose into everything. So it is a good thing that we also have those who understand his way of thinking and can pass on to him our thoughts on matters which concern us. Because, you see, we already know whom we want for the next Odemo.'

Akinyode spoke very slowly, unable any longer to prolong the silence that hung upon his answer. 'Well, you must remember, I am only a teacher. I don't know about these matters. Those in Lagos –'

His father snorted. 'Those in Lagos, yes, we know about those in Lagos. Of course we must get in touch with those in Lagos, and it is you who must do it. The matter concerns you more than those in Lagos.'

Now he was truly alarmed. 'Concerns me?' For a moment his thoughts went wild, his lean face jerking between the two men. Surely they did not mean . . .

His father read his thoughts precisely. 'No. Do you think Jagun would be talking to you if he meant *that*? But it touches you. It touches the House of Lígùn. So get yourself and your friends together. Because we know all those who think it is their father's private throne, and they will bring the seat of government in Lagos into this matter.'

Akinyode badly wanted time to think. 'We still have some time. The king may survive another ten, even twenty, years.'

The two older men looked at each other. The father made a dismissive

---

* The secret talk.

gesture but Jagun laid a hand on his arm and laughed. 'You sent him to the mission seminary, so don't complain.' He turned to Akinyode. 'Tisa, Ifa has had its say on the matter. Do you think we would speak on such a matter without consulting deeply into the heart of knowledge?'

The teacher sensed vaguely that he had just been administered a rebuke. He shrugged. 'I suppose the same Ifa has approved the successor you have in mind?'

Jagun grinned his approval. 'You are a quick pupil, Tisa. We will talk more about it on the way to Iya Agba.'

'Yes, let's go now,' Josiah urged. 'Your grandmother has something to show you.' His demeanour had changed and Akinyode looked at him with more apprehension, refusing at first to move.

'What is it?'

'I said she has something to show you. You think you will find out what it is by standing there?'

The little notebook of precepts, prefaced in capitals by that very first motto which had accompanied him on his enrollment journey to Ilesa, also contained excerpts from church sermons, proverbs, analects, jottings, moral observations, snippets of vital information such as overseas college and university addresses, page references to articles in journals which had engaged his professional and other interests. There were even a few verses, copied from Cudeback's letters or directly from books. The notebook remained his constant companion. As usual when he opened it, he let his eyes linger on that first page, where, over eighteen years before, he had inscribed the lines from Archdeacon Howell's farewell sermon: 'He has no future who fails to affect his present.' It was his last attendance at St James's Church before his departure for Ilesa, and it had seemed to him that the preacher addressed his sermon to no one else, just to him alone. It stamped a special mandate on his departure, coated it in an aura of special designation which remained with him all through college and even through his career. He often assessed the activities of his friends, their plans, through these special lenses placed before his eyes by the unsuspecting prelate. Even Damian, the would-be printer turned farmer turned would-be railway worker, settling finally into the driver's seat of a timber lorry – even Damian's progress had been viewed through this singular perspective. Everything Damian had ever done, from his first act of running away from Benin to this one, becoming Node's driver – had not every act been guided by his resolve to 'affect his present'? His feat of self-transformation from Damian to Wemuja had merely capped this firm resolve to direct his life.

And this it was that produced in him the greatest disquiet. Compared with Wemuja, was he truly in full control of his present? His friend Sipe stood in a class by himself, a being resolved to affect not just his own present but that of everyone within affecting orbit. So, Akinyode, he demanded of himself, did you even choose to be a teacher? Or did you just settle into it because that was what was expected? And now the affair of his grandmother . . .

He soon found the reference he sought and laid the notebook beside the pile of dated journals. They made up his Ìsarà library – two improvised Peak milk cartons which housed the precious source material for planning and decisions that required his utmost seclusion. The disputations might take place in Abeokuta, but it was to Ìsarà he came to sort matters out in his own mind, away from the uneven sessions of bantering and earnest debates and business schemings among The Circle. The visit to his grandmother had upset him, moved him in quite unexpected ways, rousing him to an accelerated sense of urgency, yet inducing a contrary state of enervation.

His father and Jagun had looked on, impassive, while the slight figure acted out what she called her final rites. 'This is the way I wish to be buried.' The two older men looked at each other and evinced no further interest; they had seen it all too often; it was what they brought him here to see. She now lay on her back, having sat up on their arrival. 'This mat, now, say it is a bolt of white brocade, you know, the kind I still keep at the bottom of my box, though that is now somewhat yellowish with age . . . you will roll me up in the cloth, like this' . . . and she pulled up the mat on either side, covering her emaciated frame up to the chest. 'And then you lift me up and put me in the coffin. Don't bother to put any dress on me, I just want to be wrapped up as I've just shown you. And let me tell you something else –'

Jagun interrupting, 'Iya Ile Lígùn –'

'I haven't finished.'

'Iya, your grandson merely came to tell you of the new house he's building for you.'

'Then he can occupy it. And the other thing I was going to say. Don't you dare perform any Christian worship over me. You will dig the grave just outside there, in the courtyard –'

Josiah threw up his hands. 'You see, she won't listen.'

Jagun tried again. 'You cannot stay here, so no one is burying you here. Since your husband left us, your in-laws have been asking to take back their brother's house.'

'In the courtyard, you heard me.'

Akinyode knelt by her side. 'Iya Agba, why don't you simply come back to Abeokuta with me.'

'What for? So you can bury me in that foreign land?'

'Then stay with your son,' Jagun pleaded. 'How often do you want him to beg you to go and live with him?'

'I am not living with another man's wives.'

Josiah flung his arms to heaven. 'You hear her? Another man's wives! This is me, your son Josiah. Josiah! Another man's wives, she says. And all this because I became a Christian. Have you seen any of my wives living under my roof?'

Akinyode rose and dusted his knees. 'She has become used to living alone.'

Josiah snorted. 'She's stubborn. Stubborn as the very day she gave birth to me. Did she not insist she would go to the market even though I was already halfway out of her womb?'

Laughing, Jagun asked, 'How do you know? You were hardly present.'

'Well, I heard my baba say it often enough.'

'Perhaps when the new house is ready,' Akinyode suggested, 'and we take her to see it . . .'

'Of course, of course,' Josiah mocked. 'As long as we're prepared to carry her. You will ask her to do her "final rites" again, then seize her when she is rolled up in the mat. That's the only way you will get her out of here.'

Iya Ile Lígùn, who they thought had fallen into one of her frequent slumbers, spoke up. 'Who is talking about a mat? I said, the white brocade. What sort of death do you think I will die that you want to use a mat on me? Did you ever see me in the courtyard of *agemo*?'

Jagun began to herd them out. 'Let's go, let's go. This one will grow ears from even beyond the grave.'

Akinyode stared hard at the smoke-rimed rafters, thinking of this new imposition on his resources. No one had discussed it with him. It was assumed; of course Tisa would build the house for his aged grandmother. If he did not, who else would? There it was. Those *iyekan* of his late grandfather were claiming back their family house. There was hardly any point even contesting this in the Customary courts. Both Jagun and his father knew where the rights lay and had decided on the only remedy: a new cottage – and, since it would be built by the 'foreign' son, a cottage with corrugated iron sheets and a cement finish, not the familiar mud-plastered two-room affair, its floor blackened with *eleboto*.* Yet even that

* Dung plaster.

258

'simple affair' cost money. As for the elders in this matter, it went beyond putting a roof over his grandmother's head. Was he not a grown man with his own family? At the moment, visits to Ìsarà meant that he stayed with his father, while his family took over his mother's house. Now he would have a house of his own, two or three rooms to begin with, expanding as resources came to hand. They had it all worked out. Akinyode knew that Jagun would call on him the following morning, take him out to 'show you something.' His cunning hand would describe a circle over an untended piece of land. 'There it is, Tisa, it is yours to do as you wish. Your father saved it for you. God will provide the "strength" to complete it for your children.'

He tried hard to project himself through the next ten, no, even five, years. Would Aké have become a distant, even resented, interlude? His hand groped for the lever of the kerosene lamp and turned down the wick. Now flickering on his retina was Sipe's handwriting, the vistas he conjured up so lavishly with all his madcap projects, even as Sipe remained stubbornly bound to prosaic earth. How much longer do I console myself with merely fleshing out those alien worlds evoked by exotic names, the smells, the textures and sounds? He conceded that Sipe and he – indeed all ex-Ilés – burned with the desire to affect their present, in some form or other. There was no 'other' in Sipe's own motions of change; those motions led in one direction only – 'to be free of the drudgery of salaried work, to become a man of independent means.' And his passionate harangues, shifting from rebuke to mockery to challenges to boastfulness: 'You can all stay put and continue to wonder what kind of ferns will grow in the gardens of Laniero or what ornamental trees line the avenues near Alessandro of Milano. Just leave the rest to the Resolute Rooster. He will help you get at the contents of those warehouses!'

Was Sipe right?

At thirty-two, married, with two infant children . . . The housing was free but there were those basics – clothes, food, social demands, soon it would be time for books and school uniforms. Surely it was not too early to give due weight to these thoughts. He thought of Morola in Aké, probably fast asleep by now, or else adjusting the baby's wrapper for the twentieth time that evening. That one had come hard on the heels of the first, only fifteen months in between. Even his father had cautioned him against a repeat: Three years at least, that is how we brought you into the world. Do you want her milk to dry up on her? Go sour? And you call yourself a teacher – is that how the missionaries go about it? Chastened, he resolved to pay greater heed to those intervals in the future. And of course there was the problem of her health; his father had strong ideas about that and was already 'taking steps.' He would pursue it to the exclusion of all else, perhaps even follow him back to Abeokuta on his return journey. He would not entrust such sensitive matters to a mere messenger. That was the other thing – whatever he had done, and whatever there still was to do, it all meant money.

It was still a long way to the New Year but it was not too early to begin stock-taking. The New Year Resolution – a quasi-religious chore – could wait, although he already had a fair idea what that would be. The last resolution, now winding down with the year, had succeeded even by his stringent standards – there was no self-reproach on that score. He had saved well above the goal he set himself, and this was quite apart from his monthly contribution to the Syndicate. But that contribution was routine. If the Great Adventure was to be realised, however, yes, Sipe undoubtedly had the right approach. Again he uncovered in himself a sneaking admiration for the Tempter – the man had no doubts whatsoever. And he moved! Even as he presented a new idea to the ex-Ilés, he had already tried out variations of it in practical terms. The greatest irony was that often it was he, Akinyode, who opened a path to him, quite unwittingly. The teacher would be struck by a new item, an essay in a journal, a letter to the editor, and would quote it to the young entrepreneur in the normal course of a discussion, little thinking of the commercial aspects of the tract. That, however, was precisely what Sipe did see. Gradually, even he began to acquire the habit. Soon he was actually suggesting business ideas to Sipe and trying out a few of his own. The trouble with Sipe was that he could not remain satisfied with half measures, with part-time interest or the casual investment 'on the side.' He wanted his entire circle to abandon their jobs, transfer to Lagos, which was the land of the 'bold and the daring,' and take the plunge into – for him – the certainty of success.

No, not yet, though God knows, that Mephistopheles had already taken over a portion of his mind. He reviewed his own attempted ventures of the year, always keeping in the forefront the difference between his friend and himself: His ventures were not an end in themselves but a means to a medley of ends, all under constant review. Certainly a higher degree, studied for and awarded overseas. Return at least a bachelor of arts. Or law. A bachelor of law, just like his father-in-law. Divinity was also a possible beginning – B.D. And afterwards? Perhaps become an official of the teachers' union. Or principal of a secondary school . . . contribute a book on methods of education, something special, unique, some new scheme for the development of childhood intelligence, a study from which the white education inspectors who visited their schools might even benefit, might acknowledge as something novel in the history of educational systems. Why, he could even return to teach in his alma mater, the training seminary in obscure Ilesa, so often confused with the bigger Ilesha between Ife and Oshogbo. Well, was that not part of the mission of the ex-Ilés, 'to put our own Ilesa on the map, to rescue from obscurity this cradle of our intellect and maternal bosom of our professional family.' At least, so exhorted the Right Reverend Beeston.

I enjoy teaching, he said softly into the night, repeating it with emphasis. True, a few over-pious articles in *The Nigerian Teacher* tended to put one off the profession for ever; Soditan was content to admit that he simply found teaching congenial. And he enjoyed being one of the family, a new family begun at the teacher training seminary, one which increased all the time through numerous encounters with odd and scintillating minds. Wade Cudeback, that far-flung member of the family, trundling through Ashtabula in his jalopy – were such encounters not part of the rewards of his profession? And the others on home ground: stodgy textbook fanatics, stereotype characters, brilliant eccentrics, and earthy individualists. That Eyo Ita, for instance, his first-ever meeting with an intellectual from the Delta Region, a supremely self-confident man, patronising in his approach to white officialdom. He could not think of a more capable choice for the magazine of the Nigeria Union of Teachers. The erudite Miss A. Taylor – why he did not know, but he never thought of her name without the initial. Easily the sensation of the union's last conference, having barely returned from England, where she had bagged a master's each in the arts and the sciences. And she threw her energies straight into the union, the light of battle in her eyes – education, education for the entire protectorate! Was this perhaps what he looked forward to, the inspiration of the vision of his own return to the country after the Great Adventure, after the 'return of the Argonaut with the Golden Fleece'? If one could pick out a turning point in one's life at such a young age, that, Akinyode felt, would be it – the annual conference which brought such giants together. And the drama! A bullish Daodu taking on the headmaster from Awka, who had come wrapped up in a single-minded mission from his people. 'Two orthographies for the Igbo language? Do tell us, we here in the union, tell us what sets the Igbo language apart from Hausa, Yoruba, Itsekiri, Idoma, etc., etc. This union calls for the standardisation of Igbo orthography in conformity with what exists for the languages I have just listed. Right, speak to us in both Igbo orthographies and let us hear the difference!' Then the confused though stubborn response of the poor headmaster as he strove to fulfill the mandate imposed on him by his electors. For a while, the Reverend I. O. was content to let him splutter; then he sprang up to deliver the *coup de grâce*. 'Your position, let me suggest to you, is not really that of holding out for two orthographies, but of arguing for the retention of the one which you prefer. In short, everything you have said, sir, points to a partisanship, not to a conviction on the need for two orthographies. May I suggest therefore that we are on the same side? You accept the position of the union, am I right? That obstacle overcome, we can proceed to speak with one voice, letting all Babel loose when the choice comes to which orthography should be adopted.' And the assembly proceeded to their resolution, calling on the government director of education to move at once on the issue and regularise the situation.

Daodu also swinging the union fully behind him on the matter of local composers. Daodu loved to talk, of course, but even more remarkable, he knew how to listen! And he could never resist the urge to relive the victories. 'Ha' – rubbing his hands together as he stopped afterwards for tea in Soditan's home – 'that seals it.' He visibly preened himself. ' "On the Banks of Allan Waters" must now compete with "*E se rere o.*" That's all we ask, let all melodies contend! Pity you didn't meet the union's patron, Adeniyi-Jones, afterwards, but I have warned him I shall be bringing you. It is important that he meets the rising stars of our educational firmament. And I'll be interested to know what you think of him. We must keep up our assessment of these older mentors or they will fall asleep. Yes, tell me, at least you heard his address, what did you think of it?'

All in all, yes, he found himself in agreement with the white-haired patron – the school as the 'factory of humanity,' in which 'teachers are the artisans.' The young teacher wished he had stopped there, not gone on to propose to that gathering of 'artisans' that the competent teacher 'be like a candle which lights others, while consuming itself.' Now that was what he, Head Teacher Akinyode Soditan, Jebusite of the clan of Ile Lígùn, Ìsarà, Remo, had no intention of being. Nor did he observe anything in the expressions of his listening colleagues which suggested that they also intended to 'consume themselves.' Certainly nothing in the demeanour of the dapper 'Triple E,' Mr E. E. Effiong – an Efik to boot, which conferred on him the right to advertise himself as 'Quadruple E' if he thus chose – nothing in that gnomish face suggested any desire towards such self-immolation in the name of his profession. His face was weathered stone throughout the patron's flight into hyperbole. Effiong was the geography teacher in Abeokuta Grammar School and was rumoured to be on his way to becoming the first African member of the Royal Geographical Society. Nor did the Asaba representative, Mr Onyah, seem any more enamoured of the Jonesian doctrine – but then, he was a special case, and encounters with him were reputed to be guarded. The Colonial Office had its eyes on him, it was rumoured, because of his radical, even subversive, ideas. He had declared that the Nigerian teacher's first duty was to replace the 'educated mind' – which he declared was the same thing as a 'colonial mind' – with a 'cultivated mind.' For fifteen minutes the intense personality had lectured the assembly on this all-important difference, leaving his colleagues more baffled than ever, and mostly at a loss to see why the Colonial Office was afraid of him. Daodu was among the exceptions; he invited him to join his staff any time he chose.

It was nearly a year since that conference, but the euphoria had yet to wear off. Was he not the same obscure head teacher who had launched the battle against the age-test for admission into primary schools? Daodu and Miss A. Taylor had added their determined voices, and together they had carried the day. The union had been duly impressed. In a country where birth certificates were a rarity, young Soditan had argued, how do you assess the age of an aspiring pupil? The head teacher's 'success' was blown up out of all proportion in Ìsarà. It provoked a rash of messages that he come home immediately and be welcomed as a worthy envoy of Ìsarà. The elderly ones, his father's closest friends, also wanted him back, but only to undergo various rites for protection. Enemies, enemies . . . your son is rubbing shoulders with the high and mighty, so bring him home, Josiah, bring him home and have him prepared for that wicked world. Do not leave him naked among strangers!

And those who were not strangers? Those who were anything but strangers? Each day brought a new relation, the dependent of a casual acquaintance or colleague, each with his own need, her own dependency. Go to Josiah's son, he's there. He will know what to do, and if he cannot do it, he knows who to summon to your aid. You can stay with him for a while until you find a place of your own. This was a phenomenon he could not fully fathom. Unlike Sipe, he pursued a quiet life. A taste in well-cut clothes, yes, that was common to all the young men in and outside his circle; beyond that, no outward expression of opulence. He had purchased a brand-new Raleigh bicycle, on which he sometimes partly rode the forty miles to Ìsarà. This again was nothing. He threw no parties, celebrated anniversaries only with his closest friends. So where had it all begun? How did the invasion begin, where would it end? He could understand if he was

263

like Sipe, who possessed the talent of making the mere prospect of a shilling shimmer in the eyes of others like a hundred pounds already in his palm. Yet whenever he visited Sipe, he found no hangers-on, no distant relations arrived in the middle of the night with baggage and dependents. Was there some secret amulet which Sipe buried in his front porch to deflect all intending guests? He wished he could find the secret. He knew he had better find the secret before the old year ended, that dangerous period when people made plans and involved others like him, who were always the last to know!

The Great Adventure – yes, that was also a solution. Away in one of those overseas colleges, he dared any of his tormentors to turn up on his doorstep. But that required the means, the wherewithal. It seemed one only journeyed back to the beginning – to Sipe Efuape and his enterprising genius, bursting to fulfill itself and enrich himself and his selected friends.

Impulsively he turned up the wick again, sat up, and began to rummage through his library, turning the well-worn pages, thumbed and flagged and underlined in red and black. The night was clearly one that would not quickly yield to sleep, so he set the kerosene lamp on the window ledge. Rumours of war. One in every five of those journals, dog-eared, sometimes even termite-nibbled, hinted at the inevitability of war – it was the other intrusive element, very unsettling. How could one even plan beneath the threat of a global war? Would they become a prize to be fought over? In whose hands would the protectorate end? For now he merely sought out a context for his business options, flicking the pages till he found what he was looking for – that 'statistical talisman,' thus mocked Sipe, 'which you have hung around your neck for an entire decade to ward off every straightforward business decision!'

It contained the phrase that appealed so much to his instincts for security in certitudes, not Sipe's breezy lunges towards all speculations that merely hinted at profit. There it was, the key expression to every speculation. It stood out starkly, bold and challenging – 'mathematical exactitude.' Now that was the key. Only this made sense. If one could plan with mathematical exactitude, then all business enterprises became rational endeavours, no different from a salaried job, which yielded a return precisely on a specified day of every month. He had first encountered it in an old copy of *The Elders Review*, under an expression which neither he nor anyone else in The Circle even knew existed: 'Reflections on the World Depression.' Really! Was Ìsarà depressed at that time? Not that he or any native of Ìsarà knew of. Was the Northern or Southern Protectorate part of this Depression? But the real bone of wild contention had to do with the fascinating claim of mathematical exactitudes in farming activities. For the teacher, only some form of security in such expectations could protect one against failure, or indeed against Sipe's propensities for speculative ventures. Surely this was one way which was truly guaranteed to 'affect the present'? *We are about to complete an entire year of general worldwide depression. The 'dark day' was that of October 24, 1929, which made the world cycle of trade stagnation complete, for it was on that day, after vain attempts had been made to put off the impending gray, that American industry found itself face-to-face with a crisis.* . . . How many times did he have to wave this warning in Sipe's face – don't keep tying our prospects to these world industrial seesaws! See what happened to 'the world' in 1929! Bombarded with signs and predictions of global war, he had resurrected that ancient 'talisman' to contest Sipe's plans. But Sipe was unmoved. The way he planned their future, the downfall of those world giants would even guarantee a 'killing' for their own business schemes. 'One world's Depression is another world's buoyancy – did our world here even know of that Depression?' The logic failed to persuade the teacher, or indeed any member of their Syndicate. He skipped rapidly through. . . . Yes, there was also Mussolini's reference to that Hauptmann fellow, whose books he had then ordered but never received: *We have only to recall the poem of Gerhart Hauptmann, the great German dramatist, who pictures the poor hand-weaver trying to compete with the crushing loom.* Well, if he did travel overseas, he would certainly track down Mr Hauptmann, the unknown writer who had provoked his revisit to Iseyin. Wade Cudeback too could claim some of the credit, but it was that Hauptmann reference that took his thoughts straight back to Iseyin. As for the villain Mussolini, he must have a humane side to him after all if he could be moved by a poet's depiction of the 'poor weaver.' Were they any poorer than the weavers at Iseyin, he wondered anew? He experienced an overwhelming urge to find the poem, again relishing his excursion to Iseyin, so different from those school journeys through the town when he had not yet learned to *look*. Were there other crucial aspects of local industry which St Simeon's had trained them to ignore? The passage he sought was on the next page, heavily underlined in red and black: *This year we celebrate the twenty-fifth anniversary of the foundation of the International Institute of Agriculture by His Majesty King Victor Emmanuel III of Italy on the initiative of the late David Lubin, economist and merchant, of San Francisco. This institute collects daily, even hourly, from all parts of the world, by telegraph and radio, governmental information from official sources on the crop conditions of the various countries. After their tabulations, the experts can state with mathematical exactitude what the world supply of wheat will be in any current year.*

Of all the debates ever embarked upon by the ex-Ilés, this had proved one of the most intense, certainly the most prolonged. The implications were taken personally; after all, there was hardly one of them who did not have an ongoing farming occupation within the family. If wheat, why not maize? Groundnuts? Cocoa? Even Osibo, whose fastidiousness made him look down on farm work, was drawn into partisan positions. This was too vast, too hyperbolic a claim. Drug production, yes. Iron and steel ingots, maybe – all it required was to assess the potential of new mines, anticipate the exhaustion rate of ongoing ones. But farming? Farming was a hazard at best, a slave of the vagaries of rain and sunshine, locusts, kwela bird, foot-and-mouth disease, the black-pod blight, and fungoid parasites. Yet here was this European supranationalist claiming that all the variables could be anticipated! Even Onafowokan, who taught algebra and geometry at Igbore, felt that this was not merely an impossible claim; it was sacrilegious. No wonder there befell America the plague of the Great Depression, from which – note – the African peoples were not only spared, but of which they remained blissfully unaware! If that was not a divine punishment, then the Seven Plagues of Egypt were not divinely inflicted. Both Mussolini and that man Lubin were saying, in effect, that there was no God. Harvest was a season, a God-ordained season, not a mathematical piece of exactitude!

To Akinyode, however, there were crucial down-to-earth considerations tied up with Lubin's institute. He still hesitated over a commitment to a small cocoa farm which his father had then been negotiating on his behalf. So he waved the letter from his go-between, Oderinde, at the others and demanded a hearing. 'Argue all you want,' he urged. 'What I would like us to do is find some means of profiting from Lubin's institute. Why don't we simply agree that Benito Mussolini should have said mathematical *approximation* instead of exactitude? Right? Approximation. Of course even the mere gathering of accurate statistics from all over the world is formidable enough. And our society definitely believes in God – or gods. That means we also believe in what we call an act of God – which is the same as reverses of human expectations. Right? After all, Job is there as a warning; so are those fat and lean years following each other and playing havoc with Mr Pharaoh's granaries! So none of us will ever claim that farming is an exact science – I mean, who can actually predict the harvest in any given year?'

The Circle mulled this over; it seemed a reasonable compromise. And they prided themselves in always giving even the devil his due. So one after the other, with a last-ditch resistance here and there, they took off their hats to the late David Lubin and conceded their envy of the International Institute of Agriculture. Ogunba accepted the task of writing a letter on their behalf to 'Akede Eko.' It would demand that the colonial government set up a branch of that institute in Lagos, which would cater to the protectorate farmers in an approximate way, not infringing on the whims of the gods with any provocative assumptions. But even an approximating centre was needed at home. What was the sense of going to Italy or San Francisco in order to find out – even by telegraph – the quantity of maize, cocoa, cassava, or timber Ìsarà would produce the following year?

For Efuape, the entire exercise was a waste of time. Another timid, drudgery-enamoured venture! Did it make sense to run a postage-stamp-sized farm which had to be overseen in one's absence anyway? He pooh-poohed Oderinde's scouting mission, snatching the letter from Soditan's hands and reading it aloud. Did Soditan think that Lubin's institute had time for dwarf ventures like this 'microscopic patch of land in the tropic jungle'? Mussolini was far too busy to be bothered with the like of Yode's piffling amateur cocoa plantation. And the passionate but fragmented syntax of Oderinde only added ammunition to his artillery as he shot it down in jeers! *For such a flourish and fructful cocoa farm to be going for a mere fifteen pounds is nothing short of a Christmas miracle from God.* In that letter Oderinde had also threatened that if the teacher did not come to see the farm, latest in three weeks time, *I will come in personal to see you because, as for this matter, if the mountain has not coming to Mohammed, Mohammed will then go to the mountain.* 'Well, my dear pupil teacher, does this Mohammed plan to bring the cocoa farm along with him? It will fit into the pocket of his *agbada* without difficulty, I'm sure!' All mathematical exactitudes and approximations vanished in the uproarious laughter.

Unmoved, Akinyode continued to nurse that prospect. Cocoa was constantly in the news. And it held, he admitted, a deep childhood attraction – rows of cocoa trees with their luscious pods were embedded in his earliest concepts of earth as green and golden spaces. The gold was wealth, there was no denying that. The richest farmers he knew had cocoa farms. And there was the authority of his friend Opeilu, a produce inspector, who would sometimes bemoan his job, which was to weigh and grade the riches of others in the shape of cocoa seeds. The proposed farm was at Ifo, some thirty miles away to the south. Transport service to Lagos was reasonable, and from Aké, Ifo lay midway on the route to Lagos. That was definitely part of the attraction. But cocoa?

Again he resorted to his information bank, selecting one journal from the more recent pile, which lay segregated on a shelf above his bedpost, directly behind his head. Along the way to the sought-out page, war intervened yet again, rearing its head through warnings by the League of Nations over the matter of Eritrea. But why, why? the head teacher demanded. And that proposal – arbitration – what did this mean? Mussolini lived in Italy, Haile Selassie in Abyssinia. What was there to 'arbitrate' when only one could be an intruder in the other's territory? Ogunba was right, the drums of war were already being sounded, only the dancers still hesitated. Akinyode proceeded to the essay signed 'A Produce Broker.' Its message was simple but negative: The best days were over for the cocoa industry in the Gold Coast. Soditan's dilemma was how to balance this with the strong demurrer entered by the editors of the journal themselves. Now that was the nub of the matter. In between the two, the adventurous cocoa grower must himself take a position, launch forth towards his fortune or withdraw his horns, as Sipe would say, 'like a frightened snail whose antennae had felt the sheerest touch of adverse reality.' *In printing this article, it is probably desirable that we should make it clear that we do not agree with the writer.* Probably? What else is the job of editors but to assert their own opinion on such crucial issues? Akinyode could never overcome the irritation he felt at this editorial coyness. The editors were British, which probably accounted for it – they had this tendency towards apologetic, even tentative, language in straightforward matters. A disagreement meant a second opinion, and journals are meant to record opinions. He succeeded in overlooking this quirk for now and continued: *The main reason for the suggestion appears to be one of doubt as to the ability of the Gold Coast farmers to increase their efficiency. This is a challenge to which, we hope and believe, the Gold Coast farmers will reply.* Challenge, yes, but – and there the teacher entered his . . . not so much disagreement as qualification – everything still depended on demand, as any market woman would impress on you. This was where David Lubin played such a dominant role in all his speculations, but only, alas, in a wishful way. If, if, if! If only he could find out, with or with as near 'mathematical exactitude' as possible, how much cocoa was being produced in the world at any given time, then indeed he could take a decision on Oderinde's find. But to enter the competitive world of cocoa just like that – well, maybe Sipe would. Certainly not him. That was one sure way of ending up an involuntary producer of fermented cocoa wine. And how many people outside Ijebu really drank that stuff?

Well, if not cocoa, what then? Cotton? Not unless he wanted to live in the far-off north. He tried to think of some of his townsmen who lived in the cotton belt – Kano, Sokoto, Katsina. Famade, perhaps, his tailoring friend? He was well placed to make enquiries for him. Or Oye, the ex-serviceman – he would jump to attention on receiving a request from his old mentor. The problem was finding out the situation of world supply and demand. And there was timber, but seriously now, like Node, not with any more romantic thoughts of books and backyard paper mills à la Ashtabula. Yes, timber was gradually proving itself. The colonial government burrowed deeper and deeper into the interior like soldier ants, opening up virgin areas. New brands of heavy-duty lorries appeared on the roads, laden with mahogany, afara, teak, iroko . . . He revelled for some moments in a picture of himself riding, Wemuja-style, on the back of a giant log, an endless log which began in his own concession in Ìsarà, was felled with a thunderous splash all the way across the creeks of Epe, on a waterfront where the flying sprays would reach Efuape's house and shatter his complacency – yes, Mr Rooster, here I come, you didn't think I had it in me, did you? – then smashing against the other side of the Atlantic and bouncing down the Reversing Falls, where his friend Wade Cudeback's contemplation would be rudely broken by this sight beyond the marvels of his Magnetic Mountain. What would the man say as his pen pal coolly stepped off the back of that if-all-the-trees-were-one-tree monstrosity from the heart of Ìsarà's forests, as yet unpenetrated by man or machine? What would be his greeting? Mr – no – Prince Soditan, I presume? Merchant prince, of course . . .

The teacher pulled himself up abruptly, alarmed at himself. Akinyode, what is going on in your head? Has Sipe finally taken over your mind? This is worse than daydreaming, this is madness! Where, for a start, do you obtain the capital? Even a second-hand motor lorry is beyond the savings of a lifetime for a pupil teacher with a wife and two infant children and an extended family that acknowledges no limit! What do you do for capital?

And what of the looming war? If there is war and your meagre capital has taken flight to some commercial centre of a beleaguered nation, that is it! Fii-oom, good-bye! Even if it is not cash, you use up your savings or take a loan to obtain the timber, float it down the Niger or Ogun River and onto the high seas. You sit down to await cash on delivery. War begins. Sea routes blocked by Adolf Hitler. End of life savings. This again was a key difference. Sipe saw the war as OPPORTUNITY! *You read only the negative articles, Yode, only the negative ones. Don't you know a war brings about demands, creates its own needs? An entire industry springs up to support the madness of war. Rubber, for instance. Have you thought of rubber? This is the time to acquire a rubber plantation or two. Forget your David Lubin – war needs food, cash crops, iron and steel, even the gum arabica which you so Jebusitically boil in your backyard, you will be amazed how it will shoot up to astronomical heights both in demand and prices. Soap! Have you forgotten the article you showed me in* The Nigerian Teacher *on the soap-making industry? Ask yourself, why does a teachers' journal bother its head with soap-making? The British who edit that journal are looking for cheap supplies. They want to turn you all into cheap labour, earning a pittance, for their war needs. But if we go into it in a businesslike manner, manage a factory which guarantees a regular supply, not depend on the whims and leisure caprices of a bunch of exhausted teachers . . . I don't say it has to be soap; in fact I hate soap factories – have you ever visited one? The fumes are poison, they cling to your clothes. You feel you need a wash as soon as you are out of there. But we don't even have to manufacture soap; we become the middlemen and leave all those journals like* The Nigerian Teacher *to encourage the home amateurs, then buy from them and deal directly with the big companies – UAC and Lever Brothers and others. The sky is the limit, so why keep looking over your shoulders at the approaching war? Look at the silver lining for a change . . . In fact, it is no silver lining but a rich seam, waiting to be mined by the fearless . . .*

Admit it now, Soditan murmured to himself as his eyelids finally began to droop and he turned the lampwick down for the last time that night, it was not . . . no, he intended to be scrupulously fair to himself . . . it was only partly the travelogues of Cudeback and his chance encounter with the Mussolini-Hauptmann dialogue which spurred his bicycle excursion to Iseyin. Animating him also was the son of Efuape, Sipe, the merchant adventurer to whose commercial urgings he had sought a more modest counter. If Sipe could venture all the way to Italy to trade in worsted wool, albeit by mail, he would see what Iseyin, a home of weavers nearer to hand, could provide. No one had expected the soft-living, Lagos-besotted Sipe to accept the challenge thrown at him, but the Resolute Rooster surprised them all, accepting both the challenge and risks of the journey. Alas for the son of Efuape! A few days to setting-out, he developed a stubborn boil, as he put it, *right within that parting in the lump of flesh which God, the true inventor of bicycles, had shaped to fit athwart the saddle of the bicycle.*

Akinyode rode and strolled alone through the dusty streets of Saki, glimpsing, through gloomy mud interiors, busy looms festooned in coloured threads, flashing shuttles and pedals packing the steady-spun lines from spindles into the famous Saki fabric on upright frames. *As I pushed my bicycle slowly through the main street of weavers, having dismounted*

the better to savour the smell of dyes and bask in the industry of our ancient craft,
I felt like a two-legged spider strolling through arcades of multicoloured webs.
How Wade Cudeback would respond on receiving this first-ever adventurous challenge to his own thrilling correspondence, Akinyode had yet to find out. But a copy of the letter to his cousin 'Saaki' Akinsanya had already elicited a most envious response, uncharacteristically effusive. It was further reinforced by a threat that the schoolteacher's next exploration would not take place without him. Sipe, on his part, could not decide if it was the receipt of the letter from his would-be travelling companion which had *made my boil over with such disappointment that it erupted, to my great embarrassment, as I was at that moment reading your missive aloud to a group of visitors who had come to sympathise with my predicament.* Or was it, he proposed, the fact that among his audience was their friend Dr Otolorin, for he had called *not simply to sympathise, but with a wicked scalpel ready to lance the troublesome boil, and had only paused to listen to the contents of your mettlesome epistle.* The boil, Sipe confessed, began to loosen its stubborn consistency on the appearance of Otolorin's scalpel and proceeded *on its own volition, to do that which I had so fervently prayed for these past four weeks. Such is the power of fear, my dear Yode, and the terror which even a human boil has of a doctor's knife.*

But it was nostalgia, unquestionably, which took him beyond the planned limits of the trip. From Iseyin he found that his bicycle wheels turned inexorably towards Ilesa. The motor road was not fully opened and the frequency of lorries meant that he could pay for space for both himself and his bicycle, which rode tightly strapped against the side of the lorry. For several long minutes after he had cycled from Ilesa's improvised motor park to the seminary, Akinyode stood before the gates of St Simeon's, uncertain whether or not he really wanted to pass through. For the first time he became uncertain of his attachment. Was it all imagined? Was it yet again an emotion which he felt he *ought* to experience? The compound was silent, which he expected, as it was vacation time. He paused and listened, half-expecting to hear the drone of the Reverend Beeston's motorcycle as it raced dangerously round the gate pillars – a favourite act of his. What would he say to him? How would he judge the progress his pupil had made since he quit these grounds for the last time and took on Beeston's role for other trainee teachers in Aké? And the rest of the staff? Was Dr Mackintosh, the music teacher, still on active service?

Akinyode pushed his bicycle through the gates, headed for the open field behind the principal's office, where Dr Mackintosh had undergone his sad experience of cultural defeat. 'A knowledge of classical music is indispensable to the cultivated mind,' he preached, as he embarked on suiting some action to his words. The experiment had begun modestly enough; a few students were singled out, young Soditan at the fore of those who had shown some musical aptitude. Every Sunday morning – that is, those Sunday mornings when Dr Mackintosh succeeded in rousing himself from a Saturday-night stupor induced by visits to a notorious corner of Ilesa township – he would lure his victims into his living room, serve out cups of tea, and crank up his rusty gramophone. He prefaced his choice of records with a brief lecture, shut his eyes, raised his forehead to the ceiling, and proceeded to intone the range of emotions which he expected his pupils to undergo as the strings of violins or massed choral voices suffused his living room. His eyes were invariably shut as the record played, his head nodding gently to the imaginary baton of the conductor – this was when his pupils attacked the saucerful of shortbread biscuits, the main attraction of the Sunday-morning sessions for the majority.

Akinyode wheeled his bicycle thoughtfully across the lawn, the neglected grass tickling his ankles. Any moment, it seemed, Dr Mackintosh would appear, clutching an armful of Bakelite discs and humming a Bach fugue, totally oblivious of his surroundings. He would probably look at him with reproach, as it was he, Akinyode, who had most disappointed him when he took his music experiments out onto that very lawn to embrace the entire colony of seminarians.

Et tu, Soditan?

And poor Akinyode had felt so sad for the good-natured Mackintosh; the guilt made him wince afresh each time he heard his music drifting through St Simeon's fields from his bungalow. The buildup towards the advertised concert! The trayloads of sandwiches, buns and cakes, teas and lemonades, prepared by the teachers' wives. Chairs and benches dragged from schoolrooms and the chapel. Special guests from the rival training school, St Andrew's in Oyo, all come for the event of the term, a treat from Mackintosh's collection of classical records. The chairs on the front row for teachers, the benches to the rear for pupils. And Mackintosh had also invited the touring inspector of education to participate in the experiment of imparting classical music appreciation to young Africans and weaning them from their crude though vigorous music. To this end he now took his place among the students, his physical presence echoing his living-room commentaries and narrations on the motion of the music, its colours and textures, caressing the scenery it evoked, not too remote from what they all knew, and of course there had been photos of Scottish hills and dales in Dr Mackintosh's living room . . .

272

'Imagine a river flowing . . . the wind gently swaying the willows . . . sunlight glinting on pebbles as a trout threads a silvery path through the ripples . . .'

The benches hardened against some sixty-odd buttocks. Slowly, Akinyode became aware that the night was filled with menace. He prayed hard, staring across the lawn at the wooden chapel with its wide low-slung windows, a tar-coated structure that never failed to remind him of the police barracks at Ibadan past which he trudged on his journey to the seminary. He then turned his concentration on the pale, animated profile whose ghostly arms furtively sliced through and enfolded the night air as he conjured up nostalgic images of homeland. The music washed over attentive heads. Akinyode gritted his teeth, tensed his muscles, and prayed.

The night had been specially chosen – full moon. There was also a working light provided by a hurricane lamp placed near the phonograph itself, next to a large *araba* tree. The tree cast scattered shadows over the assembly. A light breeze fanned their faces and the grass felt cool on their bare feet. From time to time a bat squeaked across their heads, arousing a genuine interest for the duration of its passage. An assistant had been detailed to change the records and re-crank the gramophone while Mackintosh introduced the next item on the musical fare.

'And now think of mountain peaks, and snow falling gently through fir trees. Then, this next movement, you will imagine a storm which has been brewing in the distance. It now approaches, sweeps through the mountain gorges. The scattered fleeces of white clouds are framed against an inky-dark heaven – behind it all is the frown of an angry God. When the cymbals clash . . .'

And the black heads dropped, one after the other, sank onto their chests, oblivious now to Mackintosh's unspoken programme notes. The local clouds then shifted from the face of the moon and revealed the pride of Dr Mackintosh slumped in various postures, heads on adjoining shoulders, on their own laps, sprawled over benches. Some had taken advantage of their well-to-the-rear positions and given up the struggle completely. They abandoned their benches altogether and spread out comfortably on the cushioning grass. A few snores actually punctuated the second movement of Schubert's Third. Not one, and this was what broke the heart of Dr Mackintosh, not one Simeonite was left awake that night, not even one, he murmured over and over again as the music stopped and he gazed, horror-stricken, at the philistinic motley.

But it was the presence of Akinyode Soditan, seated right next to him yet oblivious to the world, which broke his heart. He had shown the greatest promise, and Dr Mackintosh had remarked him to his colleagues. Soditan's eyes were wide open, fixed solidly on the *araba* tree, the last in the line of objects which he had commandeered that night to save him from the waves of sleep that threatened his sorely tried eyelids. At first Mackintosh had permitted himself to grasp at this small crumb of consolation as he rose and surveyed the field of prostrate bodies. Turning to his favourite pupil, he ordered: 'Soditan, wake up these savages!'

But Yode remained in his ramrod position, eyes staring but unseeing, and Mackintosh knew that the very worst had indeed happened. He touched him on the shoulder, and young Soditan keeled over, then began to scramble up in fright, not knowing where he was. The Scot let out a heartrending sigh, as one who felt that he had indeed drained his cup of gall to the bitter dregs.

Et tu, Soditan?

II

EFUAPE

Misty dawn in the riverine town of Epe. A young tax inspector put finishing touches to his battle strategy and nodded with satisfaction. Sipe, son of Efuape, had long identified the main obstacle to his grand design – the solution was to disarm that individual, and the rest of the ex-Ilés would follow his lead. It was time to abandon piecemeal, tentative action. Crumbs! Yes, that was it, crumbs! It was all that had so far fallen in their hands while others made off with the body of the feast. Did the Arimojes of this world possess two heads? No. Just one, like them, like every other human being. If anything, if one went by what each head contained, that *ara oke** probably had even less than one – was the man not completely illiterate? Yet it had not prevented him from becoming a millionaire – or so it was rumoured. Rumour or not, no one disputed that his feet were on the highest rungs of the ladder of wealth. His houses were vast palaces; the number of motor lorries that bore the sign ARIMOJE TRANSPORT SERVICES – even in that rudimentary stage of the motor vehicle in West Africa – was the envious talk of the country. Not bad, not bad at all for an illiterate. Perhaps that was the trouble with himself and The Circle – they were crippled by too much literacy.

Certainly Akinyode was. He, Sipe, had far more sense of the world. Since his abrupt departure from the teacher training seminary, so many years ago that the pain of it had utterly vanished, his reading horizons had been confined to mail-order catalogues. His favourite was Lennards, from whose glossy pages he conjured shimmering vistas of an opulent future. The magic wand took various shapes – patent leather or tanned leather shoes, ties, ready-made suits, wind-cheaters, felt hats, watches, fountain pens and assorted stationery, handbags, vanity cases and toilet accessories. When he dipped into journals of the kind that had seduced the mind of his friend Akinyode Soditan, it was only to seek out the advertisement pages, those foreign companies forever seeking raw materials or agents to dispose of their own products. And of course the shipping notices – that was crucial to his reputation: Whatever Sipe promised by a certain date would be delivered on that very date, or earlier. His Christmas cards and New

* Country bumpkin.

277

Year calendars, for instance, complete with envelopes, arrived at least a month even before the orders of the C.M.S. Bookshops. Sipe canvassed for his orders – which expanded all the time – mainly from the young professionals, a few businessmen also, but mostly office clerks, teachers, and college students. His clientele was flung across the country, from Lagos to Port Harcourt and Kano, so he was careful to commence his contacts very early, order, clear, and mail those seasonal cards and gifts to their destination in time to avoid the postal rush at end of year.

But these were small, dilettante beginnings; now it was time to move on and win more territory, challenge the Lebanese and Indian traders who monopolised the cloth trade. Go to Ereko, Idumagbo, Ebute Metta, and Isale Eko – whose rosy faces did one see smirking in the shadowy interior of shops, shelves bursting with rolls and rolls of chiffon, voile, gabardine, worsted wool, and every kind of apparel and their accessories? It was these Middle Easterners, keeping a sharp eye on their local shop assistants as they measured out the cloths to local customers. The jewellery shops also belonged to them. Everything well-turned-out ladies or gentlemen of refinement required to hold up their own in society, the Lebanese and the Indians reaped the profit thereof. Well, it was time for the Jebusite to match the Levantine in enterprise, and this was his message to those vacillating seminarians.

Akinyode was the problem. No sooner did Sipe succeed in firing their imagination with a BOLD NEW PLAN, than the schoolteacher would embark on some diversion for extending the debate – at the end of which, the will to act in concert would peter out. Always he brought up something or other he had just read, in the same journals – the irony of it! – on which Sipe depended for his business aspirations. For the teacher, even the abdication of King Edward of England had only prompted a whole new series of considerations. Suppose it led to civil war in England? Would their investments be guaranteed protection? From then on, it was an entire afternoon spent discussing the English War of the Roses while Sipe fumed silently. Oh, he also took part in reconstructing and arguing details of that war, but at least he had the grace to be angry with himself afterwards. For the rest of The Circle, however, it was a Sunday afternoon spent most profitably. Profitably! Did these friends of his understand the meaning of profit? And so a meeting which he had expressly summoned to look into the logistics of locating abattoirs to supply tons of dried bones to a firm in Birmingham was frittered away with purely speculative manoeuvres of some incomprehensible battles fought by figures encased in iron and steel across some remote English plains! Who cared whether there were intriguing parallels between those battles and the Kiriji or Ijaiye wars of Yorubaland? What was it to him if the famed Dahomean 'Amazons' could have taught the House of York or Lancaster a lesson or two in military tactics? They did not even touch aspects that truly concerned them in those Supplies Wanted columns of the journals which had provoked the meeting! What, for instance, was the nature of the products for which the bones were needed? Was it perhaps something they could themselves manufacture on their own? Bones were required for *something* – what was that something?

And the Belgian bonds – Hypothek and Creditbank – Efuape had primed his friends' expectations and they were all ready to fill out the application forms. Investments guaranteed, on good authority, to quadruple in value within two years. But trust the teacher to run into a reference to an ancient indictment by a British knight who had uncovered unspeakable cruelties by the Belgians in the Congo! So, up came the moral issues. Arguments that swung backwards and forwards and ended in nothing! How do we know for certain, Sipe had insisted? The European powers were rival territory-grabbers – could anyone deny that? Roger Casement was an Englishman – could they be certain that this campaign was not simply anti-Belgian propaganda? And in any case the man was long dead, hanged for a traitor. Whoever heard of civilised people cutting off ears and hands for failure to fulfill the supply quota of cassava and rubber and whatever else? Did they think that those Belgians had never read the fable of the goose that laid the golden egg? Self-interest made such action illogical! It was far too improbable. Did the British cut off anyone's ear in their West African colonies and protectorates? Well, he had bested Yode in that argument – at least the teacher failed to produce a convincing counter. But his triumph was short-lived, it proved no more than a Pyrrhic victory. The Circle resolved that the teacher write to England for further details – which of course took care of the closing date for making that most enticing investment. Yode, Sipe ruefully concluded, was a cunning procrastinator!

This time, he would take the wind out of his sails, take them all by surprise. He would insist no more that they all abandon their jobs – his new plans now permitted them to wear their chains of slavery, so beloved of them, poor timid souls! No more insistence on the immediate hire of imposing premises with a blazing signboard which would announce the entry of EX-ILÉS ENTERPRISES into one of the main commercial streets of Lagos. No, they would not even hire a store. No overhead. There would be no risky investments. The key to this new operation was so simple:

Employ a full-time agent who would operate from his own home. In case of an emergency – let us say, the arrival of a large order which could not be immediately distributed – Sipe's living room would be converted to a temporary warehouse. The essence was a rapid turnover: advance orders from clientele – arrivals of goods – immediate distribution, but this time on a nonstop basis. Their employee would act both as clearing and forwarding agent. Then watch the progress for a year. The first line of business was already decided by him – clothing, and Italian clothing at that. He had made the contacts, his suppliers were ready – only the capital was missing, and a fair proportion of that was already guaranteed. Sipe felt he had earned the right to give himself full marks for his new strategy and the groundwork that surely guaranteed its success. Yes, success, that eloquent conqueror of misgivings, would, without further urging from him, make even Yode 'cast his chalk of slavery at the blackboard and take his place among the adventurous heroes of our time.' He flicked through the thin file of letters from his prospective partners in Italy, his already buoyant spirits further uplifted by the names that rang in seemingly familiar accents to his Remo ears. Morigi? *Ha, mee r'igi, ere r'emi ri.* Benito? *B'eni to se, be ra mi se.* Milano? *Emi Sipe re mi lano.** One more year as a wage slave. If the others could bear it, so could he. But only one more year; after that, the local government council in Epe would have to find itself a new tax inspector.

There remained only one unresolved question: what to do with the Spirit of Layeni! Impulsively he called out, 'Mrs E.'

'I am nearly ready.' And his wife peeked out through an opening in the curtain that separated the living room from her bedroom, hair halfway piled up above her head, smelling lightly of the effects of the hot iron. Sipe glanced up, was startled yet again by her beauty and saddened equally by her continuing childlessness. He caught his breath, lost his nerve, and muttered a reminder of the departure time of their ferry. The advice he had suddenly thought of seeking from his spouse was swept aside as he gazed upon her loveliness and chafed at the luck that married its desired fulfillment. And he reasoned also that to bring her into the orbit of the Spirit of Layeni, even through knowledge of his plans, might jeopardise the remedies she undertook for her cure. One never knew what might happen in these matters. Invocation of such spirits could destroy those very planes on which her cure depended. So Mrs E. withdrew her head and

---

* Do I see a tree? No, I see no trees, only profit. Beni to? As one who can do it, so does one proceed. Milano? Indeed it is I, Sipe, who blazes the path.

returned to her toilette. He shook his head at the lopsidedness of Fate. Time, Sipe, give it more time. . . . He took out the Lennards catalogue and marked a shimmering frock, which he would order now for her next birthday. His spirits rose again and he decided it was time to clip the pink carnation on the wide lapel of his gray worsted suit . . .

They had set out for Otuyemi's wedding early enough, taking no chances, but the day which had dawned over such rosy vistas now seemed resolved to end in total disaster. Worst of all was his feeling of incongruity in the stranded company in which he found himself; a three-button suit of worsted wool set Sipe apart from the other passengers who huddled in the shade of the broken-down lorry. Their loud to mumbled variations on the themes of anxiety and resignation had long ceased to divert him; the letters he had begun to compose in his mind to the bridegroom to explain his absence, and of course to the ex-Ilés recounting the day's misadventures, lay suspended in midphrase. On the dirt road between Ijebu-Ode and Iperu at midday, trapped in his brand-new catalogue-order suit complete with a silk-lined waistcoat, the once proud ensemble now sadly shrouded by the dust of voyage that had seeped steadily through floorboards and loosely welded joints – it was difficult at this moment to find those witty turns of phrase with which he delighted to challenge his friends. The wilful vehicle had, naturally, chosen the most arid sector of the road for its final rebellion, far from the lush forest and vast stretches of cocoa and kola-nut plantations through which they had earlier driven with such confidence. Now there was only scrub and hot November wind. When he took out the breast-pocket handkerchief which he had folded into a fleur-de-lys that morning, after applying its regulation drops of Yardley's Olde English Lavender, he was not surprised to find a handful of dust fly out from its folds. No, it was decidedly straining the mind to attempt to order his experiences in that inclement hour.

Still, the time had to be occupied somehow, and so it came about that, without actually setting out to do so, Sipe began to 'bring his books up to date.' It was an exercise which came with the training for his abandoned profession, and one which he undertook with moderate frequency, far less often than, for instance, the schoolteacher. This resumption only made him more dejected. His card, even before he reeled off his myriad undertakings for detailed assessment, read, 'Poor. Below expectations.' He pronounced the verdict only just audibly. Yet such was the heartfelt gloom his voice conveyed that his fellow travellers thought that the judgment had been passed on the efforts of the sweaty, grease-stained driver and his mate, who still wrestled chunks of engine parts from beneath the vehicle, clambered through the bonnet, and re-emerged through a hole in the floorboard of the driver's cabin – all to no avail. The passengers were inclined to agree with him but found the remark rather unhelpful. A motor vehicle was still largely a mystery, and breakdowns were simply part of its God-given character. In any case, as they looked him up and down, they could not help wondering what he was doing in a passenger lorry at all, even if he had occupied the 'first-class' compartment, that is, the front cabin, separated from the driver by a token wood partition. His appearance placed him firmly among the occupants of those few cars which had passed them along the road.

Sipe's self-recriminations knew no bounds, taking on himself the blame for his predicament – even including the breakdown of the vehicle. There was nothing he could have done about the ferry that had broken down in Lagos the previous day, yet he felt that he ought to have anticipated this and made alternative arrangements. He had gone to the pier in all confidence, Mrs E., as he fondly called his beautiful wife, dressed with matching elegance beside him. On such mornings Sipe experienced what he called pure happiness, a sense of soulful enlargement as he relished the frank stares of admiration from the townspeople of Epe. The direct route between Epe and Ijebu-Ode was cut. The ferry would have taken them to Ikorodu, where a Morris Minor car and a Ford pickup had been chartered to take the guests, their finery untarnished, to the society wedding. The pier itself had contributed an additional sense of achievement – 'the beginnings of bigger things to come' – as he stood on the new-laid planks, the supports still smelling of tar. Within mere weeks of his transfer to Epe from Lagos, he had persuaded the District Officer of the urgent need to replace the shaky embarkation pier. His argument was sound: The Resident would soon visit, inaugurating the new local governments –which really meant a few lucky ones – carved out from the former Ijebu-Ode administrative territory. A new pier, duly publicised by the Epe Descendants Union resident in Lagos, would place Epe at the top of the list of towns to be so honoured. It was the last sensation of pleasure Sipe would obtain that day. The ferry, which so reliably plied between Lagos, Epe, and Ikorodu every other day, had had its propellers twisted into a shapeless hulk by a drifting log the previous night and had barely limped into Lagos. At Ikorodu the motorcars waited for the pair as long as was reasonable, then departed with the other guests. Dejected, Sipe escorted his wife back to their home. They had both decided to make the best of a bad job – Mrs E. would stay home while Sipe, unencumbered, undertook the epic journey on behalf of both.

Sipe prided himself on his resourcefulness. Within an hour he had obtained a canoe with outboard motor – road transportation from Epe was now out of the question. He would go first to Lagos and hope that there would be a lorry or pickup travelling towards Ijebu-Ode. Sipe disembarked at Ebute-Ero, where he not only found a lorry but obtained the seat in the front cabin, easily displacing a produce inspector who was still hesitating over the extra fare. They made good speed and his spirits began to rise. And then the engine coughed once, twice, a few times more, began to hiccup with increasing violence, and finally shuddered to a halt. The passengers all disembarked and waited. Sipe at first stood at the rear, ready to flag down any passing vehicle. The afternoon grew longer. Not a lorry passed them, and the few cars were full. A motorcyclist did stop and Sipe was momentarily tempted to buy a ride to Iperu on the pillion. Another look at the rider soon changed his mind, however – whatever little gloss remained on his suit would be fully extinguished by the dust before they had gone half a mile. And the lorry engine did begin at the time to give some hints of resuscitation, raising hopes in the breasts of the passengers. The sun glowered down as the minutes dragged by. The younger ones of the travellers had long taken refuge beneath the lorry itself; others sought varying degrees of relief within or beside it. Incredibly, a nursing mother had constructed quite a passable shelter with the aid of her headtie and wrapper and the meagre shade cast by a scrub that the early harmattan drought had somehow overlooked. It was her resourcefulness indeed that had first triggered off the urge to share the day's reverses with Akinyode. *My dear Yode,* he began, *never let it be gainsaid – necessity is indeed the mother of invention, and I did make her acquaintance today, in the most unlikely of places. And a mother, let me hasten to add, is the master of necessity.* It was a good opening, he thought. The teacher, overwhelmed by that opening salvo, would first put the letter aside, mix himself some ginger or lemon juice, and sink back in his armchair to relish the rest of his narrative.

Long after that letter had been abandoned, Sipe observed a most unusual increase in the traffic. It was decidedly out of place. The roads between Ijebu townships and Lagos constituted his familiar beat, and he had never, in the years since he saw his first motorcar, never seen such a frequency of motor traffic outside Lagos. At first he had been merely annoyed to find that they were all going in the wrong direction, that is, away from his own destination. And then he paid attention to the passengers – such as could be discerned through the dust – and saw that the men were variants of his own sleekly outfitted figure. Evidently another wedding. It took a while for Sipe to recognise in their exhausted, not anticipatory, bearing that they were not going to another wedding; they were coming from one! And then, as he identified a couple whose clothes he had himself helped to procure for the occasion, the crushing truth descended on him – they were all coming from *the* wedding. It was all over. The church ceremony, the photographic session, the reception. In another hour or two the bride would be ceremonially extracted from her parents' home while the bridegroom, waiting in his own home with impatience, would undergo the customary badinage.

Sipe felt thoroughly ill-used; how on earth would he explain his absence to Otuyemi? And who, at such short notice, had Otuyemi found to propose the toast of the bridegroom? For a moment he took consolation in the fact that he had not, after all, defaulted as best man, then corrected himself. If he had been the best man, he would have slept in Iperu the previous day, overseeing all the arrangements. His posting to Epe had, however, derailed that proposal, and Otuyemi had been quite understanding. But to fail in the end even to turn up and liven up the occasion with one of his memorable speeches, sparkling with wit and skeetering just on the edge of the naughty, that gall he found bitter and excessive. As he watched the passing motorcars trailing one another at careful intervals to avoid the cloud raised by the preceding vehicle, he added a comment to his abandoned letter: *I felt, my dear Yode, like one of the foolish virgins in that biblical parable*.

Homeward bound – Sipe finally crossed the road to the other side and caught a market lorry on its way back to Ikorodu – he took out two sheets of paper from his inner breast pocket. One contained what looked like a shopping list, the other a series of questions and answers. At the bottom of the sheet was a question, in capitals and in his own handwriting, which summed up his dilemma: DO I PROCEED OR NOT?

The teacher training seminary at Ilesa was now little more than a recollected idyll of youthful comradeship, though Sipe still enjoyed answering to a famous name bestowed on him at that institution. The question he now addressed to himself was: 'Do I still deserve this title? Have I demonstrated, in recent times, that control of any situation in which I happen to be, anywhere, anytime? Or have I permitted myself to be tossed here and there, drifting like that foolish log that messed up the propellers of the Epe–Lagos–Ikorodu ferry? Where is the young Efuape who threw the Right Reverend Beeston into such spiritual turmoil with the fast and furious ideas that he presented to that worthy gentleman, mainly ideas for the enhanced status of the products of St Simeon's? How disturbed that college principal had been when he had confronted him with the news that students of St Simeon's would no longer refer to themselves as Simeans, nor would they accept in future to be addressed as such!

Akinyode, ever the browser in exotic texts, had stumbled on the word 'simian.' Until then, its existence was unknown to any student in the seminary. It did not even exist in their prescribed *Elementary English Dictionary*, and they had to wait until night, when a volunteer squad, led by Efuape, broke into the staff library and borrowed the much bigger *Oxford Dictionary*. There it was, horror of horrors! Then followed the question: Had the white teachers known this all along? Had they furtively enjoyed a racial joke at the students' expense all these years? It was not like Sipe to await the resolution of such questions or to give his tutors the benefit of the doubt. He marched straight to the principal's office and announced to him a decision that had not yet been taken. That was the young Efuape, the man of resolution, whose favourite phrase was: 'If we must do it, let us do it with instant flash and flair.' Was it now that same Sipe who could not even organise the elements to get him on time to a wedding which – the cruellest part of it all – he had almost single-handedly planned, even to the courtship of the bride, which he undertook on behalf of the irresolute Otuyemi? Could such a weakling conjure up the Spirit of Layeni?

Reverend Beeston's revenge, which came not long after, had been painful at the time. There was first that gentleman's suspicion of this brash young man who answered to the nickname Resolute Rooster, to which the shameless youth, stepping jauntily across the lawns or classroom corridors, would – depending on his mood – respond, 'Thaz me – Cock of the Walk!' The principal had overheard this ritual exchange more than once and pondered long on the moral health of such an individual. There was something suggestive about the appellation, so he summoned his student to his office one day and questioned him closely – his background, his leisure occupations, his future ambitions, his favourite reading. Sipe supplied nothing but candid replies, which, however, sounded incomplete to the principal. Something had to be wrong about this confident youth who even managed to look uniquely dandified in the drab Anglican-ethic uniform, which was designed to abolish individuality. He resolved to keep a close watch on Efuape for the rest of his career.

That period proved to be mercifully short, from the principal's point of view. Of his class, Efuape ranked among the top three students; only he, Akinyode, and Egunjobi shared the top position on any consistent basis.

Among that circle of friends, however, Otuyemi was a poor performer, and Sipe thought nothing of helping him with his homework. From homework to class tests to examination was a progression that developed without much thought. Efuape was trapped passing his friend his answer sheets to copy. Hauled before the gleeful principal, Sipe stared silently at the pictures of former principals of St Simeon's hanging above the head of the incumbent, his gift of gab sent on abrupt vacation. Reverend Beeston was vindicated. This lapse was proof of what he had always suspected – any youth who answered to the name Resolute Rooster had to have something innately evil in him. To that worthy priest's eternal frustration, however, the movement of the answer paper had been detected only on its homeward journey, that is, as Sipe tried to retrieve it, sliding it inwards with his toes, out of view, he thought, of the invigilator. He refused to confess where it had been. The three students sitting to the left, right, and rear of him were questioned at length, threatened with the eternal perdition of their souls if they shielded the culprit – all to no avail. They had been truly hunched over their answer papers as regulation demanded. Otuyemi agonised over his own position, set off more than once to confess his part in the escapade, but was waylaid by Efuape and finally silenced by his eloquent sermon. Two heads might be better than one, he argued, but certainly not on the guillotine. Otuyemi had never heard of the guillotine but it gained his attention. Moreover, Efuape drummed it into his head that he was leaving St Simeon's to fulfill his destiny, which was to play John the Baptist to their financial Saviour in whatever form he might appear and launch them on his dreamboat headed for the perilous seas of Enterprise, and since Fate had laid its finger on him to be their Sindbad the Sailor, to take them on the Golden Road to Samarkand and revolutionise their lives in the manner of the merchant princes of antiquity, and no revolution was ever complete without its martyrs – preferably on the guillotine – he, Sipe, son of Efuape, willingly laid his head on the scaffold and would rise like a phoenix from the ashes of defeat to return through the portals in a gleaming motorcar and blow dust in the face of the Reverend Beeston, who would never boast of his own motorcar in all his life, you just wait and see, and you, Otuyemi, must therefore remain and bear witness to history fulfilling itself and be content to be recruited into the army that would lay siege to the fabulous kingdoms of wealth – just join up as soon as you struggle through your certificate here, and you can even come to me for extra lessons during your holidays. The catalogue of bloody precedents from myth, history, and hearsay bludgeoned Otuyemi into submission, to Efuape's immense relief.

He packed his bags, departed from the hallowed gates of St Simeon's, 'a fallen angel, a fashion-wise Adam, banished through the gates of our earthly paradise,' preached Reverend Beeston the following Sunday. But young Efuape did not return home to Ìsarà. He went straight to Lagos and began to look for work. When his colleagues returned home on their next holidays, the Rooster was firmly established as a clerk in the tax office at Yaba, his charm and confidence having captivated the European chief inspector of taxes. It was a coup without parallel in the history of the young products of St Simeon's. Without a proper certificate to speak of, with no testimonial save one written by yet another friend of his own age and social status – but composed by Sipe himself – the young man landed a white-collar job at no less a salary than twenty-four pounds per annum, with paid annual leave, promotion and advancement scales, and a pension at the end. It was higher pay and brighter prospects than the normal St Simeon's graduate could expect. Akinyode and Otuyemi organised the party of the year for Sipe, who had once again lived up to the name of Resolute Rooster, turning such a serious reverse to maximum advantage.

As the wind whipped his face and the dust filtered in through every permissive cranny of the homebound vehicle, Sipe admitted to himself that he had never known himself so irresolute. Naturally, he never intended, not even for a moment, to make a living out of the career of a civil servant. His present job was only a base for future operations. Scheme after scheme had passed through his mind with a rapidity that was only checked by one simple issue: capital. A working capital and a minimum guarantee of success. In the process of seeking the former he had stumbled on the forbidden path that would lead most rapidly towards the latter. They had all heard of such things. Even at St Simeon's there were fellow students who resorted to stranger methods to achieve the desired examination results: special black powder, rubbed in the centre of the head while secret incantations were muttered; answer papers touched with a special talisman from the Orient; furtive visits to the cemetery at night, leaving behind pouches of bones and earth, over which were pronounced a magic formula from the Sixth and Seventh Books of Moses. A brilliant scholar in his own right, Efuape had scoffed at such credulity. Now his foot was poised over that dread terrain, and his erstwhile scepticism was receiving knocks from the beckoning hand of lucrative advancement.

A 'Benefit Fund' was the earliest child of his fertile brain. 'We band together, put aside a percentage of our salaries regularly, place it in a post-office savings account or a bank fixed deposit. It accumulates a steady interest. In an emergency or in case of a venture to be approved by all members, any of us can withdraw a portion of that sum.' To Ogunba fell the task of drawing up a constitution. Referred to Sipe for further vetting, it returned unaltered, except for the name itself. 'Benefit Fund Club' had progressed to 'Cooperative Society.' From 'Cooperative Society' it was one short step to an 'Investment Syndicate,' with outlines of an unmistakable business company pencilled into the margin. Only a few minor changes, Sipe insisted, only some minor tidying up, replacing the fuzzy edges with a more dynamic outlook, shifting from a Boy Scout mentality to that of a full-grown combatant. Finally there was no holding the young tycoon.

'Let us give up this *esusu* mentality,' he harangued them at the next meeting of the 'board of directors,' which consisted of all six contributors to the now-eclipsed Benefit Fund. 'Do we or do we not want our independence? Then why these half-measures, my comrades of St Simeon's? Here we are, young, energetic, the hope and backbone of a burgeoning colonial territory. The future spreads itself before us like a feast for the brave, so why do we hesitate to throw off the shackles of salaried existence? Our pioneers await us. They have trodden the path of thorns and climbed the rocky prospects. From these heights they reach out to take us by the hand and aid our ascent. One after the other they abandoned their white-collar jobs – postal clerks, sanitary inspectors, council officers, miserable accountants, hospital orderlies, petty surveyors – name it, you will find their vacated places, some of which you and I now occupy with shaming complacency . . .' And Sipe reeled off the names of the 'young heroes,' none of them quite as successful as the illiterate Arimoje, but all now meeting their erstwhile employers on equal terms, including the white ones. His oratory was heady stuff, the ex-Ilés admitted, but their prudence remained unshaken. They would go with him as far as the Benefit Fund, but the word 'Syndicate' proved its own downfall – it sounded too businesslike, they complained.

In frustration Sipe had turned to an outsider. Onayemi was a childhood acquaintance with whom he had attended primary school. Onayemi dropped out early, went to work as a house servant in a District Officer's residence in Ikare, moved on to Lagos, where he served as salesman to John Holt for a year. He then started business for himself, supplying kola nuts and palm kernels to a branch of Lever Brothers. Onayemi, now a moderately successful businessman, was ready to invest in Sipe's projects. And the proof of his seriousness was his insistence on a certain 'mystic service' which had ensured the success of his own enterprise. Without it, Onayemi would never think of embarking on a new venture, nor even expand an existing one. This 'service' involved the invocation of the spirit of an unseen guardian – in his case, the ancestor Layeni.

The head teacher, despite some misgivings, had entrusted to him the sum of twenty-five pounds, 'to be invested as you wish' or treated as a loan to be returned without interest. Despite this boost, Sipe still required Onayemi's promised contribution – and his business experience. And this partner would not stir until the spirit had been evoked: 'Don't you see,' he patiently explained, 'if we go ahead without invoking this spirit, we may lose the entire capital.' To Sipe's still-practical mind, this was the most twisted form of commercial reasoning he had ever encountered. Yet everyone he spoke to – guardedly, always feigning a disinterested curiosity – everyone assured him that there was no wealthy man or woman who ever attained success without some such procedure. Sometimes it was worse, some really hideous ritual that required the use of parts of the human body. Invoking a spirit was cleaner. Although more dangerous, it threatened no more than the actual participants. The medium was the most exposed; he required special fortification, which more than justified the demand of a rather high proportion of the capital, never a straightforward, fixed sum. And of course the rewards were guaranteed to come in direct proportion to that first investment, which would in turn affect, proportionately, all subsequent ventures. This, Sipe's quick mind deduced, was to discourage the kind of escape route that had suggested itself to him – to lower the initial outlay to next to nothing, then increase it after the spirit had given his blessing and could be shrewdly abandoned. Cunning, calculating spirits, he thought. Or perhaps one should say mediums.

Next was the thought of what would be Akinyode's reaction. True, the teacher had left the direction of the enterprise to him. As for the choice of making his contribution an outright loan, Sipe had rejected that completely; the profits must be shared equally. His mind did not conceive of losses. But Akinyode would balk at what might appear to him as some kind of satanic rites. Should he simply go ahead and list the medium's fee as a legitimate expense – which indeed it was? Like a promotion exercise? Onayemi's medium as public relations officer to the spirit world? The concept was not all that ludicrous; a medium, after all, is an intermediary. The spirits need cajoling, a little bullying, elements of seduction – yes, it was no different from a public relations exercise. But suppose the spirit was invoked and it advised against the project altogether, how would he then explain the loss of a third of Akinyode's capital? Also, when the next venture began, would they again . . . NO! On that point at least, Sipe was quite resolved. If Onayemi was so much in thrall to Layeni, he would simply have to take what was left of his capital and quit the Syndicate. The spirit could have one bite, no more. Yet even regarding that first and only bite, the Resolute Rooster found himself most uncharacteristically irresolute.

Efuape re-read the contents of the paper. Onayemi had prepared the conjuring brief, based on his prior experiences in this kind of affair. A date had been computed as a propitious night – two earlier appointments had been shelved, again because of Sipe's vacillation. To help him resolve his doubts, his business partner than prepared a list of preliminary questions, which he had taken to the medium in Odogbolu. He had written them down, then taken down the medium's responses. Sipe's daring did not extend to the spirit world; at no time did he plan to be present at the 'service.' So he settled for this method of communicating 'by double proxy,' a twice-removed correspondence with the spirit world. No one could now accuse him justly of consorting with 'dark powers,' if indeed the more sinister spirits were involved. Efuape reviewed the questions and answers for the twentieth time, finding yet another reason to be sorry that he had missed the wedding. That was the occasion he would have seized to probe Akinyode's reactions indirectly, merely showing him the questionnaire and the answers, then asking casually if he thought that such a procedure could be considered satanic in any way. It would have been the best way to approach it. Now he would simply have to take his own decision. It was not possible to travel to see his friend before the new date, and Onayemi had warned that the medium could not guarantee another propitious night in the immediate future. The sheet was carefully dated September 19, and the hour entered – between five and six P.M. Even the subject of the interview with the medium was stated and underlined.

Invocation of the Spirit of Layeni. On the Questions of the Proposed Mystic Services by T. S. Onayemi

Questions presented to the medium:

1. Is it wholly profitable if this (Name of Business) is done and should there be no course of shortening one's life?
2. What of sacrifice of commission to be duly offered every month?

Across the second item Sipe had drawn a thick line. Onayemi had mentioned nothing about sacrificing any commission on the business to any spirit. When he tackled him on this, his would-be partner explained that it did not refer to their venture since this was not commission-based. Patiently, he outlined the differences.

He, Onayemi, had started out as a salesman for John Holt and had had to sacrifice his commission every month to the medium for the first year. He had included the question specifically to assure them both that this claim did not apply to this new venture. But what, asked Sipe, had he lived on during that period? What did he earn, in effect? Onayemi explained mysteriously that being a salesman was a many-sided affair – beyond that, he would not elaborate. The regular commission was mere bonus, a pittance, and the Spirit of Layeni was more than welcome to it. Firmly, Sipe shook his head as he leapt over that section. Pittance or no pittance, under no circumstances would any spirit extort a full year's commission from him. Onayemi was a good businessman when dealing with mortals but he had yet to learn how to drive a hard bargain with guardian spirits. He moved to the next item:

3. Is there any rule which can cause any ineffect on its part?
4. What do you aware of the ingredient whether they are strong enough to be compounded or not?

Sipe could not resist an indulgent smile. It proved something – he was not quite certain what – but a large proportion of successful businessmen were either illiterate or semiliterate. He turned to the second sheet of paper, which contained the answers to the first. It was headed:

Paper II. *Reply or Rejoinder of the Spirit to Questions as Numbered in Paper I.*

What a punctilious civil servant this Onayemi would have made! Obviously wasted in the private sector, but no doubt he kept good books in his business. Sipe already knew the answers by heart but went through them again:

Question 1. No least course to regret the experiment.
Question 2. Inconstancy of this will issue serious fruits.

And in brackets, Onayemi had added: *Time – New Moon – Sacrifice*. That of course did not concern their own enterprise, and Sipe emitted a sigh of sympathy as he pictured poor Onayemi expending his commission on goat, yams, palm oil, or whatever, dutifully carrying them to the medium as *saara* every full moon. Or did the medium insist on hard cash? Of course he would, come to think of it.

Question 3. Provided a clean room is dedicated to it and avoid two persons to salute the spirit.

This, Onayemi had again explained, referred to the suppliants. They could all be present at the service or they could select a representative. In the former case, only one person could salute the spirit when it made itself manifest. Sipe snorted – thank you for nothing. He had already made up his mind not to be anywhere near the 'service' chamber. It was Onayemi's familiar, so let him go as their representative. The details did not interest him in the least; he had no curiosity to meet the guardian spirit of commercial enterprise, or indeed any being from another world, in any shape or form. Even foreigners did not interest him; the white skin was as close as he wanted to get to the world of ghosts. So let Onayemi bring in the results and take care of the procedure. Paper II continued:

Question 4. Powerful. But the 'Ruling Spirit' has to append his own personal prescription to compound with it for its benefit (spirit).

That 'prescription' which Onayemi had evidently obtained as a result of further consultations with the medium, was then listed in a footnote:

1. Living Partridge (or dead)
2. Living Lilly (Compulsory)
3. White young pigeon
   Turn to powder some days before the experiment. Carefully wrapped with white cloth with virgin earth from the graveyard and throw into deep water citing or calling:

Thereafter followed a curious symbol, which evidently only the medium, and perhaps Onayemi, would be able to decipher, cite, or call. Sipe merely labelled it CURIOUS SIGN – in capital letters. The page was then certified with what again struck Sipe as a most inappropriate punctiliousness, considering the shady world into which they were about to venture: 'Cited by me, T. S. Onayemi.' The signature that followed was as polished and impressive as any he had ever encountered in the seminary, and that included his friend Akinyode's masterpiece, or indeed any that graced the myriad items of official correspondence that came his way during his years in the civil service. It seemed to have been cultivated as a conscious redress for a deficiency in what Osibo, the pharmacist dispenser, would often refer to as 'the graces of the literate.'

For the first time in his life, Sipe dozed off in a moving vehicle. Unable to resolve his dilemma, the entrepreneurial mind took refuge in a troubled sleep which was peopled by white colonial officers sitting in judgment over their prize tax officer. Why, they wanted to know, had he kept white pigeons in the office filing cabinet? He assured them that Onayemi could explain everything as soon as he returned from Odogbolu. In the meantime, if they cared to read his deposition they would understand that nothing had been done without formal authority of the chief medium, who had been personally ordained at the Anglican seminary, of which he was a faithful adherent. He was asked to produce the said deposition, and while he went to his desk, a prophet from the Cherubim and Seraphim Church of the Assembly of God danced in to a riot of tambourines and announced that he had come to bear witness and give testimony according to the Lord. Sipe, he swore, was a perjurer who stood in mortal danger of his soul. His wife was the true faithful, a member of his flock, whom he had tried to cure of barrenness, the poor unhappy woman. Sipe, to give that devil his due, unbeliever though he is, had indeed brought her to him, though again his sins must be pushed in his face, he paid only sporadic visits to the church. Frantically Sipe searched for his deposition to give the lie to the prophet, but when he opened a drawer he found only stacks and stacks of that CURIOUS SIGN whose recitation was to accompany the sprinkling of the white powder from the (compulsory) lily. The next drawer contained the partridge (dead), while the white young pigeon, which he last saw on the desk labelled Exhibit I, flew out of the third drawer, circled the room, and landed on the ceiling fan. Desperate, Sipe took out the sheets of CURIOUS SIGN – yes, he read it in capital letters – and distributed them to his judges. And what is this? they all screamed! Is this a joke? The prophet had evaporated at the mere appearance of the CURIOUS SIGN.

Smugly, Sipe rounded on them. Right, he said, now we know who the Antichrist is – you saw him turn tail, didn't you? By their tails – and cloven hooves – we shall know them. He stopped laughing when he saw his judges merely stare stonily at him. Don't you understand, he screamed! This is ancient Hebrew – the original language of the Bible. No true Christian would dream of conjuring up spirits in any other tongue. The inspiration had come from – he did not know where. It had to be divine. He felt supremely confident. I assure you there is nothing satanic about it; on the contrary it is one of the oldest rites known to the CHOSEN PEOPLE – he said that too with capitals. They continued to stare, faces frozen hard, including the one in the middle, whose flared nostrils now betrayed the features of Reverend Beeston hiding behind the mask of the District Officer, wreathed round and round in garden creepers and flowers. Sipe watched him narrowly; now that he was being unmasked and deflowered he felt surer of himself. Beeston, he was certain, knew no Hebrew – Greek maybe, but no Hebrew. *Eloi eloi lama sabachthani!* It worked. His persecutors came to life once more; the chairman announced that the panel would shift the sitting to Odogbolu, where they would interrogate the medium in person. So Sipe informed them that the ferry had broken down. Of course they could send word to the Resident – he had a personal yacht and might be willing to oblige. As for the roads, that Epe-to-Lagos so-called road was one long stretch of marsh. Even in harmattan, he warned them, it was constantly waterlogged – again that touched a nerve. Don't tell me about waterlogged roads, screamed Reverend Beeston, leaping up, mask and petals completely peeling off his face. What do you know of the pioneering spirit? We opened up this godforsaken hole, and by God, if we have to close it up again just to get to the bottom of this business, we will. Let's go, gentlemen. I know this uppity native. I deal with his type every day. Onward – Christian – Simeans!

And Sipe felt himself seized by white arms that undulated the length and breadth of the hall, turned into long sea serpents, and this seemed out of place. Everyone knew that the sirens known as Mammy Wata existed only in the Delta creeks, and Epe was a long way from there. Unless of course the log that fouled up the propellers of the Lagos-bound ferry was no log at all but the salt-encrusted seaweed plaits of the Mammy Wata's hair or her swishing tail caught in the boat's propellers as she dived deep down in Epe creeks to clamber among the logs of timber floating down the Niger from the torrid interior – not that he ever intended to deal in timber, far too clumsy, and the lorries broke down so often before they even reached the waterways, which were more disguise than blessing. Leave that to Node, paralysed Node, to whom timber and tuber were one! You think you know it all, he screamed, you think you know it all, you have it all worked out, but how wrong you are! So the sinuous arms bounced him up and down, saying, No, we don't, but we know all about you. Nothing is beyond you. You have tried usury, otherwise known as money-lending, speculated in land, which always shifts under your feet, and not content with forging and fermenting local brew, called medicine, for foolish syndicates, you now consult astrologers. Oh yes, we know all about your visit to local herbalists, pretending that you want a cure for your childless wife but taking notes in notebooks, filling pages with those remedies for hernia, piles, *igbona*, fevers, *lukuregbe*, *sobia*, common dysentery, ringworm, oh yes, we know all about them. Call yourself a Christian and you have not learned to bear your yoke with humility and wait for God's time which is the best as every simple child could tell you. Beauty is all in the eye but a child is a man's wealth, and where is yours, you cheap inspector of taxes, where is your offspring, the product of your loins, and you with seven years of marriage to the local beauty envied by all but succumbing to your dashing roostery figure of a man. The arms shrank to normal and dropped him so suddenly, like rebellious waves, that his stomach leapt upwards to his throat and he complained to the leering Beeston: Look, forcing your ordination on me will not pay your dividends. I am the one and only Mephisto-Rooster, son of Efuape, so watch it or you won't even know what hit your simian face, you albino ape. Don't think we didn't know you had been laughing up your sleeve these many years, but we found you out, didn't we? Issuing us only bowdlerised dictionaries while you kept the one with the secret of the tongue and clamped the Sixth and Seventh Books of Moses under your bed so we could not learn the secret. I can do without you, Beeston, I tell you I can do without your type. Beeston's face was really ugly, hibiscus red as the face of Mephistopheles bearing off the damned soul of Mr Faust, poor curious soul ruined by too much reading, which of course the teacher would defend, popping up beside the District Officer with his sad censorious demeanour – No, no, no, you must not say that, Rooster, too much reading never made Jack a dull boy. On the contrary, a little learning is a dangerous thing, drink deep, etcetera, don't you agree? Sipe's face fell. Oh no, don't tell me you are on their side. No, no, no, no, the teacher assured him, and we'll have dinner in a moment, you must be hungry. Sipe's stomach lurched painfully as fez caps on the police-shaven skulls butted him in the stomach for insulting the Resident. Another seized him beneath the armpits and the Right Reverend Beeston leapt up, crouched on the table, and revealed what he had always known –

there it was, a long curved tail ending in a quivering arrowhead. So the Resident screamed, Blind him, blind him, he has seen what should not be seen. Out! Out! Drag him out! His two-tone tan leather Saxone shoes were ripped to pieces, dragged against the floor, caught between the wooden beams of the courtroom floor. They lifted him bodily, threw him into the waiting lorry, and the engine roared to life, roared and roared and suddenly all went quiet.

'Genturuman . . . genturuman. *Akowe*.' The driver shook him with amused patience. 'Akowe, you no go get down? We done reach Ikorodu.'

When Sipe eventually reached home, long past midnight, he did succeed in taking off his jacket by himself. It was Mrs E., however, who took off his waistcoat and unlaced his Saxone shoes. There was nothing she could do but leave him to sleep in his worsted wool trousers, which, however, lived up to the catalogue guarantee and did not become rumpled or lose their crease by the following morning. One of his last thoughts as he crashed into bed was yet another footnote to his abandoned letters: *PPS. If ever I come face to face again with your beloved principal Reverend Beeston with his favourite theme – Sweet are the uses of adversity . . .* And suddenly he stopped, a beatific smile spreading all over his face. Layeni or no Layeni – he was certain now, more than ever, which line of business would engage their fullest attention. Those cars that passed him on the road, filled with the wedding guests – what made them all look so much alike? Indeed, come to think of it, was it not that same punishing worsted wool outfit he himself had been wearing under that scorching sun? That damnable Reverend Beeston – he appeared resolved to haunt his existence after all, but he had to give the devil his due – even Beeston's banalities appeared to have some ring of truth. Did missionaries make good businessmen, he wondered, just before he fell asleep.

III

LÍGÙN

Mariam shifted the bolt of mat in the corner of the room listlessly, without even looking down into the vacated space. To her husband, Josiah, the lone witness of her futile search, it was clear that she had no further interest in the result of her motions or, at least, no further expectations, and Josiah lost his temper.

'That makes some twenty times you have lifted that mat. Just what are you searching for?'

In a helpless tone which matched her gestures Mariam murmured, 'I have told you, the cabin biscuit tin. The one with the flower print.'

His irritation rose even higher. 'I know it's the tin. What is inside the tin?'

'But you know. The usual knickknacks . . .' and her voice trailed off into the practised murmur, which disappeared upwards into the bared roof. For by now she had climbed onto a stool; her indigo-dyed fingers raked the top of a wall and the junction of rafters but failed to make contact with any likely object. So she came down again and returned to a large basket which she had already gone through, and emptied its contents on the dung-plastered floor, polished black as her own skin. She began to separate the contents of the basket, carefully, shaking out the pieces of cloth. When she felt the back of her neck burning from Josiah's fierce gaze, she conceded. 'And a little money.'

Unappeased, Josiah snorted. 'A little money. How much?'

Mariam's hand paused midway into its next probe, her spine snapping straight abruptly. 'Oh yes, the lamp stand in the bedroom. Maybe . . .'

This time, Josiah screamed. 'You searched it last night. I watched you. You dug in every crack of the wall and nearly tore out the bamboo beams! And if it is that same biscuit tin you've had since I foolishly married you, I cannot see any hole in the wall which is large enough to take it!'

Mariam gestured helplessly. 'I can't think where else to look.'

Squatting on the bamboo bench, on the edge nearest the door, Josiah looked out and nodded a grumpy greeting to an early passerby. He had said nothing when the frantic search began the night before, roused from his sleep by her movements, squinting at her. When he next woke up in the morning, the search turned out to have merely taken a pause for the night. He could not even recall her lying down during the night, only that when he opened his eyes in the faint glimmer of a yet distant dawn, he had glimpsed her through the doorway, crouched – he grinned – like an evil bird, as her puffed-up cheeks blew alive the breakfast fire. But then she would break off, look around her in response to a new idea, or leap up in the middle of stirring the corn-pap or lifting some firewood, dash to the newly thought-of hiding place, and proceed to violate its peace.

From his recumbent position he continued to watch her for a while, then he got up, ignoring her entirely as he walked past into the courtyard, picked up a calabash of water, and flushed the last of the drowsiness from his face. After all, it was her cottage. If she chose to break it apart, that was her affair. Until her movements became unbearable and he wished he had not picked the previous night to be so liberal with the palm wine. His legs had felt heavy afterwards and he had succumbed to the invitation of the mat. Josiah liked his morning peace: a seat by the door, or a position by the window with his elbows on the broad lintel, chewing-stick idly traversing a set of teeth which gleamed from time to time in greetings to a passing acquaintance. Not like this morning, with flying arms dipping into and scratching at innocent hollows and receptacles.

Josiah sought consolation, reached into the depths of the pouch of his *agbada* and mentally dared her, as she glanced past him, to approach and look for her missing object in that vast pocket. He took out his snuffbox, slowly opened the lid, keeping a bemused eye on his distracted companion. Happily, she returned to her cooking. Years of practice nested the shallow tin snugly in his palm while short powerful fingers of the same left hand secured the cover. He pinched a few grains – it was too early in the day for a large dose – and flattened them into paste in the centre of his tongue. As he closed the tin carefully, his mood appeared to have improved and he leaned back to enjoy himself. His sneeze came on cue and he felt better still.

'There is one place you haven't looked.'

Mariam fell cleanly into the trap. She spun around. 'Where? Where?'

Josiah stabbed the empty air through the doorway. His fingers pointed unwaveringly in the direction of the pit-latrine: 'There!'

Mariam cursed herself, then cursed the man under her breath. Aloud, she merely complained. 'Don't you think it's too early in the morning for that kind of play?' Unable to think of a fresh place to search for the moment, she turned to pay some attention to the frothing pot on the fire.

300

Josiah nodded in solemn agreement. 'So it is. And now answer the question you have been dodging like a five-year-old: How much is this missing money that is driving you mad?'

'It is not even my money,' she wailed.

'Oh God, protect me from this woman! Mariam! I said, how much money have you lost? I know it is not your money. I know it is not your money because you would not be dancing around like a scalded cat over your own money. I know it is not your money because if it had been your money you would have asked me straight out: Did you borrow the money I left here? I know it not your money because you do not keep your own money in that ancient biscuit tin. If you kept money in that tin it could only be because you did not want to confuse it with your own money. I know where you keep your own money, woman! So, for the last time . . .'

Mariam slowly stirred the *ogi*, a mere reflex action, born of daily preparations, but her mind was far away. 'How will I tell them? This is not *oju lasan*.* Nobody entered this house. Nobody even knew the money was kept with me . . .'

Josiah opened his mouth to speak, closed it, and got up. He quietly gathered up his farm implements – he had stopped there the previous evening on his way from the farm – threw his work clothes in a heap into a basket, and left the home of his senior wife without his breakfast.

Mariam remained by the fire, stirring the porridge, her mind far away from her surroundings. The bottom began to congeal, and finally the smell of burning brought her back to earth. She shrugged, pulled out some of the wood to reduce the heat. She did not mind the acrid taste; indeed, the burnt layer, browned and hardened dough like flat sour cake, was a delicacy in which she indulged from time to time. But for the business of the missing money, the monthly contribution of *esusu* by her women's self-help group, she would be peeling off that layer right now, scooping it out through the frothing pap, and setting it aside for herself. But this mystery . . .

The sum was staggering. Even if it had not been a strictly women's affair, one of those secrets kept from everyone, including – indeed, especially – husbands, the sum was too huge to reveal as casually as Josiah had demanded. It could affect the chance of getting it back. Mariam felt only a slight twinge of conscience for thinking in such direction, Christian believer though she was. But these things did happen. Converting to the faith did not stop them happening. And she knew that one of the first

* In the normal course of nature.

301

questions the *onisegun* would ask might be: 'Have you told anyone?' Well, she had in a way, but she had not really 'told' Josiah. She had been careful not to mention the amount, or its source. It was fortunate that the money was not men's business, any more than its disappearance was the work of a sneak thief rather than someone's 'doing.' Her mind had already run through a list of those who might wish such a loss on her and work hard to bring it about. And then Tenten . . . could he have something to do with it? There were far too many reasons why she had to be careful. How often had she seen the *onisegun* shake his head regretfully, muttering, 'What a pity. What a pity. It makes things very difficult. If only you had not mentioned it aloud. If only you had kept it within. Now, you see, you have dispersed it with the mouth. That is going to make it more difficult, very difficult. What the human mouth scatters . . . well, I don't have to tell you.' Mariam grew more hopeful. At least she had not 'scattered' the missing money. Wherever it was, it would stay intact. She would seek help from those who knew about these things.

The timing troubled her. Was it by chance that the money chose to vanish just when the matter of Tenten hung over her head? Far too many of these related events, as if some force had determined to put her to the test. Like Job. Tenten's death had shaken her. He was her only brother, which made her now the closest surviving kin. There were relations in Sagamu; she would send word to them. Ajike would take the message, a trustworthy girl from Node's compound, quite grown-up for her age.

Then her mind turned to her son the schoolteacher. He would laugh at her, of course; he did not understand these things. Well, he did know of them. He was raised in full knowledge of the dangers of the world and the many ways to avoid them. One could not succeed all the time, of course – the missing tin was one example. Tenten's few possessions of any value were also in the tin, and the heirloom jointly owned by them. Still, everything had a remedy of its own. It was only a question of knowing where to look. Nothing ever happened by chance; money painstakingly put aside by one's own female group – all petty traders, weavers, food-sellers and so on – such money did not simply fly through the roof. There were always those for whom such schemes spelled envy, those outside the self-help scheme and with no will – or means – to start one of their own, and even well-off ones, whose comfort would be destroyed at the mere sight of the success of others. That was why the members swore to keep it a secret, even from their children. One never knew. It wasn't only that a child might innocently blurt out the secret. Some children were actually born that way, unwitting instruments of the evil in others. Mariam said a silent prayer of gratitude that her womb had never brought forth such a monster.

The thought of the son, doing so well in his teaching profession, cheered her up immensely. She was even happier to recall that the period of training was definitely over. Ilesa had been much too far away. Now he was nearer home, settled into married life, two children already, and doing very well at work. Only the continuing illness of his wife cast a shadow over their happiness, some stomach ailment which kept coming back. Still, if they stubbornly refused to try local remedies, what could she do? Josiah kept trying. Perhaps she ought to write him a letter. In any case there were many things to discuss: the cocoa farm; his plans for his junior brother – too bad, all the reports suggested that that one was not doing well, not doing well at all. Neither at his profession, nor in the evening school arranged for him, since he was too old to be admitted into a regular school. Oh yes, and there was the matter of the palm oil – now that had been pending much too long, nearly three years and it still wasn't over, not for her husband anyway. Gifts should not provoke contention, least of all gifts on the occasion of a newborn child. The sooner that was laid to rest, the better. She would get the son to speak to his father on that matter. And a new year was approaching.

She got up then, set down the porridge pot, and flicked the ladle to get rid of the drips. She cleaned the ladle further with her forefinger, and her tongue pronounced it pleasantly burnt. Just as well Josiah had left without eating – he hated burnt *ogi* and found her taste perverse. A final glance around the room just to make sure there was no cranny she had overlooked, and she picked up her sponge and soap and headed for the mud-walled space which served as bathroom. She entered, pushed the sheet of corrugated iron in position to serve as a screen. In a moment, the soothing feel of the night-chilled water had begun to improve her outlook on a new day.

Fatuka, her favourite letter-writer, grumbled at being dragged out of bed, but Mariam was unmoved. That was the only warp she knew of in Fatuka as an efficient working man. It was sad to see a grown man still lolling about in his wrapper, chewing-stick in mouth, when half the world was already at work and some farmers were even sheltering from the sun's ferocity after a hard morning's labour. It made no difference that Fatuka's duties required that clients come to see him in his own house, where the verandah served as office. He should conduct himself like any of the clerks in the Treasury office, don a shirt and a pair of trousers, and be dutifully at his desk awaiting clients. Instead, Fatuka merely interrupted some mundane chore such as warming up some food, buying breakfast from the passing hawker, or washing his clothes; the worst part of it was the casualness with which he asked his clients to wait while he completed such unclerical chores. On this particular morning, Fatuka had barely dragged himself awake.

'But you wrote your son only last week,' he grumbled.

'What is it to you?' she countered.

'He sends you too much money, that's your problem, Mariam. If he didn't, you wouldn't have so much to waste on letter-writers.'

She pretended to get ready to leave. 'Well, if you want me to waste it on someone else . . .'

'No one else will take you.' He laughed. 'They are all afraid of Teacher. If they make a spelling mistake or commit what he calls a grammatical error, they know they'll be in for it when he comes home.'

'And you are not afraid, I suppose.'

'Not me. I write in Yoruba, not like those others who want to show off their English. And I'll tell you something, the day even your son decides to challenge my Yoruba, I will show him who has stayed home in the home village and who only comes back three or four times a year to taste *ebiripo*.'

By now Fatuka had gathered up his pen, inkwell, and writing pad, adjusted the fold of his wrapper, and planted himself in front of his desk. '*Ise ya*. Shall I tell you what you wrote about the last time?' She knew he was teasing her, referring to an exchange in the distant past.

He dipped the nib in the inkwell and hung it over the pad. Mariam's gaze traversed the distance between her and her son, and her voice sounded almost disembodied. 'Ile Lígùn . . .'

Fatuka dropped his hand. 'How often do I have to tell you. Look!' And he thrust the pad in her face. 'Don't you see this corner is already covered with writing? And on the opposite side, do you see that? *Omo mi owon.** As the clerk will tell you in any government office, I have opened a file for you. This is your special writing pad, for you and for you only. To save time, I have written your address on the top of every sheet. Look, look.' He flicked through all the sheets. 'See? There are only three people in this village who have their own writing pads with me. Fadeke Alaso, and you know what a busy trader he is. And that stubborn mule Node.'

Mariam nodded sympathetically. 'God take pity on him.'

Fatuka shrugged. 'Did he take pity on himself? A stubborn fool, that's

* My dear son.

304

what he was. His son went to do business with the Saro, sent one letter, one letter only, and then not another word.'

'It must be twelve years now.'

'Fifteen years. Fifteen! But he kept writing to him, wasting his life savings.'

'Why did you write for him, then? Why did you not stop?'

Again Fatuka shrugged. 'You know how it is. At first, it seems only right. You also hope the son will return. I mean, we all grew up with Ba'tunde. By the time you are sure he is never coming back, it is too late to persuade the old man. You know how abusive he can be. Each time I wrote his letter I told him my thoughts. Once he even threatened me with his walking stick. Well, it is all over now. Poor Tenten was the one who could tell us what he tried to say, and now he is gone.'

Fatuka began to scribble beneath the address. 'So now, the date is in. So is "*Omo mi owon.*" Let's get on with your letter.'

Mariam tried to compose her thoughts again, shifting her gaze this time onto the pen and pad, but seeing neither. Her mind, by habit, was preceding the letter to its destination.

'*Omo mi owon,*' Fatuka repeated impatiently, but he knew very well that she could not begin to speak to a son whom she had not yet conjured into her immediate presence, within sight and hearing. At last she was ready.

'*My dear son, I send you many greetings, and especially for the care you are taking of your junior brother. I am told he is ill with* sobia, *but that the worm has begun to emerge. I am glad of that. Remember that just as Iya Jeje is, that is, your own child, so should Foluso be to you. Grown as he is, he is only a child. He does not know better, so don't worry about the other troubles I know he is causing you.*' She sighed with relief. That thorny problem was neatly taken care of. She could now proceed to weightier matters.

'*I am informed that the boy has lost a bit of weight. Tell Iyawo not to let that worry her. Now, know your father has been using the matter of the palm oil sent to you and your wife to abuse me. Your father says it was a kerosene tin and I kept telling him that it was only a keg. Your father was not at home that day, so how would he know? I was the one who received it. I don't know who told him it was a kerosene tin. Olorunise has not been back home since he went on transfer, so he could not have said such a thing to him. Who then is claiming it was a tin? The keg is here; I still use it to keep cooking oil. I show it to him but he does not want to listen. So anytime we quarrel he brings it up. He says, "That is how you took half the oil sent to your own son." After two years! He is a strange man, your father.*

Anyway, enough about that. I forgot to add – sobia *sometimes brings a fever*

305

with it, so tell Foluso to take some of that agbo *we made for Iya Jeje. He should not wait for the fever to begin.'*

Mariam fell silent, thinking rapidly and hesitating. She had to ask for help, and she needed to let her son know why. Was a letter not the same as scattering the matter with her mouth? Fatuka's case was more easily resolved; he was only a medium. And unlike what she sometimes heard about other letter-writers, he was *opa awo** itself when it came to keeping his clients' secrets. That was indeed what he had teased her about when he asked if he should remind her of the subject of her last letter to her son. On that occasion she had forgotten whether or not she had passed on some news, so she enquired – naturally, she thought – of the only person who could tell her, the letter-writer. The pompousness with which he had rebuked her! Like the bishop who sometimes came to deliver the sermon. Or even like one of those clerical officers at the Treasury announcing penalties for lateness in paying market rates! 'Iya Foluso! You engage me to write your letters, not to memorialise the content of your personal affairs. When I have completed that assignation' – and he made a sound like one expelling air, then with his hands consigned the air into a deeper void – 'that is the end of the contraction of business matter for me. I am not just an ordinary letter-writer. I am a coffeedetial secketries.' Since Mariam could not read, she had missed the proclamation which affirmed his claim to all of Ìsarà in blazing colours on a board outside his window:

ADEbabs FATUKA – LETTER-WRIter aND COFFEEDetial SECKetries.
ALL ePIStolARY and DocUMental MATTERS UNderTAking.

But she knew that the sign-writer was her brother, the late Tenten, on whose recommendation she had first approached him.

That exchange had already put her mind at rest; this medium could not be regarded as a scattering agent. As for the letter itself, by the time it reached her son, she would have seen the *onisegun*. No harm could be done by letting her son know at this stage.

'My son, there is some trouble I must now tell you about. I have lost a large amount of money. It has given me great concern as I have never lost anything like this before. It is the esusu *money from my women's group, and as you know, I have always been the keeper if the person whose turn it is does not want to take it yet. There were also some heirlooms and other small items in that tin, you know*

* The staff of secrecy.

306

it, that tin with flower decoration which I have had before you were even born. And it has disappeared without trace. Anyway, I am looking into it with all the remedies I can muster, but first, I need some help from you in the matter of Tenten's burial because I have no one else to turn to, and the missing money has added to all my troubles.'

She felt better. A sense of loneliness reduced meant even that her problems were nearly solved. She placed the modest fee on the table. It was time to turn her mind to other matters that Tenten's death had provoked. She watched Fatuka continue writing for a while and knew that he was sending her greetings to the teacher's wife and to both the children. From her file Fatuka retrieved a ready-stamped and addressed envelope, sealed the letter with a ritual finality, and handed it to her. She rose, adjusted her shawl, and bade the letter-writer good day.

Fatuka let her walk the length of the pathway, then made the usual bet with himself: Would she head straight for the postbox or would she first look for a chance traveller to Abeokuta? As he watched her turn first into the tailor's shop to make enquiries, he sighed. Nine years her letter-writer, and he had yet to persuade her to accept a plain envelope, keeping the stamp apart in case the letter found a personal courier – which was quite often the case. Her son no longer bothered. Whenever he found Mariam's letter awaiting him on his desk, he would first check the stamp. He soon became adept at easing off the ones that came unused.

The girl, Ajike, returned long after dark, just as an anxious Mariam was preparing to set out again for Node's household in order to consult with Ajike's mother. Now she stared at the dust-covered waif, her mind reluctant to accept the result of her mission to Sagamu, where the remnant clan of Fadebo was still to be found. The girl had brought back nothing but the tidy bones of rejection. No evasions, no excuses, no vague promises, not even those meagre strands of meat a woman could lodge between her teeth and pick upon to string out hope. Her relations had not even tried to get rid of her awkward messenger with a lie whose bitter truth would be only too apparent at the receiving end: 'Go ahead, tell her we may even get there before you. I have to wait for So-and-So to return from a journey to Kontagora; she keeps the family purse and will know what to do' . . . and so on. No, these broken branches of my family tree, she thought matter-of-factly, they have simply tossed back the bundle in my lap. But she would not give up immediately.

'You are sure it was Carpenter you saw?'

The girl remained firm. 'Mama, I know Carpenter very well.'

'And he said . . . ? What exactly did you hear him say? Try and remember the words he spoke. How did he put the message – try and remember, Ajike.'

The girl repeated everything. 'Brother Carpenter was in his workshop when I arrived. I greeted him and I gave him your greetings just as you told me. Then I delivered your message about Tenten. Before that he responded very well and asked about everyone at home. But when I gave him your message he raised his voice at me. He said, "Well, what does she want me to do? The only farms we go to are the *akuro* beside the streams and those are miles away. The soil is burnt here; people travel far to get anything to sell in the market. They will be away for days." '

The girl stopped but Mariam egged her on. 'En-hen?'

'So I asked, "What shall I tell Mama Foluso?" It was then he said, "Are you blind, or do you see any customers in my shop? Tell her when you get back how many customers you saw ordering tables or beds or buying furniture. Not even coffins. Nobody seems to be dying in Sagamu, whatever they choose to do in Ìsarà." Then he picked up his *buba*, put it on, and went away, leaving me in the workshop. I waited for a long time for him to return. When I began to fear that I would miss the last lorry home, I left for the motor park.'

'That was when you saw him again, *abi*?'

'Yes. He was sitting in the beer shop, drinking with some men. And the last lorry had left, so I had to take bicycle transport, then walk the rest of the way.'

Mariam nodded. A well-brought-up girl, she thought appreciatively, could be relied upon to deliver a message faithfully. She knew that everything had happened exactly as Ajike had described it. Her mind shifted beyond her through the open door and she asked aloud, of no one in particular, 'So who will bury Tenten?'

The girl began to shift from one leg to the other. The evening harmattan chill was setting in and she had clearly sweated from the long walk, mostly uphill. When she sneezed, Mariam remembered that Ajike ought to be returned quickly to her home. She undid the knot in the corner of her wrapper and brought out two *onini*, which she handed to her.

'You did very well, Ajike. Take this. And greet your mother for me. I'm on my way to thank her myself.'

The girl curtseyed quickly and left, Mariam shouting a parting admonition after her to take her damp clothes off as soon as she arrived home. Ajike liked this elderly woman who lived by herself and sold all sorts of *wosi-wosi*. Often she would take it on herself to pause by her window and ask if she had any errands to run. She knew of her son, too, the next thing to an *oyinbo*, who taught in Abeokuta, perhaps the source of those rare items which she displayed on a rough table outside her window. Why didn't she own a real shop, Ajike wondered, skipping across the broken gutters on her way home.

Left alone, Mariam continued to stare through the door. She got up at last, went to the corner where she had stacked her merchandise for the night, and picked up a tin that contained the previous day's sales. It rang with the hopelessness of its meagre contents, the exact sum of which she knew already. That did not prevent her from taking off its lid, staring at the few coins, then replacing the tin in its place in a corner of the laden tray. As her eyes encountered the dung-plastered floor, she slapped the back of one hand into the cup of the other repeatedly and asked again, louder than before, 'So, who will bury Tenten?'

Carpenter was the head of her cluster of blood relations in Sagamu, yet he had dismissed her plight so offhandedly. Not even a promise to summon a family meeting. That said it all. Her new family in Ìsarà had done its part; she could ask no more of them. As soon as they learned of Tenten's death, Node's household had levied two shillings from each adult towards *egunsale*.* She knew only too well how little was the profit they made from their petty trading, even at festive seasons – harvest, New Year, and the Muslim festivals. Two shillings was a big hole in their savings, there was no doubt about that, even for someone like Tenten, who had looked after Node since that unlucky farmer became paralysed. It was Tenten who brought about this intimacy with Node's household, turning himself into Node's arms, legs, tongue, and even mind since Node became totally disabled. Even so, she was touched by the promptness of their aid.

The women had brought the money as soon as they heard. She received them in that same room and watched as they solemnly piled the shillings on a mat at her feet – twenty-two shillings in all. Node had sent nothing, but she understood. With Tenten gone, who else was there that could read his thoughts, follow the faint tremor of his lips, and understand their message? Only she, Mariam. It was only when the shillings, the dark brown colour of *robo* – her mind sought out the strangest irrelevancies – only when the shillings began to pile up did she shed tears for Tenten, as if the loss of her only brother had finally come to her at the sight of this aid towards *egunsale*.

This was her new family, quite different from the Christian fellowship

* Pre-funeral rites.

with whose members she did the monthly *esusu*. These were mostly wives from Node's compound, and his sisters also from their married homes. With them she undertook the forty-mile round-trip trek doing the markets between Ìsarà and Abeokuta, where they camped in her son's compound. Even before Node's illness, trade had pulled them together, being such close neighbours. Then Tenten pulled them closer still. His sign-writing venture had attracted only two patrons – the results showed very clearly that he was neither gifted nor more than barely literate. The palm-wine shack was the other patron, after Fatuka. Tenten had begun by working on her husband's farm but found his nature too cantankerous, so he moved in with Node and became his right-hand man on his farm. This was the new family she had found after her own disappeared to Sagamu and abandoned her to her marriage with Josiah. Raising her face to the women as they grouped around her in her living room, she had not felt bereaved. They said little, and that was mostly to do with the message they would take to *osugbo*. The eldest wife of Node undertook that errand – Tenten was ready for burial. And not just the burial for a nobody. None of the rites that were his due should be skimped. Tenten had people of his own.

And then the shocks began. First, *osugbo* declared that Tenten was not their death. It was not possible! Mariam could not believe her ears. 'Not *osugbo*'s death? What did they mean? That Tenten was not one of them? Since her own conversion, she had striven to bring her brother also into the Christian fold but had finally accepted failure. That was when she saw how Tenten had taken charge of Node in his helpless state – not even a mother hen looked after her chicks the way her brother had looked after Node. He had been avoided, abandoned by others who called themselves his friends – and they were Christians. So Mariam ceased to pester Tenten, left him to his pursuits, which, from what she saw, did not appear to be short on 'charity' or 'love thine neighbour,' any more than the activities of those of her own Christian faith. And perhaps it was from that new outlook also that she found she had begun to listen for the drums of *osugbo*, as if she sought to understand the message of their ponderous throb.

She shocked her church group finally, in the schoolroom where they held their Bible class. The catechist was expounding a Bible passage when he stopped, pointed a trembling finger through the window at a stern-faced, silent procession clad in indigo wrappers and patterned shawls, heading for the *osugbo* house near the *aafin*.*

'Your Christian mission,' he exhorted his flock, 'remains unfinished as

* Palace.

310

long as such pagan sights as these defile your gaze in Ijebuland. Your faith is sham unless you bring them into the fold of our Lord Jesus Christ.'

'Why?' Mariam demanded before she could stop herself. 'They do no harm.'

It was the longest silence ever, and Mariam found herself the centre of unaccustomed turmoil in the Bible class. Catechist Aderounmu, transferred to Ìsarà barely three months before, began to wonder if he had been thrown, unprotected, into the very tower of Babel. He would have been totally devastated if he had heard what Mariam, at first a little cowed by her outburst, then somewhat recovered, muttered under her breath: 'After all, Yode's father is also a Christian. Yet he says that the church bells only sound in the ear, while the drums of *osugbo* resound in the pit of one's stomach.'

After this, however, her momentary rebelliousness dissipated of itself and she began to murmur explanations. She apologised. It was all clearly the voice of the devil which spoke through her. The class was relieved and reassured. And when she added, truthfully, that it was the unchristianly conduct of some of their own Christian fellowship that had troubled her, the catechist was convinced that it had indeed been no more than a momentary aberration. Mariam bowed her head to receive his admonition and agreed to pay a fine of threepence.

So now, this same *osugbo* dared deny that Tenten was their death! Whose death was her brother's then, and who would bury him? The church?

In a sudden burst of energy, Mariam took up her headtie, turned it into a sash around her waist, and went bareheaded into the night.

Node, three-quarters paralysed, spent most of his nights and days in a specially woven cane-and-wicker chair. Josiah's son had sent it, the handiwork of his pupils. Its design had been inspired by an illustrated article in *In Leisure Hours* which advocated the use of local materials for 'sensible, cheap, and durable native furniture.' The article did not lie. The reclining chair had become glossy with unbroken occupation while Node's body converted itself to its curvature. Node's son Ba'tunde then had it copied by a local artisan, shipped the copy to Freetown in Sierra Leone, where a prospective business partner was setting up a factory for the manufacture of 'durable furniture made in native styles but with European elegance.' Ba'tunde wrote one letter, then washed his hands of the nuisance of a paralysed father. But first he broke into the cripple's secret cache – Node believed neither in banks nor in the post office savings scheme

311

– and made off with nearly the entire life-savings of the helpless father. Node became even more dependent on his wives – and on Tenten, his principal farmhand. He took it all, like his paralysis, with an unnatural calm, which was not shared by the rest of the household.

His paralysis especially. This was undoubtedly the work of an enemy within. Only Node, whose mind evidently had also been affected by his stroke, could even think that it was a failure of his body all of its own. He had, moreover, the example of his father before him; he had also succumbed to the same affliction. To cap it all, he was one of the convertites who religiously believed in the good Lord's 'Vengeance is mine.' Not so his wives, whom, despite his conversion, he had refused to disperse. His youngest, however, was the one acknowledged in the church register. And the others, supported by neighbours and relations, all knew that she was the agent through whom his enemy had worked this evil. And they knew, even more confidently, who this enemy was.

Tenten, and quite early too, broke through the carapace that first encased Node's mind. His stubborn patience earned him the language that was forced through the patriarch's twisted lips, and he learned also how to speak to him in turn. Thus Tenten it was who let Node know, barely in time, that the 'agent' had been identified, and that justice had been plotted against her, his youngest wife, Binutu. The other wives and his relations had met and consulted. The result was unambiguous – the hand was the hand of Alarade, his closest friend; and the agent was Saanu's mother. So Binutu was dragged forth and faced with her accusers. Yes, she admitted it, she had indeed slept with Alarade; Saanu was not even Node's child, but her lover's. Their affair had begun a long time before, since she began to trade in Lagos, staying, as was right, in the household of the best friend of her husband. But to act as agent to harm her husband? No! She demanded any test they could think of – the truth would reveal her innocence. They locked her up, confined her to a room while they debated her sentence.

The news travelled quickly to Binutu's relations in Ode. They came to Ìsarà in the dead of night and set up camp, facing the home of Node. Their demand was simple: They wanted Binutu given back to them, with her child, both safe and sound. Node's side replied that this was a crime committed against a son of Ìsarà; Ìsarà and Ìsarà alone would decide what to do. The accusers let it be known that Jagun, against whose word as mouthpiece of Ifa no one dared voice a doubt, had himself confirmed their findings. What did Ode mean? How dared they interfere? The town seethed with rumours. Node's compound became a war camp under siege.

Node raced against time, and it was lucky that he had Tenten as ally. What passed between them both no one knew for certain. But Tenten went back and forth between Node and the house of *osugbo*. Finally, five days after it all began, he returned with the spokesman of *osugbo* himself in tow. The case was not unusual, he declared. Quite simple. The earlier consultations were indeed accurate: Binutu was the agent, no question at all about that. But why had no one thought of also consulting the same Ifa to find out whether or not she had been, as was common, an unwitting agent? 'You all rushed off with half the message; you failed to probe further, to find out whether or not she had brought the thing of her own will, with her own knowledge, or whether Alarade had used her without her knowledge! Has none of you ever heard of *magun*, for instance, which a man can place on his wife? He does this without her knowledge, to protect her chastity and punish the intruder on his private land. Do you think that *magun* is an only child? How stupidly you have all behaved!' The priest chastised them thoroughly, made them so crestfallen that even the matter of Binutu's infidelity was somehow forgotten. Well, not entirely forgotten, simply accepted as one of those sins that prove fortunate in the end. For Node was now incapable of producing more children, so who could fail to see the hand of Fate in a wife's infidelity which had resulted in a child!

And thus peace returned to Node's corner of Ìsarà. *Osugbo* fined Binutu two fowl, a bolt of white cloth, and a keg of palm oil, which her relations gladly paid before they departed for home. In addition she had to go through cleansing for the evil that had been placed upon her. She made *ekuru* and served it through the town. Messengers were sent to inform Alarade in Lagos that his present abode would have to become his permanent home unless he was prepared to undo the heinous injury he had so treacherously inflicted on a trusting friend. The child, Saanu, belonged of course to the man whose roof still sheltered Binutu as wife. And there the matter ended.

Mariam replayed the drama through her mind as she trudged through a black night, pockmarked by oil lamps and slashed by weak wedges of hurricane-lamp light through open doors and windows. Node would have the answer to this riddle, of that she was certain. Even without Tenten, he would know just what to do. Like her brother, Mariam had also acquired an ease of communication with Node; the only difference was that while Tenten had appeared to read his mind, she had to place her ear against his lips, then somehow make sense of the belchlike spurts which issued through near-immobile lips. When Tenten was compelled to stay on the farm for days at a time, Node's household would often turn to her for help when Node's wishes became impossible for them to understand. Yet Tenten, Tenten who moved back and forth between *osugbo* and Node's household during the crisis of Node's paralysis, that same Tenten it was whose death, they claimed, was not *osugbo*'s. So who would bury him? Her mind flew to many possible answers. Had Tenten, for instance, died still 'owing' them? There were stories, never really resolved. If it was not *osugbo*, there was always some other cult, stubbornly awaiting the closing of the balance sheet before they would even permit relations near the corpse. They took over the body, even the house, if he owned it. And that was that. A new initiate could promise many things – it all depended what he craved: wealth, recognition, children . . . even longevity. Everything had a price and that price did not exclude even the life of an innocent. Every preacher knew a hundred such stories, each one with its own bloodcurdling details. The listeners had long learned to accept the frequent change of details for each dire event – after all, was there ever smoke without fire? The details were considered trivial. Mariam regretted now that she had not stayed closer to her brother; maybe she would have gleaned something to help her understand why he was now untouchable to the *osugbo* after his death.

When she placed her ear close to the lopsided opening between Node's lips after posing the question for a third time, she was astonished at the simplicity of the answer which she deciphered from those jumbled sounds.

'Didn't you know? *Osugbo* cannot bury Tenten. He is an albino. The rites for an albino's death are forbidden to them.'

Mariam exploded angrily. 'But why did they not simply say so?'

She understood the contortion of face to mean that she should again place her ear close to his lips. 'Who did you send?' he asked.

'Iya Ajike.'

A throaty chuckle came through Node's lips. 'You mean you sent one of you? Hm. See how foolish you women are? You expect *osugbo* to tell you what they can or cannot do? Of course all they will tell you is: He is not our death. If they tell you they cannot perform the death rites, the next thing you will want to know is why.'

'Well, why not?' Mariam insisted.

'You see? Now go to the *ogboni** – I mean, let Josiah go. Either Tenten is their death, or they will tell you who must receive him as theirs. They will do what is needed.'

Mariam sighed and took her leave, then headed for Josiah's home. From

---

* An ancient conclave of elders.

a distance she could see a glimmer of light issuing from the cottage and she breathed a sigh of relief. Josiah played many roles in Ìsarà's affairs, not all of which she understood, only that it often meant long hours into the night, meeting at the home of a chief, in the palace, or in *iledi* itself. Josiah had forsworn *osugbo* after his baptism, but that did not prevent his taking his seat at their meeting place when the affairs of Ìsarà brought the elders together in the courtyard of *osugbo*. She breathed a silent prayer to God that Josiah would cease altogether from accompanying them into the inner recesses. There, she knew, was where the danger lay. Then there was the matter of the other wife. Mariam shrugged. At least she did not have to seek him there tonight. Josiah took everything the wrong way these days. Something, she did not know what, had been eating him of late, making him more grumpy than usual. Their marriage had never been easy but lately it had grown tempestuous. Every little thing resulted in a quarrel.

Josiah sat on a raffia bench, squinting in the light of an oil lamp into a book held close to his face. His spectacles were the consequence of his adventure into the reading world, and the sight stopped Mariam in her tracks. She had not known that Josiah had begun to read. Clearly the efforts of her son whenever he came home on holidays had begun to yield results. Half-bitten pieces of kola nut lay strewn on the bench beside him, a certain sign that whatever Josiah was doing caused him great effort. But it was the sight of her husband hunched over a C.M.S. hymnal companion, looking for all the world like an owl with those spectacles, that brought some light relief into Mariam's mood. She stood, stared, and a chuckle escaped her, which she promptly stifled.

Josiah had heard, however, and looked up angrily. Mariam then knocked unnecessarily on the side of the doorway. 'Can I come in?'

'What did you find to laugh at? Did an *opidan** precede you here to keep you amused?'

Mariam refused to rise to the bait. She entered fully into the room and came straight to the point. 'Baba Yode, only you can talk to the *ogboni* over the matter of Tenten.'

'I no longer enter *osugbo*,' Josiah lied, and turned back to his book.

'You don't have to. Jagun is your friend and you visit him at home. He can speak to them for me.'

Josiah shook his head. 'I am a Christian. I even hold a title in the church. Just think how it would sound when it is found out that I took my in-law to *ogboni* for burial.'

---

* A magic-performing masquerade.

'And what of me? Am I not a Christian too? I am his only sister. Am I now to abandon his corpse?'

'Hn-hn, you see the difference. You are his blood relation. Everybody will understand. In my own case –'

'Did you not marry me? What does that make Tenten to you?'

'*Iyekan*, not *ibatan*. The burial of Tenten is a blood matter. I can have no hand in it.'

Something was not quite right. Mariam recognised the stubborn streak, but accompanying it was a plain irrationality which could not survive any form of scrutiny. She thought of calling on Barbarinde, the neighbouring goldsmith, to intervene in the discussion, so certain was she that Josiah was not making sense. How could he refuse to act as simple intermediary between his wife and the elders of *osugbo*? She had no living relations in Ìsarà, no uncles, not even a distant cousin. So who was she supposed to turn to when such a matter came up? Yes, that would be the best course. Let a man take her part in this matter. As she turned to go, however, another thought struck her. Perhaps there was a simpler reason for Josiah's stubbornness. And for his recent moods, come to think of it. Feigning innocence, she said, 'All right. I shall find someone else to be the father of my family. So will you give me your *egunsale* now, or shall I let the women come and collect it tomorrow?'

Mariam knew she had hit home when he flung the hymn book aside and leapt up angrily. 'Do you understand nothing of what I am telling you? *Egunsale* is what they are going to use to make all the *etutu* and other things which you know are forbidden to me. And you still want me to put money into something like that? Just take yourself away. If you want to bury Tenten in my backyard, I shall dig the grave myself. We will say a prayer over him. But *ogboni*? I did not lead him to *iledi* when he was alive. So I am not taking his body there, now that he is dead. Now get back to your house and leave me in peace.' He turned his back on her and stormed off into his inner room, flinging back at her a reminder to leave the door ajar 'to your sister witches.'

So Mariam knew that her guess was correct; Josiah was stone broke. 'I will have to write to your son,' she said.

Nodding vigorously, he turned round. 'You should have done that to start with instead of trying to make me do something unchristianly. Write and tell him to send you money for the *egunsale*. He is far removed from it all. I doubt if he even knows what *egunsale* is, so he won't be committing a sin.'

'All right,' Mariam agreed. 'I shall write him another letter. Do you want me to ask that he send something for you too?'

The barb went home and Josiah reacted as she expected, furiously. 'Did I tell you I needed money? And even if I did, who are you to help me ask for money from my own son? Just go about your business, woman, and let me be.' He stormed into his bedroom, pulling down the matting which served as curtain. Then he stood behind it and watched Mariam's growing grin, grinding his teeth in frustration since he could not do what he really wished, which was to rush out, grab her by the neck, and fling her out of doors. How would he face the parish priest if she chose to make a report of such a simple matter between husband and wife? His mind reached out then to his son the schoolteacher. He was not only married to one wife; he actually shared the same roof with her. Did he ever undergo such trying moments, Josiah asked himself? And how did he cope? He, Josiah, could at least seek consolation in the home of his second wife. Come to think of it . . . Josiah went round the house and picked up his farming tools. He would leave for work the following morning from the house of Desinwa, his second wife.

Two elderly men emerged from the shadows before her cottage when she returned. They bore a staff which she recognised – it belonged to the *olifan* – and she wondered why she had not thought of them. They greeted her as the wife of Josiah, mother of Akinyode and Foluso, and the one born after the man once known as Tenten. Then they asked her if she had missed anything.

Strange, she found that their presence did not surprise her at all. If anything, she felt she had anticipated some such visit, and when she told them about the missing tin, she was not astonished by what happened next. The shorter man flipped his shoulder shawl aside and beneath it was the missing tin. He held it out to her, its flowered patterns still discernible though its once-bright colours were now faded to a pale brown, monochrome with age.

'Is this what you missed?'

She nodded.

Holding out the box to her, the man continued. 'We have removed only what is not yours. Look inside the tin. If you wish to dispute what has been taken, now is the time to tell us.'

Mariam found that her hands trembled somewhat as she took the box and prised open the lid. She did not bother to undo the knot in the piece of cloth in which the *esusu* account was tied; even the shape confirmed that no one had tampered with it. But the family heirlooms were gone, and so was a small packet that contained an *iyun* bracelet and a copper ring which

317

Tenten had long ago given her for safekeeping. She looked in turn at the two impassive faces, which, in the dim glow from surrounding cottages, looked like dark skulls on which the white, tight-fitting caps appeared to float. The evening had turned chilly, as with most harmattan evenings, and she shivered.

'No,' she said softly. 'Everything is here which is mine.'

This time the other man spoke. 'We cannot bury Tenten but he is our death. We have sent for those who will bury him. Send the *egunsale* to us at *iledi* and all the rites will be performed. Later, someone will take you to where he has been buried.'

He hit the ground with his staff once, then turned away. Soon there were only the two slouched shadows receding into the night.

IV

TISA

The head teacher was a firm believer in cause and effect, so when a sigh emerged from the depths of his disputed soul and the slouched form of the Genie of the Bottle followed, he assigned credit where credit was due: His sigh had indeed produced the apparition. *Aje ku l'ana, omo ku l'oni; tani ko s'aimo pe aje lo p'omo naa je?** Come to think of it, was the Genie himself not a kind of *aje*? The teacher savoured the thought, stored it away with a smile for future airing among his fellow ex-Ilés. And he did not imply the Genie's physical appearance but the genus: Genie. And no puns intended, he frowned at his invisible audience. The Genie's presence at that moment provided its own answer to the question: Which side of the disputed territory would such a blatantly biased intrusion reinforce? The urge to escape from his desk for the rest of the day, and not simply for a dinner break, now gained the upper hand.

Earlier, his chances had been even, though desperate. Alone in his makeshift study, that is, the famed corner of his front living room into which Soditan sometimes gave the appearance of having been stamped from adolescence, he had battled against the ambush of the dying year, his mind near-jammed by the log of accumulated chores. From time to time he would taunt himself, audibly, not simply muttering aloud. The teacher did not believe in wasting breath and when a crisis stirred his spirit into protest – or admonition – he would address himself directly, volume trimmed to the solitary audience, punctuation supplied by his habit of sucking in air with his tongue from behind the ridge of the upper teeth. Such deliberate monologues also served to rehearse his voice in preparation for reading the Sunday lesson. It was now Saturday afternoon, quite late. If his work had gone according to plan, he would by now be in the emptied schoolroom, moulding his voice around the selected passage, noting sections for stress and perfecting different tones for a variety of

---

* The witch cried last night and the child died at dawn; who dare claim it was not the witch that murdered the child?

subtle inflections. Unlike some other lay readers, the teacher did not believe in bravura renditions, or indeed any form of vocal ostentation.

For some moments, he pretended that the Genie was not there. The battle was already lost, he acknowledged, but at least he would spend a little time frustrating his intruder. It was futile to deny that the rout had begun much earlier. The mean blow beneath the belt – slightly above, to be precise; the teacher was well tutored in the human anatomy and did not encourage imprecision – that blow had been sneaked in under a feint of aromas which came from the direction of the kitchen. His acute sense of smell had already identified the advance guard of crayfish and peppers simmering in palm oil. Accurately, he anticipated the composition of the next wave of assault; his nostrils twitched and his stomach sounded a gentle drumroll. The crayfish stew's simmer merged with an agglutination of black-eyed beans, which had been left to consolidate their potency all afternoon, studded through and through with chunks of lean smoked pork and *odunkun*. The aroma cut through his study with impudent ease, clinging to the ceiling mat, investing the front room so thoroughly that the teacher could no longer pick up a file or a school report without absorbing the dense fumes through his fingertips. And so he sighed, and the Genie appeared, soundlessly, as was his wont, raking the inner recesses of the teacher's modest home with his steel-rimmed pebble glasses, his gaze coming finally to rest on the hallowed corner, benevolently, a wide beam slashed across his normally lethargic face.

Graciously, the teacher conceded that the Genie's presence was quite superfluous; his will to continue his work was already fully subverted. To his caller, however, he said, not looking up from his desk, 'You are not here. I merely sighed and you appeared. All I have to do is sigh again and you will vanish.'

But it was not a sigh that escaped from the teacher but a repeat of the long, low rumble from his stomach. The visitor looked startled, glanced questioningly, then with understanding, in the direction of the kitchen. Still, he made a mental note of the event, for it was most unusual. The teacher, he knew, was a being of such precise habits that his stomach should not rumble like that of mere mortals. His eating schedule, like his work, was planned to the last detail. One made way for the other on the designated minute, permitting no encroachments from exigencies. The Genie's nose, a much celebrated landmark even beyond the city limits, described a half-arc in the air. A massive outcrop which engaged in games with his spectacles, its upward jerk was timed to arrest the downslide of that contraption. One could see that it was a much-practised manoeuvre.

His ears were just as impressive, broad coco-yam-shaped leaves, as fibrous-looking and almost as large. He had a skin of pure anthracite, contrasting so remarkably with that – unusual for an African – aquiline nose. His gaunt, tall frame enabled him to reach any shelf in his pharmacy without the aid of a ladder, packing case, or stool. And now his shuttlecock of an Adam's apple worked in sympathy with his own surrender to the message that had pervaded the sanctuary of his friend. Unlike the teacher, however, he felt only contentment and undisguised anticipation.

'I take it then,' he smiled, 'that Madam is home, and that you shall, in a short order of things, cease from thy labours?'

The teacher ignored him, so he let himself into the room, reaching effortlessly down to manipulate the latch at the very bottom of the lower half of the twin door. Inside the room, he stood over the teacher's table, his head brushing the low ceiling. Still the teacher refused to look up; he knew full well what the Genie's next utterance would be. It was not long in coming:

'Me-e-e-e-to-di-ko!'

For the pharmacist, the teacher's tyrannising stacks of files, school registers, circulars and memoranda, account books, inkwells, and rubber stamps and pads constantly presented an organising sleight-of-hand. It was evidence, he would remark, of a meticulous industry, an exceptional gift of those rare individuals with tidy instincts. He was not alone in his opinion. The teacher's desk, whether at home or in school, was a tableau of inanimate queuing. The pharmacist had no inhibition over restating the obvious, and no visit to the teacher's home was ever begun until he had performed the ritual of professing some variant of his admiration. This time, he spiked his eulogy with an equally familiar barb:

'No one can take it away from you, my dear Yode. I have said it before and will forever say it: Your desk, even at its busiest, manipulates the eye to perceive an order of the same quality as that conveyed by your noble garden to the cultivated eye.' His eyes twinkled with mischief. 'The difference, I suggest, is that while one is redolent with Nature's lavenders, the other only smells of gum arabica. Please . . .'

He raised his hand to stop the teacher's expected reaction. 'An illustration only, my dear Yode, nothing but a comparison. I said nothing of the spirit of frugality, of Ijebuism, the fact that blood must out, and so on and so forth – no. I merely compared two different states of order, and their accompanying odours. Talking of which . . .'

He sniffed, ostentatiously this time, and jerked his head in the direction of the kitchen, then turned to flick with his long finger at the pile of papers immediately in front of the teacher.

'Naturally you will wish to work until Madam announces that the table is laid and dinner is on the table. I have, on the other hand, closed shop for the day and have sauntered here for an evening's leisure. As a considerate person, I shall leave you to continue your labours in tranquility.' He dived down suddenly and picked up a journal from a pile in the basket. 'Is this the latest? I suspect, regrettably, that I have fallen behind in my subscription. I have not received the last two or three issues.'

'Find out for yourself,' the teacher retorted. 'As for dinner, I shall ask my wife to boil you some gum arabica.'

'Of course, of course,' the Genie said soothingly. 'I have no doubt that in her practised hands even gum arabica will prove more than palatable.'

He sat in the armchair and eased out his legs to their fullest length. The teacher cast a glance towards the windowsill on which the contentious jar of yellow viscous fluid with brown and black impurities sat conspicuously. He was quite unrepentant over his preference for this local product, which he made from the secretions of rain trees lining the broader paths of the parsonage. The fact that the school could obtain heavily discounted supplies of imported jars, with brushes, from the missionary bookshop did not deter him. At every handwork lesson, he supervised the pupils also in making their own gum and improvising brushes. The heavier glue for carpentry work was boiled from compressed slabs of resin, imported; that much he had had to concede. Their own product lacked the strength needed to hold the wooden joints together. But gum for paperwork, papier-mâché models for geography lessons, or indeed lampshades or fibre projects? No – he preferred to spend the school money on more worthwhile items.

Knowing that he had at most another half hour to work gave a renewed spurt to his flagging energies, and he bent over his desk, shutting out the presence of his visitor. In that half-hour reprieve he attempted to deserve some of that reputation which earned him the nickname corrupted from 'Methodical.'

First he tackled the draft balance sheets of the school accounts. That was a chore he hated, not so much from the nature of it but because he dreaded to make a mistake. He could leave it to the school secretary; in fact, until two years before he had always left it to that employee, whose task it really was, contenting himself with merely vetting his arithmetic. Two years ago, however . . . he shuddered over the memory of the downfall of that diligent servant of the diocese, who proved to have been more diligent in his own cause.

Next it was the turn of the class registers. The pharmacist was right; they were stacked in a distinguished pile, each edge so precisely matched with the next that they could be taken for a single thick ledger. It was his duty to close the register for the year with a diagonal line across the space below the last entry, write his comments within the right of the two triangles thus created, and seal it off with his signature. The signature was another source of marvelling; across the lined page it looked like an ornamented cluster of music notes, appropriately perhaps, since music, like gardening, was one of his passions. The comments entered – they had of course been carefully drafted in advance, and reviewed at least half a dozen times in the past week – he replaced the registers in their previous position, cleanly stacked as before.

On their return journey, his hands bypassed the Christmas cards. They would wait till the following day, which, being Sunday, did not admit of the work he was then doing. The signing of Christmas cards, with insertions of special sentiments where appropriate, was a chore which could not be considered unseemly on God's ordered day of rest. He moved on to the file of letters to parents, which were arranged in different categories. Some were straightforward replies to normal parental enquiries – these were the easiest. Stern warnings to fee-defaulting parents followed; he signed them rapidly, first skimming through to ensure that their messages were exactly as persuasive, or stern and uncompromising, as he wanted them to be.

The musical flourish of his signature beneath the next group of letters would provide no music to the ears of their recipients. These were terminal, the result of teachers' meetings, earlier warnings, and even summons to the affected parents – a pupil caught cheating at examinations, stealing, incurable unhygienic habits 'which endanger the health of others.' One or two cases of premature sexuality. The chronic dunces, 'whose places would be better occupied by others with proven aptitudes.' In some cases, recommendation that the rejected pupil would be 'best apprenticed to a trade where his scholastic abilities would never be tested.' Even as he signed these letters, he prepared his plans for evading the descent of relations, guardians, and go-betweens. Would there ever come such a day, he wondered, when they would understand? Such decisions were part and parcel of the business of teaching. Each classroom had its numerical limit, and there were always new pupils queuing to enter all classes at different times of the year. Parents came on transfer from other stations. Sometimes a school would be closed down – usually in a remote station – for lack of teachers. The bright ones among them had to be given preference; it was only just.

Now take young Odebambi. He leaned back in his chair, holding up the letter for a final scrutiny. An obviously talented pupil, but only in subjects that held his interest. The strange thing was that those subjects took turns, so that, in the end, he demonstrated not merely potential but brilliance in nearly all his subjects – history, geography, grammar, arithmetic, and so on. Even handwork. But would he do it all at once? Not Odebambi. Cajoling, field punishment, extra hours after school, floggings – nothing worked. Do not spare the cane, I beg you, the father would implore. You are his parent here; flog him for me until he learns some sense. Well, no one could accuse Soditan of shirking his obligations in that respect. He applied the rod and also applied, one after the other, all the 'tried and tested' methods outlined in Reverend Hackson's *Manual for Teachers*. The term's examinations took place and Odebambi scored the highest marks in his current one or two favourite subjects, failed dismally in others; in short, an overall Fail. This was his second year in Primary III. Very rarely did the school permit a third chance in the same class, and Odebambi would perhaps have qualified to be such an exception.

He had one handicap, however, and it was one which the boy could not overcome. His father was a first cousin to the head teacher. It was just too bad, Soditan sighed. He returned to his position over the desk, dipped the ebony-handled pen into its inkwell, and slowly signed the death warrant. Below the signature he wrote, 'Sorry, coz., there is really nothing more I can do.'

Soditan's mood lightened almost immediately after, as he turned his attention to the loose music sheets lined up beside the registers, a flicker of amusement even passing over his face. He had now to select the songs both for the music hour during the next year and also for the school march – but it was not this which brought about his amusement. His forearm flexed involuntarily as he remembered the pupils' impertinent variation on that year's marching song. Well, boys will be boys. He tried not to be a hypocrite, recalling his own schooldays, but – discipline is discipline. Surprisingly, the first hint of the mischief had come from Adeturan, the Primary II teacher, who was held in awe because he suffered from the sleeping sickness. His bouts were so acute that sometimes, when he began to write out a sentence on the blackboard, his students watched the sentence disintegrate into a nonsense squiggle and trail off the edge of the board, leaving Adeturan struggling to recover his balance. Adeturan had his good points, however. He wielded a willing cane. And it was his normally comatose hearing that first detected the extra syllables inserted in the refrain, so that instead of:

> Boys wanted, boys wanted
> Boys of muscle, brain, and power
> Fit to cope with anything
> These are wanted every hour.
> Boys wanted, boys wanted . . .

the young, lusty voices belted out:

> Boys, won ntedi, tedi
> Boys, won ntedi, tedi . . .

The crime was established, but the rest was not so easy. The miscreants were practised ventriloquists, and when the teachers walked close to the ranks of the marchers, the insertions disappeared in their immediate vicinity but continued farther down the line. Both sides pretended that nothing untoward was happening. The officiating teacher called out orders, drilled them into formation for the march into the assembly hall, and acted as if the parade were word-perfect.

The pupils escaped detection for a while. Their downfall came because they could not resist amplifying the new text with some physical action. It was the same Adeturan, whose determination so much overcame his sleeping bouts, who finally uncovered the clue. There was a telltale variation in the movement of the felons. If one looked closely, a few trunks here and there tilted forward – only a fraction of an angle – on the final accented and legitimate beat, then augmented that tilt by an additional jerk forward on the unauthorised 'tedi.' A few compulsive dancers went further; they did a swivel at the end, with a somewhat suggestive wiggle of the buttocks, especially as they marched up the flight of steps leading into the schoolroom for morning assembly. So the head teacher stationed Mr Adeturan on the inside of the entrance, and as each 'tedi' dancer passed through those portals, Adeturan neatly jerked him aside and waved him on into the far corner of the schoolroom. The others, completely masked by the front marchers on the upper steps, had no suspicion of the fate of their comrades. One after another, they were apprehended and herded together to await their fate. The bag – Soditan smiled with satisfaction – was twenty-three, three of them girls.

The head teacher was not without a sense of humour. He stood them at attention in his small office, then ordered 'About turn!' They formed a quadrangle, facing the office walls, which now appeared to be lined by quivering khaki statuettes. Next the order was given for them to mark time to brisk 'Boys won ntedi.' On the 'tedi, tedi' they had to *te'di* to the full, touching their toes. As they had their faces to the wall and dared not turn round, they had no way of knowing whose turn it would be to receive two strokes on the two accented beats as the head teacher – assisted by Adeturan, who could be relied upon to stay wide awake at such official duties – wheeled briskly round the proffered buttocks, laying on solid strokes. It was difficult to keep accurate count among twenty-three buttocks, so some received more and others less than the intended half dozen. But there was nothing abnormal about that; collective punishment made no pretence at even-handedness – that much he had learned to accept in his own pupilage.

Akinyode finally made his choice for the new year. One was 'Just Before the Battle, Mother' and the other a local air by Kilanko. The latter brought back the sense of triumph he had experienced during the hard-fought battle to introduce 'native' compositions into the school curriculum. What seemed obvious to him had not been so obvious to the schools board and those who gave directions from Lagos. Happily he had received vigorous support of Daodu, the formidable Reverend I. O. Ransome-Kuti, who had lately become the secretary-general of the National Union of Teachers. His booming presence had routed the conservatives, and Mr Kilanko himself was led in, to loud applause, to perform his music before the Teachers' Congress. The missionaries, he reflected, had been far more accommodating about the innovation, but the director for education had not even wanted to hear of it.

Akinyode became pensive. Yes, there were these tiny triumphs, but were they enough? Fulfillment, he enquired – silently, because there was a listener in the room besides himself – fulfillment, what does it mean? He glanced swiftly round his modest dwelling – did these walls completely circumscribe his future? Was Sipe right, Sipe, who read only timidity in his elected profession? And his young wife – perhaps she should not have had the second child so soon . . . those incessant stomach pains – was she really content with being the wife of a pupil teacher, even a head teacher highly thought-of at such a young age? There were much older teachers who had not been considered worthy of his level of responsibility. He recalled again the shock that had accompanied his letter of appointment. And his father had been cautious: They will try to kill you, he warned. If they can, they will harm you. So you must come home first and let us prepare the necessary protection. Protestations were unavailing, but then he . . . Do I really believe? And afterwards, did I not walk feeling safer, return the stares of those older men with confidence? Have I ever since been afraid to shake hands with them, not even caring what kind of dye-blackened rings they wore on their fingers? It was not the envious ones who could impair his future, no, but what of the future itself – what prospects did it hold for one in a primary school?

Abruptly he put aside the music sheets, lifted out of planned sequence a file marked PERSONAL and leaned back in his chair once again, holding up some sheets of lined notepaper clipped together. The handwriting on them had an attractive vigour, a marked contrast to the soft elegance of that of the teacher.

'What,' he demanded of the Genie, 'what shall I do about Sipe?'

'Oh. Mephistopheles?'

The ex-Ilés had attended a performance of *Faust* at the Roman Catholic seminary. Such treats were rare, and the ex-Ilés, as was their habit, made of it an 'occasion.' The dandified group struck the rest of the audience dumb with admiration. They barely recognised their neighbourhood pharmacist; the head teacher, with Ogunba and two others of his staff; Opeilu, the produce inspector (on casual leave from Adio for the occasion); Sotikare, the town clerk; and Akinsanya, the trade unionist, who had joined them from Lagos to grace this rare treat of European opera. The credit for their stunning entrance and presence in that hall belonged almost exclusively to their 'outfitter' and social organiser, Sipe, the master schemer and adventurer. After the night's musical induction into the world of high-risk dare, high stakes, and damnation, Sipe, by common consent, was stripped of his erstwhile name, Resolute Rooster, and conferred with that of the archetypal Tempter. As usual, Sipe wore the new name like a carnation, playing variations on it as the mood seized him. This letter in the teacher's hand, for instance, had been signed, Resolutely yours, Mephisto-Rooster.

'Has it occurred to you,' Akinyode continued, 'dispenser of foreign potions that you are, that this Sipe is actually the most conservative, homebound, parochial country-boy Jebusite of the lot of us, and yet he always introduces these alien, seductive vistas into everybody's life.'

'Just business,' remarked the Genie.

'That is the point. To him they are nothing but prospective trading partners. He sees no difference between, let us say, a Belgian firm and an Italian.'

'Well, is there?'

'Maybe not. But if I had to choose between a Gunter Henklehacker – or whatever the name is of that machine-spare-parts factory he proposed last year – and these Italian firms, I would definitely choose the Italians.'

'You, Yode, are a romantic.'

'That's what he says. And he says that's why I shall die a teacher, and as poor as a church mouse. He says it in one breath, then tries to save me from myself in the next mail. But wait, listen to the names – Signore Porta Agostino Beila & Co., Messrs Instituto Ameriale Laniero X Italiano, via Alesandro Manzoni, Milano. Montanari Caro, Esq., 12 via Morigi . . .' He paused suddenly, then began to chuckle. The Genie watched his host's laughter become uncontrollable until tears appeared in the corners of his eyes. As he wiped them off and gradually recovered his breath, he began to splutter: '*Motan'nari, kaaro o. Wo r'igi? Are. Wei r'igi. Mu suuru. Sipe a ko' gi ru e. Waa ri'gi, waa ri kunmo!*'* As Osibo made out his meaning, he held his sides. The laughter waxed so furious that they did not hear the little girl enter and stand in the doorway, making the pharmacist nearly jump out of his skin.

'Good God. Look at her, just like a fairy. Does she want to give me a heart attack?'

'Sorry, sir. Good evening, sir.'

'Yes, what is it, Bose?'

'Mama says food will soon be ready. She says she hopes Mr Pharmacist is staying to eat.'

'Of course, girl. What do you think I've been waiting for all this time while your papa was working. Tell Madam I shall be ready whenever she deigns to summon us to the dinner table.'

The girl left. Chuckling in spurts, the Genie continued: 'But you are right, you know. You don't know how right you are. Sipe will shave clean their heads. In a straightforward way, I mean, not crooked. Sipe plays straight. But he will shave their Italian heads just the same.'

'Oh yes,' agreed Akinyode. 'But you do see what I mean. Their names sound like Yoruba names. Look at this Benito Paserelli . . . *B'eni to pase r'eni!*† Padua . . . look, even that one – *p'adua . . . B'eni to p'ase r'eni p'adua.*' He paused suddenly. 'Why does that sound familiar? Padua . . . Padua . . .'

'If you don't know that, Mr Schoolteacher . . .'

'Really. Should I? We never teach Italian geography, you know. Only that of the Empire.'

Osibo shook his head. 'Padua. If you don't recall it, you will need an

---

* Montanari, good morning. You say you can see wood? Wait. You are yet to see wood. Be patient. Sipe will load your back with timber. You will see wood, you will taste the cudgel!

† As one who can feast us into a state of exhaustion. As one who feasts us so dead tired, we fall to prayers.

adua to make me stop when I start to broadcast this ignorance to the world.'

'Wait wait wait . . . Padua . . . Padua. Oh dear, where where where? History. Let's see. It has to be history. The treaty of . . . ?'

The dispenser shook his head. 'You are in trouble.'

'Not history? What other subject could it be? Religious knowledge . . . something about the popes? Look, ours is an Anglican school. Did they teach you about popes at school?'

The pharmacist shook his head, firmly. 'Not religious knowledge. And you have only one more chance. You miss at the next attempt and I will tell you.' He rubbed his long fingers together and gloated, 'And you know what that means.'

The teacher suddenly exhaled a deep breath of relief. He had been looking out of the window, concentrating hard, when he saw, emerging from the gates of BishopsCourt, the ample figure of the circuit preacher's wife, whose presence in St Peter's Church the previous Sunday had created such a stir. She had insisted on sitting in the very front pew, which, like two or three others, had its own side doors with latch and was the exclusive seating right of one of the oldest families in Egbaland. The politics was local; it was not a matter in which the teacher had felt obliged to dabble. As sidesman, however, he had had to act, bringing all his diplomatic powers to bear on the circuit preacher's wife even while the husband, sitting in the choir stalls, pretended that nothing unusual was going on in the elevated transept. Akinyode offered the woman his own sidesman's chair with its narrow bible-and-hymnal podium. It was all one unit, down to the kneeling platform, unpadded. This had the distinction of such exclusivity that she was soon mollified and proceeded to occupy her new status. Until she tried to squeeze her bulk into the single-piece contraption, clearly built with a more frugal frame in mind. Then a new commotion began. The event was not lost on the organist; he rose in the sidesman's estimation by playing so loud that only a handful of the congregation – and even this was limited to the occupants of the transept pews – had any notion of the scale of the disaster.

The Genie had noticed the change in his demeanour. 'Well?'

'Providence is kind. I knew I deserved some divine reward for my handling of last Sunday's – er – situation.'

'Make your guess.'

'Shakespeare. *The Taming of the Shrew.*'

'Damn damn damn! But what's all this about Providence?'

'Look out of the window – keep your head low! Don't let her see you.'

Osibo raised his nose to the level of the lower door.

'It is the woman?'

'None other.'

'And that went into that contraption you normally occupy?'

'She tried to.'

The Genie nodded slowly. 'Now I know what Jesus saw before he pronounced his "verily, verily" on the camel and the eye of the needle.'

The teacher's wife came in to cut short their mirth, bringing the dispenser to his feet. He took her hand. 'Good evening, my dear Mrs S. My guess is that you have come to summon us to dinner?'

'I am sorry I took a little longer than I had planned.'

'Don't give it a thought, Mrs S. Don't give it a single thought. Your husband has kept me fully entertained, after he took his nose out of his desk, of course.'

The Genie stood up, plonked the open journal down on the table, face down. 'There's another of your countrymen in there. Let's talk about him after dinner.'

The teacher could not retain his curiosity and he turned over the journal, a recent issue of *In Leisure Hours*. The face in the picture that stared up at him was cut from a different cloth than were the imagined shop-corner salesman faces of a Beila or a Paserelli, though he did share a common Christian name with the latter. This Benito was that no-nonsense face whose antics on the continent had formed the theme of impassioned discussion within The Circle, cropping up again and again as his latest manoeuvres or pronouncements came to their notice. Some, like Sipe, had interest only in the fact that this alien enigma had been photographed sitting astride one of the most modern motorcycles to roll out of the Italian motor industry. Could they not import Italian machines? For nearly ten years this face had popped in and out of the news that filtered through to West Africa, appearing even in *The Nigerian Teacher*, but mostly in *The West African Review*. Was he a diabolical tyrant or simply a MOUTH? What drove the man? Was it greed or power? The Circle debated Mussolini endlessly.

The teacher discarded the journal and led the way to the dining room. 'At heart,' he said, 'he is only another one of them.'

'Of course. He's Italian, isn't he?'

'No, I mean – another businessman. Trader. He is busy looking for markets for expansion, just like everybody else.'

Osibo did an about-turn, snatched up the journal, and stabbed the picture with his long forefinger. 'Take a good look at that face. Does that look like the face of a haberdasher? Can you see that one dealing in gentlemen's apparel – shoes, ties, shirts with detachable collars, two- and three-piece suits in worsted wool? This is a man of iron and steel, sir. If Sipe moves near him – which he never will, not even by correspondence – this man will chew him up.'

Akinyode admitted that this was not in dispute. The ex-Ilés had long ago accepted that Benito Mussolini was not a figure to be trifled with. And he continued to haunt their discussions, thanks in the main to the editors of *The West African Review*, who, in their Gold Coast colony, appeared also to find his personality irresistible. He emerged sometimes as the very antithesis of those euphonious names of Sipe's partners – calculating and domineering. What had he not done to bring Haile Selassie, the lone African emperor, under his dominance? The diminutive ruler cried for help to the League of Nations – in vain. Step by step, Mussolini proceeded to harry him into the Red Sea. Some claimed that he had routed the Abyssinian forces by the foul use of poison gas. The soldiers breathed it in and simply keeled over without firing a shot. 'Activity,' the scoutmaster, undertook to commence recruitment for a brigade to fight Mussolini, confident that the colonial government would give its blessing. He was acquainted with several veterans of the last war, he declared, and could field a company of West African Volunteers within a week. Prominent on the wall of his living room was the framed reply he had received from the colonial secretary. The matter, declared the letter, was being effectively arbitrated by the League of Nations. Activity still waved the letter round the town, and it was difficult to decide whether this was an act of pride – that he had actually received a letter from an official in the governor's office in Lagos – or that the lukewarm letter provided proof of collusion among the colonial powers. Even after he had framed the letter and hung it up prominently in his home, his visitors found it impossible to resolve the nature of his invocation of that august piece of recognition.

'Have you noticed something?' the teacher remarked, turning the journal at different angles. 'He does bear a resemblance to I.O.'

Osibo looked down over his shoulder. 'I.O.? You mean our own Daodu?'

'Yes. Take a good look. Same disciplinarian expression. They would make a match, I suspect. Daodu could handle him. If anyone can, it is Daodu.'

For a long while, Osibo contemplated the photograph. 'You may have something there. Maybe it is Daodu who should be sent to confront him in the League of Nations.'

A soft voice broke through their scheme for high diplomacy. It was

Akinyode's wife, retracing her steps to express anxiety about the dinner slowly congealing on the table.

'Let's go, let's go,' urged the teacher. 'Or we'll get blamed if the food has been burnt.'

Laughing, they proceeded to the table.

'You know,' the teacher resumed, 'I never did obtain those books from Foyles in London.'

'Which ones out of many?'

'The ones by the German writer Mussolini referred to in that speech. No, not the one you were reading just now – a much earlier speech in *The Elders Review*, more than five years ago. I spent a fortune on stamps sending reminders.'

'But Foyles are usually so reliable.'

Surgically, Akinyode sliced his *eko*, spiked it with a piece of crayfish, plastered it with bean pottage, and rounded it off with a rind of pork. It finally had acquired the desired shape and submitted to its onward transfer to the mouth. He chewed methodically, integrating his speech into the normal working of his jaw muscles.

'My suspicion, Mr Pharmacist, is that those books did not arrive for the same reasons that Activity was dissuaded from forming his volunteer brigade. Sabotage. Or censorship, if you prefer.'

'I don't understand. Who was the author?'

'It is not a familiar name; I only read of him that once – Gerhart Hauptmann. You see, he is German.'

The Genie frowned. 'Well?'

'Don't you see? The British, Italians, and Germans have always been rivals, even when they collaborated against us with one another. Remember how we used to argue the possibility of Mussolini reaching for one of the British possessions if he failed to grab Eritrea?'

'Yes, but –'

'Now, if you were the British, would you have encouraged your subjects to have access to the nationalist propaganda of your potential rivals? You wouldn't wait until hostilities actually broke out before sealing up the minds of your colonial subjects against the voices of competitors.'

'Could be. Sometimes I think they even carry it into the field of medicaments. Hardly ever did we run into German drugs during our training.'

'Oh yes, they kept the boundaries tightly closed once we were carved up. No trespassing. No poaching. Honour among thieves. You never see any German teachers – in fact, any German professionals in any field in this corner of the protectorate. Only priests. And those are confined to interior missions.'

Osibo chewed his food thoughtfully. 'You think this writer . . . er . . .'

'Hauptmann. I don't know if that is the current way to pronounce it.'

'All right. Do you think he might be a dangerous writer, then?'

'I wouldn't know. I never read him. But he is German. He may be a strong supporter of Hitler. Like Mussolini, Hitler wants more slices of the continent. Well, let's hope that when they really get down to business they'll be so exhausted that they'll all go home and leave us alone.'

Startled, Osibo looked up. 'Surely you don't mean that!'

'Why not? Oh, I don't mean pack up lock, stock, and barrel. It's too late for that anyway. But look, how would you feel each time Empire Day comes round, and you have to prepare your pupils for the schools' parade in Ibara, teaching them to sing:

> Victoria, Victoria
> *Aiye re I'awa nje!*
> *O so gbogbo eru d'omo*
> *N'ile enia dudu.**

We've been colonized, agreed. But really, sometimes I feel that is carrying things too far!'

The young wife ate little, contenting herself with ensuring that both husband and guest tasted from every dish. Nor did she take part in the conversation, though she listened intently. When she paused in the motion of refilling their glasses, arrested by a remark being made at that moment, the Genie could not resist noting her attention with approval.

'Madam, I see, shows keen interest in the vicissitudes of our world?'

She smiled shyly while her husband responded, 'Ah, you don't know what I have to put up with. She is not Daodu's niece for nothing. In the end, maybe she is the one we shall send to confront Hitler while her uncle takes on Mussolini.'

They laughed uproariously. The food sank rapidly, and soon gleaming patches showed in the interior of the white porcelain. This always sprang the wife to action; she seized the bowl and went to the kitchen to replenish it. The dispenser seized one such opportunity to whisper: 'The first

---

* Victoria, Victoria,
  What a life of ease we owe you!
  You turned all slaves into free beings
  In the land of the black peoples.

question I should have asked, but you were then busy. How is Iyawo? Do the pills agree with her?'

'There has been some improvement. She still has those bouts of pain but . . . yes, definitely some improvement.'

'And the cramps?'

'Not for over a fortnight now. I think the pills worked for those cramps.'

'I have a new consignment from Lagos. German, as a matter of fact.'

'German? How —'

'I have contacts. Sipe is not the only businessman, you know. I am really interested, professionally. Some say French medicine is the best. Others say German. No one ever says English. Not one mention of Italian medicine either, come to think of it. Well, what do they say across the border, I mean, in the French colonies? Do they believe there that English medicine is best? Or Italian?'

The teacher smiled. 'The pasture on the farther bank of the river . . .'

'That's it exactly. Always lusher than the one behind one's backyard. I really must find out. We shall see if the British are really keeping the superior things from us. It will be a rough road, but I have made up my mind. A colleague in Lagos has opened up the channels.'

With a mischievous grin, the teacher asked, 'Where do we come in in all this?'

Osibo was puzzled. 'Come in? Who?'

Mrs Soditan returned with the replenished dish.

'We. You and me and all the rest. Before you began to stock your pharmacy with all that *oyinbo* stuff, didn't we have our own curatives?'

Osibo shook his head, firmly. 'No, thank you. I am not getting drawn into that argument all over again.'

'But we did. And still do. All I am asking is your professional opinion. Does our medicine come after the Germans? In front of the British or French? Or don't we rate at all?'

The pharmacist transferred a full serving-spoon load of bean pottage to his plate, passed some into his mouth, and masticated vigorously, staring stubbornly at the wall.

'Just an informed opinion,' the teacher persisted. 'If you don't answer I shall send my father to you the next time he comes round with his potion for my indigestion.'

The wife remonstrated. 'Dear, let him eat his food.'

'Madam, don't plead with him. Let him continue to pose his combative questions. I remain mute, firm and impregnable as Olumo rock. Let him continue to waste his breath.'

'But why should any of our local herbalists not come to your shop with a bottle of his concoction and ask to become your supplier? No, not even to stock it, just to ask you for a professional opinion. Right? What' – and he raised his gaze to the ceiling, conducted an invisible orchestra with fork and knife as he posed the question – 'what would be so unusual in two professional colleagues exchanging learned opinions on the art of the apothecary?'

The Genie fell for the taunt. 'It would not be two professional colleagues but a pharmacist and a jujuman. A trained chemist and a mumbo-jumboist.'

'A-ah, but which is which? Let us ask ourselves in all sincerity: What does the local herbalist think of Osibo, the dispenser of white men's medicines?'

'Dear, your food. And do let Mr Osibo eat.'

'No, no, madam. Let him be. I knew where he was heading all along. Some people simply do not like progress. We shall ignore them and persist in our march towards civilisation.'

'But you do stock *Gbogbonse*? That is a local product invented, if I may mention with modest pride, by an Ijebuman . . .'

'*Gbogbonse* is produced in Lagos under hygienic conditions, bottled and labelled according –'

'A-ah, I knew it. The label maketh the drug.'

'Labelled according to accepted pharmaceutical usage. It is not a mixture of the powdered nest of the praying mantis with drops of chicken blood and lizard's –' He quickly caught himself.

'Lizard's what?' Akinyode insisted.

'Not at the dinner table. And certainly not in the presence of Madam.'

'All right, but don't say I didn't warn you. Sipe will reap all the benefit of your prejudices. His latest proposal includes starting a patent-medicine store, dealing mostly in local potions.'

'What?'

'Aha, I thought that would shake you up. He is already securing premises in Yaba. So, if we end up stocking medicines that are not fit for human consumption –'

'You don't mean it. Seriously, now.'

'I shall show you the letter. It's all there. Worsted wool from overseas, patent medicine of our own manufature. He's worked it all out. He is going to make us rich men whether we like it or not.'

The pharmacist glared at the schoolteacher for some moments, heaved a deep sigh. 'Well, I suppose if there is no other way of stopping you reckless young men from becoming murderers –'

'Good. Sipe plans to come over during the holidays. He will be glad to learn that he now has a consultant pharmacist.'

Osibo shook his head somberly and returned to the business of eating. Mrs Soditan smiled secretively while the teacher tried to conjure up a mask of innocence; it did not fool his wife.

Pa Josiah's letter lay on the table between them, an unsought and unwelcome marriage test – or perhaps simply a test of faith. Their visitor was gone, the table cleaned, and they were finally alone. Soditan and his wife sought each other's thoughts in the dim light of the kerosene lamp, the wife more desperately than the man. He appeared far less troubled; if anything, his thoughts had ranged much farther away than the immediate challenge posed by his father's letter. What he sought more, indeed longed for, was the resumption of the steamy, raucous debate with his circle over the entire question of cures. The debate was unending; they returned to the same subject again and again, never resolving anything but feeling mentally elated afterwards. As he glanced round the compound, however, he reflected that they were probably all asleep. Indeed, his was the only lamp still flickering in that compound of some twenty families – mostly teachers like himself, but with a sprinkling of court clerks, a pharmacist, the catechist, and one other government employee of indeterminate functions. In his household, the only sound that broke the silence came in the form of angry spasmodic grunts from the direction of the curtained door of his wife's bedroom, produced by the second child of their five-year marriage. The mother knew at once that he had got his legs tangled up as usual in the bedclothes, so she got up and went into the room. It was a warm night like most others, but she would as soon dream of exposing a newborn child stark naked to the rain as leave the covers off a sleeping child. Even in burning heat, COLD – she thought of it in menacing letters – cold was the eternal enemy of infants and must be kept at bay with wrappings drawn up to the chest. Soditan had long ceased to argue, but the baby did not give up the disputation.

In the bedroom, she gently disentangled his limbs, keeping a firm hand on the chest so he would not spring fully awake. It worked, it always did. He continued to sleep peacefully until the next bout of wrangling. In the front room, the husband marvelled at this unending ritual.

When she returned, she found that he had picked up his pen and was dipping it thoughtfully in the inkwell, wiping the excess against the rim. She read the decision on his face correctly and remarked, 'Father will think it was I who refused to come.'

'I shall make it clear that the decision was mine. In fact, I shall not even admit that I discussed it with you. Come to think of it' – his face opened wide in a mischievous grin – 'what are you talking about? I do not even know what you're talking about.'

She refused to be sidetracked. 'Oh, he won't say anything. But you will see it in the way he sulks at me when next we visit.'

'That's if he doesn't show up to take up the fight in person.'

Then his mood changed abruptly, betraying a deep underlying concern. He stared hard at her for some moments, then demanded, 'But how are you *really* feeling? Really really.'

She spread out her hands and shrugged. 'It is still too early to tell – I no longer jump at these improvements in my condition. It always waits a few weeks, then starts all over again.'

'So you don't feel this has been different from the other treatments?'

'I don't know. I really don't know. I only hope and pray it is. I haven't felt any pains so far but . . . well, I don't know. We'll just have to watch and pray, that's all.'

'Your appetite has not fully returned,' he insisted.

She laughed at that. 'That's what you think. You weren't home when I had my *amala* this afternoon. That was why I couldn't do justice to our supper together.'

'That never used to stop you, not a small afternoon snack.'

'Oh, it was late. I thought you would be returning late, not before evening, what with the meeting of your Auxiliary Committee.'

'That turned out to be more routine. We didn't take up the financial matter I told you about. The accounts were not ready.'

After that, they both fell silent. He kept the pen poised over the writing pad, his mind busy on the best phrasing to mollify his father; the letter had to be ready for the courier who would leave very early in the morning. As he began to write he pursed his lips as his mind returned to yet another nagging thought.

'Anyway, we must wait quite a while before the next child.'

She understood. Deinde had come quickly after their first child, a daughter. And those pains had begun soon after Deinde's birth; for Soditan the two things remained connected. In vain she reminded him that this was nothing compared with the pace at which other women gave birth, so rapidly that the nurses would sometimes joke that the new pregnancy must have taken hold on the eve of the last labour pains. In her case, it was over six months after the birth of Tolu that she had again become pregnant – they had not planned it so but . . . She shrugged. It happened, so, it happened. And there was certainly nothing complicated about that birth. The pains were longer than expected, but, no, no complications.

The result lay peacefully – for now – on the large bed next door, and besides that troublesome seizure which sometimes wrenched her insides and went on for days, she foresaw no problems with the next. Her husband continued to write, speaking at the same time, shaking his head in continuing bafflement.

'Not even that white specialist from Lagos. And the Massey Street Hospital with all its modern medicine. So where does one try next if it starts all over again? All these tests and drugs and injections – *otubante!* what exactly have they been treating? I think it is nothing but trial and error. They don't know. They simply don't know.'

She seized her chance to return to his earlier remark. 'They are all agreed on one thing – at Sokenu, at the Catholic Hospital, the consultant who came to McCutter's – they all say it has nothing to do with Deinde's birth.'

'So what do they say it has to do with? They know what it isn't. Now let them tell us what it is. The medicines they keep giving you, what are they supposed to treat? The hospital cards don't tell me anything. Uncle Segun, with all his training – he is just as baffled. All right. I'll tell you what I am replying to Father. You are not going to Ìsarà for now – we are both agreed. In principle, we are going to stick to this European treatment.' He nodded emphasis. 'In principle. It's over a year now, and that is a long time to be kept anxious. I simply do not like it. After this last course, we wait and see. We'll see if the miracle has finally happened. I shall give it one week, a month – but only if the pain doesn't start all over again! If it does, Father will be set loose to place his *ebo** right against the church gates if that is what his *onisegun* recommends.'

The wife looked worried. It was difficult sometimes to divine his true intent. 'Are you sure we would be doing the right thing, dear?'

He grinned, pleased to find himself on favourite grounds. 'Oh no, *we* won't be doing anything at all, right or wrong. It is Father who wants to do something, so let him do it. He is not going to force any medicine down your throat, and what he does won't stop us going for fresh consultations with any European clinic or specialist anyone recommends. Only this time, I am withdrawing the monopoly.'

She shook her head in continuing doubt. 'This pagan business . . .'

* Ritual offering.

340

'Pagan? Why pagan? All right, what if it is pagan? Tell me, don't Christians make *saara** on occasion?'

She sensed she was losing grip on the central issue. The battle light was already in the head teacher's eyes, and soon there would be no stopping him. She had grown familiar with that sign of the flaring nostrils – oh yes, Soditan's adrenaline had begun to pump, ready to take him into the early hours – into the next week, indeed, if he could find stimulating opposition which also possessed his staying power. Still, this was something she felt strongly about, so she braced up for a fight, however brief.

'Let me say this, dear. The way I see it, *saara* is a kind of thanksgiving. A child has been ill, recovers, so we make *saara*. Or, let us say, after a successful childbirth. People have a good harvest, or they arrive safely after a long journey . . . all that is different. What Father is saying in this letter is something else; *etutu* is like a secret ritual.'

'Why secret?' He pushed the letter towards her. 'Where does it say so in the letter?'

'Oh, you know what I mean,' she protested.

'No, I do not know what you mean. There is nothing secret about it. Or we can go to Ìsarà if you like – that would take the secrecy out of it. He has invited us – or rather, you. So, go and find out what it's all about. If he embarks on anything that contradicts your Christian teaching, you withdraw.'

She threw up her hands in desperation. 'I am trying to be serious, dear. This is a serious matter –'

'So am I,' he protested, 'So am I. The old man says he wants to make *etutu* for your recovery – there is nothing secret about *etutu*. It is less secret than a surgical operation. Those doctors, do they allow anyone in the theatre when they start cutting up people and sewing them up and removing their insides?' He paused. A new idea had occurred to his mind, which now entered its playful mood. 'Come to think of it, we don't even know what they do with those organs they remove, do we? How do you know they don't use them to make some white man's *etutu*?' He raised his hand to forestall her protestations. 'Hm-hm, you answer only if you know exactly what they do with those organs. They don't replace a thing; all they do is cut things out. Right? What happens to those organs?'

Confidently she said, 'Yes, I'll tell you. They put them in bottles in some kind of preservative – that's right, formaldehyde. Probably to study them. I have seen rows of those jars with my own eyes.'

---

* Ritual feast.

341

That checked him only for a second. 'Including amputations? You have seen legs and arms, even tiny hands and feet, in those pickle jars?' Then the grin reappeared. 'But tell me, when you go to the market and see all those dried snakes and lizards, mice, monkey skulls and pickled bats and so on, what are they for? And why do these Europeans look down on them as instruments of devilish rites?'

'You are changing the argument,' she accused. 'You are twisting everything. I don't know which ground you are standing on right now.'

'That's because I haven't landed,' he cried. 'Be patient. I am going to land in a moment. Let's go back to *etutu* for now. We will say that it involves slaughtering a goat. The officiating priest takes bits and pieces out of it – you do know that, of course. Certain parts of the animal are reserved for him as of right. Very specific they are in these matters. Nobody else can take them. Other parts belong to, let us say, the Baale, or the chief of the compound, the head of the family. If there is an *abiku** in the family, his or her part is equally guaranteed. To the celebrant himself belongs this or that chunk, while others still are distributed to friends and neighbours. The helpers make sure no one does them out of their own allocation. Right? Now let's return to the white officiating priest – or if you like, the surgeon. What does he do with his own portion, those bits and pieces which no one else sees? Not *everything* goes into those jars! Amputations, for instance – what happens to those limbs?'

Morola did not hesitate. 'The surgeon eats them, of course. He takes them home and gives them to his wife to cook.'

Soditan sank back in the chair, deflated. 'I must have told you that one before.'

She shook her head. 'No. But I am getting used to the pattern.'

'I shall have to take out a patent. When I see Sipe he'll advise me what to do. A man can't have his wife stealing his best lines.'

She laughed. 'Let me leave you with your letter. And if it's a ram, don't forget we could do with some meat in the house.'

'You think I'll forget that? I want half the entire beast. You forget who is going to bear the cost in any case.'

'Oh yes,' she sighed. 'And that is the other thing, dear. These things cost money, and what you have spent so far is hardly child's play. The hospital bills –'

Soditan sat back suddenly. 'Ha! How could I have overlooked that? I know why you are so dead against Father's kind of cure. With European

* A child that repeatedly dies – mythical.

342

treatment, you eat all the medicine by yourself. In our own, we all get to share in it. That's it! Selfish woman. And me fooling myself that your appetite has not yet returned!'

She shook her head with a despairing finality. 'I am going to bed. Your letter – don't let the courier miss the early morning transport.'

For the husband, it would not be bedtime for a while. Mopping-up operation, he called it, as he completed and sealed the letter, then turned to grapple with outstanding matters on his desk. The annual school report came first. Sighing, he drew thick lines over most of the draft composition – clearly the young trainee teacher, eager to impress, had decided to engage in an essay competition, or an article for *The Nigerian Teacher*. The item on Ogunba especially he rewrote completely. Ogunba, his favourite colleague, was leaving, the one teacher he always considered irreplaceable. He now stressed the urgency of replacing him, certainly before the commencement of the new school year.

The official part over, Soditan let himself sink into doleful thoughts; the impending loss of his friend had long oppressed him. The weekend afternoons, spent alternately in each other's home . . . the rare privilege of a friend whom one could actually take for granted. He cast his mind round others in The Circle, shook his head. With none other did he feel this special bond, neither within The Circle nor among the inner sect of the ex-Ilés, those children of Ìsarà who had also trained at Ilesa and called themselves the first rank of trained exiles from Ijebuland. Ogunba was a personal loss. Even if he were sent the most efficient, most experienced ex-Ilé, could he again, whenever his duties took him from his station, could he ever leave his station again without a twinge of unease? With Ogunba in charge, Akinyode admitted, he would sometimes take an extra day on his journeys, confident that the affairs of the school were in capable and trusty hands. That was it – trust. That really was it, that deep *trust* which bound them together.

It could not be helped, but the head teacher felt cheated. Ogunba was going to take charge of a school in Ijebu-Ode. That was the only consolation, the tiny crumb of solace. Ìsarà was close enough to Ijebu-Ode, so he could look forward to more delightful holidays in Ìsarà. And was it not typical of his friend to leave the elder son, Jimi, behind in his care, so that his schooling could continue under his tutelage? 'I don't know how good that Ijebu-Ode school is, but I know it will take us years to bring it up to this standard even if we were together; how much more with me alone . . .' It was Ogunba's way of admitting the wrench he also felt at his departure. I really am absurd, Akinyode admonished himself, as he found a film of tears dimming his sight. He hastily completed his notes, which again urged the mission to arrange Ogunba's replacement quickly, certainly before the school reopened in January, otherwise, 'the task of maintaining our standard of education in this school cannot be achieved.' He turned to the next item with some relief.

Akanbi Beckley was a truculent eleven-year-old, much too old for the Standard III Elementary, which he had barely managed to attain. Spoiled by a wealthy father, one of the 'established' families in town, he should indeed have been expelled from school three or four times over, but interventions from above managed to thwart the teacher's iron code. What he would not accept, however, was that in matters of discipline the same kind of intervention should be countenanced. Akanbi often stayed behind at school to perform some physical chores as punishment – scrubbing the school floor or cutting grass on the playing fields. It was no more than others underwent for like offences, but of course young Akanbi would first refuse to touch anything, sometimes keeping up his defiance until dusk. His father (or mother) would come to fetch him, and the process would continue the following day. Akanbi would stand in the alotted field, banned from classes until the punishment – plus its accumulated interest – was fully carried out. This process might persist for a week, since the head teacher was never known to remit a sentence, once delivered. Finally, the father would come with Akanbi to school, having cajoled him and brought his birthday forward by several weeks or months, then stand over him while he carried out the task. Two or three times a year this comedy was played. Then Akinyode decided that he had had enough.

The teachers had chafed and fumed. They could not resort to the far less protracted form of punishment – flogging – because the doting father had obtained from one of his doctor friends a certificate of ill health. Young Akanbi's constitution was declared extremely fragile, unable to withstand the shock of corporal punishment. Since one of Akanbi's favourite sports was engaging in physical fights, especially in the classroom – fights from which he usually came off best, since he always chose his opponents very carefully – Akinyode had quietly registered his own opinion on that subject.

The day of reckoning dawned at last, not unexpectedly, as school drew to a close. This was Akanbi's open season. He would commence his round of crimes and refusal of punishment near the end of term, after which the holidays would intervene and the whole episode, he reasoned, would be forgotten. He was very wrong about that, but Akanbi's little mind could never stretch to embrace past lessons concerning the head teacher's infinite patience. On this occasion, however, Akinyode was not even prepared to adopt his usual measures. These involved withholding the miscreant's class report or refusing his fees for the following term until the punishment was served out in full, usually in the final days of the holidays, with papa in attendance. This time, as soon as the fracas broke out, with Akanbi's unique vocal register penetrating the partitions between the classrooms and distracting other pupils who were dutifully sitting their examinations, Akinyode summoned both teacher and pupil to his office. He asked no questions. He simply reached into the corner of his office and ordered the teacher: *'Gbe pon!'*

The teacher stammered in confusion. Was their H. T. out of his mind? He did not even recall that such a role had never before been given a teacher – the norm was to make one of the bigger boys carry the victim piggyback – so preoccupied was he with the enormity of the event. This was the delicate egg no one dared touch. Mr Soditan flexed the cane while Akanbi gave him a look of utter contempt. The head teacher further underscored his intentions by locking the door to his office, then turned round and repeated, 'Hump him! Are you deaf?'

The child with the delicate health put up the fight of his life. It did not save him. His arms were pinioned round the neck of the teacher as he was hoisted onto his back while he twisted and wriggled, tried to kick his mount, the head teacher, the walls, and the ceiling. Soditan thereupon took the tiny head in one hand, yanked it round to face his own, and spoke above his screams.

'Now, it is in your own interest to lie still. If by chance this cane misses you and hits your teacher, when I have finished, he will himself give you three strokes for every one that touches him. Anywhere he pleases. You understand me? I will not be carrying you. I will simply hand him the cane and he will give you a general flogging. I hope that is clear.'

Young Beckley, seeing that he was clearly doomed, began to whimper and beg. Too late. Akinyode gave him, as he was fond of putting it, 'twelve of the best,' then sent him back to class to complete his interrupted papers. When he reached home that day, he took a shower, ate his supper, and selected a very stout cane, which he placed beside him in the front room. Then he sat down to await the storm.

He was surprised that it took so long to arrive; Beckley Senior also probably believed in having his supper before embarking on a confrontation. He had, however, also taken time to have his son examined by his doctor and had received a written report on the state of his back and his little bottom. Armed with this potent document, he stepped onto the raised concrete entrance of the head teacher's house and was astonished to be received with fussless courtesy. Soditan rose and opened the door for him.

'I've been expecting you, Mr Beckley. Please take a seat.'

Mr Beckley eyed the teacher with undisguised hostility, which he extended to an inspection of the front room. The left half of his face, especially the region between his left nostril and upper lip, squeezed itself together to indicate his disgust at being compelled to be in such surroundings. He faced Akinyode squarely.

'I think what we have to say to each other will not require my sitting down, thank you very much, Mr Head Teacher. All I want to know from you is whether you wish to deny that you were responsible for inflicting those inhuman injuries borne home upon his back by my son Akanbi. Not surprisingly, he is now seriously ill, confined to bed, and may even have to be hospitalized. I have come merely to hear what you have to say in your own defence.'

Soditan sighed, resumed his seat, and leaned back comfortably.

'I hope you have no objection if I sit down myself, Mr Beckley. Actually, I think this may take some time. I would seriously urge you to sit down.'

'I am NOT sitting down, Teacher Soditan. I am asking you very simply – did you or did you not inflict those inhuman injuries on my son?'

The teacher did not immediately reply. He took out a folder from under a stack of papers, opened it carefully, and began to turn over the sheets.

'Your son, I think I am correct in saying, is Akanbi Beckley. This file contains all the reports which his teachers have made on him over the past four years in two classes, as he spent two years in each class, where a normal pupil spends only one –'

Mr Beckley exploded. 'I did not come here to ask for a school report on my son. Did you or did you not savagely attack the child, knowing full well that his health is most delicate at the best of times? That is the only issue I have come to discuss with you.'

Soditan closed the filed and carefully put it back in its place. 'I thought,' he began, 'that this was to be a sort of parent-teacher meeting. I was under the impression that you were so concerned about your son's future that you decided to encroach on my private hours and impose on me for a few minutes' discussion. Since, however, this is not the case and this still happens to be my house' – and with that Akinyode brought out his cane from its hiding place – 'I will give you five seconds to remove yourself. At the end of that, I shall proceed to do to you what I have unjustly done to your son. Because you see, Mr Beckley' – he rose slowly from his chair – 'it

346

is you I should have flogged, years ago. Then perhaps we would all have been spared the disgusting nuisance of your delinquent dullard of a son.' By the end of his speech, Akinyode had squeezed out of the confined space behind his desk, his eyes glinting like a fanatic's. Beckley spluttered, raised his arm in a warning gesture, but finally let himself to be persuaded by the mad gleam in Akinyode's unblinking eyes, fled the house and the compound without a backward glance.

The result now stared Akinyode in the face: Beckley's letter of complaint to the school board, with a covering memorandum from the schools inspector. The matter had become formalised: Every exchange was being forwarded and copied in triplicate. It was likely – and this was nothing less than he had anticipated – that the bishopric in Lagos was already in possession of the facts. Beckley's connections were of the very highest. In a separate folder lay Akinyode's ultimate response: his letter of resignation, which lacked only his signature and the date. But that would come only as a last resort. It was prepared as an expression of his stand in the matter of young Beckley. This far, the folder said, I am prepared to go.

He took up his pen and prepared a draft response to his query. It stated the facts very simply and reiterated his view that Akanbi's conduct merited instant dismissal from the school; he had been flogged as a lesser punishment. Finally, he wanted to know in writing from Mr Beckley how he would like his son to be treated in the future. Beckley, he wrote, must anticipate every conceivable situation based on his son's past conduct and the moral welfare of the rest of the school. He set the draft aside for further ideas in the morning. A smile played on his face as he tried to imagine Sipe's reaction when he came to learn of the episode. Working for the likes of Beckley – I told you! Abandon that post! As for teaching itself, I don't know what you see in that thankless, graceless, unrewarding profession . . .'.

He turned to the folder marked PERSONAL – FOR REPLIES. News of the death of his cousin Akinsanya's father continued to plague im. The reply was written, but should he visit him in person? But for these year-end chores he would already be on his way to Lagos. To Lagos? His cousin could be at Ìsarà that very moment, then be on his way back to Lagos while he sat in an Ìsarà-bound passenger lorry. He decided to await news of the funeral plans. And if his work load lightened rapidly, why not a visit to Lagos. Saaki would appreciate it. And he must not forget his lemons this time.

Tailor Famade wrote from a new address at the Nigerian Railways, Kaduna Junction, where he had gone to set up a tailoring service. He was beginning to get worried about the influx of tailors. Word seemed to have gone round that Kaduna was becoming quite a fast-growing civil service and business enclave, what with its increasing importance as a junction for the two main rail lines – from Enugu in the east and Lagos to the south. A new barracks for the West African Frontier Force had also recently been opened. They required uniforms; so did the police, which had been proportionately expanded. Every two-bit tailor, he complained, was heading north with his Singer sewing machine. Trade was expanding at the same time, and a number of wealthy traders required new *buba* and *agbada* outfits. He was surviving, having got into the main chance early, but the encroachments were becoming quite heavy and determined. He was thinking of coming down in the New Year to have Akinyode's advice.

A letter from a former teacher-trainee under his instruction brought a twinge of regret. *My dear old pedagogue*, she began. What a mischievous bundle of seductive energy she had been! A trainee teacher, she had been attached to his school for some months for practical experience; he had ended up wondering who was the teacher and who was the pupil. Pretty, provocative Olarounpe was one of the most capable trainees that had ever come to his school. She hardly ever required help or needed supervision. After her practical sessions she would write up her notes and bring them to him in person – then the game began. A little difficulty encountered, she would claim, in her English class; she could not make her pupils master the rules of Direct and Indirect Speech.

For instance, 'I set the class this simple exercise, and I was most disappointed by the results: *Put into Indirect Speech the following sentence: The teacher said, "What I most admire in a man is discipline and dignity."* ' Looking at him in a way which neither Direct nor Indirect Speech could ever hope to convey. Then wistfully, 'I have a feeling that the results will always be the same, disappointment?' But most unnerving of all was when, under the pretext of translation problems in the Yoruba class, she left him, in her own handwriting, the passionate speech of spurned love by Kako's wife in Fagunwa's *Ogboju Ode!* That, he admitted, had made him sweat. Now the letter in his hand resumed the tease: *I am still as weak as ever in my Direct and Indirect Speech. I wonder if I should come for a refresher course with my dear pedagogue but fear the results will never change.* Then, as a dutiful afterthought, *I nearly forgot, do give my love to the fortunate Mrs S. and the entire family. My very best wishes for a Happy Christmas and for the New Year.* The season was her excuse for renewing this correspondence, subtly restating her attachment.

Soditan sighed, turning the letter over and over in his hands. Deep in the pit of his stomach, he knew that this inconclusive affair would continue to haunt him for a while. Sipe, who was his main confidant in such matters, chided him for his cruelty and swore to uphold Olarounpe's interest as long as she showed interest, and as long as her claims did not try to monopolise the rights of the many 'butterflies which flutter around your deceptive, coy candle that hides its flame under a bushel.'

Despite his inner convictions, he leaned out of the window, struck a match to Olarounpe's letter, and watched the paper curl up, charred, letting it drop only after nothing was left of the white-lined 'love-blue' sheet. He regretted now that he had not addressed to her one of the Sipe-ordered Christmas cards, then again decided that it was a good idea not to have done so. He turned his attention to the remaining item for the night, the hard nut which he had deliberately reserved for the quietest hours of the day – an address to the Owu National Society. Heaven only knew why he had succumbed to this hazard of proposing a toast to the Owu elite. He considered himself a poor substitute for J. S. Odunjo, whose textbooks were in such wide use in the country. In any impromptu debate the teacher could hold his own, but delivering formal speeches always gave him stage fright. Reading the lesson in church was easy, but addressing an audience of mostly strangers? What did one say? In the first place, he was not even an Owu, he was not related to Owu by blood or water. He had, in effect, been blackmailed into accepting the dubious honour. J. A. Ladipo, the headmaster of Igbore High School, was Owu, and Soditan had requested his services at the prize-giving ceremony of his own school. It was a special occasion for which Soditan wished to gather all the local heavyweights. He needed them as balast to offset the presence of the principal guest, Mrs Melville Jones, wife of the director for education. Ladipo, ever the blunt Owu man, put it to him quite directly:

'Ah, God is good. J. S. O. can't come to honour our gathering after all in December and we desperately need somebody who is close enough to his stature. You agree to come and do us the honour; I agree to come and help you balance Mrs Melville Jones at your own do. Agreed?'

The teacher was so taken aback by the opportunism of the man that he found that he had shaken hands on the deal before he knew it. And now he could not even think of a theme for his speech. He had given himself today as the absolute deadline for the first draft. His notes on Owu history lay beside him; they included even some bloody clashes with the Ijebu, that is, with his own Remo and Ìsarà ancestors.

But first, the joke to break the ice – he had that ready selected. No sensible speaker plunged directly into his subject; a joke must oil the way.

An immaculate script which never deserted him, even in the drafting stage, began to cover the paper: *I was taken aback to find myself asked to be the proposer of the toast of the Owu National Society in place of the well-known educationist and textbook author J. S. Odunjo, at these famous educational premises. I felt I would not be a good substitute, more so when I recollected the story of the Viennese scientist who, with as much pride as could be conjured, announced to his audience: I have discovered a substitute for human blood. After a brief silence, a man from within the audience shouted: You can see that we all here very much doubt it. And don't imagine the income tax people will be fobbed off with that!*

The pencil paused. His original idea was to link the story with his own unpaid appearance there or with the Owu's reputation for hardheaded business. Or else find some connection with the reputation of the Ijebu for being tightfisted. And the story – transpose the story to an Ìsarà herbalist, perhaps? An Ìsarà herbalist announces that he has successfully concocted a substitute for blood. The hardheaded Owu man consults him after falling off his bicycle and losing a lot of blood . . . No, the roles should be reversed. An Owu herbalist invents the blood substitute; then an Ìsarà man falls off his bicycle and consults the Owu man for treatment. On being offered the blood substitute . . . what happens next? Enter Sipe, who works in Inland Revenue. No! Better still, that glorified tax collector should be the one to fall off his bicycle. Come to think of it, was he quite certain he had read the joke? Wasn't it likely that it was from Sipe's unlimited repertoire of stories? No, he felt reasonably certain that it had come from a book, although he could not remember which one.

He turned to his notes on Owu history and character. Begin all over. Given: The Owu are known to be tough, hard bargainers, but they do not appear to come even remotely close to the Ijebu reputation for extracting money from stone. Or blood. Yes, take blood . . .

Fifteen minutes later Soditan admitted failure. At least, deferment, until The Circle could meet and help him out. Jokes, he admitted, were not really his forte. They did not spring to his mind with that spontaneity which he admired in others. So he left a gap for later inspiration and proceeded to the substance; there was no shortage of material in the history of Owu people. But first, perhaps a little more on the theme of his own inadequacies, then contrast them with the virtues of Owu people? *I do however consider myself highly honoured to be asked to speak here, being neither Egba nor Owu, being blessed with neither a sweet tongue nor a good voice. Since you must have known all of this before asking me, I hope you will overlook the inadequate manner in which I set forth what little I have unearthed to redress my ignorance of the many achievements, not only of the Owu National Society, but of Owu people themselves.* He read it over, permitting even his strict judgment to admit that that was as good a transition as he could hope to make between preliminary remarks and the main burden of his speech. Next, to reap the harvest of his diligent research: *The Owu National Society, founded some years ago, no doubt from patriotic reasons, is a society fit to be compared with a tree which has strong roots in the ground and shoots out so many branches at the top. There are, of course, many societies with your own aims, ambitions, and branches, but ask yourself which of them has achieved a fraction of what you have achieved since the few years of your birth! Is it not within living memory, evergreen memory, the part you played when a decision was taken that the late Olowu of Owu would henceforth go and collect taxes from the farm? By your unity and steadiness of purpose you put an end to such a step that was fraught with danger to peace, containing as it did a threat of repression to the poor peasants of Owu. Can anyone deny the role you exerted in the selection and installation of the present Olowu . . .'* Soditan paused, a little bit uncertain. Would this not be considered an impertinent interference by an alien in the affairs of Owu? He had no means of ascertaining if all of Owu were quite united behind the decisions of the Owu National Society. After all, the former Olowu must have had his own supporters. Again the pencil paused for some minutes. In the end, he left a gap for the achievements of Owu and went into the safer grounds of Owu's role in the Ijaiye wars. The next instant the pencil was flung down. Safer? Was it really that much safer? The Ijaiye war was a war which could awake bitter memories in some of the immediate descendants of the tragic participants of that war. A glancing reference, perhaps, just to insert a historic sense – no more. He filled out the remaining space on that page, took a fresh one, and embarked on the controversial character of Owu people. It was time to draw on his little notebook of quotes, some ready ticked for this address.

Owu people have earned a high reputation, one which makes them frequently contrasted with their neighbours, of sticking to their guns, never being scared to utter their conviction of the truth. Thomas Henry Huxley, the great educationist, it was who said, 'Every word uttered by a speaker costs him some physical loss and in the strictest sense, he burns that others may have light. So much eloquence, so much of his body resolved into carbon acid and . . .' Oh dear! Was that much different from Adeniyi-Jones's approving description of a teacher as a 'candle which lights others, while consuming itself'? Would his use of Huxley's quote not suggest that he agreed with that patron of the teachers' union, whereas the truth was that he, Akinyode Soditan, most emphatically did not? No, he must not appear to select for praise airy attributes that he himself considered extravagant to expect in the commitment of a teacher. Akinyode began to wonder if he had not taken on more than he could chew. Still, he found that he had already put together nearly two pages. He returned to the records of the young society for guidance in directions of a less controversial nature. Such as? Pity he had never seen an Owu masquerade, or more accurately, he did not know which of the masquerades that paraded the streets of Abeokuta were from Owu quarter. Some comparative remarks – Owu versus Ìsarà masquerades, perhaps – would have moved his address to areas of culture. Culture would be a less risky subject. He went over what he had written and took his decision: He would leave in the early sections to spike things up a little – a bit of political ginger did no harm – but for the rest, deal with the Owu National Society through its cultural life. . . . He yawned, replaced his files and writing materials in the planned order of resumption for the following day, and retired to bed. On the whole, he reflected, it had been a day well spent. He was well ahead of his working schedule.

By dawn the courier was rendered superfluous. When the maid opened the front door in the morning to sweep out the dust, she let out a scream that took Soditan clean out of his early-morning dream and sat him bolt upright in bed. Simultaneously, he heard his wife's voice raised from the adjoining room. 'Who is that? Who screamed just now?'

The maid's foosteps came pounding into the parlour, then stopped. Morola could hear the heavy panting as the girl tried to recover some measure of control.

'Bose, is that you?'

'Yes, Ma.'

'What were you screaming about so early in the morning?'

'An old man, Ma. He was sitting right against the door.'

A loose pair of slippers slapped their way into the front room and their owner voiced his umbrage at the maid. 'Is the girl mad? Who is an old man? It is your father who is an old man. Get me some water to drink, you fool.'

Later she would tell her mates that she had opened the door that morning to find a *sigidi** squatting by the door. It was all very well to punish her for screaming, she complained, but she dared anyone, anyone, even Teacher, who was the most unflappable man in the world, she dared

* Incubus.

352

him to open the door in that early-morning half-light when it was neither dark nor dawn, encounter a waist-high object in *agbada* propped against the wall, and not think it was a *sigidi* which had been placed there during the night. Oh yes, she declared. Anyone would have screamed and taken to his heels. It was a wonder she had not fainted. Mama would most certainly have fainted, she with her frail health.

She had good cause to be apprehensive. The head teacher's wife had already decided her punishment; such loss of control admitted of no mitigating circumstances. For his own part, Teacher Soditan, who had been subscribing to the publications of the Rosicrucian Society and sometimes experimented with some aspects of its regimen, regretted that he would have to miss his morning meditation that day. He recognised the voice at once, even though he refused, for some moments, to believe his ears. When he emerged from the bedroom, still trying to fasten his coverlet round his waist, his father, Josiah, was comfortably seated in an armchair in the parlour. The maid returned at the same time with a glass of water that spilled onto the tray held in her trembling hands.

Soditan walked slowly into the room, prostrated himself carefully and took a chair opposite his father. Then he waited while Pa Josiah drank his water.

'I did not mean to wake the household – this foolish maid. I thought I would sit there quietly waiting for the house to wake. In fact I dozed off. I haven't been to sleep all night. And then she screamed in my ear. Did she think she was seeing a spirit?'

'Never mind the girl, Father. Has something happened at home?'

Josiah refused to be mollified. 'Screaming her head off like that! She nearly scared me to death!' His baleful glare followed the girl's departure. 'Iyawo nko? I suppose she is awake too, and she really ought to have as much rest as possible. She has to stay home for some time, get plenty of rest, you understand? Forget all her trading up and down for a week – that is what Jagun says. She needs to be strong.'

Soditan looked puzzled. 'How did you know she was back? Even in your letter –'

'Efuape's son told me. He sent his wife home ahead of the New Year, with some goods just cleared from the harbour in Lagos. Everything works together at the right time, just like I always tell you. How do you think I got here so early? The transport that brought Sipe's wife and goods was a produce lorry going to Omi-Adio to collect a load of palm kernels. It was to leave Ìsarà hours before dawn, so I decided to follow my messenger here. The driver didn't even charge me anything.' He chuckled admiringly.

'Efuape! There is nothing that one can't get away with. Diverting a whole government vehicle to Ìsarà on the way to Adio. That boy will either end up a millionaire or end up in prison.'

'Didn't he pay for the hire, then?'

'Of course,' Josiah said. 'But, you know, private arrangement. Bringing me here without paying was the *eni** – he knows how to drive a hard bargain, that boy.'

'He takes risks,' Soditan commented. 'But he was born lucky. Well, what about breakfast?'

'All in good time. I didn't come here just to push my message, you know. Something happened. If Efuape had not arrived, you would have seen me later today anyway. You see, last night, Jagun sent for me. I was with him till about two o'clock this morning. I haven't had any sleep at all.'

'About that matter, Father –'

'I know, I know. I already know what objections you would have. Don't think I didn't anticipate all your doubts.'

'I have written it all in the letter. Do you want me to read it to you?'

'Wait, just wait. I am telling you that something else has happened. Jagun sent for me to tell me that he had seen something. Just in the normal course of consulting – not for anyone, just for general well-being. And he came across something which he recognised as touching me. He sent his servant for me and we looked at it together. Don't say anything. Just wait until Iyawo wakes up and I shall ask her some questions. Then we shall see.'

Soditan spoke as gently as he could. 'Of course, Father. You ask her anything you want. But I have to tell you, we don't think she should come. Anything you want to do over there, that's fine. I won't even try to stop you. But Baba, you know how we think already, so why involve us in this thing?'

'Wait, I tell you. Wait until you've heard what we found. It is quite weighty. You say I am trying to involve you? Not me. Blame the person who really involved you.'

He turned in the direction of a noise and saw Morola emerge from her bedroom.

'Ah, Iyawo. I knew that *alakori* of a maid must have woken you up!'

Morola knelt before him. 'Papa, you are welcome. And don't worry about my being woken up. I was already wide awake.'

---

* Bonus.

'Then you should not have been. And I don't want you doing all that travelling around for a while. You have to keep your feet in one place.'

'Anything you say, Papa. What of breakfast? I shall go and prepare something.'

'Sit here.' Josiah's voice had gone very soft as he patted the chair beside him. 'We'll get to breakfast soon enough. I want to ask you some questions.'

Morola cast a quick glance at her husband, who shrugged slightly. She took her seat and waited.

'Tell me, Morola, do you share your shop with anyone?'

She shook his head. 'No. No one at all. The shop is hardly big enough for me.'

'Not even the pavement?' he asked. 'There is no woman who displays her wares anywhere close to your shop? Someone you allowed to –'

'Oh, the pavement. Yes. There is a woman there. I allowed her to place her *ate* there. Sometimes she is still selling long after I have closed up my shop.'

Josiah glanced triumphantly at his own son. '*Alate. Iya alate.** That was what Jagun saw. One *iya alate* whom she brought there herself.'

Morola tried to correct him. 'No, I didn't bring her . . .'

Josiah shook his head indulgently. 'You don't understand. You did. She doesn't pay you rent, does she?'

'Oh no, God forbid.'

'That's it. You brought her there. She is there because of you. Because you gave her permission. *Iwo ro gbas'ile. Ota ile de ni.*'†

Akinyode broke the silence that ensued. 'And Jagun holds her responsible?'

'No question at all. The letter I sent you, I said that we had already found that Iyawo's illness was not *oju lasan*. That was obvious. We didn't need to look into anything to see that. Twelve months in and out of hospitals, and no one knowing what it is. All those clever overseas doctors? But we looked anyway, just to make sure. Then, last night, Jagun sent for me – I told you. When we looked together, it was there, and Jagun read it out. I tell you, when *awo*‡ wants to take a hand, it takes a hand. Ask yourself. Your wife was in Lagos, that is what we all thought. Efuape's wife brings news that she has returned to Abeokuta. That same night, Jagun sees something. Then it so happens that Efuape's lorry is waiting to

* The woman with a tray (of merchandise).
† It was you who brought her indoors. And she is an inside enemy.
‡ Divination.

355

go on to Omi-Adio, passing through Abeokuta. A child can see it all. It is not just that it was time that something should be revealed; it meant that it was time something should be done. The evil work of that woman is itself ready to be undone. Its power is on the wane.'

Soditan smiled. 'Well, in that case –'

Josiah rounded on him. 'In that case you are about to talk like a child. Leave everything as it is, right? Wasn't that what you were about to say?' He shook his head in annoyance. 'I keep reminding you – I knew what I was doing when I let those people baptise me. It wasn't that I meant to turn my back on everything I knew, just you keep that in your mind! Twelve months! Up and down, in and out, here and yonder. Do you think I can sit all that time with my hands folded? And now that we know what has been going on, you want us to leave things to take their own course?' He paused, turned from one to the other. 'Just why do you think these things are revealed to us at all? Why? If they could take their own course for good, without our own participation, why would they be revealed at all? So that we can boast and feel clever for having known? Oh no. *Awo* is far too busy for that kind of indulgence!'

Soditan gestured surrender. The contest had been merely symbolic, anyway. Josiah had to be kept somewhat at bay, just sufficiently to make him understand that his son was resolved to lead his own life, no more. He respected his father's stubborn will; they were both alike in that respect. The difference was that the teacher disliked open clashes and would walk a circuitous route to avoid them. Not so Josiah.

'All right. What do you want us to do? Of course,' he casually added, 'as you yourself have just advised, Morola won't be travelling anywhere for some time. I am glad you reinforced what I was telling her only last night. So, whatever you want us to do here, we shall do. If it is to be in Ìsarà, then it must be done on her behalf.'

The elder man glared at the son, a suspicion stealing over him. Could it be that he had trapped himself? Not for the first time, he was compelled to cast baleful thoughts in the direction of that Ilesa seminary, which he held responsible for the slippery tongue his son had acquired when it came to an argument. Of course he had to get her to Ìsarà. Going to Ìsarà was a different matter from running up and down on trading errands. In fact, the point of saving her strength was to save it for the visit to Ìsarà and a full *etutu*, with all that would entail. Well, he would just have to be cadgy with this son. Seminary or no seminary, he Josiah was still the head of the Ile Lígùn.

'I have the list of things I am taking back with me.' He said it with

356

finality. It was clear that the old man was in no mood to permit any new grounds for argument. He ticked them off on his fingers. 'A shawl, one she has used since it was last washed. In other words, I don't want one fresh from the washerman. Also one of your own discarded slippers.'

'My slippers?' Soditan thought it was a slip of the tongue.

'Yes, your slippers. A very old one, worn through at the sole. He says he prefers one through which the sole of your foot has actually touched the ground.'

The son laughed. 'Suppose there isn't one?'

Josiah's reply was unsmiling. 'Then you will simply have to make a hole in one, put your foot in it, and walk round the house. Stop asking me these foolish questions. I also want one of the coverlets you use for your children.' He dug into the pouch of his *agbada* and brought out a scrap of paper. 'Here is a list of the other things – snails, two doves, alligator pepper, and the rest of it. Morola must buy them from the market with her own hands – I am sure you will find them all at Itoko.' He handed the paper to the wife, who cast a hurried glance over the list.

'Yes,' she nodded. 'I am sure I can find them.'

'Good. While you are getting them, I will wait for you in the shop so I can get a good look at this woman. She can thank her stars that we are all Christians now. If she had tried this when I was as I was, I would be doing more than just taking a look at her. Now I have to settle for simply protecting my own and rendering her powerless to do further harm.'

Morola stood up. 'Shall I get breakfast now?'

'That is a good idea,' Josiah consented. 'But first I need a wash.'

'I'll have some water for you in the bathroom in a moment.'

She left the two men together. Josiah leaned back in the chair, a feeling of partial achievement leaving him somewhat dissatisfied. Still, the battle was not yet over; he would find some way of ensuring that his son did not hide her away during this New Year season, as he did the last one. Not that it mattered that much; Jagun had merely wanted to take a look at her, and pass his hands over her head, the hands which had carried out the *etutu*. The teacher, on his part, remained watchful; it was too early to breathe a sigh of relief that all had gone so smoothly. His father was not the kind to give up that easily.

'So, how is Foluso doing? Does he appear to improve at all?'

Akinyode threw up his hands. 'It's the same as I reported to you the last time. The evening classes are a waste of money. And as for the tailoring trade he is supposed to be learning, his master complains of him every day. He is not serious.'

'*Oloriburuku!*'* He let out a long hiss. 'Did he ask you before making that request he sent me in his last letter?'

The teacher frowned. 'What request?'

'A wife. He wants us to find him a wife. That idle one who has no work, no trade to his name, no money to even feed himself, he wants us to find him a wife. To condemn some poor girl from a hardworking family to a life of hunger.'

'He asked you for a wife?'

'If I had not been in such a great hurry, I would have brought the letter with me.'

'I don't think that boy is well in the head,' the son observed at last.

'Forget his foolish head. Let's talk of better things.'

'Pity. I had to send him to Lagos with some things for Saaki. I would have liked to see his face when you mentioned that wife business.'

Josiah waved off the subject impatiently. 'He will meet his deserts soon enough. I am glad you mentioned Akinsanya because I have to tell you that he did nobly over his farm. He sent a pound to pay labourers when I was ill for some weeks and couldn't go on the farm myself. But for him, we would have lost most of the harvest. Too bad about his father. You will come for the funeral, of course? All of Lagos will come to Ìsarà, I am sure.'

'I am waiting to be told the date. He will have to fix his car now; he's been having problems with it or he would have brought Morola back himself. He sent a note through her though,' he added, smiling, 'asking for fruits.'

'Fruits? Is he also trading in fruits in Lagos?'

'No. To eat. He has developed this craze for fruits, and just when he gets to Lagos, where they are so expensive. He has gone mad on things like oranges and lemons especially.'

Josiah shook his head dolefully. 'I feel sorry for our people in that Lagos. I feel really sorry for them. They should come home more often than they do. And tell Akinsanya to take care with those white men. They say he is secretary of a union for people with whom he is working. Isn't that dangerous for him? You do remember what we last spoke about?'

Soditan smiled. 'You know Saaki. He is like Sipe – in a different way. He was never meant to lead a quiet life.'

'Not like you, enh?' the older man teased.

Soditan waved a hand in the general direction of the compound. 'All this

* Ne'er-do-well!

358

place is noisy enough for me. And it keeps one more busy than you can imagine.'

Josiah nodded. 'I know. I know. Your friends give me all kinds of good news. Oh, and talking of your friends –'

The maid interrupted to announce that water had been placed in the bathroom. Josiah got up, waited for the girl to be out of earshot.

'Yes, talking of your friends. Don't lend them so much money.'

Soditan was flabbergasted. 'Who told you that?'

'I know. I hear these things. They couldn't try it with someone like Sipe. But they take advantage of you.'

'Oh, Sipe. He told you?'

'Who said he did? Hasn't he also borrowed money from you? He has eyes on business even though he too is working for government. But these people all know you have a steady job, you don't risk money in all sorts of dubious ways. They know you save steadily, so they know you always have some money in hand. And of course, you lend it to them. You don't know how to say no. That's right. Just like your father.'

The son made disparaging noises; then he spoke, rather shyly. 'Well, I don't know. I was actually thinking of coming to ask for your advice. It's about Sipe. He wants me to go into business with him.'

Josiah stood open-mouthed. 'Efuape? Sipe asked you? I thought he had too shrewd a business head for that. He knows you have no head for business.'

'Oh yes, he does. But he wants me to invest. He will do all the hard work.'

'A-ah. That sounds more like him. What sort of business?'

'Anything. He has so many ideas, that's his trouble. But first he wants us to form a syndicate and put aside money for whatever enterprise we decide on.'

Josiah thought over this for a while, then shook his head sadly. 'I don't know. I don't know what advice to give. I have never tried that route myself. I have no head for it. But I can't help thinking sooner or later you will have to start thinking of earning something outside your teacher's salary. The children will grow up. You will want to send them even farther than St Simeon's. That is the way it was. We all pray that our children go farther than we did, and we try to help God answer our prayers. And if others of your own group start sending their children to study overseas and you can't, you won't forgive yourself. Isn't that the way your mind is working?'

The teacher nodded. As usual, his father had read him accurately. The old man grunted, 'Hm-hm,' as if to say, 'I thought so,' then went off for his bath. As usual, he had avoided giving an opinion on the real issue, one way or the other.

V

HOMECOMING

First to call was the widow, Mrs Esan, taking the fight to Akinyode for leaving Morola behind. She had travelled directly from Saki with bales of *eleto eto* cloth and, with great pride, samples of the Saki variant of the imported velvet *petùje*, whose influx on the market had threatened the local weave from Iseyin and Saki. A former trainee teacher under Soditan, she had imbibed some of his resentment at the claims of this cloth, which the Lagosians had named, with such disloyalty, 'the cloth which eclipses *età.' Età*, that noble cloth whose warp and weft spun the very fabric of the history of the Yoruba! Isolated in the Women's Training College to which she had been posted, she thought often of this outrage wrought against the local product by the insensitive elite of Lagos. It was bad enough that this so-called *petùje* should command outrageous prices yet be so much sought-after, but to lord it, in addition, by the sheer power of naming, over a passive product of undisputed worth – this was augmented thievery, aided and abetted by the shameless children of the house! She was in charge of homecrafts at the training school, and aided by the weavers of Saki and Iseyin, she set up her looms in the school, unravelled the velvet impostor along patterns borrowed from the disparaged *età*, then filled them in with cotton yarns, based on the original colour motifs. The result was lighter, more porous, and therefore more suited to the climate. She named it *èye età*. She had come home with two full sets of *bùbá, ìró*, and *gèlè* for herself and Mrs Soditan, sewn from this cloth. Its outing was to be at the New Year in Ìsarà, and what a sensation they would have caused, just the two of them in *èye età*. Now she was faced with bitter disappointment.

'She is in hospital,' Soditan informed her, quietly.

Mrs Esan was immediately contrite, accusing herself of every crime in the world, as if she should have known in advance. This was followed by renewed alarm at the state of Morola's health. Had no solution been found even now for her recurrent illness?

'She is recuperating,' Soditan explained. Her illness was finally diagnosed – it was pneumonia all this while, suppressed from time to time by the prescriptions but never fully cured. It all came to light when she returned to the maternity clinic for routine testing . . .'

'The maternity . . .'

Soditan's smile carried a tinge of sheepishness. 'Yes, I'm afraid she is pregnant again.'

And Mrs Esan dropped her bag, took off her headtie, flung it round her waist in a loose knot, and began to dance, accompanying herself with her voice.

> *Mo fe e su're o*
> *Aa se*
> *Mo fe e sure o*
> *Aa se*
> *Iku o ni wo'le to wa*
> *Aa se*
> *Arun ko ni wo'le to wa*
> *Aa yun aa yun a bi rodo*
> *Aa se*
> *Aa bi aa bi a bi rodo*
> *Mo fe e sure o . . .**

In vain did the uncertain father-to-be try to shush her, succeeding only when, now fully carried away, she threatened to extend her joy into the street and join up with one of the roving bands of masqueraders whose treble voices identified them as children. Akinyode shut the door firmly on her and proposed instead a glass of Dimple. Restoring the sash to its proper use, Mrs Esan accepted a glass of pineapple juice instead, toasted the expected child, recited an endless litany of blessings, and predicted the sex on the spot.

'It's a boy, you will see. And you can only name him Obatunde.'

'Sit down, sit down,' Akinyode urged. 'What is happening in Saki? I felt annoyed with myself afterwards. I should have written to tell you I was making that bicycle tour –'

'Yes, just imagine my feelings! I would have stayed behind to welcome you. Oh, I felt so cheated! I had kept some salt, too, but had no one through whom to send it. Since I have only a maid living with me, I always have surplus from my ration. And I had cartons of Guinea Gold and

---

* I wish to pronounce a blessing
  So be it
  Death will not cross our threshold
  Illness will not cross our threshold
  Our wombs shall grow big and rounded
  Our wombs shall deliver again and again . . .

Capstan cigarettes. Those are the favourites of the *akowe*. Bicycle brand is everywhere, I think – no problem there. You know Saki is near the Meko garrison, so the soldiers usually sell us their unwanted rations. Or maybe they steal from stores – that's their own worry. Those favourite brands are scarce now, so I kept some for her. I've left them with Mama at 'Gborobe.'

'I shall take them with me when I go back. Thank you.'

'I haven't been able to obtain the black thread she wanted – the flat-packed kind for braiding hair. Only the spindle type is available. She wrote me months ago saying she had run out in the shop – she should come over, Teacher. As soon as she is better, let her come and stay with me. Then she can choose all the things she wants. There is so much scarcity down here, but we don't do too badly upcountry, you know.'

'I'll tell her,' Soditan promised. 'As soon as she can travel, she will pay you a visit.'

Mrs Esan sipped her juice thoughtfully. Exhausted perhaps from her gyrations, she gradually sank into a pensive mood. It was a good while before Soditan had to admit that her mind had travelled elsewhere, as thoroughly as during her earlier outburst of joy.

'Is there something the matter?'

The visitor sighed. 'I don't know, Mr Soditan. I simply get worried sometimes. You know, we who live on the way to Meko, we see all the movements of these soldiers. We feel the war a lot more over there, perhaps more than in Lagos. And those of us in the trade – even we part-timers – we know how everything is affected. Farmers know it, business is undependable. And the training schools – educational, technical, or whatever – when the students leave, there is no job for them. Even secondary school learners. Well, Teacher, the question I have been asking myself is this: Whose war is this? What is our stake in this quarrel between white people?'

Soditan smiled ruefully. 'I wish I could tell you. All I know is that we are caught in it. Unfortunately, we cannot even choose between two evils; one of them has already enveloped us.'

'And afterwards?'

'Afterwards, Mrs Esan, I think you will find that people like Onyah, Akinsanya, Mrs Kuti, Enahoro, are right. You should read *The West African Pilot* if you can get it in Saki. And the *Daily Times* also. They sometimes echo what Mahatma Gandhi says on the other side of the ocean – they are in the same boat as we are, you know. One way or the other we all have to choose our destiny – ourselves. The war will bring things to a head – for the colonies, and the colonisers. That is what they are saying, and I think they are right.'

'But that is the very thing which troubles me, sir. Will these people let go of us? I read what many of our own people have to say about the win-the-war campaign, why they are supporting it. They give that very reason, that the war will set us free. I like to believe it; sometimes I say it myself. But you see, sir, it is that very hope that takes my mind to the many things the white people themselves have written and said. Will this war help them to change their mind? That is my question. Will they have a change of heart? Do you remember, sir, when you used to send me your old journals?'

Soditan nodded.

'Well, I used to copy out some things before returning them – I won't say from whom I acquired that habit!' Her laughter filled the room as she dug into her handbag and brought out an envelope. From it she extracted two sheets of paper, both copied in her handwriting. 'You'll be surprised how many of your former students imitate you in that respect – and in other ways too, but I won't tell you which. One of us reads his Bible religiously every night, then follows it with a passage he stole from your notebook – night after night, the same passage, his wife tells me. He sneaked into your office when you were out – he was much too scared to ask your permission.'

Soditan shook his head to dispute the last point, but she stuck to it. 'Oh yes, we were all a little scared of you, sir. Except maybe Miss Olarounpe.' Her eyes danced wildly with mischief. 'Do you still hear from her?'

'Sometimes, she sends her old teacher the occasional Christmas greetings.'

'Oh no, not so old!' she protested, smoothing out the sheet and holding it to the light from the window. 'Shall I read it to you? I am certain it is from *The Elders Review*, although I did not make a note of the source at the time – not a pass mark, I must say, but I was too emotional over the matter, so I forgot. May I read it, sir? It will help me practise my English – my pronunciation, I should say. Out there, I have no one to keep me on my toes. I can bomb the English language worse than Hitler and no one will complain.' She cleared her throat self-consciously and began to read: ' "The average West African whom I have met is a good chap. I love him. But he has his limitations. He is a merchant, an electrician, a farmer, or a grocery boy; within his bounds he is excellent – but only within those borders. Occasionally, he shines as a lawyer, a doctor, or a padre – but only very occasionally. You never find the West African who can invent a big business, such as a steamship line, or a bank, or a railroad. The white man steps in there. The average West African is no more fit to govern his own colonies than the average English member of Parliament of today is to handle any part or portion of the British Empire. If the African were allowed to try, and we, at the pull of our silly sentimentalists, withdrew the home stiffening, how long would it be before chaos reigned? Five years? One? Six months?" '

She looked up. 'Does it ring a bell, sir?'

Akinyode nodded. 'Of course it does. That is a constant theme of the colonial tune. Surely you know that.'

She nodded vigorously. 'Yes, of course, sir. In fact –'

'Wait. I even think I remember that particular article. That was quite a long time ago. There was heavy correspondence on it afterwards – mostly from Sierra Leone.'

'There was. And most of the letters were from other colonial officers who took that writer's side. I wanted to reply myself but it was around that time you stopped sending me journals.'

Akinyode looked rueful. 'I'm sorry I didn't keep it up.'

'Oh no, there is nothing to be sorry about. You did your work; it was up to us to carry on as best as we could. But then we get married, have children, acquire extended families with all their problems. But you see, sir, afterwards something happens, like this war. And one's mind goes back to things one had forgotten, and all the old questions return. If you don't mind, I'll skip the middle and read you the last paragraph. Here it is now. The man says, "The West African would be well-advised to hug his present vassalage, and indeed pray for it to be firmer in points. Nobody who knows has the smallest idea that the West African Negro can govern himself efficiently. We are not long removed from the blood bath and the crucifixion tree of Benin city."

'So, there you are, sir. Somewhere in between, the man even says that he couldn't care a bean if virile nations take us over, just like property, that if native West African rule were set up, it would be . . . please, let me just find that place . . . yes . . . he says it would be a "blood-and-iron affair" which would apply "whips and scorpions with a steady hand." The long and short of it, Mr Soditan, is this, to my way of thinking. If these people have already made up their mind about us, why should we worry about who wins their war and ends up with us as property?'

Soditan walked over to her, took the lined, handwritten sheet, which shows its nine or ten years' aging, and reread the entire extract himself. He felt strangely moved. 'And you copied it at the time?' he asked.

'Yes, Mr Soditan. You see, you underlined it. In red. If I had the magazine in my hand now, I would point exactly where the paragraphs were on the page, even if I was blindfolded.'

He laughed. 'And you want to tell me that in between trading in *eleto eto*, dried fish, yams, and *gari* together with my wife, plus your teaching schedule, you actually found time to recollect these . . . er, jottings and engage in battle with colonial powers?'

'And the matter of Abyssinia, Mr Soditan. What sort of place is that League of Nations? Yes, they should be called that. They are all in league against us, the black people!'

Soditan nodded slowly. 'When you next come to Abeokuta, tell your partner to take you to meet Mrs Kuti. You know Beere, don't you?'

Mrs Esan's eyes sparkled. 'Who doesn't, Teacher, who doesn't?'

'I am sure the two of you will have a lot to say to each other.'

'Ah, sorry, sir. I forgot to give you this.' She handed over the other sheet of paper. 'Please find time to read it, and let me know what you think. I tried out parts of it at the synod last week, in Lagos. I hope you won't disown me when you learn of the reactions. Please look it over for me before I send it to *The West African Pilot*. I really would appreciate your corrections, Mr Soditan.'

'All right. I will.'

She stood up, looking elated. 'Now I must go and catch my home customers. They are all waiting for their Christmas stock and if I don't get rid of what I've brought before the Lagos people come in –'

'Of course, of course. I am only sorry again that Morola could not come. I know you would have done your rounds together.'

'I'll manage. And I've kept her own goods separate. I have sorted out the ones which are for New Year sales; I'll sell them for her and send her the takings.'

Soditan watched her depart, then remained by the door looking out into the village as dusk gathered. He felt very strange after the visit. He could not remember when he had exchanged so many words with the woman alone; usually she came to see his wife, who was perhaps her major trading partner. Beyond a comment or casual exchange over some immediate event or news, they had not spoken much together since she completed her practical teaching course under him and was sent off to Saki. There she met and married her husband, a native of Ondo, also a co-teacher. He contracted tuberculosis and later died. For a number of years afterwards she would not even return home, so terrified were people of the disease and its reputed contagion. To make matters worse, they had lost their first two children, although not to the same disease. Later, as a year passed, then two, and it became clear that she had not fallen victim to the disease – which, it was widely assumed, she must have caught from her husband through living together as man and wife – her return became easier and she reintegrated herself into the community, fully. But to have noted and kept that article, which had so outraged him at the time, yet divided his feelings on the cautionary grounds of that dire prediction, the 'whips and scorpions,' stolen from the Bible . . .

He looked up and saw the familiar figure of his erstwhile colleague Ogunba coming up the road and felt a surge of childlike happiness. Ogunba suited the tranquil part of him; they would meet, greet, and simply sit, commenting desultorily on any subject that happened to cross their minds. As the figure drew nearer, however, he saw that it was not Ogunba at all but his cousin, who so much resembled him as to be sometimes taken for his brother. He drew level with the door and stopped.

'Sir, my cousin asked me to come and greet you.'

'Where is he himself?'

'Still in Ijebu-Ode. He hopes to be here tomorrow.'

'He will have to pay a fine. I hope he knows that.'

'He knows it. And he sent it ahead. This is yours, sir.' He handed over a small raffia bag. Opening it slightly, Akinyode beamed with delight, taking out the little packets of seeds, which were neatly labeled in capital letters.

'Gossypium Brasiliense . . . Ishan type Gossypium . . . South African U4 . . . Vinifera Afri . . . Hey, this is what Akinsanya's son promised to send me from Achimota. He must have sent it through your cousin, that's all.'

'I am only the messenger,' the cousin grinned.

'All right, wait till I see him. If he thinks he can pass this off as his fine . . .'

'He'll be here tomorrow,' the messenger promised.

'Yes,' Akinyode grumbled. 'Leaving me to cope with Efuape all by myself.'

A mere trickle to begin with, the human flow through footpaths and surrogate roads would swell gradually into a torrent over the remaining days before the New Year. Ìsarà was filling up. The native sons and daughters came on foot, in lorries, and on bicycles which served more for porterage of personal belongings than for human conveyance, vanishing into bulging sacks, tins, covered baskets, and boxes, weighed down on both sides like donkeys. Singly and in family groups, lorries disgorged the returnees at the motor park. A few vehicles struggled bravely up the sole laterite road, which pierced the very heart of township, past Node's compound and onto the field of bamboo poles which served as the central market, coating the last vestiges of green in an all-pervasive rust. There were a few cars also; their entry brought admiring heads out of doors, peeking through windows, eager to know whose son had finally brought the wealth of Lagos or Kano into Ìsarà – never mind that the motorcar may have been hired for the journey. It was the difference that mattered; someone had actually aspired to a private sedan; the reflected glory enhanced the status of the town.

The push-trucks had the hardest time of all. Every foot gained up the hill had to be secured by thick wooden slabs before it was lost to a backward roll. When the pusher's feet slipped, a disaster was almost inevitable. And it was the traders who needed the trucks, so the loads were predictably heavy. Patiently, the hirer, usually a woman, walked beside the tensed, muscular figures, caked in dust and sweat, and clad – when they were not half-naked – in the most outlandish gear, usually copied from a favourite figure in the cowboy film going the rounds of Ijebu-Ode or Sagamu. The headgear was always the most distinctive; their cheerful banter was incomprehensible to all but one another since it was a unique dialect of Lagosian Ijebu twanged through the nose in the manner of their favourite stars. Clearly they were strong, but it was mostly their humour that got them up the hill.

A patronizing smile broadened on Wemuja's face as he perched on the bonnet of the Commer near Node's compound. Self-consciously he alternated between picking his teeth and puffing on a clay pipe, a new acquisition which he had made only a few weeks before from Mariam's stock. His scoutmaster hat was thrust forward over his forehead, his eyes narrowly calculating whether or not the space left by his Commer on the choked road would suffice the *omolanke*, or would he need to wake up his apprentice, Alanko, to move the vehicle out of the way? Certainly he, the Master Driver, was not going to stir himself for a mere push-truck. As the crude contraption inched nearer, he made his decision. After all, it was nearly a month since Alanko had his last driving lesson. He shouted over the wall of Node's yard, slid down the bonnet onto his bandy legs, and strolled off towards the palm-wine shack near the marketplace. That, he shrugged, was how his own master had taught him. Whenever a chance occurred for a manoeuvre of some five or ten yards, his mentor simply threw the keys at him and left him to sink or swim.

A festive anticipation pervaded the streets, the households, even the churchyard and the marketplaces, where the goods already on display were clearly *oja odun*, not the humdrum, everyday affair of basic needs. The push-trucks had not creaked up the hill for nothing, nor motor passengers paid the extra fare to tempt their driver to risk stalling his engine up the sheer cliff face of the only motorable road into Ìsarà. Already rival explosions of cap guns could be heard outside the houses – homemade 'cannons' devised by the local blacksmiths: The metallic cup was filled with matchheads scraped off matchsticks, a nail was rammed into the cup, and the charge was detonated by striking the nail against a stone or a concrete wall. The larger the charge, the greater the explosion; sometimes the entire weapon split all the way down and had to be taken back to the blacksmith for repairs. And the same children donned their masquerades, took to the streets, jigged from house to house, accompanied by their band of stick percussion and tin-can drummers, though some actually boasted the occasional talking-drum, usually borrowed according to size. They danced as if possessed, inventive, while others augmented their fervour further by loading up, sneaking round to the nearest wall, and detonating their weapons. The dancing grew even more frenzied as the chorus threw its challenge to adult powers – a challenge unanswerable at this universal season of the year – urging halfpennies from reluctant pockets:

> *Olopa ko le mu wa.*
> *Odun to de la nse.**

Far, far different was the dance of the adults. The mood of levity of groups which drummed past the house of the regent, Olisa, for instance, was on the surface only. More than one war fever had gripped Ìsarà. The capers in the open grounds raised more than dust, and the masquerades emerged for a far deeper purpose than to enliven the days of waiting for New Year revelries to commence. *Orin ote*, the songs of intrigue, had taken the place of the usual sounds of *sakara* and *agidigbo*. Familiar tunes and lyrics were changed or amended subtly as each band of strolling minstrels approached certain frontages or encountered the relations of marked individuals. The Odemo was long dead. The battle for succession was now joined. The war being waged in faraway Europe was relegated to a background noise as rival bands, armed to the teeth with *agogo, sekere, omele, gangan*, and *dundun*† took to the streets.

> *Aafa, a gbe'ke yan*
> *Labalaba oluwo*

* No policeman can touch us.
  It is this festival that we celebrate.
† All musical instruments.

371

Aafa a gbe'ke yan
Oko iya Talatin. *

Not that Hitler's war was ever permitted to be totally forgotten. Sipe Efuape's first port of call was Pa Josiah's home, where his problematic son would be found, he swore, probably digging a deep hole for his savings to prevent them falling into the hands of the 'big bad wolf' from Germany. Akinyode, a smile on his face, watched him drive up the hill in his borrowed Morris, consoled by the fact that he himself had arrived in Ìsarà three days before the seasonal invasion began and had at least enjoyed the very last spaces of tranquility Ìsarà would offer for the rest of the year. Sipe stepped out of the car and smoothed down his *buba*, his glance swept the surrounding houses casually to savour the admiring looks cast in his direction, then he strode grandly into Pa Josiah's living room, over-whelming it completely with his vitality.

'So, you got to Ìsarà before me.'

Akinyode shrugged. 'As usual.'

Sipe looked up at the ceiling, inspecting the house minutely before settling himself into a seat.

'He seems to have missed,' he concluded.

The teacher stared at him. 'Who did? What did you hide here anyway that you kept looking for?'

'Hold in the ceiling. Hole in the ground. You mean Hitler hasn't bombed Ìsarà yet?'

When the laughter had subsided, Sipe proceeded to upbraid him. 'But really, Yode, you are just too much. I write to you on serious, straightforward business matters and what do I get? All sorts of procrastination. Seemingly erudite but merely pedantic wigwagging –'

'Oh-oh-oh-oh!' Akinyode held up his hands, palm forward to mime a shield. 'My head, Sipe, my head! You are breaking my head.'

'No, no, this is serious. What am I to do with you? You are stuck in that backwater called Abeokuta and your temperament has become one with her rock of ages. Nothing can move them – same with you.'

'Lagos, for me, is –' Akinyode began.

'Forget that! Why do you like to travel backwards? I know why! So that you don't have to face the real issue. I have already given up the whole idea

* Chief Priest, vaunting his hunchback
  Butterfly with horns
  Chief Priest, vaunting his hunchback
  Husband of the mother of Talatin.

372

of your coming to Lagos. I tried, yes. But finally I said to myself, Sipe, son of Efuape, give up on that man. He is a stick-in-the-mud, a man of inexhaustible excuses and self-justifications. He will not move. All the efforts you have made on his behalf, all the openings you have obtained for him with the aid of friends, greasing that palm or using "long legs" here and there – oh, did I tell you that that fellow ended up in jail?'

'No. What happened?'

'He overreached himself. Tried the same trick once too often. Imagine, pretending to collect bribes on behalf of the European supervisor. Anyway, this applicant was a messenger in Joe Allen –'

'Saaki's territory?'

'Yes, that is where our slippery Aiyedipe made his mistake. Ten pounds from an ordinary messenger! How much would a messenger earn in a whole year, much less talk of saving such a huge sum. Anyway, the fellow found the money, paid him, and began the long wait. Come today, come tomorrow . . . three months, then four, five, six. He got desperate, naturally – At least give me back my money, he kept crying. Doesn't the song say *"Orisa*, if you cannot save me . . ." '

' ". . . leave me at least as I was." '

'A-ha. Well, to cut a long story short, the messenger and would-be clerk took his case to Saaki. Hm. You know our man. He fired a formal letter directly to that supervisor in his hottest English, made it double-barrelled by signing S. A. Akinsanya, Secretary, Lagos Motor Workers' Union, and Secretary, Nigerian Youth Movement, then took it personally to the man.'

'Ho ho. *Sangba tu s'epo!*'*

'Precisely. The supervisor quickly called the police. The end of it all . . . eighteen months. And another wasted opportunity.'

'Yes, it's sad. When someone in such a position throws away his future just like that!'

Sipe looked at him with his perfected mocking tilt of the head. 'Who are we talking about?'

'Aiyedipe, of course. Who else?'

'You! You, you, you! I am talking about Akinyode *omo* Soditan! That was another job open, free for the taking. Vacancy created instanter – Aiyedipe out, Soditan in. Senior accounting clerk, Lagos Town Council. You would be right in the centre of action, where all sensible men with an eye to the future congregate.'

---

* The bean-cake has scattered in boiling oil.

Akinyode stood up and moved to the cupboard. 'I have some Dimple left from the bottle Opeilu sent me.'

'Oh yes, go ahead. Change the subject. Who wants you in Lagos, anyway? Wasn't that the very point I began to make? There is no longer any need for any of you to come to Lagos. But is that the same thing as refusing to *invest* in Lagos? What is wrong with investing in Lagos?'

The teacher smiled and Sipe sneered as they both gave the answer at the same time. 'The – war.'

'So why do you continue to bother this born provincial?'

Sipe sighed. 'What a pity. What a pity.'

He continued to shake his head, recollecting the many lost opportunities. He had himself bought property, indifferent to Hitler's bombs which might choose to fall on Lagos. If Lagos was indifferent, then so was Sipe, son of Efuape. Until the governor began to pack out of his residence, he considered his investments safe. He had taken only one precaution – removed what money he had in the post office savings account and transferred it to a proper bank, advising all the ex-Ilés to do the same. The post office savings could be commandeered for the war effort, compulsorily acquired in return for war bonds. That was one of the few advantages of working in government service – one gleaned such bits of vital information and acted in time to forestall such awkward developments. There were a few other pleasant by-products too, all of which he did his best to share among his intimate circle. Somehow Sipe had long since come to the conclusion that none of the others were worldly-wise, that he had been uniquely chosen to help them find their way in an inhospitable world.

As if reading his thoughts, Akinyode, handing him a glass, a bottle of soda, and the whisky, enquired, 'Anything going in "private treaty"?'

Efuape hissed. 'What is private treaty to you? Do you know how many chances you've wasted?'

'Don't worry. It's not for me; Osibo says he might be interested.'

'Private treaty' was another unwritten bonus of working either in government service or within or near Lagos. It brought an enterprising mind – not just everyone – into contact with government and licensed auctioneers under whose hammer passed landed property. Private treaty meant prior arrangement, with the public hammer only providing the formal show. The auctioneer took his cut, and so did the middleman, if there was one. Sipe had succeeded in putting together a treaty or two; the rewards had been sufficiently lucrative to enable him – aided by the same contacts – to do a private treaty on his own behalf. The result was a modest bungalow in Ebute Metta, one wing of which had, until a few weeks before, born a signboard announcing the birth of his long dreamed-of COASTAL HERBAL INSTITUTE. The dethronement of that board – which Sipe swore was only temporary – was the result of concerted efforts of the Medical Association and the only slightly less prestigious body called the Qualified Dispensers' Association. That argument which ran light-heartedly in the head teacher's home in Aké between Osibo and Soditan had finally been transferred to the public ring, carried into a realistic confrontation with the young entrepreneur. A herbal institute? What sort of a monster was this supposed to be? Sipe could only rage in the background. As a civil servant he could not even enter the fray directly, since he had acted against his terms of employment by engaging, in the first place, in private enterprise. Everyone did it, of course – who wanted to retire on a niggardly government pension? The essential thing was not to get caught. A front managed the business, erecting barriers of files to camouflage his principal. The affair rankled deeply in Efuape. Not once, however, had Akinyode even linked Osibo with the actions of his professional union. Now Efuape slowly put down his glass, staring at the teacher as if at a madman.

'Did you say Osibo?'

'Which one?'

'The same. You know, the Genie of the Bottle.'

'And you want me to help him to a private treaty?'

'Sure. Isn't that your favourite hobby? Lucrative hobby, I should add.'

Sipe appeared to pick his words with difficulty. 'You – want – me – to help – that – dispenser?'

'What is the matter?'

'Did he actually send you to me? Or are you just asking this all on your own?'

'Sipe, what's wrong with you? What has he done?'

'What has he done? What have they not done, all those Europeans and their black quacks calling themselves Doctor this and Dispenser this and that? Have you forgotten . . . ?'

'Oh.' Akinyode, belatedly remembering the unfinished warfare. 'Well, even so. What has it got to do with the Genie?'

Sipe waved his hands furiously, as if to ward off the subtly gathering forces of assault which he could already divine in Akinyode's mind. 'You can forget everything already seeping into your mouth. This is no joking matter and I am not listening to your arguments. Tell your Genie he can squeeze himself back into one of his dispensing jars, preferably one of

375

those labelled "Poison." That is, if his European nose can fit in. Typical. Only a person with a nose like that will choose to be a dispenser anyway; it fits the white company into which his job takes him. No – don't say anything. What is wrong with our medicines? They all turn up their noses at our native medicines – what did their grandfathers use to bring them up? Dare they come to Ìsarà and tell me not to set up a herbalist shop in Ita Oba? Do they dare close down the herbalist stalls even in Ereko market in Lagos? No. They cannot. They know their fathers' heads will end up in the *salanga** behind the nearest compound. But a proper shop in Lagos is too good for herbalists, not so? The streets of Ebute Metta are too European for black man's medicines!'

Akinyode sipped his whisky and water slowly, waiting for him to wind down. 'Have you done?'

'No!' He exploded. 'Do you know, my clerk and the agent were both arrested! They were taken to the CID and interrogated!'

'You wrote me. You bailed them out, didn't you?'

'And they were charged to court . . .'

'Oh. I didn't know that . . .'

'That happened last week! But they don't know who they've taken on, oh no, they don't! They are fooling with the son of Efuape – God willing, a millionaire in his own right before white hair makes its appearance on his head and long before the first spot of shiny skull begins to show.'

'Resolute Rooster!'

'Cock of the Walk.'

'Mephisto-Rooster.'

'Death to the Beestons of this world and their native allies. Anathema and Maranatha!' And his mood changed abruptly, dissolving in self-deprecating laughter.

'Wait, wait, wait. I missed that. What was that terrible curse you just pronounced?'

'Anathema and Maranatha! Plus fire and brimstone and the Seven Plagues of Egypt!'

Akinyode shook his head. 'I know the others. But which one is Maranatha?'

'I don't know. But we had this magician who performed in Glover Hall. And that seemed to be his all-powerful conjuring code. Apart from the regular "Abracadabra" and "I conjure you in the name of" and so on.'

* Pit-latrine.

376

Akinyode tested the phrase in his mouth, chewing the words. 'Anathema and Maranatha! He must be from India.'

'They all claim to come from India. Or at least to have trained there. Anyway, those dispensers will find that Ìsarà medicine is stronger than theirs. We will shrink them down to size, seal them up in their own medicine bottles, and float them back to England.'

'All right, all right. You know Osibo had nothing to do with it. It was obviously government action. If Uncle Segun had been home, he might have prevented it. He works with the General Hospital, so he has influence in government circles.'

'That Rosicrucian? He only eats vegetables, you told me.'

'And what has that to do with herbal medicine? If anything, it should make him more sympathetic.'

Efuape ruminated. 'Maybe. Maybe. All I know is that he is almost the opposite of his brother, I.O. Anyway, what news of the dandy? England must suit him – he can have all the tea parties he wants. And bow ties. Still, I don't envy him. I only hope he is dodging the bombs in London. People like him don't bother with protection before they leave. They don't bother to arm themselves with *egbe* and the like.'

They fell silent. The war was both remote and near. They had been part of crowded scenes at the harbour, had looked in on preparations when a son of Ìsarà, or indeed any friend or colleague, joined the select band of those who would leave 'in search of the Golden Fleece.' The prayers were now more fervent and frequent, no longer the routine send-off services at home or in church, the parting benediction was far more passionate as the well-wishers were finally persuaded to descend the gangway and the boat began to weigh anchor. The thanksgiving services that welcomed them back were riotous celebrations of the heart, not merely hymns of pride at the numerical growth of the local challenges to European control of Nigerian life.

His face clouded and solemn, Akinyode said, 'Suddenly, Ashtabula is full of new perils.'

Outside, the haunting chant of a girl selling *ebiripo* floated in their direction. But it was drowned moments later by a more aggressive tune, and as both men picked out some words, they realised that the faction of the regent was on its way to pay Pa Josiah's house a glancing visit. Akinyode shut the window that looked out on the road but left the top half of the door as it was, open. The revellers' passage was mostly good-humoured but the challenge was undisguised. They paused directly outside the house, pounded the road on jubilating feet, as if already assured of victory. The name of their candidate was sufficient motif for their improvisations: How, indeed, could an elephant be shifted by a child?

> *Atari ajanaku*
> *E mi s'eru omode*
> *Eni ema a m'erin yi'se*
> *A r'orun bo, a f'ina bori.**

But not even this ongoing skirmish succeeded in banishing for long the other, whose reminders had become woven into daily existence. And it was not simply the usual run of rumours, which once brought the war to Lagos and, later, Meko.

After the first bombs fell on London, the war effort was stepped up even more intensely in the colonies, a spirit of patriotism for the colonial powers calculatedly whipped up, even taken to a competitive dimension. The Spitfire Fund, for instance: rallies, concerts, exhibitions, dances, and plays organised to raise funds to purchase a Spitfire fighter for Britain. Both within their hometowns and operating through their town unions in Lagos, Spitfire Clubs vied with one another to prove themselves loyal subjects of the crown and defenders of British possessions. The Residents, the District Officers, toured the country, encouraging the numerous events, announcing the progress of the collections, and spurring others to greater efforts. Spitfire badges were distributed to the deserving; the more successful organizers were honoured with invitations to tea parties at the Residency.

The dissidents were censored. The intrepid Mrs Esan seized her chance to declare that the war would free Africans, that Africans 'can set the Thames on fire.' It happened during the 'free session' of the synod in Lagos, after the official business of the gathering was over. She had begun harmlessly enough, delighting her listeners with her imagery of the institution of marriage as the union of the shuttle and the loom. As she warmed up, however, asking into what role the African family should fit in the war, the assembled prelates became restless. Glances were exchanged with increasing intensity, notes were passed. The presiding bishop tugged at his round collar but there was nothing anyone could do until the well-

---

* The head of the tamer of forests
  Is no load for a child.
  Whoever will turn aside an elephant's stride
  Will first visit heaven, he must wear fire on his head.

378

known trader-teacher of Saki completed her thesis and sat down to restrained applause.

The war even bred expectations. Would government really pay the rumoured 'war bonus' of forty percent of the salaries of civil servants? A twenty-six-thousand-pound outright grant to teachers was no rumour. Denounced by Onyia as grossly inadequate – it was meant to compensate for the sharp rise in cost of living – it was yet to be shared out. And in any case, shared out on what basis?

And salt turned to gold dust.

It was a mystery. How could common salt suddenly vanish from the markets? Where it was available, its price had jumped tenfold or more. And finally, it was now being rationed. Salt! Rationed? How could such a thing happen? Not even in those ancient wartimes was such an event recollected, and this was a war thousands of miles away. Was salt also part of the war effort? Was salt used to manufacture guns and Spitfires? Or could it be gunpowder?

But the tailors were doing well. In a different corner of Ìsarà, Tailor Famade was awaited in vain; he would not be home this New Year as there was far too much money to be made. Over two hundred tailors, he wrote, had been hired by the government to make army uniforms. He would simply have to celebrate the New Year another time, not this year, thank you. This was boom time for his trade and he would not be a proper child of Ìsarà if he threw that chance away to come and feast at home. The war might end the following week, and then would he not bite the fingers of regret?

It was boom time also for enterprising lorry owners. Private lorries were seized to transport goods and soldiers, and there was compensation at thirty shillings a day. And so began the scramble to hand over lorries. Bribes to the police, to government officials, by lorry owners: Seize mine, please, won't you please seize mine? Food prices, the cost of utensils, clothing, farm implements, even of local foods, rose until the pulpits rang with denunciations. Money is the new idol; the spirit of religion is dead in us! Why, why is this war bringing out the worst in us? So what would it do to those who are actually engulfed in it – will those mothers now begin to sell their children for a quick profit?

And there was panic within some Ìsarà households. That Osode should join the army was only expected. He was heavily in debt and there was no other course for him. Mind you, he had astonished even his loudest enemies; his first paycheck was sent to Akinyode to pass on to some of his creditors; so was the next. And he wrote, enclosing a picture of himself in full uniform, braids and all, proudly announcing his promotion to the post of ammunition storekeeper. While the rest of the country scrounged for salt wherever they could, Osode revealed that there was no shortage of that commodity in the army. He sent the head teacher a bag and promised to send more if needed. Books were what he needed in turn; he was also seizing his chance to study shorthand in the army's vocation school. He wanted to increase his vocabulary. Would his friend the teacher kindly send him any unwanted books?

But that was Osode, always a wild one, which was no wonder, as he had a drunk of a father who had even sold his family land (including farmland) in order to remain in Lagos and crawl from bar to bar. But what would one say of the son of the Reverend Opelami, a well-brought-up son, lacking nothing, who had even graduated at Yaba Institute of Health and was obviously destined for greater things! Everything was prepared, his admission to a higher institution in Bristol confirmed. His passage was booked, a new wardrobe prepared by the 'London-trained, etc., etc.,' men's outfitters in Broad Street. Even the farewell services had been held – both in Lagos and Ìsarà. All that was left was for the liner to dock in Lagos and young Opelami, escorted by a galaxy of his father's friends, relations, and their relations, would be consigned to the merciful hands of God of the high seas. Only . . . Opelami went mysteriously AWOL, and it took a letter from Osode, his childhood friend, to reveal that he was with him in Kaduna, enlisted in the infantry. The wise heads of Ìsarà shook their heads; no, there was no doubt about it. Envious enemies of the family had done it. They had worked at his head and turned it in the wrong direction. *Efun!* Even a child could see it – *efun!*

'I suppose,' Akinyode enquired suddenly, interrupting the directions of their individual reveries, 'I suppose you would have thought of publishing?'

Sipe's snort of dismissal required no elaboration.

'The reason I ask,' the teacher persisted, 'is that I received a very interesting proposal from – you will never guess who.'

'It can only be a woolly-minded teacher like you. Look, I have given it plenty of thought. Leave publishing and printing to the government and the Church Missionary Society. Publishing is no way to real business for people like me.'

Akinyode sighed. 'D. O. Fagunwa doesn't think so.'

It sat Sipe up with a jerk. 'Fagunwa? The *Ogboju Ode* man?'

Akinyode nodded. 'The same.'

'And he wants to set up publishing?'

380

'No, not quite. But he has put forward a – well, something a young entrepreneur like you might want to consider. At sixpence a copy, he believes he can provide a background to the war, just to help our people understand what is going on. And of course it can become part of our history textbooks, proving – maybe – as popular as his *Ogboju Ode*. Just a small pamphlet. So he is looking for a printer. He already has the backing of the Resident of Oyo province, but that one cannot guarantee the use of the government printer.'

Sipe's shake of the head was quite dubious. 'Hm. I doubt it will prove that popular.'

'Even from the pen of a famous writer like Fagunwa? And he plans to do it bilingually, you know, English and Yoruba. And that is only to start with. Later, it will have other bilingual versions – English-Ibo, English-Hausa, maybe even Tsekiri and one or two other languages. He'll call it *Iwe Itan Ogun*.' Soditan paused. A smile broke out on his face, mischievous. 'We should recommend Mrs Esan to him, I think – you know, she could write the foreword.'

'*Eparipa!*'

'Well, just an idea. Two warring heads in a book on war – why not? Anyway, he is thinking of an advance subscription drive – he cites the example of Dr Azikiwe's *West African Pilot*, which already had a sale of five thousand copies guaranteed before he printed the first copy.'

Sipe snorted, derisively. 'You see, you are all the same – teachers, fabulists, and innocents. You are comparing a war pamphlet with a newspaper? Who really cares about the war? Oh, just because we are all doing what we can for the victory of the Allies – heh, you think people like Onyia and Esan and that Saro man Clinton are in the minority? You can count the son of Efuape among those who swear that this war will give Africans and Asians their freedom!' He sprang up, tiptoed to the door, and glanced melodramatically to left and right. 'But don't say you heard it from Sipe's own lips because he will deny it and swear on his grandfather's bones! The law does not recognize hearsay or – indirect speech.' And he threw his head back and rocked back and forth in uproarious laughter. 'Do you still hear from her, by the way?'

The door was flung open and a compact tornado erupted into the room. Neither of the two young men expected Pa Josiah. Seasonal homecoming, as this was, generally meant that he would abandon his home completely to his son and his friends, taking refuge with his wives in turn, but mostly staying with Jagun. Especially in the first few days of reunion, when they all moved from one house to the other, drinking the spoils of their prolonged sojourn away from home and swapping tales. Josiah's forehead was creased in violent furrows as he swung from one figure to the other and released a compressed snort, then jerked his head backwards to the figure of Jagun, standing in the doorway just behind him.

'They are laughing,' he said. 'They have come home for New Year and all is well.' He marched into the room, fixed them both with baleful eyes. 'You have cause for merriment, not so? You don't even care that war has broken out beyond these walls?'

Sipe and Akinyode exchanged puzzled looks, which seemed to infuriate the old man all the more.

'Yes, war!' he virtually screamed. 'While you sit there talking grammar – and you, Akinyode, you, whom I relied on to warn them in Lagos, did I not tell you the matter was getting desperate?'

Hitler! Was he in Lagos already? Chaotic thoughts raced through the teacher's mind. Well, he was right, after all. By now Hitler's storm troopers were probably sequestering Sipe's 'private treaty' properties and carting off the occupants to slavery. The agent and clerk would wish they had not been bailed out after all by the Resolute Rooster. The police cells seemed suddenly safer. There was only one thing he could not understand: What was he supposed to have done to halt this Teutonic invasion?

Sipe's mind had raced even farther. Once again, he had failed to anticipate! So much for careful planning, so much for all the gibes at the cautious Yode. Next came the question: How soon would Hitler's conquering hordes march into Ìsarà? To make matters worse, he was still based in Epe, and if there was one thing they had all learned, it was that the first target of an invading force was the harbour. After Lagos, Epe had to be next. He had not built a house in Epe but had already secured a piece of property – and on the waterfront. Indeed, Sipe's next project was a simple canoe with outboard motor, nothing like the Resident's yacht nor a simple canoe with outboard motor, semidetached, but still an integrated vessel, the model of which he had seen in Epe's burgeoning shipyard, and on which he had made a modest down payment. Now it would be commandeered, just as the British had seized the lorries, only – if Hitler's reputation was to be believed – without even the mention of compensation.

'Well, are you just going to stand there staring at me like *ileya* rams? Get inside that tin-box motor you have left outside my door and let Lagos know what is happening. The Olisa faction has installed its Odemo!'

Yelps of disbelief, horror, and anguish were rent from his bewildered audience of two. Jagun had come fully inside the cottage; he led Pa Josiah to a seat by the window and sat on the chair just vacated by Efuape.

'They have. It is true what you just heard. It happened this afternoon.'

The elder Josiah hissed a trickle of snuff-black juice through his upper teeth onto the floor. 'Yes, the regent. The one we named regent after the death of the Odemo. But I know where he got his courage – it is that senile old man Agunrin Odubona, calls himself Agbari Iku!* Odubona, who doesn't even accept that the railway or motor lorry exists in this world!'

Sipe raised his hands. 'Enough, Baba, we will leave tomorrow. Awobodu will still be in Lagos. And Akinsanya. We will round up our friends in the newspapers and cry havoc in the ears of the governor himself!'

'It is an abomination,' Jagun persisted. 'They could not even perform the proper rites. How could they? But Olisa took his creature into *iledi* . . .'

'Who?'

'Who? Erinle, of course.'

'I just wanted to be sure it was still the same person.'

'Who else could it be?' Josiah snapped. '*A nki, a nsa, o ni oo m'eni to ku!*'†

'His supporters have sung past the house,' Akinyode explained, as if to mollify him, 'but we still could not assume that Erinle would agree to such an illegal step. It is so foolhardy –'

'It is worse than foolhardy. Erinle has committed *eewo*.‡ To put on the regalia without the correct rites! He thinks he is riding on the reverence we all have for Agbari Iku, who supports anything that is toothless like him!'

'We will leave before dawn,' Akinyode promised, nodding towards Sipe. 'Tonight, we will meet with the others. Some will go to Ibadan and report the matter to the district commissioner. Another delegation will visit the Resident – everything will be arranged; leave it to us, Baba. In fact, we should start thinking of a lawyer. I can see the whole affair ending up in court.'

Sipe spoke next. 'There is only one thing. The whole town knows who Olisa's candidate is; we've all known that for some time. But all we have regarding the choice of the other side is mere rumour. The last we heard was that five names altogether were sent to the kingmakers, including Erinle's. Who are the other four?'

'The other four?' Jagun stared, open-mouthed. 'We farmed past that stream a long time ago.'

---

* Death Skull.
† We call out his praise-names and recite his lineage, yet you continue in ignorance of the identity of the deceased.
‡ Taboo.

383

'You mean you don't know?' And Josiah regarded his own son with unbelieving eyes.

'All you said, Baba, was that the matter concerned us in Ile Lígùn. That we had an interest in the outcome.'

Jagun looked at Josiah, who threw up his hands but nodded assent. 'All right,' he said. 'Come closer.'

Ray Gunnar was a young middle-aged Trinidadian of Indian origin and adventurous bent. He woke up mid-ocean one morning in October 1939, overwhelmed by a belated realisation that he had committed the greatest error of his life. The torpedoes had so far ignored him, but news of their depredations came daily over the radio and were reinforced by daily emergency drills on board in which both crew and passengers were compelled to participate. Over the wireless he had also heard the torrential harangues of the man with the unique moustache, and even though Gunnar did not speak a word of German, he had become convinced that this little man, a total stranger, had a personal, single-minded design against his life. Gunnar's dreams became sessions of emotional torture, from which he often woke up screaming and sweating, invoking the aid of his personal *obeah* and the hundred and one deities of his forgotten ancestry, which was Hindu, for the security of his existence.

England, the 'mother country,' was – if all reports were to be believed – herself quaking under this menace, so who was he, a mere deckhand, barely above the status of a stowaway, to refuse to take this threat of annihilation to his very existence seriously and personally?

His presence on this cargo boat – which took also a dozen and a half steerage passengers – was clearly a result of compulsion: Ray Gunnar had only that choice or a stretch in prison, for reasons he preferred to forget. But the violent contractions of his stomach on that sea voyage soon made him look back with longing to the abandoned prospect, which certainly did not include flying bombs and torpedoes on the wide-open seas. Before he got to Liverpool he had made up his mind that the return journey home would be his last. When his ship docked, however, and he felt the firm, secure contact of good mother earth beneath his feet, he knew that he had sailed on his very last voyage for a long time. Ray Gunnar jumped ship. The Liverpool air was a dirty fog but it smelled infinitely healthier than the mists and squalls of the open seas, whose depths were constantly threaded by invisible torpedoes seeking out his heart and no other, no matter where he chose to hide himself within the bowels of the boat.

To Ray Gunnar, making friends was second nature; no one who tended his life with such disarming candour and affection could fail to evoke sympathetic feelings. He was especially drawn to West Africans, who were not much different from the Trinidadian blacks, whose cultivation had landed him in that small trouble with the police. A series of menial jobs took him to the black centres one after the other – Birmingham, Hull, Glasgow, and eventually London. His West African acquaintances were fascinated by his store of scratchy but authentic calypso records, and he also appeared to have an inexhaustible supply of a brand of marijuana which, they swore, was more aromatic than any they had ever smoked. In return, when he decided to move to London, his African friends provided him with a letter of introduction and the address of the West African Students' Union, a home from home for the increasing band of African students in London.

Ray Gunnar was impressed by the organization of the students. No less than an authentic princess, the daughter of a paramount ruler in Yorubaland, the Alake of Abeokuta, held the office of the union's treasurer. Its secretary-general, a brilliant, articulate lawyer called Ladipo Solanke, actually held liaising meetings with important officials at the Colonial Office in Whitehall, and their news journal did not hesitate to castigate British colonial policies in incredibly robust language. As for the League of Nations, a debate on the conduct of the League of Nations towards Abyssinia in its dispute with the premier of Italy, Benito Mussolini, literally took his breath away. Some were self-declared communists. One Nigerian prince had fought with the International Brigade. 'Hats off to Hitler' was the title of a lecture that Gunnar attended. The students obviously did not fear the wrath of the British government. Nothing was sacred to them, and to tell the truth, Gunnar was more than a little bit intimidated by their lack of regard for the sensibilities of their host government.

Before long, Gunnar had obtained a job as cleaner and general odd-job man at the African hostel in Camden Road, London. He got to know the students very well, their problems and their ambitions. He had of course long since made a stunning discovery: The preeminent obsession of the West African, both in Britain and at home, was – studies. It did not matter the subject or the end qualification: London matriculation; bachelor's or master's degrees; higher, elementary, or primary examinations in the various professions – law, medicine, pharmacy, accountancy, economics, etc. The West African paid vast sums to famous and reliable correspondence schools like Wolsey Hall, Oxford, but even more to fly-by-night schools which simply collected the cash and fed the students useless instruction papers. Such schools, unlike the accredited ones such as Wolsey, did not even mark course papers or assess the students' progress.

Gunnar was very interested in the potential of this educational hunger. He studied the wording of advertisements placed by correspondence schools and tried a few tentative compositions himself. He was impressed by the results. He took a bus to the opposite end of London, Kennington, and paid for a post office box. Then he had leaflets printed, which he stuck on the notice board of the African hostel, left on dining tables, in the common rooms, and under the doors of the students' bedrooms. Avoiding the journal of the students' union itself, *WASU*, he obtained the addresses of other journals, such as *The West African Review* and *The Nigerian Teacher*, and invested some of his accumulated savings in advertisements on their pages. Then he sat back, carrying out his humble chores at the hostel, running private errands for students and visitors alike, while he waited for the postal orders to flow in.

It was purely by chance, as he browsed through old copies of *WASU* in the reading room, that Ray Gunnar learned that a great Negro bass named Paul Robeson had actually visited the student centre during those years of his duels with the Trinidadian police. Paul Robeson had then delivered a speech which still formed a subject of enquiry in students' letters to the editor and was variously described as 'invigorating,' 'a cultural manifesto,' 'a summons to the black Renaissance,' etc. What had become of this great project, they demanded? Gunnar's chick-pea eyes popped out of his head as he read the rollcall of African elite who had graced the occasion and who in turn graced Paul Robeson with the accolade Babasale, in effect, the Grand Patron of the Union. His wife also earned the female equivalent, Iya Egbe. So Ray Gunnar laid his mop and pail aside, tracked down the famous speech in the sparse library of the reading room, and studied it. The great man had not minced his words, nor did he confine himself to misty rhetoric, no! Paul Robeson actually launched a project, and this project touched a creative chord in Ray Gunnar: Robeson would create a Negro Theatre in the West End of London.

Theatre was a field to which Ray Gunnar instinctively felt he was born – his life, after all, had been nothing but theatre. In his next advertisement, therefore, 'Professor' Gunnar was pleased to announce that the Ray Gunnar Inter Correspondence School would also provide courses in all theatre and cinematic skills and was setting up an actors' school in the very heart of London. But it would serve more than actors and future film stars; Gunnar's school would teach 'confidence, public personality, poise, and public speaking, to lawyers, preachers, executive officers, princes, and

386

politicians.' At the bottom of the advertisement was boxed a quote from Paul Robeson's speech:

> Out of these traditions will grow with spontaneity and power an art perhaps comparable with that of Elizabethan England – but unique art, Negro art, yet as far removed from the Negro art we know as modern British poetry is from that of Chaucer. I do not think this is an impossible dream.

Ray Gunnar then wrapped up his copy with a ringing annunciation in bold print:

THE DREAM OF BABASALE, PAUL ROBESON, HAS FINALLY ARRIVED! BE PART OF IT! CREATE THE GREAT NEGRO CULTURE!

In faraway Sierra Leone, Gold Coast, Liberia, or Nigeria, no young reader of this advertisement had any doubt at all that the school project was the authentic product of Paul Robeson's brain. The R. G. school also promised scholarships, for which application forms were available for the modest sum of one guinea – postal orders only.

For most aspirants, their contact with Ray Gunnar began on the pages of the journal and ended with their dispatch of the fee for an application form. There were, however, the exceptions. These were the stagestruck cases whose thirst for the boards could not be assuaged by the eloquent silence that followed the dispatch of their one pound, one shilling. They accompanied their fee with passionate pleas, expressing their readiness to stowaway to London if a scholarship was not forthcoming and to undertake the most menial of jobs to keep alive during their training. Ray Gunnar sympathized, offered them the desired scholarship, which, however, required further deposits 'for the completion of formalities as required under British law.' In many cases, though it sometimes took up to six months to a year, the deposits would be painstakingly saved and sent to Ray Gunnar Inter for Drama.

Efuape was too earthy an individual to be affected by the malady of the stagestruck; nevertheless he had long realised the business potential of theatre in an entertainment-hungry Lagos. Having watched a few Christmas and Easter 'cantatas' and the odd historical play or biblical story dramatised by amateur groups, counted the heads of the audience, and estimated the production outlay, he began to give periodic thought to exploring this avenue of obtaining capital for his greater ventures. Moreover, he had watched Akinyode's efforts in Aké, as his versatile friend assembled a team to prepare the pageant celebrating the one-hundredth anniversary of the entry of the first missionary into Abeokuta, an event that would last two days and promised to be elaborate. It would involve almost all the articulate adults of Abeokuta and even their children. Sipe had also taken to heart the stirring performance of *Faust*, when he had been one of the young blades who created such a sensation among the audience. Again, the observant young man had noted the arithmetical lesson of the audience multiplied by the entrance fee minus the probable cost of production.

Fascinating as Aké's centenary pageant developed, it was the drama of Akinkore, the librettist, that mostly intrigued him. Sipe had taken his annual leave during preparations for the pageant. Spending most of that time with the teacher, he had obtained a ringside seat at the unfolding of this drama and been bemused by the intricacies revealed in the nature of the dramatic muse.

First, the organising committee (appointed by the Anglican diocese) met and selected what should be the highlights of the drama. The first visit of the Reverend Henry Townsend was accepted as the starting point but it was his second visit, in company of Reverend and Mrs Gollmer (reduced to Goloba in Egbaland), which would form the centrepiece of the drama. It was this second visit which led to the establishment of the churches; and even more significantly, the visit took place at a perilous moment for the Egba, who were then at war. Such potent ingredients of history could not be celebrated with a mere thanksgiving service, and it was indeed this fact which had led to the commissioning of the pageant.

The head teacher tracked down the wandering minstrel, Mr Kilanko, to assist him in composing the music. Various individuals had been marked down for various roles – Osibo, the dispenser, was, for instance, a natural for one of the white visitors; his long face and hooked nose eliminated most of the competition. So did the light-skin complexion of the shy, normally retiring court registrar from Igbore, Bandele Dosumu. And Sipe, bored with merely watching his host pump the pedals of the harmonium and issue instructions on numerous details, accepted a small role as the ghost of Chief Sodeke, who died just when news came from Badagry that the nasal preachers were on their way to Egbaland, their purpose being to establish a Christian mission. Sipe would have to take casual leave for the performance week and travel back for the event, but Akinyode rehearsed him in this newly created role before his departure.

The search for the librettist was easy: Akinkore, a health officer with creditable experience in the writing of Christmas and Easter cantatas. He embarked on his assignment with enormous enthusiasm, drew up a vast list of dramatis personae, unearthing minor characters whose involvement everyone else had forgotten, even inventing others in order to accommodate new aspirants to the Thespian crown. Chiefs, civil servants, tax inspectors, nurses, policemen – all were ordered to stand by. The Egba nation had need of them! This was an event which would resound not only in Lagos but in the Home Office in London. Akinkore split up the times and places of action in the best professional style:

Act I, Scene i: at Badagry.

Act I, Scene ii: at Ado.

Act I, Scene iii, had as yet no location but this was compensated by the subtitle: OKUKENU INSTALLED THE SAGBUA OF EGBA IN PLACE OF SODEKE THE BALOGUN OF EGBA.

Act II, Scene i, continued the action: in Abeokuta Town.

Act II, Scene ii: at the Town Hall.

Act II, Scene iii: a divine service at Oso Ligegere's house.

The final scene was presumably somewhere in Abeokuta because its synopsis was given as: REV. AND MRS TOWNSEND'S DEPARTURE FROM ABEOKUTA ON THE GROUND OF MRS TOWNSEND'S ILL HEALTH.

After which, Akinkore seized up. Overwhelmed perhaps by the wealth of historic detail, his mind ceased to function. At meeting after meeting of the preparations committee, Akinkore turned up with the same sheet of paper, except for once when, in a sudden explosion of creativity, he was able to reveal progress in two specific areas. First, in Act I, Scene iii, he had scratched off 'in place of' and replaced those words with 'to succeed.' The synopsis of that scene therefore read: OKUKENU INSTALLED THE SAGBUA OF EGBA TO SUCCEED SODEKE THE BALOGUN OF EGBA.

The second development was truly dramatic. Akinkore finally presented a sample of typical missionary dialogue – as he explained to the meeting. It was now only a question of fitting this sample to the general action, situations, and even unforeseen events, and the play was ready. The sample dialogue was duly read to the committee by the dramatist:

REV. TOWNSEND (*to Chief Ogunbona*) – Good afternoon, Chief Ogunbona. Information has just reached us at Badagry that the Egba people are at war at Ado, and as we have an intention of proceeding to Abeokuta very shortly, we therefore decided to visit you. We are also very sorry to hear that our friend Sodeke is dead.

Akinkore insisted that this was how the nineteenth-century missionary spoke to Egba chiefs, and there was no one who could gainsay him.

389

Akinkore then disappeared again for two weeks, and all the news that could be obtained about him was that he was ill. He, however, sent a message that he had created a new character – the ghost of Chief Sodeke.

When a crisis meeting was summoned three weeks after the creation of the model dialogue for Reverend Townsend, all the dramatis personae, it was clear, were now struck mute by a historic virus caught from Akinkore's muse. Since he caught it first, he was unable to attend the meeting. His confinement was spent mostly wondering why Christmas and Easter 'cantatas' dealing with God, his son, magi, and saints should be so easy to write, but not an episode of Egba history dealing with mere mortals, like chiefs and misssionaries.

Akinyode Soditan, composer and chief impresario, took it all with calm resignation. 'Perhaps he should have undertaken the Ray Gunnar course,' he sighed.

'What is that?' asked Sipe.

'Oh, haven't you seen his adverts? He runs one of those *gbogbonse* correspondence courses. As a matter of fact, our union has been asked to investigate him.'

'Is he a phony?'

'We don't know yet. Daodu wrote to the director of education on the matter. We are waiting for his reply.'

Sipe departed for his station in Lagos soon after, somewhat sad that he had had to abandon his friend in the middle of such a crisis. Still, the teacher seemed quite capable, and he had taken over the role of the librettist as well. Efuape also penned a few verses – plus music – of the kind of lugubrious threnody that he felt should emerge from the throat of the Ghost of Sodeke when he appeared to the Egba army camp in Ado. He had become rather taken by the spirit of the whole enterprise, much to his surprise. He was even more surprised that his friend found his song unsuitable, eventually excising the Ghost of Sodeke from the pageant altogether, as being neither founded in history nor essential to the drama. Since he did not believe in wasted effort, Sipe stored away his lyrics. Long before the two-day epic of the missionaries in Egbaland could materialise, they formed the cornerstone of Sipe Efuape's own debut on the Lagos stage – in the 'native opera' titled *Ali Baba and the Forty Thieves*!

Sipe had, however, been greatly troubled by the phenomenon of Akinkore. With such a panoply of events spread out before him, how could any man simply dry up, his mind refuse to function? Unable to resolve the mystery and determined to avoid such a set-back in his own case, he wrote to Akinyode for the reference of the journal whose professional offering he had referred to in such a flippant manner. Perhaps Ray Gunnar held the key to theatrical success. A guinea was a reasonable investment, in any event. So Efuape bought his postal orders, cut out the application form, filled and mailed it, but also commenced preparations for his own strictly business theatrical venture. Weeks passed without a word from Ray Gunnar. Sipe gathered his troupe together – these consisted largely of his office colleagues, the agent for his private business, two or three ex-Ilés and their lady friends, plus a local Lagos runaway member of the Tunde Young juju orchestra who was seeking wider fields of fulfillment.

Assisting Sipe with backstage management was a young Lagosian who had simply drifted in during rehearsals. A clearly starstruck youth, he never missed a film show in Lagos or on mainland Yaba and Ebute Metta. He haunted all the performance halls and collected cigarette postcards of film stars, Shirley Temple being his favourite. Soon he was handling the publicity for Efuape's company and managing the front of the house. He had access to many of the 'expatriate' Yoruba of Lagos society and guaranteed their attendance when the music drama *Ali Baba*, tired of waiting for the expertise of Ray Gunnar's school, finally took to the boards. Young José Santero, as de facto manager, had, however, taken over the pursuit of Ray Gunnar and had indeed entered privately into the second phase of correspondence with him. The scholarship prospects threw him into a fever of anticipation, with which he also infected his fellow Thespian Kolawole, the runaway musician from the Lagos band. The financial success of *Ali Baba* was stunning, and it owed much to the dedication of young Santero, and his plans for his own future.

As the Morris trundled its way to Lagos, Sipe turned to Akinyode and gave him advance warning of an additional chore they would tackle once they had taken care of the main business of the succession.

'Do you know the Santeros?'

'Oh yes, I've heard of them. There is a branch of the family in Abeokuta.'

'Good. It's not too bad actually, this unexpected trip to Lagos. We can kill two birds with one stone.'

'Which is the other bird?'

'I'll tell you when we have finished with Akinsanya. I tell you, the gods are taking our side over this matter. But let's plan our campaign. First, Akinsanya, how exactly do we tackle that one?'

'Yes. We should decide that before he gets a chance to be difficult.'

Sipe smiled. 'Oh, I am leaving you to deal with that. He's your cousin, after all, so you take care of him.'

'Why do you think I brought the lemons? While he is salivating at the sight of them, I shall let go at him with both barrels.'

'Good. Still, I wish Job had arrived in time to come with us. He seems to know just what to say to cool down that fiery head of his.'

Akinyode chuckled out loud. 'Job is right. What was his affliction the last time he wrote?'

'His wife. Before that, it was boils. With an *s*, you know. Not for him a solitary boil, even though it sprout within an embarrassing divide, like that of Sipe, son of Efuape. No. Opeilu would be content with no less than plural boils, preferably accompanied by piles and maybe *sobia* as bonus. Then a clash with drunken soldiers from which he rescues himself by reciting Psalm 21 . . .'

Sipe cast a sidelong glance at his companion, reminding himself that this otherwise tedious journey provided the best chance for sounding out the teacher on the matter of the Spirit of Layeni. No distractions or possible interruption. Akinyode could indulge in his favourite sport of arguing for the sake of argument till he was sated. But at least he would know at the end of it all where the teacher stood. Then he could proceed to take his own decision.

There were also any number of other matters, far weightier, which he sought to preview with Akinyode before they came to formal airing at the seasonal gathering in Ìsarà, when the other ex-Ilés were home from Kano, Port Harcourt, Saki, Samaru in Zaria, Lagos, and everywhere! The change of status of the colony districts to Native Administrations was one – five new administrative units from Ijebu-Ode district alone! Ìsarà now belonged to Remo. But not even this momentous event agitated Sipe as much as the planned road between Ìsarà and Ibadan. All the work that the Ìsarà Road Committee, spurred on by the Ìsarà Auxiliary Society in Lagos, had done was being frustrated by the Alake of Abeokuta. He had ordered the surveyor to work on the route between Asa, Fidiwo, and Ìsarà instead of Asa, Ipara, and Ìsarà, as decided by them. They were the ones who collected funds, wrote petitions, made the preliminary surveys, and mobilised public opinion, especially in the newspapers. But the Alake single-handedly decided to re-route everything through Fidiwo, leaving out their close kin in Ipara. That was a major fight for which Sipe had braced himself, and he meant to deal hard with the ex-Ilés of Abeokuta when he had them all under one roof in Ìsarà. Perhaps their closeness to the Alake had sapped their will; well, he would remind them that they were

Afotamodi, firstly, daily, and lastly. They were born in Ìsarà and would return home to die. This was war; no other attitude would do. He felt like pouncing on Akinyode there and then but decided that this should wait. He would conserve his energy for a massed onslaught. Or maybe begin on the return journey, when he would have the support of Awobodu and Akinsanya, though that one had become too involved in national politics and trade union activities to pay sufficient attention to what was happening at home. Well, he was in for a shock. The thought of the jolt which was coming to him from the clear sky gave Sipe a thrill. After this, let him dare give second place to the affairs of Ìsarà!

Events were moving too fast, Akinyode thought. Would they even have time to go through the plans for the maternity clinic Otolorin had helped him design for Ìsarà? There was always the problem of priorities. The Lagos group, he knew, was obsessed with the Ìsarà–Ibadan road. This was only a logical extension of their even more ambitious plan to link Lagos, Ikorodu, and Ìsarà by a year-round, all-weather motorable road. The pace of events had outstripped all routine programmes, however; it was doubtful if even the usual rounds of convivial gatherings would take place, or the ritual reviews of the year and planning for the new. This was beginning to look like a New Year for children only; he now regretted that he had left his children behind. At least they would have enjoyed the seasonal reunion with their cousins and age-mates and wallowed in the indulgence of their aunts and grannies while the men tackled this immediate hard-eyed business of local politics. Still, he gave silent thanks that Morola's illness had been finally diagnosed. His father and Jagun would have schemed their way into making her undergo their *etutu*, and once she was in Ìsarà, all the advantage was theirs. Then his grandmother – three days already he had been in Ìsarà, but he had kept walking right past her cottage each time he set out to visit her. That macabre performance was something he never wanted to see again. Instead, he had gone to the plot of land on which he proposed to build his own house, stood there for long stretches of time, planning the building in his mind, costing it, setting a timetable for its progress. Pity Ogunba had not arrived before his father's eruption into the house. He would have been on this journey also. No matter, he intended to place the construction of the house in his charge, now that he was in Ijebu-Ode, much nearer home than Abeokuta. Opeilu was the one whose arrival most of them awaited with some impatience. Even more than Efuape, he was at the hub of economic trends because of his job as produce inspector; he could predict the pattern of price fluctuations, he knew what commodities would become scarce or prove a glut on the market and how the war affected everything. Opeilu would advise him whether to buy corrugated iron sheets at once and store them or wait until prices came down. And bags of cement, nails, even the treated timber . . .

'You know,' Sipe began slowly, 'it's all very well to laugh at Opeilu's misadventures, but sometimes I can't help wondering. And then, of course, his remedies for getting out of scrapes and illnesses. I mean, Yode, I ask myself sometimes, one hears so much about the Sixth and Seventh Books of Moses. Have you never been curious what they actually contain?'

'Of course. I once tried to order it from that same Ray Gunnar. He has a sideline in educational and oriental mystery books and so on.'

Sipe nodded grimly. 'Yes, he would. Anyway, even if the books exist –'

'No question at all. I am sure they do.'

'Well, what could be inside them beyond what is already in the Bible? And if one uses verses in them to conjure good luck or riches, would that be any different from, er . . . well, from Opeilu, for instance, reciting Psalm 21 anytime he is faced with danger?'

'What of the other things he's done to counter his wife's – well – plots against him? Hardly what you would call biblical remedies!'

'So? Isn't one permitted to fight fire with fire?'

Relaxing after a spirited and successful defence of Oduneye before Bishop Vining in Aké parsonage, Opeilu had good cause to be proud of his loyalty to his friends. Oduneye was convicted of keeping shoddy accounts, but beyond that – he was innocent on all counts. Vining went even further: He accused his main accuser, D. Kuye, of a vindictive attitude, 'unchristianly and ungodly.' Vining had been so impressed with Opeilu's objective concern that he asked him to spend the night in BishopsCourt so that he could consult him on a number of decisions. The Location Committee would not meet again until Passion Week of the New Year and there were transfers to be made before then. Opeilu, as produce inspector, travelled a lot and worshipped wherever he found himself. His gentle, benign face, lightly marked by a childhood attack of smallpox, was familiar to most of the parishes in the south, especially those served by the railway line. He was known to be above church politics and was therefore often invited to arbitrate internal wranglings. But it was the first time he had been asked to testify for a friend, and by a white bishop at that. Bishop Vining began to unburden himself, asking advice. Oduneye, for example. It was clear that he could no longer remain in the Ibadan diocese; he had far too many enemies. Did Opeilu think he would be happy in Abeokuta? Or should he go farther afield to Ondo? Reverend Alalade was old and had earned his pension. Vining would make recommendations to the Patronage Board – did Opeilu think the decision right? And then there was Archdeacon Phillips, who did not wish to go to Abeokuta for love nor money. Opeilu was close to the head teacher in Aké – would he discreetly find out why there was such bad blood between him and the Director of Education, Melville Jones? Reverend Adegoroye was being difficult. Igbara-Oke was a good station – why didn't he want to go? He had even threatened to leave the Church if he was transferred from his present station. You mustn't take offence, Mr Opeilu, I hope you won't take offence, but our African brothers in Christ sometimes strike me as being deficient in their sense of mission. Are you not all one people? Why does an Ifo priest fight tooth and nail to remain within shouting distance of his hometown? We go wherever we are sent, in England. After all, look at me. I was sent all the way to West Africa from across the seas – of course I obeyed. We must all go wherever our mission is needed. Even the Methodists are having problems, from what I gather. Young Mr Ogunbayo has just resigned from their mission, and all because of his transfer to Ilesha. Somebody must serve the Methodists of Ilesha, not so? Oh oh, you mustn't think that I am painting a gloomy picture of everything. We have quite a good number who can hardly wait to pack their portmanteaus and head for their new positions. Mr Okusanya set a very good example, for instance; he heard the news of his transfer to Owo just as he returned from vacation and he simply picked up his bags and went. Of course, he is not a prelate – you know him, don't you? He is the new principal of the teacher training college. Perhaps teachers are more adventurous than prelates – do you think that's the truth? Ogunba left willingly for Ijebu-Ode, didn't he? I received Mr Soditan's letter asking for his replacement. I gather from other sources that they are very close friends; they certainly made an excellent team in St Peter's. But that's the point. We need good workers as pioneers. Tested workers. The same thing goes for the cloth, of course – that is what I wish they would understand. Look at the way I. O. Ransome-Kuti has taken Abeokuta Grammar School by the scruff of the neck. He's performing the same miracle there as he did in Ijebu-Ode. A remarkable man, a remarkable man. He is Soditan's in-law, isn't he? By the way, I hope people were not too upset that I couldn't personally officiate at Elliot's wedding. It was the event of the year for Ibadan, from what I gather. Bishop Akinyele told me all about it, gave me a copy of his sermon. Over two thousand people, bicycles jammed all over the place. And of course quite a number of motorcars. Well, I hope they didn't forget the Spitfire

Fund; that is the kind of God-given chance for the war effort – very well-to-do modern and professional Nigerians. Quite the cream of the Nigerian cream, wasn't it . . . ?

Opeilu did not mind. He felt a deep serenity sitting with this white benevolent face, which seemed to glow as dusk gathered in BishopsCourt. It had been a hard day but he felt satisfied with what he had achieved. His only regret was that Soditan had already left for Ìsarà; it would have been pleasant to spend the night with him and recount the day's battle over Oduneye's case, into which he had been brought as an impartial witness and, of course, as a man with some commercial expertise. He was never really at ease with the Europeans, but Vining struck him as almost native to England with his easy familiarity with everyone and a boundless, gossipy energy. He appeared ready to indulge himself in the respite of talking to someone outside his normal field of engagement, all night long if that was possible.

And so, Opeilu recognized, was he. BishopsCourt was a different world from Ekotedo quarters in Ibadan, which he had to pass through every day on his way to work. Ekotedo was the notorious sector of Ibadan, patronised by prostitutes and now, of course, by soldiers in search of amusement. The drunken street scenes through which he had to pick a careful course when he returned late from his produce shed in Adio, he was certain, must have something to do with the frequent eruption of boils and other afflictions on his body. And it had been a trying year, which did not really do much good to his general state of health.

If only his own problems were as trivial and easy to unravel as the minor infraction of Oduneye – a technical one, at that. But his work involved great personal risks; he had begun to wonder if the protections on which he depended would really survive a determined assault. The war seemed to bring out the beast in everyone. Forty-eight bags of salt at a blow, snatched from the store right under his nose! The labourers thought he had left for the day because he had locked up the store and his office. So he caught them red-handed – forty-eight bags in all, and the mastermind was none other than his assistant. He thought of how much that would have fetched in the open market, when even a fairly senior officer like him had to manage with the official allocation of a pound and quarter each fortnight. And only last week the government announced that this would be further reduced to four ounces. Now, how was a normal family with all dependants supposed to manage with that? And that was without reckoning with friends who were not in the government service and therefore received no allocation at all. The profiteering on the open market had really reached unbelievable proportions. Even so, forty-eight bags – the attempt was bold! Well, so was the punishment. Three years for Mr Kadiri Toye, plus two for the assistant inspector of police with whom he had planned to subvert the course of justice. The labourers were freed – that seemed quite just; they were, after all, only obeying the orders of their superior.

But then, soon after, the entire store was burned down. The arsonists were yet at large. Had it been part of the main plan? To burn down the store so as to cover up the fact of the missing bags. Or was the burning down an act of revenge for the apprehension of the villains? Was it a warning to him? It was no wonder that he began to cough afterwards. Probably he had breathed in too much of that unhealthy smoke – all those fumes from God knows how many different commodities. Still, it was a relief when he went to the doctor and he found that he had not contracted tuberculosis, as he had feared. TB was rumoured to be raging through the country at the time; perhaps it was the soldiers who brought it with them and were spreading it.

The soldiers! They were the greatest menace. It was possible – maybe they were behind the arson. The inspector, or even Toye himself, could have instigated them. After all, did they not break into the warehouse at Ilaro on their way to Meko when they were being transferred to the border town, supposedly to stem the rumoured invasion? Nobody bothered anymore about the kegs of palm oil and bags of *gari* removed by the soldiers. Life was at stake, and anyway, who cared about looted shops when even the government warehouse could be raided by soldiers. His dysentery, which followed that unresolved attack, had lasted two weeks, continuing even after the rumour of invasion was scotched and some of the loot recovered from the soldiers.

Those soldiers had become the bane of Opeilu's life. His most scary fever had begun after their display in the seedy passages behind the cinema in Ekotedo. Nothing but physical exhaustion could have made him take the shortcut, but it had seemed safe enough at that moment. A number of late-night drinkers were out on the street, but there was no sign of soldiers. He was halfway through the passage when they burst out of the Starlight Konkoma Bar, staggering from wall to wall, all fifteen to twenty of them. There he was, trapped, and if he hadn't quickly recited Psalm 21, he would never have seen the obscure doorway, which could hardly hide a child, but he had forced himself flat against it anyway, praying like mad and psalming soundlessly. One of them gave a shout, which must have been an order because they all tried to gain some form of balance, then began to unbutton their trousers. Another shout and they all began to urinate, against the walls, into the passage, on themselves, so drunk and unbalanced were they. But the strangest sight was still to come.

When the next order came, they buttoned up – that is, those who still remembered that their 'objects' were still dangling out, because some were so eager to obey the next command that they forgot. And that order, it appeared, was that they should take off their belts. And they began to flog one another! Opeilu knew all about *egungun* festivals, he had seen all types of masquerades, and he knew that there were those outings in which men held flogging contests, using palm stalks and the springy *atori*, applying the whips only to the legs, which were usually covered anyway by thin trousers. But these soldiers were applying the buckle end of the belt to one another – and everywhere! Blood flowed copiously, but on they went, nonstop. Those who collapsed were simply left lying in their urine puddles. The exercise – for what else could one call it? Opeilu had demanded in his letter to the teacher – the exercise lasted some three quarters of an hour. Onlookers had gathered at a distance from the centre of action, but there he was, trapped in the middle, nothing between him and the certainty of death on discovery but the narrow space in that doorway and the power of Psalm 21! When they were finally wearied of the exercise, their 'panic-sowing and alarming show of barbarity,' they flung their empty beer bottles against the houses, shattering them against the walls and smashing windows, then hauled up their wounded and staggered to their barracks, singing at the top of their voices.

Opeilu's fever was prolonged, even though he had to report to work every day. He wore a thick scarf around his neck, and a generous whiff of mentholatum surrounded his presence. Only his illness had prevented him from dealing more severely with his new assistant, who had taken over from Kadiri. This new Bolaji was incompetent. His grading of cocoa beans and palm kernel was so atrocious that he, Opeilu, had to do it all over again to avoid scandal. In fact, it was so bad that he suspected him of taking bribes. But what really riled Opeilu – and what he suspected had probably made Bolaji last this far in the civil service – was his disloyalty to his colleagues. Only this individual, as far as he knew, had refused to join the civil service union. He refused to sign the membership circular and seemed to take pride in being a yes-man. Without stooping to such tactics, he, Opeilu, still had the best report in the handing-over notes of the European head of Oyo division. Thank goodness for Otugbile, whose staunch alliance offset Bolaji's depressing presence. Yes, Opeilu had finally realised that Bolaji was the main cause of his recurring migraine. He was not accusing him of doing anything deliberate – no, not yet. But one could not help observing a link. He certainly did not suffer from migraines until Bolaji assumed duty at his station . . . And suddenly Opeilu realised that he was in a unique situation from which he had not yet profited. Perhaps some other psalm would prove even more potent than Psalm 21 against the likes of Bolaji. He opened his mouth to enquire, but the bishop beat him to the draw.

'Well, then, Mr Opeilu. Who is going to be the next Odemu of Ìsarà? Or is it a secret?'

Their knocking went unheard, so Akinyode opened the door and entered. They had heard raised voices from the moment Sipe parked the car against the raised pavement in front of the house and cut off the engine. Akinsanya lived in Denton Street, not far from the edge of a lagoon inlet with its brackish water and mudskippers. Fish traps lined the bank, a few yards from the cemetery at Alagomeji. The lagoon border – one could hardly call it a shore – oozed forth a black sludge, as if every sea-plying vessel discharged its wastes of oil and tar into that marshy bay, which curved through from Ereko waterside on the island to the depot of Zarpas Motor Transport, a mile and a half from Iddo railway station. Across the stretch of mudflats one could see the boats and the timber pontoons heading out to sea to join the vast oceans, heading towards ports that would turn them into Spitfire frames and ship hulls for the war against Hitler. Children raced across the road, trying to catch the soft-shelled crabs which sidled out from their dank holes, crossed the street, then raced back to their underground shelters for safety. A short distance away, an Aladura church had already commenced its evening service, with bells and chanting, swinging incense burners, and the slap of bare feet on concrete floors. This part of Yaba was a different township from the main body of Lagos, as if it were a waterlogged Ìsarà, completely remote from the island itself with its violating sense of noise and motion. Its sole link to the island colony was Carter Bridge, a replacement for the old Bailey Bridge constructed by the West African Royal Pioneers. It gave off such an air of eerie desolation in the evenings that children stayed close to their doorways, playing their games within sight and hearing of elders in the house. And the story was told – so complete was the dependence on Carter Bridge – of one of the earliest Lagosians to attain a position in the senior grades of the civil service, who once attended a party on the island in his brand new Austin sedan. It was his first drive at night over the bridge. He returned home late, drunk. His wife put him to bed, took off his clothes, and left him to sleep it off.

The following morning, the civil servant woke up but refused to leave his bed. It was long past the time to prepare for office but he remained asleep – at least so thought his wife until, alarmed by the lack of movement in the room, she looked in to see in what state her husband was. To her astonishment he was wide awake; he lay on his back, eyes wide open and staring at the ceiling. The poor woman became anxious; was the man ill? She moved closer.

'Darling, are you all right? Are you going to miss work today altogether?'

The man turned his head towards her slowly, appeared to recognize her, and beckoned her to come closer. She moved forward with trepidation. 'Shall I call for a doctor . . . ?'

The husband's response was quite emphatic – no. He took her arm, invited her to sit beside him on the bed. Gently, with the weight of one divulging a secret, the details of which he was as yet uncertain about, he confided: 'I am still trying to recollect the route, but do you know, dear? Between our mainland and the island there is actually an alternative route. I used it last night. One doesn't need to go over Carter Bridge at all. And it's quicker. It takes less than a quarter of the time one would normally take using Carter Bridge. The trouble is, I cannot recall how I gained access to that hidden route.'

The wife did not remain puzzled for more than a few seconds. Then her eyes popped. She rose slowly from the bed, stood rooted to the spot for a few more moments, then let out a soft sigh and keeled over backwards in a dead faint over her husband's body.

They could distinguish two voices in the inner room as they stepped unnoticed through the front room, a sparsely furnished and narrow room with framed photos hanging on the wall, and a few more of obviously superior technical finish on a round table in a corner. Soditan spotted the latter group at once, stepped round the leather pouffes neatly arranged on the perimeter of a fibre mat, and picked up the photograph of a smiling young man in a heavy overcoat. He stood in front of a fountain, while an equestrian statue on a plinth towered over him and pigeons fluttered through a soft gray haze, some of them perched on his outstretched arm as if in dutiful response to a request from the photographer.

'Look at S.O.,' he said, holding out the framed picture to Efuape. 'The one he sent me was taken on a pier; he said it was Brighton.'

'Hn-hn. Whose turn is next?'

Akinyode did not answer the question. 'This must be the famous Trafalgar Square. Or Piccadilly Circus. He's probably written it on the back.'

Sipe replaced the photograph on the table, sighed. 'What annoys me about young Awokoya is that he won't cooperate. All I ask from him is a short list of reputable firms; instead he sends me descriptions of snow. Who cares about snow!'

A wistful look came over Akinyode's face as he glanced around at the other photographs on standing frames on that table. Each background was alien. It bore a forelorn air like some unattainable distance, despite determined smiles on the faces of the subjects. The structures were like nothing that existed in Lagos; the streets were broad and looked antiseptically clean, unwelcoming. Glancing round the parade of these doubly exiled ex-Ilés, he sighed.

'Ashtabula podium.'

Checked in his stride, Sipe cast a quick glance around the display. 'Ah, yes. All those who have braved the seas and come to harbour.'

Akinyode jerked his head in the direction of the voices. 'Shall we wait or join them?'

An angry voice rose from the other side of the closed door. 'Bowen has to go. I don't care what their teachers do in their own public schools. But no European comes here and attempts to sodomize an Ìsarà son and gets away with it. That King's College must be cleaned up once and for all.'

'I assure you, Mr Akinsanya, the matter has been officially reported.'

'When? When? Every day he stays in this country is an affront!'

'I am sorry, sir.' The other voice was very subdued. 'But it was the only thing I could do . . . I would not affront your sensibilities for anything –'

'No, no! You are still taking it personally. Look, McEwen, it was decent of you to come to me and admit that you have given him refuge. You did a Christianly thing and I do not hold it against you. Do get that clear. But the Ìsarà union has lodged a formal complaint and demands action. I am speaking now of official action, and you can take my words to the education department. We would do the same if such an abomination had affected any other pupil! And I can tell you right now that the Nigerian Youth Movement has also taken up the matter! Bowen must leave the country. How do we know how many others he has attempted? Perhaps even succeeded with! Sodomy! Is that the kind of civilization these Europeans want to inflict on us?'

'I understand, Mr Akinsanya, I understand. It is all most unfortunate. We are trying to avoid a scandal –'

'Who wants a scandal? You know the man who left here just now? That was J. V. Clinton of *The Eastern Mail*. If I had wanted the matter to reach Calabar by next week, all I had to do was tell him. Not to mention the *Daily*

Times and *The West African Pilot* closer to hand. We want Bowen off these shores, that is all. But if the education department drags its feet, then there will be a scandal!'

There was a scraping of chairs, followed by a sigh of resignation. 'All right, Mr Akinsanya. I shall pass on your message.'

'Be sure to state it as a condition. Bowen goes or I cannot guarantee what will be our next line of action.'

The door opened and the owners of the two voices emerged. One was a wiry, light-complexioned man, obviously a mulatto. He held a trilby in nervous hands and, although quite young, was clearly balding down the middle of his head. As they came out, the other, somewhat paunchy, as black as the other was off-white, broke into a delighted shout on seeing his visitors. His massive head was split by a grin as broad as a generous slice of pawpaw. He wore a loose shirt over a local-weave wrapper bunched up at the waist, and this lounge ensemble was topped by an *ikori* cap which swung down over one ear, flapping in his excitement like the loose patterned slippers on his feet.

The man called McEwen took one look at the pair and cast a worried glance back at his host. Akinsanya understood and hastened to reassure him, though it was not quite the kind of reassurance he sought. His face had lost its smile and he spoke quite sternly.

'If you are wondering if they overheard, you needn't worry. Because I shall tell them anyway. These are close friends. They also have sons who will probably find their way to King's or any of the other government schools in the country. And I already told you, this assault was against a son of Ìsarà. Nobody tries to make a woman of an Afotamodi, Mr McEwen. Nobody.'

A faint plea hovered in McEwen's eyes as he took a polite leave of the two men. Akinsanya waved him good-bye at the door and turned, with evident relief, to his townspeople.

'Was that McEwen of the secretariat?'

Akinsanya nodded yes. 'You know him?'

'By correspondence only. We've been dealing with him over this matter of the teachers' war bonus. The government seems to want to back out.'

'Let them dare! And as it happens, I have news for you. Pity, you just missed Clinton. He sailed from Calabar expressly for that purpose. He wanted to talk to Kuti. Sit down, sit down. Let's stay out here. I took that man into my study only because of the dirty matter we had to talk about. I'll get some glasses – oh, did you bring me any lemons?'

Sipe and Akinyode exchanged glances. 'They're in the car. When we have spoken, I'll decide if you deserve any.'

Akinsanya stopped dead in his tracks, inspected their faces carefully. 'Yes, come to think of it, shouldn't you both be at home already? In fact, Sipe, I ran into H.O.D. only yesterday and he told me you detoured through Lagos to see him on your way to Ìsarà.'

'Hn-hn. I wanted him to intervene in the matter of Santero.'

'So, how is that going? Is the mother going to bail out that scapegrace?'

'I don't know yet. Anyway it's been overtaken by events. I have since thought up a way of breaking the deadlock. During this very last night, in fact.'

'Wait a minute, wait a minute. We'd better take everything one at a time. First, the drinks. Johnnie Walker or Haig? And there is Keo of course – both brandy and sherry.'

'No Bristol Cream?' Sipe pretended to be hurt.

'Leave my sweet tooth alone,' Akinsanya barked and went into the study. He was back a moment later with an armful of bottles. From a cupboard stuck high on a wall of the living room, filled with porcelain plates with intricate designs along the rims, he extracted three glasses, darted back again to fetch a jar of water and bottles of fruit juices. Then he stood, legs apart and hands on the waist, surveyed the array, and proceeded to nod with satisfaction.

'Right. We don't have to get up for a while. If you came back all that way after settling yourselves in Ìsarà, the matter must be serious. Ah, wait . . .' He dashed back into the study and returned with a letter, and a piece of paper. 'Clinton left this for I.O. He also wants to spend New Year with his family, so he could not afford to miss the ferry. He had hoped he would catch Daodu here in Lagos – somebody told him the synod would not break up until tomorrow. Imagine that! Something which finished last week! But we discussed what is inside the letter, and I took down some notes. In fact, I am going to undertake the same exercise for my union; it is such a brilliant idea. Let the Colonial Office contest the power of statistics if they can.'

'Well, what is it about?' Akinyode demanded.

'It's all in here' – slapping the notepaper. 'He wants the teachers' union to prepare a list of the ideal menu for a family of teacher, wife, and two children. The menu must contain – it's all listed down – all the necessary vitamins, protein, proper quantity of carbohydrates, roughage, salts, etc., etc. It's to be used in what would be a union pamphlet of advice on nutrition. It will have the backing of the Medical Association, of course –

they must endorse it! Then we itemize the average cost of rent in the given area of the respective branches, clothes for the whole family, etc., then total up everything. In a parallel column you will tabulate the average earnings of different grades of teachers. And don't forget emergency expenses such as medical bills, etc., etc. Now, the *Mail* for its part will gather market prices of the essential commodities in different areas of the country . . . You've got the general idea?'

Sipe applauded loudly while Akinyode nodded thoughtfully. 'Yes, I think I know what it is aimed at. The Colonial Development Fund.'

Akinsanya nodded vigorously. 'Correct. It is not only the *Times* and the *Pilot* which are now read in England, you know. *The World Review* even carried an editorial from the *Mail* only last month. Clinton is anxious to influence decisions over there. Of course, we will use the same method, in a slightly different way, to work on the motor firms. Our problems are different. These are private firms. But the *Mail* will run the series over three, four, even six, months, covering one area after another. I like the man's project. It has method.' He slapped the arms of his chair. 'So, the union man is finished. What brought you two back?'

Akinyode took a deep breath. 'Saaki. What is happening with the youth movement?'

'Oh.' He sounded somewhat disappointed. 'Is that what brought you all this way?'

'It is connected. But tell us, first, what is the position?'

'All right. Here is the latest. We were all pretty riled by that editorial in the *Pilot* – but you know all of that. What you may not know is that Ernest Ikoli has been to see me. He even wrote letters – I'll show them to you later. For me personally, I have put all the provocation behind me, but, well, we have the "hotheads." And while they say they will take their cue from me, whenever they get together on their own they become more uncompromising. Zik has also made overtures. I agree with him; the good of Nigeria should come first. But he has to call his own hotheads to order.'

Sipe said, 'In short, for now one could say that you are not really playing an active role in the movement.'

Akinsanya hedged. 'The movement is active, that's the important thing. I have enough on my plate, fighting these private firms for new conditions of service.'

Again, Sipe and Akinyode exchanged signals and the teacher pressed home the point. Ìsarà needs you. And it has become now a matter of urgency. The trouble has already burst.'

Akinsanya's mind shot straight home. 'Over the succession?'

'You guessed right,' Sipe confirmed. 'The Olisa has jumped the gun. He has installed Erinle and even handed him the regalia. Saaki, charity begins at home, if you don't mind me stating the obvious. You have to forget the movement for a while – and we are not speaking just of the movement, all the politics attached to it. You have to come home and face this crisis with us.'

Akinsanya was puzzled. 'I don't understand what the movement has to do with the situation in Ìsarà but . . . look, certain elementary steps should be taken right away.'

'We've taken them,' Akinyode assured him. 'We came to Lagos while a different group headed for Ibadan to see the district commissioner. Amoda, Olusoga, and Sowole went; the Akarigbo's clerk accompanied them. My father said that the Akarigbo had earlier mentioned his suspicions that the Olisa might actually take such an illegal step; he said he warned him and thought he had given up the idea. Erinle is an ambitious man. He is weak, so he can be led. This thing is really Olisa's doing. He does not really want to give up being regent, so he wants a pliant material like Erinle as king.'

'We must brief a lawyer too . . .'

'Sowole's team have their instructions. Our choice is Prince Adedoyin – we are going to pass by his chambers after seeing you. The Sowole will come straight to him from Ibadan and report the result of their meeting with the district commissioner before returning to Ìsarà. They will also confer with you.'

'Good. That seems to have taken care of everything. Jagun and others will of course mobilize Ìsarà people and I will interact with our descendants' union in Lagos. Fortunately, I had not quite made up my mind to come home this New Year. I may got to Achimota, look up my son, 'Kitunde.'

Sipe's smile was thin. 'You will have to do more than that. You must demand audience with the Resident and state Ìsarà's position. Then the most crucial role of all . . .'

'Go on.'

Akinyode looked him straight in the eye. 'Can't you think what that is? Something only you can take on.'

Akinsanya cast his mind through every possible step that needed to be taken in this long-simmering crisis, which had now burst open. 'No. Every ground appears to have been covered by someone.' And then he burst out laughing. 'Unless, of course, you want me to volunteer for the throne.'

And his laughter suddenly dried up, watching the unblinking stares of his two friends boring into his face.

'Oh,' he exclaimed, and went on repeating, 'Oh. Oh, oh . . .'

'You see.' Akinyode spoke gently. 'That is why you must leave politics for a while. That is father's message to you.'

'And Jagun's.'

'Yes. The majority of the kingmakers agreed on you a long time ago. The others we heard rumoured were merely wasting their time – and money. And you have the support not only of the Akarigbo of Remo, but of the Awujale himself. And Chief Ladega in Ibadan. Of the Ìsarà chiefs, we have already told you of Jagun. There is also the Apena – we don't have to tell you. But you know how things are. If you continue to terrify the government with your politics, the Resident will be instructed to get under these people and turn them round: Do you want such a troublemaker as a brother Oba? – that kind of thing. Our chiefs can be quite fickle; even a child knows that!'

Sipe stood up and made towards the array of drinks. 'Well, Saaki, it has made my day just seeing you lose your power of speech. Yode, while he is looking for it . . . Haig's? Or the Johnnie Walker?'

'Everything combines together for good for the righteous man,' Sipe pontificated, steering the Morris over Carter Bridge into Lagos Island. Akinyode stared at him in surprise. This level of sermonizing was most unusual in the young tycoon. He attributed it to the feeling of elation which must have developed as a result of the meeting with Akinsanya, and the effect of seeing his face after they had sprung the surprise. But Sipe tapped himself on the chest and said, 'Me. I am talking about me. The Righteous Rooster. When I think of the entire saga of Ray Gunnar . . .'

Akinyode nodded slowly. 'So. You are now the Righteous Rooster.'

'Yes. Haven't you noticed? I have not talked or thought business for the past twenty-four hours. But now, we are on our way to settle a business affair. Amicably. And all because of these dramatic developments. Well, drama calls to drama, I suppose. This time it will serve the interest of our friend Saaki. That is what makes me feel righteous.'

'Virtuous, I would have said.'

'Have it your own way, Mr Pedantry. "Seest thou a man righteous and diligent in his works, he shall stand before kings, and not before mean men." '

Akinyode placed a hand on Sipe's brow. 'No. There is no sign of a fever.'

'But better still, young teacher, than standing before kings is the thrill of helping a king to his throne. I have not felt such a rise of excitement since I made a hundred and twenty pounds on negotiating three private treaties in a week. As the deal rocked this way and that and finally began to clamber up that last crest of near-certainty, I found myself in a state of unparalleled ecstasy.'

'Sipe, please. Don't let us count our chickens yet.'

'I know. There is many a slip twixt the cup and the lip – you see how inspired I am this morning – but look at even you. You've lost the Micawberish dillydallying which you normally exhibit in the face of straightforward choices. You have taken to the engines of intrigue like one born to the art. That is why I am certain of success. I know this is only the first blow in a long battle, but you see, I am already tasting victory. You are going to see the old Rooster, a butterfly emerging from a long sleep induced by temporary uncertainties. Yes, I must confess a secret I have carefully kept from you all this while – you, Akinyode, you had infected me somewhat with your spirit of cautiousness, but now – I am myself again!'

'Well, I am happy for you.'

'Denton Street! That is where Saaki lives – have you thought of that? You think that is a mere coincidence? Denton! Don't you remember Denton, the agent who tried to bribe the Awujale? Denton! The one who tried to get the Awujale to sell Ijebuland for a thousand pounds. And Saaki lives in the street named after him! Now let any of you dare sneer at destiny after this.'

The car drove through Idumagbo, turned through the rutted streets towards Tinubu Square, and negotiated the narrow passage created by the corners of two houses which were evidently built before there was any thought even of horse-drawn carriages.

'Oh, that reminds me. Opeilu had to grease his way with nearly fifteen shillings before he got his building plans approved in Mapo Hall. They dribbled him here and there, queries sprang up from nowhere, from the Town Planning Office. His file would vanish for two, three weeks at a time, "gone for the final approval." But approval where? He swore he would not grease anyone's palm – remember?' Akinyode nodded. 'Well, I heard from him two or three weeks ago. He said he had to choose between the rashes on his skin and a temporary retirement of his principles.'

'How is his body responding to that new situation?'

'No, not body. His soul. He went to Aladura church the next Sunday to make atonement. So far, no news of his rashes. Well, here we are. I don't think this will take long.'

Sipe drove through the massive gates of a walled compound, a wrought-iron arch over the pillars at its entrance. It was a sharp contrast to the streets through which they had just driven and also to the majority of houses in the neighbourhood. Vines clambered over broken trellises, wisteria and bougainvillaea smothered the walls in a profusion of colours. The expanse before the main building was filled with neat rows of royal palms, wild apple, guava, and pawpaw. The manicured lawns almost duplicated those of the parsonage at Aké – which, however, had none of the majestic palms, so suggestive to Akinyode's present frame of mind of an awaited royal procession. The style of the building was distinctly Brazilian. A wide wooden verandah surrounded the top floor, its support beams at diagonals to the wall. There was ample space all round the house on every side, and a row of outhouses with low wide doors lined the wall of the compound to the left, facing the house. Sipe gestured towards them.

'The stalls. Once each one was occupied by a thoroughbred. Now only two horses remain. The family still races one but the other is just a household pet. Spotless white. I've seen young Santero exercise it along the beach.' They climbed the steps and Sipe applied the heavy knocker to the door. 'What you see before you, Yode, is – debt. The entire house is papered with debts. Only pride keeps them going. Everything should really be up for sale. I know one of their money-lenders. What we should do is pick up this mansion stone by stone and rebuild it in Ìsarà for a new palace.'

The door swung open into a gloomy anteroom, smelling of a mixture of camphor balls, mustiness, and freshly cut flower. The maid was dressed in a black skirt over which she had tied a waist-high apron. Her eyes assessed them coldly; then she appeared to recognize Efuape.

'Oh, I . . . do you want to see Mama?'

'Yes. Tell her it is Mr Sipe, son of Efuape?'

'Please wait.' And she waved them in the direction of the stuffed sofa, covered in thick purple velvet, its wooden back topped with carved figures like misericords on a baroque pew.

'So this is his background,' the teacher remarked. 'Then why did he do it?'

'It reeks of impoverishment, Yode. Beneath it all, nothing but proud penury. But it isn't that which does it. Young Santero is no different from our own Sotolu, for instance. Look at how that one threw away such a cushy job in Army Supplies. I ask you, how could a young man of his age be so greedy? Sardines, whisky, gin, cartons of milk – powdered and evaporated – it was nearly a full lorry-load of nothing but luxury items. And he stored it all in his father's house. In his own father's house! If the elder Sotolu had not been so respected in the community, so far above suspicion, who would have believed he was not acting in collusion with his son?'

'I still don't understand. How could he have hoped to get away with it? The hoard was too much.'

'Oh, easiest thing in the world. Just continue doing what he was doing, put the word out that he had special goods, and sell them off bit by bit. He was only caught at the second attempt. That was when the police went to search his house.'

The maid re-entered, held aside the heavy green baize curtains, and announced that Mama would receive them now.

A lineup of portraits of the Santero ancestry confronted them as they entered the vast reception hall. In massive frames of faded gold-and-cream rosettes, they dominated the reception hall of the Santero family house, redolent of a different time, a different space. The largest portrait was also dead centre; it was that of the Senhor himself, Alveiro Miguel Domingo de Santero, who had brought back the clan from slavery in mid-nineteenth century. New floors and wings had been added to the house since then, porches were attached to the main entrances and the hanging verandahs widened, but this reception room with its raised dais beneath ancestral portraits had remained virtually unchanged for nearly a century. It occupied most of the ground floor and was surrounded by corridors that were generous in space and permitted a constant flow of air in every direction. The portraits behind the raised dais of this main room were dressed, without exception, in formal attire. Alveiro was himself dressed in the full regalia of the Grand Order of the Lodge, his hat perched on a round table to one side. Others wore mainly frock coats, a top hat settled in the angle of a carefully extended arm. A variety of orders dictated details in other portraits – a medallion, a mace extended outwards, a shield in the background emblazoned with the words 'Order of the Knights of St Patrick.' Lace trimmings in varying tints of white, yellow, and brown, ending in a knotted rosette at the top of the portrait, singled out those who had passed away. It was possible to tell the order of their departures both by their distances from Alveiro at the centre and by the degrees of brown-rimmed yellowing which the white lace trimming had acquired with age. The living appeared to require no such adornment.

Madame Santero was the last surviving sister of the last male descendant of the Senhor. She sat in a high-backed chair directly beneath Alveiro's portrait, a small, intensely dark woman with hair pulled back tightly in a white bun, which rested sideways on a crochet-work antimacassar. On either side of the chair were round low tables with flower vases surrounded by yet more family portraits, this time of the younger generations. Weddings, christenings, mounted polo players, horse-racing and pavillion scenes – the Santeros were synonymous with horse racing in Lagos and Ibadan. Indeed, it was part of the Santero legend that the family introduced horse racing into the southern part of the country.

Madame Santero gave the appearance of a diminutive queen holding court among subjects who had briefly excused themselves but left behind their shadows. She waved her two visitors into chairs on either side of her and raised her eyes in question at the one she did not know. Sipe introduced him.

'Mr Akinyode Soditan, school principal from Abeokuta.' School principal sounded more impressive than head teacher, and Sipe felt a need to balance this splendour, however decayed.

She held out a fragile hand and Soditan took it. He hesitated for a moment, wondering if the old lady would prefer him to raise it to his lips, as he had sometimes observed among the white officials and their wives. Even some of the Lagos 'been-tos' indulged in the practice, and Madame Santero was obviously of that returnee stock from Brazil. He settled for a brief handshake and a bow, murmured the usual 'Pleased to meet you,' and hastily took his seat. She came straight to the point.

'Well, Mr Efuape, what have you decided?'

Sipe exhibited surprise. 'Mrs Santero, I thought it was your family which had to decide. When we last spoke –'

'No, no, young sir, I made our position quite clear. We are going to stand by our son, whatever you decide to do. We do not deny what he did, neither do we condone it. But I made it clear that I simply do not have the money to refund what he . . . what he stole from you. And my family is tired of rescuing him from the mess he creates for himself. You understand, Mr Efuape, we obviously cannot pay. So it is you who must propose some arrangement. Do you still wish to press charges?'

'The case is already with the police.'

'I know. But it can be withdrawn. Please, let me remind you of what I said. My son is not dishonest –'

'Mrs Santero –'

'No, not really dishonest by nature. He gets into scrapes, yes. The point I am making is that he did not misappropriate your theatre funds just to

410

spend them. We have the proofs in the post office receipts – he sent most of it in postal orders to that con artist in London, this mysterious Ray Gunnar. You must, after all, accept some of the blame yourself –'

Sipe's voice rose to a scream. 'I, Madame?'

'He would never have learned about him if you had not assigned him the task of recovering your money from Ray Gunnar. That is how he was caught in Gunnar's web. José has always been stage-struck.' She rode over Sipe's gasps, wrung out by what he considered the greatest injustice of his life. 'But all that is neither here nor there. I am only trying to tell you that the case may go on forever, because we definitely intend to subpoena this Ray Gunnar. And that means awaiting the results of investigations in London. The police have to find him first.'

'It is a lot of money,' Sipe murmured.

'I know,' the lady said gently. 'I am aware of that, Mr Efuape. I am sorry that José is such a romantic fool. He already saw himself as a film star.'

A long silence followed while Sipe appeared to think. 'I take it you cannot even think of paying it back by installments. We could come to an understanding.'

'I wish I could do that. I wish I had the means to guarantee that. But I know the repayments would be irregular.'

Akinyode sat up with a jerk at the next pronouncement, which emerged with unmistakable finality from Efuape's lips. 'In that case,' he announced, 'I will take the white horse.'

Mrs Santero's eyes flashed for a brief moment, either with anger or with shock; it was difficult to tell. Then they went soft and gentle, and a sad, brave smile hovered round her thin lips. 'Bahia.' Her lips trembled slightly as she turned round to look at the photograph of the ancestor directly behind her. 'That's the last in the breeding line of the first Bahia, which came with him from Brazil. He named him Bahia. He wanted his descendants to have a live remainder of their other home in Bahia.'

'It is a handsome horse,' Efuape commented. 'Your son brought it sometimes to Glover Hall. I have watched it being exercised on the marina beech.'

'Do you like horses, Mr Efuape?'

Efuape shrugged. She turned to Akinyode. 'What about your friend?'

Startled out of his bewilderment, Akinyode stammered that he was not a wild one for horses but that he did admire the species.

'And are you going to sell it to offset your loss, Mr Efuape?'

'Oh no. A king is going to ride it – into Ashtabula.' And he grinned at Akinyode.

She frowned. 'A king? Ashta . . . ?'

Sipe nodded. 'Yes, a king. An Oba. Ashtabula is a place my friend here knows more about.'

' A *future* Oba,' Akinyode amended, but Sipe repeated firmly, 'An Oba.'

Mrs Santero reflected only for a few moments. 'And this will be in full settlement?'

'Complete settlement.'

The lady exhaled a deep breath. 'So be it. It was really José's horse; no one else rode it. I think it is only just.'

'I believe so, Mrs Santero.'

'In that case, perhaps you can get your lawyer to draw up the terms of settlement . . .'

Sipe succeeded in astonishing Akinyode one more time that day. He reached into the inside pocket of his coat and brought out a legal-looking document tied with a red ribbon. 'I have it here already. A friend, Lawyer Otusanya, prepared it for me last night – in Ìsarà. Everything is in order.'

She did not take her eyes from his face as her arm reached out to take the document. Again the faint smile played over her face. 'So. You knew what you wanted all along.'

Sipe smiled in turn. 'What else could one think of, Madame? I had actually asked a mutual friend, Mr H. O. Davies, to look into the matter for me – act as intermediary, you understand? I had not planned to see you so soon myself. But then certain events intervened to promote a new idea – only last night. I think it is the best solution all round.'

Her hand moved towards the bell on the side table. The silvery tinkle sounded unearthly in the gloom of the reception hall. The maid appeared.

'Bring my writing set.' The maid left. 'I suppose your friend here will act as witness?'

'It is convenient he's here.'

The maid returned with a pad built into an inkstand, two pens lying in grooves near the edge. She took it and placed it on her knees.

'Now bring the sherry decanter and three glasses. I'd like to drink with a man who can teach José such an impressive lesson.'

VI

ASHTABULA!

Exhausted but filled with euphoria, Sipe turned the gray Morris at last up the sheer cliff-surface that controlled all motorised entry into Ìsarà. Soditan was somewhat pensive. They had called on his uncle, the carpenter, in Sagamu, and now he wondered if this had not been a mistake. Soditan was rapidly developing an instinct for the sheerest threat of new responsibilities; in his mother's brother, he detected just such a threat. The man had to be fetched from his favourite workplace, the drinking parlour at the motor garage. He turned up, his speech slurred, yet sufficiently clear to convey his plans of sending his two 'wayward' children to his famous nephew in Abeokuta, to imbibe a little of his tested discipline. Soditan very firmly advised him to postpone such a scheme indefinitely, warned him that if they arrived without his approval, he would send them back on the next lorry. Yet he feared that this would not be the end of the matter. If the carpenter continued to drink his business dry, the children themselves might turn up on their own, or be sent not by the carpenter but by a concerned relation.

The carpenter went into a torrent of excuses, barely understandable, but related to Tenten's death and a message from his sister Mariam. Teacher was not to believe whatever his mother said; he had not even been home at the time and only returned to find a message left by some girl, who obviously mistook his assistant for himself. Anyway he had been told of Teacher's stout assistance and may heaven bless his efforts and didn't he always go on his knees in Sagamu and pray that his own children would grow up to be like this son of Ìsarà of whom everyone was so proud? Akinyode did not even know that Mariam had turned to her brother for help at the time; he wondered why she had wasted precious money sending a message to such a feckless being. Still, what was he doing there himself? Even if the project that took him there was to be a secret from Ìsarà until the last moment, were there no carpenters nearer Ode to whom he could give the commission? He shrugged. One had to keep trying. If the business could be assisted from time to time . . . it was not too much in the way of duty for a nephew. And it was in his own interest. If he did not lend a hand

and his young cousins arrived on his doorstep, destitute . . . well, which was the greater evil?

Soditan gave the instructions to the assistant, sketching out in minute detail the contraption he wanted built on the back of Node's lorry for the awaited event. They left some money for wood; the rest would be paid after the frame was mounted on the lorry – probably in a week. While he busied himself with the carpenter, Sipe wandered through the workshop, his gaze fixed on the stacked cabinets, wardrobes, and all-purpose cupboards awaiting customers. In the interior store there were a few coffins stacked on trestles, awaiting orders before being given their finishing touches. Briefly he wondered if the Syndicate should invest in the carpentry trade but deferred a decision until after the kingship tussle was settled. And he stored away the skill with which Akinyode had made his sketches; perhaps he could persuade him to turn his hand to designing for the new enterprise – if that route was pronounced lucrative after he had made his enquiries.

They found Josiah in Mariam's cottage, washing his hands after a meal of *eba* and *ikokore*. He waited impatiently while they greeted Mariam; she cleared away Josiah's plates and the calabash of water, then went to prepare food for the newcomers.

'We saw him,' the son reported.

'Hn-hn?'

'He accepts the decision of the kingmakers.'

'And the rest?'

'Yes. He will do as we asked. No more fight with the government.'

The older man waited. The two emissaries fidgeted and exchanged glances. Josiah looked at them with amusement, appearing to enjoy their discomfort. Finally he said, 'You have not told me the rest.'

Sipe spoke, somewhat plaintively. 'Baba, you know our friend. He agrees to keep quiet until the Resident has settled the matter in our favour. But he says he hopes the elders of Ìsarà are not expecting in him a deaf-and-dumb king. Because if they are, they should search in another house.'

Silence followed. Then a low chuckle began in the hidden regions of Pa Josiah's chest, welling out into gusts of laughter that shook his entire body. He slapped both hands on his thighs and rose, still shaking. 'I knew it. I told Jagun. If they think that the son of Akinsanya will stop fighting those white men forever, they have mistaken their man.' His laughter stopped abruptly. 'But he must not breathe – Feem! – until we have won the battle. Not even to fart, you understand?'

Hastily Sipe reassured him. 'Oh no. We have his word.'

'And the other contacts you promised to make – the lawyer, our people in Lagos . . .'

'We left nothing to chance,' Akinyode said.

'Good. I'll take the news to Jagun.'

At the door he turned. 'Oh yes, Sipe. Jagun has something for you. I heard all about your troubles over the native-medicine store you are trying to open in Lagos, so I spoke to him.'

'Oh, thank you, Baba.'

'Far too many of our own people don't wish their own kind any good or success. That is why the black man is not making progress in this world. As soon as it looks as if someone is forging ahead, when they see the skin on his body glistening . . . oh, have you heard of Opeilu's cousin, Sorunde?'

'Yes, we heard.'

'Well, that is an example for you. Not even one month to enjoy his promotion to assistant inspector, they had to send him to join his ancestors. But there is a God in heaven; sooner or later his enemies will find that out. Now you make sure you see Jagun; he will give you something to hang over your shop. He says, give it six months at the most and that licence will be in your hands.'

'Thank you, Baba. I will talk to him.'

'He went into the matter, I don't have to tell you, as something that touched his own person. This time, Lagos people will find out whether or not our fathers had their own kind of power. And if they think it died with them the moment white men stepped on our soil . . . You see for yourselves to what straits we are now reduced? I have to wait on the white intruder to decide who is going to sit on the throne of my ancestors. Are we not even supposed to learn from the past? Look at the Oyo and Ibadan – I am talking of the Kiriji wars. At the end of it all, who did they invite to come and make their peace? The white man. The missionaries. And we are all paying a heavy price for that till today. Now that is the situation Olisa is shamelessly provoking all over again, as if they have no history in his father's house!'

'But Paa,' Efuape demanded, 'is it not also the fault of us Ijebu? Surely we have a share of the blame.'

'Oho, the grammar people have come. O ya, tell me. In what way?'

'Well, didn't Awujale Tanwase sign that treaty with the white man? When he wanted to change his mind, it was too late. Carter said to him, an agreement is an agreement, so he brought soldiers to collect his debt.'

'En-hen. How else do you want the white man to narrate the story? That is what they taught you about that affair when you went to school, not so? You should sit down with Agunrin Odubona someday – when all this is over – and hear what he has to say. The war was before my time, but he took part in it. And he met this man Carter in person. In Lagos. Ìsarà sent him to accompany the Awujale's men when they took their peace offering to Carter. We all remember. But he is now senile, and Olisa takes advantage of that.'

A commotion was developing outside. Two men, babbling in excited voices, emerged from the dark, shouting Pa Josiah's name. They stopped when they saw him in the doorway and greeted him with a hurried prostration while the elder panted out their message.

'Jagun sent us to find you, Baba Tisa. Very bad things have happened on the farm.'

'What sort of thing? I was actually on my way . . .'

'They have just brought in the body of Jagun's in-law Ba'tola. There was a big fight at Oripe farm; Olisa's men went and attacked them. Ba'tola was macheted to death. Many otherrs were wounded on both sides – they were taken to the hospital at Sagamu.'

Josiah stood stock-still, his eyes boring through the dusk. 'So,' he breathed at last. 'Erinle wants to wear the king's slippers with bloody feet? So be it. Take me to Jagun.'

'You cannot see him now, Baba. He has gone into *osugbo*. He wants you to handle the trouble at the farm because – and this was his message to you – he is going where he cannot be reached.'

Josiah hastily pushed his way through the messengers and stood outside, beyond earshot of his son and his friend.

'Give me the rest of the message.'

'What he said, Baba, was that Olisa is fouling up the town only because he has the support of the Agunrin Odubona. So he says he will call him home, all night if need be.'

'He said that?'

'Those were his words. He will come out, he said, only when the old man has finally answered.'

Josiah was silent for a long moment; then he spoke softly, as if to himself. '*Olorun a gbu'se.*'*

He turned precipitately, almost bumping into two figures who had emerged round the corner of the house, directly behind him. The bigger one was Sotikare, the court clerk from Lagos; the smaller was Ogunba. Pa

---

* May God grant success to his endeavour.

Josiah barely acknowledged their greetings before he disappeared in the direction of 'Gborobe, from where he would send for the men he needed. With Jagun in total seclusion, the mundane duties had clearly been left to him.

Sotikare pushed his way up the step, filled the doorway with his bulk. He glowered down at the two friends, who sat sombrely before the dishes Mariam had prepared for them, untouched. Then Akinyode caught sight of Ogunba, partly hidden by Sotikare's body, and moved forward to greet him. The quiet but severe voice of the court clerk was a lash across his face, freezing him dead in stride.

'I hope you are all satisfied!'

Ogunba tried to remonstrate with him; it was obvious that they had been arguing all the way to Mariam's house. Sotikare waved him aside and plunged into violent denunciations. 'I thought young Akinsanya had more sense, and if he did not, that he had friends who could lend him some. An intelligent man like Saaki, he starts competing for a primitive institution like obaship, and you, his supposed friends, actually encourage him. You bring him to the level of ignorant men like Olisa and Jagun.'

Soditan's face was grim. 'Go on. Don't be afraid to include my own father in that list.'

'I did not refer to Paa.'

'You should. If there is a conspiracy, he is at the very heart of it.'

'We don't have to bring personal emotion into this.'

Sipe laughed out aloud. 'Who is bringing emotion in it? Just look at you.'

'It's a disgrace, that's all I have to say to you. And if you have any love for your man you should tell Akinsanya to pull out his candidature – immediately!'

'But why?' Ogunba demanded quietly. 'All you have said so far is all you've been saying all day.'

'You are all educated men. How could you involve yourselves in such a matter? It should be beneath you.'

'Akinyode turned to face Ogunba, dismissing the court clerk with the suggestion of a hiss. 'Where have you been? What kept you in Ijebu-Ode?'

'This very affair. I heard rumours that our man had been chosen –'

'You mean you knew before we did?'

Ogunba laughed. 'What do you people know in Abeokuta?'

'Ho ho, listen to this runaway? He hasn't even settled down in his new station and he's already become the ear of all Ijebu!'

Sotikare walked away from them and sat apart, staring gloomily through the window and murmuring under his breath.

'So when did you hear?' Sipe demanded.

'Not that long before you did. The kingmakers sent an emissary to the Awujale to report Olisa's move. Of course he had known months before what the Ìsarà kingmakers had decided. But when Olisa crowned his own man, it blew things out into the open. I went to see him. He has sent for Olisa and his backer – that old man they called Agbari Iku. And then I stopped to see the Akarigbo – he agreed to summon an emergency meeting of Remo Local Council.'

'When?'

'They met this morning. I waited to bring you the decisions but had to leave while they were still at it. My cousin will bring the news first thing tomorrow morning.'

'Good. Very good.'

Sotikare's voice cut through their elation. 'I hope the council finds a way to bring Babatola back to life. Not to mention those others who will be the sacrificial lambs over such a primitive contest.'

Sipe spun round angrily but Akinyode restrained him, got up instead, and went to stand over the simmering hulk of Sotikare. 'Look, er . . . Sotikare. We are all ex-Ilés here, so we can speak the same language and speak it frankly. State your objections in clear terms. What do you have against Akinsanya's selection?'

'The whole thing smells. He is lowering himself . . . an ex-Ilé.'

'We've heard that. But what exactly do you oppose – the entire idea of obaship? Or is it that you think it is okay for illiterate people but not for a Simeonite?'

'The entire thing is too primitive.'

From the other side of the room, Sipe swore out loudly.

'Why don't you and Ogunba start eating?' Akinyode said. 'I have just one more question for our civilised clerk.' He faced Sotikare directly. 'Now tell me, what do you feel about the throne of England?'

'What?'

'You heard me. The throne of England. Is it primitive? Did King Edward abdicate because he found it too primitive, or was it simply because of woman trouble?'

Sotikare ignored the loud laughter of the others, a look of disbelief stamped on his rotund face. He managed to stammer out at last: 'Are – you – comparing the throne of England to – this throne of – Ìsarà?'

'Why not?' all three chorused.

420

Sotikare rose. 'Now I know you are all lost. You actually compare – I mean, are you people serious?'

'Well, one is obviously bigger,' Akinyode conceded amiably. 'It even boasts of an empire. We all have to dress up our pupils ever Empire Day and march and sing songs of praise to the English throne and all its forebears, Queen Victoria included.' He turned to the others and raised his arms in a conductor's pose. 'One – two – three!'

> Vikito-ria, Vikito-ria
> *Aiye re l'awa nje*
> *O so gbobo eru d'omo*
> *N'ile enia dudu.*

Sotikare glared at them rolling in laughter after they had ended their cacophonous rendition. But it was mostly Akinyode to whom his attention was directed. 'You know, I am seeing a side of you I never suspected before. I always thought you were more sensitive to things of this kind. Look at you, a man has just died . . .'

'Sotikare, we all regret that death. But do you know how many of our people have died to preserve the British throne? Those who have now joined the army for this war at least made their own choice – thank God for small blessings. But whose throne are they really fighting and dying to preserve? It is certainly not that of the Odemo if Isàrà!'

'Talking of the war,' Ogunba said, 'the radio predicted this morning that the war will certainly reach Senegal. Something about treachery by one Admiral Petrain.'

'Hm-hm. It creeps nearer and nearer,' Sipe agreed. 'Let's eat our dinner before Hitler snatches it from our mouths. Come on, Sotikare.'

'I don't want to eat!'

'It is *ikokore*,' Soditan warned, taking him by the arm. 'We can eat and plan how to stop the violence before it spreads. You will come in useful there.'

'I've told you, I want no part of it.'

'As court clerk to the British crown,' Yode said soothingly, 'your voice will carry plenty of weight.' He led him to the bench and sat him down before the dishes. 'And you are already close to the Rokodo House – Erinle's people, from where Olisa made his choice.'

Ogunba nodded in agreement. 'We mustn't leave things to Jagun and . . .' He chuckled, glancing at Akinyode.

'And my old man, you are right. We will have to tell them that Akinsanya is one of ours, and he must not be made part of any violence.'

'You see, Sotikare, something which seems to have escaped you – everything is being transformed. Adjustments are being made to a new age, and the obaship is only one of the institutions that are affected. It is wrong to think that the former Oba were "illiterates," by the way; that is very, very wrong. Very narrow-minded. Akinsanya is merely representative of a new breed. Of course, if you are saying that the whole thing should be scrapped . . .'

'No, I never said that.'

'Well then,' Ogunba continued, 'as long as that position is there, let's make sure that we help to fill it with an enlightened person.'

'Talk to the Rokodo family,' Soditan said. 'Let them see that violence will only bring the full weight of the government down on Ìsarà. And it is wartime. Any excuse to send in the soldiers in order to "keep the peace" – the government will grab it. Remind them of Carter's war against the Ijebu. Some of their elders were eyewitnesses to what happened to the Ijebu. Ìsarà may not be so fortunate this time – not like that war, which we fought outside our borders. The soldiers will come in. Ask people who live in and around garrison towns and they will tell you what evil that means. It is a question of who the people want; let the people decide it. Use the right language to them. Ìsarà has never been subjugated in all its history. If we use our own hands to open the gates to an army of occupation, our ancestors will curse us from their graves.'

'And their children. And unborn generations,' echoed Efuape.

'All right, all right. You don't have to preach at me. I was the one who first denounced the violence, wasn't I?'

'Of course,' agreed Soditan. 'I was merely making suggestions because, you see, you must find the right way to talk to those stubborn old men. If you go there and speak grammar, they won't listen to a thing, least of all our man Agbari Iku – that's if he can still hear a thing. But you try reminding them of the judgement of their ancestors, etc. Make them see THE CURSE already hanging over them like a dark cloud over their roof – drought, famine, plagues, even Hitler dropping down from the sky on satanic parachutes . . .'

Mollified, Sotikare even permitted himself to join in the laughter. 'You should have been a lawyer,' he spluttered.

'No, no, preacher,' Ogunba corrected him. 'I have always said his place is really in the pulpit.'

Sipe opened up the dishes and passed his hand over them with a flourish. 'Bless this food o lord for christ's sake amen do we eat this congealed mess now or never?'

422

As they moved to take their places at the table, Ogunba touched Soditan on the arm and unobtrusively drew him a little distance away from the others. 'I sent my cousin to Sagamu – to the hospital. He returned with news that two of the injured have since died. The doctor is a family friend, so I have sent back word that he should keep it quiet for as long as possible. I have not told anyone. And he'll bring back news of the council's decision. He has my motorcycle so he should be back with the first light of dawn.'

And then it was the turn of a neglected Christmas and New Year spirit to intrude with a reminder of the season, which had vanished from their minds under the pace of events now moving the sleepy town closer to the brink of civil strife. It took the form of Wemuja, dressed in a two-tone cowboy affair, complete with shimmering tassels down his long yellow sleeves and aquamarine pantaloons. On his head was perched a purple conical-shaped paper cap and around his waist was a silver-studded belt complete with leather holsters and chrome-plated toy pistols. Only his face was anything but festive. He came into the room and stopped dead, confused by the presence of Soditan's friends, who had paused in various stages of transferring food to their mouths or masticating. They all stared at the apparition in amazement, looking at Soditan for some kind of explanation. Only Efuape turned his back on the eruption, burying his face in his plate.

Wemuja swallowed rapidly, his precipitate entrance – and whatever it portended – totally overwhelmed by the gathering. Soditan decided to help him out, before the paper hat, which he had now taken off, was shredded in his powerful fingers.

'What is it, Wemuja?'

'I . . . er . . . sir, Head Teacher, sir, we heard. We heard the news where we were playing band. I came right away to let you know, Brother Babatola was my friend. I have people, sir, in the motor parks. I can get fifty of them together even if I go there tonight. And I have the railway people. They never forget me. I can take Pa Node's lorry and go and collect all of them to come here. If you want, I am ready to go now.'

Soditan smiled. 'Thank you, Wemuja. I assure you we will need your timber lorry very soon. I already have plans for you to go to Sagamu. But not yet. I will let you know when.'

The master driver's face relaxed into a satisfied grin, swiftly followed by a spasm of anguish as he remembered what had caused his presence there. 'Thank you, Teacher. What these people have done, God will not forgive them. Man will not forget and God will not forgive. Good-night, sirs.'

And he turned on his heel and left the house. Only then did Sipe look up from his plate, shamefacedly. Akinyode took one look at him, darted a glance at the figure of Wemuja slowly disappearing into the dark. He shook his head, and his eyes returned to Sipe and framed the question. Sipe nodded sheepishly.

'Guilty. He saw it in my mail-order catalogue and begged me to order it for him. Cost price, I swear. No commission.'

It was routine work to Goriola, who had carried out this chore a thousand times in his career and in hundreds of households. His gangling figure was a familiar sight in Ìsarà, as it was – albeit on different weekdays – in Ode, Ipara, and a few clusters of cottages in between. Thursday was Ìsarà's day, though not with strict regularity. sometimes Goriola would disappear for a month or more; a fellow worker had been taken ill or had gone on leave, and he would cover his beat in Isonyin or even as far afield as Igbajo. No matter, sooner or later his figure rose above the hilltop on a Thursday, perched on his gleaming bicycle – he always stopped just before entering a village, and gave the crossbars, the handlebars, even the spokes, a careful wipe, taking off every speck of dust. Then he took out the bicycle lamp from its protective nest in the saddlebag – even though the lamp was never required, unless sometimes on the very last mile or two of his journey home, and then only if he had stopped on the way to quench the thirst which came with his pedalling exertions. The lamp slotted in position, he pushed his bicycle up the hill and freewheeled down on his first target. His route was chosen carefully to ensure that his first appearance in town did not involve any unseemly exertion.

It was the children who usually first spotted the khaki pith helmet framed against the sky, followed shortly by a youngish face which was set in a conscious official-duty sternness. It pronounced every household guilty until proved innocent. Next followed a disproportionately long neck which, everyone remarked, must have been his main qualification for the job of sanitary inspector. It enabled his face to peer round tight corners, pry underneath beds and into cupboards, reach between rafters, and negotiate awkward shelves. Then followed a bristling white collar, its flaps nearly as wide as those of an *abetiaja*. En route, it had been protected by a white-dotted red bandana carefully tucked into the space between the collar and the neck. The collar was held together by the fattest knot ever seen in Ijebuland, while the maroon tie itself covered nearly all the exposed sector of the shirt and vanished into the regulation khaki jacket with gleaming brass buttons, bearing the crest of His Majesty's Government. Goriola's shorts were so wide that they appeared to be abbreviated

424

versions of the local *kembe*, and the feet that rested authoritatively on the bicycle pedals were encased in white canvas shoes whose soles were holed through six years of careful usage.

When the children saw him, they set up a cry: '*Wolé-wolé! Wolé-wolé!*' It was a signal for the women of the household to rush about as if suddenly stung by bees. Chasing the carelessly discarded leaves and other debris in the compound, scooping up the neglected excrement of a child, and screaming at older children to check that the waterpots had been covered up. Brooms flashed up and down the wall corners, darting into the rafters and slapping furiously at windowsills. Indigo-pots in the yard were covered up – never mind what the teacher once said, that mosquitoes never bred in dye-pots, how could they? The pots, half-sunken into the ground, were quickly covered up by flat iron sheets and wooden planks, while efforts were made to throw fresh earth on the indigo puddles and trickles formed by drips from the hanging cloths. In the dark corners of houses where the waterpot was stored for coolness, the damp on the floor was wiped dry, the water itself keenly probed for evidence of mosquito larvae – the very worst crime in the sanitary inspector's manual. Any suggestion of a wriggling motion and the pot would be emptied, the telltale larvae stamped into earth.

Goriola never hurried. His practice was to vary his choice of the first victim from visit to visit, and he would sometimes prop up his bicycle against one house, only to walk through the passages to begin his inspection at another. And he began by ensuring that his own appearance was beyond reproach. 'A sanitary inspector,' he would say, 'must firstly pass his own inspection sanitarily.' He saw to it that his rather willful shirt collar had both flaps in place beneath the lapel of his jacket, then walked round to the saddlebag, took out a notebook to which a pencil was attached by a string, then struck a pose which he had consciously adopted from his hero, the head teacher, who had obtained the position for him in the first place. The young sanitary inspector would stand stock-still, then turn slowly round in a complete circle, carefully surveying the neighbourhood and deciding, it seemed, which would be the first doorway to receive his frame. His mind made up, he caught the dangling pencil in one swift move, wetted the lead point between his lips, and wrote down the name of the selected houseowner. This ritual never varied. Faces peeked at him from behind half-closed doors and windows, spied on him from the dark entries into the rutted passages, and even, in the case of children, looked down from treetops. Nothing moved on the outside of houses – it was too late for any careless occupant to start sweeping over dogs' faeces, tins, and food scraps which had been unhygienically ignored. In the interiors of houses, however, all was frenzied activity. Goriola's ritual, he would privately admit, was a last-minute concession to lazy housekeepers. After the five minutes' grace thus provided, any delinquents could expect no mercy. Notebook, summons, court, and fines. Knowing that he had to compensate for his youthful appearance – at twenty-nine he still looked like a twenty-year-old – he developed various strategies to bolster his authority in face of the patronising pleas of mostly older delinquents. One of them was the reputation for never rubbing out an offence once entered in his notebook, which acquired for him the name of Mr No-Gbebè. The ex-Ilés, however, had long bestowed on him a name more suited to his appearance and also closer to his own name. He did not mind; on the contrary it made him feel a special relationship with the teacher's select circle of Ìsarà's indigenes.

On this unusual Thursday, there were no children to announce his appearance. He coasted downhill as usual and pressed down the chrome-plated bicycle stand with his foot. He sensed something different in this familiar neighbourhood but could not really place it. He shrugged it off, proceeded to execute his slow-motion rituals, and marched, somewhat thoughtfully, towards the Rokodo compound. He knocked, then frowned. There was none of the usual rustle of last-minute whispered instructions, flying brooms, and scurrying feet, no furtive scraping of congealed food from the bottom of a forgotten pan or pot. Goriola turned his gaze in the direction of the other houses, caught a face or two in the act of rapidly withdrawing, and was somewhat reassured. If there had been an untoward happening, such as a death in the household, one of the neighbours would have come forward to inform him. So he knocked again, this time announcing himself:

'*Wolé-wolé. Emi ni o*, Mr Goriola.'

Receiving no answer still, he reached over the gate and found the wooden stop, lifted it from its slot, and entered the passage between the immediate houses, which led into an open space. The compound was empty; a quadrangle of silent walls receded behind covered verandahs and houseposts; closed doors and windows confronted him. The Rokodo compound looked completely deserted. Goriola shrugged, flicked up the notebook with a much-practised gesture so that the pencil landed on the pad, against which his thumb pinned it, then proceeded to inspect what he could in the open compound.

The indigo-pots were grouped around a sparsely leaved *odan* tree, which appeared itself to be the centre of the compound. He smiled grimly as his gaze instantly took in three pots which were wide open. There was worse. The entire household gave the appearance, almost, of a place that had been hastily abandoned. A charred cooking-pot lay tilted on an open-air hearth near one of the houseposts, while a mound of rubbish decorated the far corner, under the eaves, as if an effort had been made to sweep up the compound, but for some reason the pile had been overlooked. Goriola picked his way through baskets and other litter of a normal, busy enclosure, walking towards the cluster of half-buried pots that had first attracted his attention. He ducked under a dirty *agbada* which hung from a cross-pole, and then his nose crinkled in disgust at the spectacle occupying the space between the trio of open pots – a potsherd; it could be the usual offering one found at crossroads, or perhaps it was a special *etutu*. He wondered, for the first time, if the *odan* tree was a household deity whose festival was perhaps being celebrated on that day. The potsherd contained some whitish food which could have been *lafun* but was so liberally covered with palm oil as to defy any certainty. There were also kola nuts, split open; a giant snail, impaled through the shell and through the potsherd into the ground; cowries; a quantity of black powder in a tin. Three *ado* tied together with a palm frond completed the picture, except for nine *onini* – the inspector counted them very carefully, wondering what coins from the white man's mint had to do with such a primitive offering.

Pondering whether or not this mess, which was already attracting a swarm of flies and ants, should also be entered in his notebook among his list of offences against household hygiene, Goriola turned away and caught sight of his reflection on the still surface of the indigo fluid. Tucking his notebook under his armpit, he seized the chance to adjust his tie and smoothe down the lapels of his jacket. That objective attained, he restored the notebook to his hand and stood still for some moments, inspecting the result. He remained in that position for longer than he had planned. The quiet of the compound slowly seeped into him. Perhaps the reflection of his helmeted face, framed against the sky, across which a few wisps of clouds idly floated, and the exertion of the five-mile ride to Ìsarà also aided the creeping lethargy. Goriola became lost in thought; the seconds lengthened into minutes. And then he experienced, he thought, a momentary hallucination. Another face had appeared behind his and, in a flash, yet another. But all thoughts of hallucinating vanished when he felt a touch on the nape of his neck which was different from the feel of his accustomed sweat-soaked bandana. And swifter than thought was the cold feel of water enveloping his head – preceded by a *plop* as his helmet fell into the dye-pot – and he knew that his head was forced again and again into the

427

dark depths of the dye mixture. When he came up again for air, Goriola screamed. It was answered by a blow to the side of his face which sent him sprawling backward to land on the votive potsherd, smashing it and leaving a wide red swathe on the back of his khaki uniform.

Goriola was not a strong man, but he had the advantage of height, and, for once, his uncoordinated body became an advantage. As more men poured out from the various doorways and the seemingly silent, empty compound became animated with screams, curses, blows, and the tearing sound of his precious uniform, Goriola fought for his life. From the heart of the nightmare that appeared to engulf him, a government employee on official duties and in broad daylight, he succeeded in making out a few coherent voices.

'I told you they would come.'

'This one is only their spy. Grab hold of his arms!'

'You're done for, foolish *ami*. You think we all sleep in Rokodo House?'

'The *etutu* drew him like a pig to slaughter. You saw it, didn't you?' He got here and he couldn't move.'

'No. He was uttering incantations to render it useless.'

'Get the rope. Knock him on the head if he won't keep still.'

Goriola struggled like a maniac, screaming for help at the top of his voice, both to neighbours and to Jesus, son of God, yet praying silently to wake up from what he still hoped was a nightmare. He felt his clothes ripped off piece by piece, his baggy shorts were already in shreds as his assailants sought to pin him down, clubbing him, while his head did its best to dodge the blows and the blood from his wounds mingled with oil from the smashed potsherd. It was when he saw the flash of a cutlass in the hands of one of these unknown assailants, however, that he found himself suddenly possessed of a superhuman energy. Flinging off the two men who clung to one arm pinioned behind his back, he leapt up, crashed unseeing through all the human obstacles around him, and fled through the gates of the compound, indifferent to the array of missiles that flew after him – pots, pans, stones, a hoe, which caught him in the small of the back, the snail, which flew past him to land on the gate as his hand found the latch . . .

Once outside, Goriola hesitated, unable to decide which way his safety lay. Then he saw a group of sober-looking men, neatly dressed, coming down the same hill he had so calmly ridden down some moments earlier. He turned uphill towards them. Sotikare, Ogunba, and Opeilu saw the half-naked madman rushing uphill at them and stopped in their tracks. It was Ogunba who first recognised the unlucky sanitary inspector.

'Hen! It's Young Gorilla!'

Sotikare stared hard but shook his head. 'Goriola? Impossible.'

The fugitive also recognised them, stopped, and stared at them imploringly, his jaws trembling from their roots in a futile effort to explain, or perhaps to ask them to explain, what was happening to him. Finally there emerged a rasping 'Save me, please. Save me.' Opeilu pulled him gently behind them as the crowd poured out from the Rokodo compound after their victim and soon came up to where they stood; there were nine or ten wild-looking men, none of whom the three friends could recognise.

Above their shouts Sotikare succeeded in making himself heard.

'Have you people gone mad? What do you think you are doing? And who are you?'

A babble of voices ensued. With great difficulty the small group was however able to make out their accusations. This man had been caught spying and uttering incantations in the Rokodo compound. Indeed, they were now certain that he had 'left something' there. After all, he was within the compound a very long time; he could have buried it anywhere, before he moved to the centre, where he could be seen. The passage between the gates and the open space, for instance – nothing would satisfy them unless he went back with them and uprooted what he had buried in the ground. Oh yes, they were waiting for him. They had waited all night for Jagun's people, who they knew would be coming to avenge Ba'tola's death. They had sent away all the women and children and laid an ambush for the fools. It was lucky for them they didn't come at night – to be dealt with as one deals with burglars and other night-marauders. They waited until morning, then sent their spy, this shivering object, who deserved to be castrated. He was burying charms and uttering spells over the indigo-pots and the 'protection' they had themselves placed there against enemy forces. Anyone who thought he could walk into Rokodo House, disguising himself as a sanitary inspector, as if he was dealing with children –

Sotikare interrupted. 'Where is Chief Odubona himself?'

The assailants stopped and seemed to really look at the three men for the first time. They became somewhat wary and appeared to turn to one among them, as if to identify him as their spokesman. The hefty, cicatrixed individual pushed his way forward.

'And who is asking for Agunrin?'

Sotikare's party eyed him carefully, shifted their gazes from one to the next, then exchanged glances with one another. 'You people are not from here,' Opeilu remarked.

'So what? We are Erinle's people from Ode.'

Opeilu nodded slowly. 'I see. And Erinle asked you to come from Ode to guard his house in Ìsarà.'

The man grinned. 'In Ìsarà, the king cannot have relations from neighbouring towns?'

'Of course, of course,' Ogunba said. 'For all we know, Erinle may even have relations in Hausaland. But is the Agunrin home? It is he we were coming to see. We have a message from Lagos. This man here' – and he pointed to Sotikare – 'is from Lagos courts. He has a message.'

The attackers seemed to pull back. They looked at one another. 'What are you going to do with that spy? We caught him red-handed, didn't we?'

'I have just told you. This is Mr Sotikare, court clerk from Lagos. When we have seen Chief Odubona, he will decide what to do about those who attack a government official.'

The spokesman's voice took on an aggressive whine. 'But we caught him breaking into the house. He thought it was empty –'

'You could have killed him,' Opeilu reminded them. 'You were trying to kill him.'

'Where is the chief?' Ogunba repeated.

The spokesman shrugged. 'We were only told to watch the house. But I heard someone saying they had to go to a meeting at Olisa's place. That is all we know.'

'Go back to the watch you were given,' Sotikare ordered. 'The people of Ìsarà don't want you on their streets. Bear that in mind.'

For some moments both groups did not move. By now the street was filled with clumps of people, standing silently, keeping wary watch on the scene. The dark countenances of the men betrayed little emotion, but the ominous way the sleeves of several *agbada* hung down left no doubt about the presence of hidden weapons, waiting to be produced if matters came to a head. For a long moment, only the continued anguished panting of Goriola punctuated the silence. It was difficult to tell on which side the hidden weapons would be drawn, so uncommitted appeared the expressions of the watchers. There were many more who remained behind their doors, lurked behind walls, and crouched in the warrens of those compounds, awaiting a signal, no matter what form it took.

Finally the men from Rokodo House turned at the prompting of their leader, walked back to the compound, and closed the gate. Opeilu gave a sigh and turned to the man they had just rescued.

'Ah, Mr No-Gbebè, what a thing to happen to you in our Ìsarà!'

'What is going on, Mr Opeilu? Just tell me what is going on?'

Ogunba stared at him in surprise. 'Where do you live that you haven't heard?'

'Heard what? Is it not the same Ìsarà to which I've been coming on inspection since . . .'

Opeilu took his arm. 'Come on. We'll take you to the clinic . . .'

'My bicycle . . .'

'I'll get it,' Ogunba volunteered, and walked down the hill towards the machine.

'My helmet is also in there.' And then he appeared to become aware of his appearance for the first time. He turned his arms over and over, staring at them, then at his half-naked and bleeding body. 'Look at me! Look at me! Look what they did to me.'

'Come on. Forget your helmet for now. We'll get treatment for you. Didn't you know that Ìsarà is at war? The fight for the throne is out in the open.'

'Yes,' Sotikare added. 'And there is no time to lose. First the battle on the farm – so many wounded, and Ba'tola dead. And now this, right in the heart of the town.'

'When Jagun hears of this . . .'

'Maybe he shouldn't – at least not yet.'

'How will you prevent that? You saw those looking on. They were eager for blood. In a few moments it will be all over Ìsarà. People will start arming themselves . . .'

'Then we can't waste any more time. The Agunrin is the one we must tackle. He has the longest memory, and that is what fuels the violence. Memory can be a dangerous thing in a stubborn old man.'

Ogunba returned, wheeling the bicycle. 'Can you ride?'

The battered inspector tried to flex his limbs. The action produced only a groan and Ogunba stopped him. 'Try to get on the saddle. We'll push you to the clinic.'

They assisted him onto the saddle; then, with two of them holding the handlebar on either side and the third pushing from the rear, they set off for the clinic, filled with sober reflections. They had reached the crossroads at Orelu quarters when Opeilu stopped and turned to the patient, whose face was now visibly swollen on one side.

'Young Gorilla, I know it is hardly fair to ask this of you, I mean, after what you've been through. But if you could bear your pain for just a short while longer –'

Sotikare interjected eagerly. 'Just what I was thinking. We should confront Olisa with this. His fellow elders should see the work of his hands with their own eyes.'

Ogunba nodded slowly and turned to Goriola. 'I wish it had not happened but . . . and you are not even of Ìsarà . . .'

Goriola shook his head to disagree, only to hunch his shoulders from the pain. He half-raised his hands towards the source of pain but stopped just short, afraid even to touch himself. So he attempted to grin, producing at best a grimace. 'I have been through the worst already.' His tongue appeared to work on the inside of his cheek for some moments. 'Wait,' he said, and he turned his head to one side and spat. A gob of blood flew out, together with a tooth. 'I thought so. Anyway, you can't really say I am not now part of Ìsarà, because that is my blood on that soil. And I don't think it is all palm oil you will find on the ground where I fought those ruffians just now. Only, I . . . I . . . think you may . . . have to . . .'

Sotikare caught him as he fainted. 'Poor Gorilla,' Ogunba murmured as they stretched him out by the roadside. He jumped on the bicycle and pedalled furiously to find Efuape and the only car accessible to them in Ìsarà.

That the meeting should take place in Olisa's house and not in the Rokodo House was more than sufficient hint of the futility of their mission, if they chose to be discouraged. The three emissaries were buoyed, however, by a sense of their role in the making of history. Where else, for instance, in the entire history of the Yoruba, had a king been chosen by the spectacle of two main contenders seated in an open field, their supporters lined up behind them, visible to all the world? Of course, there had been the earlier murky passages of intrigue, of pressures and treacheries, even of bribery. But that in the end it should come down to what, in effect, was a simple open election? Why, even the legislative council of the nation, now undergoing its fifth decade of experimentation, did not allow such a broad participation of the people. Akinyode could be forgiven, Ogunba argued, for comparing the moment with the era of the Greek *demos*. If the Oyo people had thought of the example which Ìsarà was now about to set, the Kiriji wars, with all their attendant suffering, destruction, and the final humiliating European intervention, would have been avoided.

Not for nothing, however, was the Olisa known – though somewhat uncharitably – as the *asin*.* His ruse to empty the Rokodo House was impelled by the need to keep Agunrin Odubona a virtual prisoner, inaccessible to the opposition except under his control. Odubona, agreed by most to be over a hundred years old, was not know to have uttered a

---

* A species of rodent, small but poisonous.

432

word in human hearing for the past ten years of his life. Old and gnarled as the bunched open roots of the *odan* tree, he was the last surviving tome of Ìsarà, and indeed of Ijebu, history from before the settled phase of missionary incursion. He lived with his memories, a still-active but closed circuit within the tight-skinned independency of his head. The Olisa was his sole link with the present; he translated reality to him, and even this, for Odubona, was already more than a healthy intrusion upon his peace.

Erinle, the king-elect, would not appear. To meet with mediators or representatives of the Jagun faction would be to admit that he was not truly a reigning king. And for even greater safety, Olisa, who was painfully aware of Erinle's low level of tolerance for such conflict, had sent him off to Abeokuta, where he had taken refuge with the Sodade family. There he was safe from pleas and summons, from do-gooders and peacemakers who would weaken his resolve and compromise the Olisa's masterful strategies. The lone spokesman for the Rokodo House was thus Agunrin Odubona, Agbari Iku, whose stature however transcended any one ruling house but was indeed the collective will of all of Ìsarà. To be seen with Odubona, night and day, to ensure that the word was spread throughout Ìsarà and beyond that Agunrin had actually 'sought shelter' under his roof, was a decisive blow, he felt, for any challenger to his choice.

The sitting room had been carefully arranged, the reception planned to the last detail. Agunrin alone would speak for the Rokodo, and Olisa chuckled loud and long at the ploy. No one could then truthfully report to the Akarigbo or the white Resident that the Rokodo had refused the path of peace. No one would accuse them of not listening. The emissaries would talk to the venerable but dumb. When they had finished their speech, he, Olisa, would rise as regent, thank them, assure them that, as they themselves had witnessed, their father had listened intently to what they had to say. When he had digested their message thoroughly, he would send for them again and give them his reply.

Olisa installed Agunrin in a high-backed chair against the wall to the left of the doorway, so that very little light fell on him. If he fell asleep, no one would notice. Agunrin could sleep on a stool or bench without once falling off or losing his balance, even in advanced age. Let these white-educated peacemakers talk their heads off; they might as well speak to his iron-and-bronze *ogboni* staff and hope for a reply. But he could say to all Ìsarà, to the Awujale, the district commissioner and other interfering busybodies: As the regent I was present when our Baba gave them audience. No one seeks peace with more fervour than a man who has suffered through wars in

433

defence of the soul of Ìsarà. The rest is up to the other side, who refuse to listen to reason . . .

The callers had also agreed on their own strategy. Opeilu would speak first. It had not taken much to persuade him, on arrival, to replace Soditan, who reluctantly agreed that he was disqualified from such an arbitration role because of the open partisanship of his father. Efuape was adjudged to be no diplomat – even by himself. Opeilu frankly enjoyed the fast-growing reputation he had acquired as a dependable mediator, impartial, deferential, inspiring trust; had the Bishop of Lagos himself, the Right Reverend Vining, not employed his services to settle the odd dispute here and there among his wayward flock? His personality suited the role – nothing flamboyant; his voice deferred naturally to the sullen mumbles of the elders. And afterwards, between kola nuts and a calabash of wine, there were produce tips to be extracted from him. What were government plans regarding cocoa, for instance? Would the price go up? Were companies buying up kernels? Dried peppers? How would the war affect the thirst for palm oil? On his part, Sotikare exuded official menace, the quiet, spectacled surrogate for the hovering presence of the white men's courts, baliffs, police, and even jailers. Least desired, even to Olisa's faction, was the threat of another expeditionary force, the tramp of alien soldiers, this time on Ìsarà soil, home, perhaps, after severe mauling from that man Hitler and eager to take out their humiliation on the innocent heads of the Afotamodi . . .

None of the elders present had forgotten the consequences of the stubborn pride of the Ijebu in the past. The old man who now sat passively listening, his cheeks collapsed into each other with loss of flesh and teeth, a veritable death mask, the Agunrin Odubona, had fought in nearly every battle and skirmish on the Ibadan–Lagos route through the latter decades of the nineteenth century. Beneath his shaven skull, gleaming with *shea*-butter, an active memory recalled the days when, as a young emissary from Ìsarà to the court of the Awujale in Ijebu-Ode, he had instigated the resolve that no missionary-educated youth should be allowed to return and settle on Ijebu soil. The Egba and other inland peoples were free to absorb them and ruin their customs and beliefs; they were at liberty to corrupt their children and desecrate their ancestral shrines with the manners of returnee slaves who wore European suits and ties, smoked cigarettes, and walked shamelessly in public with their wives, even holding hands. Such habits had to stop at the gateway in Ijebuland. His fingers, now turned into desiccated claws, still tingled with recollection of the numerous raids in which he had participated on that crucial route into the interior, controlled by the Ijebu. What terror had they not unleashed, aided by their ferocious allies, the Mahin!

The Egba had ruined everything. Their *ifole** had not gone far enough – every Christianised dwelling should have been gutted! Even if the Saro were their returnee brothers, freed on the high seas by the white men and replanted in that faraway place called Sierra Leone, they should simply have embraced them, loaded them with gifts, and sent them back. Did they not see right away that these sons had changed? They were no longer the same flesh and blood that was spirited away. They had become conceited, contemptuous of their past. They settled in that new place, mingled with the white people, and became successful. Good for them. But they should have stayed in their white settlements and sent money home, returned from time to time for reunions, even festivals, but not to settle! This was the plan adopted by the Ijebu, faced with the menace of pollution. That was the wisdom they adopted, and how right they had been proved . . .

'The rains of the past season cannot be sucked back into the sky, no matter how much farmland was eroded away. And anyway, do we also give back the harvest we have reaped in the meantime? We know the trouble that man Carter caused us . . .' Opeilu's voice fell harmlessly on his ears until the name Carter grated upon his hearing . . .

Kata-kata! Agunrin's skull-face permitted itself a small toothless grin, which Sotikare saw and misinterpreted, thinking that Opeilu's quiet speech was working in the right direction. No, Agunrin was merely remembering the day he finally came face to face with Nemesis – though he did not know it then – in the person of Carter. When that aggressive presence was announced, Agunrin turned round to his elders and said, 'Ah, here comes Kata-kata,' and the name had stuck from then on. Even the Awujale would say, deliberately, 'Ah, Mister Kata-kata – ah, sorry, Mr Carter,' and his audience chamber would erupt with laughter. Agunrin's face turned grim. Yes, Kata-kata had had the last laugh. His predecessor, Moloney, had proved easier to handle, although he was quite a cunning fellow. Was he not the one who sent one Denton to the Awujale with a bribe of a thousand pounds? Just sign here on the paper, his agents said, just sign here, we promise you no one will know about it. Mind you, nobody really got to the bottom of the truth. Did Awujale Tunwase really take that money? Certainly his chiefs rejected the presents which the

---

* A resistance campaign against colonial/missionary presence – literally: house-smashing.

435

Denton man tried to offer them in public, and that was what began the trouble. The emissary went back to the king of England, so they said, and claimed the Ijebu had insulted his king. Well, what of it? Had the man not insulted their own king by his conduct? Trying to bribe the paramount king of all Ijebu to sell out his people just to let in the white man and destroy their lives. Was that not the father and grandfather and great-great-grandfather of insults?

'*Eyin re bare eni . . . eyin r'ologbon eni . . . eni boje l'aiye wen.*'*

Yes, this young man made sense but where would these people stop? How many years now since Kata-kata brought war to Ijebu? Forty? Fifty? And was this Odemo they wanted to inflict on Ìsarà not their way of finishing off what they began forty years ago? Was it not enough that the missionaries now strutted through the proud land, their churches and schools everywhere, their products mincing on feet suffocating in thick socks and leather through their council halls? Was it not enough that they had to obey laws imposed on them by Kata-kata and his black servants? Must they now permit one of these godless ones to come and sit on the throne of Ìsarà?

'Akinsanya will abide by your wishes, the wishes of the people of Ìsarà. He knows the white man but he belongs to Ìsarà. He has sworn to preserve the ways of Ìsarà while carrying our voice to the highest councils of the land, and beyond the seas. . . . The Ibadan, Egba, the Ekiti, the Ijaiye or Oyo never defeated us in war. They will not now mock our defeat at our own hands.'

Yes, he had been one of the four Agunrin who took the peace offering to Kata-kata in Lagos. Four Ogboni went with them, three Pampa, and eleven Parakoyi. The man had demanded a powerful delegation to bring the humiliation of Ijebu to him and sign a treaty which declared the routes open to every Christian riffraff and company agent. Ten sheep they took, a small bag of *iyun*, but what was the result? It only boosted Carter's pride, and what a tongue-lashing he had given them! Insults. Abuse. And then, most daring of all, his soldiers had pointed guns at them and ordered them to put their thumbs on the paper. What was in it? They could not read it. And anyway they did not care. Their mission, which he, Agunrin Odubona, had agreed to, and only with the greatest reluctance, was to present their peace offering and assure Kata-kata that no one had wished to insult his king. But after the man's speech, had everything not simply

* You are our elders . . . you are the custodians of our wisdom . . . ruin must not come to Ìsarà in your lifetime.

scattered? Even the most appeasing of the Awujale's delegation swore that the man had gone too far, and not one of them would put their hands to the wretched paper.

'So you see, our fathers that you are, we urge that you accept the Resident's proposals. . . . Let all of Ìsarà gather together, every man, woman, and child behind the man of their choice.'

Yes, as Kata-kata wanted us to do. Throw open all our roads, the lagoons, the rivers, our ancestral pathways, to the desecration of aliens. Why not our bedrooms and our daughter's thighs? Yes, why not? A 'Lagosian' king sitting on Ìsarà's throne, just as those two so-called Ijebu from Lagos had been called in to do what we would not do. Well, they claimed to have Ijebu blood in them but in what nightmare of the Afotamodi was a name like Otumba Payne ever conceived? Or Jacob Williams? And were they not the two Lagos dwellers whom Kata-kata brought in to sign the paper which they, the emissaries of the Awujale, would not sign? And they had dared break the kola to celebrate the treachery. Abomination upon abomination! They, the mincing spawn of tainted Ijebu blood, had not only signed, for Ijebu, the paper that the emissaries would not touch, they also had taken the kola nut and broken it. For this white man who dared come to their own land and order them not to collect toll from Christian travellers and traders!

'No one is urging you to accept anyone as the new Odemo. We merely urge a peaceful way.'

Peace. Yes, they always say that. The missionaries brought peace. Their god was the prince of peace, they said. Yet their bishop from Ibadan, that Togiwe* – if only Ijebu-Ode had cut off his head! – Togiwe came and provoked them. Deliberately. Pity he had not tried it in Ìsarà! Right from the gates of Ijebu-Ode he began to preach. He insulted their worship, cursed their gods, damned their king, and predicted the end of the 'heathen' Ijebu. Yet they let him go. Well, maybe they were right. That preacher had been sent in as a troublemaker. He wanted the white man to say this time that not only his king but his god had been insulted. Then he could come in finally with his army. Well, that did happen in the end. So, they might as well have cut off his head and denied him the joy of their defeat. Peace! They told him that Togiwe kept dancing in the market-place, dancing on one spot like a man a snake has bitten, dancing before the gateway of Ijebu-Ode even as the crowd booed him, dancing with his book held high in his hand, waving it round and round like a flag before an

* Tugwell.

437

attack. Why are you dancing? the people asked him. Is the man insane? And he told them he was dancing on the spirits of their pagan forefathers, on the bones of our heathenish gods . . . screaming obscenities at the Ijebu-Ode people. But they only laughed at him and let him go. Yes, they let them go! They forgot one thing he preached. Yes, an Ìsarà trader coming home from Lagos had witnessed the scene and he rushed home to warn them. Christianised too and wearing trousers and tie like the others, but he had not fully lost his soul. He was no traitor, like the others. And he said Togiwe had pronounced a famous curse on them, conjuring in the name of one Newton and so betraying the secret of their future plans: 'The sword of steel goes before a sword of the spirit.' And the trader rushed home, more fearful, he confessed, than he had ever been in his life. And was it not he, Odubona, who had been sent to accompany the trader to the Awujale with the message: 'Did you hear what that Reverend Togiwe said? Well, a war that trumpets its advance does not kill even the lame. We are ready in Ìsarà. Send word to Ode, Ipara, Odogbolu, Isoyin . . . As for the Mahin, they need no urging. Ibadan should know that we have no animosity against them, but now is the time to choose. Either they expel the missionaries or they will get no more salt, and no more ammunition, either. And if they want our friendship, they should send Your Highness the heads of Togiwe and his companion Harding, the man of ill omen.' Yes, that was Ìsarà's message to their fellow Ijebu.

'Ìsarà has been fortunate. Our fathers, uncles, are still living, who fought in the last war, but it was fought away from our borders. We have never known the tramp of aliens on our soil. Agunrin Odubona, I bow my head to you, you are the veteran of veterans, *ogbologbo ajagun*; if there is anyone in this town who knows what it means fighting against the white man's soldiers . . .'

Yes, let such a man come forward and stand before me, the old man's aggressive cheekbones challenged, while his cheeks sucked in air like an antique pair of blacksmith's bellows. Kata-kata brought Hausa soldiers, he even sent for soldiers, they learned later, from the Gold Coast. They had all heard of the Ashanti, fierce, stubborn warriors; perhaps there were some of them among Kata-kata's army – the Ijebu did not care. They showed the invaders that there were warriors also in Ijebuland. The defeat was bitter, but then, it was not for want of resistance. The Egba had long since caved in. The Ibadan thought they had scores to settle – well, it would soon be their turn. As for the Ondo, whom they had also urged to carry out their own *ifole* – how sad that all these people proved so deaf, so blind to their fate. Even the Ijaw, with whom the Mahin had so much in common. They were river people like the Mahin; the Mahin carried out their trade with them over the same waters, they even shared some customs. Yet the Mahin reported that the Ijaw all but worshipped the white man and his ways. What was it that made some so different from the others? Had those Ijaw also been corrupted by Lagos and Saro returnees like Otumba Payne and all the others? People who actually put their hands to paper which their own fathers would not touch? Was this Akinsanya not part of that breed? A king should be like a huge *iroko*, casting a protective shade over all his subjects. Who ever heard of such a tree being nourished on foreign soil, then transplanted home on the eve of coronation? Was this how the white men chose their kings?

'. . . that is all we urge on you, with all deference due to you as our father. We have not come to preach the virtues of one man against the other. Let the people choose their own king. It is the new way of doing things, and the government in Lagos has given this plan its blessing. So has the Awujale . . .'

Th Agunrin's head jerked up violently, and sounds issued from his throat. The effect on the hearers was startling, like the scratch of grinding stones on which coarse sand has been sprinkled.

'Aaa-wu-ja-le!'

The Olisa ceased abruptly to affect boredom. His ears prickled and the hairs rose on his skin. Ten years at least, that voice had not been heard. He turned in his seat, his gaze transfixed by this figure, whose voice even appeared to command the timbre of an ancestral mask.

Again Agunrin spoke: 'Aaa-wu-ja-le!'

Ogunba it was who broke through the paralysis that had taken hold of the chamber. In a shaken and uncertain voice he said, 'It is so, Agunrin. I met the Awujale myself. And the Akarigbo has summoned Remo Council and their decision has been taken. What Olisa has done was fully condemned, and Erinle was fined twenty-five pounds. He has also been forbidden to parade himself in the king's regalia.'

But the ancient warrior did not appear to have heard. His eyes seemed to be on the verge of bursting out of their sockets, and as if impelled by a force greater than could possibly emanate from his wiry yet weakened frame, he spat out the name of his paramount king: 'Aaa-wujale Tunwase!'

Mystified, even alarmed, glances flew across the room. Olisa spoke slowly. 'Baba, Tunwase is long dead. This is a new Awujale on the throne of Ijebu-Ode.'

Apprehensive eyes remained trained on the ancient warrior as he thrust forward his trunk, like a snake about to strike, or a bird taking off from a leafless tree branch at an acute angle, to spike an insect on the wing. They watched him change course abruptly, reach for his *ogboni* staff propped against the wall beside him. He pulled himself up slowly, his hand hovering over the bronze *edan* which formed its headpiece. His fingers twitched convulsively as they grasped it, stopped there some moments, then slid slowly down the iron stem while his body sank, ever so slowly, into his earlier seated posture.

'*O ti fo n'oju!*'*

The *ogboni* staff came to rest on his right shoulder. His hand continued its slide downwards until it was stopped at the knee, still clutching the stem. His head fell towards his shoulder, coming to a gentle rest against the staff. His heart then ceased to beat.

Jagun came out of *osugbo* some moments later, summoned by violent knocking on the outer gate. He took one look at the dishevelled messenger, who sought to regain his breath and transmit the weighty news he had brought from Olisa's house. Jagun raised his hand to silence the messenger.

'I know. Take the news to the other chiefs.'

The messenger saluted him and ran off. Jagun adjusted his shawl, raised a grim face to the sky, and walked homewards. It had been a long night, spent in solitude in the house of divination. His expression was that of a man who regretted a task accomplished, but knew that it was all for the public good.

Wemuja stood regally before the gates of Node's compound in the very early hours of dawn and, from his vantage, surveyed the city of Ìsarà still folded in a silence of sleep. Countless times he had stood thus, but today, even the barely visible outlines of the cottages wore, it seemed, a special garb. A sheen from some of the newly installed corrugated iron sheets provided the only illumination, creating false contours that made the village curl in upon itself, like a fat caterpillar, waiting to be nudged awake by his giant feet. At such moments, the only being lawfully awake in the whole of Ìsarà – he did not count the night guards – waiting for his apprentice, Alanko, to complete the ritual washing of the Commer, when he would then take over command of the monster and ride out of the dormant domain, Wemuja felt that he was the true king of Ìsarà. He stuck

---

* It is smashed beyond redeeming.

his unlit pipe between his teeth, nodded, and announced to the dewy air: 'This life, it is good.'

He took in huge, luxurious gulps of the fresh air and turned towards the shack of Dekola, the blacksmith. The smith was not an early riser, but his apprentice would be crouched by now against the forge, blowing embers awake from a cloak of cinders. Wemuja's route to the stream where the Commer took its morning wash lay past the forge. Since he discovered this, he made a ritual of stopping by the forge, picking up an ember with the heavy pair of tongs, and lighting the half of a Bicycle cigarette which he had saved from his last smoke the night before. Its usual storage was behind his right ear, even when asleep. The apprentice had learned to expect him, and Wemuja always found the door unlatched. The lorry driver's exotic appearance more than made the boy's day. Every visit, he picked up the tongs and held out the glowing charcoal to his visitor's cigarette stump, first greeting him with a quick semi-prostration. Today, however, the apprentice was stumped; never before had he seen Wemuja with a pipe this early in the morning. Wemuja relieved him of the tongs, dropped the proffered coal, and fished in the furnace for a more suitable lump for his pipe. Squinting over the bowl to drink in the admiration of his sole observer, he drew in air and soon the pipe was smoking smoothly. He handed back the tongs and then astonished the boy further by fishing in his pockets for two *onini*, which he handed over to his server. Patting him on the head, he said, 'For *saara*. On behalf of the king to come.'

Until his figure was swallowed up in the dark the boy stood at the door, staring at his hero turned philanthropist. Wemuja strolled downhill, seemingly oblivious of the new raptures he had engendered in the soul of a burgeoning lorry driver. When he got to the stream he received Alanko's greeting with studied condescension, gestured that he open the bonnet for inspection. He checked the radiator, oil, and battery level with more than his usual gravity, wiped his fingers on the grease-cloth offered by his assistant, and walked round the vehicle, kicking the tyres to test their pressure. Satisfied, he climbed into the driver's seat, checked the gear to ensure that it was disengaged, then nodded to Alanko, who had taken up his position at the front. At the fourth crank, the engine roared to life. Wemuja depressed the throttle, let the engine roar for about a minute, eased it off gently, and listened intently. His eyes were shut in concentration as his body sensed the tiniest vibrations of the vehicle. Alanko had meanwhile drawn out the crank, rushed to the side to await the next order, which would normally be to remove the wooden blocks from beneath the rear wheels. To his surprise, however, Wemuja merely gave the engine one final roar and turned off the ignition. He then took off his scoutmaster's hat from its hook behind the driver's seat, adjusted it over his eyes, and settled back into his seat as if he meant to indulge in a little more slumber.

Alanko waited some moments, wondering what to do. Finally he asked: 'Oga, we no go start?'

Wemuja removed his clay pipe from his mouth, tipped his hat fractionally up in his practised Rod Cameron manner, and said, 'Today we are not carry timber.'

'A-ah. You mean we no dey go anywhere at all?'

Wemuja looked down at him as if at a retarded child. 'Who say we no dey go somewhere? You no see me fill de tank yesterday?'

Alanko scratched at the arid tufts on his head. 'But just now you say . . . all right, if we no carry timber, wetin we go carry?'

'His'ry,' Wemuja replied. The tone was the nearest he could muster to match Opeilu's, whom he had overheard the previous day. 'We dey go carry his'ry.'

And with that he pushed the hat fully over his eyes, a gesture which Alanko normally associated with those afternoons when Wemuja doused his energy long enough to permit himself a brief siesta.

Alanko gave up, returned the crank to its hole in the engine to await whatever moment was appropriate for setting off to carry history. Before he could follow his master's example, however, and snatch a few moments' rest, a pair of headlamps swung round towards them from the direction of Losi, picking out the harsh grains and laterite veins of the hillsides before settling into the farmed flat stretch on the borders of the stream. Its lights sailed over browned strips of plantain leaves, lumpy green kola-nut pods, grazed the low-lying cocoa plantation, and raised new speculative thoughts at the sight of those lustrous pods, swollen to twice their normal size in the artificial light. The contrast between this outlying belt around Ìsarà and the built-up higher ground was never more insistent than at dawn when a swathe of ground mist rose, a suspended girdle, neatly dividing the two. Tangled among parasites, the euphonious *asofeiyeje** merely affirmed the sheer extravagance of the fertile basin, for it seemed that only a soil which was truly generous, even prodigal, could name such a fruit for birds alone. It was the cocoa pods however which set Efuape's brain at work all over again, until he rebuked himself, wondering how he could even think of business at such a time. A day like this, he counselled himself, should be

* Fruit for the birds' delight.

reserved for giving thanks to God and praying for his support in the momentous undertaking. Row after row of the gold-flaunting dwarf trees leapt in and out of the headlamps and not once again did Efuape permit himself to dwell on the tonnage rate of cocoa on the world market. When he pulled up beside Wemuja, however, his wayward mind recalled that the timber man had once remarked on the rich texture in the higher soil of Ìsarà, similar to that of his village in Edo. And there, a small-time chef had become a virtual millionaire from his red-brick factory . . . well, later, muttered Sipe, son of Efuape.

Wemuja whipped off his hat as the car pulled up behind the Commer and gave his best scoutmaster salute.

'All set, are you?'

'Good morning, Mr Sipe. We all standing by.'

'Good.' Sipe came out of the Morris holding a torch. He climbed onto the back of the lorry, directing the light at the platform. 'You are sure it will be steady on this thing?'

'We are going to nail it down well, Mr Sipe. And then we use ropes which hold down even timber.'

'Of course,' Sipe conceded, feeling more reassured with that information. He was helped down by the two men and he stood thoughtfully for some moments, trying to make his mind up about their next movements.

'All right,' he decided, finally. 'You go ahead to Sagamu. I still have to call at Odogbolu. See that you supervise the carpenter yourself. Because it is not even morning, don't you imagine that he won't be drunk.'

Wemuja laughed. 'Trust me, Mr Sipe. I am not bad carpenter myself. If necessary I take hammer and nail and do the job.'

'As soon as I finish in Odogbolu, I'll join you. Then we proceed to Lagos together.'

'All right, sir. Safe journey.'

'You too, drive most carefully. We have more than enough time.'

Wemuja grinned. 'I know what today is, Mr Sipe. I just tell Alanko myself, I said, we are going to carry his'ry.'

Efuape's tone was a teasing rebuke. 'We-mu-ja! I thought you were supposed to be a man who could keep secrets.'

'Me, Mr Efuape, do you doubt me? Ask him yourself if he know anything. He was asking questions, but even though he is my assistant, do I tell him anything? I just say to him, we are going to carry his'ry full stop, so shurrup and don't worry me. That's him standing there, ask him if you don't believe me.'

Efuape laughed and slapped him on the shoulder. 'All right, all right, I

443

was just teasing you. Not that it would have mattered. After all, you are both heading out of Ìsarà.'

'You mean he can tell me now, sir?' Alanko chipped in.

'If he wishes. He is your master, after all.'

Efuape drove off, hoping to find Onayemi.

If anyone had told him twelve hours earlier that he would divert his journey through Odogbolu at an unholy predawn hour, Sipe would have retorted that there was no more time for any diversionary antics. True, the main tasks had been accomplished, but there still were possible slips, as Opeilu continued to caution them, 'twixt the lid and the cup,' which brought Soditan on the offensive as usual, insisting the word was 'lip,' not 'lid' – until they were both persuaded to leave the argument to the next dictionary that could settle the dispute. Both made sense, Efuape arbitrated, but of course, 'a saying is a saying and some are born incurable pedants.'

'Let us go over the arrangements once more,' Opeilu pleaded. 'No slips, no regrets – and that is original! We are agreed there are not too many crayfish sellers, so their group should merge with others in the dried or smoked fish line, be it *apasun, ebolo, panla* etc., etc. – let them form one group. The other change is the dyers' guild. They will now join the procession after it has passed the Koranic school. Everybody got that? Regarding the hunters, they have now been supplied. They have sufficient gunpowder to restart the trade war our Odubona lost to the missionaries last century. . . .'

Soon Sipe was alone in the fast timber forests through which the rudimentary road had been driven – by the enterprising Ijebu, he reminded himself with satisfaction. The snag over the Ibadan road still rankled in his breast, but was that not one of the hopes he had set on Akinsanya's ascension? Yes, a strong man who would stand up to the Alake, never mind that the Alake was far higher in royal ranking. Saaki was like Daodu, he would battle for any rights he believed in. No browbeating this trade unionist by anyone, black king or white colonial servant. Over the Morris's noisy interior, he chuckled to himself – that Yode, he concluded all over again, he surely was a close one. Sly even. Imagine concealing from everyone all this while that he too had consulted the Spirit of Layeni – or some relation of that shade, never mind how distant.

'But I did not conceal it,' Soditan had protested. 'You never asked me. It simply never came up.'

The death of Agunrin intrigued them. Yet what should be strange about

444

the death of an old man, reputed to be over a hundred? True, there was the small detail of his voice, which, everyone recalled, had dwindled progressively into a hoarse, uneasy whisper that sometimes appeared to have journeyed from the depths of a densely forested gorge, then given up altogether. That was at least ten, maybe twelve, years ago. Then the eerie moment when the old man found his voice – or was it his? No one remembered any longer how the warrior's voice had sounded either in his prime or in advanced age. But even the man of Lagos, Sotikare, had admitted that it made the hairs on his arms stand on end. As for Opeilu, his stomach ulcer ran riot and had to be sedated with six wraps of *eko* taken with *ekuru* and palm oil stew from which all trace of pepper had been excluded.

Agunrin Odubona's death lured them all out of the straightforward rules of scheming and intrigues and, for Sipe especially, came a reawakened interest in the project he had merely suspended. In turmoil after the warrior's death, the House of Rokodo had no more will to resist plans for a peaceful show of strength – and Ogunba had given full credit to the powers of Jagun.

'He had a hand in it. He removed that silent obstacle.'

Dinner the last night at Sipe's house marked the end of a week-long intensity of furtive motions and rehearsals. Now there was nothing to do but await daybreak and unfold their unabashedly emotion-harvesting designs. From *osugbo*, the nightly throb of heavy drums reminded them that the rites for Odubona's funeral were not yet over; conversation was easily dominated by his death, the first such experience for the three emissaries – to witness the passage of a soul. With the exception of Opeilu, the others were also mortality virgins, but more contentious was the actual manner of Odubona's exit, given the grim pronouncement of Jagun when he withdrew into seclusion.

'I would have been better persuaded,' Sotikare scoffed, 'if your Jagun had exerted this so-called power on Olisa. That old man already had both feet in his grave.'

'I don't know,' Soditan countered. 'It's only common sense to strike at the weakest point in an enemy's defences. Olisa was tougher material. Maybe Jagun needed a whole month to – call him home.'

'Stop playing the devil's advocate,' Sotikare said irritably. 'Do you realise what you're all saying? You are accusing an innocent man of murder.'

'No-o-o. Conspiracy with Nature perhaps . . . an acceleration of her tempo . . .'

'How? How? Tell me how. By poison? Did he even move near him? No. Your supposed murderer locks himself away in seclusion and – yes, does what? What exactly does he do?'

'We don't know. No one here says he does.'

'Ha! Yet you persist in suggesting that Jagun did it!'

'May have done it,' Efuape corrected him.

'No.' Ogunba shook his head stubbornly. 'I believe he did it.'

'Then you must be able to say how he did it.'

'There are more mysteries in this world, Horatio . . .' Efuape intoned.

'Oh, go away!'

'. . . than are dreamt of in your legalisms.'

Sotikare shook his head in despair. 'If only Reverend Beeston knew how much he wasted time.'

'Why do you say that? Didn't his own Shakespeare also believe in ghosts and charms, etcetera?'

'You're right.' Soditan nodded. 'So, Duncan's castle or Odogbolu shrine, what's the difference?'

Sipe pricked up his ears. 'Odogbolu? What do you know of Odogbolu?' His voice was tinged with suspicion, as if Soditan's remarks had been a subtle dart in his direction.

'What shouldn't one know of Odogbolu? Where else in Nigeria would you find spirits which actually *read* English?'

'Oh, come on . . . !' Sotikare began.

'This is not hearsay. I can personally testify to it.'

'Where? When? Do you seriously mean . . . ? How did you . . . ?'

Soditan raised his hand. 'One at a time, one at a time. It was – let me see – yes, some four or five years ago. With Efunsewa, before he went overseas. He asked me to accompany him.'

'So what happened? Go on, go on, what happened?' Efuape was by now on the edge of his seat. Soditan laughed.

'Hey, look at Sipe! Why are you so excited?'

'Never mind Sipe. Just tell me what happened!'

'It was simple really. Efunsewa wanted to know how he would fare in the U.K. What to do and what not to do, what to take . . . the usual stuff. The medium had instructed him to write everything down on a piece of paper. So, we entered the shrine. The medium – he remained invisible throughout – told him to put the paper under a piece of stone. He did. Well, I know you won't believe this, but the voice – it came from behind those walls – answered all his questions one by one. In the very order in

446

which they were asked. He read out the questions – not exactly read but he summarized them pretty well, and replied to them.'

Sotikare snorted.

Ogunba tweaked his nose at him. 'It's true. I was present the second time.'

Opeilu was alarmed. 'You mean you risked it a second time? Oh. Maybe you recited Psalm –'

'What risk? It was all straightforward. The first time it was a bit frightening, I must admit. The atmosphere of the place . . . it was intimidating. But I had resolved to go back. In fact I made the appointment before we left – you have to, you know. Some periods are simply not appropriate. I prepared my own list of questions.'

Opeilu's eyes twinkled. 'Was he right about which of them you would marry?'

The dinner table broke out in laughter. 'Maybe Morola had already nailed him at the time,' Sotikare suggested.

'Or how many he would end up marrying.' Sipe began to tick off an imaginary list. '*Obiren alaran*. Indirect Speech . . .'

'Hm! Ola-rumpus!' Opeilu chuckled long and loud.

'Then the floral codes – Bougainvillaea . . .'

'A-ah, that was a thorny affair . . .'

'Bachelor's button. Cana Lily . . .'

In his best baritone, Sotikare began to sing, 'Behold, the lilies of the field . . .'

Soditan's lips went prim and he folded his hands across his chest. 'Right. Finish off the story yourselves.'

They cajoled him. He relented. 'Only, don't let me have any more of this pot calling the kettle black. You, Sipe, especially. *Oo l' enu oro.*'*

Sipe threw up his hands. 'Why pick on me?'

'Just you shut up. Now where was I?'

'You went back with Ogunba.'

'Right. And if you really want to know, I asked the obvious questions any young man would ask. Would I be successful in life? Would I go to the U.K. or not? Should I invest my money in stocks and shares or start up a business of my own?'

'Hypothek and Creditbank,' Efuape grumbled aloud. 'Sabotage by the ghost of Roger Casement, R.I.P.'

Soditan continued, as if he had not missed a beat. 'And of course,

* You haven't the mouth to comment.

teaching – do I stick to teaching? Is Sipe a reliable friend or is he the devil in disguise?'

'I knew it. I knew that was coming . . .'

'I haven't given the answers yet,' Soditan protested.

'I don't want to hear. No, I don't want your made-up answer.'

'Ogunba can back me up.'

'Sure he will. Which party would the housefly endorse if not the one with the sores?'

'Thank you, Mephistopheles. Now I shall tell you all what Yode truly asked,' Ogunba said. 'Seriously. Are you ready for it?'

Ogunba's demeanour arrested their attention. He was not joking. In any case, Ogunba rarely told stories. He would laugh at them but he seemed incapable of actually inventing a story for laughs. So they watched him cautiously. Whatever it was he tried to recall struck them as a long-hidden puzzle, teased out by this recent occurrence which, like the other, he could not explain.

'It is true,' he said at last. 'Yode's first question was: Would he be successful in life.' His frown deepened further. 'And you know what the medium replied, it was very strange. He said, Find Asabula.'

There was silence, then Sotikare spoke. 'Asabula. But isn't that Yode's correspondent – no, the name of his town?'

'Minus the *t*, yes,' Opeilu observed.

'Yes.' Ogunba nodded. 'I heard it distinctly. Asabula, not Ashtabula.'

'A half-literate spirit after all,' Sotikare mocked.

Efuape remained undeterred; he tried to work out a meaning. 'Axabula . . . asabula . . .' He shook his head. 'So much easier work making something out of those Italian names.' He tried again. 'Asabula . . . Sakabula . . . abula . . . are you sure you got the intonation exactly right?'

'Allowing fully for the ghostly echoes . . . definitely Asabula.'

'So it could not mean "the hawk has facial marks"?'

Soditan smiled. 'We thought of that.'

'We thought of every possible twist. Nothing made sense.'

'Why should it?' demanded the court clerk. 'Oracles speak in parables, don't they? Maybe it has no more meaning than "Abracadabra." Have you thought of that? "Abracadabra" in ancient Odogbolu dialect, now fallen into disuse.' And his stomach heaved with chuckles.

Opeilu had remained thoughtful. 'It could be mind-reading, you know. There are some genuine mind-readers among our herbalists and *babalawo*. That unseen medium was probably all-seeing. He watched and studied you from the moment you entered, reading your minds.'

448

'But that's the point,' Ogunba explained. 'We returned to Abeokuta the same day, trying to puzzle out the word all through the journey. We were so exhausted, so we parted company at the gate – I wanted to go to bed right away. I had hardly pulled off my shirt when Yode came running up to my quarters, screaming my name. He was waving a letter in his hand, an overseas letter.'

'No, don't tell me,' Sipe began.

Yode nodded. 'That is God's truth. I saw the mail on my table as soon as I stood in my doorway. Lying on the top was this overseas letter, the very first from Wade Cudeback. It was the first time I had ever heard of Ashtabula. So you see, that name did not yet exist in my mind. It was not there for the medium to read.'

An unusual sound had begun earlier outside, a low rumble that rose and diminished in intensity, a purr from a feline throat, not menacing at first, almost soothing in fact. Opeilu was the first to hear it, and he raised his hand for silence. It drew nearer and nearer, seeming to retreat, then swelling in volume until it took on the semblance of a warning of thunder, only steadier, smoother, carefully controlled. They looked towards the door, then at one another. The earlier possibility, that this could be an unusual motor engine, had been dismissed. Each one had a feeling that he had heard it before, that it signified something, but the memory had become faint, tenuous. As the now powerful roar transferred, it seemed, from the outside dark and encroached on the lit interior space they occupied, booming against the rafters and circling their heads, its meaning broke through the distance of childhood and, one after another, sheepish grins appeared on their faces.

'Have we really become such total expatriates?' Sipe lamented.

'*Oro*. Imagine that! I no longer recognise the voice of *oro*.'

'Well, how often did we hear it, even in those early days?' Sotikare paused, troubled. 'But why . . .'

'Odubona's death, of course. The grand climax, I suppose.'

'Which may last all night,' Sotikare grumbled, rising. 'Me, I am off to bed.'

'Keep your head down,' Soditan advised. 'Don't let *oro* snatch it off into the night.'

'You worry about yourselves,' Sotikare shot back.

'Yode is right,' Sipe agreed. 'We'd better see you home. *Oro*'s wind may sweep you into the darkest void from where there is no return. We will wake up in the morning and look in vain for our court registrar. Vanished. Gone with the wind.'

'Is it me you are trying to scare?'

'No, no,' Soditan reassured him, taking his hand, while Efuape seized the other. 'In fact, what we shall do is take you right to Igbo'ro and leave you there. When *oro* returns at dawn and finds a stranger at his very doorstep . . .'

'I said I was going home. I prefer my own bed.'

'*O ya*. Let's carry him . . .'

They hooked their arms firmly under his armpits, and hoisted him over the doorstep and into the night. Their laughter overwhelmed the now-retreating noise of the bull-roarer. Sipe stood on the doorstep, shouted advice to the struggling Sotikare. 'When *oro* tries to seize you for breakfast, just send a *habeas corpus* to Lagos on its wind. . . .'

In the contrasting silence which enveloped the house after their departure, even Sipe conceded a faint unease. He ensured that his windows were shut and his door firmly bolted. He hesitated as his hand reached for the kerosene lantern, then laughed at himslf. Before turning down the wick, however, his eyes went to the calendar and he was startled to recall what day of the month it was. Under the pressure of events he had forgotten all about the 'consultation.' Only two more days, and then the appropriate opening would be gone.

There was still time, fortunately. A detour through Odogbolu, see Onayemi and authorise him to reopen negotiations with the Spirit of Layeni. Enough time to team up with Wemuja in Sagamu, carry out his mission in Lagos, and Onayemi would then meet him at the gates of Ìsarà with the answer to the new question which so stubbornly occupied his mind. Sipe smoothed out a notepad and unscrewed his catalogue-order fountain pen. A smile of satisfaction (and virtuousness) wreathed his face as he tried to imagine the sigh that would be wrung from his erstwhile trading partner when he unfolded the notepaper and found, instead of the agreed theme of a business shopping-list, a single question which read:

'Will S.A. Akinsanya, popularly known as Saaki to his friends, the trade unionist currently living in Denton Street, Ebute Meta, will this Akinsanya be Odemo of Ìsarà?'

He read it over more than half a dozen times. He was about to put it away, intending to give it a very last lookover before setting out early dawn, when a sudden fear struck him and he again unsheathed his pen. Before 'Odemo' he now inserted the words 'the next,' smiling with self-satisfaction at his narrow escape. He, Sipe son of Efuape, was not the man to permit ambiguity to any spirit of Odogbolu, literate or illiterate, and in whatever language. And, just for good measure, he underlined 'the next.'

That Pa Josiah, that hard-laterite embodiment of the stubborn core of Ìsarà, should panic, even for a moment before his breakfast, only affirmed what even children sensed as they rose from their sleeping-mats: a tension in the very air of Ìsarà, a complication of their normal Christmas and New Year treats and larks, and the open faces of the grown-ups. Iya Ajike, Node's wife, had risen early and discovered that Wemuja was missing. Then she called out to Alanko and found he was also gone. There had been no plans for transporting timber, and even if there had been, such plans would have been cancelled on a unique day. So she rushed to Mariam, and both invaded Josiah as he cleaned his teeth on the chewing-stick. For Mariam, it was a welcome excuse to intrude on Josiah. She had tried and failed to see him for over a week, and an urgent matter weighed on her mind.

'Wemuja?' Fear, anger . . . it was impossible! And yet that was where his thoughts leaped instinctively; he did not even have to think about it. Wemuja was the only stranger in town. Agunrin was dead and his funeral rites approached their conclusion. *Oro* had wailed its famished circuit through the night, sending shivers through women and making children pull coverlets tighter round their heads. Josiah had never been part of *oro* cult but that did not mean he did not know where *oro* fed, and on what. . . .

And then Josiah cursed himself for a fool and told the women to go home. There was nothing to worry about. He had recalled all the to-ings and fro-ings and conspiratorial sessions between his son and Efuape, and, of course, Wemuja. He knew that it all had to do with bringing Akinsanya to Ìsarà but he did not bother himself with their plans. Wemuja's dawn disappearance obviously had something to do with their furtive schemes; what a state he must be in to think that anyone would dare touch Wemuja! Or even that *ekan* weed he called his apprentice. His mood improved almost immediately; he shook his head and took some snuff to restore his nerves.

Mariam lingered after the departure of Iya Ajike. 'I think you should call on Iya Agba. I know you have been busy with affairs of the town but I saw her yesterday. She did not seem to know me. I think she is fading.'

'Tonight. I shall see her tonight.'

'Don't leave it till too late. . . .'

'I said tonight, after the meeting. Do you think I have not had enough to do without going to watch her funeral antics?'

451

'I am going to cook her food now. I shall tell her you will be along later. Pray she may recognise you when you get there.'

Through a bright red mist, that speciality which Ìsarà shared with few other towns or villages in the South, the late *akuro* farmers began to drift homewards from their farmsteads, anxious to arrive early to take their places where their loyalties lay. Rumour was their travelling companion, rumour welcomed them into town. Under the curfew imposed by *oro* – was anyone still foolish enough to think that Agunrin's death was natural? – a faction had sneaked into Ìsarà charms-potent *igun* men from Badagry. Under cover of the noise of the bull-roarer, the drums of *gelede* had sounded and its masks beamed a discriminating sorcery through the critical roads and passageways of Ìsarà. When the District Officer stepped on Ìsarà soil, he would find that he was defenceless against the alien spell. He would perform just what the faction demanded of him. He would see three but would count three hundred, see a tree and attempt to enter it as he would his own house. Seasoned as Ìsarà was in her own ways with the forces of rain and wind, of earth and sky, and the secret words that bound them together, the *igun* were in an otherworld class by themselves; nothing could stand against their invocations. And the secret departure of Efuape's two-vehicle motorcade at such an unearthly hour had also been observed. So the Olisa faction warned their supporters to be alert. It only confirmed what had long been suspected, that Jagun would import a private army to drive Erinle from Ìsarà. When the District Officer arrived, he would find only one candidate and his supporters. The alien stalwarts keeping guard within Agunrin compound now paraded their own street openly, diverting all human traffic to other routes – no hostile shadow was to fall on the walls of the main figures of the contest. Even the children's tin-can masquerades vanished from the streets, but their glad rags, it seemed, had been transferred to treetops. For there they were, high among the branches of Ìsarà's scattered baobab trees, leafless, strips of clothing where *oro* had perched at night. And the women did not look up at them, while the older children pointed them out to the younger ones and narrated dire tales of their efficacy, skirting the trees or turning back to find another route.

The field of contest, the open grounds in front of the Native Administration court, were prepared early by prisoners brought in a station wagon from Sagamu. They came with hard-back chairs and a baize-covered table, with soft-cushioned armchairs and an awning where the District Officer's party would sit and listen to both parties. They were supervised by a foreman from the Public Works Department under the watchful eye of their prison guards. The guards' were not the only eyes that watched.

Olisa's clutch of *onisegun*, his medicine guards, watched from one side, silently muttering incantations, gesturing towards treetops and rooftops, in the direction of the moist valley and even at their feet. From time to time they made motions of spitting in the wind in all directions of the compass. Jagun contented himself with strolling vaguely past the field from time to time, putting on an unconvincing show of minding any business except the present. Only the most watchful eye could see a movement of his lips when he drew parallel with the dais, but all could see that he took off his shawl from the left shoulder, let it drag on the ground for a few steps before slapping it back into place. His gestures with the fly whisk went beyond merely brushing off troublesome flies, but no one could really accuse him of any sinister devices.

The sun rose higher in the sky. The Native Administration police with blue-dyed baggy shorts, red cummerbunds, and brown fez caps had begun to take up positions when a cloud of dust announced the approach of yet another vehicle and derailed all the self-conscious, guarded motions of the populace and their division into clans. Even the motley guards momentarily lost their alertness. Never before had a three-legged monster appeared on the streets of Ìsarà. The motorcycle half was ridden by one of their own people, but the low-slung pod which shuddered on elastic springs contained a white man in safari suit, complete with pith helmet. The combination came to a stop by the dais, and the policeman dismounted. Olisa's medicine guard retreated, moving backwards slowly at first, then turned homewards in a precipitate rush to spread the news. Olisa, in council with Erinle, nodded grimly. So the news was true after all. Moments later another emissary arrived with a report that removed any lingering doubt. The policeman had been overheard; he had asked for directions to the head teacher's home. Olisa turned to his *onisegun* and told them to prepare charms to deflect the now inevitable bullets; the contraption was undoubtedly the advance guard of reinforcements which Sipe Efuape had sneaked off at dawn to obtain.

Josiah's scouts were even swifter. When they told him a policeman and a white man had asked the way to his home, he dragged out his son and, ignoring his protests, marched him off to his mother's house to hide. 'At least wait here until we find out who they are. You forget Erinle has been staying in Abeokuta; he could have plotted something against you there. Why should a white man come looking for you today of all days?'

It did not make sense, yet is was possible. 'By the way, watch out for anything strange in Iya's behaviour. Your mother was talking some nonsense about her not recognising people anymore.'

Akinyode could only insist that Ogunba be informed at once, and resigned himself to spending a few hours under his grandmother's roof. He found her asleep and tiptoed past her mat, praying fervently that she would not put on her funeral performance for him when she awoke and found him tamely seated there.

When Josiah returned to his house, the motorcycle and sidecar were parked by the door, surrounded by milling children and a few grown-ups. The policeman kept them at a respectful distance.

'Your visitor is inside,' a neighbour informed him.

'Whose visitor?' he snapped. 'The one your grandfather sent me?'

But first he took the precaution of peeping through his own window. There, seated in his favourite chair, looking totally at ease as if he had lived there a hundred years, was a man so pale, even to hair, including the hair on his skin, that he seemed to have been moulded from cotton fluff. A few freckles on his forearms were the sole exception. Yet he looked sturdy, was probably of his own height. He sweated abnormally, constantly mopped his face and the back of his neck. Josiah would have assessed him harmless but for one curious fact. The stranger had brought a notebook with him and there he was, making notes. It was this that Josiah found alarming. The man inspected the interior of his home with unnatural intensity and, as any feature struck him, put down something in the book. It confirmed Josiah's worst fears and he turned and fled, muttering to himself as he heard the amazed cries of the excited crowd:

'Take him home since you are so fond of uninvited guests.'

Now he had to find Jagun wherever he was.

Yode waited but no one came. An hour passed, then two. He had not even brought his pocket watch. He was grateful for one thing, however; although his grandmother had stirred once and even muttered in her sleep, she did not wake up. Perhaps he would be spared her show altogether. He moved stealthily around the cottage, hoping to find even a neglected Bible with which to occupy his time. There was nothing. He stood by the window, looking at the sky. The source of drumming that broke the silence was easy enough to identify – it came from the direction of Ago Aro, from where Erinle would emerge with his supporters, chant and dance towards the field, exuding confidence and hopefully attracting waverers to his side. The teacher felt a twinge of pity for Erinle, so confident was he in the outcome of that afternoon's gathering. Had the regent himself not committed the unspeakable folly of writing to Akinsanya and conceding that he, Saaki, enjoyed the greater support? Yet he wanted him to step down for Erinle 'in the interest of Ìsarà.' For Olisa had sought to remind Saaki that Ìsarà was not Abeokuta, it was not Lagos, it was not even Ondo. Ìsarà had always gone her own way, protected her own ways. What Ìsarà needed was a king steeped in its oldest traditions, not one who hobnobbed with city operators and alienated civil servants and fired angry letters at the white men. Ìsarà simply wished to be left alone. Wily Saaki . . . he had promptly dispatched a copy of the letter to the Resident.

In the isolation of the cottage, Ìsarà and its frantic manipulations of the past few days seemed suddenly remote. Indeed, before he had spent the first hour, Akinyode found himself sinking into the illusion that this was an unseasonal visit after all. Nothing was happening, or else nothing was happening here, it was all – elsewhere, it was another time. He was again alone in Ìsarà out of season, where nothing disturbed his peace beyond the munch of grass tufts between the gums of indolent sheep and goats, transfixed in wall corners by solid shafts of heat.

With a twinge of guilt, his mind went back to his other home, to Morola and the children. How soon did the midwife predict the expected child? Well, at least the illness was over. She would miss this Ìsarà New Year, but then, it really had not been much of a New Year. The next would be different, that would really be a double celebration if all went well today – which it must. It had to. Ìsarà needed Saaki. It was no generation thing. After all, even Jagun, indeed Apena, Ladega – a number of Olisa's fellow chiefs were, if anything, more fanatical on the choice. And his popularity was not in question . . . especially with women, Yode added, wondering why no one had remembered that but chose instead to saddle him with that reputation. No matter. It meant also that kingship would suit him – at least, that aspect of the palace image. For the rest, the real challenges, well, the ex-Ilés had accompanied him this far, they would remain with him the rest of the way, keep him on his toes. Abeokuta was too far ahead in every way. He faced the truth squarely – Ìsarà was still backward. What the ex-Ilés needed was a focus for all their schemes, someone with a real vision – well, at least the drive, the experience of organising. Between them they would provide the vision. . . .

Akinyode turned round at a new sound. His grandmother had sat up on the mat. He could not explain it, but at that moment he was seized with a terrible premonition and he leapt in her direction, kneeling down beside her in the same motion. Almost at once she tilted slowly sideways. He caught the bundle of twigs that her body had become and let it down gently, straightening her limbs and then closing her eyes.

For a long time he knelt there, staring at the form turned lifeless before his eyes. Then he pulled the coverlet over her body, and covered up her face.

Akinyode rose, let his eyes journey round the room. It had always seemed so small, so sparse, and now it was truly empty. He tried to gauge his feelings and found only a simple sadness, no lacerating anguish, only a sense of a freshly untenanted space in his concerns and thoughts of that home which was Ìsarà. He wondered how it would affect his father, but he knew that he would never reveal the extent of his bereavement, except perhaps to his friend Jagun.

Over the heated air now came unmistakable sounds of *sekere*, pierced by bugle notes. Again, Erinle's. They all knew he had brought a royal bugler from Abeokuta, as if that would make up for his loss of the usurped regalia, or the paucity of heads he would muster to his side. But what could be the nature of events which brought a policeman and a European to seek him out? Was his father right? Something cooked up with intriguers from Aké? Was the Alake taking sides? Or was it some powerful Olisa supporters from Lagos?

He glanced again at the stilled bundle on the mat, indulged his thoughts in wondering if she was ever aware that the Odemo she knew was long dead and another, and perhaps a different era, was now in the making. What, anyway, did all that matter to her? She would meet her Odemo over there, wherever there is, and maybe they would look down on the current performers and shake their heads, patronisingly. They had been through it all. Akinyode walked to the window again to see how high the sun had risen. If it was not three o'clock, it would be very close. Their tryst had been planned for three, at the very spot where the motorcade had moved off in the morning. Perhaps Sipe had already arrived. And Saaki. Yode strained his ears to catch any motor sounds but realised that even gunshots from that area would be blanketed by the thick vegetation on the intervening slopes. He shut the window, unlatched the door, and looked out carefully. Locking the door behind him, he slipped into the lesser-used paths and skirted the town towards 'Gborobe stream.

Wemuja's appearance was loudly incongruous. He had changed into his cowboy suit topped by the scoutmaster hat and was grooming a spotless white horse as one born to the job. He saw the dubious expression on the head teacher's face and hastened to reassure him.

'These are just my job clothes, Mr Yode. A man has to suit to the part, that is my belief, especially on an occasion like this. I am the one looking after the chief's horse.'

'Have the others arrived?' Yode was anxious to know. 'Efuape, Mr Akinsanya . . .'

'All present and correct. They went into *igbale*. . . .'

'What *igbale*? What do you know of *igbale*, you just-come Edo alien?' Wemuja laughed aloud. 'Mr Teacher sir, *egungun* is coming out today. Royal *egungun* is coming out and then we will know who is who in this Ìsarà town. So the masquerade has gone to dress up, and if you want to know where, it is that former maternity clinic which has been taken over, and that is now the headquarters. I have been resting the horse after its journey. . . .'

'Better go and tell them I am here.'

Wemuja's mouth opened in astonishment. 'But they are waiting for you over there.'

'No. Tell them – just tell Mr Efuape I am here. Tell him to come quickly.'

Wemuja caught something in the tone of his voice and became anxious. 'Anything wrong, Mr Yode? Any trouble in our absence?'

'No. At least, we don't quite know what it is. . . .'

Wemuja's face had changed to dark clouds. 'If it is those Olisa people again, Teacher, I have told you to let me –'

'No, no, no. We don't really . . . look, just you go and find Sipe. . . .'

An approaching motorcycle drowned out his remaining words. It was Ogunba's young cousin who had been posted as lookout on the road from Lagos. That gave the ex-Ilés' rally at least two hours' notice, since lunch had been planned for the commission at the Residency, where they would also spend the night after completing their task in Ìsarà. Everything appeared to be on schedule so far, so the meeting might actually begin as planned.

'They arrived half an hour ago,' young Ogunba reported. 'I waited until they actually started lunch.'

'Well, our group seems to have shifted base,' Soditan began, but a squelch of tyres on the soft road announced the approach of the Morris. Sipe leapt out, his eyes blazing with excitement. 'Where have you been? Where have you been hiding your head?'

'You changed the arrangements. When did you switch to the clinic?'

'We had to. What else did you expect us to do? We couldn't very well invite your guest into the heart of this jungle.'

'What guest?'

Sipe looked stumped. 'What guest? Isn't he here yet? He left Lagos hours before we did. He said he would go ahead of us.'

457

'Sipe, who are you talking about?'

Efuape held his head. 'Oh my God, he's missed the way. By now he's probably in . . .' He stopped abruptly. 'No, he couldn't have. A policeman drove him, we found one who was once stationed at Ode. Your man rode in the sidecar.'

'Oh. A sidecar has been reported, yes. . . .'

'Then he's here. How come you haven't seen him?'

'Seen who? I fled. Baba thought they had come to arrest me.'

'Arrest you? What for? Wait, wait, wait a minute. Are you telling me you haven't caught up yet with your friend Cade Woodenback . . . or whatever he calls himself?'

'Wooden . . .' The teacher stood stock-still. 'Who did you say?'

'You know, your friend, your pen pal.'

'Here? Wade Cudeback?'

'That's him. He arrived on the mail boat over a week ago but he'd taken ill in the high seas. So he stayed with the education secretary while recovering.'

'But, but how –'

'Let me finish. He began enquiries about how to reach you, and Melville Jones contacted Saaki. That's all. The man isn't fully himself yet but he insisted on setting off when he heard you were here.'

But Soditan only repeated, 'Wade Cudeback! Within the protectorate?' And then as a light broke through his mind, he shouted, 'Ho! He must be sitting in Baba's house this very moment!'

Sipe's mind stayed on the stolidly practical. 'Then let's make a start. We shall simply pick him up along the way, with the rest of the procession.'

And so, with only minor variations, the centenary pageant that had floored the librettist, Akinkore, in Abeokuta was replayed through the troughs and serpentine streets of Ìsarà. Spirited as Olisa's procession attempted to be, it proved no match for the sheer spectacle of the Jagun faction, led by what Sipe dubbed their secret weapon, the thoroughbred Bahia, his white-maned head tossing above the hill from where Goriola normally made his grand descent, until his mishap.

A moment stayed with the rider. It would remain with him throughout that day. As he was assisted onto his horse on the blind side of the hill over which they would first appear to the carefully installed groups, his mind rehearsed the routes and functions which had been mapped out for him and he was struck by the elaborateness of planning, and the prodigal resources expended for this contest. As the folds of his *agbada* were carefully draped over the horse's flanks and over the horn of the chased saddle, his face fell in unaccustomed humility and his voice broke slightly.

'*Ha! Emi re wuwo l'owo wen to 'we?*'*

They saw that he was overwhelmed. Akinyode, however, looked his cousin in the eye and spoke for all: '*Si ko je k'Ìsarà wuwo n'owo re.*'†

Akinsanya nodded slowly, his far gaze a solemn pledge. Then he brightened up abruptly, hitched up his shoulders, and kicked the sides of his horse, impatient to begin. Wemuja wrapped his stubby fingers round the horse's bridle, and the procession moved forward.

Saaki's face, a black sun against the sky, was topped by an *abetiaja* of stiffened white damask, its triangular flaps bristling above his ears in severely symmetrical folds, their tips at right angles to the ears. No one had, until then, seen an *agbada* made entirely from *èye etù*. The huge embroidered robe shimmered in soft contours with the motion of the horse. Wemuja, self-appointed equerry, obeyed his instructions to the letter. Dressed now in a simple *buba* and *soro*, with *ikori* cap, he brought the horse to a halt at the very crest, while groups of hidden supporters poured out from every side to swell the triumphal entry. Saaki raised his extra-long whisk and acknowledged the tumultuous greetings, his face eclipsed from time to time by huge *sekere* tossed ever higher by the competitive musicians.

Across the heaving rump of the stallion, Efuape and Soditan winked at each other and smiled with satisfaction at this first detonation of the hidden caps. This part of the affair was assured. The rest was in the hands of the commission. And perhaps right within the pocket of my *buba*? Sipe asked himself. For hidden beneath his *agbada* was a sealed envelope from Onayemi, and he found that he feared to open it, to come face to face with the prediction of the Spirit of Layeni!

The route had been deliberately chosen, boldly past the Rokodo House, but only after that faction had left for the meeting place. The symbolic defiance was sufficient, there was no need to mar the resplendence of their progress with unseemly scenes. Yode answered the question in Wemuja's look, nodded, and they proceeded slowly down the hill.

Akinyode Soditan turned his attention to Saaki's ramrod figure on the horse, yes, this was indeed homecoming. But would he truly 'return to sender'? The tasks were daunting. Beneath the finery that surrounded them, the teacher was only too aware of bodies eaten by yaws, a fate that

---

* Ha! Is it I who weigh so heavy in your hands?
† You simply ensure that Ìsarà weighs heavy in your hands.

seemed to overtake an unfair proportion of Ìsarà inhabitants. The children's close-cropped heads did not all glisten in the sun; tracks of ringworm ran circles through stubs of hair. The mobile clinic which served Ìsarà and other towns in Remo district was infrequent. Sometimes, an expectant mother would deliver her baby on the roadside, having set off too late to reach the maternity clinic at Ode. Within that crowd, Akinyode's eyes caught sight of a goitre round a woman's neck, the size of a pawpaw; he knew the woman. The ex-Ilés had once gathered funds to send her for an operation in Sagamu but she would have none of it. If anyone was going to cut her up, let it be done, she said, within Ìsarà. Dysentry took the lives of far too many infants, even before they were weaned. It was a symbolic reminder, the clinic that had closed down for lack of staff. It was a good thing that Sipe had turned it into the headquarters from which Saaki would make his bid for the crown. There was no running water; not one faucet had ever been installed in Ìsarà. The streets, swept abnormally clean for this day, were often like the interiors of far too many homes which remembered the feel of brooms only at the approach of Goriola. . . . Ah, yes, Saaki's shoulders might look straight enough; Akinyode saw them already bowed under the load of expectations. 'Am I that heavy in your hands?' he had exclaimed with touching gratitude. It is Ìsarà, Saaki, which, alas, will weigh heavy in your hands. Must. And you dare expect no gratitude, only more demands, more expectations, and miracles, yes, nothing short of miracles. But no gratitude. That emotion, Akinyode felt often, did not exist in Ìsarà dialect.

And yet despite that suspicion, and in spite of the divisions and present bitterness, Ìsarà had that sense of community, quite unlike Abeokuta. When their procession joined up with Olisa's at the meeting place, with a wide space between to proclaim the division to the wide world but not, he hoped, to enshrine it, all of Ìsarà would be there, a feat which would be impossible in Abeokuta. Indeed, where in Abeokuta could one find a band of ex-Ilés who could so routinely scheme in concert towards the day they would massively 'return to sender'? No, Abeokuta was too vast, its ex-Ilés had no knowledge of Ìsarà's poverty, no instinct of the 'sender' as that mutely demanding, irritating entity from which they had all dispersed. The rockland city of the Egba was a kestrel with outspread wings, Ìsarà a wood-pigeon scrambling out from the shell of time. . . .

Battered by the noise, but inwardly elated by the result of weeks of careful planning, Soditan's mind took refuge in many directions. He was dying with curiosity to see his fellow teacher who had travelled thousands of miles across the seas – for what? An obsessive interest in that 'dark continent' he had merely read about? Or was it a general thirst for knowledge? Knowledge at first hand, that impossible teacher's ideal? Well, whatever he sought here, this was one outing to beat General Montcalm's ghost fields, the Reversing Falls, and Salem's witching house all rolled into one. . . .

Wade Cudeback! Soditan stopped so abruptly that the group behind bumped into him and propelled him forward. Yes, of course, there was such a difference. Cudeback travelled for pleasure, not necessity. But Ìsarà was bereft of choice; she pushed out her sons and daughters, firstly to be trained, then to earn a living. The aridity was all-embracing; Ìsarà could not provide a living. The starkness of it shook him. He knew a few other peoples with that itinerant reputation – the Ogbomosho, for instance. Anywhere along the coast of West Africa, you would find them there. So perhaps to a lesser degree, were the Ijebu. He could not speak for the Ogbomosho's reason for self-dispersal but he knew now, for a certainty, what made the Ìsarà such exiles. There were no factories, not even small businesses, no institutions, nothing of note that would draw in the curious or make the existence of the indigenes a productive adventure.

Did Akinsanya know this? His *abetiaja*, its sharp triangular ends still stiffly parallel to the ground, began to look more like a chunk of the cactus which Ìsarà's hardy soil sprouted on odd hillocks and in the occasional backyard. The teacher made a note to pass this on to him as warning – not that Saaki was likely to forget his mission. Still, it might come in useful. If Saaki slackened or tired, or began to live only for the pleasures of position, it would be time to vary the ancient saying for him – an *abetiaja* is never made of velvet, and no one compelled you to wear it.

And it soon became clear that the homage was cast wider, that it embraced more than the rider. As often as a group surged forward to touch the horse, or Saaki's robes, a figure, or groups of two or three, emerged quietly at Soditan's side, beaming or giggling, manifesting their personal forms of pride and gratitude, sometimes, a claim of simply belonging.

'Do you still remember me, Teacher? You trained me at . . .'

It became routine, every few steps. Faces he had not seen for years, they had responded to the summons by telegrams, by couriers, grapevine, and newspaper notices, even by episcopal circulars – there were several ex-Ilés who had taken the cloth. Opeilu simply took them in charge. Some arrived that very day, in time to swell the ranks; the ex-Ilés had cast their nets far and wide. Some faces merely shouted 'Teacher' from within the crowd and waved until he responded and they were satisfied that he had recognised them. Others raised up their children above the milling heads for him to see. And there was Mrs Esan standing slightly apart, nodding with quiet satisfaction. He waved a grand approval towards the triumph of her *èye età* on Saaki's back. Their discussion ran through his mind and he felt himself warmed by an inner glow, acknowledging that, as if by accident, he had stumbled on the secret of fulfillment.

Could it be – he returned to the shrine at Odogbolu, to the medium whose enigmatic pronouncement had defied all understanding – could this be what it all meant? Ask a foolish question and you get a foolish answer? When you ask a spirit if you'll find success in life, you should first tell it what you mean by success. That game played on you by grown-ups as a child: Go to your Uncle So-and-so and bring me some *arodan* . . . and the child goes to that uncle, and the uncle shakes his head dolefully, no, he has no *arodan*. But he encourages you to try his friend, who probably has it. That friend, alas, only regrets that he lent his last piece to his brother, so to the brother you proceed . . . then his cousin . . . until at last – don't say you heard it from me but – try your next-door neighbour, who returned from *arodan*-land only yesterday and is sure to have plenty on him. On to Mr Next-door-neighbour, who exclaims, But your father has just dropped by to pick up the last bit! Somewhere along the way, certainly by the very end, you discover yourself that *arodan* is just a nonsense word, that there is no such thing, and another lesson is implanted. Well, maybe spirits also play games with humans, especially those who pester them with foolish questions. . . .

Node had been brought out to watch the parade. Mariam stood by his side, among the women and children of his household. Node, on whose timber lorry the horse had ridden from the home of the Santeros and whose blessing could only be conveyed by Mariam. Saaki halted briefly, bowed and silently pledged to obtain one of the wheelchairs in use in Lagos General Hospital for the paralysed man. Then to the gate of *osugbo* amidst gunshots, swelled at every passage by tens of newcomers.

Jagun waited with the *osugbo* elders to sacrifice a ram and smear its blood on the horse's forehooves. They entered the last stretch of crude terracing, the horse's hooves raising hard clacks, as if to counterpoise the optimism of the cheers. Then to Josiah's home, Ile Lígùn, where bowls of water were thrown on the ground before them. An hour or so earlier, the mystery of the strange caller had been explained to Pa Josiah, so he now stood side by side with the guest and the rest of the ex-Ilés against the three-legged transport that had brought him from Lagos. Wemuja did not need to be told; he tugged at the bridle and the horse came to a halt, the crowd nearly impossible to control as they sought to catch a glimpse of the intruder from over and beyond the seas who had come to seek out an Ìsarà son – and on such a singular day! Did it augur well? The feeling was – it had better!

As he set eyes on the visitor, Soditan was mildly disconcerted to find that the white teacher in no way resembled his handwriting, neither did he emit the slightest aura which evoked the places and adventures he so richly conveyed in his letters. Saaki gave Wade Cudeback a massive wink as Soditan stepped forward to shake hands with him. The Ìsarà teacher had decided on the form of greeting he would use for this encounter. It would certainly raise a laughter of approbation from the ex-Ilés and his guest, break the ice and set everyone at ease. But Wade Cudeback beat him to the salute: 'Teacher Soditan, I presume?'

In the few seconds of grace provided by the knowledgeable laughter, Soditan thought rapidly. His reponse, he would later acknowledge, emerged in spite of himself. Astonished, he heard himself say, and with a feeling of inner composure:

'Welcome to Ashtabula.'

V. S. NAIPAUL

A Million Mutinies Now

'It is literally the last word on India today, witness within witness, a chain of voices that illustrates every phase of Indian life . . . with a truthfulness and a subtlety that are a joy to read. Something like love enters the narrative – a real feeling for the land and its people'
Paul Theroux, *Literary Review*

'Brilliantly enjoyable . . . I loved the old Naipaul for his sardonic wit. The new one is to be loved for his sweetness of nature, amounting almost to sanctity. Everybody should read him'
Auberon Waugh, *Sunday Telegraph*

'The most notable commitment of intelligence that post-colonial India has evoked . . . He is indispensable for anyone who wants seriously to come to grips with the experience of India'
Joseph Lelyveld, *New York Times Book Review*

'With this book he may well have written his own enduring monument, in prose at once stirring and intensely personal, distinguished both by style and critical acumen'
K. Natwar-Singh, *Financial Times*

MARK HUDSON

Our Grandmother's Drums

'West Africa. Blinding white light, dust and scrub, salt flats and mangrove swamps, a village called Dulaba in the Gambia. People are scratching a living out of rice, groundnuts, millet. At the appointed time, the women beat their grandmothers' drums and go to the bush for the circumcision rituals. No man is allowed . . . To Mark Hudson, a casual visitor, Dulaba in 1985 was a place of fascination, its stark landscape vivid with the presence of its women. What were their lives, bounded by Islam, by female circumcision, by the necessity to work in the fields and to obey first their mothers and then their husbands?

'Out of his year in Dulaba has come a wonderful book. Reading it is like watching a picture being painted . . . A moving, even majestic book'
Listener

'A travel book of quite exceptional distinction'
Norman Lewis

'I have rarely read a book of such passion and honesty . . . full of dark moods and chaotic exhilaration'
Roger Clarke, *Sunday Times*

'A powerful evocation of village life written in simple and beautiful prose'
Weekend Telegraph

'An arresting and fascinating work'
London Review of Books

JUNICHIRÓ TANIZAKI

The Makioka Sisters

Tanizaki's masterpiece is the story of the extinction of a great family through pride and over-refinement. It is a loving and nostalgic recreation of the sumptuous, intricate upper-class life of Osaka immediately before World War Two. With surgical realism and precision, Tanizaka lays bare the sinews of pride, and in the finest qualities of the Japanese tradition, brings a vanished era to vibrant life.

'Junichiró Tanizaki may well prove to be the outstanding Japanese novelist of the century . . . His greatest book, *The Makioka Sisters* (1948), was written during World War Two as a way of reliving and preserving the happier past. It is the story of the attempts made by a declining merchant family to marry off Yukiko, a daughter who is the quintessentially Japanese heroine: inwardly stubborn though outwardly passive, spiritually self-sufficient though materially dependent, maddeningly unwilling to enter the light of day but determined to manipulate everyone from her shadowy retreat'
Edmund White, *New York Times Book Review*

'It is an extraordinary book, which can truly be said to break new ground'
New Yorker

LOUIS DE BERNIÈRES

The Troublesome Off-spring of Cardinal Guzman

'A thoroughly enjoyable and almost dazzling tale of a small South American town that defends itself against a modern version of the Spanish Inquisition . . . packed with quizzical, breathtaking events'
Spectator

'A novel of prodigious imagination, it proves that de Bernières is a writer abundantly gifted, outrageously funny, so pithy, succulent and d'Artagnan in his ease, so sure and accessible that he is bound to be underrated. His Latin America transcends the magical realist conventions . . . Louis de Bernières turns black comedy into something even darker, more profound and frequently sticky'
Scotland on Sunday

'. . . like a spoof of every fashionable Latin American novel, a carnival of pain and pleasure, violence, tenderness, high jinks of every sexual sort, quaint customs and quainter jokes'
Financial Times

'An extraordinary feat of imagination . . . Though de Bernières' scathing satire is aimed unambiguously at Church and State his points are never less than beautifully rendered. A sensuous, often farcical and ultimately optimistic argument for spiritual sanity'
Time Out

'A cocktail of fable, farce and lyricism, shot through with sobering tragedy . . . Whatever you might make of his theology, Mr de Bernières writes superbly. This is a breathtaking read: moving and hilarious'
Catholic Herald

AMY TAN

The Joy Luck Club

'A brilliant first novel, *The Joy Luck Club* is the story of four mothers and their first-generation Chinese-American daughters; two generations of women struggling to come to terms with their cultural identity. Tan writes from the heart, cutting sharp edges with wit, wisdom and a gentle and delicate precision. From the wealthy homes of pre-revolutionary China to downtown San Francisco and the age of AIDS, the novel covers a remarkable spectrum and reveals the private secrets and ghosts that haunt, torment – and comfort. Completely compelling'
Time Out

'In this honest, moving and beautifully courageous story Amy Tan shows us China, Chinese-American women and their families and the mystery of the mother-daughter bond in ways that we have not experienced before'
Alice Walker

'Pure enchantment'
Mail on Sunday

'In this deft and original debut, Amy Tan shows that she is both a consummate storyteller and a writer whose prose manages to be emotionally charged without a trace of sentimentality'
Sunday Times

R. K. NARAYAN

A Malgudi Omnibus

Swami and Friends
The Bachelor of Arts
The English Teacher

Here are three of R. K. Narayan's most famous and best loved novels, all set in the imaginary Indian town of Malgudi. These irresistible works provide the perfect introduction to a universal world of humour, sadness, wisdom and joy.

'Narayan wakes in me a spring of gratitude, for he has offered me a second home. Without him I could never have known what it is like to be Indian'
Graham Greene

'The hardest of all things for a novelist to communicate is the extraordinary ordinariness of human happiness. Jane Austen, Soskei, Chekhov: a few bring it off. Narayan is one of them'
Spectator

'No writer is more deceptively casual, or less fussed about the Eternal Verities, or more unerring in arriving by delightful detours at his destination – which is seldom a terminus because life keeps bobbing on'
Guardian

ALBERT FRENCH

Billy

The tale of Billy Lee Turner, a ten-year-old boy convicted for the murder of a white girl in Mississippi in 1937, illuminates the monstrous face of racism in America with harrowing clarity and power. Narrated in the rich accents of the American South, Billy's story is told amidst the picking-fields and town streets, the heat, dust and poverty of the region in the time of the Depression. Albert French's haunting first novel is a story of racial injustice, as unsentimental as it is heartbreaking.

'I kept trying to think of a writer who has done a better job of capturing clear, powerful and authentic language, the landscape, the people . . . the air itself. I kept searching for comparisons and I kept coming up with masters of the art, from Aeschylus to Ernest Gaines'
David Bradley

'*Billy* is a book that will stay with me in my dreams'
Tim O'Brien

ANDRÉ BRINK

Rumours of Rain

Winter in South Africa – a time of searing drought, angry stirrings in Soweto, and the shadow of the Angolan conflict cast across the scorched bush.

Martin Mynhardt, a wealthy Afrikaner, plans a weekend at his old family farm. But his visit coincides with a time of crisis in his personal life. In a few days, the security of a lifetime is destroyed and, with only the uncertain values of his past to guide him, Mynhardt is left to face the wreckage of his future.

'As complex and powerful as the African continent itself'
Books and Bookmen

André Brink, twice runner-up for the Booker Prize, and author of *An Act of Terror*, *A Dry White Season*, *An Instant in the Wind* and *Looking on Darkness* (all available in Minerva), is South Africa's foremost political novelist. He is currently Professor of English Literature at Cape Town University.

GITA MEHTA

A River Sutra

'This book is a delight. Written with hypnotic lyricism, this is seductive prose of a high order. Gita Mehta has written a novel which defies easy categorisation: its central character is India's holiest river, the Narmada, mere sight of which is salvation. The narrator, a retired civil servant, has escaped the world to spend his twilight years running a guest house on the river's bank. But he has chosen the wrong place: too many lives converge here. Minstrels, musicians, ascetics, monks – everyone has their own story to tell . . .'
Time Out

'The simplicity of the plots makes it difficult to express the joy that one has in reading them. All India seems to be there . . . I have a feeling, indeed a hope, that *A River Sutra* will become a classic, revered and enjoyed by young and old'
Daily Telegraph

'A mesmerizing novel by a writer of prodigious gifts'
Miami Herald

'Superb, profound, apparently effortless storytelling'
Independent on Sunday

AMIT CHAUDHURI

Afternoon Raag

'Enchanting, studded with moments of beauty more arresting than anything to be found in a hundred busier and more excitable narratives . . . Chaudhuri has proved that he can write better than just about anyone of his generation'
Jonathan Coe, *London Review of Books*

'If there is such a thing as a betting certainty, it is that Chaudhuri will win the Booker prize before the century is out'
David Robson, *Sunday Telegraph*

'Those who are always acclaiming the "poetic prose" of Ondaatje would do well to study Chaudhuri's language. Again and again, he produces the perfect adjective, the stupendous adverb . . . radiantly exact'
James Wood, *Guardian*

'As elegant and economical as the best poetry . . . Chaudhuri's book is an astonishing accomplishment . . . which seems to float tantalisingly above the usual demands of fiction'
Julian Loose, *Sunday Times*

'This immensely subtle novel both estranges and gently strokes the surface of English and Indian life. I know of nothing in English fiction that begins to resemble it'
Tom Paulin

A Selected List of Titles Available from Minerva

While every effort is made to keep prices low, it is sometimes necessary to increase prices at short notice. Mandarin Paperbacks reserves the right to show new retail prices on covers which may differ from those previously advertised in the text or elsewhere.

The prices shown below were correct at the time of going to press.

☐ 7493 9931 7	**An Act of Terror**	André Brink	£7.99
☐ 7493 9985 6	**Rumours of Rain**	André Brink	£6.99
☐ 7493 9147 2	**Explosion in a Cathedral**	Alejo Carpentier	£5.99
☐ 7493 9970 8	**Afternoon Raag**	Amit Chaudhuri	£4.99
☐ 7493 9705 5	**The Name of the Rose**	Umberto Eco	£6.99
☐ 7493 9878 7	**The Call of the Toad**	Gunter Grass	£5.99
☐ 7493 9080 8	**Balzac's Horse**	Gert Hofmann	£4.99
☐ 7493 9174 X	**The Mirror Maker**	Primo Levi	£5.99
☐ 7493 9792 6	**A River Sutra**	Gita Mehta	£5.99
☐ 7493 9727 6	**The English Teacher**	R. K. Narayan	£5.99
☐ 7493 9966 X	**Lucie's Long Voyage**	Alina Reyes	£3.99
☐ 7493 9710 1	**The Makioka Sisters**	Junichirō Tanizaki	£6.99

All these books are available at your bookshop or newsagent, or can be ordered direct from the address below. Just tick the titles you want and fill in the form below.

Cash Sales Department, PO Box 5, Rushden, Northants NN10 6YX.
Fax: 0933 410321   Phone: 0933 410511.

Please send cheque, payable to 'Reed Book Services Ltd.', or postal order for purchase price quoted and allow the following for postage and packing:

£1.00 for the first book, 50p for the second; **FREE POSTAGE AND PACKING FOR THREE BOOKS OR MORE PER ORDER.**

NAME (Block letters) ....

ADDRESS...

....

☐ I enclose my remittance for ....

☐ I wish to pay by Access/Visa Card Number

Expiry Date

Signature ....

Please quote our reference: MAND